THE COMPLETE DEVILBEND DYNASTY SERIES

KAYDENCE SNOW

SONDER PUBLISHING PTY LTD

LIKE YOU CARE

PROLOGUE

The cable tie around my wrists was so tight my fingers were going numb. The pole they'd tied me to dug into my back, the cold metal and the evening breeze making me shiver.

Or maybe I was shivering from fear.

They'd never gone this far before, never hurt me this badly.

I sobbed, the flood of tears stinging my sore cheek.

The knife was small—just a little switchblade thing—but it looked sharp. A shudder raced down my spine as the tip was dragged gently down my throat, the middle of my chest, my belly.

For the first time, I wondered if I would actually survive this night. Were they really about to kill me? Did their hatred really run that deep?

Movement in the distance caught my attention. Someone was sprinting toward us across the football field.

My heart soared . . . then I recognized him, and it plummeted again.

He stopped just a few feet away, breathing hard, his wide eyes taking in the whole fucked-up scene. He couldn't hide his reaction; his beautiful face gave it all away—surprise, horror, disbelief, disgust . . . was that anger I saw next?

I couldn't be sure of anything anymore. My soul was being torn to shreds, and my mind was going with it. I had no idea what he'd do next.

Would he join in and help them destroy me?

Would he stand by and do nothing, let it happen?

Would he walk away, like a coward, so he wouldn't have to watch?

Or would he defend me? Save me?

Knowing what I'd just learned, what it would mean, what it would cost, did I even want him to?

He took a step forward, and I braced myself to find out if the boy I loved would be my salvation . . . or if my heart would be torn to shreds right along with my mind and soul.

CHAPTER ONE

The tennis ball thunked rhythmically as my cousins got into a lengthy rally. It wasn't even midday yet, but the sun was already unbearable, reflecting brightly off the blue of the tennis court.

Donna and Harlow were in pristine tennis whites right down to their shoes, their skirts swishing around their tanned thighs as they lunged for balls as though competing at a world-class tournament. I was in shorts and a tank top, my flip-flops abandoned under the chair—nothing pristine about any of it. I didn't know the first thing about holding a tennis racket, let alone hitting the ball.

My cousins lived on a property big enough to hold a tennis court *and* a pool. I lived in an apartment off a hallway that always smelled like curry. This was not my world, but these girls were the closest thing I had to friends.

The rally broke, and Donna grunted a "yes" as she pumped her fist.

"Are you two nearly done?" Amaya yelled from the chair next to me before taking a sip of her watermelon juice. She went to Fulton Academy with my cousins and lived on the next street. They'd been friends since preschool, so she was always around when I was around. Not that I minded. I liked her confidence —if only some of it would rub off on me . . .

"Yeah, some of us would like to get in the pool," I added.

"We need to finish this," Harlow ground out before crouching down, waiting for her sister to serve.

Amaya and I both groaned and slumped down in our chairs. We were in the shade of a massive umbrella, but it felt as if the sun was beating right through it onto the top of my head. I drank the rest of my own watermelon juice, loudly slurping up the last dregs of the sweet liquid through my straw.

Amaya finished hers too, dropped the empty glass on the table between us, and reached for her phone. She changed the song, the new beat thumping out of the little portable speaker, then stretched her arms up over her head. Her perfectly straight, almost black hair hung down the back of the chair, shining like silk. Her long brown legs were toned and perfect.

I wished I had her beautiful skin. I wished I had anyone's skin but my own, especially the skin on my face.

"How was your summer, Mena?" Amaya asked, giving me a genuine, friendly smile. It was the question I'd been dreading all morning.

The three of them had spent most of the summer at some camp with their other rich friends. I'd spent the summer on the cramped little balcony of my apartment, doing elaborate makeup looks and then wiping them off again—when I wasn't working at the diner.

"Pretty chill." I shrugged and hoped she'd drop it.

"Did you do anything fun with your friends?"

Your friends. Not *your other friends* or *your friends from school.* Did she not consider me a friend?

I pushed the choking feeling down and worked hard to keep my expression neutral. "Nothing worth mentioning." *Please drop it.* "I can't stand this heat anymore." I groaned. "I don't know how those two aren't melting."

My cousins were still whacking the tennis ball, sprinting up and down the court.

"Ugh, I know. They're gonna get heatstroke." Amaya took a cigarette out of her pack and lit it.

Seizing the opportunity to avoid the topic of my nonexistent friends, I slipped into my flip-flops. "I'm gonna go get another drink and jump in the pool."

Amaya waved me away with the cigarette held between her elegant fingers. "Hey, you maniacs!" she yelled as I walked up the path toward the house. "We've had enough. You have until I finish this smoke, and then we're getting in that motherfucking pool, or so help me . . ."

My cousins started shouting back, but I could no longer discern what they were saying. I smiled to myself as my shoulders relaxed. I loved hanging out with these girls, but I really didn't want to talk about my life. It was easier to just pretend.

I walked through the Meads' massive house, my flip-flops slapping on marble tile as the AC cooled my flushed skin. My aunt Emily was sitting at the island in the kitchen, flipping through an interior design magazine and sipping on a coffee made for her on the professional espresso machine in their butler's pantry.

She looked up at me and smiled. Donna and Harlow got their blonde hair and athletic bodies from her and their round eyes from their dad.

"You girls having fun?" She brushed my hair off my shoulder as I leaned on the counter next to her.

"Yes." My returning smile was genuine. My mother's sister had never made me feel invisible. She'd also never made me feel awkward about my face or treated me differently because we didn't have the kind of money she had.

"Where are the others?" She glanced behind me, in the direction of the tennis court.

"We're all gonna jump in the pool soon. I just came in to get more watermelon juice." I rolled my eyes and chuckled. " After your daughters are done battling it out for the top spot in the Australian Open."

"In this heat?" She shook her head. "Do I need to go tell them to knock it off?"

"No, no," I rushed out. I didn't want her to catch Amaya smoking. "They're wrapping it up."

My aunt nodded and smoothed my hair again. "OK. Oh, by the way . . ." She hopped off the stool, her understated perfume wafting toward me as she breezed past in a tailored shirt and khaki shorts, not a hair out of place. She picked up a MacBook and coiled-up charger off the side table. "We got Donna and Harlow new laptops for school, so I wanted to give you this one. It's been reset and all that jazz."

"Oh." I took it reflexively, the sleek metal cool in my fingers. "Thank you . . ." I trailed off. I really was thankful, but I knew Mom didn't like me taking things from my cousins. My dad would be fine with it. He knew my aunt's gifts came from a good place, and he wasn't too proud to accept the help. But my mom . . .

My aunt saw the uncertainty on my face. "Don't worry about your mom. I'll talk to her. You need a good computer for school."

Her tone brooked no arguments, so I nodded. My current laptop was clunky and constantly crashing—often midsentence as I worked on an assignment. We couldn't possibly afford a new one, so I hadn't even mentioned it to my parents.

Aunt Emily took the laptop out of my hands again and set it on the bench. "You go on out to the pool. I'll have the drinks and a snack brought out to you before I head off to lunch."

"Thanks, Auntie Em."

I did as she said, making my way through the open-plan living area, out through the French doors, and down another manicured path toward the pool. I would much rather have just gone to the fridge and gotten the damn drinks myself than deal with the awkwardness of having a servant bring things, but there was no point arguing with my aunt.

The pool was as ostentatious as the house, with curving edges, natural stone paving, and lush landscaping, complete with stunning views of California's natural landscape. Umbrella-shaded loungers lined one side, towels already placed neatly on each one. I toed off my flip-flops and whipped my tank top off over my head as voices preceded the arrival of the others.

The girls walked up before I could get my shorts off. Donna and Harlow spotted me, and matching evil grins pulled at their faces.

"No," I said as firmly as I could, throwing my arms out in front of me.

They shared a look and sprinted directly for me. Neither one seemed to give a shit that they were still fully clothed in their tennis gear as they tackled me into the water. All three of us splashed into the pool in a tangle of limbs and hair.

"Oh man, that's refreshing," Harlow yelled as we surfaced, spluttering and laughing. They waded to the edge of the pool and got out, removing their sodden tennis shoes.

"You guys are such dicks!" I smacked the water on either side of me, but I couldn't help the smile tugging at my face.

"Hey, you wanted to get in the pool," Donna teased, and I flipped her off. Somehow, her short, sleek haircut still looked neat and cute even plastered to her head.

"You *did* want to get in the pool." Perfectly dry and unruffled, Amaya flipped her shiny black hair over her shoulder, lit another cigarette, and unhurriedly lowered her perfect ass to one of the loungers.

The sisters headed to the pool house to get their bathing suits, shedding wet white clothing as they went.

"Whose side are you on?" I arched a brow at Amaya as I headed toward the ladder, the denim tight around my hips. The shorts would be a pain in the ass to get off.

"Mine." She shrugged. "Always mine."

Just as I reached the ladder, a servant in black shorts and a collared T-shirt came down the path, carrying a tray laden with drinks and snacks.

I ducked my head and pushed off the ladder, diving back under the water. Better to deal with the wet denim for a few more minutes than deal with someone I didn't know looking at my gross face.

I surfaced at the deep end and took big gulps of air, facing the verdant plants on the other side of the pool.

"He's gone," Amaya announced. She had stripped down to a white bikini that practically glowed against her smooth dark skin, her black hair gathered into a messy bun on top of her head.

I sighed in relief and swam back to the ladder. She gave me a warm smile as she waded in at the shallow end. The girls knew how self-conscious I was of my face, but they also knew I didn't like talking about it.

Donna and Harlow came back out wearing swimsuits that probably cost more than my whole wardrobe, with geometric mesh cutouts, and joined us in the pool.

"I wish you went to our school, Mena." Harlow pouted.

"Yeah, senior year would be epic with all of us together," Donna agreed. Donna was born eleven months before Harlow, making them as close in age as sisters could be without being twins.

I nodded before kicking my legs up to float on my back. "Me too."

I'd have given anything to go to their fancy private school, where I'd actually have friends. But I was stuck at my shitty public school, where I wished I didn't exist—on a good day.

We spent the rest of the day by the pool, listening to music and talking, the girls telling me about their time away. We had lunch brought to us and hardly left the loungers other than to cool off in the water.

We all took photos on our phones, but when Amaya went to post one with all four of us squished into the frame, drinking watermelon juice through straws, I made her promise not to. I didn't want anyone seeing the repulsive thing on my face, and I really didn't want anything online that could be used against me. They argued with me, but I was pretty stubborn on this front, so Amaya ended up posting one with just the three of them. As usual, she added #DevilbendDynasty to the caption.

They'd started using the phrase last year, after we found a stack of photo albums in the Meads' attic—our moms and grandmothers, generations of Devilbend women, in social clubs, at charity functions, sticking together, supporting one another. I knew the girls wanted to include me in the sentiment, but I wasn't dynasty material—I was just a poor, ugly girl with no future.

My mom picked me up on her way home from work, coming inside to catch up with her sister while I squeezed in every last moment with the girls. I was pretty sure they argued about the laptop, but it came home with us, so my aunt must have won.

The carefree, light feeling I'd had hanging out with the girls was pushed out of my chest with every mile that took me farther away from them. As the manicured lawns and immaculate, tall fences gave way to tightly packed concrete buildings on the fifteen-minute drive home, some of that concrete settled on my shoulders, my reality weighing me down.

"Did you have fun with your cousins?" Mom asked as we parked in the lot behind our building. It was the first thing she'd said since we got in the car, both of us lost in our thoughts.

I sighed. "Yeah."

"Well, don't sound so enthusiastic about it." She chuckled.

I didn't answer, and she was too tired to prod me any further. My mom had the same blonde hair as my aunt Em, but I got my thick, light brown hair from my dad. I also got his pale blue eyes. If only I had some of his height too. He towered over both my mom and me—but then, most people did.

After dinner and a shower, I went out to the balcony to let my hair air-dry.

The sun was beginning to set, casting everything in a warm yellow-orange hue. Even the shitty side of Devilbend—with the squat apartment buildings, the run-down park, and the shady area near the train station—looked kind of pretty in this light.

But it was an illusion. Under the golden light and summer shadows was hard concrete and graffiti, people struggling to survive, and *me*. I'd had an amazing day, but it made the evening even more bitter by comparison. *Back to reality.* Tomorrow I'd have to go to work at the diner—I'd picked up as many shifts as I could during summer. Then on Monday, it was back to school.

I rubbed the side of my nose and sighed, wishing for the millionth time I could scrub the ugly mark off. Wishing I could change just one thing about my life.

That was impossible, so I decided to paint the pretty sunset onto my face in the form of a smoky but vibrant eye makeup.

"Motherfucker!" My chair scraped against the balcony floor as I leapt up to avoid getting splatters of foundation on my white shorts. The bottle had just slipped out of my hand and smashed on the table. "Fucking *fuck*. God *damn* it!"

I growled in frustration as more than fifty dollars' worth of goop, perfectly matched to my skin tone, went oozing over the edge.

"You all right over there?" A deep male voice came from the balcony next to ours, a shadow shifting behind the bamboo screen my mother had put up for privacy.

"Shit." I froze, heat spreading up my cheeks. That was all I needed—some asshole to tell me off over my potty mouth.

CHAPTER TWO

"Yes. I'm fine. Just dropped something. Sorry about the cursing," I scrambled to reply, hoping he wouldn't demand to speak with my parents.

He chuckled, sounding more amused now than concerned. "I don't give a flying fuck about the cursing." His voice was smooth—like the ocean on a calm day. Mellow and even on the surface, but underneath . . .

I smiled and relaxed my shoulders. "Well . . . fucking great then." I rolled my eyes at myself.

"Must've been something important."

"What?" I frowned, inching closer to the bamboo screen.

"The thing you dropped?"

"Oh!" I'd almost forgotten about the foundation. "Yeah, it was . . . expensive and . . . er . . . never mind."

I suddenly felt shy. I didn't want this random stranger with the beautiful voice to know I'd been that upset over makeup. I didn't want him to think I was conceited.

"Fine. Keep your secrets."

I could hear the smile in his voice. It made me smile too, but I ironed out my expression so he wouldn't hear it. "Why would I trust you with my secrets? You're a stranger. You could be an axe murderer."

His laughter trickled through the tiny gaps in the bamboo and wrapped itself around my shoulders, sending a little shiver down my spine.

"I'm not a stranger. I'm your neighbor. You can trust me," he said.

I realized I was just standing motionless in the middle of my balcony, staring at the bamboo partition. I reached for the roll of paper towels on the table and started cleaning up the mess. "Never trust someone who says *trust me*," I quipped.

"Touché." He chuckled again. "I'll just have to earn your trust the old-fashioned way."

"A cavity search?" I paused mid-wipe. Had I really just said that to a random?

But he didn't even pause before answering. "I was gonna say drug screening, and you jump straight to finger in the ass? Brutal!"

"I don't fuck around." A laugh escaped at the end, part of it slight hysteria from the rush of relief that he hadn't taken offence.

"No, you do not, neighbor."

I couldn't get enough of his smooth voice; his relaxed, casual tone was putting me at ease in a way I never had been with a person I'd never met. Was it the screen between us that allowed me to talk to him without feeling self-conscious about my face? Or was it *him*?

I couldn't tell how old he was just from his voice. Not elderly, that much was clear, but was he my age? A college guy? Maybe he was in his thirties and married with three kids. I really hoped I wasn't flirting with an old dude.

Was that what I was doing? Flirting?

I cleared my throat and deposited the last of the dirty paper towels into a handbasket, then wiped my hands with micellar water to get the foundation off. "So, you just moved in?"

The apartment had been empty for months. Their balcony was right next to ours, but that didn't make us neighbors exactly. Our apartment was the last one at the end of the hallway on the eighth floor. Theirs was the last one at the end of their hallway, but we had to use separate entrances to the building. There were five entrances total—twelve floors of cramped apartments, thousands of people literally living on top of one another.

"Yeah, yesterday. Although I'm questioning the decision."

"New neighbor scaring you off? Am I the one giving off axe murderer vibes now?"

"Hah! Nah. It's the smell."

I frowned and silently sniffed at my underarms. I'd just showered. I smelled like strawberries. "The smell?"

"Yeah. The whole apartment smells like feet."

"Ugh, gross!"

"You have no idea! Every single room. Even the kitchen! If it hadn't rained last night, I would've slept out here."

I laughed. "Have you tried, uh, cleaning it?"

"Yes, thank you, smart-ass. We only got the keys yesterday. My dad had to work all day, so I did what I could on my own. Shampooing the carpets seems to have helped."

He hadn't mentioned a wife and kids! I did a little fist pump. He lived with his dad, but that didn't mean he was my age. Oh god! What if he was, like, twelve, and he was just one of those kids whose voice had dropped early?

"Well," I said, "I hope you get the feet smell out. It's a shame we didn't meet sooner. I could've told you this was a shitty place to live."

"We've had worse. Trust me. Plus, if we hadn't moved in here, I never would've gotten to talk to you."

I bit my bottom lip to hold in the grin and leaned back in the chair. I had no idea what to say to that.

The sun had set; with my window of natural light for makeup application gone, I started to pack everything into my case. After the zip made an obnoxiously loud sound, he cleared his throat and spoke again.

"I'm sorry. Was that . . . weird?" Gone was the casual confidence.

"No!" I rushed out, then took a breath to calm my tone. "Not at all. Sorry. I just . . . got distracted. I like talking to you too." I cringed.

"Good." I could hear the smile in his voice again.

"So, you move around a lot?" I blurted to fill the silence.

"Yeah. We . . . my dad's . . . yes, we move around a lot."

Maybe he was as nervous and flustered as me. Why did that make my chest feel all warm and fuzzy?

The kitchen light flicked on inside. Mom or Dad would be checking on me any minute now. I didn't want them to know I was talking to . . . whoever this was.

"Shit. I gotta go."

"Oh, OK. Nice talking to you!"

"You too!"

I ducked inside and closed the sliding door behind me just in time.

"I was just about to come check on you, Sweet Chilly." Dad leaned on the kitchen counter and chugged a glass of water. My full name was Philomena Ann Willis. At some point, before I had a say in it, my parents had started calling me Sweet Chilly Philly, and it stuck. The girls called me Mena. The assholes at school called me . . . *Ugh!* I pushed the thought out of my head. I still had a few days before I had to deal with *them.*

I smiled and poured myself a glass too. Mom was snoring lightly on the couch.

"I'm going to bed," I said.

"This early?" We both glanced at the time on the microwave: 9:38 p.m.

"I've got work tomorrow." It wasn't a lie. One of the waitresses had called in sick, and I was more than happy to take the double shift. It would help me replace the foundation I'd just lost.

"Early one?"

"Yeah. Can I get a lift?" I'd get there half an hour early if Dad dropped me off before heading to work, but it would be better than walking and taking the bus in this heat.

"Sure thing."

"Good night."

"Night." He waved me off, heading to wake up Mom.

The next day, I got home from my double shift around ten. Mom was already drifting off on the couch, but she startled awake when I came in and offered to heat up the casserole they'd had for dinner.

"No thanks. I ate at the diner." The pay was shitty, but at least Leah—the owner of the aptly named Leah's Diner—fed us when we worked long shifts. Leah had been friends with my mom in high school, and they'd reconnected when we'd moved back to Devilbend just before I started high school. Just before my life turned into hell on earth.

Actually, high school wasn't hell—it was more like limbo. It wasn't constant daily torture, although there was some of that too. No, it was punishment through alienation. Unless I was being sneered at, laughed at, or having something thrown at me, I didn't exist.

Most of the time I preferred it that way—preferred that people didn't look at me. Didn't look at the hideous birthmark on my face. But fuck, it was lonely sometimes.

The purple birthmark started at the inner corner of my right eye, pooling out down the side of my nose and the top of my cheek like spilled wine—which was probably why they were called "port-wine stains."

It wasn't raised or bumpy; it wasn't a rash or an infectious disease. It was just something I was born with. Something I couldn't escape. Something I *hated*. Most people stared. Some clearly thought it was contagious, shrinking away from me. The kids at school just used it as fuel for their ridicule.

I took a quick shower, then brought my lotion out to the balcony. As soon as the sliding door was closed and I'd settled myself on the little chair, I heard movement on the other side of the bamboo.

"Neighbor?" There was that ocean voice, immediately making me smile.

"Hey, stranger," I called back, propping one foot on the railing so I could rub lotion into my leg.

"I was just about to head to bed. Glad I caught you. Long day?"

"Yeah. I pulled a double shift." I didn't say where I worked—there was still a chance he was an axe murderer.

"That's rough." He sounded unsure; some of the ease of our banter from the previous night was gone.

"It's OK." I fought to keep my tone casual. "I only work part time, so I'm happy to take the extra shifts when I can." I moved on to my other leg.

He sighed. "I gotta get a job."

"Yeah? What do you do?" This was the part where he told me he was a professional whatever and way too old for me.

He laughed. "Whatever I can. Although it would be nothing if it were up to my dad."

"Really?" Hope blossomed. Most adults didn't let their parents dictate what they did for work, right?

"Yeah. He'd prefer I focus on . . . other things."

I frowned. Neither of us spoke. That was vague and weird.

"It's getting late. I better go." As he moved, his balcony light threw his shadow over the bamboo screen. He was tall, broad shouldered.

When I didn't speak, he did. "Cute toes."

And then he was gone. The sound of his sliding door closing made me shake my head at my idiocy. Why hadn't I told him good night or something? But hey, I sure was glad I'd let my mom paint my toes that deep red on the weekend. They did look cute.

The next day, I got home just after lunch. Mom and Dad were both at work, and there was nothing to stop me from racing through the apartment like a maniac, changing out of my work uniform and into a T-shirt dress, and launching myself onto the balcony. He wasn't there. I waited all afternoon, going inside only for snacks. The sun was setting and I was packing up after my second makeup look when the slide of a balcony door made me pause.

Someone settled in on the other side of the bamboo screen. My heart leapt into my throat, and my hand froze over my makeup bag, several brushes clutched in my fist.

Then I rolled my eyes at myself and let the brushes drop with a clatter.

"Hey, stranger." This time, I let the smile show in my voice.

"Oh, hey!" He sounded a little surprised. "You're early tonight."

"Didn't work this afternoon. Been sitting out here for hours." *Shit!* I cringed. Now I sounded like a creepy moron who'd been waiting for him all day.

But he didn't skip a beat. "I would've come out sooner, but the smell of feet has finally vacated the premises, and I got dragged into a particularly frustrating campaign on Halo."

"Well, I'm glad to know the stink is gone, but, er, what's a Halo?"

"Oh!" His laugh this time was a little nervous. "It's a video game. But not, like, a kid's game or whatever. It's got a parental advisory and everything. It's super violent, actually. Not that I like it for the violence! It actually requires strong problem-solving skills and . . . I'm rambling."

"Yeah, a bit." I laughed.

"Sorry. I just didn't want you to think I was a kid or anything."

Fuck. How old was he? I was so damn confused.

"I still watch SpongeBob SquarePants on Saturday mornings," I blurted, "if I'm not working. There's just something comforting about cartoons and cereal, ya know?"

"Yeah. Takes me back to a time when everything felt right with the world and I didn't have so much to worry about."

"Yeah . . ." I was a little surprised he understood so immediately. What heavy shit was he dealing with? Was it as bad as the reason I was dreading going back to school? Was it worse?

The following day I had the late shift and was kicking myself for not telling the boy next door I wouldn't be home in the evening. Then I was rolling my eyes for assuming he cared enough to notice I wouldn't be around.

Work was busy—the Saturday night dinner crowd keeping us on our toes, especially considering it was the last weekend before school started. I didn't get home until almost eleven. The apartment was dark and quiet, and my dad went straight to bed after picking me up.

I didn't even bother changing—I just went straight out to the balcony.

"Neighbor?" His voice came as soon as I closed the door. It was softer than usual.

"Hey." I smiled, matching his quiet tone. I guessed we were both aware of the thousands of sleeping people in close proximity. "You're still up."

"Yeah . . ." He didn't sound as happy as he usually did. Maybe it wasn't the late hour keeping his voice muted. "I've been sitting out here for hours. I'm kind of avoiding my dad—he's in a mood. I wanted to hear your voice."

That warm feeling in my chest intensified even as my brows drew together. His ocean-deep voice had dropped even further, hinting at tumultuous currents underneath.

I pushed aside the chair I usually sat in and lowered myself to the ground, leaning back against the wall. This was where he usually sat—they'd only just moved in, and I had a feeling there was no patio furniture on their balcony.

We were practically shoulder to shoulder, only the flimsy bamboo between us.

"Are you OK?" I asked.

Silence.

I pressed my hand against the bamboo.

After another beat of silence, I felt pressure against my palm, then, slowly, heat spread through the thin screen. He was pressing his hand against mine.

"What's your name?" he asked, his voice almost a whisper.

He'd ignored my question, but that was OK. Some questions were too hard to answer.

I chewed on my lip but didn't want to keep him waiting too long. Even though I hardly knew him, the urge not to disappoint this boy was strong.

"Mena," I said. I wasn't sure why I didn't tell him my full name. It wasn't that I didn't like it, but I was more myself with him than I'd ever been with a new person. The only people I could remotely consider friends called me Mena, and they were the only ones I could truly be myself with. I wanted to be myself with him.

"Mena," he repeated.

"What's yours?"

He didn't hesitate for a second. "Turner."

I opened my mouth to tell him we weren't strangers anymore, but the sound of his sliding door cut me off.

His hand disappeared, and I curled mine into a loose fist, as if trying to hold on to the warmth.

"Turner?" an older, gruffer voice said. "Who are you talking to?"

"No one." He shuffled away.

I tried not to feel hurt.

"I heard something," the older man—probably his dad—said.

"Maybe it was the neighbors."

The door opened, then closed, and he was gone.

I wrapped my arms around my legs and leaned my head back against the wall. Goose bumps rose on my arms in the chilly night air, but I couldn't seem to make myself move.

CHAPTER THREE

My feet sped up, trying to match the hammering rhythm of my heart. I had to take a deep breath and force myself to slow down. It was only a fifteen-minute walk to school, but at the rate I was going, I'd make it there in five. I wanted to spend *less* time there, not more. But my legs hadn't gotten the memo and kept trying to break into a sprint.

I didn't want to feel like this.

I growled and made myself stop, closed my eyes tight, and forced a long breath in through my nose and out through my mouth, gripping the straps of my backpack until my knuckles were as white as the stars swimming in my vision. After a few moments, I steeled my resolve and moved forward at a steady pace, trying to distract myself by counting the steps in my head.

The tail end of summer meant another perfectly sunny California morning, but I wished it was cloudy and cold so I could have an excuse to hide inside a hoodie all day. I hoped I would go unnoticed regardless, that it would be the silent treatment. Being ignored was much better than how the first day of junior year had gone down.

I tried to push the memory away, but it forced its way into my mind, as insistent as the hot sun on the back of my head.

First day of school had been hot last year as well. I'd fought to slow my steps then too, but there had been a hint of excitement, a tiny sliver of hope, driving the nervous energy that day.

I'd spent all summer—every moment I wasn't working or hanging out with the girls—learning how to do makeup. I'd watched countless hours of YouTube videos and spent half my pay on new products, brushes, pallets, and all kinds of things I hoped would make me more normal in the eyes of my peers. By the end of the summer, I'd gotten pretty good at it, even practicing on Donna, Harlow, and Amaya.

That day, I'd applied an understated look. My birthmark was covered, my lashes accentuated, my lips natural. I thought I looked pretty good.

I was a fool.

I should've known—in high school, the only thing worse than being different is making an active effort to change the thing that makes you different.

I'd walked into school with my head up, smiled, made eye contact; I even gave Jessica Miller a little wave as I stopped at my locker. Most people shot me surprised looks, not really knowing what to make of the new me. A few even reflexively smiled back.

By lunch, word had spread. No one had said anything to me, of course, but they'd all been talking behind my back. Oblivious, I went into the girls' bathroom off the science wing corridor.

I came out of the stall to find four girls leaning against walls and sinks, watching me with amused smiles. Madison and her friends.

I froze, like a gazelle that had just wandered into a circle of leopards.

"Been holding that all morning?" Steph chuckled, tilting her head. "Sounded like an elephant pissing in there."

"Or a man," Bonnie added, crossing her arms and leaning against the tiles next to the mirror. "Do you pee standing up like a man?"

"Her name *is* Phil." Steph giggled. It would've been a cute sound if they all weren't looking at me with promise in their gazes.

No, no, no, please no. It wasn't supposed to be like this. This year was supposed to be different.

I dropped my gaze to the stained beige tiles and walked to the sink, drawing my shoulders forward to make myself as small as possible. All I could do now was be quiet and hope I could get out of there fast.

"That's it, isn't it?" Steph giggled again. "We've been calling you Phil this whole time, but you really *are* a man, aren't you?"

"Those tits must've cost a fucking fortune, then." Kelsey spoke for the first time, her tone bored, her eyes on her phone. I was dying on the inside, and she was double tapping pics on Insta. *Bitch.* Her comment probably came from jealousy. She was super-model thin but flat chested, and I was comfortably filling out a D cup. Not that I'd ever say that to her out loud. It was easier to silently wait it out. They'd get bored eventually.

"Oh my god." Bonnie giggled, and the others all laughed with her. "Did you—"

"No," Madison cut her off. The laughter died. No one dared interrupt Madison. "She's not a man."

I shut the water off. Steph was blocking my access to the hand drier. I decided to just leave with my hands wet.

Each girl took a step closer to me, as if they'd practiced it, as if they instinctively knew I was about to bolt.

I froze again, tried to calm my breathing so my boobs would stop heaving. I didn't want any more attention on them.

Madison kept speaking. "Can't you see Philomena's turned into a woman? Look how beautifully she's done her makeup."

Her voice was so steady, earnest even, that my eyes snapped up in surprise. She gave me a warm smile, her own makeup impeccable. Her linen shorts and V-neck hung on her perfect frame as though they'd been made for her. She tilted her head slightly and took a strand of my hair, gently twirling it between her fingers. I'd gotten up half an hour early to put a slight wave in my usually dead-straight hair.

I cleared my throat. This had never happened before. I had no idea what to do. My instincts were screaming to get the fuck away from these monsters, but Madison was saying nice things with a perfectly straight face.

"Your hair is so soft," she whispered, twirling more of it around her manicured finger.

After an extended silence, I cleared my throat again and managed to croak, "Thanks?" It came out sounding like a question.

Madison gathered more of my hair into her hand, tangling her fingers in it, and a heavy dread settled in the pit of my stomach. Her fingers scraped my scalp, and she yanked, making me wince.

The others shifted—predators scenting blood.

Madison laughed. It started out as a light chuckle and quickly turned manic, her wild eyes inches from mine as she laughed literally in my face.

"Thanks?" she mimicked. "Fucking pathetic." She punctuated her words with another yank. I cried out and instinctively reached up to wrap my hands around her wrist.

The others moved, pulling my hands behind my back.

Tears stung my eyes.

"You're not a man, Phil." Madison shook her head, her eyes narrowed. "But you're not a woman either. You're fucking *nothing*. And we can't have you walking around, *lying*, pretending to be *something*. You think covering up that hideous thing on your face makes you better? You're a fucking joke. And we can't have anyone forgetting that, can we?"

No one said anything. My labored breathing echoed off the old, chipped tiles. The side of my head where Madison was still pulling on my hair stung like a bitch, and my neck was starting to hurt from the odd angle. A tear slid down my cheek.

"Can we?!" Madison shouted into my face.

"No." I closed my eyes—the next best thing when I couldn't move my head to lower them.

"Good." She released my hair and patted my head as if I were a dog.

My eyes flew open as the bitches holding me pushed me against the sinks.

Madison walked to the back of the bathroom slowly, calmly. She gripped the handle of a mop that had been left in a bucket in the corner and turned back to face us. What idiot of a janitor had left that out? Bonnie giggled again, as if someone had handed her a puppy. Kelsey took a break from her scrolling to snap a picture as Madison raised the mop out of the bucket.

It splatted on the tiles. She dragged the sodden thing across the bathroom.

"No. Please." I started to struggle, but I had no chance. There were four of them, two of them holding me down. The edge of the sink dug into my lower back as my shoulders pushed against the mirror. "I'll take it off. Just let me go, and I'll take it off right now. Please, Madison, *please*, don't do this."

She stopped in front of me and flipped the mop so the shaggy, dripping head was level with my face. The abrasive smell of bleach hit the back of my throat.

I sobbed, pleading with them to stop, to let me go, but it was pointless.

They held me down as Madison shoved the mop into my face. I coughed and spluttered, the bleach making it hard to breathe, making my eyes water and sting. She roughly wiped at my face with the scratchy, disgusting strings until she was satisfied the makeup had been removed.

The mop clattered to the ground moments before they released me, and I collapsed next to it, sobbing, pushing away from them. But I had nowhere to go; the sinks were already at my back.

On their way out, someone dumped the rest of the filthy gray water over my head.

I gasped and spluttered again, the smell making me gag.

The door closed behind them, and I was alone once again.

I refused to look at myself in the mirror when I finally gathered the strength to pick myself up off the floor. I just wrung out my ruined hair and washed up with clean water, splashing it onto my face over and over.

As I turned the tap off, the door opened again. I flinched and turned to face it, chastising myself for stupidly not getting the fuck out of there before they came back.

But it wasn't them. Jessica Miller stopped in her tracks, her eyes widening as they took in my appearance, the mop and bucket, the water all over the ground.

She'd smiled back that morning, but now the status quo had been reestablished. She lowered her head, turned around, and walked back out of the bathroom without saying anything.

In some ways, that hurt even more than what those bitches had done to me.

I knew in that moment that nothing would ever change. Not until I left.

Last year, I'd had hope that if I tried hard enough, I could fit in, make people forget why they hated me.

This year, I'd given up.

With a heavy heart, I rounded the corner, and Devilbend North High School came into view—patchy dry grass and cracked pavement framing the low brown building with bars over the windows.

I arrived with just enough time to go to my locker and get to my first class. Keeping my head down, my hair draped over the birthmarked side of my face, I sat off to the side about halfway back—not in the back with the assholes who thought they were cool and rebellious, and not in the front with the kids who were constantly called on to answer questions. I didn't speak to anyone or look at anyone who wasn't a teacher. I did my best to remain invisible, and I managed to get to lunch unnoticed and unscathed.

"Hi, Phil." Madison's voice was so close I almost flinched, but I somehow managed to calmly put my books away and close my locker, revealing her pretty, made-up face as she leaned on the lockers next to mine. Kelsey was behind her, on her phone; the others milled about nearby, mostly ignoring me.

I turned to leave, but Steph and Bonnie blocked my path. Clearly they were paying more attention than I thought. I sighed and waited. The corridor was packed. They weren't above doing something mean to me in front of other people, but even they weren't stupid enough to pull a stunt as bad as the bathroom incident when teachers were close by.

"Where are you going? I'm just trying to say hi." Madison stepped around her friends to stand in front of me.

I kept my gaze on her purple kicks and said nothing.

After an extended silence, she leaned in and spoke low, close to my ear. "How was your summer?"

I kept my mouth shut. There was no right answer. If I replied, it would be thrown back in my face. If I tried to defend myself and was as much of a bitch to her as she was to *literally everyone else* . . . I shuddered to think.

"Nothing to say?" Madison tapped her foot as I remained still. "Good. We don't want a repeat of last year, do we? That bleach really fucked with my nails."

With a snicker, she led her sheep away, and I walked off in the opposite direction. At least we agreed on one thing—I didn't want a repeat of last year either.

I spent lunch in a back corner of the library. Food wasn't technically allowed in there, but if I was quiet enough between the bookshelves, no one noticed. I ate my sandwich as I scrolled through my Instagram feed, which was mostly filled with makeup pics and baby animals. I followed every person doing makeup I could find, but I never posted anything, and I had no followers. I was a lurker, too scared to post any of the hundreds of pics of my own makeup I had hidden on my phone.

Despite the horrible thing Madison and her friends had done to me, I hadn't abandoned my makeup hobby. There was something cathartic about focusing on a single task and being able to see the finished product—about pretending to be someone else for the few minutes before I wiped it all off again.

On my way out of the library, I heard that confident tone, the ocean-deep quality that wrapped around the smooth timbre of his words. For the first time that day, I lifted my head and looked for the guy I'd spent hours talking to on my balcony. The hallway was packed with students making their way to class, and I couldn't see him anywhere.

Then I rolled my eyes and remembered I had no idea what he looked like.

It was just my pathetic heart hoping against hope that I might have something positive at school for a change. I didn't even know if he went to school. He was probably older and way out of my league.

I dropped my gaze again and wished for a hoodie for the millionth time that day.

As I settled into my seat for my last class, I heard it again.

I was just reaching into my bag to grab my English textbook when that voice made me pause, hunched over, my hand tightening around the book's spine.

"Yeah, we moved to Devilbend last week," he said. There was no mistaking it this time. It was definitely Turner, and he was definitely walking right past my desk.

"Yeah, nice."

I clenched my teeth. *Jayden.* The only person who made my life hell as much as Madison.

"You gonna try out for the team?" Jayden asked.

"Which team?"

The two chairs in front of me scraped, and they sat down. I straightened and placed the book gently in front of me, keeping my eyes on the desk but straining to listen.

"Oh, yeah." Jayden laughed. "The football team."

"Yeah, I'll think about it." Turner sounded friendly, pleasant, like any guy having a normal conversation with a new person.

I chewed my lip to hold in the sigh, fighting to keep the scowl off my face.

Mr. Chen came in, demanding the class's attention, and Turner and Jayden stopped talking. When I was certain everyone's focus was on the front of the room, I slowly raised my eyes.

My heart thudded in my chest. He sat directly in front of me, Jayden on his left. There were those broad shoulders I'd seen only in silhouette, the white cotton of a collared T-shirt stretched over them. He had dark blond hair, cropped short at the base of his neck but wavy and growing just past his ears on the sides. He needed a haircut.

He reached up to scratch the back of his neck, and I nearly jumped as I looked away. But not before I noticed how long and strong his fingers looked, his nails square, the muscles in his arms flexing from the movement.

I made sure to look only directly at my desk and the teacher for the rest of the class, as I usually did. All I needed was for someone to notice me staring at the new guy.

It was lucky it was only the first day and we spent most of the class going over the syllabus, because I hardly heard a word Mr. Chen said.

I was in so much trouble.

CHAPTER FOUR

I went straight to the balcony after school, but he never showed up. It was probably for the best—I had no idea what to say. I just had an irresistible urge to speak to him.

I couldn't do it at school though—they'd find a way to ruin it. Of course, once he realized who I was, what I looked like, the flirting would stop, but I wanted to at least stay friends. That meant ignoring the fuck out of him at school and staying out of his way.

I still caught glimpses though. Anytime I heard his voice in the halls, I couldn't help looking up. He was friendly, talkative; I saw him chatting to several seniors and even a few juniors, but I never hung around long enough to hear the conversations.

He didn't come to the balcony for several nights, and I started to think maybe he'd already realized who I was. But that wasn't possible.

I was so determined to avoid him at school I didn't get a proper look at his face until my shift at the diner on Wednesday night.

He came in with his dad—a taller, frownier version of Turner with gray hair at his temples. They sat in a booth, thankfully not in my section.

Chelsea took their order while I stared at the beautiful boy so clearly out of my league. He had that defined jaw—not square exactly, but strong—and a heavy brow. Gone was the smiling, open guy who talked to everyone at school. This Turner matched his dad's posture, leaning forward on the table with his shoulders hunched, his brow furrowed. I couldn't even tell what color his eyes were.

As soon as Chelsea walked away, they leaned back into each other, but not before Turner cast those dark eyes about the diner, as if checking for anyone listening in, or maybe looking for someone.

I turned away to clear a table.

"Philly, can you pour table three's coffees for me?" Chelsea caught me just as I unloaded a tray of dirty dishes. "I'm busting for the toilet."

She ran off without waiting for a response.

Shit. I picked up the coffee pot and swallowed around the ball of anxiety lodged in my throat. My gaze stayed on the ground as I approached their table.

". . . you sure?" Turner's dad's voice was as deep and gruff as it had been on the balcony the other night.

"Yeah, Dad. But it hasn't even been a week. I'm still learning the layout—" Turner cut himself off as I poured the coffee. He glanced up at me, my every nerve aware of him in my periphery as I hoped like hell my hand wouldn't shake and spill coffee all over them.

"Thank you, miss." His dad gave me a small smile. I smiled back and nodded, the effort not to look at Turner directly almost crushing.

Then I walked away and avoided Chelsea until they left.

On Friday night, I walked out onto the balcony hardly even expecting him to be there. Maybe the feet smell had come back and they'd moved.

"Hello?"

His voice made me jump, my hand flying to my chest. "Fuck. You scared the crap out of me."

He chuckled. "Hey, neighbor."

I drew my cardigan closer, hunching against the light breeze, and smiled. "Hey, stranger."

"How was work?"

"How'd you know I was at work?" Had he seen me? Maybe heard me talking to another customer? Fuck!

"Uh . . . lucky guess? It's late and . . . I swear I'm not an axe murderer, Mena."

Oh god—my name on his lips, uttered so casually and confidently. I wanted him to end every sentence he spoke to me with my name.

"No, you're just a stalker, Turner."

He laughed lightly and shifted, knocking the bamboo screen. It was getting a little cold, but I moved the chair out of the way and sat next to him, against the wall.

"So? How was work?" he asked again. His light was off, and I couldn't even see his silhouette. I reached up and flicked my light off too. For some reason, it felt easier to say what I wanted to say in the dark.

"Work was fine. Same old." I chewed on my bottom lip and blurted it before I chickened out. "How was school? It can be hard being the new kid, but I have a feeling you're handling it just fine."

There was a beat of silence. My heart hammered in my chest, my throat, my whole damn body.

"Now who's the stalker?" He sounded amused, if a little wary.

"It's not stalking if I have a legitimate reason to be there."

"So, you go to Devilbend North High? What year are you in? Shit! Are you a teacher? I mean, not that it matters—to me. I wouldn't care. Although that would be technically illegal, I guess. But I am eighteen, if that makes any difference." As abruptly as he'd launched into his rambling, he cut himself off.

My head swam a little, even as the grin spread over my lips.

He cleared his throat. "Did I just make shit really awkward?"

"What would technically be illegal, Turner?" I wasn't sure why I was making this conversation even *more* awkward for him. Maybe I liked seeing a hint of him being just as nervous about this as me—at least in this moment. He was so damn confident and self-assured the rest of the time.

He took a deep breath—he was so close, just on the other side of the screen. "It's illegal for a teacher to have a relationship with a student, isn't it?"

"Is that what this is?"

"Maybe it's what it could be. Maybe it's what I'd like it to be."

So fucking confident. So *not* what I was or ever would be. My smile drained away along with any excitement I'd had about this conversation, leeching out of me and into the cold concrete under my ass. "You don't even know me."

"I know enough that I want to know more. Can I see you?" The bamboo screen shifted, his perfect fingers gripping the edge.

"No!" I shot my hand out and covered his, keeping the screen in place.

"Why?"

"I . . . I can't . . . you don't . . . I'm just not ready, OK?"

"I don't understand. Mena, are you OK? I was joking before, but are you actually a teacher at my school?"

"No. I'm a student."

The relief was palpable in his sigh. He released his grip on the screen only to push farther past it and take my hand.

As his perfect, warm fingers tangled with mine, he asked, "Mena, what's this about? Why don't you want me to know who you are?"

Because you'll stop talking to me. "It's complicated. I just want you to know me —the real me—before you know who I am."

After a beat of silence, we both chuckled.

"Yeah, that made more sense in my head than it did coming out of my mouth," I said, glad that some of the heavy tension had lifted. "Look, this is all pretty new, and I like you . . ."

I took a deep breath, hardly believing I'd been that honest with a boy about how I felt.

He jumped in before I could keep speaking. "I like you too. A lot."

I squeezed his hand, running my thumb up and down his, taking a moment to get my shit together while I jumped around and screamed on the inside like a fangirl at a BTS concert. "Enough to be patient with me? I know this is weird. I just . . . I think it could be kind of fun?"

"Easy for you to say. You're not the one being stalked by someone who's probably in the CIA."

I laughed. "I think you mean the FBI. The CIA isn't supposed to operate on home soil."

"Why do you know that? The evidence is mounting."

"A friend of mine said it a while back, and it just kind of stuck." Harlow spent so much time on the internet I wasn't entirely sure when she slept, but she was full of random-ass facts.

"Oh? And what—" A low thrumming noise cut Turner off. His hand tensed around mine as all the lights went out. "What the fuck?"

"Chill. The electricity just went out. Happens about once a month on this side of town—sometimes more often in the summer. The grid is old and unreliable. It'll be back up in ten minutes."

"Seriously? What a pain in the ass."

"You get used to it."

The sun had gone down an hour ago, and the night was overcast. Without the glow of the moon, it was pretty much pitch black. And I had at least five minutes before the lights came back on.

I extracted my hand from Turner's and got to my feet.

"Wait, Mena—"

"Shh!" With the electricity out, there was no background noise either. My parents were asleep, but we had to be extra quiet, just in case. "Stand up."

"Did you just shush me?" he whispered, sounding amused, but he shuffled and did as I asked.

I gripped the edge of the bamboo screen and unhooked it from the nails holding it to the wall. When I rolled it aside, there was nothing between us but the metal railing separating his side of the balcony from mine.

My eyes were adjusting to the heavy darkness, and I could just make out his silhouette. I reached out and tentatively placed my hand on his arm. It was ridiculously hard, like warm rocks under his skin.

He responded to my touch immediately, reaching out and placing his hands on my waist.

"Oh, hey, neighbor," he whispered, leaning in.

"Hey, stranger," I whispered back, moving my arms up to his shoulders. Why was every part of him so damn solid? And why did I want to run my hands over every inch of it? And why was being so close to him making a heavy, pressured feeling appear low in my belly? "I know we can't technically see each other, but I hope this makes up for it a bit."

His hands flexed, and we leaned into each other more.

"Yeah, this makes up for it." His breath fanned over my face. He was so close I could almost make out the lines of his jaw, his straight nose. But none of the details. And if I couldn't see the color of his eyes, I was pretty positive he couldn't see my birthmark.

My boobs pressed against his hard chest, and my breath hitched. He smelled like fresh rain and something warm and comforting—amber, maybe.

"Fuck, you smell good." *Zero filter*. I closed my eyes and cringed, but he just pulled me closer, his hands moving to my back, the railing digging into my hips. I hated that damn railing.

"You *feel* good. Can I kiss you?"

"Please . . ." I didn't even have time to consider how desperate I sounded. The word was barely out of my mouth before he closed the miniscule distance between our lips and kissed me firmly.

He sighed and moved his lips against mine in a determined but gentle way. His body was hard and lean, but his lips were pillow soft.

It didn't take long for the kiss to intensify. I don't know if he darted his tongue out or if I sucked on his bottom lip first, but then our tongues were involved, and little gasping breaths were coming out of my throat.

The thrum of the transformer on the corner snapped me out of the moment, adrenaline coursing through my veins as surely as the electricity was rushing through the wires. I knew that sound—I had about five seconds before the lights turned back on.

"Fuck." I pulled away abruptly, and he grunted, his body following mine, his hands gripping my clothing.

"Shit. Sorry." He let go immediately, and I shoved his shoulders until he was safely on his side of the balcony. I yanked the bamboo screen across just as the streetlights below once again bathed the world in artificial light.

I chuckled through shaky breaths, the exhilaration of having kissed Turner, then gotten away with what I'd just pulled, still igniting my every nerve. "That was . . ."

"Yeah . . ." he breathed. "Are you sure you don't work for the CIA? That was a little too perfectly timed."

"FBI, remember? And I never denied it."

He laughed, his voice lower, huskier—it sent desire shooting through my body again. I wanted to feel his lips against mine as he made that sound; I wanted to feel it reverberate through his chest. I clenched my thighs, suddenly aware of the moisture in my underwear.

I had to get out of there before I broke down and did something stupid—like show him my face. "I have to get to bed."

"Wait." The urgency in his voice pulled me up short. He shuffled around for a moment, then shoved his hand through the narrow gap between the bamboo and the wall, his phone clutched in his perfect fingers. Fingers that had been digging into my back moments ago, holding me against him as he . . .

I shook my head. *Focus, Philomena!*

His screen displayed the keypad.

"You want my number?" I asked. "How . . . old school."

"I mean, I'm happy to connect on Insta or Snap or Twitter, or even Facebook, but you're determined to maintain your secret spy identity, and I'd like to talk to you outside of this balcony from time to time, so . . ." He wiggled the phone at me.

I took it and entered my number, saving it under "Neighbor." "Good night, Turner."

"Sweet dreams, Mena."

Naturally, I didn't sleep a wink that night. I'd never experienced such a high. Sure, I'd kissed a few guys before at some of Amaya's parties—I'd even liked one enough to get to second base with him in her pool house—but I'd never stayed up all night replaying every single thing a boy had said to me. Not to mention the kissing—*oh god*, the kissing!

Every time I thought about it, I either grinned or bit my lip to keep from making a frustrated/excited sound.

The pressure between my legs didn't abate—if anything, it intensified to a constant dull throb. I rolled onto my front and pressed my face into my pillow, dragging my hand down my body and between my legs as I imagined Turner's perfect, strong fingers pushing my panties aside. I was so worked up it didn't take long before I panted my release into my pillow, biting it to keep silent.

Only after that was I finally able to sleep.

The Turner-induced euphoria lasted well into the next day. It was harder than usual to keep my head down and avoid contact with everyone when all I wanted was to spread my arms wide and shout to the whole world how amazing he made me feel. I had to bite the inside of my cheek to keep myself from grinning when I passed him in the hall on the way to second period.

I was putting my books away in my locker at lunch, smiling as I thought of how his lips had felt against mine, when my locker door slammed shut. I flinched back, only narrowly avoiding getting my arm or head smacked by the metal.

My smile fell, all thoughts of Turner replaced by fear.

"What the fuck could you possibly have to smile about?" Jayden leaned against the locker next to mine, frowning as though he were doing long division without a calculator.

Jayden was Madison's boyfriend—as if that wasn't the most predictable fucking high school scenario. The mean girl dated the dumb jock, and they liked to make other people's lives miserable so they could feel better about themselves. *Groan.*

Jayden had started at DNHS the same day I had. We could've been friends—comrades in being the new kids at school. Madison had been a bitch to me from day one, making lame jokes about my birthmark that half the class laughed along with. Jayden had actually treated me like a human being for a few days. We had lunch together, shared awkward fourteen-year-old chitchat. Then one day I saw Madison and her friends talking to him at lunch. Then he tried out for the football team. Then he ignored me for a solid week. When he sat down next to me at lunch the following Monday, I was happy, excited to have my friend back.

"How was your weekend?" he'd asked.

I smiled and started to tell him, but he cut me off before I could get one word out. "Oh wait!" He half turned in his seat, and that's when I realized Madison and her friends were watching us, tittering on the sidelines. "I just remembered—I don't give a shit."

They all burst into laughter. Jayden's eyes flicked between what I'm sure was the devastated look in my eyes and the popular kids howling like hyenas. I guess that was his initiation—publicly making me feel like shit.

After that, Jayden and I settled into a new routine. I avoided him as much as all the other assholes, and he pretended I didn't exist in the most obnoxious and oxymoronic way possible. He routinely bumped into me and loudly said, "What was that? There's clearly nothing there, but I just tripped." Or he looked right through me and took a deep inhale, then said another moronic thing like "Do you guys smell that? I don't see anything, but something smells like *loser*." Naturally, everyone laughed at his brilliant jokes.

He'd spoken directly to me only a handful of times—incidents I wished I could forget.

I fought to keep my breathing under control, focusing on a spot at the bottom edge of my locker where a bit of the bluish-gray paint had chipped off. Hoping he'd just go away.

He leaned in, his face close to my cheek, and said in a light, conversational tone, "I asked you a fucking question, Phil."

"Nothing," I replied as calmly as I could. *I* wasn't allowed to ignore *them*.

"That's right—you're nothing. You may as well not exist."

Then why are you talking to me, idiot? I so wished I was brave enough to say some of the things that went through my head.

Lucky for me, Jayden was easily distracted.

"Hey, new guy!" He turned away, relegating me back to phantom status.

"Hey, man."

Turner. I lifted my gaze toward the voice before I even knew what I was doing.

For one glorious, torturous moment, our eyes met. In a world where I was invisible, he looked directly at me and he saw me, a slight frown marring his strong brow. He'd saved me from whatever fucked-up thing Jayden had planned without even knowing it.

I looked away quickly as Jayden slung his arm over Turner's shoulders and led him away, leaning in to speak to him.

I grabbed my bag and beelined for the picnic table at the back of the science building. It was in a dingy spot, and one of the benches was split, but no one ever went there. I sat down heavily and dropped my head on my arms, unable to eat the sandwich I'd made myself that morning.

The churning in my empty stomach persisted until school let out. As I trailed into the hot afternoon sun along with the other students, I once again spotted Turner. My heart stuttered, and I couldn't help slowing down. He looked so beautiful, his messy hair shining like gold in the sun, his broad shoulders relaxed, his brilliant smile wide.

But who was he smiling at? I frowned as Jayden thumped him on the back and Turner extended one hand.

The man standing with them was a little shorter than Jayden, but he had the same build, the same dark brown hair, the same olive complexion. His gray suit stretched over his back as he reached out to shake Turner's hand.

Why was Turner shaking hands with Jayden's dad? Why was the older man even here?

I couldn't hear what they were saying, but it looked harmless enough. Except I knew how rotten Jayden was deep down. Could the rancid apple really have fallen that far from the tree?

Before I could move closer to listen in, Jayden happened to look over and spot me. His already tight smile fell into a frown, the look one of pure derision, and I realized I was blatantly staring.

I dropped my head and rushed in the opposite direction of home, resigned to taking the long way back—just in case Turner saw me and got suspicious.

I had to be more careful. Meeting Turner was the best thing that had happened to me in a long time—I couldn't risk any of the assholes at school finding out and ruining it.

CHAPTER FIVE

There were about ten minutes left until lunch ended, and I resisted the urge to text Turner. We'd exchanged numbers a week ago, but I was keeping the texting strictly to outside of school. God forbid anyone notice me interacting with another human being. We talked every night though, if not on the balcony then on the phone.

He kept asking when he could see me again, and I kept deflecting with coyness and jokes about keeping the mystery alive, but I knew this would have to come to a head eventually. He'd probably lose interest before I got up the courage to show him who I really was.

I sighed and drew my knees up, leaning my head on the row of encyclopedias as I opened Instagram to distract myself. I was studying a makeup look with a watercolor effect on the eyes, wondering which products the artist had used, when I heard my name.

"Mena, Mena, Mena." It was barely a whisper, but it was definitely Turner's voice. How the fuck had he figured out who I was?

Eyes wide, I looked around, but all I could see were the rows of books on the shelves to either side of me and a cart at the end of the row I was hiding out in.

Fuck, was I starting to hallucinate?

"Middle name?" he mumbled, sounding more confused. His voice was coming from my right.

Slowly, as soundlessly as possible, I lifted onto my knees and peered through the narrow, uneven gap in the books.

He was standing on the other side; my eyes were about level with the top button of his jeans. Twisting my head, I could just see the bottom of last year's yearbook as he slowly turned the pages and cursed under his breath.

I covered my mouth to hold back my laughter. He was trying to figure out who I was, sweet, infuriating boy.

Balancing the yearbook on one hand, he reached the other above his head and leaned on the bookshelf. His T-shirt rode up, revealing his hips, the toned muscles in his lower abdomen, the trail of light hair disappearing into the top of his jeans. I had an urge to shove all the books out of the way so I could run my hands through that hair, maybe lick one of the hipbones peeking out next to it.

"Hey, bro!" Jayden's voice was like a bucket of icy water poured over my head. I recoiled and barely caught myself before I smacked into the opposite bookshelf.

"Hey, Jayden." Turner sounded friendly, but I knew his voice—there was a hint of annoyance there too.

"What the fuck are you doing in the library?" Jayden laughed, as though the very existence of libraries was preposterous. I allowed myself an eye roll.

"Some of us know how to read." Turner's voice was light, as if he was laughing *with* Jayden and not *at* him. I still wanted to kiss him for the dig at that asshole's intelligence.

"Fuck you, asshole." Jayden laughed, not sounding the least bit offended. "Come on, I've been looking for you. Coach wants to talk to you."

I heard the yearbook getting shoved back into place, and then they started to walk away. I frowned. Turner hadn't mentioned anything to me about who he was making friends with at school, but if he started hanging out with them, that would really fucking suck. Couldn't he see how fake and mean they were? I wasn't the only student at DNHS whose life was made miserable because of those dicks.

I was just the only one who wasn't allowed to make friends with other misfits —because I didn't exist or matter, as they liked to remind everyone.

I sat back on my heels and tried to quell the panic. Maybe if I came clean now, told him who I was and how they treated me . . . but what if he thought I was pathetic and stopped talking to me? What if he already knew and was just in on some elaborate prank?

I squeezed my eyes shut and tried to push that last thought out of my mind— it was too painful.

"Hey, pipsqueak." Jayden's voice sounded farther away, but it still made me open my eyes, my body primed to go on the alert at any sign of him. "Dad's picking you up after school, so don't waste time after the last bell, all right?"

A small voice murmured in response, and then the sound of the library doors opening and closing announced that they'd left.

A moment later, a skinny girl rounded the corner. She saw me sitting on the ground and froze, clutching her open bag to her chest. She was clearly a fresh-man. She had that deer-in-the-headlights look that starting high school put in everyone's eyes. Her dark blonde hair was cut short, and she had knobby knees under her cute blue shorts. When she grew out of this awkward stage, she'd be gorgeous. And since she was Jayden's sister, she'd probably be a total bitch too.

Jayden had never mentioned having a sister, but we were friends for only a grand total of three days, and I'd been avoiding him like the plague ever since.

"Did you drop something?" her soft voice asked, even as she averted her gaze.

"Huh?" I frowned, then remembered I was sitting on the ground. "Oh, yeah, kind of." My dignity. My sanity. My sense of self-preservation.

I shoved my phone and the remnants of my lunch into my bag, rose up onto my knees, but paused before I fully got to my feet.

The girl had buried her chin in her chest, and her eyes were watering, seconds away from spilling fat tears down her innocent cheeks.

"Hey, what's wrong?" I shuffled forward, the worn carpet scratchy against my bare knees.

She shook her head. "Nothing."

I took a chance and placed a gentle hand on her shoulder. She jumped slightly at the contact but didn't shrug me off. "Doesn't look like nothing."

She took a lightning-quick glance at me. Whatever she saw must've been enough to crack her defenses just a little more.

"It's just . . ." She breathed hard, and the tears spilled over. "It's just overwhelming. I feel like I'm drowning, and I don't know what to do."

I sighed. I didn't want to feel anything for anyone even remotely related to Jayden, but she was so vulnerable, so broken. "I get it. Starting high school can be hella scary. Everyone feels like this from time to time, OK? Even if they don't show it. It does get better."

It hadn't gotten better for me. It got worse. But she didn't need to hear that. She just needed someone to tell her it would be OK.

She bit her lip. If anything, she looked sadder, but her tears were drying up.

"What's your name?" I asked, rubbing her shoulder lightly.

"Jenny," she mumbled, her voice a little steadier.

"Hang in there, Jenny." I gave her a reassuring smile. "You can do this."

She met my eyes. She didn't smile back, but she did give a little nod.

The bell rang, and her eyes widened. "I can't be late."

She zipped up her bag, swung it onto her back, and turned to rush away.

I grabbed my own bag and got to my feet just in time for her to turn back and wrap her gangly arms around my waist.

"Thank you," she mumbled into my T-shirt, then ran off before I even had a chance to hug her back.

I saw her again at the end of the day, along with another, unfortunately familiar, face. I didn't know what it was about Jayden's dad—I hadn't even met him—but I'd taken an immediate dislike to him, probably because he was related to Jayden. Or maybe I was just jealous that he could stand in front of the school and shake hands with Turner in front of everyone, while I had to keep my very identity secret from the boy I liked.

As I made my way through the parking lot, I watched him out of the corner of my eye. He was leaning against his car and reading something on his phone when Jenny walked up. She reached for the car door, but he stopped her so he could grab something off the front seat. Bending at the waist until they were at eye level, he pulled a cupcake out of a paper bag and held it out with a big smile.

She was facing away from me, so I didn't see the happiness the sugary treat surely brought to her face.

Maybe I'd misjudged Mr. Burrows after all.

When was the last time my parents got me a cupcake for no reason, let alone picked me up from school? I had to walk even when it was pouring down rain. It wasn't their fault—they both worked hard—but still, it wasn't fair.

Jayden bumped my shoulder, nearly making me drop my bag, as he barrelled past me toward his family.

I turned and hastened away, both happy the sad little girl was having her day brightened and bitter that an asshole like Jayden had anything positive in his life. Why shouldn't he suffer the same way he made me suffer every day?

After school, I needed to focus on something other than Turner, so I got my makeup out with the intention of trying to re-create that watercolor look I'd seen on Instagram. I quickly realized I didn't have the right kind of eyeshadow and decided to do a dramatic vintage look with killer winged eyeliner instead.

It had been a dramatic day, so it was only fitting.

With a full face of makeup, I spread my books out on my bed and started on my homework. I worked on an English essay, then reluctantly moved on to a Statistics worksheet.

Halfway through my fourth question—and about fifty percent sure the previous three were wrong anyway—the sound of the front door opening provided the perfect excuse to stop.

I stretched my arms over my head and walked into the kitchen to find my mom depositing several grocery bags on the counter.

"Hey, Mom. Is Dad working late?" They both picked up overtime whenever it was offered. That usually resulted in takeout for dinner—my parents liked to cook together as they talked about their day. I used to sit at the dining table and do my homework, or when I was little, they'd give me something nonessential to the meal to chop.

"Yeah." She smiled at me, then paused. "Oh my god, Philomena, you look stunning! When did you grow up?"

She stroked a lock of hair hanging over my shoulder as she inspected my makeup.

"Thanks, Mom." She was so busy, so overworked and tired, it was rare for us to talk like this.

"I'm making pulled pork tacos for dinner. Wanna help?"

I shot her a skeptical look. She was full of energy and in a suspiciously good mood, but it was nice, so I chose not to question it. "Fine. But only because you buttered me up with your compliments."

"Great! Can you unload while I freshen up? Thanks!" She didn't wait for a response before disappearing into the bathroom.

"Child labor . . ." I grumbled as I started putting things away.

She came back in a pair of my sweats, her hair up in a messy bun and her contacts replaced with glasses. We were the same size, but my mom was a little shorter.

Mom chatted about her work, the gossip she'd heard from the ladies she had coffee with every Saturday afternoon, and the movie she'd fallen asleep during the other night. She asked a few questions about school and my friends, but I'd perfected dodging those questions a long time ago. Instead I told her about the math homework I was struggling with and the few things I did with my cousins and Amaya.

My parents had enough on their plate without worrying about me. What would be the point in telling them I didn't have any friends at school? They couldn't afford to send me to Fulton Academy, and there were no other public schools I could get to in under an hour on public transport. I was better off gritting my teeth and getting through it. Not counting days off, I had only 174 days of school to go. I was on the home stretch.

"You know what we haven't done in a long time?" Mom said as we laid everything out on the table. "A girls' day with your aunt Emily and your cousins."

I smiled. "Yeah, we should definitely organize that."

When we moved back to Devilbend, my mom and her sister had started organizing girls' days for us. My mom hadn't really kept in touch with my aunt before we moved back—I wasn't sure why—but Auntie Em seemed really happy to have us living so close. She invited us over all the time and had encouraged us girls to become friends.

We'd go to parks and have picnics, go for hikes, or even take the hour-and-a-half drive into San Francisco and spend the day there—although my mom didn't like that too much; it was expensive. I didn't see what the issue was when my aunt was happy to pay for everything.

"That smells amazing." My dad toed his shoes off at the door, back just in time for dinner.

"Gross!" I gagged as my mom gave him a big hug and kiss.

We sat at the dining table to eat for the first time in weeks, and the TV even stayed off. Dad was exhausted, but Mom was in the best mood I'd seen her in for a long time. I figured it had something to do with a class she kept rambling on about. It was run by BestLyf—I knew nothing about them other than that they had a tall building in downtown Devilbend and employed a lot of people from the nicer side of town—and Mom had attended her first session over the weekend. It sounded like self-help bullshit and was likely to go the route of the yoga class she'd taken at the community center, or the pottery class she'd taken with Auntie Em, or the stack of adult coloring books she'd brought home one time. None of those things had lasted, but they'd each given her a brief period of excited energy.

When I went back to my room, my math homework was still sitting on my bed, mocking me in all its half-finished glory. I sent Turner a text whining about it and then packed up all the books, deciding to get up early and finish it tomorrow.

After sending the girls a pic of my makeup, I headed to the bathroom to wash it all off and get ready for bed.

I got a little pang of excitement when I returned to see my phone flashing with notifications. I didn't get a lot of messages. Usually it was Mom or Dad telling me they were working late or asking me to do a chore.

I turned the light off, got into bed, propped my phone on my pillow, and settled in for some scrolling before trying to sleep.

The messages were from the girls, gushing about how good I looked and how flawless my makeup was. Amaya begged me to post them on Instagram every single time I sent a pic, and tonight was no different.

In between chatting with them, I scrolled Instagram, obsessing over makeup that was way better than what I could do and trying to ignore the fact that Turner still hadn't replied.

Under a pic of some artfully arranged makeup brushes, there was a post from the "DNHS Confessions Page."

"The new guy—Turner—is fucking hot!"

Usually I scrolled past, trying not to read what they said, but Turner's name caught my attention. Like a masochist, I tapped on the page and scrolled through the recent confessions. No one knew who ran the page, but the description read, "Send us your Devilbend North High tea, and we'll spill it for you! Oops!" Students sent in anonymous comments, gossip, and bitchy things, and the page posted them all, unedited. I had a feeling Kelsey ran it. Something like that would require someone mean-hearted to keep it going, and that bitch was always on her phone.

There were several posts about how hot Turner was and what people wanted to do to him. There were common ones like "Anna cheated on the science quiz" or "Meg and Josh were making out in the back of the admin building even though Josh has a girlfriend." The juicy gossip was interspersed with just plain *mean* comments. At least one per day was about me. "Phil looks particularly fat today," "Is that thing on her face contagious?" and so on. It was a running joke for people to then comment with some variation of "Who? What are you talking about?"

I growled and locked the screen, dropping the phone on the bed beside me and rolling onto my back.

Why was I reading that shit? Why was I doing that to myself?

Those people weren't my friends. I didn't like them, and they definitely didn't like me. But it still hurt to read comment after comment about how fucking worthless I was as a human being.

I'd tried to switch off from it completely once. I deactivated my accounts and embraced being as invisible as they all liked to joke I was. It was bliss . . . for about two days. Then I opened my locker at school, and a sea of paper came flying out. Hundreds of printouts of posts, comments, and taunts I'd avoided while offline smacked me in the face, quite literally.

"We saw you deactivated your accounts, and we didn't want you to miss anything important," Kelsey had said, a self-satisfied smile on her face.

"Can't believe you're going to keep killing trees when you can read all this online. Don't you know we're in a climate crisis?" Madison's threat had been clear—get back online or keep receiving printouts.

Defeated, I cleaned up the mess before one of them reported it to a teacher and got me in trouble. Then I reactivated my accounts. What else could I do?

And if I really thought about it, I'd missed the makeup accounts I followed, not to mention talking to the only people my age who didn't treat me like shit— the girls.

My phone vibrated next to my thigh, and I picked it up reflexively, my heart kicking up a notch, as it did every time. I never knew if the notification would bring a mundane message from one of my parents or an anonymous suggestion I end my own life.

It was Turner.

Turner: Sorry I didn't reply sooner. It's been a crazy day. I had to help my dad with some-thing. Did you get the math homework done?

I smiled and responded immediately, not even caring if that looked as if I'd been up just staring at my phone, waiting for him to message me. I was so happy to hear from him.

CHAPTER SIX

I poured salt into the shaker and passed it to Chelsea. She screwed the top on while I did the next one, both of us taking our time, leaning on the end of the counter.

Barry, the cook, was out back having a break, and Leah had taken the night off. Tuesday nights were always quiet, so a good part of my shift was spent refilling the salt, pepper, and sugar shakers and restocking the takeaway cups, along with general cleaning and tidying. And of course, gossiping with Chelsea. Or rather she'd gossip, talking a million miles an hour, while I dropped in the occasional "OMG!" or "Are you serious?"

She used to talk a lot about her boyfriend and his friends, but they'd broken up recently, and now she talked more about some new course she wanted to do.

"Sorry, what was it called?" I realized I'd zoned out and overfilled the last saltshaker. I mopped up my mess as she repeated what she'd been saying.

"BestLyf." She huffed. I was pretty sure that was the same thing my mom had been talking about the other day. "You OK, girl? You seem more quiet than usual. Distracted."

"Yeah, I'm fine. Sorry. Just tired." I'd been staying up way too late talking to Turner on the balcony or on the phone. I gave her a smile, and she launched right back in.

"Well, remember the info session I mentioned a couple of weeks ago?" She waved the saltshaker lid around animatedly as she talked.

"Uh-huh." I nodded and glanced around the diner, making sure the three currently occupied tables didn't need anything.

"Well, it was so good. I mean, I only went because I had nothing better to do, and that chick I met at yoga was raving about it, and she seemed nice, but it was totally worth it. They even had sushi platters out after, and I didn't have to worry about dinner." She chuckled, and I gave her a wide smile. That girl was obsessed with raw fish. "It was the first time in, like, a month I managed to not think about Dave for more than ten fucking minutes." At the mention of her ex, her face fell.

I dropped the large box of salt and squeezed her hand. "He didn't deserve you."

"No, he did not." She squared her shoulders, and we got back to work. "I mean, I came out here for him. I left all my friends and my family back in Illinois because I thought we were in love and creating a life together. Then six months after we move here, he dumps me and moves to San Francisco! He is such a fucking asshole."

I shushed her, glancing around at the patrons again.

She cringed. "Sorry. Anyway, I've been thinking about moving to San Fran myself, just to stick it to him, ya know? But it's so expensive. And then I was thinking about moving home, but I haven't told my mom that we broke up yet, and I've kinda lost touch with my friends and . . . I dunno. Anyway, I think I'm gonna stay now. That info session really helped put things in perspective for me. I learned that it's OK to put myself and my happiness first, so that's what I'm gonna do."

"You learned all that from one free info session? Wow."

"No, silly." She grinned. We finished with the salt and moved on to the sugar. "I've been to three free info sessions, and the other night I went to my first workshop, which they charge for, but it was so worth it."

"You went to four events in two weeks?" I asked, a little surprised.

"Yeah! I mean, it's not like I had anything better to do, and I was learning so much and meeting all these amazing, successful people. I think it's lucky that BestLyf has one of its centers right here in Devilbend. Makes it possible for them to offer more events, ya know?"

"Uh-huh. Lucky. I'm really happy for you, Chelsea. It's good to see you so positive again." I didn't know much about this program, but I wanted to be supportive.

"Thank you." She beamed. "Hey, you should come. They're super welcoming to everyone. It's a really flexible program that's tailored to your individual needs, the further along you get. The main focus is always on helping you be your best self—whatever that means for you."

"Uh, yeah, maybe . . ."

The bell above the door dinged, saving me from having to awkwardly avoid going to whatever motivational self-help crap Chelsea had gotten involved in.

"I got it." I rushed to the door before she could say anything else.

Donna, Harlow, and Amaya walked in wearing their school uniforms, looking cute in their knee-high socks and so pretty. I'd never look that pretty. The table of college guys in the corner watched them with unconcealed interest.

"Well, hello there, fair maidens." I gave them a mock bow. "Welcome to our humble establishment. How may I be of service this evening?"

Donna and Amaya chuckled, but Harlow jumped right into the ridiculousness with me. "Your finest table, wench. We're weary travelers in need of a warm meal to fill our bellies and a pitcher of your best mead."

"Who you callin' wench, bitch?" I dropped the act and stepped forward to give them each a hug before leading them to a booth.

"That uniform looks amazing on you." Amaya tugged on the edge of my stained blue apron.

I gave her a skeptical look. "Please."

"I'm serious. The apron cinches you in at the waist and accentuates your curves. I'd kill for half your boobs." She grabbed her own admittedly smaller boobs and looked down at her modest cleavage. The table of college guys started squawking and carrying on, nudging each other like a flock of seagulls.

We all rolled our eyes at them.

"What are you guys doing here?" I asked, changing the topic.

"We went shopping after school and thought we'd grab dinner before heading home," Donna said, perusing the menu.

"Oh, OK. What can I get you?" I pulled my pen and pad out of my apron pocket, fighting to keep my smile from shaking. I knew they did things without me, had their own lives—how could they not when we went to different schools and had other social circles? Or rather, *they* had other people they hung out with. I was just alone all the time. It still hurt to be reminded of it.

"You mentioned you were working tonight, so we thought we'd come see you," Harlow added. My smile became more genuine.

"I'll have the cheeseburger with a side of fries and a strawberry milkshake, and do you guys wanna share the loaded nachos?" Amaya looked up to find us all staring at her. "What?" She dropped the menu and crossed her arms. "I'm fucking hungry."

I had no idea how that amount of food would even fit into her tiny stomach, but I recovered first. "Hey, no judgment. The nachos are really good."

The others ordered, and Donna asked when my break was. I put their order in and, when it was ready, told Chelsea I was taking my break and went to sit with them for a little while.

I stole some of their nachos, Amaya playfully batting my hand back, but the ding of the bell over the door yanked my attention away.

Jayden's dad walked into the diner in a suit but no tie, the top few buttons of his shirt undone. He was off the clock.

He paused at the door and scanned the room, then smiled and walked forward when he spotted someone. *Chelsea.* I frowned, completely tuning out the girls as I focused on their exchange.

She smiled widely, as if he'd just handed her a million dollars and not a folded-up scrap of paper. She slipped the paper into her apron pocket, and they spoke briefly before Boyd extended his hand. Chelsea took it, and he covered her hand with his other one, holding on for an inappropriately long time while leaning in to speak into her ear.

Then, as unexpectedly as he'd appeared, he walked back out the door.

What the hell was going on? Was Chelsea having an affair with Jayden's dad? My stomach rolled at the thought. He was at least fifteen years older than her, but it would explain her sudden good mood and positive outlook. Was he even married though? I'd never cared to learn about Jayden's family life.

"Earth to Mena!" Harlow waved a hand in front of my face as the others laughed.

"Huh? Sorry!" I snapped out of it. I had enough problems of my own to worry about, and I didn't want to waste what time I had left with my friends thinking about anyone with the last name Burrows.

We talked shit, discussed the latest episode of the webtoon we were all reading, ranked the college guys in order of hotness. My break was over way too soon, but it was nice to spend time with them and feel normal for half an hour.

"I would've said to just hang out with your friends, Philly, but . . ." Chelsea smiled apologetically as she picked up two plates from the servery.

"It's all good." I waved her off. A few more people had come in for dinner, and we really couldn't slack off anymore.

The girls hung around a bit longer, then came to say goodbye when there was a lull.

"It was so nice to see you guys." I held on to them each a little longer than I had saying hello. I hated saying goodbye, even though I knew I didn't mean as much to them as they meant to me.

"Same. Come over on the weekend." Harlow bounced on the spot, her big headphones jostling on her chest.

"Yeah, we can have another pool sesh before the weather turns to shit." Donna rolled her eyes.

"I gotta work." I huffed. The weather was already getting cold. Fall was beginning to turn the leaves golden, and I needed a cardigan to sit out on the balcony in the evenings.

"What about during the week?" Amaya asked.

"Homework, and I don't have a car . . ." I couldn't get to their place on the nice side of town without a car, and my parents were never home early enough to drive me.

"God, I keep forgetting. I'm such a bitch." Donna looked guilty. "We'll come pick you up one night. We'll sort it out later, OK? Get back to work."

"Sounds good. I can tell you about this guy I've been talking to."

"What?!" Amaya stopped midturn and faced me again. "Way to bury the lede."

"Yeah, we've been here all night, and you only mention this now?" Harlow whacked me on the arm.

Donna's eyes just sparkled, her smile brilliant and greedy. She wagged a finger in my face. "You're not getting away with this. There will be questions, missy. So many questions."

"And I will provide answers," I promised. "But I really gotta get back to work. Bye!"

I rushed away without waiting for a response. When I looked over my shoulder, Donna was dragging the other two out the door as they glared at me.

I held in a laugh and went to clear a table. It was nice to have them so interested in something going on with me—even if it was more because of the boy-related gossip than anything else. But as my shift came to a close, I started to worry about what exactly I would tell them. "Oh, I started talking to him on my balcony, and he goes to my school, and I've seen him (he's really hot, BTW—way out of my league), but he has no idea what *I* look like. Also, we've kissed. Also, I'm pretty sure I'm falling in love with him."

Fuck my life . . .

The next time I saw Turner, the sight of his broad shoulders, encased in a dark gray hoodie, stopped me in my tracks before I made it around the corner. I'd spent so much time silently observing him I'd know his build, his mannerisms, anywhere.

I just wasn't expecting to see him at the bottom of the back stairs in the dingy end of the English and humanities wing. The last two classrooms had busted windows or other issues and weren't even used. I went out of my way to take these stairs from time to time to avoid bumping into Madison and her friends, or Jayden and his friends. I could count on one hand the number of people I'd seen in this part of the school.

"Just tell me what to do to prove . . . please!" I missed half of what he said as I silently plastered myself against the wall, tightly gripping the strap of my bag.

I was about to walk away, risk the main stairs, but the desperation in his voice kept me glued to the spot.

". . . that simple." The small voice that responded was female. Now I *definitely* wasn't going anywhere.

"OK, then how about—" Turner's ocean-deep voice had some ripples in it now, but a sharp shush cut him off.

He resumed talking, but I couldn't make out what he was saying.

I chewed on my bottom lip and tried to make myself walk away, but curiosity got the better of me. I took a deep breath and leaned around the corner.

Turner had shifted against the railing, revealing the person beyond: the sad little girl from the library the other day.

Jayden's little sister? *What the actual fuck?*

He was holding his hands out, palms up, as if he was pleading with her ... or maybe threatening her? Her arms were wrapped around her waist, her head hanging. She looked so vulnerable—especially next to Turner's height and strength. He was easily twice her size.

Why the hell was he talking to a freshman in an abandoned part of the school, making her look as though she might burst into tears at any moment?

It killed me to even consider that the sweet, funny guy I was falling for wasn't who I thought he was, but I couldn't just stand there and do nothing ... even though that's what all my classmates had done for years as I'd endured Madison's and Jayden's torture.

I was about to bust my cover. He'd know who I was as soon as I opened my mouth. He'd had nothing to focus on but my voice for weeks.

I didn't care.

I took a step around the corner, but Turner beat me to it. He leaned down and whispered something to Jenny, his big hand engulfing her delicate shoulder, then rushed away up the stairs.

Jenny lifted her face to the ceiling and sighed, unshed tears glistening on her lashes. She lowered her head and immediately spotted me.

Her eyes widened in fear—of me? Of him?

With one hand still gripping the strap of my bag, I cautiously reached the other out to her, taking small measured steps forward. "Hey, Jenny. Remember me? We met in the library the other day."

She nodded and glanced at the stairs. The tears spilled over.

"I just want to make sure you're OK. That looked kind of intense, and—"

"I'm fine," she interrupted, squaring her shoulders and swiping at the tears on her face. "Just leave me alone."

She started to move past me, and I let her, not wanting to make her feel any less safe.

"Was that guy bothering you?" That made her stop and face me again. "Did he do something to hurt you? Is he—"

"No," she interrupted me again. "Leave him alone too. He's just ... just don't say anything to anyone, OK? It'll only make everything worse. I just ... I need to think."

She rushed off, leaving me standing at the bottom of the stairs, confused.

She'd seemed afraid of him when they were talking, but I'd caught only a glimpse of it. Was she just upset? Maybe he was trying to comfort her? He did look as though he was pleading with her at one point. And the way she demanded I leave him alone ... it was fiercer than the way she'd defended *herself*.

Was I reading this all wrong? Or was my connection with Turner making me search for any explanation that put him in a positive light?

CHAPTER SEVEN

Mom and Dad were both working late, and I didn't even attempt to do any homework when I got home. I dumped my bag at the foot of my bed and immediately reached for my makeup case. I needed to clear my head, calm my racing heart, get lost in the precision and focus required to execute a full face of makeup.

I set up in my room, retrieving the circle light I'd had out on the balcony all summer. It was getting too cold to sit out there at night anyway, but really, I was avoiding Turner. My phone had lit up with several messages from him, and it took a Herculean effort not to read them. In the end, I put the damn thing on silent and shut it in my bedside drawer.

I ended up doing a split-face makeup—definitely not something you'd ever wear in public but fun to experiment with. One side was fierce, with a strong brow and smoky eye, a defined deep red lip, and contouring around the cheeks—the bitch you didn't mess with. The other half was youthful and vulnerable, with light makeup around the eyes, soft blush on the cheeks, and a gloss on the lips—the naïve young girl who needed protecting.

I was neither.

I was both.

It spoke to my confusion and conflicting feelings about the day.

I snapped a few photos and wiped it all off just before my dad walked through the front door. While he was in the shower, I started dinner, needing something to occupy my hands and my mind.

"Er . . . you feeling OK, Sweet Chilly?" He eyed the knife in my hand with wide eyes.

I gave him a withering look and got back to chopping the pepper. "Stir-fry, right?"

"I was gonna say we should get a pizza since your mom and I both worked late, but you've already done half the work, so sure!"

He put the rice on, and we had dinner ready in no time. Dad chattered about mundane things, asking about school and work. I managed to respond just enough to show I was listening, but half my mind was still in that stairwell with Turner and Jenny, my gut churning about what I'd seen and heard.

Obviously, I wasn't the only one with secrets. I just couldn't figure out if his were going to get me into trouble.

To both my parents' astonishment, I sat on the couch with them and watched some TV for a while, then I went to bed early.

I took time with my evening routine before flopping into bed on my back, staring at the dark ceiling. With nothing left to distract me, I could no longer resist the urge to reach into my drawer and check my phone.

There were forty-eight messages in the group chat with the girls, mostly demands for more information about "the hottie you mentioned the other day."

An anonymous message told me I'd looked like shit today and should stop making other people deal with having to look at me by just killing myself. I got out of that one quickly, but my heart still plummeted in my chest.

There were three from Turner.

The first was from barely an hour after school.

Turner: Hey, neighbor. Balcony?

The second was from about half an hour later.

T: Mena? I didn't think you were working tonight. I miss you.

The third was sent about fifteen minutes ago.

T: Are you OK?

Was I? I supposed I was physically OK. Mentally, I was a confused mess. Emotionally? I didn't even know where to start.

I stared at my phone, trying to think of something to say until it went dark and locked itself. I groaned and ran my hand through my hair, then rolled onto my side, unlocked it, and replied.

Mena: I'm fine. Just need to think.

His reply was instant.

T: About? Anything I can help with?

My fingers hovered over the keyboard, my gut churning. What was I supposed to say? *Hey,* are you doing something shady with Jayden's little sister? It sounded insane, even in my own head, but I knew what I'd seen. I couldn't just ignore it.

On the other hand, if there was a logical explanation and I accused him of doing something awful, I'd feel really bad.

Every time we spoke, Turner seemed to me like a good person—I just couldn't reconcile that with how scared Jenny had looked while talking to him.

My screen went dark again, and he sent another message before I could.

T: Shit. Is it about me? About us?
　M: Kind of. I don't really know how to explain it.
　T: Fuck, Mena, what did I do? Did I say something bad? The more I get to know you, the less filter I have.
　M: No, you didn't say anything or do anything to me.

But what did you do to her?

T: Then what is it? Can we talk out on the balcony? I want to hear your voice.
　M: My parents just went to bed. I can't.
　T: Then can I call you?

Without waiting for a response, he did. I let it ring out and then replied.

M: They'll hear me. I can't talk to you right now. I just need to process some things.
　T: I can't fix anything if you don't tell me what the issue is.
　M: I don't know if this can be fixed.
　T: Fuck. You're really scaring me.
　M: I'm sorry. I'll talk to you tomorrow. I need to get some sleep.

He didn't reply for a long time. All I could think about was him in his bed, staring at his phone. Was he confused? Angry? Scared? Pissed off?

Maybe all of those things. I knew I was.

When he finally did respond, it was a simple "OK."

I put my phone away and rolled onto my other side, facing the wall, as tears pricked the backs of my eyes. He was the best thing that had happened to me in a long time. But was he who I thought he was? Or was I so desperate for human interaction that I was seeing something that wasn't there?

The next morning, I looked more like shit than usual. The lack of sleep and crying had left my eyes puffy and my nose red; even my birthmark looked worse.

Some concealer would've covered the imperfections, and a swipe of mascara would've made my eyes look more open and alert. But I just looked wistfully at my makeup case and remembered how scratchy the fibers of that mop had felt and how the smell of bleach had choked me, and I settled for washing my face with cold water, hoping that would bring the swelling down.

Like every morning, I drank my coffee on the balcony and waited for Turner. He left later than usual—I guessed he hadn't slept much either—his shoulders hunched, hood up, hands in pockets.

I waited until he was around the corner, then I left, pulling my own hood up and tucking my ponytail out of the way.

Most of the day passed in a blur as I went from class to class, took scattered notes that would probably make no sense later, and avoided Turner in the halls. I'd figured out his schedule—or at least which general area of the school he would be in at any point in the day. Usually I used this information to pass him in the hall, get a glimpse of him, hear his smooth, deep voice as he talked.

Today, I used it to keep as far away from him as possible.

Even Bonnie bumping into me and loudly declaring, "That was weird. I just knocked into thin air. Does anyone see anything?" didn't make me feel as shitty as it usually did. A bunch of kids laughed as I walked away, but my mind was with Turner.

By lunch, my stomach was still churning, which meant I wasn't even remotely hungry. But I was over feeling like shit.

School was shitty enough. I couldn't have this hanging over my head too.

I sat down in the abandoned stairwell where I'd seen Turner talking to Jenny and got out my phone to text him.

He beat me to it.

T: Can we please talk? This is killing me.

M: Yes. I was just about to text you.

T: In person. Please. I want to talk to you.

M: Tonight? Balcony?

T: I can't tonight. My dad needs me. Can I come meet you somewhere? Please, Mena!

M: Lunch is half-over. There's no time.

T: I don't care. Can't fucking concentrate on anything anyway.

M: Me neither . . .

I chewed my bottom lip and racked my brain. I wasn't ready for him to see me, but I needed to speak to him. I craved his touch, even as I worried it might burn me.

It would have to be somewhere dark.

The gym would be empty during lunch. We'd have to finish our talk before the next class came in to use it.

M: Meet me in the gym. There's a storage room at the back next to the seating. We should have privacy there.

I grabbed my bag, rushing in that direction as fast as I could. I should've waited until I was there before sending that text. Hopefully I could get there first.

The gym was empty, and I ran across the polished floor to the back corner, praying the door to the storage room would be unlocked. Luck was on my side, and the heavy door opened.

I dashed inside and took a deep breath.

Sneakers squeaked on the polished gym floor. I'd only just beaten him. Had he been close by? Or had he rushed here like me?

It was pitch black in the dank space, but light would flood it as soon as he opened the door. I hurried toward the other end of the room and around the corner, darting past the industrial shelving that held balls and mats and other torture devices high school gym teachers had used since time immemorial. The room was an L shape, with another door leading outside, providing access to the equipment from the football field.

The door opened. Light streamed in. I held my breath. What if it wasn't him?

"Mena?" he whisper-shouted into the room.

"Shut the door," I said. "Quick."

He closed the door, then cursed. "Where's the light?"

"No!" I stepped in his direction. "Just leave it. Come toward me."

"Are you fucking serious right now?" His voice had lost some of that silky-smooth quality, frustration and weariness creating ripples. But he shuffled forward.

"Follow my voice." I reached a hand out. It was so dark I may as well have had my eyes closed. If I hadn't been half-convinced we were about to break up (were we even together?) it would've been fun, seeking each other out in the dark.

My hand bumped his chest . . . and stayed there.

"There you are." He lowered his voice, his hand landing on my ribs, then shifting up to my shoulder.

I felt so distant from him, so uncertain of who he was, what *we* were. But I couldn't stop myself from getting closer. My feet shuffled forward; my other hand settled on his hip. And then we were moving as one, stepping into each other's space, hands tentative at first but incapable of holding back. My arms wrapped around his waist, and his banded around my back. We were chest to chest. With my cheek over his heart, I listened to the *thud-thud* as my breathing began to match his without my even realizing it.

For a few moments, we just stood there, holding each other. I felt at home in his arms, even though I'd touched him only a handful of times through the bamboo and kissed him only once.

His soft voice broke the silence. "Mena, what are we doing here?"

"It's called hugging." He'd torn through my defenses without much more than his touch and solid presence. My mind had calmed, the churning in my stomach had settled, and I'd reverted to our usual banter. But there was nothing normal about this situation—about me.

"I'd like to turn on the light."

"No. Please, Turner, don't." I tried to pull away, fully prepared to find an exit and run before he could see me. But he held on. His grip was firm but not insistent. I could've wrenched out of it if I'd really wanted to. I didn't want to.

His chest expanded against mine in a deep sigh, which turned into a soft growl at the end. "I don't understand this. We've been getting to know each other for weeks. I've told you things . . . I don't care what you look like, Mena. I like you —your mind, your sense of humor, how you feel in my arms. What is the big deal? Why won't you tell me who you are?"

I smiled sadly at how direct he was being. It was incredible to know he felt this connection between us just as strongly as I did.

But he'd been hanging out with Jayden and his friends more and more. I'd seen Steph and Bonnie hovering around him, giving him flirty looks. He was falling into the worst possible group, and I wasn't sure if it was too late.

"I'm sorry, Turner. I know this is frustrating for you. But once you find out who I am . . . it'll change everything."

"No." He squeezed me. "It'll change nothing. At least not for me. Are you really that insecure about your looks?"

"Yes. No. Argh!" This time I did push out of his embrace. My hands dropped to his waist, my body unwilling to separate from him completely, but I needed some space to breathe. He smelled so damn good; I wanted to give him whatever he wanted so I could continue to bury my nose in his chest and breathe in that warm fresh-rain scent. "It's not just about that. There are things you don't know. About me. About this school. I . . ."

"So tell me. Why can't you just be honest? Haven't I earned your trust?"

And just like that, I remembered why I'd been questioning everything in the first place.

"Don't act like I'm the only one keeping secrets, Turner. You can't demand honesty if you're not willing to give it."

"What's that supposed to mean?" His voice rose a little in pitch. He was getting frustrated. So was I.

My heart rate quickened, and before I could chicken out, I blurted, "I saw you yesterday. Talking to Jayden's little sister."

His muscles tensed under my fingers. He went very still, his thumbs no longer rubbing little absent-minded circles against my shoulders.

"How much did you hear?" The ocean-smooth quality that made me want to sink into his voice was gone—this smoothness was like glass. Sharp and deadly.

What the fuck had I been thinking locking myself in a dark place with a guy I suspected was . . . doing *something* to sweet, innocent little Jenny? I was a fucking moron.

"Nothing. I hardly heard a word, and I only saw you guys talking for, like, two minutes." I removed my hands from his sides and took a step back, mentally calculating if I was closer to the door that led to the gym or the one that led outside.

"Shit." He sighed, and his hands found my hips. "You sound fucking terrified. I'm sorry. Please . . . I didn't mean to be so intense. I just . . . I don't know what to say."

He sounded genuine, but he hadn't answered my unasked question. What the fuck was he doing with Jenny? I put my hands on his arms, ready to push him off if I had to, fighting the urge to pull him closer.

"What was that about then?" I asked. "I didn't hear much, but that girl looked fucking terrified."

"I know. I didn't put that look on her face. Trust me."

"Never trust someone who says *trust me*."

He chuckled, and it turned into a groan. "I can't really tell you much more about that situation—the secrets are not . . . it's not just my story to tell. But I'm trying to do something good. I'm trying to do the right thing."

"Is she in some kind of trouble?" My nails dug into his forearms. She'd defended him when I confronted her. Was it possible the fear in her eyes wasn't *of* him but *for* him?

"Maybe. I promise I'll tell you the full story when it's all over. And I hope that will be sooner rather than later. In the meantime, I have to ask you to trust me. Trust that I'm doing the right thing."

My gut was telling me I could. The idea of Turner doing something malicious was so discordant with the guy I'd gotten to know. It just didn't fit.

And Jenny had defended him.

He hadn't threatened me or even raised his voice. He hadn't demanded I keep my mouth shut. He was just asking me to trust him.

I decided to take a leap of faith and do just that.

"OK, I'll trust you, but I'll be keeping an eye on Jenny."

He released a heavy breath. "That would be amazing, actually. I can't be around twenty-four seven, and knowing she has another person I trust in her corner actually makes me feel a lot better."

I dragged my hands up his arms to rest on his shoulders. "But you have to trust me too. I know it's frustrating for you, but I need you to trust that my reasons for keeping my identity secret are not frivolous. I just need time. I've been my true self with you in every other way, I promise."

"I believe you. I'll try to be patient." He pulled me flush against his chest and kissed me on the forehead, his lips landing off-center, as he couldn't see me.

But I could *feel* him. Every hard muscle pressing against me. His strong arms holding me, making me feel safe, even after I'd felt scared just moments ago.

"Did we just have our first fight?" His shoulders shook under my hands with quiet laughter.

"I dunno." I shrugged. "Aren't fights something couples have?"

"Is that not what we are?"

"Oh . . . uh . . . you're not seeing anyone else?"

"You are?" He suddenly sounded a little worried, a little unsure. "I mean, I'm not interested in anyone else."

"Good. Neither am I." Not that I had any other options. He was it for me, and I wouldn't change that for the world. But he had girls all over school hanging off him. There was no question he'd been asked out several times already. Had he said yes to any of them?

"Good." A smile warmed his voice, and his hands started rubbing small circles on my lower back.

"Are you sure about this? You don't know what I look like." I couldn't help feeling a bit insecure.

"I'm not falling for your looks, Mena. I'm falling for your personality. And this fine body." He gave me a squeeze on the hips, his strong fingers only just digging into the area above my ass.

I laughed and dropped my forehead to his shoulder.

"Now, since we've survived our first fight"—his low words reverberated through my chest—"we really should make up."

"Oh?" I smiled into his shirt, then tilted my head to speak just beneath his jaw. "And how do you propose we do that?"

I punctuated my suggestive question with a soft, lingering kiss to the side of his neck.

His voice was as breathy as mine when he answered. "I have a few ideas."

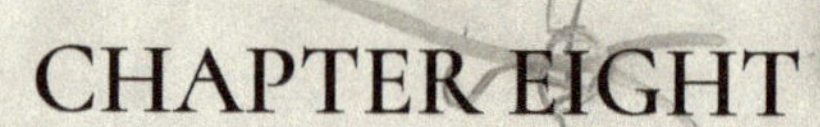

CHAPTER EIGHT

I kissed him again, a little higher, getting drunk on how his arms tightened around me every time my lips connected, how his breathing grew shallower. Emboldened by his reaction, I did something I'd been daydreaming about since I got a good look at him—I darted my tongue out and licked his jaw. Just a little lick right under his ear.

He exhaled sharply and turned his head, his lips searching for mine in the dark. I tipped my face up and met him halfway.

We kissed as if we were reuniting lovers, back together after being unsure we'd ever see the other again—tongues tangling, hands tugging at clothing. The bell rang as we started to back toward the rear wall of the room, neither of us willing to break the kiss. My back connected with the stack of gym mats, and Turner smacked one hand beside my head for balance as he leaned his body flush against mine.

He pulled his delicious lips away and croaked against my burning cheek, "We should get to class."

"Fuck that." I managed to get my hands between us and pulled the zipper of his hoodie down, stroking his chest and hard abs all the way down to the waistband of his jeans. He groaned as my hands slid under his T-shirt, my thumbs rubbing those hipbones I'd been at eye level with in the library.

Just like that day, I had the urge to kneel down and lick them, but I settled for copping a good feel. I'd never given anyone a blow job—I wasn't sure I was ready for that—and getting on my knees and licking that general area was sure to lead to a dick in my mouth.

Instead, my hands ghosted up his back, drawing him against me. The discordant thud of basketballs on polished wood only just registered—a gym class was starting. I vaguely hoped they wouldn't need any other equipment.

Turner kissed me deeply, in smooth, rhythmic strokes of his tongue against mine. His hand went to the back of my head and, finding my hair up in a ponytail, gripped the hair tie firmly and tugged. It stung for a second, and then my hair tumbled down around us.

He inhaled deeply and broke the kiss to whisper against my lips, "You smell so good. Like strawberries."

My response was an incoherent moan. I was beyond words, completely lost in the lust; the heavy, heady feeling low in my belly; the ache between my legs.

I rolled my hips against his, and his body responded, his hips meeting mine in a steady rhythm.

"You *feel* fucking good too," he growled.

I forcefully pushed my lips once more against his. I could drown in his voice, find bliss in the gritty quality I'd put there. But I needed his lips on mine.

I widened my legs, bent my left knee. He took it in his big hand and hooked it over his hip.

And then I could feel him, his hardness right there, giving me exactly the friction I was craving.

I moaned loudly. Too loudly.

The sound bounced off the walls, reminding me where we were. My sudden rush of adrenaline only added to the heady cocktail of pleasure already coursing through my veins.

Turner started kissing and licking my jaw, his mouth moving down toward my neck as his hand traveled up my front. He caressed my breast over the fabric of my T-shirt, his hand almost completely covering it, while our hips kept up a steady rhythm.

Then he was pushing up under my T-shirt, pushing my bra out of the way so he could fondle me skin-to-skin.

He groaned into my mouth, the sound going straight to my core. Maybe I was ready for a blow job after all—I wanted to hear him make that sound over and over. I wanted to be the one to wrench it from his throat. I wanted all our clothing gone. I wanted a bed instead of the stinky old gym mats at my back.

Something banged against the door, making us both jump.

We stopped kissing and froze, only our hips still rocking slightly as we panted and listened, suddenly thrown back into reality.

"I said *no* contact, Andrews! How in the hell did you two end up there?" The coach sounded mad but a little amused.

The class's chorus of laughter followed, along with a loud male guffaw right on the other side of the door. The door that stood between an entire class of sophomores and Turner and me.

"Shit." I pushed gently against his chest, and he removed his hand from my breast. I missed it already. I never wanted to wear a bra again—Turner could just walk behind me, holding my boobs in place with his big, warm hands, all day every day.

"Since you're there, grab the orange cones, would ya?" The coach shouted again.

"Fuck." This time it was Turner's turn to curse.

I adjusted my bra and ran a hand through my hair. Snatching up my bag, I rushed in the general direction of the football-field door and ended up walking right into it, bumping my knee with a grunt.

"Mena?" Turner hissed into the dark. "Fuck, what are we gonna do?"

"I'm sorry. I gotta go. Just hide or something."

"What?" He sounded panicked, but I was running on pure adrenaline now. I had to get out of there *immediately*.

I found the door handle just as the other door creaked open. Thankfully, mine opened inward, blocking me from view as light flooded the room.

I closed the door behind me and threw my hood up, thanking every deity imaginable that no one was on the football field as I powerwalked away. I'd go to the bathroom to get my shit together and kill more time before my next class started.

No one—not even Turner—stopped me as I hurried off, and I smiled, my chest heaving. I couldn't believe we'd gotten away with it. I just hoped Turner hadn't been busted.

<hr>

"Not too dark on the eyes, Philly. I want to look sophisticated, not slutty," my mom directed me as I started applying eyeshadow to her lids.

"Eew! Why the hell would I make my mother look slutty?"

We'd set up at the kitchen table, all my makeup spread out, Mom at my mercy. She'd come home in almost as good a mood as me—declared we'd get Chinese for dinner, but it would be just me and Dad, as she was going to a seminar thing, and could I please do her makeup?

I took pretty much any excuse to do makeup, so there we were.

She smiled. "I didn't mean you'd do it on purpose, sweetheart."

"So, you just think I'm shit at makeup," I deadpanned.

"What?" She backed away from my brush and opened her eyes. "No, Philomena, I was just trying to crack a joke."

I snorted and let my grin burst through. "I know. I'm just messing with you, Mom."

She breathed a massive sigh of relief and closed her eyes again so I could get back to work. "I just don't know these days. And please don't take this the wrong way, but you get in your moods, and I . . . well, I worry about you sometimes."

I paused for a second and looked into my mom's face, her eyes closed, her chin tipped up. We looked so similar, but her eyes were a little more tired, her lips marred with a few lines. She was still pretty. It didn't make sense, because I *wasn't* pretty. How the hell did that work?

I got back to work, fighting the urge to tell her everything. The messages, the taunts, the way I was ignored at school, even the few incidents where I'd actually been attacked.

But then I swallowed around the lump in my throat and shoved down that urge. There was literally nothing she could do. No point in adding further stress to my parents' already frantic lives.

"Anyway, you're in a good mood today." Mom broke the silence before I could. "It's nice to see."

"Yeah I . . . had a good day." I couldn't stop the smile pulling at my lips as I thought about what Turner and I had been doing in the storage room just hours earlier.

Mom cracked one eye open and gave me a sly grin. "I know that smile."

"You know nothing, woman. Close your eyes." I gave her a very serious look, but the smile broke out again as soon as her eye closed.

"You have a crush," Mom sing-songed.

"Mom." I laughed, then after a pause, added, "It's more than a crush."

What the hell had just possessed me to imply to my mother I was seeing a boy? Maybe I was just desperate to tell someone, bursting with the excitement Turner made me feel.

"Holy shit, my Sweet Chilly Philly has a boyfriend!" My mother squealed like a preteen and backed out of the reach of my makeup brush.

"Mother." I shot her a withering look.

"OK, OK, I'll try to have more chill," she said while bouncing in her chair.

I rolled my eyes. "I can't finish your makeup if you're bouncing around like that."

She stopped and closed her eyes again, tipping her face up. I sighed and got back to work.

After a few minutes she asked, "What's his name?"

"Uh . . . I . . ."

"Don't tell me you don't know his name." She chuckled.

"Of course I know his name." *He just doesn't know mine.* "I'm just . . . it's kind of new."

"OK, I respect your privacy. I just have to ask, Philomena, do we need to have the safe-sex talk?"

"Mom!" Now it was my turn to screech. "No. I am well across safe sex, and we do *not* need to discuss this."

"Fine." Her expression grew suddenly serious. "Just promise you'll come to me if you need to, OK? I'll never judge you or be mad if you need help."

The urge to tell her about how miserable high school was nearly overwhelmed me again. "I know. Thanks, Mom."

She smiled and nodded. "And for the love of god, don't get pregnant."

"Jesus fuc . . ." I put the brush away, done with her eyes. "Look down so I can do your mascara."

She obeyed, and I changed the topic immediately. "So, what exactly is this thing you're going to? Chelsea from work has mentioned going to the same thing, and it sounds a little new-agey to me."

"Oh, yes, I think I met Chelsea at the first info session I went to a few weeks ago. She's lovely. And Boyd Burrows runs the sessions. He's Jayden's dad—you two go to school together, right?"

"Ugh. Unfortunately."

"Oh, you're not friends?"

"Not exactly. How's that?" I held a mirror in front of her, blocking my own scowl at the mention of Jayden. I wanted to ask if Chelsea and Boyd seemed close at the last session—I was curious if that was the reason behind Chelsea's sudden enthusiasm for these seminars—but Mom would only lecture me about not gossiping, so I kept my mouth shut.

"I look ten years younger! This is amazing! Thank you."

"You're welcome." I gave her a genuine smile. I really hadn't done much—covered up the dark circles, accentuated her eyes. "You didn't answer my question about this event," I said as I started to pack up, separating the brushes that needed to be cleaned.

"Oh, it's nothing 'new-agey,' as you put it. BestLyf is a large, successful professional-development company. They have offices all over the country and run workshops and courses. That kind of thing. It's all about improving yourself while improving your skills. It's hard to explain unless you come along and experience it for yourself. It's very motivating."

"I can see that. There's not much that will get you out of the house on a school night."

"It's worth it. But I'm not sure it's going to keep happening. I've got another two events that they offer free of charge, then the next level up is paid workshops and retreats, and I just don't think we can afford it." She sighed.

There wasn't much I could say to that. Whether it was my mother wanting to improve her skills, my father wanting to spend time with his friends on a fishing trip, or me wanting to get away from my abusers—*we couldn't afford it.*

"I hope you and Dad find the money for it, Mom. I like seeing you happy and motivated."

"Thanks, sweetheart, but you don't need to worry about that." She waved her hand dismissively as she walked off toward the kitchen. "How about a snack?"

"Sure."

We spent the next half hour munching on celery sticks slathered in peanut butter. Mom managed to bring the conversation back to boys and started reminiscing about all the "shenanigans" she and Auntie Em had gotten up to when they were my age and running amok all over Devilbend.

Thankfully, Dad came home and saved me from hearing anything that would have scarred me for life, and Mom left for her meeting.

Turner wasn't home that evening, but whatever he was up to with his dad, he had time to text me occasionally.

T: I can't believe you managed to slip away without me seeing you! I'm once again convinced you work for the CIA.

M: How many times do I have to tell you—it's the FBI.

T: Maybe it's the KGB. They use beautiful women to lure men with their wiles.

M: Wiles? LOL!

T: Yes. You have incredible wiles. I'm still hard just thinking about your wiles.

I looked over my shoulder to make sure my dad was nowhere around. He was glued to the TV on the other side of the balcony door, but I still dropped my hands low in my lap before replying.

M: We definitely have some unfinished business. I can't stop thinking about it either.

T: If my dad wasn't sitting right next to me, I'd be describing all the things I want to do to you next time.

M: Change of topic then! Did you get into trouble?

T: Nah. Luckily the kid who came into the room as you ran away was someone I know—he's on the football team. He gave me shit about having a girl in there and tried to get me to say who it was, but he covered for me with the coach, and I slipped out the back door.

M: Good. I was worried you might get caught.

T: But not worried enough to hang around.

M: I'm sorry! I panicked!

T: It's OK. I'm teasing!

I went to bed with a smile on my face.

But life's a bitch, so anything good that happened to me naturally had to be balanced out by something shitty.

CHAPTER NINE

Madison must've been in a bad mood, because she seemed to have made it her mission to make my life hell all day.

She bumped into me from behind on my way to first period, making me drop my books, then declared, "You dropped something" in a monotone before walking away, as if I were gum on the bottom of her shoe.

Between second and third period, I was at my locker when the whole group walked past. Bonnie slammed my locker door on my arm, and when I wrenched back, wincing, Kelsey slammed the door shut.

"How careless, leaving a locker wide open like that." Madison was already walking away, the other girls snickering.

I rubbed my arm and flexed my fingers. That was going to leave a bruise.

At lunch, I made the mistake of walking past the cafeteria on my way to hide out in the library.

Jayden rounded the corner just as I passed the doors, his arm slung over Madison's shoulders, their friends trailing behind them. Turner was with them.

My heart skipped a beat—I wasn't sure if it was from seeing him or from fear. I hunched my shoulders and tried to slip past, hugging the wall, but it was too late.

"What is that *smell?*" Jayden waved his hand in front of his face exaggeratedly.

Madison gave me a satisfied, cruel smirk as the others blocked my path. Turner paused halfway through the cafeteria doors and turned around with a frown.

"I hope that's not coming from the cafeteria. I swear, the standards at this school are slipping." Steph tutted. Everyone laughed.

I wanted the floor to open up and swallow me, anything to keep Turner from seeing this. Hopefully they'd get bored or hungry quickly.

"I mean, everything looks clean, but . . ." Steph looked around, making it obvious I was invisible in this scenario—like a bad smell.

"What's that stuff? That gas that comes off volcanoes?" Jayden snapped his fingers. "Smells like rotten eggs. It's in fertilizer and shit."

"Sulphur," Turner supplied, his voice flat, emotionless.

It wasn't until that moment that I realized I'd been hoping he would say something, *do* something, to stop them. No, he didn't know I was Mena—the girl he'd been talking to all this time. But I hadn't thought he was the kind of person to be OK with assholes being assholes for no reason.

My heart cracked in my chest; I couldn't make myself look at him. I couldn't make myself look at any of them as they continued to pretend I didn't exist while cracking jokes about how bad I smelled.

I blocked out the rest of their words, keeping my head down as my eyes searched for a way out.

"We gonna stand out here all lunch? I'm fucking starving." Turner's deep voice was the only thing that could've made me tune back in. My head unconsciously turned in his direction, but years of habit kept my eyes low.

His right hand was in a fist by his side; his other arm lifted and flopped back down in a frustrated gesture. A small blue band circled his wrist—a hair tie. *My* hair tie.

As shitty as it felt to be standing there copping their shit, a tiny flare of warmth erupted in my chest.

They all followed Turner into the cafeteria without another glance at me, and I rushed away, gulping air, suddenly realizing how hard it had been to breathe just moments before.

After that, I was extra vigilant to avoid them and made it to my last class without another incident.

Moments after I arrived, Turner wandered in and sat in the seat directly in front of me—the seat he'd occupied since school started. It had gotten increasingly more difficult not to reach out and touch him, brush a bit of lint off his collar, run my hands through his soft, messy hair. But I restrained myself, not even looking at him too much.

Jayden sat next to him, and I tried just as hard to ignore him too, albeit for vastly different reasons.

The first half of the class was spent discussing *The Crucible*, the second half working on an upcoming assignment. Most of the students fell into silence, hunched over their books, as Mr. Chen buried his face in his laptop and typed away furiously.

It wasn't long before people lost focus, and several surreptitiously pulled out their phones. After a long and stressful day, my concentration was lacking too.

The words on the page kept blurring; I'd read the same sentence three times, and it still wouldn't register in my brain. I kept finding myself glancing around the room, forcing my gaze away from Turner's broad shoulders hunched over his desk, the short hair at the nape of his neck, the way his knee was bouncing lightly. I knew how hard those shoulders were, what that hair felt like under my palm, what a thrill it had been when that knee pushed its way between my legs.

I bit my lip to keep from smiling and shifted in my seat, pointing my eyes back down at my book. After a few moments, I looked around the room again. No one was paying me a lick of attention, so I chanced another ogling of my boyfriend (I couldn't believe I had a secret boyfriend!).

Turner shifted, extending the leg that had been bouncing a moment earlier. He leaned his head on his left hand, totally slouched in the desk that looked tiny supporting his big frame. His right hand hung off the edge of the desk, and his fingers were fiddling with something.

Those fingers . . . the things those fingers had made me feel, the places on my body they had touched, the places I still wanted them to explore . . .

My inappropriate fantasizing evaporated when I noticed he had my hair tie in his nimble fingers, twisting it around his pointer finger, stretching it out, scrunching it up. I'd tried not to read too much into the fact that he'd kept it, but I couldn't help wondering.

I glanced around the class again. At least half of them had their phones out now, and several people were chatting at their desks, abandoning any semblance of doing work. I ached to take my own phone out and text my boyfriend, but that was dangerous. What if someone read over my shoulder? What if someone took it or broke it or both? What if they started teasing me about why I even had a phone when I had no one to message?

The anxiety almost overwhelmed me, but it also pissed me off. I didn't want my life to be dictated by bullies. It wasn't fucking fair.

I didn't want to be Phil—the sad, friendless loser everyone picked on. I wanted to be Mena—the normal teenage girl who had a boyfriend she could secretly text in class. So, I pulled my phone out, hiding it behind the bulk of my textbook, and surreptitiously did just that.

M: You have something of mine.

I kept my head down, pretending to read, as I watched him in my periphery. He pulled his phone out and read the text under the desk, sitting up a little straighter.

Would he deny it? Would he be confused? Maybe he didn't put as much meaning into it as I had.

My phone flashed with his reply.

T: You left it when you ran away from me. I'm holding on to it, as per the finders-keepers rules. You can't have it!

    M: LOL! OK. Why so intense about a little hair tie?

He chuckled, glancing at the teacher before lifting his phone onto his desk. He tapped away at the screen, but my phone didn't go off. I frowned. Maybe he was texting someone else.

He shook his head lightly and tapped some more. Then he grunted and ran his hand through his messy hair before tapping at the phone a third time.

I was wondering who was making him frustrated when my phone finally went off again.

T: I like having something of yours with me since you already have something of mine.

I racked my brain but couldn't think of a single item of his I'd even held, so I replied with several question marks.

His reply was instant.

T: My heart.

My breath hitched. My eyes stayed glued to my little screen, my body frozen. He felt it as deeply as I did—this connection between us. I could hardly believe it.

In front of me, Turner shifted in his seat and blew out a big breath. He wiped both hands down the fronts of his thighs, his head bent over his screen.

I tried to think of the perfect response. Something simple and heartfelt that wouldn't come off gushy but would show him how hard I was falling for him.

Before I could find the words, another text came in.

T: Too much?

I smiled and suddenly found it easier to reply. His nervousness was putting me at ease.

M: Not too much. You have mine too.

I added a heart emoji and sent it.

He leaned back in his chair and laced his fingers behind his head, giving me a good view of his defined arms, as he sighed—the relief palpable.

"You good, man?" Jayden asked next to him, breaking my happy bubble. The soft murmurings of the class came back into focus, and I remembered where I was—shark-infested water. I couldn't show any of these people the gaping hole in my chest where my heart thudded for the boy sitting in front of me. They could smell blood in the water, and my heart was overflowing.

I tucked my phone back into my bag.

"Yeah. I'm fucking perfect." I could hear the smile in Turner's voice, and apparently, Jayden could see it.

"That is the most goofy-ass smile I've ever seen, bro. You got a chick on the hook?" Jayden nudged Turner's shoulder, and my boyfriend laughed, neither denying nor confirming Jayden's suspicion.

"Holy shit, you do!" Jayden announced a little too loudly, his exclamation masked by the bell. "Who is it? Is it Kelsey? She's been all up in your crotch since the first day of school. Is it Bonnie? She gives it up to everyone though, man. Be careful of her. Oh, wait! Is it Steph?"

We all packed up and got to our feet, eager to get home.

I waited until Turner and Jayden were making their way out, carefully staying out of their line of sight. Not even Jayden could completely ruin the buzz of Turner's adorable semi-declaration of love.

Even so, it still stung that by the time we'd made it out into the hall, Jayden had named almost every single girl in our year and even a few juniors, and my name wasn't even mentioned as a joke.

CHAPTER TEN

For two glorious weeks, Turner and I flirted unashamedly via text, sending each other messages I would have been horrified for anyone else to read. We met up in the storage area off the gym a few more times, but we had to be careful not to get caught. And I had to be careful not to let him see me.

Friday after school, it was pouring down rain but still kind of warm, in a humid way. Naturally, I didn't have an umbrella with me, so I got drenched on my walk home. After a shower, I planted myself on the balcony, resigned to the fact that my hair was going to frizz up.

Rain continued to pelt down, the afternoon sky prematurely dark due to the heavy clouds.

I thought about doing a makeup look, but that just made me feel guilty; I had a World History assignment, Statistics homework, and the assignment on *The Crucible* to work on. Plus, the weather was too humid, and the light outside was too crap. I was hoping Turner might come out to his balcony later.

I slumped in the chair, propped my feet up on the little table, and pulled my phone out. I should've been dragging my books out and starting on my homework if I was going to be tragically pining for my boyfriend on the balcony. *Oh god!* I was basically Juliet. Did that mean this love story was doomed to end in tragedy?

Apparently, I was a massive procrastinator as well as a Juliet, because I pushed all thoughts of homework out of my mind and started scrolling Instagram. I did my best to get lost in the makeup pics and cute dog videos, but ignoring the DNHS Confessions posts was almost impossible. Every time the distinctive burgundy (our school color) background popped up, a jolt of anxiety shot up my spine. I scrolled past as fast as possible, but when I started seeing Turner's name crop up, I couldn't help myself. I went onto the page and looked.

There were the usual posts about how ugly my birthmark—and pretty much everything else about me—was and how I should just put myself out of my misery. But speculation about who Turner was sneaking off to see had finally reached the wide gossip network. It was inevitable that someone would notice eventually.

One post, dated three days ago, read, "Caught a glimpse of Turner making out with someone with shiny blonde hair behind the science building at lunch. Bonnie was also mysteriously not at lunch." It made me gag, but I knew it was a flat-out lie, because I'd been pushing Turner against the gym mats in the storage room at lunch three days ago. Bonnie had probably sent it in herself.

There were several other posts in the same vein, including a few pics of the girls that had made my life hell leaning into him, whispering in his ear, touching his shoulder. I wanted to throw my phone off the balcony so I would never have to see that shit again.

"Fucking bitches," I growled, squeezing the device in my hand.

"Hey, neighbor." Turner's voice sounded a bit wary. "You OK?"

Shit. I'd been so absorbed by the bullshit on social media that I hadn't even heard him come out. "Hey, stranger. Yeah, I'm fine. Just crap on Instagram."

There was a beat of silence, the relentless rain humming all around us.

"You know none of that shit is true, right?" His ocean-calm voice was serious. "I'd tell them all I was yours if you'd let me."

You wouldn't want to be mine if you knew who I really was. The thought flew through my mind before I could stop it, surprising me a little with its intensity. My chest suddenly felt tight.

I wanted so badly to show him who I really was.

I wanted to show them all the truth.

I wanted to run away and never see any of them again.

Before I had a chance to answer, the sound of Turner's balcony door sliding open cut through the sound of the rain.

"Turner?" It was his dad.

"Hey, Dad. You're home early." Turner shifted; I could just make out the outline of his body as he got to his feet.

"Work was quiet. What are you doing out here? It's pouring. Never mind. How was today? Did you speak to her? Did you convince her?"

I kept still, frowning in confusion. Was he talking about me? Had Turner confided in his dad? I couldn't really be mad about that, but it didn't make sense. His dad sounded really intense about it.

"No, Dad. I would've messaged you right away. Let's talk inside."

Whatever it was, Turner clearly didn't want me to know. I wasn't the only one keeping secrets.

I tried not to let it get to me, but it was hard not to feel hurt when I was already in a vulnerable, self-conscious state. My feet fell to the floor, and I leaned my elbows on my knees and dropped my head in my hands. What the fuck was I doing? This needed to stop. I had to tell him the truth—the whole awful history. If he decided he didn't want me after, then I didn't want him either. The thought of losing him—not just losing him but being *rejected* by him—felt like a punch to the gut, and tears welled in my eyes.

My phone went off, and I reached for the welcome distraction.

It was my boss.

Leah: Hey, Philly. Are you free to work the dinner shift tomorrow night? Chelsea canceled on me again.

M: Again? Sure, I'll be there.

Chelsea had bailed on three shifts in the last two weeks, and I was starting to worry for her job. Leah was not happy.

L: Thanks, lovely. You're a lifesaver!

I headed inside to start on my homework, telling myself I needed the money and that taking the shift had nothing to do with wanting to delay my chat with Turner.

Saturday nights were always busy at work. Tonight there were three other waitresses on with me, two cooks in the back, and Leah floating around helping where she could, constantly cursing Chelsea's name under her breath for bailing on us.

About halfway through the dinner rush, Donna, Harlow, and Amaya came in with a group of their friends from school. I wasn't sure what they were doing on the shitty side of town, and I didn't have time to ask them; I just greeted them all warmly and seated them in a booth in my section before rushing off.

The girls had seen my birthmark plenty of times, of course, but most of their friends saw me only occasionally at parties and things. Thankfully, none of them seemed to care about it, although I did notice Nicola lean over the table and whisper to Donna, who gave her a withering look and then waved her hand dismissively. I couldn't help but wonder if they were talking about me.

I seated a couple and cleared another table before going back to take their order.

"What can I get you guys?"

"What's good?" William asked. Will had neat brown hair and had been on again/off again with Donna for nearly a year.

"Uh, the loaded nachos are pretty good, and we have a great pecan pie—it's the owner's nana's recipe."

"Hey, Mena." Drew, a guy with black hair who drove a car probably worth more than our apartment, flashed me a grin. We'd hooked up once at a party. He was nice enough, but we really didn't have anything in common. "I'll have the nachos, but when can I take you out?"

"Oh my god." I rolled my eyes but laughed lightly. He'd asked me out a few times, always in front of other people. I suspected he was doing it more to show off than because he actually wanted to date me.

"Leave her alone, Drew." Harlow slapped his shoulder. "Mena's spoken for."

"What? No." He groaned, a little over the top.

"Yeah, it's true love. You can't compete," Donna added.

"Not that she'll give us any damn details on the guy." Amaya glanced up from her phone long enough to give me a reproachful look.

"Stop," I hissed at them but struggled to keep the smile off my face. Any mention of Turner had me feeling giddy. "Are you assholes going to order or what? I'm kind of fucking busy."

"Two servings of nachos." Drew pouted. "I need to eat my feelings tonight."

I rolled my eyes at him and took the other orders.

I was elated no one had made a big deal about my birthmark, and being around the girls always made me feel good. Maybe I could even sit with them on my break—if it ever slowed down enough for me to take a break.

As I headed for the servery to place their order with the kitchen, the door swung open, the little old-fashioned bell dinging. My smile fell, a heavy weight dropping in the pit of my churning stomach.

Jayden swaggered through the door as though he owned the place, his hand clasped around Madison's. I caught a glimpse of the rest of their group before dropping my gaze and rushing behind the counter.

After placing the order, I caught one of the other waitresses as she passed. "I'm running to the bathroom," I told her, then hurried to the back before she could answer.

In the dingy toilet, I took a few deep breaths to try to slow my racing heart. With a conscious effort, I pulled the impassive mask I wore at school over my features and hoped they'd eat quickly and get the fuck out before they noticed me.

I couldn't leave the other waitresses in the middle of the dinner rush for long, so I forced myself back just in time to see Leah handing my worst enemies menus. She'd seated them in the booth directly next to Donna and her crew—in my section.

I groaned internally as dread settled around me like a heavy mist, making it hard to breathe or move or think straight. I cleared another table, kind of hoping one of the other girls would take their order—we weren't super strict on sections. But we were slammed, and I had no luck.

Having done all I could to avoid it, I sighed and dragged my feet over to their booth. My shoulders slumped, my chest caving in on itself farther with every step I took. When I reached their table, I took the pen and pad out of my apron pocket and cleared my throat, glancing up.

The flat, professional *"Can I take your order?"* died in my throat.

Seated between Bonnie and Kelsey, his elbows casually on the table, was Turner.

Fuck, he was beautiful, with his bomber jacket and his already dark eyes obscured further by the shadow of a baseball cap. He was grinning, his strong shoulders shaking lightly at something Jayden was saying across the table.

But I didn't have time to dwell on that. A full-blown tempest of panic, horror, and crippling uncertainty was writhing inside me. What the hell was I supposed to do now? I couldn't let him find out like this.

I looked around at all of them, hoping like hell I didn't seem like a deer in headlights, even though I felt like one. No one was looking at me. Maybe it had finally happened. Maybe all their jokes about me being invisible had finally translated into reality. I could only hope.

Turner noticed me standing there like a mute idiot.

"Oh, hey, sorry." He gave me a quick glance and a little smile. "I'll have the cheeseburger. Extra fries."

I responded with a tight, polite smile and jotted his order down as the others all groaned, a couple of them throwing napkins at him.

"What?" He looked confused but laughed as he defended himself from the onslaught.

"Didn't you see we were all waiting to see how long she'd stand there, not saying anything like a weirdo?" Steph filled him in.

"Uh . . . no." Turner shifted in his seat and flashed me a wary look.

I just stood there, humiliated, hoping against hope they'd just order and I could slink away without saying something.

I'd talk to Turner after work. I'd tell him everything. I couldn't keep doing this.

After an extended silence—my eyes glued to the table, my fingers gripping the pen so tightly my fingers were beginning to hurt—Turner cleared his throat.

"I'm starving. Fucking order already." He said it with a smile in his voice, but I heard the growly tension underneath.

Another beat of silence, and then Madison made a show of studying the menu, tapping one manicured finger against her chin. The others snickered.

This was taking way too long. I had two other tables waiting to order; all the other staff were rushing around like crazy. But walking away, trying to ignore them as they did me, would only make it worse.

"Is the chicken pie homemade?" Kelsey asked.

I pressed my lips together and nodded.

"What about the pasta? Is that gluten free?" Steph asked.

It took physical effort not to grind my teeth or roll my eyes. I shook my head no.

Then Madison put the nail in my coffin. "I'd like to hear the specials."

She leaned back in her seat and crossed her arms, giving me a smug look.

I hated her in that moment. I'd hated her so many times over the last few years, but in *that moment*, my hatred for her was seething and pure. She was taking my choice away. She was forcing me to expose myself to Turner in front of all of them, at work, with my only friends in the world *right there*. Donna's table had gone silent. I could feel their eyes on me, but I could focus on only one crisis at a time. I couldn't imagine what they were thinking. I was *so* humiliated.

And the worst thing was—Madison didn't even know any of these things. She just had a natural instinct for making my life hell.

With no other options, I pulled my shoulders back. I refused to do this while cowering, even though every survival instinct I had was urging me to hunch over and duck my head, scurry away like a mouse from a cat. I hoped it looked casual as I told them about the specials, my voice clear and steady—even though I was dying on the inside.

I looked directly at them as I spoke, but I didn't see them. My full focus was on Turner.

He'd been fiddling with the corner of a napkin when Madison had asked for the specials, his face turned down, one arm slung over the back of the booth behind Bonnie's shoulders. When I started to speak, he froze. Every muscle in his body seemed to tense. His jaw twitched; his long fingers wrapped around the napkin and squeezed.

He knew. How could he not?

But why wasn't he looking at me? Was he repulsed now that he knew who I was?

I couldn't stand this. I needed to be away from this whole mess. I let some frustration leak into my voice. "We're really busy tonight. What's your order?"

Several cutting looks were thrown in my direction.

"Don't rush me," Kelsey snapped.

Tears pricked the backs of my eyes. I was done. I'd send one of the other girls to deal with them.

Before I could book it out of there, Turner spoke. "Hey, neighbor," he said in that ocean-calm way, his eyes still downcast and hidden by the hat, not looking at me.

He wanted to confirm it was really me, but he didn't want any of them to know. Was he protecting me? Or himself? I so badly wanted to give him the benefit of the doubt. I'd been adamant I didn't want anyone to know about us. Maybe now he understood the implications. Maybe he was honoring my wishes.

But he'd still just sat there as they treated me like shit. This moment had been taken from me—just as they took everything else.

White-hot anger crawled up my spine, giving me the strength to remain upright.

"Oh, shit." Jayden laughed. "You two are neighbors? That fucking sucks, bro. Imagine having to look at that face even when at home."

A muscle in Turner's jaw ticked. Someone slammed something onto the table at Donna's booth. *Please, god, don't come over here.*

"You must be confused. You've never seen me . . . stranger." I hoped he got my meaning. He'd never seen me *really*—not this ugly, twisted, ground-into-the dirt side of me. Not like this.

The heat at my spine was going to my head, the rage turning to frustration and despair as the backs of my eyes started to sting. I really fucking didn't want to cry in front of everyone.

Turner rested both elbows on the surface of the table and twisted his head to look at me. I dropped my eyes before they could meet his. I didn't want him looking at me. I wanted to crawl into a hole and *die.*

"I'll have the cob salad." Madison placed the menu on the table delicately, as if we'd all been waiting for her to make up her mind. As if I wasn't standing there completely destroyed inside. Was she that oblivious? Or was she turning the knife?

The others followed her lead and rattled off what they wanted. I kept my focus on my pen and pad and collected the menus, not meeting anyone's eyes, then turned back toward the kitchen.

"Wait!" Madison held out a hand but didn't actually touch me. I paused and looked back at her.

"Who cooks the food?" she asked.

Are you fucking kidding me? Couldn't they just let me leave? I glanced at the counter. Leah and one of the other waitresses were throwing me cautious looks. They knew something was up; I was taking too long. I ground my teeth and answered in as calm a tone as I could muster. "Our cook and his assistant."

"So, you don't actually handle the food, right?"

"No." I frowned.

"OK, cool. Just checking. I wouldn't want to catch anything and end up looking like someone took an iron to my face."

The table burst into laughter as I walked off.

I couldn't look at Turner. I didn't think I could hear his deep voice joining in the laughter, but he hadn't defended me either. Maybe he really wasn't the guy I thought he was.

This was the worst night of my life.

I could handle them being assholes to me. This wasn't even as bad as what I usually had to deal with. But the fact that Turner knew everything now, that he'd just sat there and let it happen, that the only people in the world I could remotely call friends had seen me treated like a leper . . . My whole world was imploding, and the rubble was all piling down onto my chest.

As I passed Donna's booth, I couldn't help glancing up. Half the group was staring at me in shock, the other half studying the table. They were all deathly silent. Donna's gaze bored into me with startling intensity. Was she embarrassed? Upset that I'd made her look bad by association? Was I about to lose every single good thing in my life in one fell swoop?

I rushed away and put the order in, waving off my concerned coworkers with a brittle smile. "Just some kids from my school being dicks. Nothing I can't handle."

We were too busy for anyone to really push the issue.

I did my best to go into autopilot as I delivered the food and drinks to Turner's table in batches. The last was a tray of milkshakes. Once I'd deposited them on the table, Jayden didn't even try to hide the flask as he tipped alcohol into all but one of the frosty glasses. I sighed. There was no point in telling them they couldn't do that. I could tell Leah—she'd kick them all out on their asses. But that would only make things worse for me at school.

I grabbed the tray and straightened up as Madison extended one manicured hand, reaching for the milkshake closest to the table's edge. She nudged it deliberately, like a cat pushing a mug in one of those videos online. I tried to jump back, but it was too late. A strawberry-flavored, icy mess splattered all down the front of my legs and slopped into my shoes.

I gasped as the cold seeped into my clothes.

"Oops." Madison shrugged and pressed her lips together, fighting a laugh. The whole table was shaking with barely controlled laughter.

"You're so reckless, Phil. I hope that doesn't come out of your paycheck." She tutted, clearly hoping it did. "Oh well. Better bring me another one."

Still not as bad as other shit she'd done to me.

Still Turner did nothing.

Still I couldn't look at him.

Sticky with sugary milk and resentment, I turned to leave.

Amaya and Drew both got to their feet. Drew's hands were balled into fists. Amaya looked ready to explode—her beautiful face had gone red, her eyes bugging out.

My eyes widened, and in a panic, I looked at Donna. She was still seated in the booth, her posture rigid, her intense stare on me. Next to her, Harlow had her head in her hands.

I gave Donna a pleading look and shook my head. It would only make this worse if they made a scene.

"Sit your asses down," she demanded. Drew and Amaya huffed and looked between us, ready to argue. A few of the others had half risen from their seats too, but after a tense moment, they all sat back down.

I hurried off

Leah spotted me. "Oh, shit."

"Yeah." I sighed. "Can someone please send another strawberry milkshake to table twelve? I need to clean up."

"Sure thing, sweetie. Take your time." Leah squeezed my shoulder as I passed.

In the privacy of the staff bathroom, as I cleaned up as best I could with my shaking hands, I gave in to the tears. They fell freely down my cheeks, fat drops of sorrow, humiliation, and despair. How the hell was I supposed to go back out there and face them all? What the hell was I supposed to do about Turner?

I splashed water on my face even as I continued to sob, the hot tears mingling with the cool liquid. Eventually, I managed to stop crying long enough to dry off. I let my mousy hair down, hoping it would at least partially hide my splotchy face and red eyes.

Fighting fresh tears, I headed back out.

The dinner rush had passed; the diner was half-empty. Table twelve had cleared out.

I breathed a sigh of relief.

Avoiding everyone's eyes, I went to clear it. Madison's group had left an absolute mess and no tip. One plate remained untouched—the cheeseburger with extra fries.

The booth next to it was half-empty too. Donna, Harlow, and Amaya sat in a row on one side, watching me silently.

CHAPTER ELEVEN

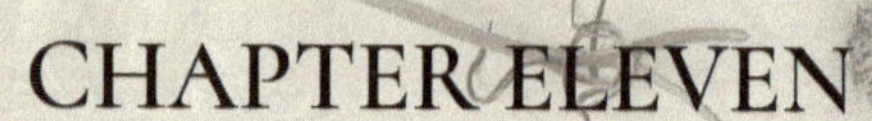

Donna had been silently pacing the length of her massive bedroom for a solid five minutes, her footsteps soft on the luxurious white carpet. She had her arms crossed, a deep frown on her face.

Amaya was leaning against Donna's desk by the window, staring at the floor intently. Harlow was on the bed next to me, her legs drawn up to her chin.

I shifted uneasily, worried about staining Donna's white sheets with my still wet and messy uniform. As if I didn't have enough to obsess over already.

The three of them had stayed in their booth until most of the other customers had cleared out. They hadn't budged while I worked. Only when Leah sent me home, an hour before close, did they get up and follow me outside.

I'd tried to tell them my mom was about to pick me up and I couldn't hang out, but Donna informed me she'd already called my mom and told her I was staying the night at their place. She marched over to her white BMW and opened the passenger door. I didn't have the energy to argue.

The drive to the nice side of Devilbend—the side with tall gates and trimmed hedges—had been tense and silent. Donna had driven fast, taking corners at unsafe speeds and gripping the steering wheel tightly.

Now we were all piled in her bedroom, several carefully placed lamps casting the opulent space in a warm, soft glow, and still no one had spoken.

My left knee bounced. I couldn't stand not knowing what was going through her head, but I couldn't bring myself to ask. I sighed and leaned my elbows on my knees, digging my nails into my hair.

My movement must've snapped Donna out of it; the sound of pacing stopped. I looked up, my body still bent over itself.

Donna stood in the middle of her room, frowning at me, her hands on her hips. "Mena, what the fuck was that?"

I opened my mouth, no idea how to answer, but what came out wasn't words. It was a sob.

Tears came so quickly and so intensely they took my breath away.

Harlow scooted closer and wrapped her arms around me, while Donna kneeled on the floor and took my hands.

"I'm sorry." Her voice sounded strained.

I glanced at Harlow to see her own eyes were glassy. Amaya was still at Donna's desk, but she was breathing hard, a look of deep worry on her face.

"Mena, I'm sorry." Donna squeezed my hands. "I didn't mean to attack you. I'm just so *angry*. I can't believe those assholes treated you like that. Please, just tell me what's going on."

I took a few shuddering breaths, and even though my heart was in my throat, I told them everything.

The ignoring and exclusion.

The mean comments and taunts.

All the shit on social media—the messages sent to me. At this, Amaya dug my phone out of my bag and demanded my password. I keyed it in, any resistance to them learning the whole ugly truth gone. She scrolled through, her eyes widening, her teeth clenching, her hand eventually covering her mouth in horror.

I told them about the printouts of screenshots when I'd tried to get off social media, about the incident in the bathroom last year. Swallowing any pride I had left, I even told them about Turner. *All of it*. Right up to how he'd done nothing just hours earlier.

I purged it all, laying my dirty, repulsive secrets at their feet to stain Donna's pristine carpet, just as my sticky uniform was staining her sheets.

By the time I'd finished speaking, I was drained, my eyelids heavy, my shoulders slumped. I sighed again and looked around at them.

Silent but steady tears were flowing down Harlow's cheeks. Amaya had one fist pressed to her mouth, her other arm crossed over her chest with my phone still in her hand.

Donna had remained sitting at my feet, her legs under her, her nails digging into the carpet. "Do your parents know about this?"

"No," I rushed out, her question drawing me out of the numbness I'd fallen into.

"Your teachers? We need to tell—"

"No!" I shot to my feet. "You think I haven't tried? You think I *want* to live like this? You think I haven't gone over every fucking possible way out in my mind? *There is no way out.*"

Donna slowly stood up as I ranted, my hands balled into fists. But it was Amaya who made the next move.

She bolted across the room and smashed into me, squeezing me tightly in her arms. "Oh my god, Mena. *Oh my god!*"

For a beat I just stood there, stunned, my arms hanging at my sides. Amaya was as tough as Donna and even more of a bitch—in a good way. I'd never seen anything get to her. *Ever.* She was stone cold. I couldn't count the number of times I'd wished I was as resilient and cool as her.

I hugged her back, closing my eyes and letting myself be comforted. Donna wrapped her arms around us both, and Harlow completed the group hug on our other side. We just stood like that for a while.

Everything was fucked up beyond measure, but at least I had them. I knew now they didn't simply tolerate me, as I sometimes worried they did; they genuinely considered me as much a friend of theirs as I considered them friends of mine. I wasn't an occasional, annoying, poor fourth wheel in their group. I was *one of them.*

"We love you, Mena." Harlow's voice sounded so small. Had she stopped crying at all? "We've got you, girl. Whatever you want to do, we'll have your back."

"Always," Amaya agreed fiercely, her words right in my ear.

"Without a shadow of a doubt," Donna added. "But, girl, what's the deal with your parents? And the teachers? Why is no one doing anything to stop this?"

"I'll explain," I said. "But . . . er . . . can I do it sitting down? I'm getting kind of hot here, guys."

We all chuckled and separated. We'd been standing in a vertical puppy pile for a good five minutes.

"How about showers first?" Amaya frowned down at her previously white skirt, pulling the fabric away from her perfect legs. Splotches of pale pink marred the pristine fabric.

My eyes widened. "Shit! Sorry, Amaya. I . . ." I was about to say I'd pay for it, but I was pretty certain I couldn't afford to replace that. Maybe I could pay for the dry cleaning.

She fixed me with a firm look. "Stop. You're not allowed to be sorry about anything tonight. I hate this fucking skirt anyway. Go. Shower."

I smiled at her.

"I'll get you some PJs." Donna headed for her closet.

"I'll get us some food." Harlow gave me a watery smile, wiping the tears from her cheeks as she moved toward the door.

After a nice hot shower in Donna's bathroom, with six jets working the tightness from my muscles, I dressed in a bamboo cotton set Donna had left on the bench for me. Somehow, it just happened to be in my size. Harlow and I were about the same height, but I was bigger than all of them—I had a feeling the girls had bought this specifically for me. In fact, I had a feeling they had a whole stash of stuff they were just waiting for an opportune moment to give me.

When I came out of the bathroom, the three of them were pulling a mattress through the door, grunting with the effort.

Harlow flashed me a grin. Her eyes were red, but she'd finally stopped crying. "We're all sleeping in here tonight. It'll be like the slumber parties we used to have when you first moved here."

I shook my head and helped them pull Donna's mattress down too. Her room was spacious enough that we could butt the two mattresses together.

We got comfy in the bedding and pillows, someone put music on, and the next half hour was spent stuffing our faces with junk food. They even had my fave cheddar cheese popcorn. I ate an entire bag by myself and chased it down with chocolate ice cream.

Just as the food coma was setting in, Donna spoke up. "Mena, why don't your parents know about this?"

I sighed. "I've wanted to tell them but . . . what's the point?"

"What do you mean?" Amaya tried to argue. "They're your parents. I'm sure they'd want to—"

"I have no doubt they'd want to help," I interrupted her. "Don't get me wrong —it's not that I think my parents don't give a shit. It's that . . . look, you guys don't understand how much easier some things are when you have money."

They all remained silent. This wasn't something we'd ever discussed, but they weren't idiots. They knew I was poor—as evidenced by the brand-new PJs I was wearing.

"My parents both work full time, and it's just enough to cover our rent, to keep the car running and food in the fridge. When they do overtime, sometimes we can do extra things like go to the movies or get a pizza or whatever. I stopped asking for things a long time ago, because I learned we can't afford them. The only reason I can buy clothes and makeup is because *I* work."

They were listening, but they looked confused, obviously missing the connection.

"If I tell my parents," I went on, "they'll have to come down to the school, talk to my teachers. They'll miss work—money we can't afford to miss out on. And then what? I can't change schools. The only other school that wouldn't take two or more hours to get to is *yours*, and they sure as shit can't afford to send me there. So why stress them out when there's nothing to be done about it?"

"OK." Donna nodded. She was trying to understand, but this was hard for her. She was a doer, a fixer. "They may not be able to let you switch schools, but if they knew the crap you were dealing with, they might be able to get the school to do something about it."

I was shaking my head before she'd even finished. "No. I've tried. No one gives a shit, you guys." I groaned and ran my hands through my hair. They were all frowning at me.

"What?" Harlow looked outraged.

"When we first moved here, my mom didn't have a job. My dad was working two just to keep us off welfare. They were out of their minds with stress. And when all this crap started . . . it's not like I was bashed up on my first day of school. It started with being excluded, ignored, then the name calling and shit talking started. I went home crying after school for a month solid. On the days my parents were there . . . I didn't have the words to tell them what was happening, and they kind of assumed I was just missing my friends and my old school—that I was struggling to adjust.

"Eventually, I spoke to a teacher. I told Mr. Young that some of the other kids were picking on me. He reminded me of my grandpa with his gut and the bushy moustache." I laughed lightly. "But he all but dismissed me, saying I needed to toughen up, get a thicker skin or some shit.

"When it escalated in sophomore year—the first time Madison shoved me into a wall and then loudly wondered how she'd just bumped into thin air—I reported it to another teacher. We were both called in. Madison denied it, putting on an innocent act. When she left, the teacher said I needed to have proof before accusing other students of serious things. She dismissed it, but Madison sure as fuck didn't. They were careful to stay out of sight of the teachers, but they made my life a living hell for a whole week." I didn't go into details. I didn't like thinking too much about that week, let alone talking about it.

"Anyway," I continued, "a couple of other kids have tried reporting Jayden and his friends too, but it never goes anywhere. The boys are too well liked by the faculty, because they're on the football team. The girls are fucking smart about how they dish out the torture, making it hard to prove. The school can't and won't do anything about it. Trying to report this shit again will just make my life even harder."

"God dammit!" Amaya growled and threw a pillow across the room. "This is infuriating. How the fuck have you been dealing with this for three years, Mena? You're, like, the strongest person I know."

I ducked my head and smiled, flattered. I didn't feel strong. I felt like splinters most days.

"Honestly, you guys, I can handle it," I said.

Disapproving looks fell over their beautiful faces, so I hastened to add, "I know I shouldn't have to. But I can, and there's only, like, 155 school days left before I'm free of it. It was having you guys see it that really upset me tonight." I fiddled with the edge of the cashmere blanket. "I didn't want you to see me like that. I didn't want . . ."

Thinking about him made the lump rise in my throat again.

"You didn't want Turner finding out like this." Harlow squeezed my knee. I nodded, suddenly struggling to meet any of their gazes.

"Fuck Turner!" Amaya crossed her arms. "He can go fuck himself."

I bit back a grin. She was so fierce in her outrage on my behalf. It was down-right heartwarming.

"Which one was he?" Harlow asked.

"The one in the baseball cap. Tall, bomber jacket, panty-melting voice, broad shoulders . . ."

Harlow groaned in frustration, and Donna said "fuck" as though she'd just smashed her favorite pair of designer sunglasses.

"Dammit." Amaya shook her head. "Why is it always the hot ones?"

I chuckled, a tiny bit of pride rising in my chest. These beautiful, smart, amazing girls thought my boyfriend was hot. Then I remembered I was pissed at him and didn't know where we stood after tonight, and my face fell.

I checked my phone—nothing. He hadn't even texted to ask if I was OK.

"What are you gonna do about him?" Harlow nudged me with her shoulder.

"I don't know." I shrugged. "Everything is just so fucked up. I want to explain shit. But then I'm so fucking mad he didn't defend me, or even say anything, and he hasn't even texted me. Like, does he even care? But then I think about all the things he's said to me, the *real* connection we have, and I feel like of course he cares! But then after tonight I'm questioning if *that* was even real. Like, what if it was all in my head? What if he knew who I was this whole time, and this is just some elaborate prank? I just . . . I feel like I'm going fucking crazy."

I growled and flopped back against the pillows.

Harlow lowered herself onto her belly next to me, her chin in her hands. "I think you just need to talk to him, get it all out in the open. Maybe he didn't say anything because he was worried it would make it worse for you."

I considered that. He had looked uncomfortable sitting there as they'd picked on me. But that could've been for any reason. Shit, maybe he had gas!

"No. Fuck that," Amaya said, and Harlow rolled her eyes. "Fuck any asshole that isn't there for you no matter what. Ride or die. He didn't ride tonight. So, he should just die. Like, figuratively. In your heart . . . but also maybe literally."

I laughed at her murderous tendencies, then sighed. "Donna? What do you think?"

Donna sat leaning against the bedframe, her legs stretched out and her hands clasped in her lap. She hadn't said anything in a while.

"I think you should sleep on it. Whatever you decide, we'll have your back. And if he hurts you, we'll fuck him up." She was so calm when she said it; I had no doubt my determined cousin would find a way to "fuck up" a guy twice her size. "But honestly, I'm more worried about the shit you're dealing with every day, Mena. You're being bullied, and I can't just stand by and let it happen."

I sat up. "Donna, please. We've been over this. You can't tell my parents. Or yours. *Please.*" I wasn't above begging.

"I hear you. We won't tell your parents, but you have to let us help."

"What can you possibly do?" I threw my hands up and let them flop onto the soft bedding. I didn't say it—I'd never say it to them—but sometimes their privilege made them think they could just snap their fingers and have whatever they wanted. The real world didn't work like that.

"Maybe we could . . . lean on them a little. Convince them to leave you alone," she suggested vaguely.

I frowned. "What? How?"

"Threaten them. Rough them up a bit." She shrugged, as if it were no big deal. As if she wasn't talking about committing crimes.

Amaya laughed. "OK, Tony Soprano. How are we supposed to do that?"

Harlow was looking at her sister as though she had a screw loose.

"We don't. We get someone else to do it for us. I could make some phone calls," Donna said cryptically.

"To whom?" Harlow chimed in. "We know the same people. None of them are hardened criminals."

Donna looked around at us and smiled. "Uh . . . I'm sure we could find a way. I'm just brainstorming here. We'll figure something out. Point is, Mena, you have to let us help you in some way. I can't just sit around knowing you're being treated like shit. I refuse to do nothing. The Devilbend Dynasty takes care of its own."

There was no point in arguing with Donna when she set her mind to something.

"As long as you promise not to tell our parents or my teachers, and you don't do anything to make my life worse, yes, fine, help away." I sighed and dropped back against the pillows.

CHAPTER TWELVE

When Donna and I managed to drag our asses out of bed around eleven the next morning, Amaya was already gone, and Harlow was still fast asleep. We made our way downstairs and had breakfast with Auntie Em, then Donna drove me home in relative, comfortable silence. The windshield wipers swooshed rhythmically for the entire twenty-minute drive as a Sunday chill playlist softly drifted through the speakers.

Donna didn't bring up any of the crap we'd discussed ad nauseam the night before until she pulled up next to my building.

"You don't have to deal with this alone anymore, Mena. We're here for you." She gave me a serious look, and I leaned over the console to hug her. She squeezed me tightly, then smiled as I pulled back. "I love you." She looked away.

I appreciated that more than she could know. I knew how hard it was for her to show emotion most of the time.

"I love you too, Donna." I moved to get out of the car, but she reached over and gripped my forearm.

"Let me drive you to school tomorrow." It wasn't a question. It was practically a demand.

I laughed. "Don't *you* have to go to school?"

"Yeah but . . . just let me, OK?"

I narrowed my eyes. "Why?"

She rolled hers. "Mena."

"OK. Fine. I'll see you in the morning."

She finally released my arm. "Great! See ya then."

I got out of the car, and she drove off.

Once she was gone, I trudged up the path toward my building. I'd put my work uniform on to go home, and I didn't really care if I got soaked—it was covered in milkshake anyway.

As I rounded the corner, I paused, my heart flying into my throat.

I hadn't expected to see Turner until tomorrow at school, had maybe even planned to avoid him a while longer. But there he was, sitting on the entryway steps and blocking my way. He had his baseball hat on, his head in his hands, his elbows resting on his knees.

As if he could feel me looking at him, he lifted his head and spotted me. He stood up, his movements lithe and quick, and came down the stairs, out of the cover of the entranceway and into the softly falling rain.

I set my shoulders, lips pursed, and focused on the door, fully determined to walk right past him.

"Mena." He reached for me as I passed. Why did his voice have to sound so rough, so broken?

"Don't touch me." I leapt out of his way, off the path and onto the patchy grass.

He stepped back immediately, his breathing hard, almost frantic. His hands flew to his head before dropping once more to his sides.

Why did he have to look so good? His gray sweatpants hung loose and low on his hips, and a black tank was stretched across his defined chest, the gray hoodie over it left unzipped. I wanted to lean into him, push my hands under the hoodie and around his waist, rest my cheek against his strong chest. How was I supposed to stay mad at him when all I wanted to do was put on my own sweats and find a couch so we could cuddle and listen to the rain?

That rain was now plastering my hair to my face; wet patches were gathering on Turner's shoulders.

I raced up the steps, but he was right on my heels.

"Wait, wait, wait. Mena, please." He sounded so desperate. I hated myself for stopping.

I turned to face him and crossed my arms. "What?"

"I . . ." He looked lost. I could only just make out his eyes under the hat—they were watching me intently, flying about my face. "Fuck. I've been sitting there for hours, running through what I'd say to you, and now it's all just . . . gone."

Hours? "Why have you been sitting in the rain for hours?"

He took a deep breath. "Waiting for you. I waited for you last night too. But then you left with those girls, and . . . I just want to make sure you're OK."

I rolled my eyes. "Whatever. That's why you called and texted last night then? To make sure I'm OK?"

He hung his head. "I wrote and deleted dozens of messages. I was up all night, trying to think of something to say that . . . nothing seemed like it was enough. I . . . I had no idea where to even start."

"A simple 'Are you OK?' would've been a good start."

"Fuck. Yes. You're right. It just seemed so . . . inadequate. I'm sorry. I am *so, so sorry*."

"For what exactly?" I tilted my head, tears stinging the backs of my eyes. This was breaking my heart. He clearly cared. He wouldn't be standing in front of me, looking as torn up as I felt, if he didn't. But I couldn't just let go of the hurt. I wanted answers. Maybe it was unfair to lay all my anger with the world at Turner's feet. But I didn't care what those other assholes had to say—they couldn't hurt me as he could.

"All of it. For what you've had to deal with. For not saying anything last night. For not doing more. For . . . fuck . . . everything. If I'd known it was you all those times, I would've said something. I would've done more. I . . ." He swallowed, faltering, but I still wasn't satisfied.

"That's your reasoning? If you'd known it was me, you would've done something? So, it's not OK that they treat *me* like shit, but it's OK if they do it to other people? Is that the standard, Turner? People you care about should be protected, but fuck everyone else? That's a pretty messed-up morality system. It's *not* OK. Whether it's me or some other desperate loser whose name you don't know, it's not OK to treat people like shit. And it's not OK to stand by and watch it happen and do *nothing*," I ground out and swiped at the angry tears now streaming down my face.

He made a pained sound and reached for me again.

"Don't." I stepped out of his reach, pressing my back against the chipped metal railing.

He turned away, his body radiating tension, and gripped his head with his hands. He took his hat off, ran a hand through his soft blond hair, and put the hat back on backward before turning to face me again.

I had an unhindered view of his face now—could see the dark circles under his eyes, the pain in his dark gaze.

"You're right. It's not OK. You have no idea how badly I want to call them all out on their shit. I don't even fucking *like* Jayden. He is such a douchebag."

"Then why are you friends with them?" I huffed. This was what it came down to. This was why I'd been so afraid to tell him from the start. I was *terrified* he'd choose popularity, image, over something real. Because I no longer doubted what we had was real. I could see it in his desperate eyes, hear it in his pleading voice. He felt as strongly about me as I did about him. But was it enough? Was *I* enough?

He growled and looked up to the ceiling before focusing his gaze back on me. "I don't want to be friends with them. I swear."

"So, stop. We have each other. We're both seniors. School will be over in a few months anyway, and none of this will matter."

He sighed and looked away. "I wish that was true. God, you have no idea how badly I wish that none of this mattered."

My heart splintered.

I wasn't enough.

Fresh tears trailed down my cheeks. I tried to swallow them down, but that just made me choke on my own heartache, so I took a shuddering breath.

Turner's eyes got watery too, and his voice wavered as he spoke. "It's not that simple. I can't just walk away. It's not up to me."

I chuckled darkly and shook my head. "What does that even mean?"

"I don't know how to explain without . . . it's not . . ."

"It's not going to work," I finished for him, dropping my gaze.

"What?" He stepped toward me again, and a sob tore from his throat. "No. That's not . . . just give me a couple of weeks. I need some time to sort it out, and then I'll tell you everything. I can explain all of this. I . . . we can just keep doing what we've been doing. No one has to know. I just need a little time."

He was pleading with me, but it just sounded like more excuses. He wanted to have his cake and eat it too. He wanted to be the gorgeous popular guy everyone liked while still having his piece on the side. Well, I was no one's side chick.

"Fuck you, Turner." I wish I'd said it firmly, with anger lacing the words. But it came out on a sob, sounding weak and hurt—sounding exactly the way I felt.

I wrenched the door open and ran up the stairs, not waiting for the elevator.

He didn't follow me.

CHAPTER THIRTEEN

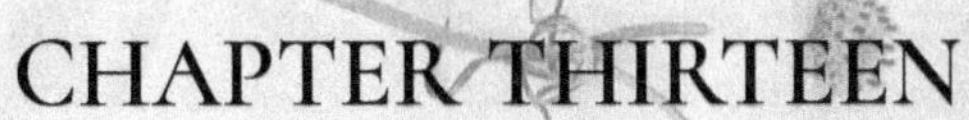

O n Monday morning, for the first time, I didn't go out to the balcony and wait for Turner to leave—it didn't matter if he saw me anymore.

Donna's BMW was waiting for me in the same spot where she'd dropped me off the day before. I was honestly glad I wouldn't have to walk to school in the light, unremitting rain.

As soon as I opened the passenger door, I was met with a cheery "Good morning!" that made me cringe. Amaya and Harlow were in the back seat, and all three of them had yelled the greeting. They looked amazing in their Fulton Academy uniforms—teal tartan skirts and matching ties, dark gray blazers over crisp white shirts. I looked down at my skinny jeans and black sweater and sighed.

"It's too early for that level of enthusiasm," I grumbled as I slid into the car. It also made me slightly worried. When they were this coordinated and excited, it usually meant they had something up their sleeve.

"Shut up and caffeinate." Harlow handed over a large takeaway cup.

I moaned before I even tasted it; I could already smell the caramel syrup. They were driving me to school, and they'd gone out of their way to bring me my fave complicated coffee I could in no way afford to have more than once a week. True friendship!

"I'll give you money next time I see you. Don't have my wallet," I mumbled around the cup.

"No, you won't." Donna took off. They always refused to take my money, and I refused to stop offering it.

We chatted about nothing important and listened to music, but it was a short drive. I didn't notice the other cars until they were pulling up next to us.

Another pang of anxiety spiked.

"Shit. What did you guys do?" I bugged my eyes out as a black Lexus pulled up on our left. I could see another shiny, very expensive vehicle beyond. They'd all parked on a diagonal right in front of the school, blocking half the parking lot and taking up space as if they owned it. Who knows, one of them probably did.

I may not have noticed the cars until it was too late, but there was no missing those extravagant vehicles in front of a public school in this area of town. Something was up, and the students wanted to know what. They were slowing down to look, abandoning their trek into the school. Some had even turned back.

"I told you I wasn't going to sit back and do nothing. We're taking care of it," Donna announced.

"Fuck. *What did you do?*" Panic laced my voice. I loved Donna for how fiercely protective she was being, but I worried she was about to make my life even worse.

"I remembered who I was and what I do best," she said, not explaining anything. "Harlow did her creepy online stalker thing to get me the info I needed, and Amaya mobilized the troops. Now it's time to remind them who *you* are."

"Mobilized the . . . guys, this isn't a war." I was fighting to remain calm and failing. No one had gotten out of the fancy cars, and a crowd had started to gather. Hopefully the security guards hadn't noticed the commotion.

"Life is war. And I refuse to lose a single battle." With that final unhinged comment, Donna smoothly got out of the car.

As if they'd been waiting for her move, all the other car doors opened, and suddenly a large group of teal-and-gray uniforms were congregating in the parking lot. Drew, William, and the rest of the crew that had been at the diner the other night were all there, along with what looked like half the Fulton Academy football team.

"Fuck my life." I groaned, took another sip of my sugary coffee, and stepped out of the car.

Several of the Fulton Academy crew waved at me, Nicola gave me a fist bump, and a couple of others gave me hugs. They were just standing in front of the cars and chatting, acting casual—as if it were completely normal for them to be in front of my school twenty minutes before the first bell on a Monday.

"Well . . . uh . . . thanks for the ride, you guys." I kept my voice low, speaking only to the girls. "And the escort, I guess. I'll see ya?" It came out like a question, but I turned to leave anyway.

"Nope." Donna stepped into my path. "We haven't made our point yet."

"What exactly is the point?" It felt as if my heart were trying to shatter my ribcage. So many people were staring, and I hadn't gone unnoticed—the only Devilbend North High student in among all the pretty rich people.

"Just chill." Harlow took my backpack off my shoulder and lowered it to the ground as she and Amaya pulled me back to lean on the hood of Donna's car, positioning me between them.

For lack of anything better to do, I took more sips of my coffee.

"Excuse me." Donna sounded sweet, but I knew that disingenuous tone in her voice. She had her sights set on a freshman, his eyes wide and disbelieving. "Yes, you. Could you please run along and find Madison and Jayden?"

The kid nodded and sprinted toward the school.

Shit, shit, shit. What the fuck was Donna up to? I was dying on the inside. On the outside, I tried to act as cool as they were. "Just those two? I mean, you're here. Might as well get the whole gang together."

"The others will follow." Amaya's face was in her phone, as always, her free hand resting behind me on the car. "It's what they do."

Well, that was ... true, but no less terrifying or panic inducing.

Within a few minutes, excited murmurs rippled through the growing crowd, and a path cleared down the middle. My pounding heart jumped into my throat. I lowered my gaze and hunched my shoulders, taking another sip.

Amaya's hand wrapped around mine. "Head up, Mena. You no longer bow to these vermin."

Her cool, disinterested mask stayed firmly in place, but there was no denying the rage in her tone. Harlow looped her arm through mine, and I took a deep breath and lifted my head. It went against every instinct I had around these people, on these grounds, but I felt stronger with the girls at my side.

Jayden sauntered out of the crowd first, Madison beside him; the others followed close behind, just as Amaya said they would. My gaze scanned their faces, and I wasn't sure whether to be relieved or disappointed when I didn't see Turner with them.

"I hear I've been summoned." Jayden laughed, raising his voice for the crowd, putting on a show. "Color me intrigued. What the fuck do you want?"

Donna smirked at us, then schooled her features into a hard mask, turned to face my tormentors, and crossed her arms over her chest. "Jayden, I'm guessing? And this must be Madison?"

Picking up on Donna's hostile vibe, Madison crossed her own arms and pursed her lips. "And who are you, bitch? What makes you think you can just roll up here and summon us like we're your subjects? This is *our* school. You don't own Devilbend."

"Don't I?" Donna sounded amused. "I'm Mena's cousin, and I thought it was time we had a little chat."

"Who the fuck is Mena, and why should we care?" Jayden chuckled, but his gaze landed on me. They knew what this was about.

"How about you get daddy to buy you a few brain cells and fuck off?" Kelsey snarled, and the girls snickered.

I was screaming internally, not sure if I should be more worried about my safety or Jayden's and Madison's. But I kept my expression smooth, drawing strength from Amaya and Harlow on either side of me.

"You sound and look ridiculous," Bonnie added. "This is the real world. You look like a bunch of preppy losers in those stupid uniforms."

"Our uniform looks better than that tragic Kmart outfit any day." Amaya eyed her up and down.

Bonnie flipped her hair and frowned. "Kmart isn't even a thing anymore. What are you, stupid?"

Amaya just raised her brows and gave her an amused, challenging look, waiting for Bonnie to put two and two together and understand the implication that her outfit not only looked like shit but was outdated.

I could see the exact moment Bonnie figured it out. The smug smile fell off her face, and her nostrils flared, her hands clenching into fists.

"That's enough of the pleasantries." Donna waved a dismissive hand. There was nothing pleasant about her tone—or any of this, really. "Let me put this in a way your subpar-educated, underdeveloped minds will comprehend. My cousin Philomena is—"

"Who the fuck do you think you are?" Madison's raised voice cut across Donna's, but whatever she was going to say died on her tongue.

As one, the entire Fulton Academy crew dropped their casual demeanor. They all pushed off the hoods of their cars and took a menacing step forward, shoulders tense, expressions stony.

My whole body went rigid, ready to spring into action, run away, do *something* when all hell inevitably broke loose. But Amaya and Harlow tightened their hold on me, keeping me in place. Donna didn't even flinch. The four of us were the only ones who didn't move.

As Donna's crew stepped up, the assholes from my school reflexively stepped back, eyes wide in surprise and fear. Some even went into a slight crouch, ready to throw down. The other students gasped, but no one left, too enthralled in the spectacle, the drama. If I hadn't been freaking out, I might have been entertained too—this was better than an episode of *Real Housewives*.

Donna spoke again, her voice clear and firm. "Don't interrupt me when I'm speaking."

She stood still for a beat, letting the silence get heavier.

That's when I noticed Turner. He walked up from the direction of home, his backpack slung over one shoulder and his other hand stuffed into the pocket of his jeans. About halfway into the middle of the crowd, he paused. Every fiber of my being was aware of him in my periphery, but I refused to look directly at him. Plus, I was worried if I took my eyes off Donna, she was going to go full terminator on these fuckers, and that really would complicate my life.

It was like watching an apex predator dominate all the other animals in the jungle. Donna was unflappable, while the others reacted before even thinking shit through.

"Let's try this again," she said. This time, no one dared interrupt. "Philomena

Willis is my cousin. I don't allow my family to be treated like shit. So that's going to stop."

"You're trying to force us to be friends with Phil?" Kelsey looked me up and down and sneered.

"Good *god,* no." I could practically hear Donna's eye roll. "No family of mine will lower themselves to your level. No, you're simply to stay away from her. Don't talk to her. Don't touch her. Don't contact her online. Don't so much as think about her."

"Or what?" Jayden was brave enough to step forward, I'd give him that. Or maybe I was mistaking bravery for stupidity.

"Or there will be consequences," Donna said, as if she were explaining something complicated to a toddler.

"Are you threatening us?" Madison sounded outraged.

"No. I'm simply explaining cause and effect. Fuck with Mena and I'll fuck with you." For the first time, a bit of bite entered Donna's tone.

"How full of yourself can you be?" Madison crossed her arms again, but she was staying back, in the relative safety of the crowd. "None of you assholes go here. You can't protect her all the time."

She threw me a smug look, and my heart sank. I refused to let it show on my face, but this was exactly what I was afraid of. The Fulton crew would all drive off, go back to their privileged lives, and I'd be left to deal with the pack of animals they'd just poked with a proverbial stick. What the hell was Donna thinking?

But I should've known. Donna never did anything without thinking it through. Without at least three backup plans.

"That's cute." I could hear the smirk in Donna's voice. "Your world is so tiny. But that's the thing. You feel powerful in a pack, pushing a girl around, walking these halls like you own this school. But there's a whole big world out there. A world in which your parents live and work. A world in which I can ruin you in more ways than you can count."

"Empty words." Jayden scoffed. "My dad works for BestLyf. You're not the only one who knows people."

"Your father—Boyd Burrows—is middle management at best. He doesn't even make enough to send you to a private school."

How the hell did she know his dad's name? I frowned, and Harlow chuckled, giving my arm a little squeeze. Of course. Harlow's stalking. But I didn't have time to think about how creepy my little cousin could be. Donna was still speaking.

"And, Bonnie, your mom works at GoodGrocer, right? Heath Preston owns that company. He and my dad are old friends. I call him Uncle Heath. And, Steph, your dad works for Mitchell Mechanics. Mr. Mitchell went to college with my mom. We had him and his wife, Darlene, over for dinner last week. Oliver

Vanderford runs Norton Corp. He and my dad are golf buddies—he even tried to set me up with his son a few times." She chuckled, then got deathly serious again. "Several of your parents work for him, right? I'd hate to have to mention to my family friends how *appallingly* their employees' children are behaving. I mean, these are family-run, respectable businesses. They can't have people working for them who would tarnish those brands."

Holy. Shit. Most of the kids at my school were in similar situations to mine. We knew how tenuous our parents' grip on financial stability was. Donna had gone right for the jugular. I almost felt sorry for them.

They all looked furious, teeth clenched, eyes narrowed. But how could they argue with that?

Then Kelsey stepped forward and propped a hand on her hip. "My parents work for themselves. You can't do shit to threaten me. You don't control every-thing, you stuck-up bitch."

For the first time since she'd started to speak, Donna moved. She took three measured steps forward, leaned in, and whispered in Kelsey's ear.

Kelsey visibly paled. Her eyes widened and looked at Donna with fear. "You can't . . . how . . ." she stammered, then turned on her heel and barreled through the crowd.

I'd never wanted anything as badly as I wanted whatever that information was—the ability to make Kelsey disappear like that? *Priceless.*

Donna raised her voice. "That's all. Dismissed."

She turned back to us, a satisfied smile on her face as the crowd all started to speak over one another.

"Remind me to never get on your bad side." I gave her a tentative smile.

"Shit, I'm your sister, and I'm a little scared." Harlow chuckled.

"I'm kinda turned on." Amaya cocked her head, and we all burst out laughing.

"Thank you, guys. I really hope this works." I gave them each a hug.

"Anytime, girl. We got you." Donna held on for an extra beat before letting go.

And then I was swallowed in a sea of Fulton uniforms as every single person Donna had brought with them came up and gave me a hug, a fist bump, or words of encouragement murmured in my ear.

Drew stepped up last, that cheeky grin on his face, and wrapped his big arms around me. His tight squeeze lifted me clean off the ground, eliciting a surprised yell from me that ended on a laugh. My legs hung limply as my arms held on to his neck.

"I'm sorry this shit is happening to you, Mena," he whispered in my ear.

"Me too," I whispered back. "Thanks for having my back. I really appreciate it."

"You got it. It was fun, actually." He dropped me to my feet and grinned before saying goodbye and rushing for his car.

Most of the crowd had dispersed while my protectors were taking their leave, but Jayden still stood in the same spot, arms crossed, glaring.

It wasn't until the cars started to pull away, their powerful engines roaring and purring, that he sneered and walked off.

I really fucking hoped this wouldn't make everything worse. Now that my defenders were gone, I was alone again, and that thought sent a cold chill of fear down my spine.

I dropped my empty coffee cup in the trash and picked my bag up off the ground. As I straightened, I noticed Turner still in the same spot, hands in his pockets. He was staring after the cars as they pulled away, his strong brow deeply furrowed.

He kind of looked as if he wanted to punch something—or someone. I knew the feeling. I just couldn't figure out what his problem was. He refused to stand up for me, but no one else was allowed to either?

His gaze turned to me, and the deep, angry frown cleared. The look in its place was kind of uncertain. If I didn't know better, I'd say it was longing that stretched across the distance between us.

He took a deep breath, readjusted his bag on his shoulder, and took a few steps in my direction.

Then his eyes caught on something over my shoulder, and he stopped with a frown. And just like that, I was forgotten again. He changed direction and speed-walked toward the school entrance.

I turned just in time to see Jenny—skinny arms wrapped around her torso, head hung low—walk around the corner of the building. Turner wasn't heading for the entrance. He was going after Jayden's little sister.

In all the bullshit that had been happening lately, I'd almost forgotten that weird situation. Part of me wanted to go after them, demand answers. I'd had enough of this shit. But I was also exhausted, bone tired in every way possible, and it wasn't even nine on Monday morning.

The bell sounded, making the decision for me, and my thoughts turned back to what I would meet beyond those doors.

Donna had bluffed those assholes like a pro. There was nothing left to do but borrow her limitless confidence, keep the bluff going, and walk in there with my head held high.

CHAPTER FOURTEEN

The next three days were blissfully uneventful. Donna and the girls got up extra early and drove me to school every morning, my sweet caramel concoction ready for me as soon as I got in the car. I walked into school and went to my classes with my shoulders back and eyes up. No one bothered me. I still kept to myself and had lunch on my own—I wasn't expecting Donna's threats to work miracles—but I no longer slunk through the halls like a wounded animal. Jayden and Madison sneered when I passed, but the rest of them just ignored me. Kelsey actively avoided me, turning to rush in the other direction whenever she saw me coming.

I'd tried to get Donna to tell me what she'd whispered to her, but she just smirked and cryptically replied that "Secrets like that only have power while they're still secret."

Figuring it was Harlow who'd dug up the dirt on some shady part of the internet, I asked her, but she was just as mystified as me. Whatever it was, Donna had found it all on her own.

Turner kept his distance. He didn't call or text, and I avoided the balcony, so I had no idea if he was going out there or not. It was so damn hard to stay away from him. I couldn't count the number of times I'd written a text only to delete it, had reached for the sliding door handle before pulling myself away. I cried about it every night, when everyone was asleep and the house was dark and silent. I missed him like crazy, and knowing he was just on the other side of the wall was torture.

But it had to be like this. Donna and the girls had lit a fire under me, and I was rolling with this newfound self-confidence thing. I couldn't be with someone who was ashamed to be seen with me.

But I also couldn't really figure out what he was thinking. He'd all but stopped hanging out with that group, though he did walk the halls with Jayden from time to time, and they still talked as if they were close in English. Turner's presence directly in front of me in that class made it impossible to focus. Now that I knew I'd never touch him again, reaching out and feeling his firm, warm shoulder under my palm was all I could think about.

I caught him looking at me several times a day, his expression neutral but his eyes blazing with perplexing emotion.

I'd also seen him speaking with Jenny two more times. Whatever they were up to, they were getting careless. But I was no longer worried he was doing something shady—something to hurt the fragile girl. She looked as if she was pleading with *him* now, and the last time I spotted them by the stairs, she'd even leaned forward and given him a tentative hug. Turner had frozen for a moment, then wrapped his big arms around her little frame and patted her shoulder gently. The gesture looked protective more than anything. I'd left more confused than ever.

By the time my Thursday night shift came around, I was exhausted from the week's emotional whiplash but feeling hopeful. There was only one day left before the weekend. I'd nearly made it.

"So, I'm going to speak to Leah tomorrow"—Chelsea leaned in, keeping her voice low as we wrapped napkins around cutlery—"but I just wanted to tell you I'm going to quit."

I dropped a knife, and it clattered on the counter. "What? Why?"

"I'm gonna miss working with you too, Philly. You were really there for me after the breakup and all that. But it's time." She smiled at me serenely, but my frown only deepened.

"Time for what? Did you get another job?"

"No. But I can't expect amazing things to happen when I'm wasting my time and energy on mediocre things. I learned that at my last BestLyf seminar. I feel really positive about the future."

Mediocre things like making money to buy food and pay rent? I wished I had the confidence to say that to her, but we weren't that close. Instead I just sighed and added Chelsea's quitting to the long list of shit my mind was struggling to deal with. Two large groups came in right after she told me, so I didn't have a chance to ask her more about it anyway.

I got off about ten, texted my dad to pick me up, then grabbed my stuff from the back room. Before leaving, I tried to talk to Chelsea again about her decision, but she waved me off and went to clear one of the remaining tables.

With a sigh, I stepped out into the crisp night air.

"Mena?"

I'd have recognized Turner's ocean-deep voice anywhere. I was pretty sure I'd go to my grave knowing exactly what my name sounded like on his lips. I squeezed my eyes shut and steeled myself before turning toward him.

He stepped away from the wall, out of the shadows. His hat was obscuring his eyes, his dark hoodie and jeans only adding to the menacing vibe.

"What are you doing here?" I asked, unsure if my heart was beating faster because he'd startled me or because I was excited to see him.

"I need to talk to you. You haven't been coming out to the balcony, so . . ."

"So you decided to wait for me at my work like a creep? You could've talked to me at school. You could've called me."

"Would you have picked up?" He conveniently ignored the bit about being seen with me at school.

"I don't know that there's anything left to say, Turner. You made your choice."

"No, I didn't." He stepped toward me, reaching his arms out. "And I have a lot to say. I want to tell you everything. I can't do this anymore. I miss you so much."

His words snaked into my chest, wrapped themselves around my heart and squeezed.

"Why are you doing this? Just let me get over you." *As if I could.*

"Well, *I* can't get over *you*, so . . . I don't even want to." He took a breath and another step closer, visibly steadying himself before speaking again. "Look, I have a lot to explain. Can I please just walk you home?"

I checked my phone—my dad would be there any minute. "Turner, I can't . . ."

"Please."

"No. My—"

"She's my sister," he rushed out just as familiar headlights turned the corner, my dad's beat-up old Toyota Corolla heading straight for us. "Jenny is my little sister."

"What?" I frowned, my brain trying to process. What the hell was he talking about? Was this some attempt to confuse me even further, somehow manipulate me into getting back together with him?

Dad's car pulled up, and Turner closed his mouth, abandoning whatever lie he'd been about to spew next.

"My dad's here. I have to go," I gritted out and turned for the car. Dad rolled down the window, the glass making an obnoxious squeaking noise, and leaned over to look at us. "Hey, Philly. Who's your friend? Do you need a lift anywhere, son?"

I bugged my eyes out at my dad as I opened the passenger door, and he gave me a little frown. When I turned to put my belt on, I jumped. Turner had followed me to the car and was leaning down to look through the window, a friendly expression on his face. I narrowed my eyes at him, but it was too late.

"Actually, I live in your building, sir, and I'd really appreciate a lift." He smiled.

My dad ignored my death glare completely. "Sure thing. Jump in."

I huffed and stared out the window, ignoring them both. The radio was on some easy-listening station, Michael Bublé's crooning the only thing breaking the awkward silence.

After a few minutes, dad eyed the rear-view mirror. "Hey, you—dark and brooding in the back seat. What's your name?" He chuckled at his own mortifying joke.

I only just resisted the urge to pinch the bridge of my nose.

"Turner Hall, sir."

"Nice to meet you, Turner. I'm Brad."

"Nice to meet you too, sir."

After another few awkward minutes of silence, Dad cleared his throat. "Soooo, how do we know Turner, Philly?"

I growled under my breath. I really wished they'd stop calling me Philly, especially in front of people. I was *Mena*. And I wasn't about to explain to my dad the clusterfuck that was Turner and me. "He goes to my school."

Turner sighed, clearly not happy with how I'd reduced our relationship to "classmates," but Turner could go fuck himself. At least he was smart enough to remain silent.

"Cool." Dad dragged the word out and turned the music up, but we were already pulling into the parking area at the back of the buildings.

We piled out of the car, and Turner turned to my dad. "Thank you for the lift, Mr. Willis."

"You're welcome." Dad thumped him on the shoulder. "And please, call me Brad."

Were they trying to be chummy? *Ugh!* That time I couldn't stop my hand from reaching up to pinch the bridge of my nose. I walked to the entrance without looking at either of them.

"Mena?" Turner's pleading tone made me turn to face him. He was begging me with his eyes.

I hated myself for it, but I was curious. With a defeated shake of my head, I turned to my dad. "I'll be up soon, Dad. Just need to speak to Turner."

Dad paused, one hand on the door handle, and looked around at the parked cars, the tall apartment buildings. "I don't know if you noticed, but we live in kind of a rough neighborhood. It's getting late." As if to emphasize his point, a car alarm went off somewhere in the distance, and several dogs started barking in response.

Turner climbed the few steps to join us on the landing. "I'll keep her safe, sir."

Dad gave him a long, serious look. "I'm not entirely convinced she doesn't need to be kept safe *from* you."

My lips twitched into an almost smile. I was simultaneously mortified and kind of happy Turner was copping shit from someone.

"I swear to god, I would never hurt a hair on Mena's head."

"No, you just stand by and watch other people do it," I cut in.

Dad's hard gaze turned on me, his brows creasing in a worried frown. "Philomena?"

I took a calming breath and gave him a reassuring smile. "It's fine, Dad. I'll be up soon."

He looked between us with narrowed eyes. "If you're not up there in fifteen, I'm coming back down." And because he was a dad, and by default an embarrassment, he raised his digital watch, pressed a few buttons on it, and showed us the timer ticking down before he disappeared into the building.

Turner and I stared at each other until the sound of my dad's footsteps faded. Then his mouth quirked up on one side. "Philly?"

"Seriously?" I ground out through clenched teeth. "If you're going to poke fun at me, I'm just gonna go."

I reached for the door, but he lunged forward and took my elbow. "No. Wait. I'm sorry. I just . . . I miss you. I miss our banter."

"Yeah, well . . ." I extracted my arm from his grip. "You said you wanted to talk, not banter, so . . . what the fuck do you mean Jenny is your sister?"

He blew out a big breath and took his hat off, putting it on backward. I wasn't sure if it was better or worse now that I could see the desperation in his gaze. "OK, fair enough. I meant what I said. She's my sister. But no one here knows that. That's why I've been speaking to her, and that's why it looks kind of intense when I do. We've . . . been through some shit. About three years ago, my mom and my sister left, disappeared. My dad and I have been looking for them ever since."

"What? That doesn't even make sense. This sounds like some ridiculous story you made up to confuse me. I just can't understand *why*."

Turner sighed. "I'm not making shit up. I wish I were."

He looked resigned, kind of sad, as he pulled out his phone, tapped away at it, and then held it out to me. Staring back at me from the screen was a young Turner. He was skinnier, a bit more gangly, but it was definitely him grinning at the camera, his arm slung around a little girl's shoulders. I frowned; the girl definitely looked like Jenny.

"Flick through. There's more." Hands in his pockets, he stepped up next to me so we could both look at the pictures on the screen. The next was of a couple, arms around each other, the man laughing while the woman looked off to the side. I'd seen Turner's dad a few times, and that was unquestionably him in the pic—the woman had to be Turner's mom. The next photo showed all four of them grouped around a cake with several candles, Jenny the center of attention at what looked like a birthday celebration. The next was of Turner and his mom. Photo after photo of what was clearly his family.

"I don't understand." I handed the phone back. "What exactly happened? And what does this have to do with anything?"

Turner checked the time. "Look, I don't know how much time we have before your dad's countdown clock runs out, but I'll try to keep it brief. Like I said, my mom took my sister and left. She tried to take me too, we got into a huge fight, and I went and stayed the night at a friend's. I had no idea she was intending to just disappear."

I held up a hand to stop him. "Wait a second. If your mom took your sister, isn't that, like, some form of kidnapping? Why didn't your dad just go to the police?"

"Of course he did. They checked with a few of my mom's friends from church and the one cousin who was all the family we had in the area, then pretty much told him there was nothing they could do. That was just before they put me into a room and asked me a bunch of leading questions about whether my dad got angry or drank or ever yelled at my mom. They pretty much just assumed he was abusive and she'd run away from him. They told him to get a lawyer and washed their hands of it—wouldn't even hear him out about the people responsible. The people that have been helping her stay hidden."

"What people?" I checked my phone. We had ten minutes.

"Look, my parents did not have a happy marriage. I mean, maybe they did when I was younger—I do remember some happy times. But by the time I was in my teens, they'd just fallen out of love. They argued from time to time, and things were tense, distant. But my dad was never abusive. I never once saw him hit her or throw anything or even raise his voice. They weren't at each other's throats—they were just making each other miserable. I think they were trying to keep the family together for us kids, but I wish they'd just broken up. Maybe all this could've been prevented then.

"Anyway, the point is, my mom was lonely, broken. Looking back on it, she had some issues—things neither she nor my dad were equipped to deal with. Those things made her vulnerable. She somehow got mixed up with these BestLyf people, started going to a few free meetings. Then she started paying to attend the more intense seminars. That caused more arguments about money. Dad thought she was wasting it, and Mom felt like it was the only good thing in her life."

"What exactly are you saying?" A heavy dread settled in my gut. I believed he was telling the truth about Jenny being his sister—the photos were undeniable. And I believed him when he said his dad wasn't abusive. I'd never heard any yelling or crashing from the apartment next door, and Turner had never said or done anything to make me think he was scared of his dad. But the story just kept getting crazier and crazier.

"I'm pretty sure BestLyf is a cult." He propped his hands on his hips.

I frowned. That couldn't be right, could it? My mom went to those meetings and had nothing but good things to say. Chelsea loved every second of the personal-development courses. Cults didn't help people be their best selves— they made you live on some secluded farm, waiting for the second coming or some shit. Didn't they?

"What are you talking about? BestLyf is a corporation. They have offices all over the country. They advertise on TV, for fuck's sake." Was Turner a conspiracy theorist?

"I know it sounds crazy, but we're not the only ones this has happened to. There's a whole network of people who have lost loved ones to that hellhole."

"Then did you report that to the police? I'm pretty sure cults are illegal."

"We did." He sounded defeated. I wanted to hug him, so I stuffed my hands into the pockets of my apron. "But after the fifth police station my dad was laughed out of, he stopped trying. BestLyf is a legitimate business in the front—they do provide legit services, but they hide behind that front and ruin people's lives. They've been at this for years. It's hard to find proof. We couldn't get any help from the police, so Dad went straight to the source. He banged on the doors of the BestLyf office in our town, demanded to see my mother. They denied she'd ever even attended a meeting. When we realized my mom and sister were no longer even in town, we started looking for them elsewhere.

"Dad did some research and found all the places they have offices, training facilities, retreats—any property that's associated with them. And we started going to these places. Dad tried to get jobs with them in different towns, but they obviously communicated well between branches, and he could hardly step onto the property before they would call security. So, we came up with a new strategy. We would go to a town where BestLyf had an office, Dad would get a job doing whatever he could find, and I would be enrolled in the local school. I'd make friends, talk to people, figure out whose parents worked for BestLyf, and try to get some inside info. Every spare second we had, we'd stake out the offices and employees' houses trying to get a glimpse of my mom and sister. When we were sure they weren't in that town, we'd move on to the next one."

My eyes widened as he told his insane yet somehow admirable story. I couldn't believe the lengths they were going to. But then, maybe I could. Who knows what I'd do for my own family? "Holy shit," I breathed. "And now you've found them."

"And now we've found them."

I turned away, threading my hands into my hair. "This is fucking insane, Turner."

"I know," he rushed out. "But this is *why*. Please, you have to believe me. This is the only reason I put up with that bunch of cunts. I want to punch Jayden in the nose half the time. But pretending to be his friend has allowed me to get closer to Jenny. I've been over to his place a few times and managed to snoop around a bit. They did a number on my sister, and she's refusing to see my dad, but she hasn't told anyone we're here, so I have hope she's starting to come around. They've convinced her my dad was a bad man—that he was the reason my mom took her and left. I'm slowly helping her remember. But we still haven't seen any sign of my mom, and any time I ask her, Jenny clams up."

"What about Jayden? Have you asked him?"

"About my mom?" He sighed in frustration. "I can't really ask him directly without giving away who I am. I've tried to bring it up in a roundabout way—asking if his mom or dad will be home when he invited the boys over, or asking what his mom does when he mentioned his dad's work. That kind of thing. But all he's said is that his mom died when he was eleven, and he doesn't like talking about it. Never even mentioned a stepmom or anything. It's so fucking weird."

He was breathing hard, his shoulders tight and his fists clenching as he talked. I wanted to wrap my arms around him and make it all better.

"I can't blow my cover yet," he went on. "I can't risk them finding out who I am or that we're even here. But having you think I don't care is fucking tearing me up inside. So, I'm trusting you, Mena. I'm trusting you with my truth."

I hadn't trusted him with mine.

He didn't say it, and I didn't think he meant to throw that in my face, but I drew the parallel myself. I'd lied to him to protect myself. He'd lied to me to protect his family.

And he was dealing with so much—an insurmountable, crazy amount of pressure.

I couldn't hold back anymore. I rushed forward and wrapped my arms around his waist. He hugged me back hard, his heart hammering under my cheek, his heavy breath in my hair.

My phone rang, and I hurried to answer it—it had been twenty minutes. "Just waiting for the elevator, Dad," I said before he could even speak.

"You better be in this apartment in the next three minutes, Philomena."

"Yes. I'm coming." I hung up without waiting for a response and stepped out of Turner's embrace. It was harder than I could've imagined—to have his arms around me after so much angst about how he really felt . . . "I have to go."

He nodded, but he looked so uncertain. "Are we good?"

"Honestly, I don't know. This is just . . . a lot. I need to process."

"OK. Yeah, of course. Just promise you'll let me know if you have any questions? I'll tell you whatever you want to know."

I nodded. I had no more words.

But Turner did. "I want you to know I'm going to fight for you. I know you need to think about all this, but I can't lose you. You're the best fucking thing that's happened to me in a long time."

With one last agonizing look at his beautiful, tortured face, I left.

CHAPTER FIFTEEN

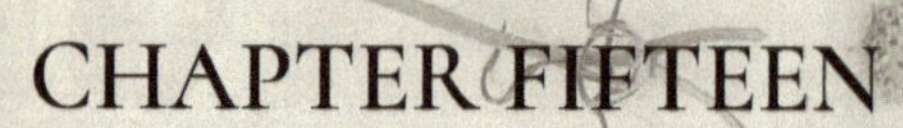

As was becoming my new normal, I hardly slept that night. Thinking about Turner used to keep me up with giddy excitement as I replayed all our interactions in my head. Lately, Turner kept me up because I was heartbroken over how shit had gone down, first because he didn't seem to care and now because of his supposed tragic story.

Around two in the morning, I gave up and grabbed my phone, hardly even surprised when I saw Harlow was online. That girl kept the weirdest times. On a whim, I messaged her. I didn't feel right telling her Turner's story—it felt too private and heavy, with too much at stake if it was true—but I couldn't just take his word for it. Even though I couldn't go into details, Harlow helped me anyway. She dug up a few local missing-person articles from three years ago, and when she looked into Turner's dad, she couldn't find anything worrying, other than complaints from BestLyf.

It all matched Turner's story.

I managed to get maybe three hours of sleep before my alarm went off, and when I saw myself in the mirror, I groaned. I looked like shit. With the girls having my back, and Madison and the others having left me alone all week, I was just emboldened enough to apply some eye makeup. Nothing ostentatious—just enough to cover the bags under my eyes. I didn't touch my birthmark, figuring it was best not to draw too much attention to the fact that I was wearing makeup.

Mom asked over breakfast if I could do her makeup that night. It was my aunt and uncle's anniversary party.

I shook my head. "Sorry. Gotta work. Have fun."

"OK, sweetheart. I'll just pick your dad up and head straight there after work then, so we won't see you after school. Drive dad's car to work—don't walk, OK?"

I waved her off, yawning as I headed out the door.

The girls drove me to school, and the giant coffee they brought me helped perk me up a bit. Thankfully, Harlow didn't bring up our late-night sleuthing. I still wasn't sure what to do about that, or how to feel about it.

I made it through most of the day in a haze, hardly paying attention in class and nearly nodding off in English. As I stopped at my locker during lunch, Madison and her friends happened to be walking past. I spared them a glance and ignored them, assuming they'd keep doing what they'd been doing all week —leaving me alone.

How wrong I was ...

Madison's eyes narrowed as she took in my face, and she walked straight up to me. Kelsey turned around and hurried off, but that still left three of them hovering around my locker.

Madison leaned in and sneered. "You can slap all the makeup on it you want, but you'll always be ugly, Phil."

Anger rose quickly and unchecked, and I slammed my locker shut. I was so done with everything the past few months had thrown at me.

"What the fuck is your problem?" I got up in her face and did not keep my voice down, did not cower or back away. I was like a different person, hands thrown out and eyebrows raised as I unleashed. "What did I ever do to you? Seriously? Why do you hate me so much? Why do you care?"

She shrugged, but the gesture lacked her usual nonchalance. She was seething. "There's just something about certain people. You can't really put your finger on it, but you can't stand the sight of them. You're just hateable, and I wish you'd do me a fucking favor and just die."

"You're a hateful, spiteful bitch, and you'll never be happy. Go fuck yourself!" I yelled into her face. I was completely lost in the rage, not thinking at all about the words coming out of my mouth.

"Miss Willis." Mr. Chen's deep voice froze me to the spot. All the fight drained out of me, and my face fell as I slowly turned toward my English teacher.

He had his hands on his hips, his expression very stern. "That kind of language is unacceptable."

"You should've heard what she was saying before you got here, sir." Suddenly, Madison sounded meek, her voice even a little watery. "She called me the most awful things."

"It's true, sir. We heard it all," Bonnie piped in, Steph nodding emphatically.

What a joke. I rolled my eyes. "Please. What about all the things you've said to me over *literally years.*"

Madison gasped and pressed her hand to her chest. "I would never—"

"Enough!" Mr. Chen snapped, taking his glasses off and rubbing his eyes with the heel of his hand. He looked about as tired as I felt as he mumbled under his breath—something about shitty pay and long hours and teenagers being the devil.

"Miss Barnes, I heard the terrible things you said too. Now, I don't know what this is about, and I don't want to." He held his hand up, stopping Madison from spewing another lie. *Of course* he didn't want to know about it. None of the teachers gave a shit. "You're both about to be adults. You're seniors, for god's sake. The younger kids look up to you. Start acting like it."

"Yes, sir." Madison nodded.

"I'm sorry." I sighed.

"I'm not done," he barked, then looked between us. "Detention. Both of you. You can take the time to think about what it means to conduct yourself with dignity. I'll see you both this afternoon."

He walked off without another word.

All three of them stared daggers at me. If this were a cartoon, steam would have been coming out of Madison's ears. I flipped them off and walked away, hoping to spend the last twenty minutes of lunch taking a nap in the library. This really sucked ass. I'd have to run home, grab my uniform, and head straight to work.

Mr. Chen slept through most of detention, leaning back in his chair with his mouth hanging open. It suited me just fine, as I was able to doze a bit too, although it was hard to fall asleep completely with Madison sending me a death glare from across the room, stopping only to text on her phone.

The moment Mr. Chen's alarm went off at the end of the hour, he eagerly dismissed us and hurried ahead out the door, his shoes echoing in the empty hall. I tried to rush off too, but Madison kept getting in my way, slowing me down until the other students were all ahead of us too.

As we neared the corner around which were the front doors—and my freedom from this nightmare of a day—the door to the last classroom flew open. I gasped, but before I could make another sound, a hand covered my mouth, and several others pulled me into the dark room. Madison calmly stepped in after us, closing the door with a quiet *click*.

My pulse thudded in my ears as I struggled, kicked my legs, threw my head from side to side to try to dislodge the hand over my mouth.

Had the others already walked out the door? Was anyone still around to hear me scream? *Oh god!* My parents weren't even home to notice I hadn't come home.

Panic choked me as I redoubled my struggling, its icy grip cutting off my air as badly as the hand over my face. I screamed anyway. The sound was pitiful, muffled by my attacker's hand.

"Would you shut her up?" Madison hissed. She was still by the door, listening, peering out, making sure we were alone.

Steph stepped into my field of vision and punched me in the gut. Her arms were as weak and useless as mine, so the blow didn't make me double over in pain, but it still hurt, startled me, made me cough.

The hand over my mouth disappeared. "Ugh! Gross! She slobbered all over me," Jayden complained.

I took a deep breath and screamed as loudly as I could.

Bonnie rushed over and slapped me, cutting the sound off and snapping my head to the side. Jayden's firm grip on my arms kept me upright.

"Shut the fuck up, you whore," Madison growled as my cheek burned.

For a few seconds, the only sound was my ragged breathing, bouncing off the abandoned walls of the dark classroom. There were no running footsteps out in the hall, no worried cries—no one had heard me scream.

No one was coming.

I swallowed back the fear threatening to take over and took a deep breath. I needed to stay calm. I needed to get myself out of this.

Madison was still by the door, and Jayden was still holding me, his grip on my upper arms sure to bruise. He seemed to be the only guy.

Kelsey wasn't with them. Whatever Donna had on her must've been way heavier than threatening poor people's jobs—and that had been going straight for the throat. Which begged the question . . .

"Why are you doing this?" My voice was croaky, weak. "What the hell are you thinking?"

"Your stuck-up cousin's threats spooked people, but we talked it over, and . . ." She shrugged. "I don't believe her. I mean, she's a senior in high school, just like us. As if she could really get anyone fired."

I chuckled darkly and shook my head. Clearly, they didn't know Donna. But laughing was the wrong move.

Another slap stung my cheek, and Madison leaned in close, baring her teeth. "Who the fuck does she think she is, coming here and threatening us? Who the fuck do *you* think you are? You're not one of them. You're poor, sad, worthless trash. And you need to be reminded of it."

Did she realize she'd just put us in the same category? That she'd all but referred to *herself* as worthless trash?

It probably wasn't wise to laugh again though. That last hit had cut the inside of my cheek, and the taste of coppery blood filled my mouth.

Steph poked her head out the door and looked up and down the corridor. "No one's around. Let's get moving." She walked out of the room, and the others followed, Jayden pulling me along roughly.

Where were they taking me? What were they going to do to me? They'd never gone this far. Even the incident with the mop hadn't made me bleed, and it felt as if they were just getting started.

CHAPTER SIXTEEN

In the week after Donna's show, I almost couldn't believe how well it had worked. They had really been leaving me alone. It was all I'd ever wanted. She'd pushed them into a corner and made it clear it was either submit to her demands or be ruined.

But that's the thing—when animals are pushed into a corner, the only thing they can do is fight. Madison and her crew were fighting, all right. But four against one wasn't exactly fair.

As we rushed through the dark hallways of the school, I tried to scream another few times, but one of them would always shove me or smack me over the head; they didn't seem too worried about it. They knew just as well as I that everyone had gone home.

I'd have to figure out some way to save *myself*. Whatever I had in my bag was useless, sitting as it was in the empty classroom where I'd dropped it. The only thing I had on me was my phone, tucked into the back pocket of my jeans. All I could do was hope they didn't discover it, and wait for a moment when I could call for help.

At the doors leading out to the football field, they paused again, checking that the coast was clear. Then we were making our way across the grass, which was still wet from the previous night's rain. The bluish-gray light of dusk covered everything in a gauzy blanket of shadows, and the chill wind raised goosebumps along my forearms.

Out in the open, I hoped there might be someone around to hear me, so I screamed again.

Jayden shoved me to the ground. The impact cut off my scream, pushing all the air out of my lungs.

"Shut the fuck up!" he roared above me, one foot on either side of my hips. "Scream again and I'll knock out all your teeth." He turned to Madison and threw his arms out. "What the fuck are we doing, Madison? This bitch isn't worth it."

Madison's tone was clipped, her rage barely restrained. "Get her ass up and get her to that goal post, now. I refuse to be threatened by her. She needs to learn a lesson she'll never forget."

Jayden sighed but did as he was told, dragging me up roughly by the arm.

They'd completely lost the plot. She was so outraged I'd dared to step out from under her control, so angry with the world and her place in it, she was lashing out. She wasn't even thinking about the consequences. All she could see was *red*.

I'd never been more scared in my life.

This wasn't about humiliating me in front of the rest of the school.

This went deeper.

"Against the pole." Madison pointed, and Jayden slammed me into the goalpost, my back crunching.

The other girls disappeared behind me and yanked my arms back. A cable tie zipped into place around my wrists.

"What do we have here?" Steph taunted as she pulled my phone out of my back pocket. I closed my eyes and sighed. That was my only chance . . .

She held it by one corner and waved it in front of my face, smirking.

Bonnie grabbed it, threw it on the ground, and stomped on it, the screen making a devastating cracking sound under her foot. "Who the fuck would you have to call anyway?"

My eyes went wide. I knew they could do serious harm to me, was preparing myself for it. But with my hands tied to the pole and no way out, for the first time, I wondered if they were about to kill me.

The panic I'd been holding back broke through, and I started crying. Sobs racked my body, and tears trailed down my cheeks.

"Please," I wailed. "Please, just let me go. No one has to know. I won't even tell Donna. Just let me go, and we can pretend this never happened."

Bonnie spat at my feet as Madison mimicked me. "Please, please, don't hurt me. Wah!" She ended on a cruel laugh, which her sadistic friends echoed. "Like I give a shit if you tell Donna. Like I give a shit what you want."

She stepped forward and shoved her thumb against my right eye. I closed it just in time, but she didn't try to gouge it out as I expected. Instead, she dragged her thumb down my cheek, smearing the makeup.

She cocked her head, surveying her work as more tears poured out of me. "There. That's more like it. Now you look like the trash you are. And since you insist on trying to cover it up with makeup, your rich-bitch friends, and this, quite frankly, rude new attitude . . ." She shook her head like a disappointed mother scolding her child. I hoped to god Madison never had children. "Well, it's time to expose you. Completely. Lay you bare, so to speak, for the world to see. The football team has practice here tomorrow morning, right, Jayden?"

He nodded and gave her a bored "yeah."

She grinned. "Excellent. Then they'll see you. Maybe a few of them will even use you. That's all that lumpy body of yours is good for anyway."

I was getting a little confused. Were they just going to leave me out here all night? I could work with that. I could try to reach my phone as soon as they left.

Like an idiot, I let hope spark in my chest.

They crushed it almost immediately.

Madison reached into her jacket pocket and pulled out something small enough to fit in the palm of her hand. Slowly, she pulled the switchblade straight, giving the sharp edge of the knife a little stroke.

The others shared uncertain looks. Obviously, she hadn't shared this part of the plan with them.

"Madison?" Bonnie was the only one brave enough to tentatively voice her discomfort.

But Madison ignored her. With every slow step she took toward me, the beating of my heart somehow ratcheted up even harder and faster. At this rate, I'd die of a heart attack.

I sobbed again and turned my head to the side.

She pressed the blade flat against the side of my nose, right at the edge of my birthmark.

"Maybe I should cut this out. It's so disgusting," she whispered close to my face as another sob shuddered through me. "But no, that would be doing you a favor. Don't wanna catch any diseases anyway."

Instead she trailed the knife down my cheek, over my jaw, and down my neck, moving to the middle of my chest.

She bunched the top of my T-shirt in her fist, adjusted her grip on the knife, and started hacking away at the fabric. She didn't stop until it was cut all the way down the middle, and then she pulled my bra away from my chest, wedged the knife between the cups, and cut that too.

The others stood by doing *nothing*, saying *nothing*, as Madison dragged the tip of the knife down my torso. Just before it reached my belly button, a flash of movement over her shoulder caught my attention.

Someone was running—sprinting across the field toward us. The sky was now nearly completely dark, only faint indigo light and the brightly shining moon making it possible to see.

He was halfway to us before I realized it was Turner. Relief warred with uncertainty in my chest.

Noticing my attention was on something behind them, the others all turned.

"Fuck," Madison muttered under her breath.

Bonnie looked as if she was ready to bolt, wide eyes flicking between Turner and me.

Madison's knife was still pressed to my belly.

Turner stopped just a few yards away, breathing hard, his shocked gaze taking the scene in.

Jayden recovered first and took a step toward him. "Hey, man. Let's get out of here and leave the girls to it."

Turner looked at him as though he'd only just realized he was there, then his eyes zeroed in on me—the cut-up clothing, my arms tied behind me, the mess that was my face.

I couldn't look away from his eyes, but I started to cry again.

I was out of my mind with fear, and in that moment, I had no idea what he might do.

Would he crack a joke, join them in torturing me?

Do nothing and just walk away, as he had every other time?

Snap out of his shock and try to help me?

Did I even *want* him to, knowing what it would mean for Jenny, for his family, for all that he'd sacrificed to get here?

Everything was so fucked up; I had no idea what the boy I loved would do next, and that almost broke me.

"What . . ." The single word fell from his lips softly, hanging in the moonlight between us. Then his eyes hardened, his nostrils flared, and he roared, "What the fuck is wrong with you people?"

Jayden dropped his friendly act and got in Turner's face. They were almost the same height. "Just walk away, Turner. This has nothing to do with you."

"Walk away and let you keep hurting her?" Turner pushed Jayden, who stumbled back. Without giving him a chance to recover, Turner threw his whole body behind a solid punch to the other boy's face. Jayden went down hard, clutching his nose.

Madison pointed the knife at Turner.

The other girls backed away, looking as though they wanted to run but were too afraid of what might happen if they did.

"Get away from him, you psycho!" I screamed as Madison swung the little switchblade. Turner leaned back, avoiding the swipe at his chest.

I pulled at my restraint in vain, the hard plastic digging farther into my wrists. My fingers were completely numb.

Turner lunged and grabbed Madison's wrist, stopping a second strike. With his other hand, he gripped a fistful of her hair and yanked. She cried out in pain, and Turner took the knife smoothly, tossing her to the ground as soon as he had it.

"Leave!" he bellowed. "Get the fuck away from her before I completely lose my shit!"

The girls backed away immediately, breaking into a run when they realized he wasn't going to chase them down like the animals they were.

Madison helped Jayden to his feet. He looked as if he was considering having another go at Turner, but any idiot could see he didn't stand a chance, especially when Turner had the knife.

Madison sneered at me. "This isn't over."

Turner stepped between us, breaking her line of sight. "Oh, it's fucking over."

Without saying another word, they walked away. About halfway up the field, they started to bicker, gesturing with their hands, but by then, they were out of earshot.

Once he was sure they were gone, Turner rushed to my side, his hand hovering around my shoulder, beside my head, but not connecting. "Oh god, Mena." He sounded pained, his soul as tortured as my body.

I closed my eyes and cried some more. I hated that he was seeing me like this, even as a forceful wave of relief coursed through me. I hated that he was hurting. In that moment, I hated the whole fucking world.

Turner stepped behind me and carefully cut the cable tie. As soon as my arms were released, I collapsed to the ground, the wet grass squelching beneath my knees.

Despite my numb fingers, I managed to cover myself with the ragged bits of my T-shirt before slumping forward and completely giving in to emotion.

I was hysterical—crying, rocking back and forth, yelling as all the pain registered over and over in my overworked mind. My knees hurt where I'd fallen on them. My hands were in agony as the blood rushed back to my fingers. My shoulder ached from when they'd shoved me to the ground. My head pounded. My cheek stung.

My soul was the worst though—my soul was in tatters.

Turner wrapped his arms around me so gently—as if worried that if he pressed too hard, I might shatter. He was murmuring something, but his words didn't register. All I could focus on was the feel of his strong arms; his fresh, clean smell; the rocking motion of our bodies.

All that mattered was that he was there. He'd been there for me in the single darkest moment of my life.

I wrapped an arm around his waist, and he drew me closer into his chest, rubbing my back, kissing my hair.

"I'm here." His words finally broke through the fog of my shock, and I stopped sobbing. "You're OK. You're safe. I won't let them hurt you ever again."

"Shit." I gripped his jacket in one fist. "Turner, what about Jenny?"

"Shh. It's OK. Don't worry about that right now. We'll figure it out."

I had to take his word for it. I could cope with only so much at one time.

He stroked my hair. "I'm gonna call the police now, OK?"

"No." I pulled back to look into his eyes—his red, crying eyes. I held my T-shirt together with one hand and stroked his cheek with the other, softening my voice. "Please, don't call the police."

He frowned. "OK, then let's find a way to contact a teacher or the principal to report them. There has to be some kind of after-hours emergency number."

I was shaking my head before he finished speaking. "No, Turner. They don't care. No one gives a shit what happens to me. Haven't you learned by now? I'm nothing. I don't matter."

No one cared about me. No one. How could this have happened to me if they did? What was the point in trying to tell someone when they didn't care to listen?

I wanted to get away from it all. I wanted to ignore the world as it had ignored me. I wanted my very existence to stop so this pain would stop too.

Turner looked angry. He huffed and shrugged out of his jacket, then draped it around my shoulder and helped me put my arms through the sleeves. "You're not nothing. You matter to me more than anything on this fucked-up world."

I stared at him. I didn't know what to say to that.

Moisture was seeping into my jeans. I shivered. "Just take me home, Turner. Please."

He gave me a searching look, then zipped up the jacket. "OK, Mena. Let's go home. I've got you."

He didn't let me even try to stand up myself. He just grabbed my broken phone, gathered me into his arms, and started to walk across the football field.

I rested my head on his shoulder and stared up at the impassive moon.

CHAPTER SEVENTEEN

I awoke with a start, but the feel of Turner's warm, comforting arms made me relax back into his side almost immediately.

"What . . ." I cleared my throat. It was sore from screaming for help, but that was the least of my worries. "What time is it?"

"Just after ten. You dozed off." He kept his ocean-deep voice low—a balm to my bruised soul.

I sighed against his shoulder and snuggled closer, staring out the window. His curtains were wide open, the moon intruding on our private moment.

The past few hours were a bit of a blur, but I'd obviously felt safe enough to fall asleep. Small victories. I remembered Turner shuffling me gently into the back of a cab, the driver grumbling about the short fare.

He hadn't let me walk when we were dropped off outside our building, scooping me right back into his arms. "Do you want me to come in with you? Talk to your parents together?" he'd asked.

"They're not home. I don't want to be alone. Take me to yours?"

He did as I asked, not even setting me down in the elevator. It seemed his dad was out too—his apartment was dark, silent. I hardly registered a couch, a kitchen as we passed.

I asked to use his shower, and he hesitated, fidgeting with the hem of his T-shirt. "OK, but . . ."

"What?"

"I know you don't want to go to the police or whatever, but can I take some photos first? Just so you have them. If you change your mind later." He eyed me warily.

I didn't want to think about why I might need them, what he wanted to take photos of. I just nodded.

The flash cut harshly through the darkness of his bedroom, and I closed my eyes. He took several photos—of my face, my wrists, my clothing. Then he shuffled me to the bathroom and got awkward again, asking if I needed help.

I'd managed without him.

I remembered thinking it felt good to be in his T-shirt and boxer briefs—comforting. We must have settled on the bed soon after.

The next thing I knew, I was starting awake.

"Are you hungry?" he asked.

I shook my head.

I wished we could stay like this forever, cocooned in the darkness, away from the rest of the world. But eventually, things started to creep back into my head—ugly, insidious things crawling over my comfort and ruining everything.

I lifted onto my elbow to look at him. "Do you regret it?"

He frowned, so I clarified. "Saving me. Putting all your hard work to find your family at risk."

The frown disappeared, and his lips quirked into a barely there, sad smile. "No. Not even for a second."

"But what about your sister?"

He rubbed my feet with his. "They still don't know Jenny is my sister. We know where she is, and we won't let them disappear again. I'll talk to my dad in the morning, and we'll come up with a plan."

"Your dad is gonna hate me." I dragged a hand down my face.

Turner caught it and rubbed my knuckles gently. "No, he won't. He's going to love you. Just like I do."

I looked into his face, suddenly lost for words. Did he just . . .

He frowned slightly before rising up onto his elbows. Was he nervous? "Mena, I could never for a second regret standing up for you. I'm going to defend you with everything I have from now on. I'll walk you to every class if I have to. I'll beat Jayden's ass every time he looks at you. I'll report every little transgression against you to the school until they're sick of me. I'm going to do what I should've done from the start. Because you mean everything to me. The world is a shitty place, but you make me happy. I love you."

So much had happened that night. My body and my soul were damaged, but my heart . . . Pure anguish had been writhing inside me; I'd thought I might never smile again. Yet there he was, pulling one out of me already.

"I love you, Turner." I closed the small distance between us and kissed him with a smile on my lips, this intoxicating feeling between us making me giddy.

It wasn't long before it turned to more. Our smiles fell away, and the kiss deepened, our tongues stroking.

He wrapped an arm around my waist, and I leaned forward, pushing him back against the pillows and pressing my chest flush with his. I swung a leg over his hips, and his other hand went to my knee. He trailed his fingers up my leg, then dipped them under the fabric of the boxer briefs to grip my ass.

I moaned and rolled my hips, seeking friction. He'd already given me *everything*, but I wanted more. My heart was full, but my body was greedy.

I moved until I was straddling him fully and ground myself against him. He was so hard that pressing too much was almost painful.

He gasped and broke the kiss, but I just kissed and licked down that sharp jaw to his neck, my hips never stopping, that heavy, heady feeling building low in my belly.

When my mouth reached the collar of his shirt, I frowned. There was too much fabric between us. I didn't want *anything* between us anymore. I wanted all of him, and I wanted to give all of myself right back.

I yanked him up into a sitting position and pulled his shirt off. He propped one hand behind himself for balance, his other gripping my hip. I stilled, and for a moment, we just drank in the sight of each other, breathing hard.

He was so beautiful, bathed in the silver moonlight streaming in through his window, all the dips and flat planes of his sculpted body accentuated. I ghosted my hands up his arms and leaned in, placing a soft kiss on his shoulder.

"You have freckles on your shoulders," I whispered against the adorable little spots, smiling. He had a few on his nose too, but they were faint, hardly noticeable unless you were nose-to-nose with him.

In place of a response, he dragged the tip of his nose up my neck and kissed the spot just under my ear. I shivered, but definitely not from cold. If anything, I was overheating.

I leaned back and whipped the borrowed T-shirt off.

Turner's eyes widened as he took me in, bare from the waist up and straddling his lap. It was clear where this was going. At least, I hoped it was clear. Did he not like my boobs? His stare had gone hard, fixed on something just below my chest.

I looked down. "Oh."

Madison must've nicked me with the knife after all. Compared with all the other injuries, the little cuts on my belly didn't really rate as something to worry about. I hadn't even registered them in the shower—although I had been in a bit of a haze.

Turner sighed and looked into my eyes. "Maybe we should slow down? Or just stop if you want to?"

"Do you want to?" I crossed my arms, covering my chest, and looked down.

He wrapped his arms around me and leaned back against the pillows. "No. I don't want to stop. Whatever you're thinking, put it out of your mind. You drive me crazy." To punctuate his point, he rolled his hips and ground his still very hard erection against me. I gasped, my body reminding me that it was still roaring to go.

"But, baby"—Turner ran a gentle hand through my hair—"I don't want to hurt you. After everything tonight . . . I just want to be careful."

I shook my head and lifted myself just enough to look into his eyes. "Don't. Turner, I don't want you to see me as some kind of broken, damaged thing. This is exactly why I didn't want you to know at the very start. I don't want this to define me."

"That's not how I see you, Mena. It's not about that. But it was only a couple of hours ago that . . ."

"Please." I didn't let him continue the thought. "I don't want to go there. I don't want to think about that right now. I want to be *here*, in this moment, with you. Make me feel good, Turner. Make me forget."

I let my voice go breathy at the end as I rubbed myself against him. His eyes grew hooded, even as I watched the indecision dance in their depths.

"Just to clarify . . ." he whispered, then moaned, his hips once again moving against mine.

"I want to have sex with you." I could feel myself blushing at the words, but I was proud I'd managed to get them out all the same.

"Fuck." The word tumbled out of his mouth on a heavy exhale, and he ran a hand through his messy hair. "Are you . . . is this your first time?"

"Yes." I bit my bottom lip. "Yours?"

He shook his head, and it took a conscious effort not to ask how many people he'd slept with. It didn't matter. In this moment, he was here, with me, and he loved me.

With gentle but deliberate movements, he rolled me onto my back and kissed me . . . and kissed me and kissed me until I could hardly breathe.

When he finally pulled his lips away, he rested his forehead against mine, our breath mingling. "It's probably going to hurt."

I chuckled. "I know. I'm not completely clueless."

He laughed lightly. "I wasn't suggesting you were. I'm just . . . I can't do anything to prevent that, but I want you to feel good first, so . . ."

He shifted onto his side, the length of his body pressed against mine, and propped himself up on one elbow. For a moment he simply stroked my cheek, then his gentle hand ran down my neck to circle each breast, caressing the undersides, trailing his fingers closer and closer to the nipples. I was breathing so hard my chest was heaving, every breath pushing my breasts farther into his touch.

Just when I thought I might die from this torture, he firmly kneaded first one, then the other, making me moan. I threaded my hands into his hair as he leaned down and took my nipple into his mouth, circling it with his tongue while his fingers played with the other.

Pleasure shot down to the spot between my legs, and I squirmed, rubbing my thighs together.

Turner responded by dragging his hot hand down my body. When he reached the waistband of the boxer briefs, I moved my hands down to help him remove them, taking a shuddering breath.

Holy shit. I was completely naked on a boy's bed. No—not just some boy. *Turner*—the boy I loved. This was really happening. I grinned at the dark ceiling, then reached for his underwear.

He lifted his head, another jolt of pleasure shooting down my spine at the sensation of cool air hitting my wet nipple. Gripping my hand gently, he guided it away from his crotch, and I frowned.

"I told you I wanted to make you feel good." He gave me a devious little smile and boldly stroked me between my legs.

I gasped, my knees instinctively widening as his fingers explored the most private part of my body.

It felt so good, but I didn't want to waste any more time. "I love you for wanting to do that, but I can't . . . uh . . . I won't be able to . . ."

He kissed my lips gently and whispered against them. "Come?"

My "yes" turned into a moan as he slowly slid one finger inside.

"You've never had an orgasm?" he asked, adding another finger.

I rolled my eyes. "I've had plenty of orgasms, Turner. On my own. But . . . no one else has been able to make me come before." Although I was questioning my doubt; the things he was doing with his fingers were making that delicious feeling build at the base of my spine. Until his hand stilled, that is.

He blinked once, then shook his head and smiled. "Sorry. My brain just short-circuited for a second. Thoughts of you making yourself come were warring with thoughts of beating the shit out of anyone else who's tried."

I laughed, then cried out in pleasure as his fingers started moving again, sliding in and out of me, creating the most incredible friction.

He dropped the smile and lowered his voice again. "Just tell me what you like, Mena."

I looked down at my naked body writhing under his touch, the erotic view of his hand between my legs, and decided to let him try. Taking a deep breath, I reached down for his hand and adjusted it until his thumb was over my clit.

"Rub here," I instructed, pushing down any awkward self-consciousness that was trying to make me feel weird about this.

"Like this?" He moved his thumb from side to side. It felt good, but it wasn't what worked for me.

"Up and down."

"OK." He changed direction immediately, and I began to roll my hips against his touch. "Does that feel good?"

"Yes," I breathed. "A little harder."

He increased the pressure and started moving the fingers inside me again, finding a rhythm that had my whole body feeling as if it were about to combust.

"Fuck." A bit of surprise leaked into my tone. "Right there. Just like that. Don't stop."

I writhed against him and moaned, surges of pleasure shooting out from my core. My back arched as the intense orgasm washed over me. One hand gripped a fistful of Turner's hair, and the other tugged at the sheets, searching for something to hold on to so I wouldn't float completely away on this wave of intense pleasure.

Turner removed his fingers and stroked me gently as I came down, my hands releasing their death grip on hair and fabric.

"That was the hottest fucking thing I've ever seen." His voice was gravelly, strained.

Still panting, I leaned up to kiss him as I pushed his underwear down. This time he let me.

As our tongues battled for dominance, I wrapped my fingers around him and stroked. He groaned and pumped his hips into my hand.

A few short moments later, he broke the kiss and shifted out of my reach. "If we keep doing that, I'm gonna finish in your hand."

Without waiting for a response, he swung his legs over the side of the bed and reached into his bedside drawer. As he opened the foil packet and put the condom on, I lightly scratched his back, along the length of his spine. He hummed and rolled his shoulders, making the muscles in his back dance.

When he turned back to me, he captured my hand and placed a gentle kiss on my palm. "Do you want to be on top?"

I shook my head. "My legs are jelly."

"Are they?" He gave me a teasing smile as he positioned himself between them.

My witty retort died on my lips when I felt him, suddenly, *right there*. He leaned down to kiss me, pushing strands of hair off my sweaty forehead as he rubbed his length up and down.

Pulling back to look into my eyes, he reached between us, positioned himself at my entrance, and pushed in slowly, his eyes hooded, his teeth gritted. He got to what I guessed was halfway, then pulled back out, only to slide back in again.

I moaned lightly, gripping his shoulders. My body was still sensitive from my orgasm, everything warm and relaxed, and I was surprised to find I wanted more. Would I ever get enough of Turner Hall? My back arched and my hips rolled, seeking more, more, more. The stretching sensation was new but felt good.

Then he pushed farther in, and pain shot through my lower body. I winced and he stilled, kissed my cheek.

"Breathe, Mena. Try to relax."

My fingers were digging into his shoulders, my abdominals clenching against the intrusion. With a deep breath and a conscious effort, I relaxed my muscles and nodded.

He pulled out slowly, then pushed back in. There was pain again, but it wasn't as bad this time, and now he was all the way in, his hips flush with mine.

He smiled at me, and I smiled back before kissing him. He rolled his hips, grinding against me until I was panting and turning my head to the side in order to breathe.

With a groan, he started sliding in and out of me, gently at first, his chest grazing against my breasts with every stroke. Then his pace increased, his movements becoming more frenzied and uneven.

I reached one hand over my head, gripping the pillow, and dragged the other down his smooth back and all the way to his ass, fascinated by the way his muscles tightened and relaxed as he pumped his hips up and down, in and out.

It wasn't long before his whole body tensed and he released a long, low moan, burying his head in my neck as he came. Chest to chest, hearts beating frantically, we let our breathing even out for a few moments.

Turner kissed the side of my neck, then my cheek, then my nose, and finally my lips. "You OK?"

I smiled and kissed him again. "I'm perfect."

His returning smile was more than a little self-satisfied, and I couldn't blame him. As far as first times went, this one was pretty damn great.

He held the condom to the base of his penis as he pulled out. I wobbled to the bathroom and peed, relieved to see just a small amount of blood; cleaned up quickly; then returned to the dark room.

Turner was back on the bed, a fresh pair of boxer briefs on. He opened his arms, and I snuggled into his side. We held each other in silence, just breathing, just *being*, as I stared at the bright moon framed by the window.

That impassive, glowing sphere had witnessed my lowest moment and my highest peak all in one night.

The night was so still and silent that the sound of a phone vibrating cut through it like a bullhorn. I glanced over my shoulder, but Turner tightened his hold on me. "They can leave a message."

His voice sounded sleepy, gritty. I was ready to drift off at any moment too.

The phone buzzed again. We both sighed and waited for it to ring out.

Barely a few seconds later, it rang again.

With a growl, Turner reached for it, then frowned. "I don't know this number."

He showed me the screen. It didn't look familiar, so I shrugged.

With another dissatisfied smile, he answered it. "Hello?"

"Turner?" It wasn't on speaker, but the panicked voice of a young girl cut through the silent room all the same. "I need your help. I need you to come get me. I'm—"

Turner's whole body tensed, and he sat up. "Jenny? What's going on?"

He rushed to the other side of the room and turned on the light, the sudden brightness making me wince. I couldn't hear Jenny any longer as Turner rushed about the room, pulling his jeans up awkwardly.

Without anything else to change into, I pulled on one of his T-shirts and a pair of sweatpants from off the floor. The pants fit well around my hips, but I had to roll the legs up several times so I wouldn't trip over them.

"OK. I'm coming to get you." He was keeping his voice calm for her, but I could hear the tremble in it. Worry churned in my gut as I pulled my sneakers onto my bare feet.

"Jenny, take a deep breath and listen carefully." He stopped in the middle of the room, staring into space as he spoke quickly but clearly. "We're going to hang up in a minute. As soon as we do, you need to throw the phone away, OK? Throw it as hard and as far as you can. They can use it to find you. Then go and hide. Do not come out until I get there."

He listened for a few seconds. I thought I could hear a scared little voice crying.

"I'm already on my way. OK? Now *go*."

He hung up and turned his wide, panicked gaze to me.

CHAPTER EIGHTEEN

I handed him a T-shirt. "Turner, what's going on? Is she OK?"

He pulled it over his head and shoved his feet in a pair of sneakers, tying them as he answered. "I don't know. She ran away from home. She's terrified." He stood and gripped my shoulders. "I'm so sorry, Mena, but I have to go get her. She's in Oak Hill Park. I'll have to sprint there."

"It's OK." I started to tell him to go get his little sister, then remembered Mom had picked Dad up on her way to my aunt and uncle's. "Wait! We can take my dad's car!"

"Yeah? OK. Let's go."

We were heading for the front door when the glint of the moon through the sliding door reminded me there was another way.

"Turner!" I yanked on his arm. "The balcony will be faster. Can you break the glass or something?"

"Good idea." He ran into the kitchen and came back out with a butter knife, tucking it into his pocket.

Out on his balcony, he reached over the dividing railing to unhook and push aside the bamboo screen, the first and now the last remaining barrier between us. With ease and athleticism, he launched himself over to my balcony, knocking the rickety little chair over, then helped me clamber across. I didn't even have time to worry about how far the drop was before I was safely on the other side.

Turner yanked on the flimsy old sliding door, shoving it sideways as much as the latch would allow. Then he used the butter knife to flick the latch up, and we were inside my apartment.

I sprinted across the room and grabbed the car keys out of the little bowl as

Turner wrenched the door open. After flicking the lock and slamming the door behind us, we tore down the corridor.

Waiting in the elevator to get down to the ground floor was torture. Turner tried to call his dad and cursed when he didn't answer.

We wedged out into the lobby before the elevator doors were even fully open. Heart hammering in my chest, I led the way to Dad's car and jumped into the driver's seat. I had to adjust it, my fingers fumbling on the bar under the seat as I cursed bloody murder.

I started the car and peeled out of the spot, the tires screeching as we took off.

"Which way, Turner?" I shouted. I knew the park he'd mentioned, but I'd been there only a handful of times and not recently.

He was already looking it up on his phone. "Turn right at the end." He pointed.

I glanced down at the clock in the dash, 10:56 illuminated in neon green.

For the next seven excruciating minutes, Turner directed me while trying to call and text his dad. I drove like a crazy person—flying past intersections, barely slowing down at stop signs, skidding around corners.

As soon as we reached our destination, I stopped the car with a lurch across three parking spots and killed the engine, and we both launched ourselves out of the vehicle, leaving the doors wide open.

"Jenny!" Turner bellowed as he ran across the grass. "Jenny! Where are you?"

"Turner!" Her high voice reached us before we could see her. Only seconds later, the young girl came running out of the pitch-black trees and into her brother's waiting arms.

I stopped halfway between them and the car, breathing a sigh of relief and resting my hands on my knees.

I couldn't make out what they were saying to each other, but Turner pushed her out and held her at arm's length, speaking earnestly while visually checking her for injuries.

I ran my hands through my hair, adjusted the sweatpants on my hips, and started walking over slowly.

". . . sure you're not hurt?" Turner's voice was somehow both stern and worried.

"Yes. Shut up. I need you to take me away. Can we go? Away from here. Just me and you," she pleaded, obviously panicked.

"What? What are you talking about? Jenny, what happened?"

She tugged his arm and tried to pull him in my direction, but he dragged her back to his side, still trying to calm her down.

Headlights appeared at the parking area's opposite entrance, snaking down the drive toward us. I frowned. Who would be out here this late?

"He killed Mom!" Jenny yelled. "He didn't know that I saw it, but Jayden knew, and then I couldn't take it anymore, and I ran away, and I think he knows now."

"Holy fuck. Who killed Mom? Where is she?"

"Boyd. It was about six months ago. Turner. She's gone." Jenny sobbed, and Turner hugged her, shooting me a desperate look.

But my focus was on the approaching car.

Dread washed over me like a waterfall as I realized why another car was in the park in the middle of the night. They were here for the same reason we were.

To get Jenny.

My suspicion was confirmed just as it articulated itself in my mind.

"Fuck. Turner?" I waved my hand to get his attention, my eyes still glued on the two men getting out of the car. They hadn't spotted us yet. "We have to go. Now."

"What?" He frowned, then looked over his shoulder.

Jenny followed our gazes and spotted them at the same time . . . and *screamed* as only a teenage girl could.

It pierced the night.

Turner and I took off at the same time, Turner dragging his little sister along with a firm grip on her wrist.

In the same instant, the two men looked over and started sprinting in our direction.

I kept glancing between the men and the waiting car—our only escape—as I pumped my legs. They were too close. They were going to cut us off.

Shit. Shit. Shit.

Turner realized it too. He pushed Jenny and me behind him, and I grabbed her skinny arm and pulled her close. She gripped my T-shirt as if her life depended on it, her whole body trembling in my arms.

As they got closer, Boyd threw an arm out to signal his son to stop running, then looked us over with his calculating gaze. Jayden's eyes widened as he glanced from me to Jenny to Turner and back again, trying to figure out how it all fit.

I suddenly felt sick.

I was face-to-face with one of my tormentors, mere hours after I was convinced he would kill me.

Every mean word, every shove, every sneer and look of disgust he'd ever thrown my way flashed through my mind. For a second my vision blurred, and I had to swallow down bile.

"Jenny, come here this *instant*." Boyd pointed harshly at the spot next to him, his voice the epitome of a chastising parent.

Jenny just plastered herself tighter against my side.

"She's not going anywhere with you." Turner's voice was deathly calm, but the tension in his body told me he was ready to explode at any second.

"Dude, what the fuck is with you tonight?" Jayden shook his head and narrowed his eyes in anger. "Give me my sister."

"*My* sister," Turner growled.

Boyd laughed lightly, the sound one of pure menace. "That's why you looked familiar. That bitch would not shut up about her other kid. The one she left behind. Kept wanting to go find you."

"What?" Jayden looked between them, genuinely confused. Did he not know? Unable or unwilling to process the situation, he stuck with anger. He took a step toward Turner and threw his arms out, looking as if he might throw a punch at any moment. "What the fuck is your problem?"

"*You.*" Turner pointed at Jayden, then at his dad. "And him."

"You wanna go? Let's fuckin' go!" Jayden beat his chest with his fist, but I kept my focus on Boyd. He was staring at Jenny so intently it was making my skin crawl.

"I already put you on the ground once tonight," Turner responded, "and I've been itching to beat your sadistic ass to a pulp. Don't test me."

They were seconds away from throwing punches. Turner could easily take Jayden, but could he take both of them at the same time? Maybe Jenny and I could make a run for the car.

I glanced in its direction. The wide-open doors were barely a hundred feet away.

"That's enough!" Boyd roared. "Give her to me right now!"

Turner didn't reply. Instead he simply rolled his shoulders and lifted his hands, ready to fight.

My heart was beating so fast I thought I might pass out.

Jenny was crying hysterically.

With an angry yell, Jayden lunged. Turner dodged him, grabbing his shirt and using the momentum to shove him to the side. Jayden lost his balance and toppled, but in an instant, he was back on his feet.

The two boys clashed, throwing punches and kicks as Jenny and I inched backward. I was too scared to make an all-out run for it. What if Boyd grabbed us, hurt us? And what about Turner?

As if to prove my point, Boyd jumped into the fight. Between the two of them, they soon got Turner onto his back.

I looked between them and the car.

Stay and try to fight two men twice my size?

Or try to run and get help?

I had seconds, at best, before Boyd was no longer distracted with beating the crap out of my boyfriend. It was now or never.

I have to get Jenny to safety.

I have to help Turner.

Indecision churned inside me, tearing my heart down the middle. My eyes flew between the open car and a hefty branch, about the size of a baseball bat, on the ground next to us.

Run or fight? Fucking decide, Philomena!

CHAPTER NINETEEN

A blur of movement sped past us, making me gasp.

Turner's dad tackled Boyd and laid into him. "Keep your hands off my kids, you son of a bitch!"

After landing a few solid punches, he rushed over to where Turner had already thrown Jayden off, and helped his son to his feet. "You OK?"

Turner swayed and shook his head as if to clear it. "Yeah." He coughed, leaning over.

Jayden and Boyd were already limping away as fast as they could, throwing worried looks over their shoulders.

Turner's dad made to run after them. "Hey, get back—"

"Dad!" Turner stepped in front of him and placed a hand on his chest. "Let them go." He looked pointedly in our direction.

His dad's shoulders slumped, and he slowly turned to face us.

Turner walked to our side. I wrapped one arm around his waist while keeping the other around Jenny's shoulders, careful not to hurt him more.

"Jenny," their dad breathed, his daughter's name falling from his lips like an anguished prayer. He fell to his knees and stared at her as if she were some kind of miracle, his eyes filling with tears. "My baby girl. I missed you so much."

Jenny turned wide, watery eyes up to her brother, and he gave her a small, encouraging smile.

"I told you," he said, the deeper meaning lost on me.

Jenny looked at the grown man on his knees in a park in the middle of the night, then slowly made her way toward him. When she stopped only inches away, he didn't make a move to touch her. He kept very still, as if she were a rabbit that would bolt if he made the wrong move, said the wrong thing.

"Daddy." The word came out on a sob, so low I hardly heard it. Then she wrapped her skinny arms around his neck. He held her as if she might evaporate in his grip and gave us the biggest, most emotionally charged grin I'd ever seen on a grown man's face.

Turner and Jenny both refused to go to the hospital, and their dad didn't argue too hard for them to go—I had a feeling he was worried about what kind of questions might be asked. The man didn't want to lose his children.

Instead we went straight home. Turner's dad—who insisted I call him Simon and kept apologizing repeatedly that I got "dragged into all this crap"—followed in his car behind us. Jenny wouldn't leave Turner's side, so they sat in the back as I drove at a much safer pace.

After we parked, Turner said he'd see me to my door. Jenny refused to go anywhere without him, and Simon declared he was never letting any of them out of his sight again. So even though I tried to protest, in the end all four of us piled into the elevator.

As the doors opened on my floor, several voices I recognized echoed down the hall. I winced and dragged my feet around the corner.

This was not going to be pretty.

Packed into the corridor in front of my apartment were my parents; Donna; her parents; my boss and Mom's friend, Leah; and two police officers. They were all talking over one another as the police officers tried to ask questions. My mom was crying, and so was my aunt.

Donna spotted me first.

"Mena!" She barreled past the others and ran straight to me, wrapping her arms so tightly around my neck I almost couldn't breathe.

"Hey," I croaked.

"I'm so glad you're OK," she whispered frantically. "I'm so sorry, but I was so fucking worried. I didn't know what else to do."

I pulled away and frowned. "What do you mean?"

"I told them." She managed to give me an apologetic wince before she was shuffled out of the way. Then it was my mom and dad cutting off my air supply.

"Guys," I wheezed. "Can't breathe."

"Oh my god." My mom held me out at arm's length. Her face was tear streaked, her hair a mess. "Is there something wrong with your lungs? Brad, we need to take her to the hospital."

"There's nothing wrong with my lungs. Would you calm down?" I bugged my eyes out.

"Calm down? *Calm down?*" She was doing the opposite of calming down. "Do you have any idea how worried we've been? When Leah called and told me you didn't show up for your shift . . . and then we came home and you weren't here, and the balcony door is busted . . . and then . . . when Donna told us . . ." She started crying again, covering her face with her hands for a moment. Then she took a deep breath and looked at me with some unfathomable emotion in her eyes.

Tears welled in my eyes too. I felt like shit for making everyone so upset—not that it was my fault. But it just rubbed salt in the wounds. The literal wounds I had on my body.

"Philomena." My dad's voice was low but barely restrained. "Whose clothes are you wearing?"

"Uh . . ." I glanced down at Turner's T-shirt and the sweats hanging off my hips. When I looked back up at my dad's face, he was staring daggers behind me —*at Turner.*

I stepped directly in front of my boyfriend, shielding him with my body, and threw my hands out. "None of this is Turner's fault. He saved me."

"Saved you?" Now my dad was confused.

I swallowed around a massive lump in my throat.

This was not how I wanted my parents to find out I was sexually active. In fact, I didn't want them to find out *at all.*

But that awkwardness was nothing compared to the anguish I felt at what I would have to do next.

"Yes. I got in some trouble tonight."

"Mena," Turner interjected, a hint of reproach in his voice as his hands landed on my shoulders. "You didn't just get in trouble. I think it's time you tell your parents the whole story."

Dad narrowed his eyes at the comforting hands on my shoulders.

I rolled my eyes. "Yes, I'm planning to. Can we just . . . go inside?"

We were all still packed uncomfortably in the dingy corridor. One of the fluo-rescent lights was flickering, and I really needed to sit down.

The radio on one of the police officers' shoulders crackled something unintel-ligible, reminding me they were there.

The other officer addressed us. "We have to attend an emergency situation, but we will need to speak to you all again. I'm glad your daughter is safe. We'll be in touch to take statements."

She smiled at my parents, and they rushed away.

Leah stepped up to kiss my cheek. "I'm glad you're OK."

"I'm sorry I missed my shift and didn't call. My phone is ruined."

"Don't worry about it." She gave me a reassuring smile and turned to my parents. "I'm going to head home too."

"Thanks." Mom hugged her before Leah rushed off to catch the elevator.

"Want me to come in with you?" Turner asked.

What I wanted most was to collapse into bed and sleep for a week solid, but yes, I wanted him to hold my hand while I had the most difficult conversation of my life with my parents. I suspected he'd be more of a distraction though, judging by the dirty looks my dad was throwing him. Plus, he needed to be with his family. Jenny was leaning into her dad's side, asleep on her feet.

"No," I told him. "Go be with your family. Get some sleep. I think this is something I need to do alone."

"Are you sure?"

I turned to face him. "Positive. Go."

He pulled me in for a hug, and I melted into his warm embrace, drawing strength from his strong arms. He kissed the top of my head and released me, then walked away with his family.

I turned to face mine.

They all filed into the apartment, and I dragged my feet after them. Donna took my hand as I passed. "Not alone," she leaned in to whisper, picking up on what I'd just said to Turner. "Never alone."

I squeezed her hand and closed the door behind us.

CHAPTER TWENTY

I dropped the mascara in the makeup case and smiled at my reflection in the mirror. I'd gone for an understated look with some subtle embellishment that made my dull blue-gray eyes pop. Turner kept saying how much he loved my eyes.

My hair was done too, sleek and straight, hanging down my back. I smoothed the front of my crisp white shirt with my hands, double-checking that I hadn't gotten any makeup on it.

It had been two weeks since that disaster of a night, and I hadn't been back to school or seen any of my classmates since. *Good riddance*. Today was my first day at Fulton Academy. My brand-new uniform fit me perfectly, the shirt sitting just right on my shoulders, the pleated skirt hugging my hips and stopping halfway down my thighs.

I frowned, wishing my thighs weren't so thick. But I pushed that thought away. I had enough shit to be nervous about without getting obsessed with how my thighs touched.

Of course, I knew the girls would be there with me, that I'd met all their other friends, that the staff had been informed of the situation at my previous school. But knowing didn't stop me from having intrusive, panic-inducing thoughts. What if the girls turned on me? What if I did something to piss them off and ended up friendless again? What if the other kids started picking on me? What if the teachers had just said what my parents wanted to hear and were actually just as apathetic as the ones at my old school? What if this was just a dream and I'd wake up any moment and have to go back to that hellhole?

I took a deep breath and leaned on the counter, staring at myself in the mirror. This was who I wanted to be—who I *was*. "You can do this Mena," I whispered to my reflection.

Part of me wanted to take the uniform off and just go back to bed, but it had been hard enough to get my parents to agree to this. No way was I going to jeopardize it.

That night, after Turner and his family left, I'd sat at the kitchen table and told mine everything.

When my mom got the voicemail that I hadn't shown up to work, Donna had suspected the worst. She'd told my parents I was being bullied and that she'd tried to help, but in the rush to get back and check our apartment, she hadn't had time to tell them the whole story.

That part fell to me. With my cousin by my side, holding my hand, I told my parents how miserable my school life had been since we'd moved to Devilbend. When I got to some of the harder parts, my voice wavering, Donna jumped in and filled in blanks. I told them what had happened that night—everything minus the sex with Turner. I didn't think that part was relevant, and I certainly didn't want to talk about it with my parents and aunt and uncle.

There was a lot of hugging and crying, a lot of questions, but no plans were made. I collapsed into bed that night and stayed there the whole weekend.

Mom and Dad didn't even complain, bringing me food and coddling me between bouts of sleep. Turner came over a few times, and I heard Dad apologize for assuming the worst of him. He even thanked him for "taking care of his little girl," and I'm pretty sure they hugged—I heard that telltale thumping that indicated a man-hug in progress. Then he went and ruined it by threatening to break Turner's legs if he broke my heart.

It wasn't until Sunday afternoon that I started to come out of the cocoon of denial and think about what would happen next. Technically, I had school the next day, but as I dragged my butt into the shower, the only thing I knew for sure was that I was *not* going back there. I was done with that place and those people.

My aunt and uncle arrived with the girls while I was in the shower, and they all rushed in for hugs when I came out. Amaya held me the longest.

We avoided the elephant in the room and ate an early dinner. It was nice to have them all there, hanging out, talking.

"Anyone want tea?" Dad headed into the kitchen to boil the water as Harlow and Donna cleared the table.

I couldn't hold it in any longer. "I don't want to go to school."

Everyone paused. Mom patted my hand gently. "You don't have to. Take a few more days off. We still need to get you to a doctor. And the police have called twice about taking a statement. Your father and I will go there tomorrow." Her eyes had gone hard, her lips in a thin line.

Dad leaned on the counter as the water started to percolate behind him. "They're not going to get away with this, Philly. Not anymore."

"Once we've sorted everything out, then you can go back." Mom gave me a smile.

I frowned and shook my head. "No. I don't want to go back at all. And I don't want to talk to the police or the school. I just . . . I'm done thinking about this and worrying about it and having it consume so much of my energy. I just want to put it behind me."

Mom's gaze filled with pity. "Sweetheart, you have to go to school. It'll be fine once we speak with the principal. I'm going to demand that those kids are expelled. We're going to press charges."

She was making decisions for me, not listening to what I wanted. I'd spent my whole life trying not to be a bother to my family, trying to grit my teeth and bear it. But something had broken inside me that night—and something had broken *out*. Maybe it was a backbone. I pulled my hand out from under hers and shook my head again. "No. I am not stepping foot in that school again. I'm done."

"Philomena," Dad jumped in. "You can't just not go to school, and there's nowhere else that's close enough."

My aunt cleared her throat and shifted in her seat. "She could go to Fulton Academy."

"It's an excellent school. We could make some calls on your behalf tomorrow," my uncle quickly added. A little *too* quickly, making me wonder if they'd discussed this already.

Donna and Harlow stopped in the middle of making tea for everyone, the looks on their faces hopeful. Amaya gripped my knee under the table. I could practically feel the excitement radiating off her.

But I couldn't let it spread to me because . . .

"Emily, you know we can't afford that," my mom gritted out.

"We'll cover everything." Aunt Emily's eyes were pleading as she leaned forward on the table. "Fees, uniform, books, excursions, anything else she needs. It's your money anyway, Eleanor."

"No, it's not." Mom folded her arms. "Our mother disowned me for marrying the man I love and then left all her money to you. I don't want a single cent of it."

"Well, she's dead now and it's my money, and I want to give it to *you*." Emily threw her hands up.

I sighed, sharing a look with Donna and Harlow. Our moms had this argument often.

"I don't want it. Why are you doing this?"

"Because I love my niece!" my aunt yelled, clearly frustrated. "Because I want to do all I can for her. Because I love *you*, you idiot, and I want to help. Why are you letting pride get in the way—"

"Screw you. This is not about pride." Mom got up and leaned on the table. If previous fights were anything to go by, this was headed downhill fast; one of them would be storming out soon, both of them in tears.

Frustration bubbled up inside me. I brought both my hands down on the table with a bang, making everyone turn to me in shock.

"Shut up!" I yelled. "God, aren't you sick of having the same fucking argument already?"

"Language." Dad pointed a reproachful finger at me from the kitchen.

Ignoring him, I stood up and pulled my shoulders back. "Aunt Emily, Uncle Richard, thank you, I'd love to go to Fulton. Mom, Dad, either it's this or I don't go."

My mom turned her anger on me. "You are not dropping out of school."

"Would you rather I keep coming home with bruises?" I yelled into her face, holding my raw wrists up. "Would you rather I don't come home at all one day?"

She reeled back, eyes wide, but I was on a roll. "I'm not going back there. You can't force me. I'll be eighteen in a few months anyway. I'll get a job and move out if I have to."

"Of course I don't want you to get hurt." Mom sounded tired now. "But things will be better once we talk to the school and the police. Maybe we can move . . ."

She looked to Dad, who was leaning on the counter, his head hanging between his shoulders. He sighed, then walked over to wrap his arm around her. My heart constricted in my chest. He was going to side with her—this was their "united front" position.

"Philomena will be going to Fulton," he said, surprising us all. "Thank you so much, Emily and Richard. We really appreciate your help."

"Brad." Mom tried to shrug him off, but he held on.

"It's what's best for her, Eleanor. You need to let this past resentment go. *Look at her.*"

They both looked at me. I fidgeted with my sleeves but didn't back down, meeting their gazes head on.

My mom's shoulders slumped, and she nodded.

Donna, Harlow, and Amaya all screamed in excitement and enveloped me in hugs. I hoped seeing how loved and supported I was by them would help Mom see that this was the right decision.

"The police are still going to want a statement about why you went missing, honey," Dad said. "That's going to make it hard to avoid the full story."

In the end, I conceded to reporting the whole awful thing to the police and agreed to let my parents go down to the school and raise hell—as long as I didn't have to go.

With Turner backing up my story and with the evidence online, the police were able to press charges, and the school board expelled the students involved. Kelsey caved in to pressure (that I was pretty sure came from Donna) and turned on her friends, taking a slap on the wrist in exchange for her statement.

It took a couple weeks to sort out my late enrollment at Fulton and get my uniform and supplies, but my first day had finally arrived.

With one last deep breath and a final check of my hair and makeup, I grabbed my blazer and brand-new backpack off the bed. The backpack was a new school gift from my aunt and cost more than I made at the diner in six months.

"Oh my . . ." Mom covered her mouth with her hand, then dropped it to give me a watery smile. "You look beautiful, Philly."

"You kind of look like your mom when we first met. The uniform hasn't changed much. You look lovely, Sweet Chilly," Dad added. They'd both taken the morning off to be there for me on my first day. I'd drawn the line when they'd tried to insist on driving me themselves.

"Thanks, guys." I smiled and pulled on my shoes.

My new phone—a top-of-the-line new school gift from Donna and Harlow—vibrated in my pocket.

"I gotta go. The girls are here." I slung my expensive bag over my shoulder as giddy excitement mingled with nervousness in my gut.

"You haven't even had breakfast," Dad chastised.

"I'm too nervous to eat." I waved him off. He huffed, but they let me leave after kisses and lingering hugs.

The girls were waiting for me at the curb, all three leaning on Donna's car and looking stunning in their perfect uniforms. Amaya's skirt was the shortest, although it might have just been her ridiculously long, smooth legs making it seem like that. Donna looked as if she owned this town and everyone in it, big dark sunglasses framed by her short, sharp blonde hair. Harlow had her hair in two messy buns, her massive white headphones hanging around her neck. She was the first one to spot me.

She grinned and cupped her hands around her mouth. "Woohoo! You look hot!"

I laughed and looked away, embarrassed but also flattered. Donna and Amaya joined in, and they all started catcalling me worse than a construction site full of unsupervised apprentices.

"Work it!" Donna pumped her fist in the air.

"Shake that ass!" Amaya turned sideways and started shaking her own, the movement of the pleated skirt making the action even more obscene.

Fighting giggles, I gave in and played along, dancing on the spot and flicking my hair.

A loud wolf whistle sounded from behind me, and a deep male voice joined in. "Work that tight body, baby!"

I startled, my heart flying into my throat before I realized it was Turner.

The girls all cracked up laughing. I flipped them off, then turned to give my boyfriend a smack on the shoulder. He chuckled and gripped my hips, flashing me that mesmerizing smile of his.

"You scared me," I scolded but melted into him, wrapping my hands around the back of his neck.

"I'm sorry." He leaned down and nuzzled my nose. A chorus of "awws" came from the peanut gallery, and I rolled my eyes, trying to ignore them. Turner lowered his voice. "Wanna come over to my place after school? And leave that uniform on. I've always wanted to defile a private school girl."

"Dammit, Turner, now I'm gonna be distracted all day."

"Excellent." He grinned and closed the tiny distance between us, giving me a firm, languorous kiss. His tongue swiped my bottom lip, and I opened my mouth to him on a sigh, completely forgetting we had an audience. One of his arms circled my waist, drawing me tightly against him, as his other hand went to my neck, his thumb tracing my jaw.

My eyes flew open, and I broke the kiss, pulling his hand away from my face. "You'll ruin my makeup."

"You don't need it."

I frowned. Today was my first day of being who I really wanted to be; maybe I needed to make a statement about this. "I don't wear it just to look pretty for you, Turner, or anyone else. And I don't wear it to hide my birthmark. I wear it because I *like it*, I enjoy putting it on, and it makes me feel confident."

He blinked once, surprised at my outburst, then smiled. "I know. I didn't mean it like that. You look beautiful with the makeup on, baby. But you look beautiful without it too. *You* are beautiful, and I love you."

I melted at his words. "I love you too," I told him before going in for another kiss.

An exaggerated gagging sound from the direction of the apartment building had us pulling apart again.

Jenny was sticking her finger in her open mouth, making the universal sign for disgust. "You guys are so gross."

This time, we laughed along with the girls.

"Don't you worry, Jenny baby," Amaya called. "There will come a day, very soon, when you think kissing boys is the exact opposite of gross."

"Or girls!" Harlow chimed in. "Whatever you're into."

Turner gave them a murderous look. "No, she won't. Shut up!"

It was adorable how protective he was of his little sister.

In the days after everything exploded, Turner had needed to have some difficult conversations with his family too.

Simon was shocked and deeply saddened when he found out his wife was dead. He'd wanted Turner and Jenny to have their mother *and* their father in their lives. On top of his own grief, it crushed him to accept they would never have that again.

Turner was absolutely devastated. He'd spent years missing his mom, fantasizing about seeing her again, working to make that happen—and now he had to mourn her absence in his life for good.

Two nights ago we'd been sitting on his balcony together when the electricity had gone out again. In the silent darkness, he told me the worst thing about it was that he never got a chance to say goodbye. His shaky inhale right after made me tear up too. We held each other long after the electricity hummed back on.

Short of taking Jenny and going on the run for the rest of his life, there was no way for Simon to avoid speaking with the police to clear everything up. Due to the fact that Jenny was Simon's actual daughter and adamantly wanted to stay with him, CPS allowed them to remain together. Jenny also told the police how she'd seen Boyd throw her mom down the stairs, that it wasn't a tragic accident, as he'd reported at the time. Boyd had been taken into custody and was awaiting charges. Jayden was too, for the part he'd played in hurting me, but he had no other family here, and it looked as if he'd be sent off to live with an uncle in Wisconsin when everything was settled.

BestLyf had been very quick to release a statement severing all ties with Boyd Burrows and condemning his actions. They weren't being very cooperative with police though, and apparently it was proving difficult to get warrants to search Boyd's office at work.

Simon and Turner were disappointed that BestLyf's involvement in their wife and mother's tragic situation—all the manipulation and deceit—would likely never be proven, but they were at least satisfied her murderer would be brought to justice. I didn't really know what to think of their adamant belief that BestLyf was a cult. Had his mom really been brainwashed? Or had she found herself in an abusive relationship with a controlling, manipulative man who just happened to work for them? Perhaps it was a combination of the two. I didn't see the point in dwelling on it—Simon and Turner were just happy it was all over.

They were ecstatic to have Jenny back, and they both doted on her. At first, Simon had considered taking his kids and leaving, getting far away from this place. Turner and I could hardly even talk about what that would mean for us, but thankfully, Simon quickly abandoned the idea.

Jenny was at the start of a long road to unlearning all the negative things that had been put in her head about her father, to healing from all that she'd seen and experienced. But her new therapist had suggested moving could be detrimental. She had friends here, familiar surroundings, teachers she liked. Plus, her mom was buried in the Devilbend Memorial Park, and they wanted to be able to visit her. So they stayed.

I'd nearly choked up with relief when Turner told me. The thought of losing him was unbearable.

I was in therapy too. We all were. So. Much. Therapy.

"Good morning, Jenny." I extracted myself from Turner's arms and smiled at his little sister. She beamed back and gave me a tight hug. We'd formed a deep bond oddly fast—shared trauma tended to do that to people.

"You look really nice in your uniform, Mena," she told me.

"Thanks. You look beautiful too."

"Thanks! Turner, let's go. I don't wanna be late." She tugged on his arm, and he rolled his eyes at me, but there was no missing the affection there.

It was their first day back at school too. Part of me wished I could be with them, walk there together, spend my days with him. But I knew going to Fulton was the right move—it was the best move for me.

"Have a good first day, baby." Turner gave me one last peck on the lips before letting his kid sister drag him down the street.

"I will. Bye, guys!" I waved after them, then walked to my friends.

They each gave me a hug and put their sunglasses on. It was a ridiculously bright morning—not a cloud in the sky. Harlow pushed a caramel-flavored cup of diabetes into my hands as we piled into Donna's car.

"And I know you haven't eaten." Amaya thrust a small paper bag at me from the back seat. I took it and peeked inside.

"The best croissants in Devilbend," Donna informed me as she pulled into traffic.

"I'll be the judge of that." I took a massive bite, then paused to moan around the soft, flaky, buttery goodness. "Fuck. This *is* the best croissant in Devilbend. Maybe all of California."

"Told you," Donna sang from the driver's seat.

"Hurry up and finish it." Amaya smacked my shoulder.

"No," I mumbled around another bite. "I wanna savor it."

"Ugh! Here!" Harlow leaned forward and yanked the drink and paper bag out of my hand. I just barely managed to snatch the rest of the croissant back and stuff it into my mouth with a glare. She just grinned back.

I chewed, and when my mouth was free enough to form words, I turned to face the back seat. "What the fuck—"

"Here!" Amaya thrust a rectangular box with a big bow on it at me. I took it reflexively and frowned. "It's your new school gift. I know the others already gave you theirs."

I sighed and smiled at them all. "You guys don't have to keep buying me shit. I'm happy just being able to hang out with you every day."

"We know," they chorused.

"Open it." Harlow waved her hand at me.

I let excitement win against the uncertainty. They were just being generous and loving on me—this was not about pity for the poor girl.

I ripped the paper off and opened the box.

Inside was a pair of sunglasses with a label I'd never dreamed I could afford. They were dark, like all of theirs, but had a slight point at the corners, reminding me of winged eyeliner. I tried them on and looked in the mirror.

"They're perfect. I love them. Thank you so much," I said and meant every word.

Amaya squeezed my shoulder.

We pulled into the parking area not long after. Before we could start walking toward the building, Donna dropped her bag and pulled out her phone. "We need to commemorate this moment."

We leaned on the hood of her car and squished in, smiling and pulling faces as she took several selfies.

She posted one immediately, and my phone buzzed in my pocket with the notification. She'd chosen one where we were all hugging, smiling widely, the sun glinting off our sunglasses. The caption was just one hashtag—#Devilbend-Dynasty.

I knew in that moment I'd always been a part of them as far as they were concerned. I was finally embracing it.

Donna and Amaya led the way, and Harlow and I hooked arms as we followed. I held my head high and waved to people I knew. I had a feeling it was going to be a good day.

LIKE YOU HURT

CHAPTER ONE

Donna

Mom was sitting at the breakfast nook alone, the delectable spread in front of her way more than four people could realistically eat. Dad must've been away for work again, and if Harlow wasn't up yet, she wouldn't be eating breakfast. Looked as if it was just us two.

Magda marched in from the kitchen, a fresh pot of coffee in hand. "Good morning, beautiful, smart girl. How you want your eggs this morning?" The woman had worked for my family since before I was born, but her heavy Eastern European accent persisted.

I smiled. "Poached, please."

She set the coffee on the table and patted my arm as she passed.

"Morning, sweetheart." Mom flashed me her perfect teeth before returning her attention to the iPad next to her bowl of granola. She was impeccable in a linen shirt dress and a full face of makeup, not a hair out of place—all before 8:00 a.m.

"Morning, Mom. You look nice. Big client?" I smoothed the front of my skirt as I sat down, running my fingers down the gray-and-teal tartan pleats. Emily Mead Interiors was in high demand, and if Mom was going to meet with someone herself instead of sending one of the designers she employed, it was probably someone high-profile.

"Thank you." She gave me another bright smile. "Yes, a potential new client, demanding to meet with me personally."

"Celebrity," we said at the same time, rolling our eyes.

I grabbed a piece of toast and started spreading mashed avocado onto it as Mom scrolled through her tablet again. A bird chirped outside, the California sun shining brightly through the open French doors.

Everything, down to the weather, was pristine and neat.

I couldn't wait to put on a pair of scuffed boots and feel them stick to the filthy floors . . .

I shook my head. I had to focus. Get through the day. It was only one day.

Magda returned with my poached eggs as I was crumbling some feta onto the avocado.

"I have my dinner with my friends tonight. Will you and your sister be OK alone?" Mom took a sip of her coffee.

I smiled around a bite of gourmet breakfast, wiping the corner of my mouth with the starched napkin. "Yes. I have some extra-credit homework to finish, and Harlow will be fine."

My sister, younger by exactly eleven months, would be glued to her computer. Friday nights were her gaming nights—nothing but her bladder could drag her away from the keyboard.

"Good. I won't be late."

She never was. Not that it mattered. I was eighteen and Harlow was seventeen. We were more than capable of taking care of ourselves—despite being raised with a permanent staff, managed by Magda, making sure we never wanted for anything. We may have been obscenely rich, but my parents had made sure we weren't spoiled. They'd instilled the value of hard work in us from an early age. We were Meads—nothing short of excellence was acceptable.

But everyone had to let loose once in a while. Dad had the frequent extensions to his business trips so he could play golf. Mom had her fortnightly boozy dinners with her friends, ensuring she was fast asleep by midnight. Harlow had her computer games.

I had my thing too. I'd be going there tonight. Just thinking about it made a rush of adrenaline shoot down my spine, like rough hands on bare skin.

Shifting in my seat, I pushed the thought away once again. No one could know about that. They wouldn't understand.

I just had to get through one more day at school, one more afternoon of homework, *one more day* of being driven, determined, perfect Donna Mead.

And then I could spend all night being whoever the fuck I wanted.

I took another bite of toast to hide my smile.

Harlow appeared downstairs just as I finished eating. Her Fulton Academy uniform was as perfectly neat and ironed as mine, but her knee-high socks were still pooled around her ankles, and it looked as if she hadn't bothered to brush her hair before tying it up. Her long blonde ponytail hung just past her shoulder blades.

My hair was a little lighter than hers, ashier, and I kept it maintained in a short, sharp style with monthly visits to the salon. It was closer to Mom's color, although she put lowlights in hers.

"There's my baby girl." Mom beamed at her youngest child, and Harlow gave her a sleepy smile back as she poured coffee into her travel mug. "Sit down and eat some breakfast."

Harlow grunted, and I answered for her. "We have to get going to pick up Mena."

Mom frowned. She liked that we were picking up our cousin, but it was warring with her typical-mom need to shove food down our throats. But I knew Harlow couldn't stomach anything solid until lunchtime—especially when she stayed up half the night doing god knew what on her computer.

Screwing the lid onto her travel mug, Harlow leaned down and gave our mother a kiss on the cheek. The big white headphones hanging around her neck were blaring some EDM shit that became audible as she got close. "Love you," she croaked.

I cringed internally. Had she been to bed at all?

Hoping to distract our mom from how tired my sister looked, I leaned over and gave her a kiss too. "Love you, Mom. Good luck with the delusion of grandeur."

She laughed as we headed for the garage. "Is it delusion if the majority of the country knows their name? Have a good day, girls."

Magda wordlessly pressed a granola bar into my hand as I passed the kitchen, shooting a meaningful look in Harlow's direction. I gave her a withering smile. I'd try, but no promises.

With a yawn, Harlow dropped into the back seat of my pearlescent white BMW 8, while I smoothed my skirt down and stepped in more carefully to avoid creases.

The garage door silently slid open in front of us, revealing a pair of long legs clad in the same knee-high socks my sister and I were both wearing—white with a teal stripe at the top. Next came a flash of creamy brown-skinned thigh, the skirt length flirting with inappropriate, followed by the top half of the most fabulous bitch I knew.

Our friend Amaya Ellis-Lahari lived one street over and rode to school with us almost every day, even though she had her own car. Us girls liked to stick together. She and Harlow had offered to take turns driving, but I shot that down. I liked to be in control of where I was going and how fast.

Amaya was scrolling through her phone in the middle of the driveway, arms crossed and hip cocked, her designer backpack slung over one shoulder. I started the car and revved the engine, but she completely ignored me, running a hand through her long black hair.

With a smirk, I disengaged the handbrake and revved the engine again, then lurched forward and slammed on the brakes just inches away from Amaya's ridiculously long legs.

She didn't even flinch.

I laughed, and she looked at me over the top of her sunglasses and gave me the finger.

After taking her time to shoot off a text, she leisurely slid into the passenger seat. "Meads."

"Hey, girl." I gave her a kiss on the cheek as Harlow grunted from the back. As I took off, my sister jammed the headphones over her ears and closed her eyes. Amaya buried her nose in her phone, and I put on some Billie Eilish.

This part of the journey was spent in relative silence, all of us trying to wake up and get ready for the day—especially Harlow.

We drove out of the estates area and took the main road through downtown Devilbend. The homes got smaller, the yards more cramped and untidy. Eventually we pulled up outside of a big, run-down apartment building.

Mena walked up the cracked concrete path and jumped into the back seat. "Morning!"

Her bright greeting made me smile. That girl had been through some horrific shit at her last school—which is why my parents were paying for her to go to Fulton with us now—but it hadn't made her bitter or angry. Mena was the kind of person whose inner beauty oozed out of her pores, her energy infectious.

We chatted and sang along to "You Should See Me in a Crown" as I drove us to school. Even Harlow perked up and took her headphones off, the massive coffee she'd finished finally doing its job.

I retraced our path through downtown, passed the turnoff to our neighborhood, and drove up the winding tree-lined road toward Fulton Academy.

Every other day, we got up half an hour early and drove in the exact opposite direction of school to pick up Mena, because she needed someone to show her she was worth it—that she belonged with us. The other days, she took the bus to our house, and we still drove in together.

I parked in a spot near the front. Even with the student parking lot almost full, everyone knew not to park in my spot.

Glancing in the mirror, I checked my makeup and smoothed an errant strand of hair back into place. Surreptitiously, I checked on Harlow at the same time. She'd retied her hair while we drove, and as we got out of the car, I was pleased to see her socks were pulled up and her shirt tucked in.

We all knew the strict uniform rules, and my sister wasn't an idiot, but I couldn't help but make sure everything was in place. I didn't want any of my girls getting in trouble needlessly.

Walking in through the grand front doors of one of the most prestigious high schools in California—if not the country—I kept my gaze trained forward. Amaya was at my side, Harlow and Mena joking and carrying on behind us. I envied how oblivious they were to all the people watching us, some wishing they had the guts to talk to us, others hoping I'd fall on my ass.

Perfection was fucking exhausting, but it was all I knew.

There was only one thing that could completely take my mind off it. The buzz of conversation around us reminded me faintly of another kind of buzz—*the kind I'd be feeling reverberate through my body tonight.*

Shit, I really needed this. It was the third time that morning I'd had to push the thought away. I had three AP classes on Fridays, and I needed to focus.

I got through my busy morning without incident and repressed a yawn as I shoved books into my locker at lunch.

"Cafeteria? Or you wanna head out to eat?" Amaya leaned on the locker next to mine.

Harlow appeared next to her. "Can we just do caf? I'm starving."

"That's because you didn't eat breakfast after staying up all night." I was kicking myself for not shoving the granola bar under her nose earlier.

"I second the caf." Mena nudged my shoulder and smiled before unloading her own books in her locker.

Mena had ulterior motives. She couldn't afford to eat out all the time and didn't like us constantly paying for her, so she always preferred the cafeteria— the option already paid for as part of tuition.

I rolled my eyes, and they landed on an unfamiliar face.

The guy walking toward us in the busy hallway was tall, his brown hair kind of wavy and messy on top but with a precise fade-cut underneath. The gray pants and white shirt of the uniform fit his frame perfectly—probably tailored, just like all the other uniforms on all the other spoiled rich kids in this place. His teal tie hung perfectly in place, but his blazer was draped over the books he had tucked against his hip.

I leaned back on the locker and watched him as he passed, his free hand tucked into his pocket, his face blank.

He didn't look at anyone. He didn't have that uncertain, worried demeanor that almost always marked a new kid obsessing over where they would fit in at a new school. Which told me he didn't give a shit about his place here, or maybe he was just putting up a brave front, a hard exterior to mask his nervousness.

His gray eyes flicked to the side and connected with mine for the briefest of moments. I didn't smile like half the basic bitches in the hall with hearts in their eyes. I didn't frown or show my confusion either. I didn't react at all, watching him with as steady and cool a gaze as he was me.

He stopped at a locker near the end of the corridor. Only seniors had their locker in this hall, so that was at least one piece of the puzzle.

"Who is that?" I asked, keeping my gaze locked on him. I may have been bad with names—something I was working on—but I never forgot a face. I certainly wouldn't have forgotten those piercing eyes, the strong jaw.

How had I gone all morning without knowing there was a new senior at Fulton? I hated not knowing things.

I wasn't delusional. Of course I couldn't control everything, but knowing as much as possible allowed me to be prepared for all scenarios. I had a spreadsheet with the names of each student at Fulton Academy, the names of their parents and what they did for work, any dirt we had on them, and any other pertinent information that was useful—or could be in the future. The girls were the only ones who had access to it, or even knew about it.

Information made the world go round. So did networking.

"That must be the new guy." Harlow shrugged. "Not in any of my classes, but I heard whispers."

"And you're only mentioning this now?" I glared at her, but she flipped me off with a sweet smile, and I couldn't resist smiling back. She entertained my need to know everything, and I distracted our parents from her weird online activities and less than impressive grades.

"He wasn't in any of my morning classes either." Mena looked at him over her shoulder. "I think I would've noticed that level of hotness."

"You have a boyfriend." Harlow laughed and smacked her.

"So? I'm only human. I can look."

"Amaya." I cut across their banter. Amaya would've already texted me if she'd known about this.

"Already on it." She was typing furiously on her phone.

New guy closed his locker and walked out of the hallway, heading in the opposite direction of the cafeteria. I didn't like having him out of my sight, but I chased after no man, and I certainly didn't change my plans for any.

Looping my arm through Amaya's so she could continue to text, I led the way into the bright, bustling cafeteria.

Tall windows lined one wall, letting in natural light, with several French doors providing access to a courtyard for alfresco dining. Along with the various seating scattered throughout the space, a lounge area in the back corner housed an assortment of comfy couches and low tables. The full-service food counter was closer to a buffet than a school lunch line and included an espresso station—complete with a full-time barista.

We waited until we were seated at our usual table, trays of sushi and berry parfaits in front of us, before Amaya leaned in to deliver her information.

"His name is Hendrix Hawthorn. He started at Fulton today but spent most of the morning in the office—something about paperwork—which is why no one's seen him much yet. He moved here from the East Coast, but I can't seem to get any info on where exactly he transferred from."

Her fingers tightened around her chopsticks. Amaya liked the lack of information about as much as I did.

"I wonder if he has any friends here," Mena mused. I left the comment alone for now. I needed to know more about him before I decided how close we would become.

"Hey, girls." Nicola joined us at our table, her bleach-blonde hair bouncing at her shoulders. She was nice enough, and her mom was a household name due to her film career—as well as a client of Emily Mead Interiors—so she hung around us at school. But she wasn't a part of my core group. Harlow, Amaya, and Mena were my soul-deep friends.

We greeted her warmly anyway. Within a few minutes, a bunch of other people joined us too, and the new guy was the topic on everyone's lips. I kept quiet, listening to what everyone else had to say. The girls at the table kept glancing in my direction, waiting to hear what I thought. One negative word from me, and Hendrix Hawthorn would not be getting into the La Perla panties of a single Fulton student.

Unfortunately, I had a feeling I'd have to tackle this one head-on and speak to him directly. There just wasn't enough information to decide if he was going to be trouble—or if he was *worth* the trouble.

Before long, the conversation moved on. William complained about Mrs. Watson's surprise quiz in Calculus, Harlow threw in a completely random fact about the Fibonacci sequence that I had no idea where she'd learned but was positive was correct, Drew loudly and half-jokingly hit on Mena, and half the table reminded him she had a boyfriend.

Business as usual.

Lunch ended, and we dispersed to our next classes. Mulling over the new guy proved to be a good distraction through the afternoon, and I pulled at the waist of my skirt only once, thinking about how I couldn't wait to change into something very different and go to my dirty little secret. *Only a few hours to go.*

I was the first one of us girls out at the end of the day, so I threw my bag into the car, put my sunglasses on, and leaned back against the hood to turn my face up to the sky. There was a chill in the breeze, but the sun was driving it away.

Hendrix Hawthorn came striding down the steps as if he owned the place. He looked casual enough, but that neutral mask was still in place, and his Ray-Bans were already over his eyes. Nicola and a few other senior girls were trailing a safe distance behind him, whispering to each other, trying to get up the courage to talk to him. Tess even adjusted her boobs to put her cleavage on better display.

I rolled my eyes behind my shades and gritted my teeth. I didn't know why his presence bothered me so much. Maybe it was the blasé attitude. Maybe it was the fact that I had no idea what his deal was, and I really hated not knowing things.

But I was never one to let things fester.

As he passed my car, I pushed up into a standing position and called out, only slightly raising my voice. "Hendrix, right?"

I glanced at the girls behind him, pleased to see they were dispersing, even if their focus hadn't left us. Most people nearby had slowed down and were throwing us surreptitious glances. They knew just as well as I did that this interaction would determine where the new guy would fit in the complex social hierarchy of Fulton Academy.

Hendrix pressed his lips together and looked as if he might just keep walking, but then he seemed to notice all the attention too. He slowed his steps and half turned his body to face me.

Well, at least he was smart enough to realize that ignoring me would be a bad move.

"Yeah." His deep voice was as disinterested as his facial expression. He stuffed a hand into his pocket and chewed on something, adding an edge of frustration to his impassive posture.

"Welcome to Fulton Academy." I folded my hands in front of myself, giving him my polite but professional smile—a smile I'd perfected at twelve years old. "I'm Donna Mead."

"Uh-huh." He smacked the gum. "I've already had the welcome speech from the people in the office."

"This isn't official business." Maybe he wasn't as smart as I thought.

He looked me up and down. "No thanks."

"Excuse me?" I raised my eyebrows.

He flashed me a grin, mashing the pink gum between his perfectly straight teeth. "If this isn't an official welcome, then it's clearly . . . personal." He leaned in as if he were sharing a secret, but I kept my back ramrod straight. *Was that cinnamon?* "And I'm not interested in getting personal with you."

My right hand twitched with the urge to slap him. Luckily, my left was wrapped around it. I shoved down the rage, removed my sunglasses, and cocked my head, giving him an amused smile. "That's really presumptuous of you. I just wanted to introduce myself. Starting at a new school after the year has already begun can't be easy. I can help ease the transition. I could make your time here very pleasant."

I left the implications hanging in the cold breeze between us. I could make his time at Fulton incredibly fucking *unpleasant* too if I wanted to.

He watched me for a moment, his sharp jaw working that gum a little faster. Then he turned to face me fully and took his own sunglasses off. "I know girls like you. You think you rule this school and that you're going to grow up to rule the world. I know exactly what you think you can control. But I don't give a shit, princess. I don't want to be in your court. I don't give a flying fuck about making friends or *getting personal* with you or your hangers-on, so just pretend like I'm not here and continue to live your perfect little life. I'm just here until I can graduate and join the real world."

He blew an obnoxiously loud bubble, jammed his sunglasses back on, and walked away from me.

He fucking walked away from me. It was doubtful anyone had heard our exchange, but plenty of people were looking, watching for a hint of what my decree would be on Hendrix fucking Hawthorn.

I resisted the urge to chase him down, scream at him, smack that smug look off his face. Instead I smiled and replaced my sunglasses, keeping everyone in suspense for a little longer.

The smile was even a little genuine. He'd pissed me off, disrespected me, and was downright antagonizing. But I had a feeling I was going to have fun breaking him.

CHAPTER TWO

Donna

Gravel crunched under my favorite pair of thigh-high boots. The red miniskirt was tight around my thighs, the sheer top showed off my lacy bra underneath, and I was wearing more makeup than I ever did in public.

But I wasn't perfect, polished Donna Mead with starched uniforms and manicured nails tonight.

I was . . . someone else tonight.

Dark Donna.

The gaudy green neon above the metal door read *Davey's*.

A smile pulled at my ruby-red lips as every step I took toward the shiftiest establishment I knew took me away from myself.

Mom had come home from her boozy dinner, and I'd heard her snoring through the door as I passed her bedroom. Harlow was on her computer and had been oblivious to anything going on around her for hours. She'd be going to bed soon, and she'd leave early in the morning for tennis while Mom slept in. Meaning no one would notice *me* sleeping in.

My Legal Studies extra-credit assignment was done.

I'd mentioned a headache to the girls, ensuring they wouldn't try to get me out.

My to-do list for next week was written up in order of importance.

Hendrix . . . *ugh!* Hendrix was tomorrow's problem.

The girls had witnessed the tail end of our conversation, and I'd told them every detail in the car. Amaya swore profusely, calling him some very colorful names. Harlow mostly laughed, amused that someone was getting a rise out of me. Mena didn't like that he'd said mean things to me, but in the same breath she hoped he was adjusting to a new school OK.

I still hadn't decided what to do about him, but as I pushed through the rusty metal door, thoughts of the infuriating guy melted away. Instead, the pumping bass sent chills of anticipation down my spine.

I paused in the entrance area only long enough to slip a fifty to Anton—the burly bouncer whom I had a standing arrangement with. Not that Davey's was that strict with checking IDs anyway. Anton was paid for his discretion as much as for my entry. He gave me a nod, tucked the bill away, and readjusted himself on his stool. I didn't think I'd ever seen him crack a smile.

The Davey's clientele was as questionable as the stale trail mix they served up at the bar, but I didn't come here for stimulating conversation or to meet my future husband. I came here to have fun—to let the loud music and edge of danger drive all other thoughts from my mind.

I swayed my hips to the music as I made my way through the middle of the room, checking out who was on the dance floor. A lot of bikers hung out here, drug dealers, hookers—basically unpredictable people with questionable morals. People who made a thrilling jolt of fear race down my spine.

When I reached the bar, I wedged myself between a couple of bikers and a prostitute named Gina (she'd spilled her whole life story to me on one of my previous visits but had no memory of it or me—so I didn't bother saying hello). I stuck my ass out, crossing my booted feet at the ankles and arching my back. My gaze stayed forward, but I could practically *feel* hungry male eyes caressing my curves.

Three busy bartenders were working the bar, but luckily Bea spotted me first.

"Hey, girl." She greeted me with a fist bump. Bea was in her thirties, had dreadlocks and a penchant for leather vests, and took shit from no one. "Usual?"

"Yes, please." I gave her a genuine grin. We'd never spoken much beyond that exact exchange, but just like Anton, I had an understanding with Bea.

She dropped a glass of what looked like vodka and soda in front of me, but it was actually just soda. Even when I ordered an alcoholic drink in front of other people, Bea knew not to serve me alcohol, and she knew to keep her mouth shut about our agreement. I slipped her a fifty as I paid for the drink, and she gave me a wink before moving on to take the next order.

I was here because it made me feel alive. I didn't actually have a death wish. There was no way I was going to risk getting intoxicated in *this* crowd.

I turned to lean back against the bar, sipping my drink as I scanned the room. There were a few guys with potential. I liked the ones who were taller than me in my heels. I didn't really care what color his hair was, what his voice sounded like.

I hardly even bothered with his name half the time. But he had to be strong, confident, with some intensity simmering around the edges. *He* had to be the one to approach *me*.

The boys at my school couldn't handle me. But these lowlifes—these criminals with dark pasts and nothing to lose—they could handle me in the best, most depraved ways.

That's why they had to be older. How could they handle me if they couldn't handle themselves? Even so, I still never went for anyone who looked older than late twenties. I had control issues, not daddy issues.

In the bathrooms, in their cars, against the rough brick at the back of the building. One guy had even taken me to the back of the parking lot and bent me over his vintage Mustang. That was a fun night . . .

I never hooked up with the same guy twice, and I never let them think they could get more than one night of fun—not that any of them were interested in anything serious.

As my gaze wandered the crowd, I spotted the only man I'd ever slept with more than once.

I knew him only as Shady—yes, I was sleeping with someone who went by Shady, which pretty much told you all you needed to know about him. Not that he ever told me what his "business" was, but he was at Davey's a lot, all the staff knew him, and he was always talking to some new face.

Like right now. Shady was standing with his shoulders slouched, one hand holding a drink and the other in the pocket of his tracksuit pants, talking to someone in a very expensive suit who looked as if he didn't want to be there.

When the suit walked away, I sauntered over.

"Donna." He smirked at me from under his baseball hat. He only knew me as Donna.

I pressed myself against his side and brought my lips to his ear. "Hey. You busy tonight?" I made my intentions perfectly clear by giving his ear a little bite.

He groaned and gripped my hip.

Shady wasn't my usual type. He was only a little taller than me, and while he was lean and fit underneath those ridiculous tracksuits, he wasn't the size of a fridge. But he had the dominant confidence—bordering on cockiness—in spades. And his cock was huge.

"I wish I could, Donnie baby," he answered, and my face fell. "But I got some important business I gotta take care of tonight. If you're still around after close . . ."

But I was already shaking my head. I was never there that long. I couldn't risk getting home too late.

"Next time." I winked at him and walked away, making sure to sway my hips a little extra as I moved to the center of the dance floor.

He'd send me a bunch of texts later, telling me what he wanted to do to me. I was already looking forward to the thrill of reading them—a little slice of danger in my normal, clean life.

I didn't always pick up when I came to Davey's. Sometimes I just wanted to dance, to thrash out my frustration with the world on the sticky floors. Sometimes I liked to sit in a corner and people-watch, wondering what these people's lives were like. Were they easier than mine? Harder? What secrets did they have?

As I walked away from Shady, I had a feeling no one would approach me tonight. Sometimes, when he was in a shit-stirring mood, I thought maybe Shady *made sure* no one approached me. I didn't know if he was actually possessive or if he just liked to fuck with me, but I didn't care either way. If anything, it amused me. And I refused to give him the satisfaction of my reaction.

I rolled out of bed sometime after ten the next day—a good three hours later than my usual wake-up time. Harlow was still at tennis, and Mom liked to sleep in and have breakfast brought to her in bed when Dad was away. He was more active, like Harlow, and usually dragged Mom out to the pool or for a walk in the mornings.

The house was silent as I made my way downstairs, yawning and enjoying the fact that no one was around to make me feel as if I had to cover my mouth.

The hour alone before Harlow got back from tennis was the only peace I had all weekend. Mom got up not long after, just as Dad returned from his work trip and insisted on a family lunch.

I spent Saturday night at Amaya's with the girls. We stayed up late, watched movies, gossiped—and discussed the Hendrix topic ad nauseam.

"God." Amaya groaned, letting her phone drop to the couch next to her. "That is the sixth text I've gotten from a basic bitch fishing for info on the new guy. Do your own damn research!"

I chuckled and ran my hands through the ridiculously soft faux fur of the cushion in my lap. Mena and Harlow were throwing bits of popcorn at each other, trying to catch them with their mouths between fits of giggles, and only half paying attention.

"No boy talk!" Harlow yelled, then launched herself to the side to try to catch a kernel.

Mena laughed so hard she had to wipe tears away before she could speak. "I don't get why everyone's obsessed with him. He's just a guy."

"Because we go to school with a bunch of thirsty bitches," Amaya deadpanned.

I laughed. She wasn't wrong. People were fascinated because he was a shiny new toy, but he'd made it perfectly clear he didn't want to be played with. *We may as well give him what he wants . . .*

"Reply to them." I gestured at Amaya's phone, and she picked it up.

"What should I say?"

"Just write . . . Hendrix who?" I grinned. "And nothing else."

Amaya nodded, already typing. "Brutal."

I spent most of Sunday doing homework, and on Monday, while most people were dragging their feet into school, I marched in with a faint smile. Every time something annoyed or frustrated me, I'd remember the loud music thrumming in my chest, the smell of beer and sweat and cheap perfume, the feeling of eyes on me as I danced like a stripper. Shady must've been in one of his moods, because I ended up not finding a guy to have dirty sex with, but it was still a fun night—exactly the break and distraction I'd needed.

With the help of a few depraved texts from Shady, my Davey's high lasted well past the weekend, and I was still feeling loose as I pulled into the school parking lot on Tuesday morning.

"What the fuck?" Amaya growled. She'd spotted the Tesla in my spot the same time I did. I came to a stop and gripped the steering wheel, taking a deep breath.

"Whose car is that?" Harlow leaned between the front seats.

Everyone at Fulton knew not to park in that spot—everyone except one infuriating new asshole.

"I'll give you three guesses." My buzz was wearing off, and I hadn't even stepped foot into the school yet.

"We'll just have to park somewhere else today." Mena squeezed my shoulder. "It's no biggie."

She didn't get it. It may have been just a parking spot to everyone else, but I knew how these things worked. If I gave them a parking spot crumb, those vultures would devour my whole carcass—scrape my dignity, influence, and power from me strip by bloody strip. I had to remain in control.

"You guys go ahead. I'll drive to the back of the lot and look for a spot."

"No way, girl. We stick together," Amaya protested immediately, but Harlow was already undoing her belt.

"I can't get another late mark. Sorry, sis!" She sounded genuinely sorry but also a little satisfied at my ire—*little sisters*.

"I'll walk with you," Mena said to me.

I checked the time and shook my head. "Thanks, girls, but there's no sense in us all being late. Get your fine asses out of my car."

I flashed them a smile to show I really didn't mind, and they got out, rushing for the front doors. There were hardly any students still outside. I had five minutes to find a spot and get to my first class.

Just as I was about to take off, the door to the Tesla opened, and Hendrix fucking Hawthorn stepped out, completely unhurried and unfazed.

I quickly put my car in neutral and pulled the parking brake, then got out too. If I had to be late, so would he.

"Hendrix." I raised my voice, letting the edge cut into the single word.

He looked over his shoulder and rolled his eyes. "What now? I'm gonna be late."

"You're in my spot." I folded my arms and glared, showing him exactly how pissed I was.

"Excuse me?"

"You." I pointed at him, speaking as though I were explaining a complex idea to a child. "Are in." I pointed to his car. "My spot."

He stared at me for a beat, then made a show of checking the ground around his car before raising his brows and holding his arms out at his sides. "Don't see your name on it."

I took a deep breath and pinched the bridge of my nose. "I've tried to be nice, but you threw that in my face. You said you wanted to be left alone, but here you are antagonizing me. Everyone knows I park here. I'm now going to be late because of you. Move your car, and don't let this happen again."

He threw his head back and laughed, his broad shoulders shaking under his blazer. When he looked at me again, the mirth fell from his features, replaced by an intense stare.

"The spots are not allocated. Much as you like to think so, you don't own this school, princess, you don't own this spot, and you will never own *me*. I don't respond well to being ordered around." He locked his car and stalked toward the school as the bell sounded, leaving my profanity-filled response on the tip of my tongue.

I resisted the urge to stomp my foot like the brat he thought I was. Instead, I got back into my car, drove to the back of the lot, found one of the last remaining spots, and took the walk to the entrance to calm myself.

I was already late, so I didn't bother to rush; no sense in ruining my appearance too. His blatant disrespect in front of the entire school—everyone would walk past and see his car in my spot—made it impossible to do nothing. And my seething rage and determination to remain in control allowed me to formulate a rough plan by the time I entered the main building.

I sent a message to the girls in our group chat. "I've changed my mind. He needs to be taught to heel."

If he was going to act like a disobedient puppy, pissing on things he thought he had a right to, then I would treat him like a dog.

CHAPTER THREE

Hendrix

I frowned at the bulletin board. I knew for a fact I'd put my name down on the sign-up form on my second day at Fulton Academy, yet there was the spot, covered in white-out with some other dickhead's name scrawled over the top.

I gritted my teeth and fought the urge to hunt down this Thomas Booth and make sure he could never walk again, let alone kick a football.

It was for the best—I'd come here to remove my own name anyway. Playing football was too close to my old life. Apparently the school was holding tryouts this late in the year because four of the players had been injured in some car accident—one was off the team permanently for breaking the coach's strict no-alcohol-during-the-week rule. The dumbasses were getting wasted and driving around Devilbend on a Wednesday night. It was something I would've done —before.

Only nostalgia had made me put my name down in the first place— misplaced longing for a life I now knew was a fucking joke. I flexed my fingers and bunched them into a fist, remembering the feel of the ball as it slapped into my waiting arms. I hadn't played in over a year, and it was all my fault. All my stupidity and carelessness and . . .

I dug my nails into my palm and forced myself to focus on my surroundings, the chatting of students as they passed, the opening and closing of lockers in the distance.

The teal tie felt stiff and tight, and I tugged at it before adjusting the bag on my shoulder. I wasn't used to the uniform yet.

A short woman with glasses and a pencil skirt hugging her generous curves stepped out of the office and reached for the form I'd just been staring daggers at. She spotted me and paused, giving me a warm smile.

"Did you want to sign up? It's not too late." She wiggled the form in front of my face.

"No thanks." I kept my voice even. There was no need to take my frustration out on the nice reception lady.

I did my best to ignore the other students as I walked to my locker.

She may not have whited my name out herself, but I had no doubt Donna Mead was the person behind its removal. It didn't matter though. I didn't belong on their stupid football team, especially if I wasn't welcome. You couldn't build a team if the team didn't get along.

I'd been at Fulton just over two weeks, and other than a few early verbal sparring matches with Donna, I'd hardly had a conversation with another person. The first few days had been a nightmare. It was a new school, all new people, the other fucking side of the country. I knew I was good-looking and tall, and now the giant chip on my shoulder gave me the edge of bad-boy danger private school girls creamed their panties for. A few guys had been friendly initially too, probably hoping I'd join the football team and help save them from a disaster season.

I'd either brushed off or ignored them all, wondering how long I'd have to endure this torture before they got the hint. I just wanted to be left alone, finish my senior year, and never see any of these stuck-up, rich assholes again.

By the end of the first day, it was clear who the "queen bee" was. Donna Mead strutted the halls with her predictable gaggle of girls and the confidence of a spoiled brat who'd never been told *no*. The guys all checked her out as she passed; the girls all glanced in her direction, as if waiting for permission to exist.

Donna was exactly the type the old me would've gone for. If this were a year ago, before I went and ruined everything, she would've been riding my dick within a week, and I would've been throwing punches at any guy who dared look in her direction as we both got off on the power of being the most popular couple in school.

A lot had changed. I had nothing but contempt for girls like Donna and guys like me now.

I hated her for what she represented, but I hated myself more for what I used to be.

I'd hoped to just sail under the radar, but it became apparent very quickly that wasn't going to happen. Antagonizing Donna was the best and most efficient way of making sure everyone left me alone.

So, I was rude to her, really embracing the cocky attitude, the side of myself I tried to push down.

I could tell she was pissed, but the stares from chicks wanting to get in my pants didn't stop. So I parked in her spot deliberately. Of course I knew it was her spot. I'd seen her park there, seen other students leave the prime space free. I got up extra early and sat in my damn car for nearly twenty minutes, waiting for her to show.

It was almost cute, the way her nose scrunched up in derision. It took a lot not to chuckle while she was berating me. That was the first time I noticed she had one green eye and one hazel. So unusual. It was distracting, watching both the mesmerizing colors blaze in fury at me. I'd planned to hang around longer, really rile her, maybe even get her to raise her voice. But I'd started to forget all the hurtful things I'd planned to say to her and walked away much sooner than planned.

It worked anyway. I'd goaded the queen of Fulton Academy into declaring war on me. I got what I wanted . . . and then some.

The next day, a group of freshman girls were standing in the parking space, blocking my car with their gangly bodies. I laughed to myself as I passed. I had no intention of ever parking there again. I'd made my point. But the parking-minders remained for a solid week, faithful subjects trying to impress their queen. Most likely she hadn't even had to ask. They'd probably only needed a vague mention of how inconvenient it was for her and jumped to her defense.

I deposited my bag in my locker and gripped my biology books with one hand, slamming the locker shut with the other.

As I walked the halls, no one looked at me anymore. Donna had made her declaration, and her loyal subjects were doing her bidding—excommunicating me.

Just before I reached the end of the hallway, some junior with a wonky tie and acne around his nose deliberately bumped into me in an attempt to knock my books out of my hand. His intentions had been obvious in his jittery steps and nervous glances, so I'd had plenty of time to tense my core and grip my books tighter. The kid bounced off me like a tennis ball.

Eyes wide, he stared up at me. I gave him a disparaging look, and he nervously shot a glance to the side before hanging his head and rushing off.

I followed his gaze. *Of course.* Donna was walking up the corridor with her short friend—Mena? The guy had been trying to impress her and failed miserably.

I rolled my eyes and went on my merry way.

It had been two and a half weeks of this. At first, all the early attention for a hot new guy had abruptly stopped. Exactly what I wanted. Then people started throwing me openly hostile scowls wherever I went. Not unexpected, and definitely something I could handle. Then losers wanting to impress Donna started bumping into me, attempting to shove me into lockers, trying to intimidate me, while the chicks—also wanting to impress Donna, although mostly for different reasons—started saying bitchy things about me as I passed. Having the entire school against me was more than I expected, but I could still handle it. There were only seven months until the school year ended, and I'd never be seeing any of these people again. What did I care what they thought of me?

I never fought back, never reacted more than to tense up and stop my ass from hitting the ground. I just sealed that impassive look on my face, turned my nose up as if none of these bastards mattered more than dirt on my shoes, and kept walking.

Inside, I was *writhing*.

Old habits die hard, and every time someone showed me aggression, I itched to drive my fist into their face, spear tackle them to the ground, knee them in the gut, do something *violent*. I knew it would make me feel better . . . momentarily. It just wasn't worth it anymore. Not after what went down at my last school.

As I neared my classroom, a football came sailing at my head. I'd seen the quarterback throw it. I caught it, not even flinching at how close it got to my nose or how my hand stung from the impact. The guy had a good arm, had to give him that. I was pretty sure his name was Drew—I'd seen him hanging out with Donna and her group.

I fixed him with a deadpan stare. *Nice try, asshole.* A smile pulled at his lips as he stared at me in shock. He was as grudgingly impressed with my catch as I was with his throw. *Suck on it—that's exactly what you missed out on by scratching my name off the sign-up.*

I let the ball bounce to the ground and walked into my classroom to take my seat, like a good little boy. As I opened my textbook, I allowed myself a little smirk of satisfaction.

The bell sounded, everyone settled, and Mrs. Shepard—a middle-aged woman with a killer rack that I'm sure was in the spank bank for half the boys at the school—started the lesson.

And my fucking pen ran out of ink. I scratched it aggressively against the paper, hoping to get the blue stuff flowing by force, but it refused to budge. My grip on the pen tightened to the point that I could feel the plastic about to snap. Dropping it onto the desk, I took a deep breath and, without even thinking about it, turned to the chick in the seat next to me.

"Hey, you got a pen I can borrow?" I whispered.

The look she gave me was so full of derision and outrage you'd think I'd asked her to get on her knees and blow me in the middle of class. It was just a fucking pen.

She looked away without even a response.

I'd wanted to be left alone, but this was ridiculous. How hard was it to be polite every once in a while?

Someone tapped my shoulder with a pen, and I turned in my seat. The chick one row back and to my right was holding out a black pen with a friendly smile.

I frowned and eyed the pen, wondering if it was laced with arsenic. She was one of Donna's girls—and I'd picked up enough from overheard conversations to know that Mena was Donna and Harlow's cousin and very close with them both.

So what the fuck was she doing acknowledging my existence?

"It's just a pen." She rolled her eyes, but with a hint of humor.

I took it and nodded. "Thank you."

"You're welcome." Her smile seemed sincere as she sat back and returned her attention to the front of the class.

"Mr. Hawthorn." Mrs. Shepard's voice had me doing the same. "Am I boring you?"

"No, ma'am." I held the pen up. "Just borrowing a pen."

She gave me a skeptical look and got back to the lesson.

I did my best to pay attention, but I couldn't stop thinking about the anomaly that was Mena. From what I'd seen, the girl was genuinely friendly and sweet. She had a purple birthmark on the right side of her nose that would've made her a target for bullies at my old school. Fulton was almost identical, but Mena was one of the most popular girls, protected by her close friendship with Donna.

It didn't fit my assessment of who Donna Mead was and what she was about, and I didn't like that. I didn't like that I was suddenly wondering what made her tick. It had been a long time since a chick had made me curious, and I didn't have time for it.

I drove home in the brand-new Tesla Model S my parents hadn't even questioned the price tag on. I resented having to take anything from them in the first place, but public transport in this part of Devilbend was a joke, so I'd caved and let them buy me one. But I'd chosen a ridiculously expensive one just to spite them, and the most environmentally friendly one to put some semblance of good into the world in a vain attempt to make up for all the bad I'd done. They'd just paid the bill, not even an angry message to their disappointment of a son.

Being sent to the other side of the country to live with my aunt was almost as much a relief for me as it was for them.

Aunt Hannah lived on the edge of the nicest part of Devilbend. Her townhouse was spacious and nicely decorated, but she didn't have the sprawling land some of the ostentatious estates boasted—the kind of property I grew up on back in New York.

I parked on the street, not wanting to block the one-car garage when she got home.

As soon as I finished shoveling a sandwich into my mouth, I changed into sweats and spent the next couple hours zoning out with the help of video games. I got so engrossed in the explosions on the TV I didn't even notice the front door opening.

"Hendrix?" My aunt's voice made me startle. She stood next to the couch, her arms crossed over her silk blouse.

I immediately ended the game and dropped the controller on the coffee table. "Hey. Uh . . . how was work?"

She ignored my question. "Have you been playing video games all afternoon?"

"Yeah." I cringed. I was eighteen and she wasn't my parent, but I was here and not with my asshole parents because she allowed it. "I'm going to do homework after dinner."

She just sighed and gave me a disapproving look. She'd looked at me with disapproval a lot in the month I'd been staying with her. It grated on my nerves, but I kept my reaction tightly under wraps. Considering the reason I was here, what I'd done, I deserved the disapproving looks.

I got up and started clearing the plates, cups, and chip packets. I liked to eat while I played. "Um . . . how was your day?"

"Fine." She followed me into the kitchen and dropped her oversized purse on a barstool.

"Cool." I nodded and pressed my lips together.

Hannah was working her way up through the ranks at some marketing company. She worked hard, sometimes doing long hours and often bringing work home, her laptop and piles of paper spread over the dining table. She was in her early thirties, had no kids, and had no idea how to handle me. I wondered, almost daily, how my parents had gotten her to agree to let me move in while I finished high school. She and my dad weren't exactly on good terms. I'd only met her a handful of times at family events—where she generally kept to herself in a far corner, scowling and getting slowly but surely drunk. But she'd been kind to me as a kid, bringing me little gifts and dropping the scowl if I happened to come up to her.

"I'm staying at Robbie's tonight." She leaned on the counter. Robbie was her boyfriend, whom she rarely talked about and I had yet to meet. "Do you need me to leave you some money to order takeout for dinner?"

"No, that's OK. Bank of Dad has it covered." I gave her a wry smile. My credit card had a very generous limit. My father may have sent me away like the blight on his reputation that I was, but he wasn't about to cut me off.

"Right. Good." She stared at the counter, and I shuffled my feet. I was glad she was finally spending more time with her partner. My guess was she'd been spending every night at home because of me, and I felt bad.

"You're not to have anyone around." She finally straightened and fixed me with a firm look. So, this was what was making her pause. She needed to lay down the law.

"That won't be a problem." There wasn't a single soul in Devilbend I would consider a friend.

"I'm not messing around, Hendrix. I need a night to spend with my boyfriend, but leaving you alone makes me nervous. I won't tolerate . . . insubordination."

If I hadn't felt like shit to my very core, her attempts at a firm reprimand would've been amusing. She was a petite woman with strawberry-blonde hair and a tasteful manicure. I had a foot and a hundred pounds on her. There wasn't much she could do to make me do anything, which made the fact that she hadn't had her boyfriend over to intimidate me even more perplexing. I admired her, really. She was taking me on all on her own. But she had nothing to worry about.

I'd spent the month since I'd arrived doing nothing but what she'd told me. She had only two rules, which she'd made crystal clear within half an hour of my arrival: maintain a B average, and stay out of trouble. The slightest hint of my breaking either rule would result in immediate removal from her home. I had no intention of letting her down.

We'd hardly spoken since then, but I'd been respectful, cleaned up after myself, gone to school, stayed out of her way. I was doing all I could to show her I was serious, but she still felt the need to remind me I was on thin ice every few days. As if she was worried I was just waiting for her to let her guard down so I could go back to being the douchebag I'd been before.

I'd avoided talking to her about it because I really didn't want to discuss the reason I was here in the first place. But I needed to man up and say something. As frustrated as I was with the constant side-eye, I knew I deserved it, so I made sure my voice was calm, contrite even, as I leaned on the counter opposite her.

"Aunt Hannah, I know my being here isn't easy for you. I don't know what you discussed with Mom and Dad—they don't really tell me anything—but I want you to know I'm not here because my parents made me. I want to be here. I want to be anywhere but . . . there, where it all happened and everyone looks at me like I'm a monster." *Because I am* . . . fuck it. I swallowed and made myself own it. "I know it's because I am. But I'm trying not to be. I'm really, really fucking sorry for what I did, and I promise I'm not interested in causing any trouble at all. Sorry for cursing."

She straightened her shoulders, and her expression visibly softened as she scrutinized me for a few minutes. "I believe you. I don't know if I would've handled the situation like your parents did, but I'm not your parent. But then, I guess you're not your father either . . ." She looked to the side, lost in thoughts I suspected weren't directly related to our current situation. "Anyway, I'm sorry if I've been a hard-ass. I'm just still trying to figure out how to navigate this."

"It's OK. I don't want you to change your life on my account. Go out, spend time with Robbie. Have him over if that's what you used to do. Just know I won't cause any trouble. I can take care of myself, and as soon as school is over, I'll be out of your hair. I'll figure something out."

"Tell you what, I'll stop being such a bitch and be more relaxed if you promise to come to me if you need help with something or if you're struggling. I agreed to this for many reasons, but I do want to be here for you, Hendrix. If I can."

I had to clear my throat around the lump that had suddenly formed there. If my parents had, even once, made me feel as supported as this virtual stranger had, maybe things would've turned out differently. "Deal."

"And I don't think you're a monster." My gaze flew up to hers, the emotions flying around in my chest too many to process. "I think you made a mistake—a very bad one that you have to live with for the rest of your life—but I don't believe you intended to . . . for things to go the way they did."

I held her gaze for a long moment, then nodded. It was all I could manage.

"Right!" She slapped the counter and literally shook the tension out of her shoulders. It was the most animated I'd ever seen her. "Good talk! Should we hug it out?" She tilted her head and gave me an awkward, questioning grin.

I chuckled. "That's not necessary."

"We'll work up to it." She waved her hand. "I'll get a stepping stool to prepare."

"A stepping stool?"

"Yeah. You're way too fucking tall. I need to assert my adult dominance by gaining a height advantage."

I let a genuine laugh bust out of my chest. "So, you're OK with cursing then?"

She tapped her chin and squinted, then shrugged. "Yeah, fuck it. You're an adult, and I have a potty mouth."

"Excellent." I grinned. This was feeling more like a nephew-aunt relationship, and a little weight lifted off my shoulders.

She left a few minutes later, and I got on with exactly what I said I'd do —homework.

My phone went off just as I started packing my books up, yawning so wide my jaw felt as if it might dislocate. I checked the message and sighed.

Heard you were in my neck of the woods. Hit me up if you need anything—even if it's just to shoot the shit over a drink.

The number was unknown, but I knew the name at the end of the text. This had the potential for trouble—trouble I didn't need, wasn't interested in, and just told my aunt I was avoiding. But even I knew not letting off some steam every once in a while could result in even worse trouble.

I decided to ignore the message for now and flopped into bed. It was well past midnight, but I still had trouble falling asleep, thoughts of a certain interesting blonde keeping me tossing and turning.

CHAPTER FOUR

Hendrix

My lunch tray was yanked out from under my nose before I had a chance to pick up the silverware. It clattered to the ground, pasta puttanesca splattering everywhere as a green apple rolled away.

"Oops." A girl with curly black hair held a hand to her mouth in mock shock, her friends snickering behind her.

Half the kids in the cafeteria froze, their full focus on the scene, just as Donna and her friends walked past.

I took a deep breath and released it through my nose. Fixing the wannabe bitch with an unimpressed look, I bent sideways to grab the sauce-covered pudding cup and—without breaking eye contact—removed the lid and licked it in a slow, deliberate move. I almost smiled at how her face slackened, her lips parting a little in shock even as she frowned in frustration at my lack of response. She was no doubt wondering what my tongue would feel like between her thighs, questioning how her brilliant plan to humiliate me had backfired so badly.

I dropped the lid onto the mess at my feet and dug into the pudding as she walked away, her shoulders tight.

Shit was escalating. In the last few days, the girls had started getting physical too. None of them dared try to shove me—they weren't that stupid—but pushing my books off desks, throwing their trash in my direction, and other aggressive moves were getting more common.

If something didn't change soon, I'd have to make a stand. I wasn't interested in being anyone's friend, but I wasn't going to be anyone's punching bag either. Even though I deserved it, ultimately, they didn't know that, so was it really penance for past crimes if my tormentors' hearts weren't in it for the right reasons?

People buzzed around Donna's table, laughing and joking, not paying any attention whatsoever to the rest of the cafeteria. The wannabe bitch was neither getting rewarded for her stunt with the queen bee's attention nor being chastised for her stupidity by anyone else. This thing had taken on a life of its own. Donna wasn't behind the continuing escalation of shitty behavior toward me, but she wasn't doing anything to stop it either.

Only Mena and Donna's sister, Harlow, glanced in my direction every once in a while, sitting at the end of the table in their own private chat.

My knee bounced under the table, but I made myself eat the pudding at a leisurely pace. Then I got to my feet, cleaned up the mess as best I could with napkins, and returned my tray to the staff, letting them know there was an accident and apologizing for the mess. None of these brats would bother cleaning it up, expecting "the help" to do their bidding even at school. I was one of these brats until not too long ago.

I left halfway through lunch, needing to get away from all those idiots even if it meant not getting a proper meal. The bag of chips I had stashed in my locker wouldn't be enough, but it was better than nothing until school ended.

Footsteps echoed behind me in the mostly empty hall, and I slammed my locker shut, preparing for whatever bullshit was coming next.

Turned out it was a serving of hot fries and not bullshit. Mena came to a stop next to me and held out the steaming offering. My mouth watered. Who didn't love hot fries?

"I noticed you didn't really eat." She was wearing makeup today, her birthmark invisible.

I arched a brow at her. "How can I be sure no one pissed on them?"

She scrunched up her face. "Who would defile the sacredness of hot fries like that?"

My lips twitched. She almost drew an actual smile from me. "Wouldn't put it past your friend."

"Donna wouldn't do that." She sighed as I took the fries. "And she didn't tell that girl to throw your lunch on the ground."

I gave her a skeptical look and spoke around a mouthful of hot potato. "She didn't tell her not to either."

"No, but Donna isn't the boss of everyone."

I snorted and gave her a withering look.

"OK, fine. She has a lot of influence around here, but . . ." Mena trailed off, searching for words to defend her cousin, just as the girl in question appeared with the other two at the end of the hallway. Lunch was coming to a close.

Donna stopped next to us and clasped her hands in front of her. I shoved another three fries into my mouth to distract myself from the exposed skin between the tops of her socks and that infuriating skirt. Who the fuck decided to put a bunch of hormonal teenagers into porn-fantasy outfits and make them spend every day of the week together? Idiots . . .

"You OK, Mena?" Donna asked as she stared at me. There was genuine concern in her voice.

Mena huffed. "I'm fine. He's harmless."

I shoved more fries into my mouth. If she only knew how decidedly *not* harmless I was . . . I should've just walked away, but instead I found myself leaning back against the locker.

Donna finally faced her friend. "Hendrix has made it perfectly clear he wants to be left alone."

I finished the last of the fries and cut in before anyone else could speak. "Thanks for the fries, Mena. You seem like a genuinely nice person. I really don't understand why you hang out with these vapid bitches."

Harlow fixed me with a scowl so deep she bared her teeth. Amaya stopped texting for longer than a few seconds and narrowed her eyes. Donna surprised me once again by leaning back just a fraction, a tiny smile pulling at her lips.

But it was sweet Mena who surprised me most. She stepped right into my space and poked me in the chest. "No. I know you're new around here, so you don't know us, and I don't really understand this bizarre feud between you two, but I'm not going to stand here and let you talk about my friends like that. You're being a judgmental douche—and not the vagina kind. The butt kind." She jabbed my chest again, and my eyes widened. I'd inadvertently unleashed some kind of attack koala, and she was coming for my head. "I'm trying to be nice to you because I think that's the right thing to do, but make no mistake—I would do anything for those three. They're like more than sisters to me. No one fucks with Devilbend Dynasty."

Without waiting for a response, she spun on her heel and stalked away. Harlow and Amaya trailed after her, but Donna remained, a smug smile on her lips as she crossed her arms.

I crushed the empty, greasy bag in my fist and straightened to my full height. She didn't even waver, somehow still managing to look down her nose at me despite having to look up to meet my eyes.

"Don't fuck with my friends. Then you'll know what I'm really capable of."

"You're already making my life difficult enough. What more could you possibly do?" I gritted out, showing my frustration for the first time.

"You wanted nothing to do with me, any of the other students, or this school." She shrugged. "I simply let a few people know."

"Yeah, well, they're really running with your suggestion now, so consider this a fair warning. If shit keeps escalating, I'm not just gonna take it lying down. I'm not expecting to be anyone's bro, but I'll have to start swinging back if it comes to it."

I dumped the greasy bag in the trash and shoved my way through the crowd. It was the most aggression I'd shown since I started at Fulton, and surprised students started getting out of my way.

It was a lie, of course. If the violence increased, I wouldn't do shit to fight back. I'd never swing a fist again, as much as I wanted to. *I'd rather die.*

The pent-up frustration had to be released somehow though. By the time the day ended, I'd snapped three pens.

As soon as I got in my car, I slammed the door shut and resisted the urge to punch the steering wheel. I couldn't go home. Video games wouldn't cut it today. Plus, I'd been slacking off with my fitness.

Because I was a good, responsible boy now, I shot off a text to my aunt.

Going to sign up to a gym. May be home after you.

Her response was immediate.

No worries. Staying at Robbie's tonight. Be safe!

The words on my phone screen melted some of the frustration from my system. *Be safe.* Not *be good* or *don't disappoint me* or *don't embarrass me.* I was beginning to wish Aunt Hannah had raised me and not the two emotionless robots I had for parents.

I drove to downtown Devilbend and parked at Exert. There were several gyms in town, two closer to where I lived, but I chose this one because it was on a busy street in the center of everything. I wanted the anonymity of a crowd.

The young guy behind the counter looked up from the computer screen and gave me a polite smile.

"Hey. Welcome to Exert." He was in shorts and a workout top with the gym branding, and his messy blond hair gave him a little bit of a surfer vibe.

"Hi. I'd like to join up."

"Great!" His smile widened, and he tapped at the keyboard before pointing to a touch screen facing me. "Just fill this out."

I filled out the form and handed over Dad's credit card, and he gave me a membership card and key fob. "We're open twenty-four hours, but the desk is only manned during business hours and evening classes. I've sent you an email with the schedule if you're interested. Can I help organize a PT session? The first one is complimentary."

"Nah, man, I'm good. Just here to work out." I was already swinging my bag over my shoulder.

"No worries. I'm Turner, by the way. Just let me know if you need anything."

"Thanks, Turner," I called over my shoulder as I headed toward the changing room.

I thrashed my body for nearly two hours, alternating cardio and high-intensity weights. I hadn't played football in a year, and with everything going on, my visits to the gym had been sporadic at best. No question I'd be feeling it the next day.

When I got home, starving, I made myself two microwave dinners and slumped into a stool at the kitchen island.

My phone vibrated when I was halfway through something resembling chicken and pasta. I checked the message and sighed. It was from that same number.

Hey, man. Wanna come out? Maybe play some pool? I'll be here all evening. No pressure.

At the bottom was an address two towns over.

I'd ignored the fucker's first message, and I knew I should ignore this one too, but the thought of spending another night in this empty house, alone, made me want to claw my eyes out.

I'd hardly had a conversation with anyone besides my aunt in nearly two months. I hadn't heard from my parents since the day they put me in a town car headed for the airport. The kids at school were on a collective campaign to make my life hell. And I hadn't spoken to any of my old friends in a long time. Most of the large group that used to hang on my every word disappeared pretty quickly after they realized I would no longer be going to school, let alone playing football —not after what I did. The rest I cut off myself. I couldn't stand to look at them. It was like looking in a mirror.

My aunt was supportive, but she was still my aunt, not my friend. Not someone I could chill with.

Shady wasn't an ideal companion—especially with a nickname like that— but he was all I had at the moment. I shoveled the rest of my dinner into my mouth and headed for the shower. My aunt wouldn't even know I'd gone out, but it didn't matter. I had no intention of breaking my promises to her. I was staying out of trouble. This was simply an excuse to get out of the house before I went completely batshit and started collecting cats and putting on tea parties for them.

When I pulled into the parking lot of the address he'd given me, I sighed. The neon name above the door—*Davey's*—glowed in the dusk. It had taken me forty minutes to get there, and it was probably going to be a giant waste of time. Shady hadn't bothered to mention it was a bar, so I hadn't bothered to bring my fake ID. I wasn't even sure I still had it.

I sent him a text.

Just got here but can't join you. Did you forget I'm underage?

I was hoping I could convince him to grab a burger or something. I really didn't want to go home yet.

After five minutes, he still hadn't replied. Then a lean guy in a black tracksuit came swaggering around the back of the building. I'd only met him once, when he came to visit his cousin in New York about six months before my life was turned upside down, but there was no forgetting that cocky swagger, the wide grin.

Everything about this guy screamed trouble. You could tell with one glance he was Shady by nature and not just by name.

I got out of the car and walked toward him.

"Hendrix, my man!" he called out, spreading his arms wide.

I gave him a half-hearted wave and a smile. We shook hands, and he pulled me in for a good thump on the back too.

"Hey, Shady. Nice to see you again."

"You too, man, you too. Come 'round back—no bouncer." He led the way, then leaned sideways as if telling me a secret. "Between you and me, this place isn't exactly too bothered with shit like that."

"Shit like . . . legal drinking age?" I raised my eyebrows with a smirk.

He laughed, throwing his head back. "Yeah, yeah, yeah. So, how you been, man?"

Without giving me a chance to answer, he started chattering away about nothing specific as we walked into one of the dirtiest bars I'd ever seen. It was dingy, smoky, and full of people who looked even more like trouble than Shady—and that was saying something. I followed him to a seating area in the back, and he introduced me to a handful of other guys, who gave me their best tough-guy head nods in greeting.

Before I could sit down, he led me away again, still talking shit. I'd never met someone who could talk so much without actually saying anything.

We settled into a couple of barstools, and he turned to me. "Had to intro you to the businessmen. It's a respect thing."

I just nodded. If those guys were legitimate businessmen, then I was a professional cupcake baker. "They own the club? You work for them?"

"Nah, nah. The owner doesn't come 'round much. That was the manager and a couple other guys. We all have an arrangement. What's your poison?"

That was all he was going to say on the matter of his "business," and I didn't want more details anyway. "Just a soda or something. I'm not drinking."

"I told you, bro. No one's gonna check your ID here." He thumped me on the back, waving a bar chick with dreads over.

Shady ordered vodka and OJ, and I got a Coke, then turned to him. "It's not that. I have to drive back to Devilbend, and I can't get in any more trouble, man."

He nodded and dropped the grin. "Hey, man, Wiley told me what went down. That's some heavy shit."

Wiley was Shady's cousin and a friend of mine from New York. He didn't go to my school, but I'd met him at some party, and we clicked. We used to egg each other on to do the stupidest shit. He didn't have a lot of money, so I always insisted on paying when we went out for food and shit, but he provided an outlet for me—dangerous access to getting into some dumb trouble. He was one of the only people who stood by me when "shit went down," as Shady said. But I'd stopped returning his calls too. I didn't deserve anyone's support, and I needed to cut ties to that life anyway.

Yet there I was, sitting in a dodgy bar with his cousin, who was already downplaying the single biggest mistake of my life. Maybe this wasn't a good idea . . .

"What went down?" I arched a brow at him.

The bar chick delivered our drinks, and he took a sip. "Yeah. You know, what happened . . . the incident."

"The incident . . ." I glared at him. "I don't need you to play it down, man. As much as my parents wish I wouldn't, I actually own my shit. You can just say it. I—"

"Hey, look," he said, cutting me off. "I'm not trying to piss you off or fish for info. We don't even have to talk about it. Wiley told me you were out this way and asked me to reach out. I'm happy to be a drinking buddy or intro you to some chicks if you wanna get laid, or you can just ignore my ass and come here whenever you like. I'll let the bouncers know you're a friend. They'll take care of you. That's it, bro. Take it or leave it."

He shrugged and took another sip. I watched him carefully for a few moments, then sighed and drank my Coke.

Maybe I'd let his words get to me too much. This lowlife seemed to genuinely have a sliver of heart in his skinny chest. And it would be nice to hang with someone without pressure—someone I didn't have to pretend with, someone who knew what I'd done.

"Sorry, Shady. I'm a little touchy."

"Forget it." He waved a hand, then swiveled on his stool to look at the dance floor. "Now, tell me. Are you an ass man or a tits man?"

I chuckled. As long as I kept a wide berth from Shady's "business" here, this could be exactly what I needed to chill out from time to time.

CHAPTER FIVE

Donna

The car was eerily silent when the girls piled into it at the end of the day. Amaya didn't launch into the day's gossip, Mena didn't crack jokes, Harlow didn't throw out any random facts. I sighed and turned the music up. I wasn't sure if they were pissed at me or worried about me, but I hated this.

We needed some girl time, so instead of turning off toward home, I continued on into town.

Amaya turned the music down. "Where we going, D?"

The use of my childhood nickname made something in my chest constrict, and I forced some levity into my voice. "We're ignoring all our responsibilities and getting something greasy to eat."

Harlow snorted. "It's Friday afternoon—you're the only one who has responsibilities."

They all laughed at my expense, and I couldn't help joining in.

We parked our asses at a Portuguese joint and shared a massive plate of Peri Peri chicken and fries. When the plate was empty, Amaya crossed her arms on the table and fixed me with a look. "Is the new guy situation getting out of hand?"

I groaned. "Maybe. He's been a giant pain in my ass since he showed up."

"I think you need to tell people to back off him," Mena said.

"I never told anyone to lay into him in the first place." I hadn't been lying when I told Hendrix I wasn't telling people to make his life hell.

"I know that, but people listen to you. They'll stop if you tell them to."

I bristled. That would feel like admitting I was wrong. "Look, I know some people have started taking things too far, but that's not my fault. He was a complete jerk to me, and he turned his nose up at every single person in our school. He's been disrespectful and antagonizing every time I've spoken to him. I'm not gonna just stand there and take that. I'm going to defend myself and you guys, no matter what it takes. He started this."

Mena looked down into her lap and frowned. She clearly didn't agree with everything I'd said, but she knew firsthand how far I'd go to protect the three people sitting at that table with me.

When we'd found out she was being bullied at her last school, I pulled every thread I could think of to make her tormentors pay. I'd called in favors I was holding on to for after college to protect her.

"He started it." Harlow mimicked my voice, and I smacked her shoulder. She pinched my thigh in response.

"Ouch!" I yanked her ponytail, and then we both burst into giggles.

"Seriously though"—she straightened her hair—"I've never seen you this worked up. He's just an asshole with an ego. If I didn't know any better, I'd think you had the hots for him."

"Oh, *please*." I crossed my arms and rolled my eyes.

"Holy shit." Amaya sat up. "Is that why you don't want to call the dogs off? You're worried the other girls will think it's open season?"

"No." My answer was immediate and firm. But now that she mentioned it, I didn't like the idea of a sea of teal pleated skirts hanging off his every move. But that was only because I didn't want him to have anyone to hang out with—as he'd insisted he didn't want. That was all. It wasn't because I secretly liked him.

"You're bullying him." Mena finally raised her gaze, making Amaya and Harlow pause in their taunting and poking at my sides.

I reeled back as if she'd slapped me. "No, I'm not."

"Yes, you are. You all are. The entire school. He may be big enough to defend himself from most physical attacks, but what happens when people decide to gang up on him? What happens when they get a group together, drag him out to the football field, tie him to the goalpost . . ." She swallowed as I shared a wide-eyed look with the other two. "Because they decide they need to prove a point. Prove *your* point."

She was describing the horrific things that had been done to her.

I reached across the table kaɴd took her hand. "I'd never let that happen, Philomena."

"Not intentionally." She slowly pulled her hand out from under mine. "But can't you see that you're doing to him what they did to me?"

I sat back and really thought about it. Was I instigating the mean, petty shit

Fulton students were doing to Hendrix? No. But did I start the campaign against him to prove a point? Yes, I absolutely did. And did I get satisfaction from how thoroughly he was being punished for treating me with disrespect? I'd be lying if I said no. It was why I'd let it go on.

But the thought of being as bad as her bullies in Mena's eyes broke my heart.

Tears stung the backs of my eyes, but I forced the emotion back. I refused to cry in front of other people.

"I think she's right." Harlow fiddled with her napkin. "We need to take Mena's view on the situation seriously, considering."

Amaya nodded. "D, we know you're not intending to bully him, but I do think we need to be wary of this escalating. Fulton is a whole other ballgame. You know that if any of those shits pulled the kind of stunt Mena went through, they wouldn't even see the inside of a police station before their parents' money took care of the problem."

"You're right." I nodded and licked my lips. "You're all right. I refuse to let him talk to me like shit, but I don't agree with how things have been escalating. I'll do something about it on Monday."

"*We* will." Harlow smiled, reminding me I wasn't alone in this . . . even though it sometimes felt like it.

"It'll be fine." Amaya flipped her long black hair over a delicate shoulder. "We just need to remind those idiots they have reputations to uphold. Nothing brings rich brats into line like the threat of embarrassing their parents."

Mena smiled, already looking lighter. "I love you girls."

"Love you," the three of us chorused.

"Ugh!" Amaya slapped the table. "Enough heavy shit. Let's go get Starbucks."

We walked two blocks to the nearest one and got giant cups of sugar and caffeine.

Out on the sidewalk, Mena sucked on her straw while typing out a text. When Harlow and Amaya joined us, she put the phone away.

"Turner is about to go on his break. Mind if we swing by his work?" she asked.

"Not at all!" I looped my arm through hers, and we took off down the street. Her boyfriend still went to her last school—Devilbend North High School—and the two of them were adorable together. But Mena worked at a diner closer to where she lived, and Turner had just recently gotten a job at a gym downtown, so they had less and less time to spend with each other. I couldn't blame them for seizing every opportunity.

As we rounded the corner and strolled toward the gym's front doors, our steps gradually slowed to a stop; each of us was staring through the window, transfixed.

My first response was a spike of annoyance—I couldn't seem to get away from this jerk!—but it was soon replaced with a grudging appreciation.

Only a small part of the gym was visible through the front window, the neat rows of machines disappearing around the corner. Hendrix was on a machine close to the glass, sitting on a bench with his knees spread wide, his arms pulling down on some weighted contraption. He was shirtless and so sweaty he was fucking *glistening*. It seemed as if half the muscles in his body danced under his skin at every movement.

"Wow," Harlow breathed, sucking the dregs of her drink with an obnoxiously loud slurp.

"I have a boyfriend, and even I can't look away." Mena tilted her head to the side, eyes glued to the show.

"You're only human." Amaya shrugged. "But fuck me. Why is it always the assholes that look like *that*?"

"Is that a tattoo?" If I'd been with anyone other than my three best friends, I would've been embarrassed at how breathy my voice sounded. There was definitely some ink on the left side of his back, just under his shoulder blade, but we were too far away to make it out.

That didn't stop us from leaning forward as one, our foreheads nearly touching the glass, as we tried to see what it was.

"You ladies wouldn't be objectifying our newest member, would you?" A deep, masculine voice made us all jump. Mena even made a little squeaking sound in the back of her throat that had us all cracking up in embarrassed laughter.

Turner leaned against the wall with his arms crossed, smiling in amusement. We'd been so entranced by the frustrating guy on the other side of the glass we hadn't even heard him walk up.

Mena was the first to recover. "You know I only have eyes for you," she cooed, rising up on her tippy-toes to give him a kiss.

He glared at us all with a thin-lipped smile and shook his head. "You four are worse than the creeps who only pretend to do weights while they stare at the women on cross trainers."

"We are not!" Harlow smacked him.

"We kinda are." Amaya shrugged, taking another sip of her drink.

I took one last surreptitious glance at the window—to make sure Hendrix hadn't spotted us, not to cop another eyeful, of course. Unfortunately . . . I mean, *fortunately*, he'd disappeared into the back of the gym.

Turner slung an arm around Mena's shoulders. "Come on. I've only got another twenty minutes of my break, and I need to get something to eat."

We said our goodbyes and left the lovebirds alone.

I hadn't planned on going to Davey's that night, but I was so agitated after I got home I couldn't even focus on my homework. Harlow had changed into sweats, carried armfuls of junk food into her room, and parked herself in front of the computer, so she wouldn't be noticing jack shit for the remainder of the night. My parents were home, but I figured if I left after midnight, they wouldn't even notice. They'd both had long days at work, and their bedroom was on the opposite side of the house.

I just had to be extra cautious and make sure it was a short visit. Everyone would be home in the morning, so I'd have to skip sleeping in, but I could handle one day of sleep deprivation.

What I couldn't handle was another week—another *day*, another *hour*—of this clawing, pressured feeling inside me.

My to-do list was growing instead of diminishing, no matter how hard I worked, and now I had the added problem of trying to figure out the Hendrix situation. I couldn't let Mena down; I just had no idea how to fix it. Not to mention I was suddenly finding myself thinking about Hendrix's sweaty muscles instead of focusing on how annoying and rude he was.

Black stiletto boots in hand, I tiptoed down the stairs and into the garage without making a sound. I didn't stop listening and looking out for someone to bust me until I was at the end of the driveway and putting my headlights on.

The leather seat was cool on my bare back. I'd kept the all-black outfit simple —halter top and short, loose skirt. Heavy eye makeup, messy hair, and no panties.

I didn't always fuck some random when I went to Davey's, but I was going to make sure I did tonight. I needed more than the illusion of freedom that came with dancing and anonymity. I needed the oblivion of a strong body looming over me, making me *feel* for a little while instead of *thinking* all the fucking time. I just needed a break . . .

The anticipation built as I drove, only speeding a little in my eagerness. I just knew I'd feel better in the morning, even if I was a little tired. I'd be more clear-headed and ready to tackle school, college applications, and Hendrix fucking Hawthorn.

I parked, tucked my keys into my little cross-body bag, and resisted the urge to sprint to the front door.

A grin spread over my face when I spotted Shady at the bar. I wouldn't even need to be here an hour. But as I got closer and saw who was on the stool next to him, my heart instantly jammed up into my throat.

Why was he ruining *every single* aspect of my damn life? Why was I being punished like this?

Hendrix was in jeans and a black T-shirt—an expensive one with the brand in bold white letters near the bottom hem. It was a loose style, but the fabric still stretched taut over his muscular shoulders and arms. Immediately, flashes of what he looked like shirtless and sweaty assaulted my mind.

I clenched my thighs against the pressure low in my belly. I *wasn't* turned on by him. My body was just already primed for sex, that was all.

But now that I was staring at the root of all my recent problems, my body was starting to make me think the solution could be to just . . . fuck him out of my system.

A group of chicks heading for the dance floor, drinks in hand, bumped me out of my stupor.

I clenched my teeth and retreated back into the crowd, then found a spot by the wall and leaned back, crossing my arms and keeping him in view.

"Hey." A deep male voice made me glance to the side. "Can I get you a drink?"

He was exactly what I'd come here looking for: tall, late twenties, in worn jeans and boots, his tattooed arms exposed. He had the confidence to approach me within five minutes of my arrival, and he'd already made physical contact, dragging the backs of his rough knuckles up the side of my arm.

"Fuck off." I shrugged him off and focused back on the problem at hand.

The big, bad man chuckled and muttered "feisty" under his breath as he headed for the bar. My body groaned in protest as I watched him walk away, but I had to figure Hendrix out first.

What the hell was he doing here? And how did he know Shady? Having my fun for the night ruined was frustrating, but his presence here could have much heavier implications. If he told anyone . . . I couldn't even bear to think about it. I had to speak to Shady and get some info, then I had to either make sure Hendrix didn't see me or find some way to make him keep his mouth shut.

My mind churned, adding more weight to the already massive amount of pressure I was there to get a break from. This wasn't fair. This was supposed to be *my* place. *My* reprieve from my life.

What . . . how . . . ugh! *Why*?!

I couldn't even think straight anymore. All I could do was glare and grind my teeth as worst-case scenarios flashed through my mind.

Shady got to his feet, did that manly handshake/slap-on-the-back combo, and disappeared into the back area. I'd never been over there—even Shady had warned me off a time or two, so I was pretty sure it was where morals went to die.

Hendrix downed the rest of his drink and turned on his stool, ready to get up, but his eyes locked with mine and he froze. A frown wrinkled his brow, then his eyes widened a little.

Well, at least now I knew this was a coincidence. He definitely hadn't been expecting to see me.

Fuck it.

I glared back, then pushed off the wall and strutted toward the bar.

I needed to clear my head before attempting damage control, and I figured half an hour wouldn't make a difference.

Hendrix settled back on the stool, watching me intently as I approached, but I changed direction just before I reached him.

I tapped tall, dark, and dangerous from earlier on the shoulder.

The man turned and grinned, leaning back against the bar. "Hey, feisty."

I smirked, he raked his eyes up and down my body, and I knew I had him.

CHAPTER SIX

Hendrix

I flopped my ass back onto the stool and gripped the edge of the bar about as hard as I was gripping the edge of my sanity.

It was really her. Donna Mead—spoiled rich bitch, queen bee of Fulton Academy—had a dark side. A dark, *sexy* side that had her looking as if she knew her way around a bar I was pretty sure was owned by gangsters.

Gone was the pleated skirt and pristine white shirt of the Fulton uniform—replaced by a black miniskirt and halter top. In place of the sensible Mary Janes she wore to school was a pair of thigh-high boots that had my cock stirring in my pants.

I surreptitiously adjusted myself and got more comfortable on my stool. No way in hell was I attempting to leave until my sudden stiffy went down.

It had taken me a few seconds to place the gorgeous blonde as she sauntered toward the bar. She was wearing dark makeup, and her short hair was in a messy rock-chick style. I wanted to run my hand through the soft strands, mess it up even more, maybe grab a fistful and pull until her mouth was turned up to mine. I'd make her tell me exactly how much of a bad girl she was.

I blinked, forcing the sudden and vivid fantasy from my mind. She was on her way over, and I had to remember who I was dealing with. Come Monday, she'd still be perfect princess Donna, and she'd still be responsible for making my life at Fulton hell.

But as it turned out, I didn't need to worry about what I'd say to her. She changed direction and went up to a guy ordering at the bar. I frowned, confused. Maybe it wasn't her after all.

But then I dismissed the thought. She'd seen me, recognized me. There was no mistaking the rage-filled glare she'd thrown my way. I'd been on the receiving end of it countless times now.

A pang of annoyance had me grinding my teeth. It was the bullshit from school all over again. She was determined to make me feel as if my very existence was of no consequence to her.

I wanted to just get up and walk out. If she didn't give a shit about why I was here, then I wouldn't give a shit about why she was.

Instead, I found myself waving the waitress over and ordering another soda.

A few feet over, the bastard who looked like an enforcer for a motorcycle club handed Donna a drink and wrapped a meaty hand around her delicate waist, leaning in to whisper something in her ear. She smirked, a devious glint in her eye, and ran her hand up his massive arm as she murmured a reply to whatever vulgar shit he'd surely just said to her.

My hand tightened around my drink as I sized him up. I wasn't sure if I could take him. We were about the same height, but I'd only just gotten back into the gym that afternoon, and he looked as if he bench-pressed his Harley every damn day.

His hand lowered to her hip, and Donna took a drink before lifting her gaze. Our eyes met, and she frowned slightly—at the fact that I was still there? Had she forgotten I even existed? *Bitch* . . .

I looked away first and mentally slapped myself. Why the fuck was I letting her get to me like this? And why the fuck was I thinking about the best way to put a guy—who I was positive was armed—on his ass? Especially considering I'd vowed never to throw another punch for the rest of my life.

Better to leave Donna to whatever fucked-up game she had going here. This was exactly the kind of drama I didn't want. That guy was *exactly* the kind of trouble I was trying to avoid.

Shady had left for the night. The vague excuse he'd given made me think he was up to shit I didn't want to know about. But I couldn't be mad. He'd spent nearly two hours with me at the bar, talking about three times as much as I did, pointing people out, giving me his opinions on movies and recent events, making vulgar commentary on the women. He'd even managed to make me laugh a few times. It had taken my mind off my problems and made the risky decision to come here worth it.

If only I'd left five minutes earlier. If only I hadn't seen her . . .

Now I couldn't leave, couldn't tear my gaze away as she finished her drink and let the biker dude lead her out to the edge of the dance floor.

Shady had pointed out a lot of people, and I wasn't really trying to remember names, but this guy's towering frame and mean mug had stood out. One of the very few times Shady had lowered his voice was when telling me to avoid this fucker—*Bronson*. He'd made it clear, in that way criminals had of speaking without coming right out and saying anything concrete, that Bronson was a murderer and basically untouchable because of the "people he rode with." Yep— definitely an enforcer for an MC.

"But don't sweat it!" He'd slapped me on the shoulder. "Davey's is a neutral place. Only a select few people are permitted to do business here, and no other bullshit is tolerated. We don't need the pigs sniffing around because some dick- head couldn't take his fun elsewhere."

He probably hadn't meant to conflate murdering people with fun, but that was Shady for you.

Donna didn't strike me as the kind of chick who did anything without knowing exactly what she was getting into, but behind all the annoyance and frustration, there was a sliver of worry deep in my chest too—*very deep*, buried behind all the other not-so-favorable emotions I had for this infuriating woman.

She may've been a bitch, but I still didn't want to see her end up dead.

I sat on the damn stool and sipped my drink, frozen in indecision.

It was none of my business. I didn't need this shit. Hell, maybe I could use it to get what I wanted from her down the road—I was pretty sure she wouldn't want her devoted followers, or college admissions boards, finding out she was hooking up with lowlifes and criminals. The scandal . . .

On the other hand . . .

I couldn't shake the feeling that something wasn't right. That guy was serious trouble. And I really didn't like how he was grinding his hips against her in time to the music.

It *really* didn't fucking help that she kept glancing in my direction.

At first, her gaze held nothing but contempt, but as the flirting between her and Bronson increased, her glances became more neutral—as if she was simply checking I was still there. By the time they were pawing at each other as though moments away from fucking in a bar full of people, her glances were . . . well, if I didn't know any better, I would've said she was looking at me with heat in her eyes. And if they were brief glances, I would've put it down to her being really into her hookup. But the way she looked at me—it lingered, our connection across the crowded room palpable. It was almost as if she wished it was *me* palming her ass, that it was *my* neck she was placing a sultry kiss to. Her eyes stayed glued to mine as she dragged those full lips up the column of his throat.

I was torn.

I didn't come here to watch my new nemesis get it on with some douche— the anal kind, as Mena had put it. But my dick was convinced I should go over there and pull her out of his arms and into mine.

I forced myself to turn away. Placing both clenched fists on the bar, I took three deep breaths of the sweaty, smoky air and focused hard on the peanut shells littering the chipped wood.

You're going to get up off this fucking stool, and you're going to march to the exit. You will not look in her direction, and you will not stop until you're in the goddamn car.

I gave myself a mental slap, then chugged what was left of my flat soda. Determined, I got to my feet . . . and my eyes immediately met her mismatched ones.

She smirked as she passed within a foot of me, her hand tucked into Bronson's as he led the way past the bar.

My whole body tensed, refusing to do as I'd just decided. Instead, I stared like a creep after them. For a second, I was worried he was about to drag her to the back—where even Shady told me to avoid. But they didn't turn down the dark corridor. He pushed open a back door, giving me a glimpse of the night sky and a dumpster as they made their way through it.

Just before the door swung closed, Donna turned her head and looked at me again.

I ground my teeth.

Leave, Hendrix. Just go. You don't need someone else's problems making your life any more difficult. Let the princess get herself out of her own mess.

Except I was pretty sure she was exactly where she wanted to be, and that made me want to throw something.

Fuck it. I gave up. I wouldn't be able to live with myself if I left and she turned up dead in a few weeks. I'd just check that she was—*ugh!*—enjoying herself. I'd make sure she left safely, and then I'd use this information to blackmail the shit out of her. There wasn't much I needed from her other than to get those bratty kids off my back, but I was going to milk it for all it was worth—payback for putting me through this mess of a night.

I made my way through the crowd, following their path past the dark corridor and to the back door. With my hand on the handle, I braced myself for what I might see—would sex or violence affect me more?

The music from the club faded as I stepped out into the night.

He had her up against the wall, right next to the dumpster, a string of condoms hanging from one thick-knuckled hand.

I clenched my teeth and let the heavy door slam shut.

Donna looked over his shoulder, but it was too dark to make out her expression. Bronson paused what he was doing and half turned his head. "Find some other place to piss, man. I'm kind of busy here."

He lowered his mouth back to her neck.

He was going to fuck her in a disgusting alleyway, where people routinely pissed? Real class act, this guy.

A breathy moan escaped the darkness shrouding them, and I suddenly realized that was exactly what she wanted. The perfect princess liked to get down and dirty with dangerous men.

I didn't even know where to begin trying to guess what her damage was, but it looked as though Donna was just as fucked up as me—albeit in a different way.

But I'd inserted myself into this clusterfuck of a situation, and I wasn't about to walk away. If she wanted to be there, I'd have fun ruining her fun.

I rolled my shoulders—preparing, just in case this got violent—then relaxed and shoved a hand in my pocket, trying my best to look casual.

Bronson turned his head and shoulders, raising his voice. "What's your problem, dude? Fuck off."

"I don't have a problem." I shrugged. "Just making sure my schoolmate here is safe."

CHAPTER SEVEN

"Schoolmate?" The biker dude sneered in my direction. In the distance, thunder rumbled.

I rolled my eyes. "Oh, you suddenly want to know things about me?"

He smirked and gripped my waist. "I don't give a fuck how old she is. Get lost, pretty boy."

"Do you give a shit that her rich daddy will have half the police in the state on your ass if you so much as touch her?" Hendrix cocked his head to the side, his voice amused.

Biker dude growled, and not in the fun, sexy way.

I was losing my patience too. "Are you gonna man up and get rid of him, or do I need to get *myself* off?"

"Listen here, you little slut." He jabbed a finger in my face while his other hand tightened into a fist, the leather of the fingerless glove creaking. "You know what? On second thought, I don't need this high school drama bullshit."

Without waiting for a response, he turned around and stomped back toward the bar, boots pounding on the concrete. I narrowed my eyes and gritted my teeth.

"You know what, asshole?" I yelled after him, taking a few steps in his direction.

His back stiffened under the leather vest, but suddenly Hendrix was taking long strides in my direction, eyes wide and mouth firm. The suddenness of the movement and the intensity of his stare made me pause long enough for biker dude to disappear back inside.

With my evening entertainment and outlet for my rage gone, I turned my ire on the jerk who had been a thorn in my side for weeks now.

"What the fuck are you doing?" I got in his face. The killer heels helped put me closer to eye level, but I still had to tip my head up.

"Saving your ass." He huffed.

"My ass was just fine, thanks. My ass was about to *get* some ass, you arrogant, presumptuous, cock-blocking *dumb*ass."

"Your ass was about to get killed. Bronson has a reputation for leaving his girlfriends in dumpsters." He wasn't backing down. We were practically chest to chest.

"I'm not his girlfriend. He was just a hookup. What the fuck do you take me for?"

"Honestly, I have no idea what to make of this. What . . ." He shook his head and sighed. "Donna, what the fuck are you doing here? What are you wearing? Do you have any idea how dangerous—"

I cut him off with a shove against his chest. It took him by surprise enough to make him stumble a step back, but I followed, getting in his face. "Screw you and your assumptions." I shoved him again, but this time he was prepared and hardly budged. "Screw you and your patronizing bullshit." I shoved hard, but his whole body was rigid, muscles tense under my palms. "I'm not a fucking idiot. I know exactly what I'm doing and who I'm doing it with. I can take care of myself."

Thunder grumbled again, making me wish I could growl like that—with the force of nature behind me.

Hendrix was breathing heavily even as he stood there, as still as a statue and as hard as one, but a muscle was ticking in his jaw, and his eyes narrowed. Something in me liked that. He'd been so dismissive of me at school, so blasé about everything I threw at him, that getting a rise out of him was like a drug. My favorite kind—unpredictable.

Like a junkie, I shoved his chest again.

This time his hands shot up to grip my wrists—not painfully, but tightly enough that I couldn't wrench out of his hold. I tried anyway, thrashing against him as my adrenaline spiked.

"Let go of me, asshole."

"I'm not going to hit you, Donna," he growled, the sound low and controlled but with menace simmering just below. "But I'm not just going to stand here and not defend myself. Get your shit together."

I leaned up and shouted right into his face, "Fuck you!"

The corner of his lip twitched, an almost smile. "I thought we established that wasn't going to happen?"

I was getting more and more worked up, basically throwing a tantrum, while he just stood there like a pillar, getting calmer and calmer. It was *maddening*.

Well, I was over letting him feel as though he had the advantage. He could deny it all he wanted, but he was attracted to me. I could see it in the way his eyes searched my face. His lips were smirking, but his eyes couldn't lie—those beautiful, intense gray eyes.

I used the leverage of his grip on my wrists, lifted up onto my toes, and kissed him.

For a second—a bare breath of a moment suspended in time—he froze.

Lightning flashed, illuminating the dirty alleyway and this thing between us. Then, as the thunder roared, he moved his lips against mine, his tongue darting out, his mouth claiming me.

He released one of my wrists to wrap an arm around my body and walk me backward.

I gripped his T-shirt, pulling the fabric as if the thin fibers could tether me to some semblance of control. I'd kissed him so I could prove something, but within seconds, he had the upper hand, and my head was spinning in the most delicious, most excruciating way.

My back hit the rough brick, and he lifted my other wrist above my head, keeping it trapped in his strong grip. His free hand went to my waist and made me arch—made my body mold to every hard, unyielding inch of his. He moaned into my mouth and kissed me harder until the back of my head ground into the wall.

His erection pressed against my front, and I wanted it inside me. I wanted *him* inside me—my body, my mind, my soul. I wanted him to consume every fiber of my being until all I could see, hear, smell was Hendrix Hawthorn. Until I forgot everything and everyone and there was only *him*.

It was exactly what I came here for—to forget, to lose myself in something for a little while . . . but part of me bristled at the fact that it was with *him*. Why was my body responding to his more than it had to any other man in the past? I'd been fighting to keep command of the Hendrix situation for weeks. Now here he was, smashing through my careful control with one mind-shattering kiss?

I took his bottom lip into my mouth and sucked. Then I took it between my teeth and bit.

He hissed and pulled away, another bolt of lightning throwing his confused expression into sharp relief.

Some of the heady weight of his body on mine lifted, and he released my wrist. But I didn't like that either. Fuck, I had no idea what I wanted with this infuriating son of a bitch. *And I hated it.*

Before he could completely back away, I wrapped my arms around his neck and kissed him again. The thunder rumbled, so close now that the ground under my boots vibrated.

Hendrix growled too, his own thunder rumbling through his chest. I could taste his blood on my lips, the metallic flavor as distinct as the need coursing through my body.

He broke the kiss again and shook his head, breathing hard.

I gripped his T-shirt, my body clinging to his even as my mind screamed. "If you want to go, go! See if I care!"

"Listen." He licked his lips. "I'm not into this rape fantasy bullshit. If you want me inside you, I'm gonna need to hear you say it."

I blinked. I was not expecting that. Not once had any man I'd had dirty sex with bothered to check if I was enjoying myself. They didn't give a shit, and I didn't even care enough to learn their names. That was the whole appeal of the situation—I was using them as much as they were using me, and the edge of danger that came with the unknown, the uncertainty, was intoxicating.

Why the fuck did Hendrix even care? "You are such a pussy. You're killing the mood."

He watched me for a beat, shadows falling over his face, then pushed himself off the wall.

I didn't doubt for a second he would leave. My hand shot to his belt to stop him. "What do you want, an engraved invitation into my cunt?"

Usually, men were surprised to hear such a filthy word coming out of my mouth, but Hendrix didn't even falter. "Any form of explicit consent will do."

I rolled my eyes. "Jesus, would you just fuck me already?"

"Is that what you'd like?" I could hear the smirk in his voice. The lightning that flashed a second later let me see it too. I wanted to sit on that smug face and ride it so he'd shut the fuck up already.

"Yes," I gritted out.

"That'll do." He'd barely said the words before he was on me again, reaching behind my neck to pull on the bow that held my halter top in place.

The two pieces of shimmery fabric fell away, and he palmed my breasts. He didn't take it slow or explore—just grabbed two firm handfuls of my flesh and kneaded, his thumbs teasing my nipples.

I threw my head back against the brick and moaned into the night as Hendrix started kissing and licking at the sensitive spot on my neck.

A drop of water hit my cheek, and my eyes opened in confusion just as another landed on my forehead. Another rumble of thunder reminded me a storm was rolling in, but then Hendrix took one of my nipples into his mouth, making me forget everything.

He teased me with his mouth before pulling away again.

"Do you have a condom?" His breath was hot on my cheek as his hips gyrated against mine.

"Huh?" It took a moment for his words to register. "Yes, in my . . . fuck. No. You chased biker dude off with them all." I groaned.

"Shit." Hendrix planted a hand on either side of my head and pressed his forehead to mine, sighing deeply.

I ran my hands down his front. He felt so good under my touch, his muscles coiled, his T-shirt getting damp from the softly falling rain. I liked to flirt with danger, but I wasn't stupid. I never fucked anyone without a condom. But Hendrix wasn't one of the degenerates I usually hooked up with. He was . . . I didn't want to think about what he was to me in that moment. I just wanted to get off with him.

"It's raining anyway . . ." He let one hand drop to his side, inching his body away.

I wrapped my arms around his waist and licked the rain off the side of his neck. "I'm on birth control and I'm clean. Are you?"

I felt him swallow under my lips. "Honestly, I don't know. Haven't been tested. And I'm not willing to take the chance. No offence, but I don't know where that thing has been."

White hot rage coursed through me almost as intensely as desire. I bit his neck, and he yelped, pushing me away by the hips.

"Offence taken, asshole." I scowled at him.

It was too dark to really see, but I could've sworn he looked amused, and his hands were still on my hips.

"Did you just bite me?" He chuckled. "Under that perfect princess mask, you're just a feral animal, aren't you?"

"Yeah. Whatever. I wanna get off, and if you're not game, then get lost so I can get on with my night." His rejection was starting to sting, and if I couldn't have him, I wasn't really in the mood to pick someone else up. I really hoped he wouldn't walk away from me—because I couldn't seem to make myself walk away from him.

He licked his lips, collecting some of the rain that was dripping down his face. Droplets fell from the tip of his nose, trailed down his neck. I wanted to lick every single one.

Just as I was about to cover my boobs back up and try to gather enough pride to walk away, he spoke.

"If the guys you've been with think the only way to get a woman off is with their cocks, I feel really bad for you—you must've been having some mediocre sex."

Before I could throw a witty response back at him, his strong hands were shoving my hips around so I was facing the wall. He pushed forward, his front flush with my back, and I had to throw my hands up against the brick to keep my balance. A shot of adrenaline raced down my spine, amping up the lust. I had no idea what he was about to do to me, and I *loved* it. This was exactly what I needed, what I craved.

He kicked my feet a little farther apart, then gripped the back of my neck.

I practically melted at his touch, my very being diluted in the steady rain and his intoxicating presence.

He trailed his hand down the rain-slick skin of my back, and then both hands were at my hips, dipping lower, down my thighs. When he reached the hem of my skirt, the heat of his body disappeared as he stepped away slightly—as his hands moved under the fabric and up my legs. He traced his thumbs along the underside of my ass before dragging his palms over it to cop a good feel. His fingers went all the way to my lower back, then back down, and he laughed softly.

"No panties. You dirty whore."

I bristled at his use of the derogatory term, the logical part of me offended. But my logical part wasn't in charge—my dirty whore part was, and Dark Donna was only more turned on by his words.

His hand appeared at my neck again, and he pushed—his touch not rough but firm, demanding—until my cheek was against the wall. My nipples brushed the rough brick, and rain pelted my bare back. Every place his skin touched mine felt as if it were on fire. I was nothing but heady sensation—putty in his strong hands.

I arched my back, sticking my ass out even farther, and he flipped my skirt up to expose me to the dark alley.

Done wasting time, he reached between my legs and stroked me firmly, and my already heavy breathing kicked up another notch. His appreciative moan hummed at my back as his fingers glided through my wet folds effortlessly. He put one finger inside, making me gasp at the sudden intrusion, then twisted it as he removed it. Another finger joined the first, and he slid them in and out of me at a steady pace.

The hand at my neck disappeared, but my incoherent sound of protest morphed into one of ecstasy as Hendrix wrapped his arm around my front. His body crowded me once again, that cinnamon scent mingling with the fresh rain. With one hand still fucking me with his fingers from behind, the other went to my clit and started stroking in rhythm.

Another clap of thunder shook the ground, and the rain beat down even harder, plastering my hair to my face as I grunted. With every punishing thrust of Hendrix's fingers, his other hand rubbed me up and down, and my tits scraped against the brick.

It didn't take long before my orgasm was washing over me as intensely as the rain. I squeezed my eyes shut, seeing stars, as I clawed at the wall, desperately seeking something to hold on to as every muscle in my body tensed up in ecstasy.

"That's it. I want your cream all over my hand." Hendrix's voice was strained and gravelly in my ear, his words only intensifying my orgasm as I writhed under his touch.

He removed his fingers and stroked me gently as I came down, my knees shaking, my breathing ragged. His hands clasped either side of my head, his fore-head rested against my temple, and his warm breath caressed my cheek as the rain washed away the slick evidence of my pleasure from his hand.

After a few moments, he placed a gentle kiss on my cheek, my neck, my shoulder—his soft, warm lips such a contrast to the sharp, cold rain. He cupped my breasts, making me gasp, then surprised me by lifting the two front bits of my halter top over my chest and backing away to tie them.

I frowned. Didn't he want me to return the favor, get him off? But I didn't really have time to think about that.

My knees buckled, but before I ended up on my ass in a dirty alleyway, Hendrix's strong arms wrapped around me and held me against his chest. His steel-hard erection dug into my ass, but he didn't rub up against me. He just whispered against my wet skin, "I got you."

What the fuck is happening? Usually, the guy would make sure he got off, regardless of whether I did, and within about two minutes, he'd tuck himself back into his pants and disappear. I was fine with it—preferred it, actually. But I found myself leaning back against Hendrix, allowing myself to relax farther into his arms.

When he bent down and scooped me up, the voice in my head demanding that he "put me down this instant, you Neanderthal" hardly even sounded convincing. I rested my head on his shoulder, breathing him in, as he grabbed my purse off the top of the dumpster and dropped it in my lap.

"Where'd you park?" he asked as he set off toward the front of the building. The words reverberated through his chest, just loud enough for me to hear over the rain.

I lifted a lazy hand and pointed to the back corner of the lot. It was nice to have someone take care of me for a change. I'd worry about the terrifying impli-cations later.

CHAPTER EIGHT

Hendrix

Even soaked from head to toe, she was light in my arms. I'd gone hard at the gym that afternoon, but I felt as if I could carry her all the way back to Devilbend if I had to.

My shoes squelched in the gravel as I trudged through the easing rain past rows of parked cars. Donna readjusted herself in my grip and turned her nose into the crook of my neck. She took a long inhale, then licked me.

My steps faltered.

My cock was straining against my jeans, demanding I bend her over the hood of one of these cars and do as she asked in the first place—fuck her raw. But I'd promised myself I was done doing risky, stupid shit, and having unprotected sex with a chick I barely knew was the definition of risky. Donna was probably on the pill and clean—she was wound way too tightly not to be on top of every little detail of her life. But her very presence here indicated a streak of recklessness too. I couldn't take the chance.

I chuckled and decided to ignore her hot little tongue on my throat and the steel rod in my pants. "What are you doing?"

"I just wanted to see if you taste as good as you smell," she murmured and scratched the back of my head, sending tingles down my spine that had nothing to do with the cold rain.

"What do I smell like?"

She sighed. "Like expensive cologne and cinnamon and . . . sex." She punctuated the sentence by licking my neck again.

I hid my groan beneath a clearing of my throat and looked around, desperate for something, anything, to distract me from this torture.

"Fuck." I stopped and turned. I'd walked right past my car.

Donna finally lifted her head from my shoulder, and just like that, she had my full, undivided attention again.

We stared at each other—only inches between us—and I forgot I even had a car, let alone where I'd parked it. Wait. Wasn't I supposed to be taking her to her car anyway?

"Hendrix," she whispered, leaning forward.

I mirrored her movement, pressing my forehead to hers. "Yeah?"

"What . . ." Her gaze bored into mine with increasing intensity. The orgasm high was wearing off, and her mind was kicking back into overdrive, trying to make sense of it all. I held her just a little closer, fully aware of what was about to happen but hoping to prolong the moment anyway.

"Shit." She squeezed her eyes shut, as if trying to wash a nightmare from her mind's eye. Then she licked those delicious lips and leaned away, no longer looking at me.

She pushed against my chest and wriggled her legs. Resisting the urge to hold on tighter was a Herculean effort, but I managed it.

"Put me down," she growled, but I was already bending down, already releasing my hold, already missing her warmth . . .

I'd known it was coming, but it still made me want to throw something when she looked at me with a sneer.

"Ah, there it is." I stuffed my hands into my pockets and smirked. No choice now but to go back to our bickering default. I wasn't about to show her how badly I wanted to pull her back into my arms when she was looking at me like that. "The instant regret. Aren't you glad I only fucked you with my fingers now?"

"There isn't a single thing about this night I'm glad about." *Ouch . . .*

As the rain petered out to a pathetic drizzle, she turned and started to walk away.

I watched her hips sway, her spine straight and shoulders back. She'd just spent time in the seediest establishment for miles, had let me fingerfuck her in the dirty alley next to a dumpster, had a face covered in smeared makeup, yet she was still walking away with confidence. As if she *owned* this place.

I took one step back and wavered. My car was a few spots away; she was nearly safely to hers. I should just leave, end this torture.

But I couldn't tear my gaze off her. And not because I was still hard and her ass looked amazing in that skirt. Despite how much of a bitch she was being to me, I couldn't help worrying about Donna Mead.

I was seeing in her some of the same shit I'd seen in myself a year ago. It had taken something truly catastrophic to make me realize it, but with hindsight, I could see there had been signs. I'd been doing all kinds of reckless shit, just as Donna was now. I didn't want her to end up where I was.

If someone had asked me that morning who I thought Donna was, I would've told them she was a spoiled rich brat with delusions of grandeur. She had everything handed to her and always got what she wanted. She was perfect in every way she could control—her looks, her grades, her reputation—and would never let anything jeopardize that.

Never in a million years would I have expected her to have a bad-girl streak. I had no idea what Donna was running from, but after what went down between us, I was no longer confused about why she'd come to a place like this. She was escaping. She was using the thrill of danger as a distraction and the high of meaningless hookups to numb whatever pain was deep in her chest.

The way she'd come at me in the alley—that first kiss had been almost violent in its intensity. It was the first time I'd felt truly alive in a long time. Too bad it was delivered by someone spiraling toward death.

I may have used slightly different means when I was spiraling a year ago, but she was chasing the same thing I'd been chasing—oblivion. It was a fucking miracle she didn't have an addiction yet. Maybe she did. What did I know?

I sighed and looked up to the stormy sky. The rain had stopped completely, and I wiped the moisture from my face before glancing in her direction again, wanting to make sure she made it to her car before I left.

To my surprise, she was walking back toward me with a determined look on her face, those killer boots crunching in the gravel.

"I thought you were leaving." I crossed my arms. I wasn't sure I could handle more of this in one night.

"I never leave loose ends. No matter how badly I want to take a shower."

"Loose ends?" I scoffed, ignoring her dig. "What're you gonna shoot me in the head and stuff my body in the trunk of your Beamer? You lack the upper body strength."

"What are you doing here?"

"What are *you* doing here? Oh, wait!" I gave her a wicked smirk. If I couldn't fuck her, I'd taunt her. "I already know. Come here a lot? How many degenerates have you fucked?"

Her nostrils flared. I was getting to her, but she managed to keep her voice even. "Hendrix, I don't have time for this bullshit. What are you doing here?"

"None of your business." I dropped any levity from my tone. If she wanted to get serious, I was ready to get serious. "I've made it perfectly clear you don't own me. I don't have to tell you jack shit."

"Fine. Whatever. I don't actually care. You don't have to tell me anything, just . . . don't tell anyone else either."

There it was—she'd hung around to make sure I wouldn't tarnish her perfect reputation.

She dropped her gaze, showing the first sign of vulnerability since she'd wriggled out of my arms, and pushed her sopping wet hair back with both hands. Taking a deep breath, she fixed me with an indecipherable look. "Listen, you have your reasons for coming here, whatever they are, and I have mine. All I'm saying is, let's just pretend we never saw each other here and be done with it. OK?"

I cocked my head to the side. "Yeah, but I don't actually give a shit if anyone finds out I was here."

Her shoulders drooped in defeat, but she kept her gaze on mine. Brave little princess. "Please understand the gravity of what I'm about to say—because I think I've only said this to about six people my entire life. Hendrix, *please*, don't tell anyone you saw me here."

I nearly cracked—nearly told her I'd do whatever she wanted before pulling her into a hug. But I was certain the affection wouldn't be welcomed, so I just squeezed my hands into fists and sighed. "I've got no one to tell. You made sure of that, remember? No one would believe me anyway."

She laughed, the sound low and devoid of humor. "You don't understand what it's like. Reputation is everything in my world. Even the breath of a rumor …"

"I understand better than you know." Spoiled rich brats in California couldn't be that different from spoiled rich brats in New York.

She eyed me up and down, the question clear in her gaze. *Who are you? What's your story?*

But I wasn't in a sharing mood.

She licked her lips. "So, what do you want then? What's it gonna cost me?"

"I don't need your money. My daddy has a platinum card too." She wasn't stupid. She'd seen my car; I went to the same exorbitantly expensive, pretentious school. But for some reason, I wanted to point out that we had some things in common, that I understood her better than she thought.

Now it was her remaining silent, watching me with a raised brow, waiting for me to fill in the blank.

There was only one thing I wanted from her—well, two, but there was about as much chance of me getting her to lift that skirt as getting Americans to use the metric system, so I went with the practical option.

"You already know what I want." I shrugged. "Call off your attack dogs. I don't need any friends here, but I'm not interested in making any enemies. And trust me, if I start swinging back, it's going to get ugly. So do us all a favor and get this shit under control."

"Done." Her answer was instant. Part of me bristled, wondering if I should've asked for more, but that was the old me talking. More would only get me into trouble. I got what I wanted. Nothing else mattered.

With a nod, I turned and walked away, forcing myself not to look back.

Monday started in much the same way it always did. I got to school, parked, walked to class. As usual, some students made a point of turning their backs to ignore me, while others openly sneered in my direction. But I made it to my first class without anyone trying to prove he was a big man by shoving me. No one smacked my books off my desk in my classes; a few people even got out of my way as I headed to lunch.

I'd been planning to go off campus for lunch but decided against it, turning right toward the cafeteria instead of left toward the doors at the end of the hall. I hadn't seen Donna all morning, and I wanted to remind her of our little chat, test if she was taking it seriously.

I walked in, head held high, and smacked my gum loudly. A few people turned in my direction at the sound, but I ignored them. My full focus was on the girl in the perfectly neat uniform, not a blonde hair out of place under her teal headband, the smeared black makeup gone.

Donna was sitting in her usual spot, Harlow on the table with her feet on the chair next to her. The other girls weren't there yet, but some of the other assholes they hung out with were.

I looked right at her as I passed but kept my expression neutral—doing the whole pointing-at-my-eyes-and-then-her bit felt like overkill. She glanced up, met my gaze, and looked away again as if I didn't matter. As if I hadn't brought her to orgasm sixty hours earlier. As if we hadn't struck a deal in the rain right after.

I had to hand it to her—she had impeccable self-control. If only that trait weren't driving her to do stupid-ass shit just to feel alive.

Not my problem. *Not my problem.*

I forced myself to look away, grabbed some gluten-free paleo salad thing and a drink from the food counter, and picked an empty table.

No one flipped my tray. No one even said anything to me.

By the end of the day, it was clear everyone was leaving me alone. Donna had done what she'd promised. As if there was ever any doubt she could accomplish whatever she set that pretty little head to.

I had exactly what I wanted.

Except I no longer had any excuse to speak to a certain infuriating blonde, and as I drove home, the victory felt hollow.

CHAPTER NINE

Mom turned sideways in front of the ornate mirror by the front door and smoothed her midnight-blue cocktail dress.

"How do I look?" she asked no one in particular.

"Gorgeous, as always." My auntie Eleanor smiled at her, then shoved her out of the way with her hip to take up the mirror. "How do *I* look?"

"Like me. So gorgeous, as always," Mom shot back.

Mom was older than her sister by two years, but they were as close as Harlow and me. I knew there was a period of time—when I was a young child—that they didn't speak. It had something to do with my aunt moving away to marry a man Grandmother didn't approve of and ending up without an inheritance, but every time I tried to dig more up about it, Mom shut me down with some version of "Leave the past in the past."

I just wanted to know everything. It was interesting: shoot me.

But Mena's family had moved back to Devilbend just before we all started high school, and our moms reconnected. They looked really similar, and even though they were teasing each other in front of the mirror, they were smiling and laughing.

"You're both stunning." Dad came down the stairs, fiddling with a cuff link. "Brad, back me up here or we'll never leave."

"Yes. Absolutely ethereal. We're the luckiest men on earth," my uncle Brad deadpanned, but I could see his lips twitch as he fought a smile.

While my mom and aunt started smacking and berating him for his attitude, Dad came to a stop next to me.

"Help me out, sweetness. I can never get the right one." He held out his right wrist, and I fixed the cuff link in place. "Thank you." He kissed the top of my head. "You girls have fun. And call us if you need anything."

"I will."

My parents had both stopped bothering to warn me to be safe and make good choices. It was a given. I was their perfect little girl. I'd make sure everything was fine, and I'd take care of the others.

It was Mena's birthday, and we were throwing her a party. She'd originally insisted on a small gathering, maybe at the diner where she worked. But when we sat down to write a list of who to invite, she was the only one surprised to see over twenty-five people on the list. The girl just wasn't used to having that many friends, and I was pretty sure she'd never had a real party to celebrate her birthday.

It didn't take much to convince her after that, but the guest list had grown . . .

During the afternoon, we'd had a family lunch together and opened presents. Now our parents were graciously leaving for the night. They planned to go to dinner in San Francisco and stay at our apartment in the city. The staff were given the night off, although cleaners would be arriving at ten in the morning to make sure the house was pristine before my parents returned. Everything was nearly ready.

As soon as our parents disappeared outside, I rushed to the back of the house, where the others had been listening out for the sound of the front door closing.

"Freedom!" I yelled, sliding across the kitchen tiles with my hands in the air.

Everyone whooped, and Turner pushed the button on the blender, getting the first batch of margaritas going as Mena grabbed glasses from the cupboard. Harlow pushed a few buttons on her phone, and music started pounding through the speaker system installed in the ceiling.

"Thank fuck." Amaya headed straight for the back patio, lighting a cigarette before she was even fully out of the house.

Harlow handed me a margarita, and I took it absentmindedly, mentally running through the checklist.

The staff had put up balloons and streamers in the main areas and cleared away some of the expensive, breakable items.

It was too cold to go in the pool in October, so the party would be in the main living area and on the patio where Amaya was smoking. A fire pit with chairs and blankets was set up and just waiting for the strike of a match.

Magda had prepared mountains of food.

I had a cake with eighteen candles ready to go in the fridge.

Drew and Will were bringing enough beer and spirits to give us all alcohol poisoning.

"Harlow, is the playlist ready to go?"

She nodded and planted her ass on the island counter next to the blender. "Yep! All of Mena's faves mixed in with some bangers!"

"Amaya!" I called out to the patio as Turner poured the drinks.

She startled me by leaning over my shoulder and stealing my untouched margarita. "No need to shout. I'm right here." She took a sip, giving me a teasing look over the salted rim.

"Guest list update," I demanded.

"Should be just over a hundred. There's always a few last-minute additions though."

Mena choked on her drink. "A hundred?! We don't even have that many people in our senior year. I don't even *know* that many people!"

"You can't have a Devilbend Dynasty party and expect under a hundred people." Amaya shrugged and took another sip.

I stole my drink back and glared at her before addressing my cousin. "It's just one of those things. If you invite certain people, certain others expect an invitation too. Then word spreads, and everyone wants to come so they can be seen at one of our parties, and it just kind of snowballs. Don't worry about it. All your friends will be here, and we'll have a great time."

"Yeah, baby. Just enjoy it. You deserve a fun night." Turner wrapped an arm around Mena's shoulders and kissed her temple.

Harlow, Amaya, and I made a loud, over-the-top *aww*. They were so cute it was making me sick. Will never made me smile the way Mena was smiling at Turner now.

I finally took a sip of the margarita, and my eyes widened. "Jesus, fuck!"

Harlow had been the one putting the ingredients in the blender when I'd gone to the foyer to see our parents off. I frowned reproachfully at her.

"What?" She smiled sweetly.

"This is really strong."

"So?"

"So let's not write ourselves off before the party even starts, OK?"

"Yes, mom." She rolled her eyes, and the others chuckled.

I glared at them but chose to let it go. This was Mena's day.

We hung out for a bit, chatting and laughing, then headed upstairs to get ready.

A few hours later, I felt as if I could declare this party a success. Music was pumping, and a dance floor had been established in the living room. The cake had been presented to the birthday girl as a hundred people sang her "Happy Birthday." People were drinking, laughing, and talking around the firepit, some of them smoking pot.

I'd hardly had time to have two drinks all night, but now I could finally take a bit of a break. My indigo dress rode up my thighs as I leaned over the island.

Amaya had helped me pick it out the last time we went shopping. It clung to my curves and had long sheer sleeves and a completely sheer back. Careful not to knock anything over, I grabbed the vodka bottle.

Someone came up behind me, beer breath washing over my cheek as their hands landed on my hips. "You look smokin' tonight, princess."

I gritted my teeth but made sure my voice was even when I answered. "Thank you, William."

When he called me *princess* it was an endearment, an attempt to make me feel special. When Hendrix said it, it was delivered with derision. But why was I thinking about that asshole now?

I poured the vodka and searched the absolute mess in front of me for some kind of mixer, trying to sidestep out of Will's grasp. "Are you having a good night? Where's Drew and the others?"

He moved up next to me and slung an arm over my shoulders. "Who cares? I was hoping I could steal you away. It's been a while since we . . . caught up."

There were a lot of people in the room. I had to be careful about my reaction.

I was probably going to marry Will. He was the son of a prominent businessman and planned to follow in his father's footsteps, and his mother was on the board of every charitable organization she could find. Our parents were friends and approved of us being together. Our life plans matched. He'd be the perfect husband, and I the perfect wife.

We'd dated exclusively for about six months in junior year, but I put a stop to that. I made it clear to Will I needed some time. It was around then that I started going to Davey's. As much as I'd made peace with my future with Mr. Carboard, I couldn't commit to it fully just yet.

We'd hooked up a few times since, but I'd made it very clear I wasn't interested in anything serious until maybe a few years into college. I needed to focus on my studies.

I *did* need to focus on my studies and my volunteering and all the other things that would help me achieve my goals. But the truth was, Will was about as interesting in bed as you'd expect. He had an average-sized penis, he liked to do it missionary, and he had no idea what a clitoris was.

Maybe I was being a bit harsh, but Will just couldn't give me what I needed.

"Hendrix?" Will sounded half-confused, half-angry.

Shit! Did I say something out loud? I wasn't even drunk. "What?"

"What the fuck is he doing here?" Will took another swig of his beer as I whipped my head around.

Sure enough, there he was, making his way through the crowd and craning his neck as though he was looking for someone. He was in tight ripped jeans and a plain white tee under a dark green zip-up jacket, his hair messy in that intentional way. As he reached the other side of the island, he spotted me and froze, his eyebrows slamming into a frown.

I stiffened, ready to shrug Will off, but then Hendrix noticed his arm around me. When his eyes narrowed just a fraction, I decided to lean into my future husband's side instead.

"What the fuck are you doing here?" He asked the question that was on the tip of my tongue.

"It's my house, asshole. What the fuck are *you* doing here?" I crossed my arms and cocked my head.

He looked even more confused "Clearly I had no idea. Otherwise I wouldn't have willingly put myself in your proximity."

"Clearly. So why are you *still* here?" I leaned on the counter, getting out from under Will's drunken slouch. He was starting to lean a little too much weight on me.

"Turner invited me. I had no idea the girlfriend he can't shut up about is Mena. Although I should've known. The two nicest people in Devilbend—of course they're together."

I snorted, failing to contain the smile. He was so right. "They're so cute together it's sickening."

"Right?" He laughed.

I wiped the smile off my face, remembering we were in a room full of people who thought we hated each other. Because we did. Will kept looking between us, trying to solve some puzzle, but he was probably too drunk to even remember why he'd come over to me in the first place.

"Go find Drew and the guys, Will. Your beer is nearly gone." I gestured with my head toward the back patio, and he gave me a smile.

"Good idea," he slurred and stumbled away.

"Good boy," Hendrix cooed after him once he was out of earshot. "Now fetch your balls."

I bit my tongue to stop myself from laughing. I didn't want to give him the satisfaction. I didn't even want him here. But this was Mena's birthday—it wasn't about me. "Fine. You can stay. But only because it's Mena's special day. Just don't steal anything."

He smirked. "Lighten up, Mead. It's a party—and you don't even have to find a way home. Have a drink or five. It might make your personality bearable."

"I was just about . . ." I looked for my half-made drink, but he was already walking away. "Asshole."

I downed the vodka in my cup straight, then spotted the bottle of OJ in the sink. *Naturally.* I poured myself another stronger one, then added the juice.

I would never admit it—not even to save the human race from extinction— but Hendrix was right. I wanted to lighten up and have a drink. I also *needed* one now that he was here.

I sipped my vodka and OJ as I mingled, trying to ignore the fact that he was in my house. Will had passed out in a chair by the fire, Drew and the others keeping an eye on him.

"Don't let him puke in my house." I pointed to him and raised my brows at Drew.

"On it." He took another puff of what was clearly not a regular cigarette and passed it to Amaya. Harlow was in a fit of giggles next to her, she and Nicola losing their shit over something on her phone. Laughter bubbled up in my chest too. I had no idea what was so funny, but their mirth was infectious.

I was about to find a spot and join them, but then I noticed Hendrix just a few feet over, talking with Mena and Turner. They looked as if they were really getting along. And the mirth in my chest died. He was in my house, with my friends, in my life. And I wanted him gone . . . but I also kept trying to remember if my room was messy or not and what he'd think of it if he made his way up there. And that was just . . . ugh! Insane!

Shoving some skanky chick in platform heels out of the way, I headed back inside and downed the rest of my drink, dropped the empty cup into the mess on the counter, and located the vodka.

With the smooth glass of the bottle clutched firmly in my hand, I made my way back outside. Keeping my gaze ahead, I avoided everyone and took the stone steps down to the path leading to the pool.

As soon as I was away from everyone's judgmental gazes, I could finally take a deep breath. The cool night air filled my lungs as I walked the manicured path, leaving the raucous sounds of the party farther behind me with every step.

It was chilly but still, and the water in the pool looked black—smooth glass reflecting the stars above. I sat at the edge and crossed my legs. The cap came off the bottle, and I took a swig, the alcohol burning my throat on the way down as much as the cool air had soothed it. The thumping bass and cacophony of laughing, talking voices in the background grew fainter with every sip.

I'd been looking forward to hanging out with my friends, having some fun now that the party was pretty much taking care of itself. But then *he* showed up and ruined everything. I couldn't think about anything else with him so close.

The way he'd worked my body at the back of Davey's just one week ago . . . if I closed my eyes and allowed my mind to go there, I could still feel his fingers on my rain-slick skin, still feel the ecstatic oblivion he'd provided without wanting anything in return.

He'd given me one of the best orgasms of my life, but it was what happened after that I couldn't seem to work out. Hendrix had taken care of me. He'd met my physical needs, then taken me into his arms and made me feel . . . safe? I couldn't quite put my finger on the warm, fuzzy emotion it had brought up.

Then, naturally, we'd argued. He'd gone right back to the asshole he'd been from the start, and I knew there'd be no repeat performance, even if I wanted one.

So, when I wasn't fighting memories of how good he'd made me feel, I was obsessing over how he could ruin me with one carefully worded sentence delivered to anyone in my orbit.

How had I allowed myself to get into a situation where a man like Hendrix fucking Hawthorn had that much power over me?

I sighed and took another swig. At least the alcohol was making it easier to not give a shit for a little while.

Setting the bottle on the ground, I pulled a cigarette and lighter out of my cleavage. I'd stolen it from Amaya's pack earlier in the night when no one was looking. I didn't really smoke, especially not where anyone might see me—not that I judged my friend for doing it, but I couldn't afford to have anyone think I had any bad habits. When people thought you had one bad habit, they tended to start wondering what others you might have. If they only knew . . .

I lit the cigarette and inhaled, then pulled my knees to my chest and stared at the still, dark water as I blew the smoke out.

The sound of someone approaching made me turn my head and lower the cigarette out of view. I was fully prepared to dump it in the pool, but when I saw who it was, I just faced forward again and took another resigned drag.

Why couldn't I get away from him? Even in my own house?

Hendrix came to a stop right next to me, his boots touching the edge of the pool, and whistled low. "Nice view."

I glanced up at him. He was looking out past the pool, taking in the twinkling lights of Devilbend and the Californian landscape beyond.

"Best in Devilbend," I deadpanned.

He folded his tall frame down next to me and draped one arm over his bent knee. Gripping the neck of the bottle with the tips of his fingers, he twirled the vodka on its base; the glass crunched against the travertine pavers. "There really is no happy medium for you, is there? It's either one extreme or the other."

I raised a questioning brow and took another drag.

"You're either the perfect princess, headed for the ivy league, or you're drunk on vodka, smoking, and going to Davey's dressed like sin."

"You think you know me?" I shook my head. He wasn't wrong, but I'd die before admitting it to his face.

"Can I have a drag?" He held his long fingers out for the half-smoked cigarette.

I sighed and handed it over. He was taking everything else anyway.

He pulled on it, squinting at me, then blew the smoke in my direction before handing it back. "You try to be what everyone expects you to be, but deep down, even you must know you can't control everything. And that thought terrifies you. But you don't know how to deal with it, so you go out and do stupid shit as a *fuck you* to the universe. Or just to prove to yourself that you can. Or just to let off steam. I haven't figured that part out yet."

Yet. As if he was actively trying to figure me out. As if he was convinced he would eventually. The arrogance . . . I wanted to punch him in the throat for his assumptions, but part of me also liked that he wanted to know more.

"You have no idea what you mean . . . what you're talking about." Shit. I was wasted. I hated how slurred my words came out, that I stumbled on them. I didn't want to show him any weakness.

"Yes, I do." He stopped swirling the bottle and put it behind him, out of sight and reach. "I didn't have your control issues, and I definitely didn't give a shit about my reputation like you do, but I used to do reckless shit in order to feel alive too. I know the high you're chasing, and trust me, it can only end in disaster."

"Is that what happened?" I let my knees drop to the side, brushing up against his leg, and leaned on one hand for balance. After one last drag, I put out the cigarette and left the butt on the ground. "Is that why you moved here? You did something disastrous? Did you crash daddy's Porsche?" I stuck my bottom lip out and mock-pouted.

He scoffed. "I wish. I . . . I'll never forgive myself for what I did."

He stared at the pool, and the mocking expression fell from my face. He was serious. And I was too drunk to deal with this conversation. My head spun, and I involuntarily tilted into him, grabbing his shoulder for balance.

Immediately, he gripped my elbow. He smelled like cinnamon, like that night in the rain, but there was a hint of cigarette smoke too. It was heady, alluring, and in my inebriated state, I couldn't stop myself from leaning in to get more of it.

My lips were inches from his, my body remembering how infuriatingly good it felt to have his body pressed up against me. I wanted him—badly, the pressure between my legs building. But in that moment, in the cold night, with the still pool water reflecting all our flaws, I realized what I craved more was how he'd made me feel *after*. When he picked me up and told me he had me, and I believed it with every fiber of my being.

"Shit." I dropped my head to his shoulder, squeezing my eyes shut, my breaths coming in pants.

He sighed and ran a hand down my spine, the touch gentle, hesitant. "You're wasted. Come on."

He pulled away, but he didn't disappear as I expected him to. He helped me to my feet, steadied me, and wrapped an arm around my waist as he slowly walked me back toward the house.

The sounds of the party got louder, the weight of my life heavier, with every step.

I pushed down the confusing emotions in my chest, blinked back the perplexing tears.

Just before the last bend in the path, I made him stop and took a step away from him, breathing deeply, willing myself to sober up. It was fine to have a few drinks, have fun with my friends—I didn't want people thinking I was a robot— but I couldn't have anyone seeing me completely wasted either.

Hendrix held on to my elbow until it was clear I wasn't going to faceplant, then let go, the last connection between us severed.

I pulled my shoulders back and ran my hands over my dress to check for dirt. Hendrix stepped in front of me, and I froze as his gentle fingers smoothed down a few errant strands of my hair.

"You're perfect," he whispered, brushing the very tips of his fingers across my cheek. I gritted my teeth to resist leaning into the feather-soft touch.

"I'll go around the side of the house. So people don't get the wrong idea." He smirked, then turned and walked away.

I watched his broad back until he disappeared into the darkness, then I walked back into the chaos.

CHAPTER TEN

Donna

I woke up the next morning hungover as fuck. But I still woke up. Harlow and Amaya were both out cold in Harlow's bed. Turner and Mena may have been up, but the door to the spare bedroom they'd slept in was firmly closed, and the faint noises coming through were a pretty good indication they didn't want to be bothered.

Did I want to sleep off the previous night's poor choices, stay in bed, and ignore the world until sometime in the afternoon? Of course. But someone had to let the cleaners in and check in with the parents so they wouldn't rush home early. So I dragged my ass out of bed at nine thirty and was dressed and showered when the professional cleaning crew rang the bell at precisely ten.

Sundays were Magda's days off, so I pressed the button to open the gate and put on a pot of coffee myself. I stood in the silent kitchen, the cold from the tiles seeping into my feet as the water percolated, and tried not to think about Hendrix.

Even though I should've stayed down there to supervise the cleaners, I took my steaming black coffee upstairs, grabbed a throw off the end of my bed to wrap around my shoulders, and went out to my balcony. It looked out over the yard and had a stunning view of the town and landscape beyond. The sunshine made my head hurt even with my sunglasses on, but I embraced the pain, letting it work with the caffeine to wake me.

The pool was visible from my vantage point, and the bright morning sun glistened off the water, making me wonder if I'd imagined how dark and still it had been the night before. Maybe it hadn't ominously reflected all my darkness back at me. Maybe my bizarre drunken talk with the boy I was supposed to hate never happened. Maybe his touch and his declaration that I was perfect—which had given me the strength I needed to go back to the party for another hour, pretend I was having a grand time before I managed to slink away to bed—had all been imagined.

I took a big sip of the bitter coffee and sighed, pulling the throw tighter around my shoulders. It was wishful thinking. I hadn't been *that* drunk, and there was no way in hell I'd imagined how amazing he smelled, how good and strong his shoulder felt under my hand.

I couldn't let Hendrix Hawthorn get under my skin. He was not part of the plan. College was my plan. A law career and a perfect reputation that would allow me to one day run for office were my plan. William was my plan.

My stomach roiled; saliva gathered in my mouth. I threw out a shaky hand and steadied myself on the railing. I must've been more drunk than I thought.

I forced several deep, cleansing breaths into my lungs and pushed thoughts of boys out of my mind. Then I sat down and finished my coffee before heading back downstairs to tackle the day.

The others shuffled into the kitchen one by one after the cleaners left, looking worse than me—rubbing their eyes, grunting in greeting, dragging their feet.

"Whoa! It doesn't look like there was even a party here last night." Turner looked around in awe, then rushed to the window to check the patio area.

Harlow put some chill music on, and we ordered in for breakfast. By the time our parents got home, everyone was showered and feeling more like themselves.

Thankfully, the evening was quiet, and I was able to get some homework done before going to bed early.

I spent Monday and Tuesday avoiding Hendrix as much as I'd warned everyone else to. Tuesday evening provided another good distraction, with the added bonus that I could accomplish something for my future and for the greater good.

After school, I changed into plain black clothes and headed straight into Devilbend's downtown for my volunteer shift with Devilbend Community Legal Center. I worked there for four hours every second Tuesday.

I mostly just made coffee, did filing, and took a few phone calls, but my two-year commitment would look fantastic on my college application, and I was gaining invaluable insight into family law. While the clinic covered various areas of practice, Tuesday night was devoted to family law appointments. Lawyers from some of the best firms in the area volunteered their time to provide advice to members of the community who couldn't afford legal help otherwise. I'd met partners and associates from the law firm I was hoping to intern at over the summer, plus I was building relationships and doing good in my community.

It was the right thing to do, but it secretly felt more like an obligation than anything else. I'd never admit it to anyone, not even to myself out loud, but these Tuesday nights had turned into a boring chore.

"Here's your coffee, Jasmin." I gave the manager of the center a smile.

"Thanks, Donna." She shoved several dirty cups out of the way so I could place the new one next to the pile of files on her desk.

I frowned but chuckled. "How many have you had today?"

"Uh . . . four? No. Six. I don't know. An even number. Are the volunteer lawyers here yet?" She was the cliché of the overcaffeinated community lawyer, with cheap suits, tired eyes, and her chestnut hair in a messy bun. But clichés existed for a reason. She was overworked. She was underpaid. She really needed the caffeine to get through her day.

"Yes, ma'am. Mr. Horowitz just got here, and the first clients should arrive any moment now. The interview rooms are set up, and I've got everyone coffee or tea. Also, here's a phone message from James. His son has strep throat again, and he won't be able to come in tomorrow."

Her shoulders sagged. "Great. Perfect. First they cut my damn funding, then three people call in sick. I'm going to have to reschedule a dozen appointments tomorrow."

"I'll do as many as I can tonight."

"That would be really great. Thank you, Donna."

"It's no problem. How bad is the funding cut?"

She winced. "Bad. I'm probably going to have to lay someone off—when I actually need to hire two more to keep up with demand for services. And donations are down. It's one of those days where the coffee is the only thing keeping me going." She saluted me with her mug and took a long drink, then frowned. "I'm sorry. You don't need me unloading all this on you. Thank you for volunteering your time. It makes a difference."

"It's no problem. On both fronts."

The little bell above the rickety glass door chimed, and I had to go welcome the first clients.

The rest of my shift passed as usual as I assisted the lawyers and made those calls, but the mundane admin tasks didn't do much to quell my frustration at how much this woman had to deal with on top of all the obstacles constantly being thrown in her way. I helped Jasmin tidy up and close for the night, and we left together just after eight.

"Thanks for your help tonight, Donna. I'll see you in two weeks." Jasmin deadlocked the front door, waved at me, and headed for the bus station around the corner.

I was parked a few blocks away in the opposite direction, so I pulled my coat in tight and started walking.

Even this late at night, the lobby beyond the glass windows of the BestLyf building was bright and lit up as I passed. DCLC's offices were in a dingy two-story building right next door, which also happened to be owned by BestLyf. I probably wasn't supposed to know that, but I'd glimpsed a rental statement once when I was doing some filing. The rent was astronomical. I understood that real estate in the heart of Devilbend was in high demand, but DCLC was a nonprofit, for fuck's sake, and BestLyf owned the biggest building in Devilbend and half the other properties on the block. It wasn't as though they couldn't afford to give a charitable organization a discount on rent for the shittiest building on the street. I guess they wanted to help everyone live their best life, but only if you weren't poor.

Glaring at the pavement as I powerwalked, I didn't notice the other people approaching on the sidewalk until a deep throaty laugh slammed me right back to Saturday night. My steps faltered, and my head shot up.

Sure enough, there was Hendrix, walking toward me with a man and a woman next to him. He had his hands stuffed into the pockets of a dark blue coat, the collar popped against the harsh wind, and his hair was even more disheveled than usual.

Our eyes locked, and we both slowed until we were standing in front of each other. His companions stopped too, throwing curious glances between us.

I recovered first, clearing my throat and shifting my feet. "Hey."

Ugh. I'd figured just walking away without saying anything at all would be worse, but . . . *Hey?* I mentally slapped myself.

The side of his lip quirked. "Hey," he said, his jaw slowly working a piece of gum as he stared at me.

The woman cleared her throat. "Hendrix? Are you going to introduce us to your friend?"

"We're not friends," we both rushed to say. Laughter bubbled up in my chest, but I kept it contained and smiled at her instead.

"Oh." She raised her eyebrows. "Girlfriend?"

I snorted, and Hendrix laughed. "Definitely not. This is my aunt Hannah and her partner, Robbie." He gestured to the couple. His aunt gave me a friendly smile, and her boyfriend waved, stomping his feet against the cold. "Guys, this is Donna. She . . . goes to my school."

For some reason, I enjoyed how hard he was finding it to define who I was to him. Remembering my manners, I turned to face them and reached out my hand. "It's a pleasure to meet you."

They both shook my hand, and then Robbie asked, "Are you all right out here on your own? It's getting late."

"Yes, I don't like you walking around downtown on your own," his aunt added. "Would you like to join us for dinner? We can drive you home after." She was genuinely friendly. How the hell was that surly asshole related to her?

Hendrix stiffened next to me, his jaw clenching on the gum. I decided to put us both out of our misery.

"That's very kind of you, but I'd like to get home. I just finished a volunteering shift at Devilbend Community Legal Center, and I'm tired. I'm parked just up ahead. I'll be totally fine." Without waiting for them to insist or ask more questions, I started sidestepping away. "Enjoy your dinner."

"It was lovely to meet you," his aunt called after me.

"You too!" I waved and tore my gaze away before I was too tempted to march back over there and demand to know why Hendrix was frowning at me so hard.

When I got home, I headed straight for my father's study at the back of the house. The door was ajar, and warm light was spilling onto the marble tile in front of it. I could hear soft voices and the clinking of ice.

My mother's soft laugh made me smile. They had evening drinks in here from time to time. Mom used to take a drink in to Dad to distract him from work until he gave up, and eventually it had turned into a nonregular ritual.

I knocked on the door as I pushed it open. "Daddy?"

"Oh, shit." Mom laughed, leaning her elbow on the arm of the leather couch in the corner.

Dad squeezed her knee and swirled his scotch with his other hand. "You must want something big if you're calling me Daddy."

I placed my hand on my chest and plastered an outraged look on my face. "Can't a girl show affection to her father without being accused of manipulation?"

"When it comes to most teenage girls, no." Mom took a sip of her own scotch.

"When it comes to you, sweetness, definitely not. You don't do anything unless it's with intention. You get that from me." There was pride in my father's eyes as he leaned back against the couch.

My parents knew me so well, and yet . . . no one knew that part of me that came alive by throwing myself at dangerous men in seedy bars. Other than Hendrix. And he'd still called me perfect.

I pushed him out of my mind and sat on the soft rug, helping myself to the cheese board. "So rude," I said around a mouthful of brie and cracker. Other than with the girls, this was pretty much the only place I'd allow myself to speak with food in my mouth.

My parents each raised a brow, waiting.

I rolled my eyes. "OK, fine." They burst into laughter, and I had to raise my voice. "But it's not for me."

"What's going on?" Dad set his glass on the table and leaned his elbows on his knees.

"DCLC is having its funding cut. Jasmin says she's going to have to let someone go, and they're stretched so thin already. It's just not fair."

Dad nodded and gestured for me to continue. I sat up straighter and met his gaze head-on. I'd never asked my parents for this much money before.

"I'd like you to make a donation. An anonymous one."

"How much?"

I laid out several levels of monetary assistance and what that would do for the center.

"That's a lot of money." Dad popped an olive into his mouth.

"They help a lot of people."

"Our charity fund has already allocated the donations for this year."

"Yeah, but we have the money, and you're in charge of the fund. You can expand the capacity if you want. Or we can make it a personal donation."

He eyed me for a few minutes, chewing on the olive. "Tell you what, prepare a proposal for me, outlining in detail the funds needed and where they'll go, and I'll consider it."

I grinned and jumped to my feet. "Thank you, Daddy!"

His answer was as good as a yes. He was just using the opportunity to get me to work on my report-writing skills, and I knew I'd crush that report.

I finished drafting it well after midnight and fell asleep instantly afterward, exhausted after a long day—but a certain infuriating guy invaded my dreams anyway.

With the donation all but locked in, I thought my frustrating week was finally turning around, but the next day made me want to throw a tantrum in the middle of Fulton Academy—let everyone see how done I was with their shit.

I was sitting between Amaya and Mena at lunch, slowly eating a roast veg salad while checking emails on my phone, when I saw it.

"Motherfucker." I smacked my fork down and gripped my phone so tightly I was surprised the screen didn't crack.

"D? You OK?" Amaya leaned in, her dark hair falling over her face and screening her concerned expression. The cafeteria was as raucous as usual—no one had noticed my quiet outburst of rage.

Grinding my teeth, I showed her my phone. She skimmed the email that had just come in, the one informing me I would not be awarded the internship I'd been working toward for the past year.

"What the fuck?" Amaya's frown deepened. "I was positive you had that in the bag."

"Me too." I got to my feet and stuffed my phone into my pocket. "Keep this in the Dynasty for now, OK?"

"You got it. Where are you going?" She waved Mena's curious glances down.

"To get to the bottom of it."

I marched out of the cafeteria, through the school, and up to the third floor, where all the faculty and admin staff had their offices.

Mr. Kirke was the Legal Studies teacher and in charge of facilitating students applying for scholarships, volunteering, and other opportunities in the legal field. I'd have bet my hefty inheritance he knew exactly what was going on here. I wiped all emotion off my face as I approached his open office door.

He was hunched over some papers on his desk, making a mess of the sandwich clutched in his hand. When I knocked on the doorjamb, he looked up over his rimless glasses and swallowed his bite of food.

"Miss Mead." He pressed his lips together. "What can I do for you?"

Taking that as an invitation, I walked into his office and perched myself on one of the two chairs facing his desk. "Mr. Kirke, I'm sorry to interrupt your lunch. I just wanted to clarify something before my next class."

"What's that?" He leaned back in his seat, crossing his fingers over his beer belly.

"I just received an email from Horowitz, Ross, and Shore informing me I would not be interning at their offices this summer. It was brief and uninformative. Seeing as you help organize the internship, I'm hoping you can enlighten me."

He was not at all surprised I hadn't gotten it. I pushed the rage down. I was the only Fulton student who'd applied. He should've had my back. "Hundreds of people apply every year, Miss Mead. There is only one position."

"I am aware of how competitive the position is. I am also aware of what they look for. My grades are unblemished, I'm taking several AP classes, I'm volunteering with a nonprofit with ties to the firm, and my planned career path is exactly what they nurture in potential interns. I am the perfect candidate. I'd simply like some insight into why I was not chosen."

I wasn't being arrogant—I was confident I'd done all the right things. I'd worked my ass off. And if there was something else that would've given me the edge, he should've told me. It was *literally* his job.

Mr. Kirke gave me a small, patronizing smile. "There were three dozen perfect candidates. Sometimes, life's just not fair. Take this as a life lesson and move on, Miss Mead."

That condescending mother—

"May I ask who the successful student was?" The information would be public within a week anyway.

"A bright young man by the name of Jacobs." He didn't even hesitate, didn't have to look up the name. How long had he known?

This whole situation was infuriating. I crossed my legs but kept my posture perfectly straight. "Mr. Kirke, I did my research, like I always do, but tell me if I'm wrong here."

He frowned slightly but nodded for me to continue.

"Horowitz, Ross, and Shore has been practicing law in the state of California and the West Coast since 1938. The internship has been running since 1963."

The bell rang, and he sighed, but I rushed to keep speaking.

"In that time, only two women have been awarded the position: Jemima Holt and Miriam Randle." I'd been determined to be the third—but I'd severely underestimated entropy, nepotism, and the fucking patriarchy.

"What's your point, Miss Mead?" His nostrils flared. I was pissing him off. Good, because I was livid.

"As you yourself said, there are hundreds of applicants each year, dozens of ideal candidates. How is it that year after year, a male student is chosen?"

He scoffed and waved his hand dismissively. "Female students don't generally have the same level of interest in studying law as male students. It's probably just a numbers thing."

"Females make up just over 50 percent of all students enrolled in law schools nationally. This number has been steadily growing over the decades, yet the percentage of women in leadership positions, *higher paying positions*, remains woefully low. Judges—27.1 percent. Deans—32.4 percent. Private law firm partners—22.7 percent. I would've thought you'd know these basic, easily accessible statistics as the Legal Studies teacher in one of the best schools in the country." He sat up, his belly digging into the desk and his face turning red, but I refused to let him get a word in. "And if this were a post-graduate position in the legal field, your argument of 'it's a numbers thing' may check out, but as it stands, it seems blatantly obvious Horowitz, Ross, and Shore is extremely biased toward male applicants when choosing their interns. I would expect an educational institution such as Fulton Academy—which prides itself on its progressive and exceptional approach to education—to take issue with such egregiously sexist practices."

"Miss Mead, that's quite enough."

"No. What's enough is your apathy, the ingrained sexism in the legal field, and no one doing anything about it."

He shot to his feet. I refused to have him looking down on me, so I stood too.

"You are not privy to the selection process at Horowitz, Ross, and Shore," he growled, "and you are not aware of how the real world works. But you will be very soon, so let me give you one quick lesson now. Women who throw around those kinds of baseless accusations against institutions such as Fulton Academy and Horowitz, Ross, and Shore very quickly find themselves unemployable. I would've thought that as a student of law, you'd know not to make accusations without proof. I'm sure you could cause a media storm in a teacup what with all this social media and the Twitter and such, but I'd be very careful who you make enemies of, Miss Mead, if you wish to have any chance of being employed after you finish college."

I immediately wanted to post, tweet, fucking TikTok about this and show him just how fast I could cause some trouble. And his suggestion that I'd be ruining all my carefully laid plans by doing so was . . . weirdly freeing? I guess I was just in a "fuck everything" kind of mood.

He gathered some papers off his desk, walked to his door, and held the handle. "The bell rang ten minutes ago. I'm late for a meeting, and you should be in class."

I was clearly dismissed, but it was probably for the best. The urge to grab his too-short tie and twist until he couldn't speak nonsense anymore was growing by the second.

"This is bullshit," I muttered as I stormed past him and down the corridor.

He let the cursing slide, pulling the door shut and rushing off in the opposite direction.

CHAPTER ELEVEN

Hendrix

My meeting with the guidance counselor was mandatory, but missing most of lunch to sit in an office with a woman who had no concept of my past turned out to be as big a waste of time as I thought it would be. When she asked why I hadn't graduated last year as I was supposed to, I told her that information should be in my file and I wasn't comfortable talking about it. I resented that it had even been brought up in such a casual way.

Then she spent a stupid amount of time rambling about college applications and areas of study while I tried to keep my bored mask in place. In reality, my skin was crawling, and I wanted to storm out of there the entire time. To her credit, she did try to ask me questions about what I wanted to do after high school, but I didn't give her much in the way of responses. Because I had no fucking clue. I just wanted to get through the school year and graduate. I couldn't bear to think about what would come after, what kind of future I might have.

I was so wrapped up in thoughts of a potential future I didn't deserve that I almost missed the blonde ball of anger barreling toward me from the other end of the hallway.

Seeing Donna made me pause and look around. Where the hell was I? Somehow I'd wandered into a quiet, locker-free corridor I wasn't familiar with. I was still getting the lay of the land—the school was massive.

"What the hell are you doing in the administrative wing, Hendrix?" Donna stopped directly in front of me and somehow managed to look down her perfect little nose—despite being a good foot shorter. She was seething.

I knew she couldn't stand the sight of me, but even I couldn't elicit *this* level of rage. What was up her ass?

I made sure not to let my amusement show as I frowned down at her. "None of your business."

Oh, she did not like that at all. She took another step closer, her chest just inches from mine, and gritted her teeth, but she didn't seem to have a witty comeback. I kept perfectly still, stifling the chuckle that was bursting to tumble out of me.

When it became apparent she wasn't going to say anything, I looked around the corridor, careful not to give away how affected I actually was by her proximity, by her sweet, girly smell in my nose. "Why's it so quiet here?"

She finally found her voice. "Because anyone who's not teaching a class is currently in a meeting."

She blew a big breath out through her nose, as if the meeting were being held specifically to make her life more difficult. Then she cocked her head, and a tiny smile twitched at the corner of her mouth before it disappeared. What a strange, frustrating woman.

As abruptly as she'd gotten in my face, she grabbed my wrist and turned on her heel. Stunned by the sudden movement and flowery scent of her shampoo wafting past me when she flicked her hair, I let myself be dragged like a naughty puppy. Shoulders back, head held high, she marched past two office doors and opened the third.

When she tried to pull me into the office, I came to my senses and pulled my wrist out of her grasp.

She rounded on me immediately. "Get inside."

"No." I folded my arms. "You're acting even more batshit than usual, and I really don't have time for whatever this is. I need to get to class."

"The bell went fifteen minutes ago. Is there even any point?"

"Of course there is. I'm very interested in Mrs. Shepard's hot take on string theory."

"Please. Like you even know what string theory is. You'd pick science over a blow job?"

"What . . . the fuck is happening?" My eyes widened, and I allowed myself a quiet laugh. Her erratic behavior was worrying, but fuck if it wasn't intriguing too. She was a bitch, but there was no denying she was hot, and I'd be lying if I said I hadn't been thinking about what I'd done to her that night in the rain. I knew what her pussy felt like clenching around my fingers as she came. And now that she'd put the suggestion into my brain, I wanted to know what her mouth felt like around my dick.

"I have a score to settle, and I need to burn off some steam. Meeting lets out in about twenty. You want your dick sucked or not?"

"How do I know you won't bite it off instead?" I narrowed my eyes.

She leaned in, lifting onto her toes to whisper into my ear. "You don't. But that's the risk you take any time you stick your dick into someone's mouth, isn't it? The danger, the teeth." She nipped me on the ear. "That's what makes it fun."

Her words made some things click into place in my mind—why she was at Davey's that night; the intense, controlling personality; why she was about to do something reckless on school property. Donna liked the rush of danger, the adrenaline of almost getting caught.

But I didn't have the time to fully consider the implications of all that. I was hard as a rock, and I was an eighteen-year-old guy. I was never going to say no to a blow job.

I wrapped an arm around her waist and shuffled us the rest of the way into the office.

As soon as I pulled the door shut, her hot little tongue invaded my mouth. She placed both palms flat against my chest and shoved me, and I let her, relaxing back against the wall as I grabbed her ass with both hands. She had a great ass under that scandalous tartan skirt.

But I lost my grip on it almost immediately as she slid down, rubbing her body down my front until she was on her knees in front of me.

I had to take a breath to steel myself. Part of me had figured she was talking shit and I was calling her bluff. But I should've known. Women like Donna Mead rarely said things they didn't mean, and even less often did things they didn't want to do.

Holy shit, this is really happening. She made quick work of the button and fly on my neat gray uniform pants as I tried not to pant as if I'd just run a marathon. I was acting as though I'd never had head before, for fuck's sake.

Although, to be fair, I'd never had head on school property. I'd gotten into plenty of trouble, did some fucked-up shit at my last school, but this was a first even for me.

As Donna pulled my pants and boxers down in one efficient maneuver, I could see what she saw in these moments of recklessness. It was a thrill; an exciting, tantalizing buzz of adrenaline made my suddenly free cock even harder.

I shouldn't have expected anything less, but Donna still surprised me a little when she leaned forward and immediately took me into her mouth. No teasing strokes of the tongue, no exploratory kisses. She just wrapped her full lips around the head of my cock and sucked.

"Fuck." I no longer cared how hard I was breathing. Her mouth, her lips, her tongue, *holy shit*—the back of her throat . . . I was lost, such a fucking goner for this complicated, infuriating, spoiled rich girl and her hot little mouth.

She sucked me off the same way she did everything else—with confidence and determination. As with everything else in her perfect life, Donna excelled at this too.

She used the perfect amount of suction, swirling her tongue around the head, working the base with her hand. The occasional scrape of her teeth made me shiver, the hint at pain and destruction.

She'd said we only had fifteen minutes, but I had a feeling this was going to be over in two. How fucking embarrassing. I tried to think of unsexy things to slow down the orgasm already building, stem the increasing pressure in my groin.

Puppies.

Algebra.

The intricacies of my Tesla engine.

The grating sound of nails on a chalkboard.

Austin's face as he—no, not that. I pushed that back into the lockbox deep in my mind.

For a moment, I worried I was about to go from one extreme to the other—go completely flaccid in Donna's mouth while she was giving me the best goddamn blow job of my life. But then I opened my eyes, looked down at her, and groaned, all other thoughts driven from my mind.

I could see down her perfectly ironed shirt, her perky cleavage and a hint of pink lace. Her lips were plumped up from the friction, her unique eyes watching me, unashamed and unabashed. She was perfect.

Her light, soft hair bounced as she bobbed her head up and down. Without thinking about it, I reached out to run my hand through it, then stopped myself just in time. Most chicks didn't like it when you grabbed their heads while they were sucking you off, in my experience.

But Donna frowned a little and grabbed both my hands, placing them on her head and digging her nails into my skin. As soon as I threaded my fingers into her hair, she let go, and her hands went to my hips.

I groaned again—too loudly, considering our location—but some noise is kind of unavoidable when the chick giving you a BJ actively encourages you to pull her hair and hold her head.

I was getting close, panting, the pressure building. My hips twitched, involuntarily driving my dick forward, and I fought to still them.

Again, Donna surprised me. She moaned around my cock, the vibrations feeling incredible. Both her hands moved to the wall on either side of my hips, and she gave me a challenging look, practically begging me to fuck her mouth.

I watched her carefully, just in case I'd read the signals wrong, but I started thrusting. She met me stroke for stroke, taking me deeper and moaning. The head of my cock started hitting the back of her throat repeatedly, but she just kept going, encouraging me with her eyes, sucking me down with her mouth.

For a few glorious moments, Donna gave herself over to me completely. The sight of her on her knees before me as I thrust my cock in and out of her mouth, her eyes starting to water a little, was addictive. Better than any porn I'd ever seen.

The feel of her soft hair in my hands, and her even softer mouth . . .

My whole body tensed, and I banged my head against the wall, bending slightly at the knees as the most intense orgasm washed over me. I couldn't have warned her if I wanted to—the climax came over me so suddenly and with such force. For a second, my vision went black, stars sparking at the edges as I exploded down her throat.

She swallowed it all, sucking and licking as I gasped for air as though I were drowning.

I slumped against the wall. My legs and arms felt like noodles as I slowly caught my breath. Donna sat back on her heels and gave me one small, satisfied smile. She looked happy with herself—as she should, that was fucking phenomenal—but she also looked more relaxed, not as worked up as she'd been in the hallway just moments before.

Without another word, she reached into her pocket, popped a mint into her mouth, then smoothed her hair and uniform before getting to her feet and walking out of the office.

"What the f . . ." I scrambled to tuck myself back into my pants and rushed after her, leaving the door wide open.

I caught a glimpse of her turning the corner at the end of the hallway and took off jogging after her. When I was halfway up the hall, several people rounded the corner and started walking toward me. The meeting must've finished, and all the teachers and admin workers were heading back to their offices. I slowed down to a respectable speed and plastered a neutral look on my face until I passed them.

As soon as I was out of the hall, I booked it toward the stairs.

"Donna!" I called out, taking the stairs down two at a time. I caught up to her just as she reached the halfway point.

She turned to me, a little confused, but didn't stop walking. "What?"

"What do you mean *what*? Are you OK?" I leaned in, keeping my voice low. She'd left without a single word. Had I hurt her? Was I too rough? "Did you not want to . . . did you change your mind or something?"

She laughed under her breath. "No. You finished, didn't you?"

I blew out a big breath. "I mean, yeah. I finished spectacularly." There was that satisfied smirk again. "But did I do something to make you uncomfortable? You just left without saying anything."

"Oh, I'm sorry. Did you want to cuddle? You'll have to get yourself a girlfriend for that."

"I don't want a fucking girlfriend," I barked, a little too loudly. Voices were starting to reach us from below—people were making their way to their next classes. We were about to be swallowed up by the student body once more. "I just want to make sure you're OK."

She finally stopped and faced me, rolling her eyes before glancing down at my crotch. "Your vagina is showing."

"What?" I glanced down, then looked at her as if she was crazy—I was starting to think she was. "I'm just trying to be a decent human being and make sure I didn't choke you out with my dick. Why do you have to be such a bitch about it?"

"I'm fine. You're more than fine. That was a hookup and nothing more, and I didn't think we needed to compare notes. Also, I didn't want to get caught in Mr. Kirke's office. So I left. Nothing else to it. Now stop acting like a pussy and wait a few minutes before coming the rest of the way downstairs. I don't want to be seen with you."

She fixed my collar, gave me a sweet smile, and walked away.

I stood there for a moment, trying to figure out if I wanted to smile or punch something.

Donna Mead was a fucking force of nature, and if I wasn't careful, I had a feeling she would knock me to my knees like a goddamn landslide.

CHAPTER TWELVE

The heat from the massive bonfire warmed my right cheek, but not as much as the heat from Hendrix's stare was warming my left.

It had been stupid to hook up with him again, get on my knees for that cocky son of a bitch. It had definitely been stupid to do it at school, where anyone could've caught us. But that was part of the thrill, wasn't it? It was a reckless thing to do, but I was enraged after my chat with Mr. Kirke, and I'd needed an outlet. He was just there, that was all. It could've just as easily been Will if he'd happened to walk down that corridor toward me.

I'd avoided him for the next few days, to make it clear it meant nothing, but there he was, invading my Saturday night. *Again.*

Even through his Jason mask, I could tell he was watching me. He'd worn plain black jeans and a black jacket, but the mask from *Friday the 13th* was iconic enough to make his lazy costume clear. I huffed and took a drink of my soda, careful not to ruin my lipstick. Mena had spent hours doing our makeup, insisting on getting it perfect.

I was dressed as Britney Spears in the flight attendant uniform from the "Toxic" video. My sister was the perfect "Baby One More Time" Britney, with the slutty uniform and her long hair in pigtails. Amaya had opted for the skimpiest Britney outfit, but the look from her performance of "Slave 4 You" at the VMAs looked perfect on my stunning friend. She was so committed to the look we'd had to talk her out of buying an actual snake to wear around her neck all night. Mena was in head-to-toe denim and had somehow talked Turner into dressing in all denim too so they could be Britney and Justin in their matching outfits.

Half the reason we'd decided on these costumes was so we could say hi to people when we arrived and declare, "We're Britney, bitch!" The first half hour at the party had been a lot of fun as we ran around greeting people we knew.

Last year we'd planned to go to some party at Nicola's parents' penthouse loft in San Francisco, but we'd ended up staying in to watch horror movies instead. Mena had worked all day and fallen asleep halfway through the first one.

This year, Harlow talked us all into going to a not-entirely-legal party. We'd driven nearly an hour out of town, into rural land, then down some dirt track to a party in a field. With every bump in the track, every ding on the outside of my car, I wondered how much damage I was doing. Should've taken the jeep Dad got for fishing trips he never went on.

There was a massive bonfire in the middle of the clearing, dark woods edged one side, and a wheat field stretched as far as the firelight could illuminate and beyond.

Easily several hundred people were there. Some of them were Harlow's gaming friends who'd invited her in the first place—a bunch of gangly nerds who hadn't even bothered to dress up. She'd introduced us all, and we'd made small talk, but it became apparent pretty quickly we had nothing in common. I was pretty sure every one of those computer geeks wanted to get into my crazy smart, adorably beautiful sister's pants.

There were college kids there, and some people from Devilbend North High—Mena's old school. At first I was surprised to see how many people there were Fulton students, but it made sense. Harlow had invited all our friends, and they would've told others, and Amaya couldn't keep her mouth shut about a party if she tried.

I ignored the tingly sensation of eyes watching me and turned to look at Amaya. She was in her element, several college guys hanging around her as she flirted and drank from the only champagne glass in sight. Literally everyone else was making do with shitty red cups. Where did she even get that?

"Donna." Harlow bumped into me, breathless. I stumbled but righted us both. She hung off me, her hands on my shoulders and her face really close to mine. "Donna, I can hear the fire," she whispered, her eyes going really wide.

I gave her a confused look. "Yeah, Harlow. We can all hear the fire. The wood crackles as it burns."

Her eyebrows rose, and she blinked once. "Oh yeah." Then she burst into laughter.

"How did you get drunk this fast?" I asked, getting a little worried. We'd only been there an hour.

"Uhhhhhmmmmmm." The guilty look on her face was almost caricaturish.

I rolled my eyes. "What did you take?"

"Just a little." She held up her finger and thumb and squinted through the gap at me.

"A little what?" I led her a few steps away from the fire and the crowd.

"Ooh, you want some? I feel *great!*" She pulled a little baggie out of her skirt pocket and held it out to me.

I took it from her and inspected it. The baggie had several little white pills in it—E. She was going to have a fucking fantastic night . . . but she was going to come down hard. I guided her over to a bunch of coolers and opened a few until I found one filled with bottled water, then stuffed one into her hand and made her look at me. "Harlow. You drink this or I'm going to take you home, got it?"

She straightened and saluted me. "Yes, ma'am!" Then her eyes wandered to something over my shoulder, and her mouth fell open. "Donna, there are freakishly tall people walking in the big grass."

"What?" I turned to follow her gaze and pinched the bridge of my nose. "You're not seeing shit. Those are performers. People on stilts." Someone—probably from Fulton, as I was pretty sure no one else could afford the extravagance—had hired a bunch of performers for the night. Several people on stilts were wandering the wheat field, coming into the crowd every once in a while, and contortionists in grotesque costumes twisted themselves into scenes reminiscent of the exorcist. I'd even seen a few very convincing "werewolves" leap out of the woods, scaring the absolute shit out of a group of girls, who sent high-pitched screams into the night. I had to hand it to whoever had done this—it had taken the mediocre rave in a field to the next level. Everyone was on edge, the adrenaline mingling with the alcohol (or drugs) as they waited for what might happen next.

"Oh. OK." With a grin, she snatched the baggie of fun out of my hand and ran off, pigtails bouncing as she barreled through the crowd of college dudes to Amaya's side. They chatted, the dudes laughed at some joke she cracked, and then she passed Amaya the little baggie.

Great. Now I'd have two off-their-faces idiots to haul home tonight. I was starting to wish I'd taken Will's offer to drive us so I could drink too. But he always got drunk at parties, and I couldn't rely on him to get us home. And it wasn't as if I'd be able to get an Uber to come out here, so . . . someone had to be responsible.

Mena appeared at my side and bumped my shoulder with hers. "Hey, you. Having a good night?"

"Yeah." I smiled at her. "You look really pretty."

"Thanks." She glanced down at the swathes of denim and gave a little twirl from side to side. Her eyes were a bit glassy, and her own lipstick was starting to get smudged. I could smell alcohol on her breath. She leaned down and fixed herself another drink from the coolers.

"You're glaring again." She chuckled.

I shook my head and pulled my gaze away from Hendrix. I hadn't even realized I'd gone back to staring at him.

"I didn't mean to. I just don't like him being here." I crossed my arms. He was standing with Turner, talking, laughing, chatting with some of Turner's friends. He looked as if he was having a good time, and for some reason, that pissed me off more than anything.

"Why?" Mena wrapped an arm around my waist and took another sip of her drink. "Things have been fine since you made everyone at school back off him. You guys haven't even yelled at each other in weeks. But he's kind of getting close with Turner, so I've been talking to him a bit, and he's really not that bad."

All my friends had seen was him being an arrogant smart-ass to me, me laying down the law, and us bickering those few times at school. They had no idea what he had over me, what I'd let him do to me, what I'd done to him. Hendrix and I were getting all twisted up in each other, and I didn't like it one bit.

I wrapped my arm around her waist too and turned us toward the fire. "OK. No more glaring. Let's talk about something else."

"OK. What do you want to talk about?"

"How about our trashed friends?" I pointed at Harlow and Amaya, who were dancing as if they could feel the music moving through their bones, heads rolling in ecstasy. They were sweaty and rubbing up on each other in the middle of the dance floor—and had the attention of half the guys at the party and a few of the girls too.

Mena laughed. "I wish I had Amaya's confidence. And Harlow's complete lack of care for what people think of her. And your . . . fuck, everything."

"You don't want to be me, trust me." It came out low, way more somber than the self-deprecating joke I'd intended it to sound like.

"Donna?" Mena frowned at me. I could see the question on the tip of her tongue—the "are you OK?" A twinge of panic squeezed my chest. I wasn't sure I could lie to her if she asked me so directly.

But Drew saved me from having to.

"Ladies!" He draped himself over us both, one arm around Mena and the other around me, his athletic body towering over us. He smelled like expensive cologne and bonfire smoke.

"Hey, Drew." I gave him a kiss on the cheek, grateful for the distraction.

"Come on, Mena—my other cheek feels left out." He leaned his head between ours and wiggled his eyebrows.

She whacked him in the stomach. "No. We've been over this. How drunk are you?"

"Not at all." He took a swig from his beer and immediately returned his arm to my shoulders, then lowered his voice. "Actually, I'm just trying to make a girl jealous."

Biting his lip, he gave Mena a look that would've had her dragging him off to find a secluded tree in the woods—if she was actually into him.

"So, your strategy for picking up is to make it look like you have two other chicks on the hook?" I gave him a skeptical look.

"Yeah, you know most girls are put off by that, right?" Mena backed me up.

"Not this girl." He grinned. "Trust me."

"What girl?" Turner appeared in front of us, blocking our view of the fire and cocking his head to the side. I bit my lip to keep from laughing. This was going to be good.

Drew grinned. "You must be Turner."

"And you must be Drew," Turner deadpanned.

"Aw. You talk about me. I knew I had a place in your heart," Drew cooed to Mena, pulling her closer as she rolled her eyes.

"Only to tell me what a pain in her ass you are," Turner shot back.

"But what an ass!" Drew dropped his arms and turned, sticking his butt out and wiggling it in Mena's direction.

Turner pulled Mena to his side and shook his head at Drew. I'd known him long enough to see the amusement in his eyes, but Drew hadn't. He dropped the clown act and cleared his throat, standing to his full height.

"Hey, man, I don't mean anything by it. I'm just messing around. I know she's taken—she talks about you all the time. You're a lucky man. Mena, am I making you uncomfortable?"

I coughed to cover up the giggle that was threatening to bubble over, but when Mena and Turner finally cracked, I gave up and joined them, all of us bursting into laughter at the wide-eyed look on Drew's face.

Mena, ever the sweetheart, put him out of his misery. She stepped forward and placed a hand on his shoulder. "I know we're just messing around. I would've said something if it was bothering me."

"And I would've made you pay." I wiped the tears from under my eyes.

"And I would've come down to that fancy-ass school to whoop your ass long ago," Turner added.

Drew chuckled and jumped right back into his default setting, covering Mena's hand on his shoulder with his. "Well, if we have the boyfriend's blessing—"

Abruptly, his face fell as his attention snagged on something in the distance.

"Shit," he muttered. "Nice to meet you, man. I gotta run."

Without any explanation, he took a swig of his beer and rushed toward the edge of the clearing where the cars were parked.

Mena watched him with a confused expression. "What was that about?"

I shrugged. He'd joined a group of guys who had just shown up—all of whom I recognized as Fulton Academy students, most of them on the football team. Two were gesturing wildly and getting in each other's faces. Drew dropped his beer and got between them, keeping them apart. Others helped him stop the fight before it started, but then it looked as if they all broke into a heated discussion.

"What the hell is *that* about?" Turner voiced what we were all thinking as we stood there, watching the scene from afar.

"I don't know, but I'm gonna find out." I squared my shoulders.

"Want me to come with?" Turner asked. "That looked pretty heated."

"No, that's OK. Thanks." I patted him on the arm. "I know all those guys. You two go have fun."

I marched off before they could argue.

The closer I got, the more apparent it became that I knew each one of them. Some were in Halloween costumes, masks, and grotesque monster makeup, but others were just in jeans and their Fulton varsity jackets.

Will was leaning on the hood of his gray Bentley, watching the others argue with a passive, if not bored, look on his face.

"Boys!" I raised my voice a little to get their attention. "It's a party. What's with the hostility?"

"Donna, baby, I got this. It's just some guy stuff." Drew threw me an easy smile, but his shoulders were tense, and he was still shooting looks at Luke and Donnie—the two who had nearly started throwing fists earlier.

"What happened?" I demanded. An uneasy feeling crept up my spine, leaving a chill in its wake despite the heat of the bonfire. This was how they'd been acting after Luke crashed his car over the summer and injured himself and three other guys on the team. His left arm was still in a cast.

"Nothing, Donna. It's fine." Luke rubbed the back of his head and turned away from everyone.

"Is someone hurt?" I folded my arms. Then someone shifted, allowing a streak of bright light to fall over Donnie's face, and I gasped and rushed forward. "Holy shit. What the fuck happened?"

His left eye was black and blue, and there were scrapes on his chin. He glanced over my shoulder and swallowed audibly, then gave a hollow chuckle. "Football is a contact sport. Shit happens." He pulled me into a hug. "But thanks for the concern."

I narrowed my eyes at him, stepped back, and eyed them all. They were acting shifty as fuck. And they hadn't played a game last night, so that made no sense. Was I seeing shit, or were the others sporting bruises and scrapes too? Maybe it was just the masks and makeup, the uneven light of the fire deceiving me.

Before I could pull my phone out and turn on the flashlight to check either way, Will pushed off the front of his car and wrapped his arms around my waist. "Hey, D. Wanna go somewhere quiet?"

He smirked and pulled me in close. His eyes weren't glassy, and he wasn't swaying. Will was stone-cold sober at a party. Something was definitely up.

"Not tonight." I pushed at his shoulders, and he let go, but then he grabbed my hand and tried to turn me around.

"OK, cool. Then let's go get a drink and find the girls."

"No." I wrenched my hand out of his. "Will, what the fuck . . ."

"Everything OK here?" Suddenly Hendrix was there, his mask sitting on top of his head and his dark eyes taking everything in. Why was he *everywhere*? And why was no one telling me the truth?

A motherfucking werewolf jumped out from between the parked cars, growling and raising its paws in the air. Some of the guys jumped in surprise while the others laughed nervously at the performer.

"Not now, asshole!" I screamed, and the guy in the suit gave me a hairy middle finger and stalked back into the shadows.

I turned on Hendrix. "Everything is fine, Hendrix! Mind your own business." Then I turned on Will. "No, I don't want to get a drink or go find a quiet place with you, William." I looked around at the crowd of idiots from my school. "You're all about as subtle as a sledgehammer. I don't know what this shit is about, but I don't like it, and I'm going to get to the bottom of it."

With that, I turned on my heel and stomped back toward the crowd and the fire and the music . . . and yet another thing I had to manage.

I came to a stop at the edge of the dance floor and looked up to the pitch-black sky, begging whatever deity was listening for strength.

Amaya and Harlow were still dancing lasciviously, but now they were also making out. It was nothing new—they kissed from time to time at parties and shit. Amaya liked to tease the boys, and Harlow liked to subvert people's assumptions about her. It was just a bit of fun, but there were a lot of people here we didn't know, and they were both high, and the college guys were dancing a little too close. I didn't want them to do anything they'd regret . . . or worse.

I caught Turner as he came past with a couple of beers. "Hey, can you get Mena home? I need to take care of this . . ." I gestured to the dance floor. Amaya was now shirtless, nothing but a delicate, lacy bralette covering her perky B cups.

"Yeah, I'll take her home. We have a designated . . . whoa . . . okay . . ." His eyebrows rose as he stared.

"Hey!" I snapped my fingers in front of his face and shoved him. "Go find your girlfriend."

He cleared his throat. "Yes. Yup. Good idea."

"Shit," I muttered as he moved away. I had no idea how I was going to get two trashed people into the car.

Once again, Hendrix appeared uninvited at my side, popping an obnoxiously loud bubble with his gum. "I'll get the little one. You get the naked one."

I glared at him for a moment. He was sticking his nose in my business again. But Turner was busy with Mena, and they were both kind of drunk, and the football guys were pissing me off . . . I really didn't have any other choice.

"Fine." I barreled through the crowd, which looked as if it was about to turn into an orgy any second now. More people had started taking clothes off, and several were making out and grinding on each other.

"Hey!" I clapped my hands next to Harlow's and Amaya's heads.

"Donna!" they both yelled, as if we hadn't seen each other in years.

"Time to go." I picked up their discarded clothing and Amaya's Louis Vuitton bag.

"Where are we—oop!" Harlow descended into a fit of giggles as Hendrix picked her up and swung her over his shoulder in one smooth move. I wrapped an arm around Amaya's waist and pulled her along.

Trying to get them into the car was like trying to wrangle several cats into a bath with one arm tied behind your back. There was screaming and uncontrollable laughter, and I got scratched on my arm. In the end, we managed to shove them into the back seat, and I turned the child lock on so they couldn't let themselves out.

I slammed the door and leaned heavily back against it, blowing my hair off my forehead. Hendrix leaned his hip next to me and laughed.

"Thanks for helping. You didn't have to do that," I said, unable to look at him for some reason.

"You're welcome."

There was a long pause. I stared out into the dark woods. Why was I always the one taking care of everyone else? Maybe I wanted to get trashed every once in a while and know someone would get me home safe.

My friends had said to me more than once I was the strongest person they knew. But that's the thing about being seen that way—you don't feel as if you have permission to be vulnerable. You don't feel as if you're ever allowed to fall apart.

I didn't know why I was letting this shit get to me in the middle of the night in a field in bumfuck nowhere, but suddenly my throat felt tight, and tears stung the backs of my eyes.

Hendrix sighed, reminding me he was still there.

Before I could gather myself, put my strong mask back on, he reached out and squeezed my shoulder. His thumb rubbed smooth circles at the base of my neck.

I grabbed his wrist, but instead of pushing him off me, I found myself leaning into him. "I'm just so fucking tired."

"I know." His deep voice had me feeling in my bones that he really did know. I wasn't talking about just tonight.

He pulled me into his chest and held me tightly, and even with my face buried in his shirt, I was suddenly able to breathe better. I took a long inhale, closing my eyes as the scent of his expensive aftershave mixed with cinnamon hit the back of my throat.

When he'd embraced me at Mena's birthday party, I was drunk. I could blame my momentary lapse in judgment on my impaired decision-making skills. But as he held me at the edge of fire and chaos, dancing and drama, I had no such excuse. Being in his arms felt so *right*.

But it *wasn't*. It *couldn't* be.

My heart hammered.

I straightened, pushed out of his hold.

Our eyes met in the dim light.

The urge to kiss him was palpable, but I forced myself to turn away, get into the car, drive off.

My hands shook the entire drive home, silent tears streaming down my face.

What the fuck was happening to me?

CHAPTER THIRTEEN

Hendrix

Aunt Hannah flicked the switch, and the multicolored twinkle lights came to life.

"Ahh. Now it feels like Christmas!" She beamed, backing away from the ugliest tree I'd ever seen. But it was also the first one I'd gotten to decorate myself, so my smile back was genuine. Growing up, we always had at least five trees spread throughout the house, and each one was professionally decorated. I'd been scolded anytime I reached for a shiny ornament.

"You forgot the main bit." Robbie waved the red-and-gold star at her. We'd met over dinner that night we bumped into Donna in Devilbend. He was actually a nice guy, and he and my aunt were good together. They were both sarcastic and liked to talk politics and had this weird kind of calm about them. It was nice being around an adult couple who liked each other. I was pretty sure they actually *loved* each other.

"Shit!" Hannah propped her hands on her hips, then pointed at me. "You. Tall, surly teenager in the armchair. You can reach."

"So can he!" I pointed at Robbie, who promptly pointed at my aunt. We both frowned at him.

"What?" He shrugged. "Everyone else was pointing. I just wanted to be cool."

It was such a lame joke, but I laughed anyway. Was this what it was like to be part of an actual family?

Without having to be asked again—another first for me—I got to my feet and secured the star on top of the gaudy tree.

It was only a week until Christmas, but everything felt different. Back in New York, the temperature would be hovering around zero, while here in California, it was just chilly enough for a coat. Back home, I'd probably be going to my hundredth charity event of the season, playing the perfect son for my perfect parents. Here, all I'd done was go to school, hang out with my aunt and Robbie, and train with Turner at the gym.

He'd managed to drag me to that Halloween party only after assuring me it wasn't being thrown by one of the kids from my school. He said Mena would be there with her friends, and realistically I knew that meant Donna would be there too, but I'd hoped the party would be big enough to avoid her. I'd obviously forgotten how fucking hard it was for me to stay away from that chick.

The air hostess outfit and ample cleavage had made her look like temptation incarnate. My eyes kept wandering over to her without meaning to, but what surprised me more was that I caught her looking my way too.

She'd made it clear after the incident in that teacher's office that I meant nothing to her, but we'd hooked up twice now—and it was *good*. Our chemistry was off the charts. Even she couldn't deny that.

We'd had a moment at her car. Another moment where unspoken things passed between us. And then that bitch ran from me again.

Why the fuck was I doing this to myself? I'd been so frustrated after she drove off that I made Turner and Mena leave as soon as I found them, basically telling them they were either coming with me now or finding their own way home.

They were silent and tense on the drive back to their apartment building, while I gripped the steering wheel way too hard and breathed through my stupid fucking emotions.

By the time I dropped them off, I'd calmed down enough to apologize. They both forgave me immediately and even asked if I was OK. Because that was the kind of people they were.

Why couldn't I be more like Turner? Calm, happy, steady.

Why couldn't I be interested in a girl like Mena? Nice, sweet, low drama.

No, I had to find the biggest bitch in town with the biggest fucking secret and make it my mission to get all up in her life.

I was seeing something in Donna I knew was inside me too. That twisting, writhing darkness had ruined my life, along with several others. I didn't want a single other person to go through what I went through. To go through what I put those people through. Even if that person was treating me like dirt on her shoe.

Still, there was only so much I could take. If Donna wanted to ruin her life, who was I to stop her?

After that party I took a long hard look in the mirror, realized I didn't need her rich brat problems, and redoubled my efforts to steer clear. For the next few weeks until Christmas break, I went to school, kept my head down, avoided her in the halls, and ate my lunch off campus or in my car. The only person my age I spoke to was Turner.

My phone buzzed on the coffee table, and I picked it up as I took a sip of eggnog. Who the hell invented this crap? And why was I still drinking it? I made a face and put the cup down, then froze as I read the message.

We won't be able to make it to Devilbend for Christmas. Your father has had a work situation come up, and I really must oversee the Christmas Eve charity ball. Have a safe holiday with your aunt. Kisses, Mom.

I gripped my phone so fucking hard the screen actually cracked, the line through the glass cutting through my mother's indifferent words. I stared at the message until the screen went black. Then I shot to my feet and stormed out the door, slamming it behind me, ignoring the things my aunt and Robbie were calling after me.

I wanted to hit someone, feel bone crunch under my knuckles. I wanted to drink an entire bottle of something expensive and let the alcohol obliterate everything. I wanted to find a chick and bury myself in her so deep this feeling would just melt away.

A flash of short blonde hair and mismatched eyes mixed with that last image, and suddenly I was thinking about fucking Donna. I growled and sped up.

I wanted to do a lot of things I used to do—things I'd vowed never to do again. Instead I walked. Even in my T-shirt and jeans, I didn't feel the cold, hardly noticed when it started raining lightly.

I wasn't sure how much time passed, but I didn't go back until I was calm, my breathing even, the urge to do reckless, destructive shit gone.

As I walked back inside, I checked the front door for damage. Thankfully it was fine. When I popped my head in the kitchen, both Aunt Hannah and Robbie had already gotten to their feet and were on their way to the front of the house.

"Hendrix—"

"Hey, guys." I cut my aunt off. "I'm really sorry about before. I'm just gonna grab a shower."

I rushed up the stairs before they could answer.

After showering and getting dressed, I checked the time. It was after nine. I'd been out stalking the neighborhood for over three hours. I'd missed dinner. They had to be mad at me. I'd have to apologize again—do it better. I couldn't handle it if Aunt Hannah kicked me out.

A knock sounded at the door, followed by my aunt's soft voice. "Hendrix?"

"Come in," I called, straightening my sheets and kicking some dirty clothes under the bed. I really needed to make more of an effort to keep my room clean.

"Hey." She plopped onto the bed. "I got a message from your father."

I sank down next to her, hanging my head. What was there to say?

"I'm sorry, honey." Her warm hand rubbed my shoulder.

I frowned at her. "You're not mad?"

She sat up a little straighter. "That your parents are dicks? Yeah, I'm pretty fucking mad about that. But how's that your fault? Not mad at you."

"I'm sorry about storming out." I still felt the need to apologize. "And I'll clean my room. And I'll do more around the house."

"Hendrix. Stop. You were upset. You went for a walk. I'm actually proud of you."

"Proud of me?" What the fuck was this feeling in my chest? It felt as if it were about to bust open, spilling blood and guts everywhere, but . . . in a good way?

"What would you have done a year ago? To deal with something that upset you?"

The booze and drugs, the horrific violence, the depraved sex. I cringed.

"Exactly!" She laughed. "You did good, kid. And I don't need a housekeeper." She waved her hand. "Just stick to what we already discussed—good grades, no trouble—and we're sweet. I'm not going to kick you out for not making your bed."

Fuck. There it went again—blood and guts everywhere. Why were my eyes stinging? Oh my fucking god! I was about to cry. I cleared my throat and pushed that shit down. Maybe I needed to go for another walk.

"So, your father said something about a work thing coming up?"

I dragged my hand down my face. "Yeah, that's what my mom said too. But it's bullshit. There's always a work thing, always a charity. It's just an excuse."

I hadn't seen my parents since they'd shipped me off to Devilbend, and we hadn't spoken in that entire time either. Most of my messages had gone completely ignored. It was OK—I knew I deserved it for what I'd done. But I'd been on my best fucking behavior. My grades were the best they'd ever been. I wasn't expecting miracles, but some part of me had been looking forward to seeing them for Christmas, away from the pressures of their lives in New York. I hadn't realized how big that part was until I got my mother's text message.

Her excuse was almost certainly a copy/paste from some other message she'd sent to get out of another commitment. I didn't even warrant a genuine explanation, let alone a phone call.

What had I expected? It wasn't as though my parents had given a shit about me before—why would they start now?

I hated myself a little for still craving their approval, their attention.

If I was really honest, that's what had gotten me into this mess in the first place.

"All right, let's hug it out." Hannah got to her feet and waved her hands at me to get up. "I think we've worked up to it."

I stood and reached for her, but she sidestepped me and jumped onto my bed. I gave her a withering look but couldn't help the laughter bubbling up.

"Height advantage." She held her arms out, and I gave her a hug, fighting chuckles the whole time. Despite being so small, she had a strong grip, and after the first-hug weirdness wore off, it was actually pretty damn comforting.

Like a champ, she didn't hang around and make it awkward after.

"We'll have a great Christmas, I promise. Even if it's just the three of us," she said as she jumped off my bed and left me alone in my room.

My phone went off, reminding me I'd need to get the screen fixed. It was another text from a person I hadn't spoken to since leaving New York.

I'm going away during the holidays and won't have service, so I wanted to get in touch and say merry Christmas early. And a happy New Year. I hope you make the most of it—for all the reasons we discussed. I truly wish you well, Hendrix.

I typed out and deleted my response a dozen times before giving up. She was probably leaving her home over Christmas because she couldn't stand to be there —because of me. I'd taken so much from this woman, and here she was, wishing me well.

I didn't deserve it, and I didn't deserve Aunt Hannah's kindness either.

I needed to remember why I was here, keep my head down, and stop getting sucked into Fulton Academy bullshit. And that meant avoiding Donna.

CHAPTER FOURTEEN

Donna

Clinking glassware and polite laughter punctuated the soft Christmas music playing in the background.

I resisted the urge to tug at the tight waist of my A-line red dress. I wanted to be wearing something dark, short, and plunging, and the only thing I wanted cutting into my waist was a strong arm. I took a sip of my soft drink, wishing it were vodka, or at least champagne.

"Can we bail yet?" Harlow yawned next to me. She was in a gold dress with red details, the two of us matching each other in all but attitudes—at least outwardly.

The cream of Devilbend society, and quite a few prominent San Franciscans, were mingling around our house, drinking mom's best champagne and eating delicate hors d'oeuvres. Our annual Christmas Eve *Eve* party was very different from the last party held in this house—the one that celebrated Mena's birthday, where we made a mess and people got wasted and I started falling for . . .

"Give it another half hour, Harls." I leaned down, keeping my voice low. "Make an effort to talk to someone. It'll make Mom and Dad happy. Then you can grab Mena and Amaya and slip out. I'll cover for you."

"Fine." She rolled her eyes. "Thanks, D."

She wandered off and struck up a conversation with an up-and-coming TV starlet who had recently hired Mom's company to remodel her entire penthouse apartment.

Mena was standing with her parents and Joseph and Vicky Frydenberg—
Will's dad and his much younger latest wife, who looked bored out of her mind.
Thankfully, Will hadn't been able to make it.

Amaya was nowhere to be seen, but her mom had the attention of several
men as she told a story over by the roaring fireplace, her infectious personality
and the ample cleavage on display keeping everyone enthralled. Like mother, like
daughter.

I smoothed the nonexistent wrinkles from my dress and got back to mingling.
Several family members and close friends had come out, but there were also
Mom's and Dad's important clients, business partners, and colleagues. Our
family Christmas would be a much more relaxed, fun celebration over dinner
tomorrow night, then presents on Christmas morning. This party was more a
way for my parents to nurture professional relationships.

Networking made the world go round, and I wasn't going to waste a single
opportunity.

The dean of Fulton Academy was there, and I'd briefly considered raising the
issue of my internship with her—along with Mr. Kirke's less than satisfactory
handling of the situation—but I just made small talk instead. You had to pick
your battles, and I knew that one was lost.

I chatted with my aunt and uncle for a bit as Harlow pulled Mena away and
they slipped out to find Amaya. Then I gave Amaya's mom air-kisses and compli-
mented her on her dress.

No one noticed my friends leave the party. I wished I could ditch too—ignore
everyone, take this fucking dress off, put on my thigh-high boots and go to
Davey's, or even just steal a bottle of champagne when the caterers weren't
looking and hang out with the girls.

But I had goals, ambitions, responsibilities. So I shoved those juvenile urges
down and headed through the crowd to greet the newest guest, my smile genuine
for the first time that evening. Jasmin looked a little uncertain, but I couldn't
blame her. She knew no one here, and the people in attendance could keep the
legal center going for another thirty years with change from their couches. Which
is exactly why I'd made sure Dad put her on the guest list.

"I'm so glad you came." I gave her a hug.

"Thank you for inviting me. You look beautiful, Donna!"

"Thanks! Come meet my parents." I led her over to my mom and dad and did
the introductions. Once they were chatting easily, I moved away.

I caught up with Uncle Heath and his wife, Serena. They'd been friends with
my parents since college and Uncle Heath had inherited his father's chain of
successful stores—GoodGrocer. When all the horrible bullying Mena had been
dealing with came to light, he immediately offered to fire the parents of some of
the kids involved, his face going red at the dinner table. I'd threatened the

assholes with exactly that, but thankfully, the bullies had been dealt with by the police instead.

"How's school going?" he asked.

"Great." I smiled. "All As and breezing through my AP classes."

"That's my smart girl. Come, let me introduce you to Suzanne Brandy. She's a partner at Paulsen and Price." He gently took my elbow and led me to a small group of people by the eight-foot Christmas tree near the bay window.

I knew Suzanne would be there, of course. I'd spent time looking over the guest list and googling anyone I didn't know. She was married to Andrew, a recent business associate of Daddy's. I'd been planning to speak to her at some point regardless.

"Suzanne, such a pleasure to see you again." Heath barged into their conversation, and a couple of people excused themselves, leaving only the lawyer and another woman I wasn't sure I knew. "This is Donna—the Meads' oldest and California's next great legal mind."

I laughed and dropped my gaze. He was right, of course, but this old-money crowd still subscribed to the idea that it was unbecoming of a young lady to be too confident or proud. "You're too kind, and you have to say that. Hello, lovely to meet you."

She shook my outstretched hand. "The pleasure is mine. I'm always happy to meet young people interested in the legal field. Your home is beautiful."

"Thank you. My mother designed every inch and managed the painstaking remodel."

"She's very talented."

"She is." I beamed.

"Heath, you know Raine." Suzanne gestured to the other woman standing with us. "Donna, this is Raine Clayton."

"The founder and CEO of BestLyf." I turned my winning smile on her and stuck my hand out. "Pleased to meet you, ma'am."

"Likewise." She took my hand in a firm, confident grip. We were about the same height, but I was in heels and she was in flats. Her chestnut hair hung loose around her shoulders, and she wore very natural makeup and understated jewelry. She could have been anywhere between forty and sixty years old—either she just had one of those faces or the plastic surgery she'd had was excellent.

We made small talk for a little while, but the longer I stood there, the more I kept seeing the astronomical number I'd spied on that rental statement a couple months ago.

"You know, Raine"—I gave her a polite smile, which she returned before taking a sip of her champagne—"I actually volunteer right near the BestLyf offices."

"Oh?"

"Yes. It's a stunning building. The lobby always looks so inviting yet professional. I have no doubt my mother would give it the interior design tick of approval."

"Thank you. That's so kind." Her eyes crinkled at the edges as her smile widened. "Where do you volunteer? I think it's so important for young people to give back to the community." The last was delivered to the small group of people beginning to gather around us, who all murmured their agreement.

"I volunteer with Devilbend Community Legal Center every two weeks," I told her. "It's right on the corner near your building. Actually, I believe you own the building that the nonprofit rents."

"Do I?" She chuckled, and everyone else did too, not that she'd made an actual joke. "I own so many I can't keep track of them all, dear. I have a team of people managing all my assets."

"Of course." I smiled sweetly. "It's so wonderful that you allow a nonprofit to rent the space. I believe it's just as important for corporations to give back to the community as it is for young people." I threw her words back at her. "If you'd allow me to be so forward, I do wonder if you'd consider looking into this particular property personally? The rent is reasonable for such a prime location downtown, I'm sure, but every penny saved could go toward helping disadvantaged members of the community. It is the season for giving, after all."

Out of the corner of my eye, I saw Uncle Heath bring his scotch up to his mouth, trying to hide an amused smile. But my focus stayed trained on Raine Clayton.

She cocked her head to the side and studied me as if she were seeing me for the first time. Just as the silence was about to extend to an uncomfortable length, a slow smile graced her face. "You're a C3, bordering on C2, *and* easily an A2 also. Remarkable for someone so young."

"Oh, I was thinking the same." Suzanne nodded enthusiastically, looking between us.

"Uh, thank you?" I laughed lightly, trying not to show how much this nutcase was confusing me. "I don't think I'm familiar with those terms."

"Oh, I'm sorry. I live and breathe BestLyf principles. I sometimes forget not everyone knows our lingo. It basically means you're confident and assertive. Not many teenagers are. The combination can come off as arrogant at times."

I frowned. Did she just call me arrogant? But she barreled on before I could respond.

"You have rare leadership talents—the kind one is born with. The kind people undertaking leadership seminars would kill to have."

"Thank you. That's very kind of you to say." She'd given me several compliments, but I itched to probe her about the arrogance comment. I wasn't arrogant. Was I? There was something imposing about her presence, despite her understated look. Or maybe because of it. But the way she spoke, so articulately and with such certainty, was a little mesmerizing.

"Raine is amazing, Donna. Her program got me from a graduate position with an unknown legal firm to being considered for partner at Paulsen and Price within five years. I've learned so much! You should look into their Young Minds program."

"Yes, I think you'd be an ideal candidate." Raine smiled at me warmly, as if she were already proud of the achievements I had yet to accomplish. "And I promise to look into this little rent issue." She waved her hand dismissively and took another sip of champagne.

"Thank you. I'll certainly look into your program." If it could fast-track my plans for the future, I'd be an idiot not to. Maybe I could escape this crushing pressure sooner and start enjoying my life before my forties. *Wow!* What a depressingly middle-aged thought to have. Where the hell had that come from?

"Donna excels at all she does." Uncle Heath gently squeezed my shoulder, the pride in his face so obvious you'd think I was *his* daughter. But Raine was now engaged in conversation with some of the other people gathered around her and was no longer paying attention to either of us.

A tall man in a dark suit walked past in my periphery, and for a moment, I could've sworn Hendrix had just waltzed uninvited through my parents' Christmas party. A quick glance told me it was someone whose name I didn't know, possibly my mom's PA, but that didn't stop the bone-aching urge to turn in his direction from coursing through my body.

The tight waist on the dress felt like a rope around my middle, holding me back from chasing him down. My breathing got shallow, and the conversation I was supposed to be a part of faded into the background.

Every time I thought about how he'd acted the night of the party—how he'd seemed to know what I was feeling and what I needed before I even said it—I got this weird panicky feeling in my chest. My mind couldn't seem to articulate what was racing through it, and my body got fidgety and restless.

I didn't like it.

It was inconvenient and unwanted. The only way to deal with it was to remove the trigger. So I'd started avoiding him. I had the girls help me keep tabs on him under the guise of keeping an eye on a troublemaker, but really, I used the information to avoid bumping into him at school.

The frustrating thing was, the more I avoided him, the worse my reaction was any time I spotted him—or thought I did.

I took another sip, trying to bring myself back to the present. I was being rude, but I'd lost all interest in this conversation, these people, and this party.

Jasmin pushed through the crowd, the worried expression on her face snagging my attention and giving me a good excuse to bail.

"Could you all please excuse me? There's something I need to attend to." I smiled politely and left, catching up to Jasmin just as she reached the makeshift bar area in the foyer.

"Can I get a scotch on the rocks, please? Actually, make it a double." She leaned on the bar heavily as the bartender moved off to pour her drink.

I nudged her shoulder. "Talking to my dad has driven you to drinking?"

"Donna." She straightened, looking at me warily.

I frowned. "Shit. It actually did? What did he say?"

"No, it's not like that. He was lovely. I . . ." She took a deep breath and gave me her customer service smile. "It's Christmas. We don't need to talk about this. Are you having a drink?"

The bartender placed a glass of amber liquid in front of her, and she took a big sip and winced slightly.

"I'm eighteen," I reminded her. "And you run a legal center."

"Ha! Yeah, right. Sorry."

"Jasmin, come on. What's going on? I'm not going to be able to stop worrying. You may as well just tell me."

She watched me warily for a moment, then took another sip of her scotch and nodded. "OK, let's sit somewhere."

Shit. A sit-down conversation. What the hell was this serious? As trepidation clawed at the base of my rib cage, I led her to a chaise lounge in the foyer, away from the party going on in the main living area of the house.

Jasmin was a direct woman—she had to be in her field of work—and she cut right to the chase. "I'm so sorry, Donna, but I have to terminate your volunteer position at the center, effective immediately."

I reeled back as if she'd slapped me. Of all the things I thought she might say, that wasn't even on the list. "What? Why? What did I do?"

"You didn't do anything. You're perfect. But through talking to your father and one of his financial advisors, I realized you or your family are behind a very generous donation we received recently."

"Oh god." I gritted my teeth and resisted the urge to cause a scene. "That was supposed to be anonymous. They shouldn't even be talking about it at a party, for god's sake."

"It was anonymous." She covered my hand with hers, her other tightening around her drink. "And they didn't mention the donation or break any kind of confidentiality. But the mention of certain umbrella companies and trusts . . . it was just business talk for them, but the names were enough for me to put two and two together. I had to make sure, so I pulled your father aside, and he confirmed my suspicion. It was a very generous, kind thing for you to do. Which is why it's so hard for me to have to let you go."

"You didn't have to ask Dad about it. It was anonymous. You could've let it stay anonymous."

"You know I couldn't do that." She gave me a look full of regret. I did know that. She was a stickler for the truth, a tough woman with a strong sense of right and wrong. It was why she was so good at her job.

"I know. I'm sorry. I'm just frustrated. But I still don't see why this means I have to stop volunteering. It's not illegal to donate both money and time, is it?"

"No, it's not. But we have our own company bylaws. We take several students as volunteers every year—most of them use it on their college applications, and along with the connections they're able to make with the attorneys who come to volunteer their services . . . the situation is rife for exploitation. We can't accept money from volunteers or their families. I'm so sorry, Donna, but your donation was very generous. There's no way in hell the board will let me return it to keep you on board for another couple of months."

The fact that she'd even considered returning the money told you all you needed to know about this woman's character.

"I'm so sorry." I wasn't even sure if that was the right thing to say.

"I'm sorry too. But listen, you don't even need us anymore. You've volunteered for over a year. I'm going to write you the best letter of recommendation that ever was, and I just know you'll get that internship with Horowitz, Ross, and Shore."

She didn't know it had already been awarded to someone else. I hadn't even told my parents. I needed this on my college application more than anyone knew. What the hell was I going to do now?

"Right. Of course." I smiled and got to my feet, my hand sliding out from under hers the same way the floor felt as if it were sliding out from under me.

The dress was squeezing all the air out of my lungs; my vision was starting to blur at the edges. I needed to get out of there immediately.

"See that man in the pale blue suit? He's had three champagnes, and I know for a fact this is his sweet spot for opening his wallet. Go schmooze him into a donation for the center."

"Donna, I'm not worried about that right now. Are you OK?"

"I'm totally fine." I squeezed her shoulder; my breaths were coming in shorter and shallower. "I'd introduce you myself, but I really need to go to the bathroom. Sorry."

I turned on my heel and rushed away before she could stop me.

Avoiding everyone's eyes, I took purposeful steps across the foyer. Joseph Frydenberg and Raine Clayton were standing in the corridor leading to the powder room, locked in an intense-looking conversation, but I hurried past, too weighed down by my own shit to worry about Will's dad having another affair.

I managed to control my steps and my breathing until I was in the kitchen with only the catering staff to witness my face falling, my shoulders slumping, my breaths turning to desperate pants for oxygen. But they were all too busy to notice me at all. I stumbled to the back door, steadying myself on the frame while clawing at the front of my dress.

I couldn't breathe. *Why couldn't I breathe?*

Rushing into the dark night, my vision flickering in and out, I walked past the patio and reached behind me with frantic fingers to yank down my dress's zipper. The pressure that had been cutting into my waist all night finally eased, and I gulped down cold air, my feet still carrying me away from the light and noise spilling out of the main house.

My heel caught in a groove between pavers, so I kicked off my shoes and continued down the path barefoot, relishing the sting of the cold night air as my dress slipped down my shoulders.

I walked to the pool and dropped the dress at my feet. My toes touched the curved edge of the pavers in the same spot Hendrix's boots had been that night.

At the thought of him, a sob tore from my throat.

More uncertainty, more confusion.

I wanted him here, but I hardly knew him. He'd probably make me feel worse, but I just wanted him to hold me the way he had at the Halloween party.

I *hated* that I wanted that, that I craved comfort from some guy. I was supposed to be strong, independent, smart. How the hell was my life falling apart this badly?

I didn't know what to do with myself. Going back to the party was not an option. Finding my friends in this state was not an option. There was only one thing to do—keep moving forward.

I stepped off the edge and into the frigid black water.

It enveloped me, wrapped its smooth coolness around every inch of my body, muted the faraway noises of the party. It wasn't *his* embrace, but it was an embrace of sorts. A muted oblivion I craved more the longer I held my breath and stayed under.

The burning in my lungs made me feel alive. I opened my mouth, squeezed my eyes shut, and screamed. Air bubbles burst from my mouth, floating up, up, up as I released all the pent-up ugliness inside me into the water.

Once I had no air left, my body reacted on instinct. My feet and arms pushed me to the surface, and I gasped, spluttering and coughing, taking air into my lungs once more. But I felt cleansed. I'd let all that other, ugly air out, and I was taking this new, fresh air in.

My limbs felt drained when I reached the edge, and I leaned on the side of the pool to catch my breath.

I needed to clear my head properly, reset, have a break. I needed Davey's. It had been weeks since I'd gone, reluctant to return after what happened with Hendrix in the alleyway. For some reason, I couldn't imagine taking any other guy out there.

But enough was enough. I just needed to not think about anything for a little while so I could get back to thinking clearly. Going to Davey's was the only sure-fire way to do that. I'd have to wait a few days, just get through Christmas, then Harlow would go into a routine of staying up to a stupid hour and sleeping half the day, and Mom and Dad would go back to work until New Year's. It would be risky, but I could make it work. After all, the risk factor was half the appeal.

Mind made up, I felt better already. And I was shivering.

I waded to the stairs at the end of the pool and dragged myself out, dripping disappointment and failure all over the travertine.

I pulled my dress on over my soaked underwear and tights, slipped into the house through a side door, and locked myself in my bedroom.

CHAPTER FIFTEEN

Hendrix

"Huh?" I glanced at Shady when he bumped my shoulder, but almost instantly, my eyes were drawn back to the good girl gone bad.

For all the effort she put into playing a party girl—the messy hair, the heavy makeup, the slutty clothes—she still looked as if she owned this dump and the whole damn town. Even that motherfucking leopard-print minidress somehow looked sophisticated on her. Some women just had that inexplicable class you couldn't hide. It was why anyone with a dick was watching her as intently as I was as she danced along to some grungy shit. Two games of pool had completely ground to a halt, the bikers at the tables drooling over their own beards as they leaned on their pool cues.

"Dude!" Shady whacked me on the shoulder this time.

I didn't hesitate to shove his skinny ass back. "What?" I scowled, and he threw his hands up, his mouth twitching into a smile.

"Are you listening at all?" He righted himself on his barstool and took another sip of his bourbon and dry.

I took a long sip of my own drink—mineral water with lemon—and tried to remember what he was talking about. I had no fucking clue. I'd tuned him out completely so I could watch her.

My eyes started to drift to the dance floor again, but I ground my teeth and stopped myself.

"Yeah, yeah. I heard you," I mumbled to Shady, hoping it was vague enough to fool him. No way in hell was I about to admit I was distracted by a quality piece of ass.

"Sweet." He sat up a little straighter. "So, you're in?"

Fuck. That couldn't be good. With Shady, he could be asking for anything from a lift home to a kidney.

"That's not what I said." I gave him a reproachful look. "I'll think about it."

He eyed me for a second, eyes narrowing in suspicion, then nodded. "All right."

Hopefully I hadn't just agreed to consider selling a pound of pills to the spoiled rich kids at my school for him. The guy had a big heart, but his sense of morality was beyond skewed.

Shady downed the rest of his drink and waved the bar chick over. I could no longer stop my eyes from looking for Donna in the crowd.

She was definitely a complication, but I couldn't seem to get her off my mind, her smell out of my nose, the feel of her ridiculously soft skin from under my palms. She was *everywhere*, and I wanted her to be *nowhere* so I could get through the next few months and get the fuck out of this town, maybe even this country.

I wanted her gone so badly, but when I scanned the crowd and couldn't see her light hair or ridiculous dress, I frowned. Where was she? I'd only looked away for a few minutes to get Shady off my back.

Did she take another guy out to the dumpsters? My teeth clenched so hard I was close to cracking one. I was half off my barstool before I knew what I was doing, but then Shady's hand appeared on my chest.

"Seriously?" he said. "What the fuck is up with you tonight, bro? I don't think you've heard half of what I've said."

The urge to pick his lanky ass up and throw him over the bar was overwhelming, but this was why I didn't drink anymore. Just as quickly as the murderous rage came over me, I leashed it, shoved it back into its cage, and slammed the door shut. I'd die before I threw another fist.

I rolled my head and took a deep breath . . . and that's when I spotted her.

She came out of the ladies' room, quickly wiping away the look of disgust that marred her perfect features. I laughed under my breath and lowered myself back onto the stool. She liked to play the bad girl, but she was grossed out by the nasty bathroom in the dodgy bar. You can take the girl out of the private school, but you can't take the privilege out of the girl.

My eyes tracked her as she made her way toward the bar, but I looked away before she got too close. I couldn't have her catching me staring like a dweeb. I wouldn't want her to get the wrong idea. As I turned away, my eyes landed on Shady's amused expression.

He looked over my shoulder, then back to me and grinned. Shit.

"Now it all makes sense." He chuckled.

"I don't know what you're talking about," I mumbled, taking another sip of my soda water.

"Her name is Donna." As if I didn't already know her name. As if I didn't know what she looked like when she came on my fingers. "But don't get your hopes up. She just comes here for a bit of fun."

"Isn't that why we all come here?" I raised a brow.

He laughed. "Yeah, but Donna . . ." He shook his head and blew out a big breath. "She's amazing in the sack, but she's fucking crazy, man. Just be careful."

Of course she'd fucked Shady. Had she opened her legs to every douchebag in this dump? For the second time that night, I resisted the urge to do violent damage to one of my only friends in this world.

"Noted," I informed him, my attention already drawn to the other end of the bar. She was leaning over it with her ass sticking out, the bar chick checking out her tits. Half the women here were into her too.

"Want me to intro? I'm not weirded out by sharing pussy if you aren't." Shady leaned forward and broke my line of sight. "Hell, she'd probably be into a threesome if you're game."

Three times—that was *three* times I'd wanted to drive my fist through his teeth in the space of half an hour. Because of *her*.

I opened my mouth to tell him to fuck off, but before I could, something behind me caught his eye.

"Shit. Never mind. I gotta go talk to a man about a dog." He downed the rest of his drink and disappeared into the crowd without even waiting for a response. I didn't even want to know what shit he was getting into now.

My view of Donna was unobstructed again. I tried really hard not to stare, but it was fucking impossible when I knew what her tits felt like in my hands. Now they were resting on the bar, and I wanted to pulverize the bar. This was ridiculous. I huffed, disgusted with myself, just as she looked up and our eyes met.

She glared at me and paid for her drink. Something inside me stirred at the anger in her gaze. The two times we'd hooked up, she was livid. It was as if my dick had learned that anger in her eyes meant action. I adjusted myself as she marched over, her shoulders back, tits and hair bouncing.

I gulped my drink, both dreading and craving whatever was about to come.

She leaned one hand on the bar and propped the other on her hip. "We hook up a couple of times, and you all of a sudden think you have the right to follow me around? Seriously?"

I turned my head but kept my body facing the bar, shielding my vital organs from her perfectly manicured claws. "I'm pretty sure I'm the least creepy guy in this dump, but whatever."

"Stop deflecting, Hendrix. Did you follow me here?"

I frowned, letting some of my frustration show. "You may be under the delusion that you own Devilbend, but in case you haven't noticed, Dorothy, this isn't

Kansas. No, I didn't fucking follow you, and I have just as much right to be here as you. Which, technically, is none, since we're both underage."

She scoffed and crossed her arms. "OK, *mom*. Just stay out of my way."

"You're the one who came over here and started screeching at me. I'm literally just sitting here minding my own business. *You* stay out of *my* way."

Her lips pursed as her breathing quickened slightly, those perfect tits swelling with every inhale. It took more than a little effort to keep my eyes off them, but I did. I gave myself a mental high five and smiled. I knew I looked every bit the self-satisfied asshole she thought I was, but her obvious fury only made my smile wider.

This was kind of fun.

"What are you doing here anyway?" She chugged her drink and didn't even wince, making me wonder if she was pulling the same trick with the soda and lemon I was.

"Same thing you're doing here." *Lies.* But she didn't need to know that. To drive my point home, I looked over her shoulder, spotted a tall brunette with waves down to her jean-clad ass, and eyed her up and down the same way every other deadbeat had been ogling Donna all night.

She followed my gaze and scoffed. "You're such a pig. Just stay out of my way."

Without giving me a chance to reply, she moved back to the other end of the bar, but I watched her check out the brunette as she passed. She had that appraising look all women had when sizing up their competition—pursed lips, one raised eyebrow, the quick up-and-down glance.

I covered my mouth to hide the grin I couldn't hold back.

This was a dangerous game Donna Mead and I were playing, but it was the most fun I'd had in a long time.

Unfortunately, the brunette must've noticed me checking her out, because she suddenly appeared in front of me, blocking my view of Donna.

"Hi." She smiled and looked at me through long lashes. Her glossy lips wrapped around a straw, and she took a long pull of her drink.

She was pretty, and I probably would've gone for it had I not still been hard for the infuriating, entitled bitch who had just walked away.

I gave her a disinterested "hey."

Her boobs pressed against my arm as she leaned in to say something, but between the loud music and my every sense acutely keeping track of Donna, I didn't hear a word. She just wasn't going away though, and really, she didn't deserve to be led on.

I looked at her properly. "Listen, can I be honest?"

She nodded.

"I'm interested in someone else. When I checked you out, I was just trying to make her jealous."

She pouted but gave me a smile. "The cute blonde?"

"Yeah." My eyes sought her out in the crowd again. She was dancing with some thirty-year-old-looking motherfucker with a beard and hand tats, but she kept glancing in my direction. Was she trying to make *me* jealous?

"She's a lucky girl."

I scoffed. "I don't know about that."

"Is she still looking?"

I glanced over her shoulder. "Yeah."

The brunette gave me a cheeky smile and leaned in, trailing a hand up my arm and across my shoulders. Then she tilted her head and tucked it into my neck. I wrapped an arm around her waist and angled my body into her. It would've looked as though she was kissing my neck and I was into it. I mean . . . I wasn't *not* into it . . . but only because I knew it was probably making Donna furious.

"You smell amazing too," the brunette said. "Such a shame."

"Thanks for being cool about it." I gave her hip a squeeze.

She shrugged and smiled one last time before turning and making her way to the exit.

Do not look at Donna. Do not *look at Donna.* Do not look at Donna.

I downed the rest of my drink and mentally patted myself on the back for not looking at Donna as I got off the barstool and headed for the exit too. It was time to go home. If Donna happened to think I was leaving with the brunette, that was her problem.

But as I skirted the edge of the dance floor, I couldn't help taking a glance.

Right away, my eyes caught the flick of her light hair as she turned, the hand-tat guy leading her toward the bar. Another guy with a low ponytail and a bit of a beer gut leaned into her other side, and she laughed at whatever he said.

She glanced behind her, and I slunk into the shadows, leaning back against the wall. Something didn't sit right, and I wasn't willing to admit to myself that I hated seeing her with two lowlifes. So I stayed and watched like the creep she'd accused me of being.

They went to the bar and ordered drinks. Three glasses were delivered—two with amber liquid and one with clear. At least she was still smart enough to stay sober.

Hand tats told some kind of joke, getting her full attention as they all laughed. While she was facing him, ponytail reached into his pocket and dumped something into her drink.

I pushed off the wall, my hands tightening into fists. What the fuck? Did no one else see that?

Of course fucking not. Everyone here was too drunk or high, too wrapped up in their own shit. Before I could bulldoze my way through the crowd and stop her, they cheered, and she gulped down most of her drink in one go. I had no idea what they'd given her, but I wasn't sure I could take them both. I just knew I couldn't let her out of my sight, couldn't let them take her from here.

This was none of my business—I'd been heading out the door anyway—and Donna was a bitch, but she didn't deserve this. *No one* deserved this.

So I hung around for a little while and watched.

She stumbled over her own feet while standing still, and hand tats steadied her before sharing a grin with ponytail. My vision went red, thoughts of tearing the fuckers to pieces assaulting my mind. But I had to keep my shit together.

Keeping Donna in my periphery, I scanned the crowd and spotted Shady at the end of the bar area. I beelined for him, bumping into drunks and bikers as I went. Donna was leaning heavily on the bar now with her head in her hands, while the two men hovered like the predators they were.

"Shady." I interrupted his conversation with a smack on the shoulder, barely sparing him a glance.

"Hendy, bro, I'm in the middle of some business here," he ground out.

I grabbed him by the collar of his tracksuit and leaned in close. "Some pieces of shit just drugged Donna. I can't take them alone. Come on, man."

I wasn't above begging, but I hoped the asshole's humanity would kick in before I had to.

Shady got to his feet and excused himself from the conversation he'd been having, ordering another round of expensive whiskey and stating he'd be right back after he took out the trash. Then he gestured to two of his buddies.

I kept my focus on Donna. Her feet started falling out from under her, and the two scum propped her up on either side and started helping her stumble toward the exit.

I rushed toward them, no longer caring if I had to take the two of them alone, no longer caring if I had to take *twenty*.

We cut them off barely ten feet from the door.

"Let her go," I growled, already reaching for her. Her eyes rolled into the back of her head, then focused, then rolled again.

"Back off, asshole." Ponytail scowled. He was even uglier up close.

"Hen . . . hel . . . h . . . ," Donna mumbled. Was she trying to say my name or "help"? It didn't matter. She was getting both.

Shady and his guys finally caught up. They didn't ask questions. They simply shoved the two shit stains out of the way as I stepped in and wrapped my arms around Donna. As I held her delicate frame against my chest, her legs gave out, her arms went completely limp, and her head rolled back.

Panic choked me; the shriveled thing in my chest passing for a heart constricted, then started hammering.

I scooped her up and pushed the door open with my shoulder. All I knew was that I had to get her out of there. Maybe to a hospital.

Shady caught up with me halfway to my car.

"How's she doin?'" He brushed some hair off her forehead. Lucky for him, both my hands were busy holding the unconscious waif of a girl.

"I don't know," I growled. "What the fuck did they give her?"

"Just a roofie."

This time I growled but no words came out. *Just* a roofie?

Shady gave me a sharp look as we stopped at my Tesla. "Chill, bro. She won't remember shit in the morning, but she'll be fine. They were trying to knock her out, not kill her. Rohypnol is a benzo—it's like she's taken a couple of xannies. It's not gonna kill her or anything."

In place of an answer, I gave him an instruction. "Get the door."

"You want me to take her, man? I'll take care of it. I've known this chick for a while." He opened the car door wide and stepped out of the way.

"No," I barked. I didn't trust anyone with an unconscious Donna, let alone a guy who went by Shady. But I forced my tone to lighten up as I lowered her gently into the passenger seat. "I got it. She goes to my school. We . . . I know her. I'll make sure she's safe."

Shady remained silent as I fastened the seat belt over Donna's limp body.

"You sure?" His eyes flicked between us as I straightened.

"I'm sure. Are you sure that's what they gave her? Maybe I should take her to a hospital."

He cringed and rubbed the back of his neck. "I wouldn't, bro. It would look hella sus, you bringing in a chick you hardly know, roofied. Aren't you supposed to be staying out of trouble?"

I didn't give a shit what kind of trouble it landed me in. I wasn't about to risk someone's life—not again.

"Anyway"—he shrugged—"it's definitely Rohypnol. We beat it out of 'em pretty quick."

I sighed, said goodbye to Shady, and got into the driver's side. Even though I didn't care what kind of questions a hospital visit would raise, I knew Donna would. No one knew about her secret little walks on the wild side, but maybe it was time they did.

CHAPTER SIXTEEN

Donna

I wasn't sure if the pounding in my head had woken me or if waking up had caused the pounding. All I knew was that I felt like shit.

I groaned, squeezing my eyes shut and mushing my face farther into the pillow. My stomach felt as if it were doing somersaults while twirling my intestines into a knot. I was so fucking hungover that—

My eyes flew open, immediately making me wince against the light, but I had bigger problems. There was no way I could be hungover, because I hadn't been drinking last night. I never drank or did drugs when I went to Davey's.

Panic clawed at my throat as I forced myself to look around. The sheets were gray, the desk under the window cluttered, a TV sat in the corner. *This wasn't my room.*

Where the hell was I?

How did I get here?

What happened to me?

Fighting the bile rising up my throat, I lifted myself into a sitting position and couldn't help groaning again. I'd never felt this crap before—not even when I had the flu last year. And that was so bad the doctors nearly put me on IV fluids.

The fact that I had no idea where I was or any memory of how I got there was beyond disturbing. I wasn't an idiot—I knew what happened to girls in shady bars sometimes. It was why I went there—the danger of the *maybe*. I just never thought I'd actually end up . . . *oh god*. I sucked in several deep breaths, fighting for air through the panic and the nausea and the hot tears pricking my eyes.

Was I raped?

I swallowed a sob and, with shaky hands, pushed the comforter and tangled sheets off myself completely. I was still in my leopard-print dress, my thong still in place. The only things missing were my shoes, but I spied them on the floor at the foot of the bed.

I shifted my legs. I didn't feel sore between them, but would I? If I was out and didn't fight it . . .

The room spun, bringing on another wave of nausea, and I lowered myself back to the pillow with a pathetic half sob, half whimper.

I had to get the fuck out of there, but I couldn't even get my body to stand.

Closing my eyes, I forced myself to take deep breaths through the churning in my stomach and the pounding in my head. I needed to get my shit together and get up.

My eyes flew open again at the sound of the door opening, but the only movement I could force my body into was rolling onto my back and turning my head to look.

"Hendrix?"

He was barefoot, in sweats and a T-shirt that was baggy even on his broad, muscular frame. One of his hands clutched a bright pink mug.

"Oh. Hey. You're up." I'd never seen the asshole look so uncertain. His eyes flicked about the room, not staying on me too long. "How . . . uh . . . you OK?"

"Am I . . ." My bruised brain was struggling to keep up, not processing information at its usual rate, but I got there in the end. "No, I'm not fucking OK. What did you do to me?"

I didn't shout—I *seethed*, spitting my accusation at him, as hot as the liquid in his steaming mug.

He threw his free hand up and stepped away until his back was to the door.

Was he trying to block my exit?

"I didn't do anything to you. All I did was bring you here, take your shoes off, and tuck you into bed." His voice was calm, low, deep.

More confusion. Why couldn't I remember anything? "Whose bed is this?"

"Mine."

My eyes narrowed. "You expect me to believe . . . that . . . I . . . you . . ."

I growled and punched the bed next to me, then threaded my fingers through my hair. I'd never been this incoherent, *ever*.

"I didn't hurt you." Hendrix's voice was still calm, but now it had a hard edge to it. "I'm not a rapist. I've done a lot of bad shit—and one awful, unforgiveable thing—but I didn't hurt you. No one hurt you. You're safe."

I lifted my head to look at him, breathing hard. An infuriating tear fell down my cheek, but there was no pity in Hendrix's gaze. He looked tired more than anything—bags under his eyes, hair a mess, eyelids drooping. As if to prove my point, he yawned and took a gulp of what I assumed must be coffee.

"You look worse than I feel," I said as I slowly sat up again. The nausea was easing somewhat.

"Thanks," he deadpanned.

"What happened to you?"

"Someone had to make sure you kept breathing all night." He looked away, took another sip.

All night? "What the fuck happened to me, Hendrix?"

"What's the last thing you remember?" He dragged his feet across the room and plonked down into the chair at his desk, backward, his arms resting on the back.

I looked down and forced myself to really think about it.

I remembered dancing at Davey's, feeling all my worries melt away into the sticky floor and the heavy bass of the music.

I remembered Hendrix, the immediate pang of irritation, how hard it was to ignore his presence.

I remembered us bickering at the bar, and then . . .

"I was dancing with these two guys." I swallowed, my gaze still on his gray comforter. "You left with the brunette. We went to the bar . . ." I trailed off and looked at him. He was resting his chin on his arms, watching me, waiting. I cleared my throat. "Bea, the bar chick—she knows never to pour me alcohol, regardless of whether I order it or someone else does. It doesn't make sense . . ."

"Bea didn't pour vodka into your soda. One vodka doesn't make you pass out cold within twenty minutes. The two lowlifes you were hanging out with roofied you."

I blinked once, slowly. When I woke up in a strange bed with no memory of how I got there, I'd suspected as much, but having him say it in plain English brought the fact home. I dropped my gaze and swallowed around the lump in my throat. I *really* didn't want to cry in front of Hendrix Hawthorn—again.

"Are you sure . . ." I wasn't even positive what I was asking. That it wasn't any other drug? That it actually happened?

"I watched them slip it into your drink. Shady and his boys beat the details out of them while I got you out of there. I was going to take you straight to a hospital, but I wasn't sure you'd want that, considering no one even knows about . . . your visits to Davey's. So I sat in the parking lot googling the shit out of Rohypnol, and when I was convinced you weren't about to die on me, I decided to just take you home. But then I started getting paranoid about what kind of home situation I'd be dropping you into. So then I fished your phone out of your purse to call one of your friends, but you have a damn passcode on it. I was gonna ring

Turner so I could talk to Mena, but by that stage, I was questioning whether to bring your friends into it at all. In the end, I decided to bring you here. To my place. I figured I'd pick up and explain if someone called, but it didn't ring all night."

Of course it didn't ring. No one even knew I was out of my bed. He finished off his coffee, his gray eyes boring into mine over the mug's rim.

He hadn't left with the brunette. He'd seen someone trying to drug me and stepped in to prevent them doing worse. He took care of me, stayed up all night to make sure I was OK . . .

I frowned at him, trying to figure it out. We'd hardly spoken, had two admittedly hot but mostly rage-fueled hookups. He'd said on more than one occasion that he wanted nothing to do with me, and I couldn't count the number of times I'd wished he'd just disappear and stop complicating my life.

He returned my frown, leaning back against the desk. "Look, believe what you want, but that's the truth."

"I believe you," I rushed out. "I'm just . . . not feeling the best."

His cloudy expression lifted, and he got to his feet. "No wonder. Nausea and fatigue are common aftereffects of being roofied. It's like an extremely bad hangover—you might be super tired for a few days and nauseated, and you might have diarrhea. I can take you to the hospital to get checked out if you want."

"No." I shook my head, immediately regretting it as pain shot through my skull. "That was a good call. No hospital. No records. No one can know about this. And please never talk to me about having the runs again. Just . . . drive me to my car. What time is it?" Eventually someone would come knocking on my bedroom door.

"Your secret's safe with me, princess. You can shower if you want." He pointed to a closed door next to his desk. "I'll get you some breakfast. I have better shit to do with my time than play *Driving Miss Daisy* today, but you've had a rough night, so I'll cut you some slack and drive you to your carriage."

Despite the horrid way I felt, the hint of a smile pulled at my lips. Snark was familiar territory for us, and it was making me feel better.

He collected his empty mug; gave me an exaggerated, mocking bow; and closed the door with a soft *click* on his way out.

I checked my phone and cringed. It was just after nine. Harlow would still be in bed, and Mom and Dad had mentioned brunch with the Frydenbergs. I'd been planning to be in bed when they left, but now I probably had two hours max before they got home. I hoped that was enough time to drive to Davey's and back.

But first—shower. I could've skipped it to save time, but I felt gross, dirty. I dragged my ass out of Hendrix's bed, doing my best not to think about the fact that I was *in Hendrix's bed*, in his room, in his house. What would he be doing if I wasn't here?

In the bathroom, a wave of nausea hit me so fucking hard I literally collapsed onto the floor. Luckily, I was close enough to the toilet that I was able to get to it before I vomited, my stomach spasming violently.

Once I was positive I was done puking, I pulled myself to my feet and found a clean towel and some dark gray sweats folded neatly on the counter. I frowned, struggling to reconcile this thoughtful side of him with the antagonistic prick I'd gotten to know and . . . er . . . just know.

After a quick shower where I was forced to use his shampoo and bodywash, I dressed quickly, pulling the sweatshirt over my head. When I paused and brought the fabric up to my nose—closing my eyes and inhaling the fresh, clean scent with just a hint of cinnamon—I froze.

The mindless act had me wondering if I hadn't been given some other drug the previous night—one that altered your personality. I scowled at myself in the mirror, wrenched the sweatshirt back off, and threw it into the far corner.

Grudgingly, I pulled my leopard-print dress back on but wore it like a tank, tucked into the too-long borrowed sweats.

I stashed my bra and thong in my purse and headed for the door, but I paused just before my hand touched the doorknob. What if his parents didn't know I was here? I didn't want to get him in trouble. I also didn't want to deal with any more human interaction than absolutely necessary.

Before I could make a decision, the door flew open, nearly whacking me in the nose. "Fuck! Watch it!"

The surprised look on Hendrix's face melted into annoyance. "Who the fuck just stands in front of a door like that?"

"Who the fuck goes barging into a room so violently?"

"It's my room."

"I could've been naked." I crossed my arms, fully aware that it was pushing my tits up—and getting way more satisfaction than I should have when he glanced down at them.

"Were you?" His voice dropped, and he smirked.

I rolled my eyes. Even if I wanted to entertain the idea of hooking up with this infuriating asshole again, I still felt like death warmed up. The shower had helped, but it wasn't magic.

"Can we get going? I need to be home before anyone realizes I'm not."

"Do you want to eat something first?"

My stomach roiled at the mere mention of food, and I shook my head, breathing through my nose.

"OK." He rubbed my back for a moment but didn't linger. In a few seconds, he'd pulled on some socks and tennis shoes and jammed a baseball cap onto his head. I wished it was that easy for girls to get ready. I wished anything was that easy for me. But perfection took time and effort.

He led me through the silent, empty house and out the front door. I wanted to ask where his parents were, if he had siblings, but I kept my mouth shut. It was a nice place, not as big or ostentatious as mine, but respectable. I supposed it would have to be if they could afford to send him to Fulton Academy.

Once we got on the road, his Tesla gliding smoothly around corners, I realized he lived only a few streets away from me. I ducked lower in the seat and sighed. I'd have to drive forty minutes to get my damn car, only to come back to essentially the same place.

He was silent until we hit the freeway, then he reached over and turned on the stereo. Metallica blasted out of the speakers, and I cried out at the pounding in my head, clapping my hands over my ears. He turned it down. I glared at him and turned it *off*.

"No music. Just . . . no anything. God, I wish the sun would fuck off." I covered my eyes with my elbow and groaned. It was a chilly winter day, but the California sun was shining as brightly as ever. *Dick.*

Hendrix's cinnamon scent hitting the back of my nose made me crack an eye open. He'd leaned over to open the glove box and was pulling out a pair of Ray-Bans, which he handed to me. They were super dark, and I jammed them over my eyes immediately.

I looked over and studied him from behind the anonymity of the shades. Once again, he'd done something thoughtful without being asked.

Who the fuck are you, Hendrix Hawthorn?

I pushed the thought away as soon as I could. He'd already thrown me off-balance. I needed less Hendrix in my life, not more. What I needed more of was control.

As I studied his profile—the slight kink in his nose, the way his jaw tensed and relaxed as he chewed his gum, the corded muscle in his forearm as he gripped the steering wheel—I realized I still hadn't thanked him. I may have decided to keep him out of my life and my thoughts, but he had saved me from something I could hardly think about without feeling as if I might vomit.

I may have been a bitch, but I gave credit where it was due.

I cleared my throat and sat up a little straighter. "Hendrix?"

He hummed in response, keeping his eyes on the road.

"About last night . . ."

"Yeah?"

"Thank you."

He shifted in his seat, but before he could speak, I rushed on. "I know you don't like me, and I don't like you, so what you did for me last night—it means a lot. You could've just walked away. I wouldn't have blamed you. I got myself into that position. But you didn't. You could've been putting yourself in danger by doing that. Anyway, I'm rambling. Point is, I know it was no small thing, you stepping in and stopping them from . . ." I had to swallow and take a breath, but I made myself say it. ". . . from taking me. Maybe raping and killing me. You may very well have saved my life, and I'm grateful."

He was silent for a bit longer.

"You didn't," he finally said, and I frowned in confusion. "What you said about putting yourself in that position—don't blame yourself. I mean, going to Davey's is stupid and dangerous, but it is not your fault that those skid marks decided to drug you and hurt you. That's on them."

"I'm not victim blaming myself, you jerk. I know it wasn't my fault. I'm trying to thank you."

"Fine. Good. You're welcome." His hand tightened on the steering wheel, and he chewed his gum a little faster.

I stared out the window, wondering briefly if it was even safe for me to be driving yet. But I was feeling better after the shower.

It wasn't long before we were pulling into the empty parking lot of Davey's. Miraculously, my white BMW was still there and not stripped for parts, despite how out of place it looked among the cracked concrete and chain-link fencing.

"Donna." Hendrix's serious tone made me pause as I unfastened my seat belt.

"Yeah?"

"Are you going to stop going? After last night . . ."

I bristled and took Hendrix's sunglasses off so I could narrow my eyes at him properly. The thought had crossed my mind. Was the sense of freedom, the brief escape that Davey's provided, worth the risk? Shit had gotten pretty real the night before. But who the fuck did he think he was to assume he could ask me that?

"I don't know," I gritted out, reminding myself he'd done me a solid and I should cut him at least a little slack. "But that's not really any of your concern, is it?"

"Jesus." He rolled his eyes. "Why do you have to be so fucking defensive all the time? I'm just trying to look out for you."

"Why? Why do you give a shit? I'm nothing to you. We're nothing. I appreciate what you did last night, I really do, but that doesn't give you an automatic right to have an opinion regarding my life."

I got out of the car, my purse and heels clutched to my chest, not even caring that I was barefoot in a parking lot probably covered in needles.

"Thanks for the ride." I tried to say it in a neutral tone, but I was so riled up and raw from everything that it came out sounding sarcastic. Frustrated with myself, and the entire situation, I slammed the door shut.

His tires threw up dirt and gravel as he peeled out of the parking lot and disappeared.

Good. I didn't need anyone else trying to control my life. I had enough of that from society, from my parents, from my own damn self.

I hobbled to my car, scrambled into it quickly, and locked the doors. It felt as if someone was watching me. I knew it was just paranoia, but it still made my heart hammer in my chest and my hands shake a little as I reached for the ignition.

I'd wanted a thrill when I started coming to Davey's, an adrenaline rush. But I never wanted this.

CHAPTER SEVENTEEN

Hendrix

I drove straight home, grinding my teeth and intentionally speeding—something I hadn't done since I'd left New York. I knew it was stupid, reckless, could send me right back there. But nothing else seemed to ease this infuriating pressure in my head, the incessant need to *do something* thrumming through my body.

I'd stuck exactly to the limit on the way there, unwilling to put Donna in any unnecessary danger—she did that plenty herself. But I'd be lying if I said it wasn't also to get more time with her.

She smelled like my shampoo, and her delicate, warm body was so close, drowning me in her scent mixed with mine. I wanted to pull over at least six times and just hold her, but I resisted. She would've kneed me in the balls and taken off with my car, and I wouldn't have blamed her. Not after what she'd just gone through.

That girl was spiraling. I didn't really know what her deal was, hadn't figured her out completely yet, but she'd been sloppy. Donna Mead was many things, but she was *not* sloppy. It had been desperation driving her, and she'd let her guard down.

Was it me? Maybe my presence had distracted her. No, fuck that! I wasn't about to blame myself for some despicable shit a couple of lowlifes pulled.

I just wanted her to stop going there before she got raped, murdered, or kidnapped into human trafficking. I'd carried her lifeless body out of there the night before. *Excuse me* for being concerned.

But no, all she saw was me sticking my nose into her business. God, she was fucking infuriating. Least of all because I wanted to *not* care. I wanted to call her a bitch, say I didn't give a shit what she did with her life, and actually mean it.

Lost in my rage-filled thoughts, I nearly shot past Aunt Hannah's house before slamming on the brakes and skidding to a stop.

Gripping the steering wheel so hard I felt as if it might snap in half, I forced a few deep breaths down my throat. When that didn't fucking work, I growled and got out of the car. Maybe blowing some shit up on a big screen would distract me.

I barreled into the house and slumped onto the couch, but instead of reaching for the remote, I found myself just clenching my fists repeatedly, thinking about how fucking helpless she'd looked passed out in my bed all night.

"Hey."

I shot to my feet at my aunt's casual greeting, every muscle in my body tense.

"Whoa." Her eyes widened in surprise, her OJ halfway to her mouth as she leaned against the wall. "Sorry to interrupt your intense scowling session there. You all right?"

"Shit." I ran my hands through my hair for about the millionth time in the past twenty-four hours. I was going to go bald at this rate. "Sorry. I . . . you just startled me. I'm fine." I forced a smile that felt fake to its core and lowered myself back to the couch. "I thought you were spending the day with Robbie."

"He got called into work, so I came home." She made her way over to sit down, took a sip of her juice, and looked at me expectantly.

"What?" I tried, and failed, to keep the irritation out of my tone.

"We had a deal, Hendrix. You come to me if you're in any kind of trouble. You're clearly not fine. Start talking, kid."

"I'm not a kid," I argued childishly.

"Then act like it and tell me what's going on."

Damn her and her logic. "Look, I'm not in any kind of trouble, OK? I promise. I'm sticking to our deal."

"Yeah, well, the deal included emotional and existential trouble, so . . ." She gestured for me to start talking.

I gave her a withering look. "I don't remember agreeing to that."

"Should've read the fine print." She took another sip of OJ. "Spill."

Her banter was a good distraction for about two minutes, but the restless, tight feeling in my body just wouldn't leave. Maybe talking about it would help. And my aunt was literally the only person I felt I could trust right now.

"I don't really know where to start."

"How about at the end?"

I laughed despite myself. "Usually people say start at the beginning."

"Yeah, but fuck them. Tell me where you just came from. Obviously it has something to do with this. Then we can work backward."

How the hell was I supposed to tell her I'd just come from dropping off a drugged girl at the seediest bar in the state? Hannah was cool, but even she wasn't *that* cool. Not to mention this wasn't technically even my problem.

"I . . . look . . . it's not really my story to tell. When I said I wasn't in trouble, I wasn't lying."

"But someone else is?"

"Not yet, but she will be if she keeps going like she is. But the fucked-up thing is that when you asked that, my first instinct was to say, 'Not if I have anything to do with it.'"

"Are you romantically involved with this girl?"

I snorted. "Trust me, there's been no romance." There'd been heat, sexual release, a pull damn near impossible to resist, plenty of hurtful words, but no romance . . .

"OK, so then why do you care so much?"

"I don't know!" I pulled at my hair again. "That's a big part of the problem. I wanted to just come here, keep my head down, get good grades, and finish high school before figuring out how to make my life *mean something* after what I did. I didn't even want to make friends. I don't want anything to do with this. But every time I see her . . . doing some stupid shit, I just want to shake her. I see that desperate, caged-animal look in her eyes, and I know exactly how she feels, even if I don't really know her at all. Because I used to feel like that. I used to have that look in my eyes."

"You want to save her from making your mistakes."

I paused, thought about it. "Yes."

"You can't save people who don't want to be saved, Hendrix." She got a knowing, almost faraway look in her eyes, and I had a feeling she was talking about more than just my current situation.

"That's just it though. I think she does. She just won't admit it. And then she makes me feel like shit when I try to be there for her."

"Does she know? About . . ."

"No." I shook my head. "No one knows, and I'd like to keep it that way."

"Fair enough. But I think you should talk to her. In a real way. Try to explain where you're coming from. Lay it all out, and then you have to be OK with what she does with that. You can't force someone to accept your help, but you can say your piece and move on knowing you did all you could."

"She won't talk to me." I slumped against the back of the couch.

"Make her." She shrugged. "You're a big strong man."

"I thought I was a kid."

"Clearly, I was mistaken."

"Did you just advise me to manhandle an innocent young girl?"

"I did no such thing. A man knows how to make someone hear him without resorting to violence or childish yelling." She gave me a pointed look.

I sighed and stared at the ceiling. She was right. I had to make her listen. This churning, unsettling feeling in my gut wouldn't go away until I did.

I got to my feet. "OK. I'll be back."

"Now?" Hannah bugged her eyes out.

"No time like the present. Life's too short. Carpe diem, et cetera, et cetera."

I grabbed my keys and waved over my shoulder as I headed right back to my car.

It took less than ten minutes to drive to her house. The big black metal gates were open wide, her ostentatious driveway curving up and around a bend. The top of the house was just visible in the distance.

I slowed down, nearly came to a stop . . . then pushed down on the accelerator and drove off again, swearing under my breath. I'd driven over here determined to make her listen, but with no idea what I wanted to say.

After pulling over around the corner, I pinched the bridge of my nose. What exactly *did* I want to tell her? I definitely didn't want to detail my whole sordid past. I wasn't ready to talk to anyone about that, let alone the girl who'd managed to get under my skin more than anyone ever had.

Nearly half an hour went by as my mind wandered off on tangents, the same frustrations looping around and around, half-finished sentences floating past. None of it felt right.

I was getting nowhere.

"Fuck it." I started the car.

Driving around the block took almost as long as it had taken me to drive there in the first place, as the properties in the area were massive. I pulled into the driveway and made slow progress up the hill, then parked away from the imposing front doors, on the other side of the fountain.

No way was I going to slink up to that front door looking timid and unsure, so I squared my shoulders, ran a hand through my hair—*again*—and walked up the stairs steadily and confidently.

I rang the doorbell and resisted the urge to fidget as I waited.

Donna's mom pulled the door open—there was no way the petite blonde in three-quarter yoga pants and a loose shirt was a servant. Plus, Donna and Harlow looked like her.

"Hello." She gave me a friendly smile, a hint of curiosity in her gaze. "How can I help you?"

This wasn't my first time introducing myself to rich, proper people or to the parents of a girl I wanted to speak to. I'd had more privileged pussy than I could count—way more practice at this than I cared to admit.

I pulled my Ray-Bans off and flashed her a grin. "Good afternoon, ma'am. I'm so sorry to bother you during the holidays. Please accept my apologies for showing up unannounced. If it wouldn't be too much trouble, I just need to speak with your daughter."

She watched me for a moment, amusement replacing the curiosity in her eyes. "Don't you kids all have cell phones for that?" She was teasing me. I liked her. Is this where Donna got her quick wit?

"Yes, we do, Mrs. Mead, but this is a conversation I'd prefer to have face to face."

"OK then." She looked me up and down one more time. "I'm guessing you're here to see Harlow?"

The younger sister appeared at her mother's side before I could respond, sliding over the highly polished marble in knee-high socks and an oversized hoodie. "Did I hear my name?" She hip-bumped her mother, then looked at me, and her eyes widened. "Ooh! Wow! This should be good. I'll get Donna."

She ran off as suddenly as she'd appeared.

Mrs. Mead raised her eyebrows and cocked her head. "Donna?"

"Yes, ma'am." I nodded, pressing my lips together.

"Come on in then." She stepped to the side and waved me in.

CHAPTER EIGHTEEN

I'd just done up the clasp on my bra when Harlow barged into my room without knocking.

"You'll never guess who's here." She grinned, jumping up onto my bed like a deranged blonde gnome.

"What? Who?" I pulled on a pair of baggy sweats and dug around in my wardrobe for an old hoodie I hadn't worn in years.

She waited until the damn thing was half over my head before dropping the news. "Hendrix Hawthorn."

"*What?*" The word was barked out, but the thick fabric muffled my voice. I scrambled to pull the garment on the rest of the way and caught Harlow's ankle, sending her flopping down onto the bed. "What do you mean Hendrix is here? I'm not in the mood for pranks, Harls."

She shrugged, looking way too amused. "Don't know what to tell ya, sis. He's charming the yoga pants off Mom in the foyer as we speak. And he *specifically* asked for you."

"Fuck." I released my sister and raced for the door, not even caring about my unbrushed, wet hair.

As soon as I'd gotten back—just barely beating my parents home from their brunch—I'd taken another shower. The previous night had left me feeling dirty and off, not to mention I couldn't stop smelling Hendrix's fucking shampoo on myself. I'd had to drive home with my windows rolled down, the frigid air cooling my rage and washing the scent from my nose.

After I thoroughly shampooed—twice—conditioned, and scrubbed every inch of myself, I'd been looking forward to putting on some warm clothing and taking a nap. Oblivion seemed like a really good idea.

But no. Hendrix fucking Hawthorn had to ruin everything.

What the hell was he thinking coming to my house? Was he really going to snitch on me to my family? Maybe I shouldn't have been such a bitch to him when he dropped me off. I really didn't need this shit right now.

I rushed to the landing, then forced myself to slow down as I descended the stairs.

There he stood, chatting to my mom in the same outfit from earlier, his T-shirt stretching over his broad shoulders.

"Hello, Hendrix." I kept my voice even and detached as I reached the bottom.

"Hi, Donna." He gave me a tight smile.

"Hendrix tells me he goes to Fulton with you girls, but he seems to have expertly avoided mentioning what he's doing here." Mom chuckled, and Hendrix's smile became more genuine.

"Beats me." I shrugged. "But please excuse us while I find out."

I pulled Harlow's tennis shoes on—the only footwear by the door that Magda hadn't collected yet—and stepped outside.

"It was a pleasure to meet you, Mrs. Mead," Hendrix told my mother, and then I heard his footsteps follow me down the front stairs.

When I reached the bottom, I turned on him and crossed my arms. "What are you doing here?" I demanded, keeping my voice low and my expression neutral in case someone was watching from the window.

He stuffed his hands into his pockets. "I just came to talk."

"This couldn't wait?"

"Until school starts again? So you can keep avoiding me? Will there ever be a good time, Donna?"

Movement in the corner of my eye caught my attention, and I looked over to see my mom and Harlow standing in the bay window, not even remotely hiding the fact that they were watching us.

I rolled my eyes and took off. "Come on."

Hendrix grinned and waved at them before following me around the house all the way to the pool area.

"OK, so talk." I cocked a hip, squinting against the sunlight glaring off the pool. It was already giving me a headache.

He huffed out a breath and ran a hand through his hair. Hints of auburn glinted under the direct sunlight, and I had the sudden urge to run my fingers through his dark hair too, see the colors shift at my touch.

"Look," he said, "I don't know why we keep ending up at each other's throats, and I'm sorry for driving off on you earlier. I just want to talk to you about Davey's."

I threw my head back and groaned. "Not this shit again."

"I don't want to argue. Just, please, hear me out."

I gave him a look, not even trying to mask my displeasure. "Will you leave if I do?"

He pressed his lips together and nodded, and I plonked down onto a lounger. Standing was starting to make me feel woozy again.

Hendrix sat down across from me and leaned his elbows on his knees. "Why do you go there?"

"Why do you care?"

"You said you'd hear me out."

"Yeah. I never agreed to answer questions."

"For fuck's sake, why do you have to be so difficult? I'm trying to help you."

"*Why do you care?*" I enunciated each word. I couldn't figure him out, and it was pissing me off. "Are you into me or something? You wanna be my boyfriend? Is that it?"

I was mocking him, but I also wasn't ready to hear his answer to that question.

I didn't think I could stand it if he said yes; everything would change.

I didn't think I could stand it if he said no; *nothing* would change.

Before he could answer, I barreled on. "Because this is never going to happen. And what's more, I'm not interested in being with someone who thinks they can control me, tell me where I can and can't go. My plan is to eventually settle down with William anyway."

"Will?" He looked somewhere between perplexed and disgusted. "That cardboard cutout of a guy? What could you possibly see in him? And what do you mean you plan to eventually settle down with him? This isn't 1876. You're either in love with the guy or you're not."

"I didn't ask for your opinion on my life choices, asshole! And I don't have to explain jack shit to you."

He ignored that and kept picking apart what I'd said. "And I'm not trying to control you. I'm trying to *understand* you, maybe help you avoid making the same mistakes I did."

"What the actual fuck are you talking about?" I dropped my head into my hands. Usually I at least partly enjoyed the challenge of verbal sparring, but today, I was just exhausted, beaten down. All I wanted to do was go to sleep. "You can't keep demanding to know deeply personal shit about me while not offering up any of your own, Hendrix."

He was silent for a long time. I just enjoyed the peace and quiet and watched a line of ants marching between the pavers near my feet.

"I moved here from New York, where I was born and grew up."

I lifted my head to look at him. He was in the same position across from me, but he was looking out at the view beyond the pool now, squinting against the sun just as I had.

"My parents are just as filthy rich and influential back home as yours are here," he continued. "I went to the best, most exclusive school on the East Coast —the only place harder to get into than Fulton. And I ruled that place. I'm not saying that to talk myself up. You know exactly what I mean, because it's the same position you're in at Fulton. People look up to you, follow your lead, want to be your friend. You can ruin their lives if you really want to. That's why I came to you at the very start—I knew if I wanted to be left alone, the quickest way to ensure it would be to piss you off."

He sighed and looked me dead in the eyes. "I know what it's like to have all those eyes on you, because I had them. I know what kind of immense pressure you're under, because I was. I may not know exactly what makes you crave the depravity and danger of Davey's, but I know that look in your eye. The desperate one that tells me you'll do anything to keep chasing that feeling you get. I had it too. Until I went too far. I did something . . . unforgiveable. Something that ruined *everything*. I just want to help you avoid it."

"What did you do?" I couldn't help myself. I had to know.

He winced and rubbed the back of his neck. "I can't talk about it. I . . . I'm not sure if I can trust you with that. Yet."

"You know I could just find out, right? You've given me enough information to do some digging. It wouldn't take much."

"I know. But I also know you like a challenge." He smiled, but it didn't reach his eyes. And he was right, damn him. I wanted to hear it from his own lips.

"Donna, I know you're a strong, intelligent, independent woman." I bit the inside of my cheek to keep from smiling at the compliment. "I'm not trying to tell you what to do. But you know just as well as I do how dangerous Davey's is. After what happened last night, that should be painfully obvious. It's just not worth the risk anymore. Please stop going there."

He made good points, but it still felt as if he was telling me what to do, and I hated that beyond measure.

"No." I sat up and crossed my arms. "I've been going there for over a year. Last night was a first, and I won't let it happen again."

"For the love of . . . just. Let's try something else. Whenever you get the urge for some danger, just come to me. We'll go speeding on highways, or I can take you to an abandoned warehouse and we can break shit if you need to let off steam."

I was shaking my head. He didn't get it.

"Is it the random hookups? If it's sex you're after, I'm more than willing—"

"Don't." I pointed a warning finger in his face and got to my feet. "This conversation is over. You've said your piece. Now leave."

Motherfucker thought he was god's gift to women and his dick would solve all my problems. The arrogance. Although . . . if he fucked with his dick as well as he had with his fingers . . . No! I cut that train of thought right off.

He stood too, putting his Ray-Bans on. "If you continue to go to Davey's, I will find out, and I'll have to tell someone."

"Tell who? Who would even believe you?"

"Your friends? Your family?" He shrugged. "I'll just keep talking until someone takes it seriously. If you die and I did nothing when I knew you were going there . . . I can't have that on my conscience, Donna."

"Oh, so this is about you and your conscience? Fuck you!"

He started up the path back to the front of the house as I stared daggers at his back.

"I'll be watching you," he called over his shoulder.

I stuck both middle fingers up at him and gritted my teeth.

Once he was out of view, I took the other path up to the house and let myself in through a back door. Hoping Harlow and Mom were still glued to the front window, watching Hendrix leave, I rushed up the back stairs and into my room. I'd just lock myself in there and refuse to speak to them until they dropped it.

Mom was nowhere in sight, but Harlow and Amaya were perched cross-legged on my bed, looking at me with expectant expressions. As if it were fucking story time at the library and they were a couple of five-year-olds.

I heaved a defeated sigh and shut the door, leaning back against it. "Hey, Amaya. What are you doing here?"

"Harls texted me that you had an interesting visitor. I came right over." She grinned.

"And you didn't think to invite Mena?" I gave my sister an exaggerated look of disappointment.

She shrugged. "I did. She had to work. But demands a full blow-by-blow when she gets off."

"Blow-by-blow?" Amaya repeated, barely containing laughter.

Mirth bubbled up inside me too, and my shoulders began to shake. "When she gets off?"

All three of us burst into laughter. For the first time that morning, I felt a little better. They were being nosy and annoying, but at the end of the day, I knew they cared. They wanted the best for me, just as I wanted the best for them.

"OK, that's enough with the stalling." Amaya wiped the tears from under her eyes and fixed me with a look. "Spill."

I dragged my feet across the room and flopped onto the bed, face-first. "I don't wanna," I mumbled into the soft comforter.

Harlow kicked my hip. "Start talking or I'll tell Mom and Dad what really happened that time I had to get stitches at the back of my head."

I turned my head to glare at her. "You wouldn't."

"D, come on." Amaya started running her fingers through my damp hair. It felt like heaven.

"It's not that big a deal, really. He's just being annoying." What the hell was I supposed to tell them? It all revolved around my trips to Davey's, and I couldn't tell them that. They'd make me stop going, or worse—try to go with me. I couldn't put them in that kind of danger.

"There had to be a damn good reason he came to our house," Harlow argued. "This is more than just your usual mutual disdain for each other."

"Just admit you hooked up with him. We won't judge you," Amaya said matter-of-factly.

I sat up. "What makes you think we hooked up?" Was it that obvious? Did other people know? God, I was completely losing my grip on reality.

They both looked at me as if I were an idiot.

"He came to your house." Amaya started listing things off while Harlow helpfully ticked them off on her fingers. "He braved meeting your parents. You were spotted talking in the kitchen at Mena's birthday." I knew that moment of weakness would come back to bite me. "You were spotted talking at the Halloween party. You thought he was hot that day we saw him at the gym. He riles you up like literally no other person on the planet. Your sexual chemistry is ridiculous, like some fanfic level of heat."

"Are you guys running an investigation or something? I feel attacked."

"Why won't you tell us?" For the first time, Harlow actually sounded a little hurt.

I had to tell them something, and it could definitely *not* be about Davey's or how spectacularly I was failing at everything lately—not until I fixed it. And we *had* hooked up; it wouldn't even be a lie.

"OK, fine, yes, Hendrix and I—" I didn't even get to finish the sentence; their excited squeals and proclamations of "I knew it" cut me off as they completely lost their shit, started bouncing on the bed, then pounced on me.

We ended up in a tangle, our heads at the foot of the bed.

"When?" Harlow demanded.

"Where?" Amaya added.

In the back of a dirty alleyway at a seedy bar just after I nearly fucked some guy whose name I don't even remember. "Um, a couple times. Once at school."

"At school?" they both yelled in unison.

"Yeah. I gave him a blow job in Mr. Kirke's office while everyone was in a staff meeting." I covered my face with my hands and laughed.

"Respect." Amaya nodded.

Harlow remained silent, a look of slight disgust on her face. "I don't need all the gory details."

"Well, I do. Is he hung? I bet it's huge. I can tell by how he walks."

"Oh my god, you're ridiculous." I laughed.

"Eew!" Harlow reached over me to smack Amaya. "Why didn't you tell us?"

"I don't know." I sighed. "It's not like it's going anywhere. It's not serious. It can't be. And I have Will to consider."

"Fuck Will." Amaya frowned. "Actually, don't. He's never been able to even make you come. I don't know why you keep stringing that wet blanket along."

"I'm just trying to think about my future."

"Is that why Hendrix was here?" Harlow asked. "He wants more—in the future?"

"Yeah. Kind of." At the end, I was still a little confused about it all. Did he have feelings for me? Or was he just on some weird crusade to stop teenagers from doing reckless shit? Thinking about it was making me exhausted.

"Can we please stop talking about it?" I pleaded. "I'm not really sure where we stand, and I don't want to deal with it right now. I have a headache, and I just wanna take a nap."

"OK, fine." Amaya sighed and got off the bed. "Movie tonight."

"That sounds great." I meant it.

"I'll text Mena." Harlow was already bent over her phone as she headed for the door.

I breathed a sigh of relief that they hadn't pushed for more info. I had to be careful, and I had to make sure Hendrix didn't pull a stunt like that ever again.

CHAPTER NINETEEN

Donna

I forced myself to take the stairs one at a time instead of bounding up them in twos. The auditorium was bursting, almost every Fulton student and staff member packed into the state-of-the-art facility for an assembly.

Ms. Perry, the headmistress, stood on the stage in a pale blue pantsuit, talking about Fulton Academy's charitable endeavors over the Christmas break. Half the students had already tuned out or were surreptitiously playing on their phones.

I was looking for one particular student.

I'd seen him file in with the others just moments before my phone had vibrated in my pocket, and I'd waved the girls in ahead of me as I checked the notification. It was an email from Stanford.

I'd read it, and immediately the walls started closing in.

I had this inexplicable urge to just . . . *move*. Leave. Get in my car and drive away. But I didn't think my shaky hands could steer effectively. And for some reason, my stupid brain couldn't stop thinking about Hendrix and the way he'd argued, *pleaded* with me to let him help.

I didn't want his help. I didn't need it . . . and yet I found myself slipping into the auditorium through a side door and scanning the blank, indifferent faces. They were so calm—bored even. Didn't they know my heart was about to burst out of my rib cage?

As I climbed, I checked each row for those broad shoulders, that messy hair, those sometimes cruel eyes that seemed to see me better than anyone else ever had.

"Miss Mead," Mr. Monroe hissed, a reproachful look in his bespectacled eyes. He was easily the hottest teacher at Fulton, but he was also the meanest. He had his hands clasped in front of him, one of several teachers standing throughout the auditorium to keep an eye on the students. "Take a seat. The headmistress is speaking."

"Sorry, sir. I'm looking for another student. I've just come from the office with an urgent message for him." The lie rolled off my tongue so easily even I was impressed, especially considering the tempest raging inside me.

He eyed me suspiciously for a moment, but I didn't falter. I was student body president, a top student, liked and respected by students and staff. I never got in trouble. Finally, he nodded. "Make it quick."

We'd drawn the attention of several students nearby, their curious gazes looking for any distraction from the boring speeches below.

My eyes finally locked with Hendrix's. He was sitting a few rows from the top, three empty seats and two juniors between him and the stairs. I kept eye contact, unable to break it if I wanted to, letting the desperation enter my gaze. He frowned and shifted forward in his seat.

I climbed farther up, watching him, begging him with my eyes.

When he got to his feet and shuffled past the other students, my heart kicked up a notch, even as some of the pressure around it eased.

I met him at the end of his row, gestured with a tip of my head for him to follow me, and kept climbing. His feet brushed against the carpet close behind mine, and the back of my neck tingled from his scrutinizing gaze.

Dear Miss Donna Mead,

Thank you for your application . . .

My steps faltered, and Hendrix's hand shot out to grip my upper arm, holding tightly. He released me as soon as I was steady, and I picked up my pace.

At the top of the stairs, he followed me inside the projector room and shut the door behind us.

I stood facing the dark room, finally allowing my chest to heave, my face to fall. This room had a professional digital projector for screenings of films the visual arts students made, as well as several bulky lights and a control panel for school plays and performances. An assembly didn't require any of those bells and whistles though, so the space was empty and silent. A few people definitely would have seen us slip in, but I was sure none of the teachers had—one of them would've come through that door by now to demand what we were doing.

"Donna." His voice was low, cautious, but curious. "What are we doing in here?"

We receive a large volume of applications each year, and as such are unable to offer a spot to most applicants . . .

I squeezed my eyes shut, taking a steadying breath that didn't steady me at all, then turned to place my hands on his chest.

"I'm taking you up on your offer," I whispered, hoping he mistook my heavy breathing for arousal and not the clawing panic inside me.

The smooth muscle under my palms stiffened as he narrowed his eyes. Just touching him, being close enough to smell that heady male scent with a hint of cinnamon, was already making me feel more grounded. But why wasn't he touching me back? I needed him to touch me.

"What offer?" His voice had gone low too.

"The one you made by the pool that day, when you demanded I stop going to Davey's and asked if I went because I wanted to get laid." I slid my hands up and over his shoulders, pressing my breasts against his front.

"If I remember correctly, that was around the time you told me to get lost." He was still refusing to touch me, but his breathing was getting heavier.

I shrugged and dragged my nose up the side of his neck. "I changed my mind. I want to fuck."

His hands finally gripped my hips, his fingers digging in. "Yeah, well"—he licked his lips and swallowed—"I don't."

"Liar." I growled, then bit his earlobe.

He hissed but didn't back away.

This game we played, this back and forth, was making me wet already. The anticipation was building, the adrenaline of an unlocked door and the entire school sitting on the other side only driving it higher. It was the perfect distraction from what I'd just learned.

One arm banded around the middle of my back, making me arch against him. His other hand threaded into my hair, and then he was kissing me. Intensely. Forcefully. His tongue immediately demanding my mouth. It was exactly what I needed. Unlike when we argued, I didn't have even a sliver of an urge to fight him. I wanted to give myself over completely and let him consume me until nothing else mattered.

Too soon, he broke the kiss and lifted his head out of my reach. I opened my eyes, panting, and frowned. "What the fuck? Don't stop."

He grabbed a fistful of my hair and pulled lightly until my head was tipped back, at his mercy. "What happened?"

"I don't know what you're talking about. Stop being a pussy and fuck me."

He smirked, then dipped his head, took my bottom lip between his own, and sucked. Just as my eyes started to close in satisfaction, he bit—not enough to draw blood but enough to send a jolt of pleasure shooting through me. But before I could tell him to do it again, he was back to staring down at me, denying me.

"Stop deflecting. I saw that look in your eyes, Donna. You looked like you'd seen a ghost—of a person you just murdered. Tell me what's going on."

I rolled my eyes and returned my hands to his front. "It's nothing. Seriously. Can we please just fuck before the assembly ends and someone comes in here?"

Did I seriously just plead with a guy to fuck me? *Ugh*! Who the hell even was I anymore? I pushed the indignation down and loosened his tie, but I got only three buttons of his shirt undone—barely a peek at the strong, muscular chest underneath—before he put a stop to that.

He wrenched my wrists away from his shirt, then pinned them both behind my back in one big hand. With my arms restrained behind me, my chest jutted forward. He stared at my tits and licked his lips. He wanted this. Why was he being so difficult?

The hand not holding me captive wrapped loosely around my throat, and I had to stop myself from moaning. But he didn't linger there. He dragged it down over my collarbones and to my left breast, then squeezed gently. His thumb brushed over my aching nipple, caressing it over the fabric.

"You want this?" he asked, his voice husky, his dark eyes looking down on me.

"Yes," I hissed impatiently. Wasn't that exactly what I'd been saying this whole time?

"Then start talking, princess. Nothing in this world is free. You and I know that better than anyone."

His hand was still working my breast, making me pant, the pressure between my legs building.

And then suddenly he went perfectly still.

I frowned at him.

"Talk," he demanded.

"Fine," I gritted out, and his hand immediately resumed its ministrations. "Uh ... I had a fight with my sister. She ... ruined my favorite sweater."

"Bullshit." He dragged his hand down my rib cage, over my belly, between my legs, but stopped with his fingers flat against my pelvis, just shy of where I wanted them most. "Try again."

"Fuck, OK." He started to rub me over the fabric of my pleated skirt. "Uh ... um ..." It was getting hard to think. "I got a C on my last math test. My parents are going to be so mad."

He chuckled, the sound reverberating through me. "There's no way in hell you've ever made anything below a B plus. Come on, Donna. I'm losing my patience."

I was just about ready to wrench out of his hold, done with these stupid games. But then his hand slipped up under my skirt, and his fingers skimmed the edge of my panties. He moved the fabric aside and teased me with the lightest of touches.

"Oh god. Uh ..."

His finger circled my entrance, gliding easily through my arousal. "Jesus, you're soaked," he whispered. "Come on, Donna, put us both out of our misery so I can drive my cock"—as he said that word, he slid a finger inside effortlessly, making me gasp—"into this warm, wet heaven between your thighs. Tell. Me."

"It's nothing. For fuck's sake. I . . . it's . . . I'm just moody because I'm on my period, OK?" I blurted.

He froze, his finger still inside me, and I realized what I'd just said. He looked down, then back up at me with a raised brow. I grimaced.

With an amused smirk, he pulled the finger out and held it up between us. His middle finger was slick with my arousal and nothing else. I wasn't due for another week at least. He held it there for a moment, giving me the finger with my own wetness all over it, then put it into his mouth. His cheeks hollowed out as he sucked on it, and he tipped his head to the side.

"Fucking delicious. But no tangy, metallic aftertaste. Try again."

"God damnit." I gritted my teeth so hard a jolt of pain shot through my jaw as I wrenched out of his hold.

"Tell me something real." The teasing lilt was gone from his voice. "I'm here, I'm not going anywhere. I'll make you feel good. Just fucking tell me something *real*, Donna."

We are pleased to inform you that we are offering you early acceptance to . . .

I cracked. There were so many things going through my mind, so many feelings coursing through my body, something had to give. I buckled and got into his face.

"Fine. You want to know what happened? I got into Stanford. Early acceptance."

"Is that not what you wanted?" he asked, but there was no confusion in his face, no judgment. He was simply asking.

I paused for a second, some of the tension draining from my shoulders. The next words came easier than I thought they would. "It's what I've wanted since before high school. But when I read that email . . . I felt nothing. Empty. No, that's not right. It wasn't nothing. It just wasn't what it was *supposed* to be. There was no excitement, no joy, no pride at my accomplishment, no urge to jump up and down and tell my friends and family." I licked my lips, staring at his teal tie, and forged on. As if I could stop at this point anyway. "I read that email, the culmination of everything I'd worked for all these years, and it felt like the ceiling collapsed. Everyone else just strolled on by, heading into the auditorium, oblivious to the fact that I was holding the entire goddamn building up over our heads, with my knees ready to buckle."

I looked into his eyes, no longer trying to hide the emotion I was feeling yet could hardly label.

He took hold of my upper arms and stepped closer, his eyes searching mine. "Thank you for telling me. That couldn't have been easy."

Tears pricked at the backs of my eyes, and I had no idea why.

"I don't want to cry, Hendrix," I told him. "I just want to forget for a little while. Just make me forget. Make me feel good."

He stared at me for another beat, the air between us getting charged. In the auditorium, a round of unenthusiastic applause went up as students carrying wind instruments filed on stage, ready to play a version of our school song.

He leaned down and whispered, "I can do that. I got you, baby." Then he kissed me—a bruising, distracting, dizzying kiss.

I moaned, but before I could wrap my arms around him, his lips were gone, and he was pushing me roughly around until his front was flush with my back.

Hot cinnamon breath washed over my ear, sending shivers of anticipation through my body. "Everyone thinks you're little miss perfect, all your ducks in a row, such a good girl. But I know you, Donna. I know the depravity you crave, the need humming under your skin."

He squeezed my shoulders, and I leaned back into him, but in the next instant, his warmth at my back disappeared.

"Take your panties off," he ordered.

I swallowed, the logical, in-charge Donna bristling at the tone. But she was already fading—along with her stresses and anxieties. Dark Donna was taking over, even if I wasn't wearing come-fuck-me boots and a low-cut top.

I reached under my skirt and pushed my underwear down my legs, purposely arching my back and sticking my ass out as I stepped out of them.

"Give them to me." His hand appeared at my side, and I placed the small piece of gray fabric in his palm.

As soon as my panties were tucked into his pocket, he reclaimed the space between us, his hands on my hips, his steel-hard erection pressing into my ass. I ground back against him, and he released a shaky breath.

"Undo the buttons of your shirt." He kissed and licked the side of my neck, and I tipped my head to give him better access as my fingers fumbled with the buttons. Another round of applause went up in the auditorium just as I managed to get them all undone, the entire school applauding my efforts.

This was so fucked, so dangerous, doing this here, behind a door that didn't lock, with Mr. Monroe literally feet away.

And I was loving every damn second of it.

Hendrix dragged his hands down the sides of my legs until he reached the hem of the skirt, then clasped the fabric and dragged them back up. My bottom half was completely exposed as I stood there in knee-high uniform socks and sensible black shoes, trembling with the anticipation of feeling him inside me.

As his hands continued up my ribs, the skirt fluttered back down, but then he was exposing me in another way. He seized the two sides of my unbuttoned shirt and yanked them apart, making me gasp. Almost instantly his hands were on my breasts, grabbing, kneading in rhythm with the grinding of his hips.

A soft moan escaped me, and I reached back for something to hold on to. My hands clawed at his pants—closed around the fabric at the sides of his thighs.

He dropped his right hand, reached under the skirt, and grabbed me between the legs as his left hand pushed into the cup of my bra. His fingers dug into my flesh, and he started to walk us forward.

"You're not a good girl at all, are you?" He was panting now, his words strained. "Sneaking out to bars, keeping secrets from your friends and family, fucking tattooed men with criminal records. You like the danger, crave it, get off on the prospect of getting caught."

I whimpered. His hands weren't doing anything, weren't rubbing or caressing or stroking me. I was desperate with need, my pussy clenching and relaxing, seeking some kind of relief. And his words only drove me higher.

Usually I hated it when he said things about me that were true, when he had me figured out. But in that moment, I *loved* every syllable. I was his, and I couldn't wait to see what he'd do with me.

He stopped us just in front of the dead control panel and long narrow window, the entire auditorium of three hundred people visible below. Any one of them could turn around at any moment. Would they be able to see us up here in the darkness?

The prospect made arousal flood through me, wetness gathering between my legs and soaking Hendrix's fingers.

"Oh, fuck," he breathed, rubbing me up and down a few times, spreading the wetness all over my thighs. "You're so fucking wet. You love this, don't you? As much as you love the danger of Davey's. Anyone could walk in at any moment and catch us. Anyone could look up and see my hand down your bra. You're not little Miss Mead at all—you're not a good girl. You're a bad, *bad* girl, Donna. And you want me to fuck you in front of the entire school, don't you?"

"Fuck. Yes."

He rubbed my clit roughly, and my eyes rolled into the back of my head.

"Holy shit." I panted, bucking my hips to meet the movements of his hand. "I'm gonna, I'm . . ." Already, the intense feeling was building, that inevitable pressure in my lower half.

I threw my head back against his shoulder and moaned. The sound was too loud. I knew it as soon as it escaped my mouth. Had someone heard? *Shit!*

The thought of it pushed me over the edge, pleasure coursing through my system.

Hendrix gripped my jaw with his free hand and turned my head, capturing my mouth with his. He kissed me passionately—tongues swiping, teeth bumping—and swallowed every sound I made as I came apart on his hand.

"Shh!" he whispered against my lips as I panted, my vision returning. But Hendrix didn't give a fuck that my knees were going weak—he wasn't going to give me a break.

"You need to keep your mouth shut or this stops right now. I can't get expelled for fucking you at a school assembly."

"Fuck you." It sounded weak and half-assed. "I can't exactly control it."

He licked my lips, then pushed me forward over the control panel. I threw my hands out, but the only area not covered in buttons and knobs was at the top, which meant I had to stretch my hands almost completely out. That left me pretty much lying on top of the thing, all those knobs and buttons pressing into my front.

Hendrix leaned over me and rubbed his erection against my ass. "I thought you were in control of everything at all times," he taunted, his voice gravelly.

I had no witty response. I didn't give a shit anymore. I just wanted him inside me.

With one hand, I reached back and fumbled at the waistband of his pants, but he slapped my fingers away and did the job himself. The rustle of fabric was followed by the distinct sound of a foil packet opening, and a few seconds later, my skirt was flipped up over my lower back.

His hands kneaded my ass, and then his hard length was at my entrance. The head of his cock entered me, stretching me, and I groaned.

He pulled out. "For fuck's sake, Donna. I'm not messing around. You need to be quiet."

I shifted and lifted myself slightly, looking over my shoulder. He was so impossibly gorgeous, his face flushed, his lips slick from kissing me, his swollen cock standing proud. I focused on his intense stare. "I'm sorry, OK? I'm not doing it on purpose. I'll try to be quiet, but you have my permission to do whatever the fuck you need to shut me up."

His eyes darkened at that, and I turned to face the front again.

Ms. Perry was back on the stage, talking about prom or a new mentorship program or . . . something. It was impossible to focus on anything other than the insanely hot man about to be inside me.

Hendrix's hand appeared next to mine as he once again leaned in close and positioned himself at my entrance. His free hand ran through my hair, and he caressed the back of my neck with his knuckles, sending shivers down my spine. The touches were gentle, sweet.

Which made the contrast of what he did next so much more intoxicating. As he pushed into me, his hand clamped over my mouth, muffling any sounds I made.

He took two slow, deliberate strokes, his body learning mine, then started to fuck me in earnest. His hips slammed against my ass mercilessly as his fingers dug into my cheek, keeping me silent.

I watched the assembly begin to wrap up as Hendrix pounded me from behind. I could see everything below, but I wasn't seeing any of it. Every fiber of my being was focused on him. His hand on my face, the taut muscles of the arm next to me, the hard, warm, wet, stretching, punishing freedom . . .

Another orgasm washed over me, heat spreading from my core all the way to the tips of my toes and fingers. Hendrix buried himself deep inside me and rolled his hips, his body collapsing over mine as he panted through his own release.

Even through the fog of my own orgasm, I was impressed at his control, his ability to remain silent.

His hand over my mouth eased, and he brushed some hair off my cheek before pressing his forehead against my temple. For a few seconds, we just breathed the same air. We just existed together in this moment, and I felt as if I were floating on a cloud of possibility.

CHAPTER TWENTY

Hendrix

With one last kiss to her temple, I pulled out and . . . realized I'd fucked up. Big time. Hooking up with Donna at Davey's and in that office was one thing—we hardly knew each other, we had this angry sexual tension going, it was hot, and that was that. But what we'd just done—it was so much more than sex. She'd told me something real, shown me a part of her soul. I'd known what she craved and given it to her.

And now, as I tied off the condom and buried it under a muffin wrapper in the trash, a tightness settled around my chest. I actually gave a shit what happened to her. I was *emotionally invested.*

Fuck.

My princess was feeling trapped in her ivory tower, and I knew exactly how she felt, what that could lead to.

Her arousal was still slick on the base of my dick, and I was already missing her warmth, her tight body writhing under mine, her labored breathing against my hand. I wanted to make her forget her life again, help her find oblivion in ecstasy over and over and over until nothing else mattered. But this wasn't some fantasy where we could just run away and spend the rest of our lives fucking in a cabin in the woods.

Donna cleared her throat as she finished buttoning up her shirt. "Can I have my underwear back, please?"

I did my pants back up, tucked my shirt in, straightened my tie, took my sweet-ass time to respond. "No," I told her with a slight twitch of my lips.

Her eyes narrowed. "Hendrix, don't be ridiculous. I need my underwear. I can't go back to class like this. What if I trip or something and my skirt goes flying up?"

"Then don't go to class." I ran my hands through my hair and brushed the creases from my uniform. The assembly had finished, and a cacophony of sound drifted in through the narrow window—students all talking over one another, feet shuffling toward the exits. We backed farther into the darkness, closer to the door.

Donna finished straightening herself up as well, her appearance as pristine as possible without a mirror or a brush. Then she gave me a firm look.

"I don't have time for this. We need to slip into the crowd as everyone's leaving so we don't get caught. Give me my panties." She reached for my pocket, but I brushed her hands away and backed up against the wall.

I could see that look in her eyes returning—the one that hardened her against the world. She was retreating, probably freaking out about all she'd told me, seconds away from running from me yet again and avoiding even acknowledging what just happened between us. But I was done letting Donna Mead walk away from me. I was done letting her walk away from her problems. I was done letting her control everything. She'd been doing it for years, and it clearly wasn't working for her.

"You can have them. In ten minutes."

"What?" She frowned and glanced at the door. Our window was closing.

"Meet me at the east entrance in ten minutes, and you can have them back. Bring your coat."

"Hendrix, I'm not going to skip class to . . ."

I didn't hang around to listen to her enraged demands. I just opened the door, made sure no one was looking, and rushed down the stairs until I was close enough behind a group of freshman girls to look as if I was exiting with the rest of the students.

I resisted the urge to look over my shoulder and check if Donna was doing the same. She was a big girl—she'd figure it out.

As I passed through the auditorium's double doors, I accidentally caught the eye of Mr. Monroe—my English teacher. The guy was the youngest staff member at Fulton but easily the most hard-ass. He had the best opportunity to connect with his students because of his youth, but I'd never even seen the dude smile, let alone crack a joke.

He frowned at me before pushing his glasses back up his nose. I had no idea what that was about, but I smiled back politely and breezed on past. The only surefire way to get caught doing something dodgy was to act as though you had something to hide.

Between going to my locker to get my stuff and walking out to my car, I questioned my decision to cut class about a thousand times.

I was breaking my vow to keep my head down, stay out of trouble, and get past my senior year without any hiccups. I was also breaking my aunt's trust.

I got into my car and sighed, drumming my fingers on the steering wheel. Maybe I should just go back inside. If I hurried, I wouldn't even be late for gym. But then Donna would be left standing on the sidewalk alone, and she'd be pissed. And hurt, even if she didn't show it. I couldn't let her down—especially after I'd manipulated her into coming.

Sighing, I pulled my phone out and shot a quick message to my aunt.

I'm skipping school for the rest of the day. I promise it's important and necessary. Can you please cover for me if the school calls?

I started the car, but her reply was instant.

Thank you for telling me. I'll give you an alibi. But I expect a full and detailed report tonight.

I pulled up to the curb at the east entrance just as Donna slipped out the door. This was where the younger students were picked up and dropped off by their parents, nannies, and drivers. The area was packed with Escalades, Audis, and BMWs in the morning and the afternoon, but it was deserted as Donna rushed down the stairs.

I expected her to lean through the window, demand her underwear, maybe sic the football team on me. But she surprised me by jumping into the passenger seat immediately and throwing her designer backpack into the back seat.

"Drive," she demanded as she put her belt on. "Your tree-hugging car's windows are not tinted. The last thing I fucking need is to be caught skipping class with the likes of you."

"Yes, ma'am." I let the dig slide and took off.

The drive was surprisingly uneventful. Resigned to her fate, Donna jammed her black sunglasses on and remained silent as I tried to figure out where to take us.

When all else fails—comfort food.

I took us to a fast food drive-through, and after a half-hearted argument about how she couldn't eat that crap, Donna rolled her eyes and got the same thing I did. Cheeseburgers and milkshakes in tow, I pulled back onto the road.

"Should've got some chickie nuggies as well," Donna mumbled, her head buried in the paper bag.

"Chickie nuggies?" I grinned. She was fucking adorable, with her delicate, manicured fingers stuffing several fries into her mouth at the same time.

"Shut up." She laughed around a mouthful and shoved some fries into my mouth too. I gave her finger a nibble before she could pull her hand out of reach, and she smacked me on the shoulder. "That's what my sister calls them. She's got us all saying it now."

"It's cute. More fries," I demanded and opened my mouth wide, angling my head in her direction but keeping my eyes on the road.

"Fuck you. I'm not cute," she protested but deposited the salty, potatoey goodness into my mouth anyway. "Where are we going?"

"Ah, good question. Very deep. So many answers." I nodded and opened my mouth again.

She rolled her eyes and shoved more fries in my face. "I meant physically, like, right now, in this car, where are we going? Not existentially, smart-ass."

"Hmm. How about . . ." We were well out of downtown Devilbend, the buildings thinning out, the speed limits rising. A sign for a turnoff caught my eye. "Oak Hill Park?"

The turn came up before she could answer, and I took it, but Donna remained silent beside me. We followed signs for the parking lot, intermittent sunlight shining down through the thick canopy of trees.

Unsurprisingly for a Thursday afternoon, the lot was mostly empty, no tourists or hikers in sight.

Donna turned to me as I cut the engine, her hands digging into the top of the paper bag. "I'm not getting out of this car or handing over your greasy burger until you give me back my underwear."

I pursed my lips to stop myself from smiling. We both knew I could overpower her if I really wanted to.

Reaching into my pocket, I fished out the small piece of cotton and handed it over. She deposited the takeout bag in my lap and pulled her panties up, shimmying into them under her skirt, then promptly got out of the car.

I followed her up the grassy hill to a nearby picnic table. The sun was coming and going behind grayish clouds—the kind that threatened rain but were just as likely to float away before a single drop reached the ground. It was fresh out here, the air chilly whenever the sun disappeared, and I was glad I'd made her bring her coat.

We settled onto the top of the table, our feet propped up on the seat. As we started to unwrap the burgers, Donna hesitated and looked around.

"Something messed up happened to Mena and Turner here," she said before taking a bite.

I paused with my burger halfway to my mouth and looked at her. "Do you want to leave?"

"Nah, it's fine." She shook her head. "I just realized where we are, that's all. Being reminded of what went down a few months ago just makes me angry every time."

"What happened?"

"Uh . . ." She picked at her burger. "It's not really my story to tell."

She was loyal and fearless—a fucking lioness personified. I took a few bites of my burger to avoid staring at her. "Does it have anything to do with how Turner reconnected with his little sister?"

I'd been training with Turner a few times a week since I joined the gym, and we'd hung out plenty. He'd told me most of how his mom and sister disappeared a few years back and how he and his dad had been searching for them, only to find his sister here in Devilbend and his mom murdered. He had a bit of a conspiracy-theorist streak, convinced that BestLyf—some corporate life-coaching company—was behind it all, but he was a really cool guy otherwise.

Donna's eyebrows rose slightly. "He told you that?"

"Yeah. That's what being friends with someone entails. You tell them things about yourself. Sometimes the things aren't very pretty."

She ignored that, and we ate in silence, listening to the birds chirping in the tall trees, the occasional gust of wind rustling the branches.

When there was nothing left to occupy our mouths, I turned to face her, lifting one knee onto the table.

She closed her eyes and sighed. "Don't."

"Don't what?"

"Please, Hendrix, don't start with trying to figure out my deep dark secrets again. We had amazing sex during a school assembly and got away with it. We're actually getting along. Can't we just leave it at that?"

"If what happened between us had been just sex, yeah."

"Oh, please. Don't tell me you're catching feelings now. I have enough shit to deal with."

She was going back to her defensive default, because that's what she always did when shit got hard or confronting. Did I have feelings for her? Fuck me, but yeah, I was probably getting there. But this wasn't about that.

"I'm not trying to put a ring on it, you psycho." If combative snark was the only language she could understand, then that's what I'd speak. "I'm talking about the desperate way you looked at me in the auditorium, the shit you told me about your early acceptance and how it made you feel like the roof was caving in, the fact that you go to Davey's and fuck dangerous men as a way to release the insane amount of pressure you feel every single day."

She blinked at me once, twice, not saying anything as her brows knitted. She was a smart girl, smarter than me, probably smarter than half the teachers at our school—surely she wasn't surprised that I'd figured her out.

"I don't know why I told you that earlier." She pursed her lips.

"Because on some level, you know that I get it. I may not understand feeling deflated after achieving a massive thing, but I definitely get feeling like the entire world is collapsing on top of you. I've been there."

"Will you tell me about it?" she asked, her eyes going a little wide. Was she scared? Deflecting?

"We're talking about you right now." OK, maybe I was deflecting too.

"Isn't that what being friends with someone means? Telling them things about yourself that aren't very pretty?" She threw my own words back at me.

"Is that what we are now? Friends?"

She sighed and ran her hands through her hair, pulling at it a little. "I don't know what we are."

I shrugged. "Doesn't matter right now whether or not we're friends. But you do have some actual, bona fide, ride-or-die kind of friends in those chicks—the ones you keep posting pics of with hashtag DevilbendDynasty." I'd witnessed firsthand how close they were, how they defended one another, took care of one another. Their friendship was real, not shallow and on the verge of backstabbing like so many rich, popular girls at my old school. "Why haven't you told them about any of it?"

"They . . . I . . . the thing is, we really are ride-or-die, as idiotic as that phrase sometimes sounds." She rolled her eyes. "But they'd try to talk me out of it, and when that failed, they'd go with me. Even Mena, who's had more than her fair share of violence, would risk getting hurt. I can't do that to them. This is *my* shit. *My* damage to deal with." *Alone.* She didn't say it, but the implication was there. This was something she felt she had to handle alone.

I dropped that topic before we started arguing again. "OK, then will you tell them about your early acceptance?"

"Yeah." She leaned back on her hands, turning her face up to the sun. It was likely to disappear behind a cloud again at any moment. "They'll be happy for me, proud of me."

"No doubt. It's an amazing achievement. But that's not what I meant. Are you going to tell them you don't want it?"

She sat up straight and narrowed her eyes on me. "What makes you think I don't want it? I busted my fucking ass for that."

I didn't say anything. I just watched her steadily. That was a knee-jerk reaction—the response she'd conditioned herself to have. But we both knew what she'd said to me in that dark little room, and I'd seen that panicked look in her eyes in the auditorium.

After a few moments, she got to her feet. Her eyes darted from left to right, distant and unseeing, as she chewed on her bottom lip.

"Your friends and family love you and support you," I said. It was more than I could say about my own, but I pushed that stabbing pain away for the moment. "They'll understand. Just tell them you don't want to be a lawyer anymore."

Her gaze shot up. "Who the fuck do you think you are to tell me what I do and don't want? You have no idea what you're talking about. I can't just change my mind."

"Why?" I leaned my elbows on my knees, fixing her with a challenging look. The sun disappeared behind a fat cloud. "You're eighteen, your whole future in front of you. You have every privilege, every opportunity imaginable. You can literally do whatever the fuck you want, and you're going to force yourself to follow a path that's clearly suffocating you?" Did I resent all this? Maybe a little. But I'd also put myself in this situation where my own future was tenuous, so I didn't really have a right to be upset. I deserved much worse.

"Fuck you, Hendrix. It's not that simple. I have plans. People expect certain things from me. I've put in so much work for this. I . . . it's . . . you . . . *ugh!*" She turned away in a huff, breathing hard.

"It's not worth it, Donna. Trust me. Life's too damn short." My hands clenched into fists, and I forced myself to release them. This conversation was making me frustrated and angry too.

She spun to face me once more, her hair flipping. "What would you know about it? God, why do you care? Just leave me alone."

I didn't exactly make the decision to tell her my deepest darkest secret, but the conversation had descended into another fight, and I was getting nowhere. She'd shared something pretty big with me in that dark little room—a truth she'd probably never even spoken aloud. Baring my soul to her, even in desperation and anger, almost came naturally.

I pushed off the bench, the nervous energy making it impossible to sit still, and spread my arms wide.

"I fucking killed someone!" I yelled, my horrific truth bouncing off the ancient trees in the park.

CHAPTER TWENTY-ONE

I stared at him as his words settled into the cold earth at my feet.

The logical part of my brain was questioning if I should be afraid. He'd been popping up wherever I went, had been demanding to know things about me, had driven me out to a deserted park alone, and then said . . . he told me . . .

I fucking killed someone.

. . . killed someone.

. . . killed . . .

Even as I wondered if I was safe with Hendrix, I struggled to accept the truth of those words. Maybe I hadn't heard him right.

"I'm sorry, what?" I tried to swallow, but my throat was so dry, so tight.

And yet I wasn't running from him; my body wasn't poised to defend itself. Yes, my logical mind had raised all the obvious alarms, but in my gut I *knew*. Hendrix would never hurt me. Not like that. He wasn't a threat to my physical safety—just my sanity.

He rubbed his eyes with the heels of his hands, then released a massive sigh as he collapsed onto the bench, his body sagging as if he hadn't slept in a month. "I'm sorry for just dropping that on you like that. I didn't mean to . . . I never wanted anyone to know, but I need you to understand the whole, abhorrent truth about me—what I am."

"You're scaring me." I wrapped my arms around my middle, but I couldn't tear my gaze away. I didn't mean I was worried he'd try to kill me—the very conversation was frightening. I was scared of what he was about to tell me, what it would change. For him, for me. For this thing between us.

But of course, he took my words wrong. He hadn't looked at me since he'd blurted out his confession, and he still didn't look at me as he reached into his pocket and pulled out his car keys.

"I won't hurt you. I'd rather die than ever hurt another person, especially you. Take the keys. Leave if you need to. I get it." He tossed them onto the corner of the picnic table closest to where I was standing.

I hardly even glanced at them. "Hendrix, tell me what happened." I didn't want to know, but I *had* to know.

He swallowed and released another big breath, his lips trembling. "Back in New York, I told you the kind of school I went to, the kind of people I hung out with. We got away with so much because our parents were so influential. The teachers were too afraid to discipline us. We all thought we were untouchable, invincible. But we all had this . . . " He shook his head. ". . . this *restlessness*. Me most of all. Something inside me was constantly screaming and thrashing, and the only time it would quiet down was when I was driving my fist through something. Or someone. Those guys and I, we started getting into fights. At first it was against each other, betting obscene amounts of money on the outcome. Eventually we started hanging out with people who were intimately acquainted with the darker side of the city—people who were more than willing to take our money and hook us up with other sad fuckers looking to beat the shit out of anyone."

He stared at the ground beneath his feet and opened his mouth a few times, but he couldn't seem to get the next words out.

That restlessness he described, the screaming on the inside—I felt that in my *bones*. I moved forward to stand directly in front of him, and that seemed to snap him out of his inability to speak.

"There was this guy at my school." He leaned back against the picnic table, his hands hanging between his knees. "He wasn't like us. He wasn't rich, didn't walk around like the world owed him something. The school was bigger than Fulton, more students. I didn't know everyone, hardly cared enough to know my so-called friends. Anyway, there were several scholarship students and . . ." He choked, his lip trembling again. "Austin was one of them. We used to get into it sometimes. He had his own group of friends—we didn't move in the same circles —but he wasn't scared of me like almost everyone else. He always had a comeback to any bullshit taunt we threw his way, and he never seemed bothered by it. Like he knew he was smarter than all of us combined, and we wouldn't matter in a couple more months. He was probably going to cure cancer or some shit. It had never gotten physical between us. The guys and I, we kept the fights discreet, off school property. We may not have cared about punishments from teachers, but we sure as fuck cared about pissing off our parents.

"The thing is, I'd been getting less and less capable of holding back that restless fury—that thing that writhed inside me all the time and was only silent when I was hurting, or hurting someone else. The most fucked-up thing is that I don't even remember what led up to it. It was after school, the guys and I had just walked around the corner, Austin was there, and one of my friends said something to him. Austin shot a comment back. I have no idea what it was, but it enraged me. I let it bring that monster out. I didn't care that we were in public, in our school uniforms, with teachers just around the corner. I just lost my shit."

He paused and looked up to the sky. Tears slid down the sides of his face, but he didn't try to wipe them away.

For the first time since he'd started talking, he looked at me. Each word that followed was a struggle, forcing its way up his throat. "I threw a punch that landed on his jaw. He wasn't expecting it and lost his balance, fell backward, hit his head on the pavement. He never got up again."

"Holy shit," I breathed, wrapping a hand around my throat. My own eyes were stinging.

His gaze was intense, as if now that he was finally looking at me, he refused to let me go until I saw all his twisted insides. "I killed him, Donna. Me. I did that."

"I . . . wha . . . how long ago was this?" Why hadn't I seen anything about it in the news? This felt like a big deal. But then I remembered that people died all the time, and usually the rest of the world couldn't care less.

"Just under a year ago. I was supposed to graduate last year, but I stopped going to school. My parents spent an obscene amount of money and called in many favors to keep me out of prison. They even managed to have me tried as a minor so this wouldn't be on my permanent record and tarnish my future." He said those last words with a sneer.

"They were worried about my job prospects and their reputation when Austin didn't even have . . ." A sob tore free from his chest, and my own tears finally overflowed. "He was an only child, his mom a single parent. They were all each other had. I . . ."

He dropped his head into his hands.

I stepped into his space, between his legs, and gripped his shoulders. My throat was so tight I had to cough before I could speak. "It was an accident, Hendrix. An awful, tragic—"

"No." He leaned out of my reach. "It was stupidity, it was pride, it was ego, it was not thinking through the consequences of my actions. I was a walking, talking cliché. It could've been avoided."

"No arguments here." He was right on all fronts. I knew guys like him—like the guy he used to be. "But you didn't mean to kill him."

I stepped closer and pulled him in again; he let me, but his hands remained in his lap.

"No, I didn't. I didn't think about him at all. I never thought about anyone else and how my actions could impact them. That's who I was. That's the guy who killed someone. I don't want to be that person anymore."

"You're not." I said it definitively, and I meant it. My arms wrapped around his torso, the urge to give him comfort impossible to resist. He leaned in to return my hug and rest his head on my chest.

For a few moments we were still. Just me holding a broken boy when I was barely keeping my own damn self from falling apart into a million incompatible pieces.

"After the trial and everything was over"—his words were warm on my chest, his tears soaking my shirt—"Austin's mom reached out to me. My parents and their lawyers and their fucking publicist all advised me against seeing her, but I went. I didn't give a shit what they thought. I was a mess, but she'd lost her son—I'd taken her son—so I was going to do anything that woman asked of me. I was ready to walk off a cliff if she demanded it. Told her as much when I walked into her living room and dropped to my knees before her, blubbering like a child. And you know what she said to me? Austin wouldn't want that."

Another round of sobs shook his shoulders, and his arms tightened around me—as if I was the only thing keeping him from collapsing completely. I didn't know what to say or do. I just held him, crying right along with him.

"Austin wouldn't want that," he repeated in a hoarse voice. "That's the kind of person I took out of this world. We talked for a long time, and in the end, she told me she forgave me. She said she couldn't go through the rest of her life carrying hatred in her heart. Then she made me promise to do all the things Austin couldn't anymore—live my life, make something of myself, leave the world a better place than I found it."

We fell into silence after that, the birds continuing to chirp and the clouds continuing to pass above.

After a while, Hendrix leaned out of my embrace, dragging both hands down his face. "I've never told anyone that. Not since it happened. Not the whole, full thing."

"Why did you tell me?" I didn't feel worthy of his deepest truths, not after the way I'd treated him.

"To make you understand why I'm being so weirdly intense about you going to Davey's, about you telling your friends and family how you feel about your college acceptance. We're so similar, you and me. And I'm terrified you'll—"

"What?" I took a step back, my anger rising again. It was too much. It was all just *too much*. "You think I'd kill someone because I'm not sure I want to study law? I would never do that."

"No." He closed his eyes wearily. "I know our situations are different. I'm worried you'll get *yourself* killed."

My phone started buzzing in my pocket. Desperate for an out from a conversation I still wasn't ready to have, I wrenched it out. It was Drew—school had finished ten minutes ago.

"Hello?" I answered, giving Hendrix my shoulder.

He got to his feet. "Seriously?"

"Hey, Big D! Where you at, girl?" He sounded as though he was in the car. He lived right near Oak Hill Park.

"I told you not to call me that." My response came out harsh—not at all like our usual light banter.

"Are you OK?" he asked.

I glanced at Hendrix, now standing in front of me with his arms crossed. "I need a lift. Can you pick me up from Oak Hill?"

"On my way."

I hung up, and Hendrix got in my face again. "You can run from this all you want, but it's going to catch up with you at some point."

"Yeah, well, that'll be my problem and not yours."

"All the shit I just told you makes no difference whatsoever?"

"That's your life. Not mine. I'm fine!" I yelled. A flock of birds took flight from a nearby tree.

"Really? You're just going to keep pretending your way into a life you never wanted? How long until you're married to fucking Will Frydenberg, in a job you despise, and the only thing keeping you going is a daily dose of Xanax?"

"Fuck you. I'm not pretending shit. You're the one driving around in an electric car, trying to fix *my* problems like doing good deeds will make you into a different person. You can pretend all you like, but at the end of the day, you're just a thug." I managed to stop myself from saying *murderer* somehow, but I still felt like shit as soon as the sentence left my mouth.

He bared his teeth, the fury in his face nearly masking the hurt my words had inflicted. "Yeah, well, you can't get off unless it's with a thug, so whatever. I may be a thug, but what does that make you?"

The sound of Drew's matte black Audi coming up the drive was like the splash of a life preserver after I'd been in the water long enough to start swallowing some. I glanced over my shoulder just in time to see him pull up, then turned back to Hendrix, already walking backward. "You're the one who told me I need to stop fucking losers. So just stay away from me."

He turned around and smacked the remnants of our lunch off the table.

Breathing hard, I turned and jogged down the hill. When I pulled the handle of the back door on Hendrix's Tesla, I thanked my lucky stars it was unlocked, grabbed my bag, and rushed over to Drew's car.

"Drive. Go. *Now*," I demanded. Not that Hendrix was calling after me or trying to catch up. I ignored the pang of disappointment that brought and reminded myself I'd just ensured he wouldn't. I usually loved it when people called me a bitch—more often than not it was just their way of saying I was being too assertive as a woman, speaking my mind too loudly, refusing to take their shit.

But in this moment, I knew I'd been a bitch to him, in all the worst ways.

Drew glanced in my direction. "You all right?"

"I'm fine. Can you drive me back to school? I left my car there."

"Sure." He pulled onto the main road. "What's going on with you two?"

"Nothing." Not anymore. Not ever. I'd made sure of it.

"Didn't look like nothing. You need me to get the guys together and take care of it? Just say the word."

I sighed and forced a smile. "You're sweet to offer to inflict violence on my behalf, but it's not necessary. I promise. I've hurt him way worse than he could ever hurt me."

I hadn't meant to say that last part, but it was true. Drew kept silent, but I could feel more questions on the tip of his tongue.

"Drew, can you please not tell anyone about this? I've handled the situation, and no one needs to know. I promise."

"If you're sure." He sighed.

"I'm positive. Hey, what were you calling me about?"

Drew and I texted, but we rarely called each other. He must've wanted to talk about something important.

"It can wait. Looks like you've had a hard enough day." He squeezed my knee and returned his hand to the gearshift.

I sighed and looked out the window at Devilbend flying by. Was Hendrix right? Would I end up in a life that felt as if it were flying past as I watched from the other side of the window?

CHAPTER TWENTY-TWO

Hendrix

My feet pounded against the treadmill as sweat poured down my face. My lungs were screaming, my heart thundering so hard it felt as though it might give out.

I gritted my teeth and kept pushing.

After Donna got into Drew's car and left, I'd driven straight to the gym, every inch of my body itching to just do *something*. It was better than punching a tree in the park, better than driving to Davey's and getting absolutely wasted, better than finding some unsuspecting dude in a back alleyway and beating the shit out of him. I couldn't punish anyone else to get this feeling out, so I'd punish my own body.

The person I really wanted to punish was *her*.

That wasn't true, not really. Yes, I was angry, furious, but I was hurt more than anything. I'd spilled my guts to her, told her the deepest, darkest moment of my life, and she ... she just ...

I grunted and swung my heavy arms a little harder, pumping my legs.

I'd told her about Austin because I wanted her to understand how fast and how horribly bad shit could turn when you were searching for an escape. No, she wasn't getting into fights with randoms as I had been, but she was spiraling in her own way—*exactly* as I had been. The only difference really was that she preferred to fuck dangerous guys and not fight them. Why couldn't she see that?

But maybe that was my mistake—I'd told her because I wanted her to change her behavior. I'd told her as a way to get her to do what I wanted her to do.

No, that wasn't entirely true either. I didn't think I'd be capable of saying all the things I'd said to Donna if I didn't want her to know them. Not because it would be a wake-up call for her, but because I wanted her to know me—every deep, dark, horrific part of my soul. I wanted her to *know me*. And still want me.

But she didn't. She'd run from me like the monster I was.

Maybe I was going about this whole thing the wrong way. Maybe she needed to hit her rock bottom, just as I had, in order to recognize that something needed to change. But how was I supposed to just sit back and watch her get hurt, possibly killed? Especially now that I'd gone and grown fucking feelings for her, like a moron.

"Hey, bro!" Turner appeared in front of the treadmill, his smile more a grimace. I frowned, wishing he'd go away, wishing everyone would just go the fuck away, but he reached over and hit the Stop button.

"Dude!" I panted, bracing myself on the guard rails. "I was . . . still . . . going."

"Yeah, well, I can't let you get hurt, so . . . how about you take a break and we talk about what's bothering you?" He crossed his arms, and the biceps bulged out. He was a fit guy when we met, but he'd gained definition over the weeks we'd worked out together.

"I'm not gonna . . . get hurt . . . I just need . . . to keep running," I ground out, beyond frustrated with how hard I was breathing. My legs were starting to shake a little now that I'd been forced to stop. Useless meat stumps . . .

"I can't let you keep going, man." Turner frowned, looking more worried by the second.

"Why?"

He sighed. "It's my job to make sure people don't hurt themselves. You're sweating so much it's dripping on the treadmill, which is fucking disgusting"— he made a face—"but also a slip hazard. Not to mention you're so out of breath you can hardly talk, and the only reason you're still upright is because of that death grip on the handrail."

I glared at him, still working to catch my breath.

When I said nothing, Turner raised his eyebrows and pointed to the changing rooms. "Go shower. I'll wipe this down for you and get you a Gatorade so you don't pass out."

I kept glaring at him as I hobbled off the machine. There was no point arguing; he wasn't going to let me move on to weights.

After I stood under the shower for a long time with my hands propped against the tiles, my lungs and heart returned to normal function. I put my school uniform back on and walked out of the shower cubicle.

Turner was sitting on a bench with his back against the lockers, tapping away at his phone. He looked up when I came out and held out a bottle of blue liquid.

I flopped down next to him and had a long drink.

"What's going on with you?" he asked. "You looked like you wanted to murder someone out there."

My spine immediately stiffened, and I stared at him with wide eyes.

He leaned away from me, confused. "What?"

I shook my head and relaxed my posture, dragging a hand down my face. For a second there, I thought maybe Donna had told all her friends, that she was warning everyone to stay away from me again. Except this time, she had a very real reason for it. But that didn't make sense. Turner wasn't acting scared and suspicious—he was concerned for a friend. Me. I didn't deserve him.

"I can't talk about it. It's . . ." I pressed my lips together so hard it almost hurt.

Turner rested his hands on his knees. "When I found out about my mom, that she was dead, that my little sister had seen the whole thing happen . . . all I wanted to do was pretend it wasn't real. I'd spent years dreaming about the day I'd get to hug my mom again, and then suddenly I found out I never would. You know, I don't even remember the last time I hugged her. It must've felt so insignificant, like there was so much certainty there'd be another one, that I didn't think to commit every detail to memory." He turned to look me in the eyes. "Anyway, point is, my little sister needed me, Mena needed me, so I couldn't just curl up into a ball and pretend it wasn't real. I had to face it. And the only way I could do that was to talk about it. To my therapist, to the police, to my dad, to my girlfriend. Every time I shared a bit of how I felt, it was a little easier to carry all the pain and the heartache."

He was telling me I needed to talk about my feelings. That cocky asshole part of me I'd worked so hard to eradicate wanted to roll his eyes and call him a pussy with a punch to his arm. But he was also, in a roundabout way, telling me that he had trusted me with his darkness, his pain, and maybe I could trust him with mine.

But there was one key difference between our situations. "What happened to your family, you were in no way to blame for that." I held his gaze, my jaw tight. "I appreciate you being so honest about all this heavy shit in your life. But my story is the complete opposite. I'm not the victim here. I'm the bad guy."

"There's nothing you can tell me that will make me think less of you."

I sighed and looked up to the ceiling. He was so wrong. I really didn't want to lose Turner as a friend, but I couldn't keep lying to him either. That wasn't friendship. Not to mention, now that Donna knew all the gory details and was more pissed at me than I'd ever seen her, it was only a matter of time before everyone knew. It would be better if he heard it from me anyway.

For the second time in a day, I told someone the full story of the worst thing I'd ever done. I didn't go into as much detail as I had at the park, and I didn't break down crying, but I didn't try to sugarcoat it either. I also told him that I'd told Donna and we'd ended up in another fight, but I didn't tell him why I'd told her—I was still keeping her secrets.

"I took Austin from his mom, just like Boyd Burrows took your mom from you," I finished. "All that pain you feel, I'm the cause of that for someone else."

Turner sat back against the locker, mirroring my pose, and released a big breath. "Did you set out to kill him? Deliberately end his life?"

"No. But—"

"Do you feel bad about what you did?"

"It's the single worst mistake of my life. I'll never stop feeling like shit about it."

"Did you learn from it? Are you trying to be a better person?"

"Every single fucking day. But nothing I do can take back the fact that I *killed someone.*"

"No, what's done is done, and you have to live with that. As far as I see it, it was an awful, horrible mistake that ended in a horrific accident. All you can do is keep living your life in a way that honors Austin's and make sure you don't willingly put any more hurt out into the world."

He stood up and faced me. "As for Donna, I don't know what's going on between you two, but she's not a bad person. Everyone calls her a bitch, but that's only because she's so unapologetic about standing up for what she believes in. She's a good person deep down. Just like you. You'll figure it out."

I stared up at him, struggling to process the casual way he was still accepting me as a friend despite it all. Tears stung the backs of my eyes as he pulled me to my feet and into a hug. We patted each other's backs, holding on for a second longer than our usual hellos.

"Thank you, Turner." All the things I wanted to say to him but couldn't find the words for, I injected into that thank-you.

He shrugged and smiled. "I gotta get back to work. Go home. Do *not* get back on that treadmill." He gave me a pointed look and walked out.

I took a few moments to get my shit together before grabbing my stuff and leaving, waving to him on my way out the door.

The sun was starting to set as I walked around the corner to where I'd parked, my head bent, my mind on what a batshit day it had been.

Apparently, it wasn't over.

I looked up to find Shady leaning against the side of my car, smoking a cigarette. He was in jeans and high-tops, a tracksuit top zipped up under his open coat. With a grin, he pushed off the car and held his arm out wide. "Hendrix, my man!"

"Shady." I gave him a fist bump and a half smile. He was a good distraction and cool most of the time, but it was a little odd he was out here, waiting for me. It put me on alert. "What's up?"

"Listen." He stepped in closer, took another drag of his smoke, and lowered his voice. "I'd love to shoot the shit, but it's freezing out here, and I got another matter to attend to."

"OK." I unlocked my car and threw my gym bag into the back before turning back to face him.

"I just need to know if you've given any more thought to what we talked about." He dropped the butt of his cigarette onto the ground and put it out with his toe.

"What we talked about?" I frowned, trying to remember the last time I'd seen him. It was the night Donna was roofied. We'd sat at the bar, talking shit, sports, movies, nothing serious. Then I'd spotted Donna, and I couldn't remember a single word Shady had said after.

"Yeah, man. There's a fight night this weekend, and the people in charge need an answer." He bounced on his toes, looking at me expectantly.

Every muscle in my body stiffened; it was a battle to relax my jaw enough not to speak through gritted teeth. "Shady, I don't remember us talking about any fight night, and I don't know what this is about, but I want nothing to do with it."

He licked his lips and flicked a glance over his shoulder, a flash of worry entering his gaze before he covered it up with a sly grin. "I know you used to be into it back in NYC. Don't you want an opportunity to put some of those arrogant pricks on their asses? Guys like the dickheads you go to school with? They'd stand no chance against you, man."

He thought he was paying me a compliment, but my blood was boiling. His cousin had been the only one who stood by me in New York after all my so-called friends turned their backs, and Shady had been good to me since I got here, but surely even he must know what he was asking of me.

"Shady, turn around, walk away, and never raise this with me again."

The sly grin fell from his lips, and his eyes darted from side to side. Then he sighed and gave me the first genuine look I'd ever seen on his face. "Hey, man, I'm sorry. You said you'd think about it when I mentioned it last. I didn't know you weren't paying attention. The organizers just wanted me to put a little sweetener on top, extra money, bitches, that kind of thing. They really want you, man. They think your history would add an extra . . . *element* to the entertainment."

They thought the fact I'd killed someone would make the fight more interesting—in case I did it again. Scum-sucking pond dwellers.

I looked over his shoulder and spotted a dark SUV parked a few cars down, the two hard-looking middle-aged motherfuckers inside not even hiding the fact they were watching us.

"What the fuck are you mixed up in, Shady?"

"It's not my scene, man." He leaned in even more, lowered his voice further. "You know how I said Davey's is kind of a neutral ground? Well, I'm not the only one who hangs out there, if you get my drift? Not the only one who does business there. These guys who run the fights . . ." He sighed and shook his head. "I try to steer clear of them, but they noticed we hung out and . . . persuaded me to persuade you, if you know what I mean." He shrugged and stuffed his hands into his pockets. "Don't worry about it, man. I'll tell them you're not interested. I'll take care of it."

I'd never seen Shady scared of anything. I knew he was into some dodgy-as-fuck stuff, that a lot of people were afraid of *him*, so the fact that he was doing someone else's bidding . . . a cold dread settled in my stomach. For Shady and what kind of danger he was in. For Donna and what she was walking into every time she went there.

"Would it help if I made it clear I wasn't interested?" I flicked my eyes over his shoulder so he knew I'd spotted our audience.

He watched me for a second, then gave a tiny nod.

I grabbed him by the collar of his jacket and shoved him back. "Never ask me that again! We're done, you lowlife son of a bitch," I bellowed.

He held his hands up and grinned at me, walking backward, then dropped a serious look onto his face before turning around.

I let the rage show on my face as I got into my car, slammed the door, and sped off as angrily as I could manage in an electric car that was whisper quiet.

The little bit of hope my conversation with Turner had given me—that not everyone would see me as a violent monster—was smashed to pieces, its jagged remnants left on the curb where I'd spoken with Shady.

As I parked the car and trudged into the house—my body sore from my punishing workout, my shoulders sagging from the crushing despair—I didn't know what to think anymore. Which side of the fence would Donna land on once she calmed down? She had said nice things when I'd poured my heart out to her at the park, but did she mean them?

On top of that, the run-in with Shady had shaken me. I kept running over the entire day's events, my mind twisting every single look, every single word, until I had no idea what was real anymore.

My aunt was on me before I even finished taking my shoes off.

"Hey." She leaned against the archway leading to the kitchen, a steaming bowl in her hands. "Want some ramen while you tell me every single detail of your day?" She grinned, then slurped some noodles into her mouth.

I dropped my school bag and my gym bag to the floor and sagged against the wall, not even trying to hide the despair on my face.

Hannah's eyes widened, and she abandoned the bowl on the kitchen island before rushing to my side. "Hendrix? What happened?"

So many things . . . but there was only one my mind couldn't seem to stop obsessing over.

"I told someone what I did. All of it. I didn't hold back."

"And?"

"And she threw it back in my face." It was so much more complicated than that, so much else had happened, but I was just so *tired*. I didn't have the energy to explain it all.

"Oh, Hendrix." She took my hand, cocking her head to the side and looking at me with pity. "I'm so sorry."

I didn't want her pity, nor did I deserve it.

"Today feels like it's been three years long. I'm so tired. Can we please talk about it tomorrow?" I begged.

She nodded and gave me a watery smile. "Come eat something."

I squeezed her hand and followed her into the kitchen. I didn't deserve her kindness either, or her ramen, but I was broken, and I'd take it anyway.

After an almost sleepless night, I made my way to school the next morning still with no idea what to do next—about Donna, about Shady, about how ridiculously complicated my life had become. This was exactly why I'd wanted to keep to myself in Devilbend. But I'd failed even at that.

I was tired and deep in my own dark thoughts, so it wasn't until walking up the main stairs to the entrance that I noticed how everyone was acting.

People were steering clear of me, but that wasn't anything new. What was new were the looks they were throwing me, the hushed whispers. Students were glancing in my direction, wide-eyed, but looking away just as fast. Some of the younger students even turned around and rushed away when they spotted me.

A heavy weight settled in the pit of my stomach. I rushed up the rest of the stairs and into the school, ready to deal with whatever fresh hell was coming my way next.

Inside the doors, I came to a complete stop, the blood in my veins turning to ice. My eyes made a slow sweep of the hall as I let it all sink in, including the looks on everyone's faces, and then I took off again.

There was only one person who could've done this.

Practically snarling at anyone who got in my way, I stalked through the school with a single-minded purpose—find Donna Mead.

I was going to wrap my hands around her delicate little neck, and not in the way her freaky ass liked. I wanted to feel her throat under my palms as I squeezed the air out of her. I wanted to feel those fragile bones snap under my hands. It was the only way to make her pay for this—the only way to make sure that bitch never hurt someone with her petty, privileged attitude again.

CHAPTER TWENTY-THREE

Donna

I tore the paper down and crumpled it, already rushing to the next one. My hands were full of large torn-down photocopied pages, and as the newest one fell to the ground, I cursed and jogged to the nearest trash can. I was only halfway up the corridor, frantically darting from one side of the lockers to the other to get them all down before more people showed up, before Hendrix saw it.

Logically, I knew it was pointless. They were all over the school, every wall of every corridor covered in identical posters that read, "Hendrix Hawthorn is a killer." The words were in red, stark against several newspaper clippings all photocopied over one another like some macabre collage.

Had someone overheard us talking in the park? I was pretty sure Hendrix hadn't told anyone else in Devilbend about it. Who could've done this? Who would go to this much effort? I racked my brain the entire time I attacked the red-and-black paper, ignoring papercut after papercut in my futile effort to stop this from happening to him.

The only other person I was certain knew was Harlow. After Drew dropped me off at my car the day before, I'd driven straight home. Magda was in the kitchen, stirring a giant pot of something that smelled delicious. She wanted me to taste it, and usually I would have been more than happy to, but I told her I had to go to the bathroom and went straight upstairs.

I was a little numb, my mind not quite able to focus on any particular thought or problem. It had all gone so wrong.

Harlow popped her head out of the bedroom as I got to the top of the stairs. "I've been calling you for half an hour." She frowned. "You OK?"

I glanced at my bedroom door, then bypassed it and went to hers instead, wrapping my sister into a hug and breathing in her smell. Her arms held me tightly.

"Donna, you're scaring me," she whispered into my shoulder.

I pulled back and cleared my throat. "Sorry. I'm fine. Do you have a minute? I need your help with something."

"Yeah. What's up?" She was still watching me warily.

I looked in the direction of the stairs. The faint sounds of Magda moving about the kitchen, the radio on in the background.

Shuffling Harlow into her room, I softly closed the door behind us. "I need you to look into something for me."

The last time I'd said those words to her, we were digging up dirt on the assholes who bullied Mena at her old school. There wasn't anything really illegal about what I was asking. I just wasn't sure I'd be able to find the information myself. And that's what I needed in that moment. Hendrix had told me quite a story, but I needed facts, evidence. I needed something solid to hold on to so I could begin to put my racing thoughts in order.

Or maybe I just needed to not deal with it alone. For once, I wanted someone with me as I dealt with something heavy.

Harlow flopped into her computer chair, and I shoved a pile of clothes off the spare chair in the corner before pulling it over to sit next to her.

She keyed in her password, and her three screens came to life. "What are we looking for?"

"I need to know why Hendrix moved here."

"Uh . . . OK. Do we have something to go on? I need a starting point. Maybe his old school."

I sighed. "I know why he came here. I mean, he told me what happened. I just want to check that—"

"You don't believe him? What did he tell you?"

"No, it's not that I don't believe him exactly. I just . . . fuck." I dropped my head into my hands. How could I articulate to my sister that I just needed to give my brain something to focus on?

"I just need more information," I finally said and lifted my head to look at her. When she simply raised an eyebrow, I kept talking. "We ditched school this afternoon, and he told me what happened last year, why he transferred here. He, uh . . ."

The words lodged in my throat. He hadn't actually told me not to tell anyone, but it still felt wrong, as if I was betraying his trust when he'd kept all my secrets. *So many secrets.*

But Harlow wouldn't tell anyone, and I needed some clarity. I swallowed and just said it. "He told me he killed someone. It was unintentional, a horrible accident, and he feels like shit for it. I just need to know more."

Harlow stared at me. "Jesus, fuck." She breathed out, then turned to the screens.

In the end, she didn't do much of anything I couldn't have done myself; it just took a fraction of the time. A search of his name and New York brought up countless results—his family was prominent in society there. That led us to the name of his school, which led us to Austin's full name and allowed for more detailed searches. There was an obituary, a few articles.

I got more details, put names to faces, but really, I didn't understand it any better. I didn't understand why he got under my skin so badly. Why I'd lost it at him even after he told me about the person he killed.

"This is some heavy shit, D." Harlow leaned back in her chair. "Did he . . . what's going on between you guys? Are you OK?"

I looked into my sister's eyes, so full of concern, and the urge to spill it all was almost palpable. But I couldn't do that. My heart quickened at the very thought of it. I was the responsible one, the one who took care of her, the one who did what she was supposed to so that Harlow could do whatever she wanted. I needed a new plan, a way out before I could say anything to anyone. I just wasn't sure what it was I needed a way out of . . .

"I don't know what's going on between us," I told her honestly. "It's more complicated than I can even explain to myself. But please, don't worry. I've never felt unsafe with Hendrix. Not even when he told me about . . . that." I pointed at the screen.

"OK. You wanna talk about it?"

I got to my feet as it dawned on me. *I'd never felt unsafe with Hendrix.* How often had I wished someone would be for me what I was for so many other people—protector, defender, confidant, safe place to land? He'd been exactly that and more from the first time I saw him at Davey's. I'd just been too busy fighting against it to realize it.

I was a fucking idiot.

"No," I whispered, my thoughts far away. I leaned down and kissed my sister on the cheek. "I just need to think for a while. Thank you."

The next morning I texted the girls, asking them to make their own way to school, and headed in early. I'd planned to wait for Hendrix in the parking lot so I could talk to him, swallow my pride and apologize, but I needed to pee, so I ducked into the school—and that was when I saw the posters. *Everywhere.*

I'd started attacking them immediately and had still barely made a dent. I'd only managed to do one hallway and the stairs leading to the back entrance.

"Donna!"

At the sound of Amaya's voice, I looked up from stuffing paper into the trash can.

Amaya, Harlow, and Mena jogged up to me. Other students were milling about too, and I glanced up at the clock. It was only another twenty minutes until the first class.

"Did you tell anyone?" I demanded, my focus on Harlow.

"No." She shook her head. "I would never . . . oh my god."

"Help me get them down," I demanded.

"Have you told a teacher?" Mena asked as the others started tearing down posters.

"No." I shook my head. I'd been so panicked I hadn't even thought of it. "I just started tearing them down as soon as I realized."

"I'll go find someone." Mena rushed off toward the office.

She'd hardly disappeared around the corner when Hendrix came storming down the hallway. The girls stopped ripping down posters as the few other students in the hall darted out of his way. He was furious, shoulders tight, eyes narrowed, scowling—and he was heading right for me.

I knew what this looked like. I rolled my shoulders back and steeled myself, facing him.

He stopped right in front of me and smacked the pile of papers out of my hand, his fist crunching around one as the rest fell to the floor.

"It's a little late for that, isn't it?" He cocked his head and leaned in. Anger was rolling off him in waves, but his voice remained low, seething. "Why bother taking them down when you went to so much effort to plaster the entire fucking school?"

I forced my own voice to come out steady. "Hendrix, I didn't do this."

He chuckled, the sound devoid of any humor. "Oh, of course. The princess doesn't get her hands dirty. You had the help do it for you."

"Hendrix, I didn't do this," I repeated, my fists clenching at my sides.

"You're fucking unbelievable." He was so close now, I could smell the cinnamon on his breath, feel the heat of his rage. "I know I got on your nerves, but all I ever did was try to help you. What I told you yesterday was . . ."

He squeezed his eyes shut for a second, beating back the pain that flashed for just a moment across the stormy pools of gray.

"You keep saying you want me to leave you alone—*fine*. We're done. You're on your own, Donna. If you end up dead in a ditch, I no longer give a shit. I'm done with you, you spiteful bitch."

He took a few steps backward, balled the piece of paper in his hands, and threw it before turning around and storming out. The ball of paper hit me in the chest and bounced to the ground harmlessly, but I flinched so hard. My whole body stiffened with the impact—of his words, his rage, his hurt, all directed at me. And I knew I deserved it. I wasn't responsible for the posters, but that pain in his face—that was my fault.

Tears stung the backs of my eyes, but I forced them back. There was no way in hell I was going to let myself fall apart in front of all these people.

More and more students were arriving every minute, most of them now throwing me confused, curious looks. Mena rushed back from the office, but several teachers had appeared already, tearing the rest of the posters down while trying in vain to keep the students calm.

The girls surrounded me, all looking worried.

"Donna, what's going on?" Amaya kept her voice low, her arms crossed.

I looked around at the chaos once more. I couldn't stand there and talk to them. I needed to do something.

Drew was standing a few feet away. One hand rested on his hip while the other rubbed the back of his neck as he took it all in. But unlike everyone else, there was something more in his eyes—fear.

I narrowed my gaze on him.

"Donna?" Harlow asked, placing a hand on my shoulder.

But I shrugged her off and marched right up to Drew.

He startled when he spotted the murderous look on my face. "Hey, D."

"Cut the bullshit, Drew." I got in his face. "Start talking."

"I . . . I'm . . ." He backed away, his eyes flying about the hall, unable to meet mine.

I shoved him, and even though he was practically twice my size and mostly muscle, he let himself stagger back a step. "Who did it?"

He sighed and leaned in. "It was Will. He—"

I didn't wait for him to finish. I had a name. I turned around and stormed toward the front entrance.

"Donna, wait! I have to tell you . . ." Drew called after me, but I ignored him and just kept going.

The girls fell into step beside me, but I didn't want to drag them into this. I didn't want them to find things out about me I wasn't ready for them to know.

"Amaya, I need to know who else knew about this and why I didn't." I glanced at her. She looked determined, ready to stand by me regardless of the fact she had no idea what this was about. They all had that same look.

She nodded and turned back around.

"Can you two find out how the faculty didn't notice this before students started arriving? And any other info you can get."

Harlow looked hesitant, but Mena pulled her away, heading back to the office.

I jogged down the ornate front stairs and rushed toward the back of the parking lot. Will parked in the back because he was always too late to get a better spot, and because it made it easier to do the other things that made him consistently late to class.

I pulled the door to his Bentley open, not even remotely surprised to see his pants down and Nicola leaning over the center console, giving him a blow job.

They both startled at my sudden appearance. Nicola flinched back against the opposite door, while Will was slower to react, tucking his dick back into his pants as he sighed. "Donna, what the fuck?"

"We need to talk," I snarled. I didn't want to talk. I wanted to hit him, punch him, kick him while I screamed all my frustration out. But that wasn't how my parents had raised me. That wasn't who I was.

Nicola scrambled out of the car and straightened her clothes, eyeing me with fear. "I'm sorry, Donna. I know you and Will . . . but you're not technically together, and I . . . just please—"

"Shut up." God, she was irritating. I opened the back door and threw her school bag onto the path in front of the car. "I don't give a flying fuck whose dick you wrap those Botox-filled lips around. Get lost."

Her eyes narrowed in anger, and she scooped her bag up and stalked away, muttering "bitch" as she went.

Will got out and fixed his tie. "Was that really necessary?"

"What the fuck is wrong with you?" I asked.

He looked at me as if I were an idiot.

"I know you're responsible for Fulton Academy's new décor." I let the sarcasm drip from my lips. "And I want to know why."

He eyed me for a second, the disinterested expression melting away into something more calculating. "You really are spreading your legs for that thug," he said, and my stomach plummeted. "I didn't quite believe it when Drew mentioned what he'd seen, but, shit, I don't think I've ever seen you this worked up."

Unbelievable. That arrogant, spoiled, useless piece of . . .

I slapped him. The feelings welling up inside me—ugly, awful, frightening feelings—couldn't be contained any longer, and the next thing I knew, Will's head was turned to the side, and my hand was stinging from the impact.

I curled it into a fist and dug my nails into my palm, using the pain to keep me grounded.

Will fixed me with a blank look, not even reaching up to hold his cheek. "You think you can hurt me?" He chuckled. "You're just a little girl, playing princesses and castles while there's a whole big, dangerous world all around you. Nothing you do can hurt me, Donna."

"You're jealous I fucked another guy, so you're going to ruin his life? How petty, William, especially considering your mediocre cock is still slick with Nicola's saliva."

"I don't have time for this." He swung his bag over his shoulder and slammed the car door shut.

"Don't you fucking walk away from me." I got in his path.

He looked at me as if I was boring him, absolutely no emotion on his face. Will was not at all what I always thought him to be. He was cruel and cold and empty. I couldn't believe I'd considered a future with him.

"Do yourself a favor and stay out of this, D. Now, unless you want to finish what Nicola started, get out of my way."

He didn't wait for a response—just shoved past me and sauntered off toward school.

What an absolute piece of shit of a human being. And he'd set his sights on Hendrix because of *me*.

A sob clawed its way up my throat, but I swallowed it, forced my eyes to remain wide open until they felt raw—until I was certain I wouldn't cry. Not yet.

The bell rang, and it was almost a relief to have something functioning the way it was supposed to. My world was crumbling around me, and I held the sledgehammer in my hands, but the bell tolled anyway.

I had no idea what to do next, how to fix it. So I pulled a calm, detached expression over my face, smoothed my uniform, and walked steadily back to school.

I sat through classes, said the bare minimum to my friends, listened to the announcement from the principal assuring us we were all safe and the culprits of this "prank" would be caught. But I didn't really pay attention to any of it. I spent the entire time going over everything in my head. Every interaction between Hendrix and me, every word, every touch, every loaded look.

I made myself recount all the horrible, vicious things I'd said and done to him. And in the end, it wasn't me who had broken him. In the end, I'd wanted to do the very opposite, but his downfall was my fault anyway.

I was failing in every single area of my life, barely holding it together on a good day, but this . . . this was the worst thing I'd ever done.

I wanted it all to just . . . stop.

CHAPTER TWENTY-FOUR

Hendrix

The glow of the TV was the only light in the room as I slumped on the couch, controller between my hands. I was half-heartedly playing with randoms on the internet when someone knocked on the door.

I didn't even glance up. It was probably Robbie, although he usually just let himself in. Aunt Hannah had gone to bed not even half an hour ago.

I'd called her right after my run-in with Donna, completely lost, and she'd left work and come right down to the school. She marched me up to the office and flipped her shit, demanding to know how this had happened, why none of the staff had noticed before the students arrived, what the fuck they were paying their security staff for.

The headmistress calmly answered all her questions while I sat in a chair, scowling at the edge of her desk. Apparently, most of the teachers and admin staff entered the school through a side door that led directly to their offices. The security guard who opened the student entrance in the mornings hadn't bothered to peek inside before walking to his post by the front gates. One of the janitors hadn't shown up to work that morning, and they were still investigating.

She'd probably paid him off, and in a way that he wouldn't even know who he was dealing with. I had to give her that—she was damn smart.

The knock came again, more insistent this time, and then indiscernible voices, hisses—someone arguing.

I rolled my eyes and focused back on the screen. I didn't want to deal with people, didn't even want to *think* right now. It was probably some kids from my school, here to play some prank, or maybe even their incensed parents come to threaten my aunt. The calls from worried, outraged parents had started pouring in as soon as we left campus. People didn't want their kids anywhere near me.

When we got home, I told my aunt everything that had happened between me and Donna over the last few days, leaving out the graphic sexual details. I blamed myself—I'd gotten myself into this mess by not leaving her alone, and I deserved those posters, really. I deserved their fear and contempt and disgust. I deserved their rejection for what I'd done. But I couldn't fight the disappointment, the hurt. I guess I was still human after all.

My aunt listened to it all and, in the end, said she was proud of me. *Proud of me.* For doing what I thought was right. She assured me Fulton wouldn't be able to kick me out, despite how loudly the other parents complained. I was getting good grades, and I'd completely stayed out of trouble. I was a victim in this situation.

That didn't sit well with me. I didn't feel like a victim—I felt like the monster they all now knew I was. But I appreciated her unflinching support anyway.

The knock came again, even louder. I gritted my teeth and glanced toward the stairs. They'd wake my aunt up if they hadn't already. The thought that it could be someone here to harass her was the only reason I tossed the controller down and stormed to the door.

"Get off my property or I'm calling the police." I put a little grunt into my voice, making it firm, threatening, but not too loud—I didn't want to disturb my aunt.

There was a second of perfect stillness and then: "Hendrix, we need to talk to you." The voice was feminine, but it wasn't Donna, and she didn't sound angry. I frowned, wishing the side panel by the door wasn't frosted.

When I didn't respond, another female voice, this one much more demanding, said with a single thump against the wood, "Open the damn door." Amaya. It was definitely her, and that first, uncertain one had been Harlow.

I shook my head and turned to leave. Maybe I *would* call the police.

There was more arguing behind the door, hushed words. Was Donna with them? Standing there with a smirk while they manipulated me into . . . into . . . *shit*, I didn't even know what else she could possibly do to me.

"We don't have time for this." Mena cut across the others, surprising me with the seriousness in her voice. "Hendrix, please open the door."

I sighed, already regretting the decision, but because it was Mena—the only one of them with some goodness in her soul—I turned back around and wrenched the door open.

It was just the three of them.

"What the hell do you want? Here to do your overlord's bidding?" I set my feet wide apart, blocking the door.

"We've been trying to call you. Why didn't you answer?" Amaya frowned. Always on the attack.

I hadn't looked at my phone since I got home. It was probably still on my bed, where I'd dumped everything before changing into sweats. "Why would I want to talk to you? And how the hell do you know where I live?"

"It's in the school records." Harlow waved that away as if it were no big deal they had access to the school records. "We can't find Donna, and we're starting to get worried. We wanted to check with everyone she could be with before telling our parents or the police. Have you seen her?"

I ignored the pang of worry that made the back of my head tingle. She didn't deserve it. Not anymore. "I haven't seen that bitch since this morning, and I don't give a flying fu—"

"She didn't do it." Mena stepped forward and gripped my arm, looking up at me with those doe eyes. I could see why Turner was so protective of her—she looked like the perfect meal for a wolf. "Donna didn't put those posters up. She didn't know anything about it. It was William Frydenberg."

"What?" I frowned. They had to be lying. But why? What game were they playing now?

"It's true. She confronted him about it, and they got into a fight. She slapped him. And Drew confirmed it when Amaya asked him. It was Will. Donna didn't know anything about it, I swear. We would know if she'd planned something like this. I would've talked her out of it."

"She's been acting weird all day," Amaya cut in before I could argue, slam the door in their faces. "She was really detached, hardly talked to anyone, just kind of went through the motions."

Harlow was on the verge of tears. "When we got home after school, she just shut herself in her room. She didn't even come down for dinner. When Mom went to check on her, she said she was sick, but when I went to her room after everyone was in bed, she was gone. Her car is gone, and she's not picking up the phone. *Please*, Hendrix, do you know where she might be?"

"Why do you think I'd know anything?" I was still a little wary, but the implications were slowly sinking in, making my shoulders tense. Mena wasn't one to lie, and I couldn't deny the fear in Harlow's eyes. Even Amaya—who I'd never seen bothered by anything—looked worried.

It could be a trick, another game, but I didn't think it was. Maybe I was just desperate for it to be true. I so badly didn't want it to have been her who'd ruined me.

"We know you two have been hooking up," Amaya answered. "We know there's more to the story, but that's not important right now."

I watched them for a few moments longer, trying to hold on to my anger, my hurt. But in my gut, I knew this was the truth. Donna hadn't done it. It was Will and . . . they had a history, maybe even a future from what she'd told me . . . they'd argued . . . she'd be blaming herself. On top of everything else.

"Fuck." I dragged a hand down my face. "I know where she might be."

I pulled on my shoes and grabbed my keys off the side table. "I'll drive, but you three need to be prepared. This . . . is not going to be pretty."

———

I white-knuckled the steering wheel, wishing for the first time I'd spent dear Dad's money on some obnoxious sports car instead of the Tesla. Not because the Tesla wasn't fast—it was. It glided through the night, practically flying toward our destination. No, it was the absolute silence of the high-tech machine that made me wish for something with an engine that grunted. I wanted a beast under me, one that growled with all the rage I wished I could let loose.

Amaya sat next to me in the passenger seat, Mena and Harlow in the back. For the first twenty minutes of the drive, I'd told them everything—how Donna and I first met at Davey's, how she'd been going there for months, the early acceptance and her constant self-destructive behavior. Every single one of their questions I'd answered without hesitation.

She'd kept my secret—it was Will who'd exposed me, I was sure of it now—and I was betraying all of hers. I wasn't sorry. I had half a mind to call her parents and put them on speaker as I let it all spill out. It was the only thing I could do until we found her. The only thing keeping my fear at bay until we could figure out if she was . . . I couldn't let myself think the worst.

I'd texted Shady before we took off, asking him to keep an eye out for her, but he hadn't replied.

The girls had all fallen into silence. Amaya was staring out the front window, watching the headlight beams illuminate the road as it whipped past. Her eyes were a little wide, her chest rising and falling with labored breaths.

I wanted to look into the back seat, but I was pretty sure the other two would be wearing matching expressions, and I had to focus on the road.

We were nearly there, and I needed to keep my shit together. I needed to figure out how to get the three girls to stay in my car while I went inside and looked for her. All three of them would certainly fight me on it, demand to help me look, but I couldn't risk them getting hurt—Donna would never forgive me.

I should've been thinking of a way to convince them, should've already started making my case as I pulled onto the dim, run-down street, but I couldn't get my mind off what we'd find.

The worst-case scenario—the one where she was dead in a ditch, as I'd practically told her that morning I hoped she would be—was too hard to even consider. But there were so many other scenarios. What if someone spiked her drink again and took her? What if she pissed off the wrong person? What if she'd gotten in an accident on the way here? What if she'd already found some biker dude with a cocky attitude and big biceps? What if they were already out in the back alley where I'd . . . where we'd . . .

What if she wasn't even there and we'd wasted precious time?

I was so lost in the worry, the rage, the abject fear of what we'd find—or wouldn't—that I nearly missed the turn. I slammed on the brakes and yanked the steering wheel toward the parking lot entrance. The sudden force sent us all flying to the side, and I reflexively threw a hand out to catch Amaya across her abdomen. But the car was the epitome of precision and safety, and it corrected my sudden moves, not even sliding out as we pulled into the lot.

Amaya covered my arm with hers, breathing even harder now.

"Sorry," I muttered. She just shoved my hand away without saying anything.

I slowed considerably as we neared the entrance. The bouncer was there, looking mean as ever as he nodded to a group of rough guys heading through the front door. The one at the rear of the group wasn't even trying to hide the gun tucked into the back of his pants. Beside them, a woman leaned over and vomited right on the footpath.

Mena made a sound of disgust as Harlow finally found her voice. "This is where Donna has been coming secretly? Jesus."

Amaya just stared, jaw tight.

I steered past rows of cars toward the dark corner of the lot where I knew she liked to park. As we approached the area, I wasn't sure if I was hoping to see the flawless pearlescent finish of her BMW in among this filth—or if I was hoping to find nothing at all.

CHAPTER TWENTY-FIVE

Donna

I took the turn into the ratty street a little too fast. Then I overcorrected and weaved from side to side until I managed to force my car into a straight line again. The adrenaline sent a hit of pleasure shooting through my veins, even as some addled part of my brain screamed that I was an idiot who'd get myself killed before I even got to Davey's.

I knew I shouldn't have been driving after drinking—I'd *never* done it before—but I was beyond caring.

After school, I'd shut myself in my room, unable to face anyone, unable to really process everything—not just that day but the last several months.

I'd failed. How spectacularly I'd failed at *everything*. I had no idea where to go from here. *Me*. Donna Mead. I prided myself on how organized and prepared and determined I was in all things. But suddenly I found myself sitting on my bed, staring out the window as the light disappeared, with absolutely no fucking idea what I was supposed to do now.

Every time Hendrix's face popped into my mind, I fought back tears. I'd failed him the most. And I knew—*I knew*—if I let those tears fall, if I gave in to the emotion, I'd fall apart, and no one would know where to even start putting me back together.

All the king's horses and all the king's men . . . the wall I'd fallen from was so, *so* tall.

When I'd realized I was sitting in pitch blackness, I reached over and turned on the lamp by my bed.

My reflection stared back at me from the dark glass of my window. I didn't like what I saw, so I looked away.

I wanted to go away. Make it stop. I just wanted to be able to breathe. To be someone else for a while.

Dark Donna . . .

I didn't even wait to make sure everyone was asleep before leaving the house; I just waited until it sounded quiet. No one even noticed me walk—not sneak—down the stairs, get into my car, and leave. No one even cared.

After leaving my house, I decided that maybe getting blind drunk was a better option than going to Davey's. I wanted oblivion, but I didn't really want to hook up with anyone who wasn't . . . I didn't want anyone but *him* touching me.

Don't think his name.

So I drove to a liquor store and used my excellent fake ID to buy an obscenely expensive bottle of scotch.

It wasn't until I was back in my car and the smooth scent of the liquor hit the back of my nose that I realized why I'd picked that particular alcohol. I never drank scotch, but I'd craved something smoky, spicy—because it was the closest I could get to the cinnamon that clung to Hendrix. That stupid gum he chewed . . . the scent always lingered, it was always on his tongue, in his kisses, on his breath as he told me he hated me.

I ground my teeth against the threatening tears and took a big swig, the alcohol so smooth it hardly even burned my throat. It just warmed my chest and belly, already numbing the pain, already giving me something else to focus on.

With every drink, I forced myself to think of other things that weren't him. Campfires, cigars, the smoked cheese Harlow and I had gorged ourselves on during our last family trip to Paris.

I didn't know how long I'd sat in my car, drinking and trying not to think about Hendrix, but nearly half the bottle was gone when I decided I did indeed need to go to Davey's. I couldn't go home, and I didn't want to sit in the car alone, crying and drinking. It was the one place that never failed to let me get lost, let me forget everything.

As I pulled into the parking lot, I made myself breathe, focus. I couldn't go smashing into parked cars. Not when I'd finally made it. Even though I was a fucking mess, that little part of my logical brain had managed to remind me to take the back streets instead of the freeway, to drive slowly. I was irrationally annoyed at how long it had taken to get here. Self-preservation was so weird . . .

I parked the car in the back of the lot where there was more room, where I was able to park across two spots at a weird angle and hit the divider without anyone noticing. Then I grabbed the bottle from the passenger seat, swung the door wide open, and hauled myself out. My vision blurred, and I took a moment to steady myself before walking toward the front entrance, leaving my car open, my purse just sitting there, the keys still in the ignition. Nothing mattered anymore.

I took another swig as my heels crunched in the gravel, my footing uneven. I'd changed into a low-cut gray top and applied dark eyeliner before I decided it actually didn't matter what I wore. My school skirt and socks had stayed on, and I'd added a pair of heeled Mary Janes to complete the weird ensemble. I was pretty sure I looked like some slutty porn version of a school girl with my cleavage hanging out and the heels on, but I didn't care.

I had no idea who I was anymore, which version of myself I was *pretending* to be. The clothes were a representation of all the lies I'd told to everyone, to myself. Of this ugly downward spiral I was on and didn't care to prevent.

The good girl gone bad . . . *rotten to the core.*

"Donna." My name. His voice, so rough, so demanding, no—*pleading.*

I gritted my teeth and took another swig from the bottle. I'd pushed the image of his tortured face from my mind so hard that now I was hearing him in my head.

"Donna!" Louder, more insistent. The sound of crunching gravel wasn't just from my own unsteady steps.

I stopped. He was here. My heart soared.

He was here. My heart plummeted into the dirty gravel at my feet.

I turned, resigned. But I didn't see Hendrix. No, the first thing my addled, fucked-up mind latched on to was Harlow.

My sister stopped, her eyes wide, taking me in. There were a few feet between us—an entire ocean, the Grand Canyon. Mena stood next to her, tears trailing down her cheeks unabashedly as she watched the train wreck I'd become, had been for so long already. Amaya was on Harlow's other side, hands on hips, breathing hard. The other two were shocked, worried, upset, and Amaya probably was too, but she was the most like me. In the moment, she was ready to take charge, ready to get answers, ready to fix the situation.

Well, I wasn't a *situation*, and this couldn't be fixed. I frowned, fighting the dizziness from the alcohol. "What . . . how did you know . . ."

That's when I spotted Hendrix. He was standing behind my friends, his face cast in shadow from one of the few lights still operational in the parking lot.

He was here. He'd come after me despite everything. *He was here . . .*

He'd brought my friends here . . .

What had he told them? Who else knew?

I narrowed my eyes, homing in on the one person who could make me feel more angry—*more alive*—than any other. I focused on Hendrix as my world fell apart.

"What the fuck have you done?" I sneered, my breathing getting faster and faster.

He blinked but didn't look surprised I was turning my rage on him.

"You've ruined everything." I seethed, taking a few wobbling steps forward.

As one, my friends moved toward me, ready to steady me, to break my fall. But maybe I needed to crash into the filthy gravel, let it scrape away all the ugly parts of me until nothing but clean, raw blood showed. I couldn't look at them.

I threw the bottle between us, stopping them in their tracks. The bottle didn't even break—just thumped to the ground and started spilling amber liquid.

Gravel dug into my soles as I tugged off my shoes and kept moving toward Hendrix on unsteady feet.

"I told you to keep your mouth shut. I told you not to tell anyone. I told you to leave me *alone*." I threw my shoes to the ground, like a toddler throwing toys.

I was directly in front of him now, wishing I'd kept the shoes on so I wouldn't have to look up to meet his resigned stare.

"I told you!" I screamed into his face.

He pressed his lips together but didn't respond, hardly moved other than the rise and fall of his labored breathing. He was barely keeping it together too.

But I didn't give a shit. This was *my* mental breakdown. He could wait his turn.

The realization that that was what was happening to me—that I was acting like a completely unhinged, crazed lunatic—was the last straw. Because that's what I was.

Unhinged.

Driving drunk.

Throwing things.

Screaming at people.

Crazy.

Lunatic.

The tears I'd been holding at bay all day burst out of me—a dam breaking. But even as I started crying, *sobbing*, I railed against what was happening to me. What I'd allowed myself to become.

"Why?" I cried as I shoved Hendrix. He hardly even leaned back at the force of my hands on his chest. "Why did you tell them? They know. They can see. I'm . . . I begged you . . ."

I pounded his chest with my fists, pulled at his sweatshirt. "You told them my secret but I kept yours!"

When the reality of the situation washed over me, I made myself look up into his eyes again. His jaw was tight, a muscle jumping in his cheek as if he was grinding his teeth, his eyes blazing with emotions I was not equipped to decipher in my current state.

But he was still there, still standing as solid as a stone pillar.

How many times had he saved me—*from myself?*

I sobbed, the energy draining out of me as I dropped my gaze.

"I kept your secret." The anger that had edged my voice just moments before drained away, and I gripped his sweatshirt. "It wasn't me, Hendrix. I didn't . . . I would never . . . I'm sorry."

His hands landed on my back just as my knees wobbled. He was finally touching me, finally holding me.

"Please believe me. Please, please, please . . ." I had no idea what I was pleading for. My voice was barely above a whisper as I sagged against him.

I fully expected him to push me off, dump me on the ground and walk away. It was all my fault. *It was all my fault.*

"No, it's not." His low voice reverberated through his chest. My whole body shook with emotion, and my knees buckled.

But Hendrix was there, his arms tightening around me, keeping me from falling.

I was heavy in his arms, a dead weight, a burden. But he'd never let me down, never wavered, even as I'd pushed him away at every step. And he didn't waver now, didn't let me fall.

His strong arms banded around my back as I clung to him, one hand going to the back of my head.

"It's OK, baby," he whispered against my hair. "It's going to be OK."

A small glimmer of peace flickered in my chest at his words, a tiny bit of sanity returning, reminding me he was here, that I was not alone, that my friends had come too.

Harlow. Mena. Amaya.

They were all here, all watching me unravel, watching Hendrix hold me together.

My addled thoughts were interrupted by my heaving stomach.

"Shit." I lifted my head from Hendrix's chest, gave him one wide-eyed look, then leaned to the side and vomited.

CHAPTER TWENTY-SIX

Donna

It didn't take me long to realize the bed wasn't my own. The light on my face was coming from a different direction from where my window should be, and the pillow was softer than mine. It also smelled like Amaya—that feminine, light perfume my friend wore.

My head ached. It felt as if someone were squeezing it between big, strong hands, every thought coming through a fog.

I remembered most of the previous night—I was never the type to lose memory when drunk, even when I polished off half a bottle of scotch. Thinking about the amber liquid made my stomach spasm, and my mouth filled with saliva.

I forced a deep breath down my nose and blew it out, then another and another, until the urge to puke subsided. There was nothing left in my stomach to vomit out anyway—I'd just be retching and feeling even more miserable.

Squeezing my eyes shut against the light, I rolled into an even tighter ball and snuggled farther into the bedding. For the first time since I'd learned to tell time, I didn't give a crap how late it was. Nothing mattered other than how utterly broken my body felt. My mind and my heart weren't much better.

After I'd started puking all over the gravel, Hendrix had stepped behind me, out of the firing line, so he could hold me. With one arm wrapped around the front of my shoulders and the other low on my hips, he held up my full weight as

I vomited the entire contents of my stomach. The sudden sickness must've roused my friends from their shocked stupor. Soft feminine hands appeared at my forehead to pull my short hair back, and someone else produced a bottle of water and a wad of tissues.

After that, Hendrix carried me to my car, and my friends buckled me in and drove me away. I hardly heard what they said to each other, hardly registered Mena giving Amaya directions out of the seedy neighborhood as Harlow ran her fingers through my hair, my head in her lap.

I managed to walk myself up to Amaya's room—thankful I didn't have to suffer the indignity of having my girls carry me up—and passed out as soon as I collapsed on her bed, totally spent in every way imaginable. Judging by the T-shirt and underwear I'd woken up in, they'd taken the time to change me and tuck me under the covers.

I sighed in frustration and threw the covers back, keeping my eyes closed. More than anything, I just wanted to go back to sleep, embrace unconsciousness, and pretend for a little longer that none of this was happening. But now that I was awake, I couldn't stop thinking, remembering, worrying. Plus, the awful pressure in my head and clammy, gross feeling in my entire body made it impossible to relax.

I cracked my eyes open and hissed at the light, then forced myself to lift up onto my elbows.

"Morning, sunshine." Amaya's bright voice was like talons against my brain. I glared at her, but it turned into a wince as another sharp pain shot through my head. My friend was sitting on the bed next to me, propped up against the headboard, her phone clutched in her elegant fingers.

"Were you watching me sleep? Fucking creep." My voice was hoarse, scratchy. Probably from all the crying and screaming at Hendrix. Also the vomiting. God, was I a mess.

"Don't flatter yourself. I was scrolling the gram while you snored. I was actually trying to decide whether to post this lovely pic of you." She showed me her screen, a sweet smile on her face. It was a picture of me sleeping, my mouth open, my face smooshed into the pillow. The one visible eye was dark with smudged mascara.

I lunged for her. "Don't you fucking dare!"

She laughed maniacally and leaned back, slapping me away.

"You started the 'beat her ass' portion of the intervention without us?" My sister's voice alerted me to her arrival, but I was too busy trying to pin Amaya under me to look. She was skinny, but she was fast.

"It stinks in here." Mena went to the window and threw it wide open; a gust of fresh, chilly air sent a shiver down my spine. My tousle with Amaya came to a natural end, both of us panting.

Amaya made a face. "Your breath is hideous."

"Come on." Harlow yanked the sheet off the bed, detangling it from my legs. "Go have a shower and brush your teeth."

"Then breakfast." Mena smiled from the window.

"Then interrogation." Amaya nodded.

"Intervention," Harlow and Mena said at the same time, making me think they'd already argued about how to approach this . . . situation. I didn't want to be a situation.

I crawled off the bed and shuffled into Amaya's adjoining bathroom without looking at any of them. Her bedroom was luxurious, with soft furnishings, velvet cushions, and everything in rich jewel tones. The bathroom was just as dark and moody, black marble and muted gold fixtures everywhere.

Avoiding my reflection in the mirror, I hopped into the shower and scrubbed my face before using Amaya's toothbrush. I also did my best to avoid thinking about how much Hendrix had told them, what they thought of me now, what they'd said to each other while I slept.

Someone had left fresh underwear and sweats for me on the bathroom counter. I changed quickly and stepped out to find my friends all scattered about the bedroom, sipping from steaming mugs. A tray with a fourth mug and a plate had been laid out on the bed—for me.

Shame burned the back of my neck as I sat down in front of it, the feeling as tangible as the droplets of water coming off my wet hair.

They'd made me plain toast and a cup of chamomile tea.

I nibbled on the toast, focusing on the food, on pushing through the queasy feeling in my stomach. No one said anything. The only noises were the occasional sips of coffee and the wind and birds through the open window. So weird for my usually loud, animated, opinionated friends.

I finished the first piece of toast and pushed the plate away, unable to stomach the second. Bringing the mug to my lips, I blew gently on the hot liquid.

I needed to get this conversation going, air out this odd tension between us just as the room was getting aired out by the fresh wind.

My first sip was pleasantly warm as it made its way down my throat. I sighed and opened my mouth to speak, but . . . I wasn't sure where to start, so I closed it again and frowned into my tea. I was kind of sick of always being the one to start the conversations, to take the lead. I felt like shit. If they wanted to talk, they could talk. I was just going to nurse my hangover.

"How are you feeling?" Mena sat down on the bed next to me, her kindness immediately making me feel guilty for what I'd just been thinking.

I swallowed and took a deep breath. "Like shit."

I looked up into my cousin's face. There was no judgment, no pity, just a readiness to listen, maybe a little worry.

"Good." Amaya took a sip from her mug. She was sitting in a magenta armchair in the corner. "Serves you right for what you put us through."

"You really had us scared, D." Harlow sounded unsure whether she wanted to scold me or plead with me. She was perched on the bench under the window, one leg propped up as she leaned on her knee.

"I'm sorry I worried you guys." I sighed. If Harlow—if any one of them—disappeared like that and I found them in the state I'd been in . . . "Last night was . . . yesterday . . ." I couldn't find the words. Because it wasn't really about yesterday. It was about months, years, *all of it.*

Harlow moved my tray to the floor and sat cross-legged in front of me. "What's going on with you? Why won't you talk to us? Let us help?"

I shrugged. "I don't know. I just . . . you all have your own things going on, your own problems. And it's not like there was some catastrophic thing that happened. It was just one thing after another piling up, and I didn't want to burden you. I thought I could handle it myself—that I *should* handle it myself. But shit just kept building and building . . ."

Amaya snorted, and a bit of frustration shot through me. I stared her down as she slammed her now empty mug on her desk and came to stand by the bed. This was just her—how she reacted to hurt—but I didn't want to deal with it.

She spoke before I could say anything I'd regret. "That's a load of shit, Donna. You didn't want to burden us? So, it's OK for you to help Harlow with her home-work and get her out of trouble with teachers, it's OK for you to listen to me bitch about my mom, it's OK for you to rain down hell when Mena was getting bullied, but we can't be there for you? You're not a goddamn robot. You can't do every-thing yourself, and it's bullshit that you didn't trust us to help you."

"What? I trust you girls with my life." I reached out and took her hand. She let me, but didn't break that hard stare. "Devilbend Dynasty is not just a silly hashtag to me. This has nothing to do with me not trusting you and everything to do with my fucked-up head."

I needed them to understand that this was all because of my need to handle my own shit—maybe because I was the oldest, maybe because of how driven everyone in our family was, maybe because I'd fallen into a pattern of showing everyone a tough, unshakeable face. Who knew why I was the way I was? It was something to figure out later, but I needed them to know it had nothing to do with how I felt about them.

"What did Hendrix tell you?" I asked.

Amaya just stared.

"A lot," Mena finally answered.

"He pretty much didn't shut up the entire ride over." Harlow rolled her eyes.

"About Davey's? Why I go there? What I do there?"

They nodded.

"About college? The early acceptance?"

More nods.

"About . . . us?"

"He was scant on details about that," Harlow said.

It was time for more honesty. I swallowed and looked at each of them. "I'm sorry I lied to you, kept things from you. I'm sorry I didn't come to you for help and support. But please, don't leave me. I need you girls."

"No one's leaving you, you idiot." Amaya finally flopped down onto the bed and squeezed my hand back. "Just talk to us."

Surrounded by my friends, I told them everything—the internship I didn't get, the volunteer position I'd idiotically lost, the early acceptance that made me realize I didn't want to go to law school, the way going to Davey's made me feel free of it all for a little while, how the danger of hooking up with hard men made me feel alive.

They listened to it all, held me, supported me, asked questions, reassured me we'd find solutions. They were exactly the kind of friends I hadn't given them a chance to be. I promised myself I'd never shut them out again. Then I promised them, out loud.

After talking it through properly, in detail, with three sounding boards—it didn't feel so insurmountable. It no longer felt as if I was single-handedly holding up an entire building. I'd speak to my parents, hard as it would be. I'd figure out what I wanted to do after high school. I'd lean on my friends more for support and guidance. In fact, now that they knew it all, I felt a little silly for how much the pressure had gotten to me, how spectacularly I'd fallen apart the night before. But they made me feel better about that too.

We sat on that bed for hours.

I even told them about Hendrix, the full story this time—how he'd caught me at the bar, how we'd been hooking up, how he'd been trying to keep me safe, trying to help me.

"Well, shit." Amaya rubbed the back of her neck. "Now I wish I'd let him come home with us."

"Huh?" I looked between them.

Harlow chuckled. "Yeah, he wanted to help us take care of you, but Amaya barked at him to back off and just drove away."

"All we had to go off was his word." Mena crossed her arms. "For all we knew, he was the reason you were so messed up in the first place."

"What's going on with you guys now?" Amaya asked. I'd told them everything that had happened, but even I had no idea where we stood. The things we'd said to each other, the way I'd repeatedly pushed him away . . . He'd come for me last night, helped my friends save me before I got seriously hurt, but that didn't mean all was forgiven. That didn't mean he'd want anything to do with me after all I'd put him through.

"I don't . . ." I bit my lip. That wasn't entirely true anymore. I knew what I wanted. "I don't know where I stand with him. If he can forgive me. But . . . shit. I really like him. More than like him. I think he might be the real deal."

"He believed us, last night." Mena rubbed my shoulder. "When we told him it was Will and not you who was responsible for the posters. He helped us find you. He still cares."

"Yeah, but Will . . . it's still my fault. I don't know if I can even ask him to forgive me for how awful I've been."

Before anyone could say another word, Amaya cursed and frowned at her phone. It had been vibrating with notifications the entire time we'd been talking, but that wasn't anything new. She had a pretty big following on Instagram. "Is Drew blowing up anyone else's phone?"

Mena and Harlow pulled theirs from their pockets. I had no idea where mine was.

"I have twelve missed calls." Mena frowned.

"Same. And no messages." Harlow looked around at us.

Amaya's phone buzzed again. She rolled her eyes and picked up. "Why are you blowing up our phones? We're kinda in the middle of—"

We could hear Drew's voice on the other end but couldn't make out what he was saying.

Amaya sat up straighter, the annoyance draining from her face to be replaced with something more serious. "We're at my place. Just come here."

Another moment of silence, then she hung up and looked at us all. "He's freaking out. Something about Will and . . . Hendrix."

I shot to my feet. "What happened?"

"I don't know." Amaya's voice remained calm. "But he was already in the car. He should be here any minute."

I rushed to the window overlooking her curved driveway, and sure enough, a few minutes later, Drew's Audi came tearing toward the house. As soon as the car slammed to a halt, Drew jumped out and rushed to the door. His footsteps pounded on the stairs, and then he was standing just outside Amaya's room, breathing hard.

"Shit." He ran both hands through his hair. "I shouldn't be dragging you into this. Never mind."

He turned to leave, but we all lunged for him at the same time, shouting over one another. Between the four of us pulling at his clothes and scolding him, we managed to drag him back into the room. He took a seat at the foot of the bed, and the four of us lined up in front of him, blocking the door.

"Drew, what is going on?" I demanded. It felt good to have that steel back in my voice, the strength returning to my spine. "Are you OK? Is Hendrix?"

"Yeah, Hendrix is fine." He waved that away, then fixed me with a look. "It's you I'm worried about."

"Me?" I raised my eyebrows, not giving anything away. Had he found out about my meltdown somehow?

"Will . . ." Drew swallowed. "Will's lost the plot, and I don't know what to do. I don't want to drag you girls into it, but I'm worried about you, D—what he might do. And I . . . I don't know how to make them stop."

He ran his hands through his hair again, and I shared worried glances with the girls. Mena sat down next to him and rubbed his shoulder, just as she'd been rubbing mine earlier.

"You're not making any sense," Amaya said. "What don't you want to drag us into?"

He released a big breath and leaned his elbows on his knees. "Last year, just before the school year ended, some of the guys and I . . . we got into some shit."

"Stop being vague," I demanded.

"Fights. We started going to these illegal fights Will somehow found out about. At first it was just to watch, make bets. But after a while, some of the guys started fighting too. It was fun at first, a rush, all that money passing hands. But the people running it . . . the opponents they were pitting the guys against got tougher and meaner, and we started walking away with more bruises and less money. And then they wouldn't let us walk away at all."

"Luke and the guys. The car accident." I clenched my fists, forcing my breathing to remain even. Over the summer, four of the guys on the football team had been in a horrible accident, and none of them could play anymore. "They were hurt in a fight and not an accident."

Will shook his head. "No. It was a car accident. It just wasn't exactly *accidental*. The people running the fights got in touch after, made it clear. That's what would happen to anyone else wanting to leave."

The words coming out of Amaya's mouth were filthy even for her. Harlow wrapped her arms around herself.

"You're all a bunch of fucking idiots," I said calmly. "You couldn't just hire some hookers and trash your daddy's yacht like regular rich assholes? You had to go and get involved in some dodgy fight club? That is the most toxic-masculinity, stupid-ass bullshit I've ever heard."

"I know!" Drew pleaded, hands splayed out. "We all lost interest pretty quickly, but they wouldn't let us leave, and now . . . I don't know what to do."

"What does this have to do with Hendrix? With me?"

"Apparently, they tried to get Hendrix to fight before, invited him, but he said no." Because he'd vowed never to lift a hand against another human being again. Despicable trash-bag assholes . . . "So, the posters exposing him—they're trying to bait him, make him angry. Someone's decided he'd make them a lot of money, that he's worth the trouble of . . . coercing. And Will seems to be in with this shit way deeper than I thought. I should've known." He gritted his teeth. "It was always Will with the information on the next fight, always Will making the first bet. I don't know what the hell he's doing, but that's why he put the posters up. It had nothing to do with jealousy over you. But now that he knows how much you care . . ."

The blood drained from my face. Even as a weight lifted—relief that it wasn't because of me Hendrix had been exposed—another heavier one settled in the pit of my stomach.

Drew nodded, as if he could see the horror washing over me. "After you laid into him yesterday, he realized that you and Hendrix—that there's something more there. And I'm worried he'll try to use it. Use you to get Hendrix to do what he wants."

Drew heaved a massive sigh, a punctuation to the clusterfuck he'd just dumped on us.

"Why haven't you gone to the police?" Amaya asked.

"Honestly? I'm scared." He rubbed his thighs, as if his fear was something to be ashamed of. "All the others are too. We don't want to get charged with anything, and we don't know if we'll get dragged down with the rest of them. Plus, I'm worried if Will finds out it was me . . . he'll tell the others and . . ." He was scared for his life. He actually thought these people might kill him. Considering the state Luke and the guys had been in, I didn't blame him. "Plus, it's not that simple. We never know when or where the fight will happen until the day of, sometimes just hours before."

Harlow stepped forward with a pen and a piece of paper. "Can you write the addresses down for me?"

Drew nodded and started to write things down as I mulled over what he'd told us. When he was done, he handed the paper to my sister, who had already situated herself at the desk and was filling Amaya's computer screen with weird windows of text.

"Thanks for the warning, Drew," I said and meant it. "But I'm not sure what we can do about it either. Maybe it's time we told our parents? There's got to be a way to get the police involved and keep you safe."

Drew nodded, but he looked solemn, drained. "I was thinking that too, but I can't really go to my dad." Drew's father had never laid a hand on his son, but he was a cold, unfeeling man who was always happy to point out failures, never successes. "I was thinking, maybe, with all your connections in the legal field . . . I don't know."

He was hoping I'd know what to do, who to speak to, how to handle this best. Because I always had answers, always had a plan, was always willing to do whatever it took for my friends.

I was tired, hungover, and sick of everyone thinking I was unbreakable. But Drew was a friend, and I had my girls with me all the way.

My hand closed over his. "We'll figure it out."

I didn't know how, but we would. Together.

"Shit." Harlow's wide eyes were scanning the screen as if to double-check —*triple-check*—what she was seeing. Then she turned to us, her hands gripping the edge of the desk. "Those addresses aren't random. I figured out what they have in common. Or rather *who*. We have a big problem, you guys."

CHAPTER TWENTY-SEVEN

Hendrix

The sheets were pooled around my hips, my wide-open eyes staring at the dark ceiling. I'd tried to go to bed after watching a movie with my aunt, but I'd just ended up lying awake, wrapped in the gloomy silence.

It had been a full twenty-four hours, and I still hadn't heard from Donna or her friends. I'd wanted so badly to follow them home, barge into the house and help them take care of her, but I knew they'd just had a bomb dropped on them. She didn't make it easy on any of us. So I gave them space, didn't call or text. But as I stared into the blackness, running everything over in my mind for the millionth time, I wondered if that was a mistake.

Maybe she was waiting for me to reach out, show her I cared. I frowned at the thought. Hadn't my actions over the past few months shown that already? Yeah, I'd told her friends shit she didn't want them to know, but I had no other choice.

It was kind of bullshit that, after everything, she hadn't even texted to tell me she was OK. But then, it wasn't as if we were together—she didn't owe me anything. And I didn't owe her jack shit either. So I'd deleted every message I'd half written throughout the day.

The uncertainty was killing me, but I was done chasing Donna Mead.

With a frustrated sigh, I sat up, rested my elbows on my knees, and rubbed my sore eyes. I'd hardly slept after coming home the night before. I was exhausted, and yet I was still completely incapable of sleeping.

Resigned to putting on another movie to drown out my thoughts, I was just getting out of bed when a sound from the window made me pause. I turned toward it and frowned. It sounded like a tap, maybe a branch knocking against the glass. Except there wasn't any wind—or any trees near my window.

The sound came again—a low *ping*, something solid but small hitting the glass. I edged toward the window and pulled back the curtain.

Donna stood in my yard, her hand raised as if she was about to throw something, but she lowered her arm when she saw me. That crazy bitch was throwing pebbles at my window even though we both had perfectly functioning phones.

I shook my head, torn between amusement and annoyance. What the hell?

She held my gaze for a moment, then folded her arms and cocked her head, silently gesturing for me to come outside.

I pinched the bridge of my nose and sighed, but when I looked at her again, I knew I'd go. I'd go wherever she wanted me, whenever she needed me. Because I had it bad for the petite blonde bundled in a gray coat, standing in my yard in the middle of the night.

After giving her one nod, I turned from the window to pull on sweatpants and a hoodie, then picked up my shoes and padded softly down the hall. I wasn't trying to do anything behind my aunt's back, but I didn't want to disturb her either.

The night air was crisp and cold, and I zipped the hoodie all the way up as I stepped out the back door. Donna turned and walked to the back of the yard as soon as I appeared, edging past the shrubs at the bottom of the property. I stuffed my hands into my pockets and followed.

Donna waited for me on the walking path that ran down the backs of the yards, along a nature reserve on the other side. She waved her phone at me, then silently held her hand out and gave me an expectant look.

This behavior was weird even for her.

"You wa—"

She slapped her hand over my mouth, cutting off my words. I was so stunned I didn't even know what to do. With her phone still in hand, she pressed one finger to her lips in a silent order to be quiet.

I frowned at her.

She ran her hand over the pockets of my hoodie, making my abs tighten at her touch, then moved to the ones on my pants. Several dirty jokes ran through my mind, making me smirk, but I remained silent. Even so, she still gave me a withering look as she located my phone and removed it.

My smile remained in place as she hid both phones under a bush and gave me another "let's go" gesture. She was acting really weird, but I still followed without hesitation.

We walked the silent path shoulder to shoulder, the half moon and occasional back porch light the only illumination.

Once the path veered away from the houses and into the woods, Donna finally spoke.

"Sorry about that. Harlow insisted on no phones."

"Uh . . . what?" I chuckled. "That doesn't actually explain anything."

"I know. Just . . . come on." She picked up the pace, and after another few minutes of walking, we emerged into a clearing surrounded by trees.

Harlow and Amaya were bundled into coats, shoulders up near their ears against the cold. Next to them, Turner had his arms around Mena, pressed in close behind her. But it was the presence of Drew—the quarterback of the football team and Will's friend—that made me pause.

Every muscle in my body tensed, ready for . . . I wasn't even sure what. I had no idea what this bizarre situation was about.

"Dark woods. Middle of the night." I made a show of looking around. "Are we planning to sacrifice a virgin or something?"

Drew and Amaya both snorted while Harlow grinned. "There's no virgins here, trust me."

"Hey, man." Turner nodded to me from across the clearing. "There's something you need to know."

I rolled my shoulders and stepped forward to join their weird little circle. Turner was my friend. I could trust him. "OK. And this something I need to know couldn't have been put into a text or a phone call?"

"No phones." Harlow's tone brooked no arguments.

"Relax." Donna rolled her eyes. "We ditched the phones, as instructed."

Baby Mead nodded but gave me an apologetic look. "Sorry. I know it's weird. But when you're dealing with corporations, you don't take chances. People worry about governments spying on us, but most government departments are running Windows XP on hardware that belongs in a museum. Meanwhile, Google knows more about you than your own mother, and *we let them*. It's willful ignorance. And it's because corporations have the money and the latest tech. So . . ."

"Riiight." I squinted at her. She had the hood of her purple coat up, her blonde hair tangling with the white fur trim. No tin foil hat in sight, and yet . . .

"Hey, before we go any further." Drew stepped forward and held a hand out. "I'm Drew. I know we haven't met properly, but I just want you to know that if D trusts you, so do I. Also, I had nothing to do with the posters yesterday. That was all Will."

I looked at his outstretched hand, then frowned at him, keeping mine firmly in my pockets. After an awkward silence, he cleared his throat and looked away. "Fair enough, I guess."

I turned to Donna. "What the hell?"

"I just wanted to warn you about . . . you have a right to know why . . . uh . . . right, I should probably explain about Will first . . ." Her eyes darted around uncertainly. I'd never seen Donna unsure about what to say.

"Oh, for fuck's sake." Amaya threw her hands up and let them flop back to her sides. "This idiot and his friends"—she pointed to Drew—"managed to get themselves involved in some seedy fight club. Now the dangerous bad men won't let them leave. Apparently, these same men have tried to lure *you* into the seedy fight club, but you have more than half a brain and said no."

I raised my eyebrows. I was pretty sure that was a compliment.

"But they really want you," Amaya continued, "because of your super violent past, and they don't like being told no, so the posters were their way of intimidating you. Will seems to be more involved than any of those half-brained idiots realized, so he was the one behind that little stunt. Drew's had enough and is worried about them dragging Donna into it, so he came to us to spill his guts. Harlow did some digging, and it turns out Will's dad owns all the properties where the fights have been taking place. He's a businessman with ties to several big corporations, but he seems to be giving a lot of money to BestLyf. Which is why Harlow insisted on no phones."

She rolled her eyes as if she thought it was preposterous that anyone would try to spy on a bunch of teenagers, and I was inclined to agree, but whatever. The phones didn't really matter right now.

"Harlow found other documents with names and dates that match previous fight nights, along with figures we suspect are the profits. Drew seems to think they're not going to stop trying to recruit you, and they may try to use Donna to do it because you clearly have the hots for her. She also has the hots for you, because all she could think about all afternoon was making sure you were warned and safe. Also, sorry if I was a bitch to you last night. I was just worried about my friend and didn't know you were a decent guy."

With a dismissive wave of her hand, she looped her arm through Harlow's and stomped her feet against the cold, apparently done talking.

Most of us gaped at her. Donna had her hand over her eyes, her short hair obscuring half her face.

Harlow was grinning at Amaya. "Holy shit, you actually said sorry for being a bitch?"

"And she called him a decent guy!" Mena bounced on her toes.

"Out of all that, that's what you choose to focus on?" Donna shook her head, incredulous.

Everything Amaya had blurted out—some of it shit I already knew, some of it making other things click into place—finally registered properly.

Without even thinking about it, I took a step forward and blocked Donna with my body, holding my arm out for good measure. "What do you mean they're trying to use Donna? Is someone threatening her?" I tried hard not to speak through my teeth, but my words still came out on a growl.

Donna slapped my arm away and stepped in closer to my side. "And out of all that, that's what *you* choose to focus on? You're the one they've already come after."

I huffed. "I can take care of myself."

"What? And I can't?" She crossed her arms.

I groaned. "That's not what I'm saying. You're a fierce independent woman and all that shit, but these are dangerous people who—"

"Is this some kind of foreplay for you two?" Drew cut in.

Everyone burst out laughing while Donna and I sealed our lips shut and avoided looking at each other.

"Can we focus please?" Turner sounded serious. "We need to figure out our next move. If BestLyf really is involved in this . . ." He shook his head. My friend was already convinced that company was evil—this would only be more proof for him.

"We don't exactly have evidence they are," Harlow hedged. "I just thought it was worth noting that Mr. Frydenberg was giving them substantial amounts of money each week."

"How do you know what kind of money Frydenberg is giving anyone?" I asked.

"It's better not to ask." Mena bugged her eyes out at me.

Harlow gave a nonchalant shrug. "I'm not a pro. It's not like I could hack into all his accounts or anything like that, so I definitely don't have the full picture. I just got access to a few folders on his computer."

"This is ridiculous." I rubbed my temples. "Why are we freezing our balls off in the woods discussing this and not going to the police?"

They ran me through the obstacles, the lack of evidence, why Drew and the others were scared to come forward.

"I'll talk to the police, man." Drew looked at me earnestly. "I just want to make sure that when I do, it counts—that my friends will be safe, that Will and his dad can't weasel their way out of it."

"We need evidence." Amaya tucked her chin into her scarf.

Everyone fell into silence, the only sounds those of animals scurrying and the flapping wings of some night bird.

I wanted so badly to just turn around, walk back home and get under the covers, pretend I didn't know any of this. I didn't want to get involved in this shit. But I already was, whether I wanted to be or not. And there was no way in hell I was going to sit around and risk Donna getting hurt.

An idea was forming in my mind, but the potential for trouble—exactly the kind of trouble I'd promised Aunt Hannah and myself I'd avoid—was pretty damn high.

"Are we being stupid not telling our parents about this?" Mena's voice was low, hesitant.

"Maybe." Donna ran her hands through her hair. "But telling Drew's dad or

Amaya's mom?" They both cringed. "Probably do more harm than good. Telling your parents or Turner's dad? They'd just go to the police. Telling my parents? Dad is friends with Joseph Frydenberg and would almost certainly confront him, maybe warn him unintentionally. I don't think it's worth the risk."

"So, what? We do nothing?" Drew sounded frustrated. Of course he was. He'd been dealing with this exact conundrum, stuck in this impossible situation, for a year. Grudgingly, I felt for the guy. He may have gotten himself into this position, but at least he was trying to get himself out.

"Donna, is what Harlow has on Frydenberg enough to connect him to the fights, charge him?" Even if she didn't want to be a lawyer anymore, my girl still had more legal knowledge than anyone I knew.

"On its own? No. We would need to show proof that the fights happened on his properties. Then the fact that he owns them, coupled with the documents Harlow found and Drew's statement, would be grounds enough to dig into his affairs further, search his properties and businesses."

"Drew, are you sure Will is involved in organizing this shit?"

"Yeah." He huffed. "It's all on his phone. I've been watching him for a while, and I've noticed a few texts, other things that would prove it. They make everyone surrender their phones at the doors for the fights, but Will somehow always has his."

"If Will was at the fight when the police showed up, would that be enough reason for them to check his phone?"

"Yeah." Donna nodded. "Anyone caught participating in illegal activity would be searched and questioned."

I blew out a big breath. "Then we make sure Will is there when the police bust up the fight."

"How?" Drew asked, but Donna was already shaking her head, giving me a reproachful look.

"We give them what they want."

"Dammit, Hendrix, no." Donna shoved me, but her hands stayed on my chest. "I'm telling you all this to keep you safe, not so you can get yourself into a danger-ous-as-fuck situation."

I smirked at her, but it didn't reach my eyes. "How's it feel, princess?"

"It's not the same." She seethed. "After what you told me . . . you shouldn't have to do this."

Donna knew how abhorrent the idea of violence was to me now, and here I was, about to throw myself into an actual fighting pit. She was trying to look out for me, just as I'd been trying to look out for her all this time. Only difference was, she'd been doing stupid, dangerous shit as an escape. I was about to do some stupid, dangerous shit for a good cause. For her. To protect her.

I rubbed her upper arms and spoke in a low voice, ignoring the others. "Better me than anyone else. My soul is already black."

She shook her head, her gaze pleading.

"You two done whispering sweet nothings over there?" Amaya barked.

I stepped away from Donna and fixed her sister with a look. "Get everything you have on Frydenberg ready to send to the police."

She nodded, and I turned to Drew.

"Keep us updated on any changes, but don't go to the next fight if you can avoid it. Just be ready to talk to the cops when it goes down."

Another firm nod.

"The rest of you, we all need to pretend like nothing's changed. Especially around Will. We should definitely not be seen together."

"Also, don't text or call each other about this," Harlow rushed to add.

"I'll get word to Donna when I have a date and location for the fight," I said. "If I don't check in twenty minutes after going in, that's your confirmation Will's there. That's when you do all you can to get the cops there."

"We'll make it happen." Turner looked determined.

"All right." There was nothing left to say, so I turned to walk back to my house. The others moved in the opposite direction—to where the path led to another street.

"I'll be home later," Donna called, then caught up with me, pulling on my elbow. "Wait. Can we talk?"

I just kept walking. "There's no other way, Donna. It's late, and I haven't slept in two days. I'm exhausted."

"It's not about that." She kept pace, looping her arm through mine.

I slowed down and peered at her. Her expression looked uncertain—almost nervous. I wanted to pull her against me so badly, kiss her little nose, which was almost definitely frozen in this weather. But I had no idea where we stood. Not wanting me to get killed was a long way from actually wanting . . . whatever. I hadn't even allowed myself to fully consider what *I* wanted from *her*.

But that look on her face . . . she didn't look as though she wanted to lay into me or use me as a distraction. It looked like something else. Something more.

"OK," I said, relenting. "But let's get out of the cold."

She nodded. Her hand slid down until it joined my hand in my pocket, and we threaded our fingers together.

CHAPTER TWENTY-EIGHT

Donna and I were silent as we collected our phones, crossed the yard, and made our way up to my bedroom. I didn't drop her hand until I was closing my bedroom door with a subdued *click*.

She was draping her coat over my desk chair when I turned around; I had to stop myself from rushing over to tidy up the mess of books and papers and pens littering the surface. The sweatshirt she was wearing underneath had a neon-pink pair of puckered lips on the front. It was so clearly not hers it made me smile faintly.

I took a few soft steps toward the lamp, then decided against it. Our eyes were already adjusted to the dark, and the curtains I'd left open earlier were letting in enough light. The moonlight made her hair look silver, ethereal, the soft angles of her face cast in gentle shadow as she looked around. Her eyes wandered to the desk, the bed, the window, everything but me.

I came to stand directly in front of her, not even sure what I wanted her to say. But she was here, and I couldn't find it in me to be anything but pleased.

She looked up at me and swallowed, reached out, then dropped her hands and balled them into fists at her sides. She was clearly anxious, but her brave eyes never left mine as she licked her lips and took a big breath.

"I'm sorry," she whispered and clenched her jaw—as if the words didn't taste right on her tongue. Or as if she was bracing for my response.

I frowned. "What for?"

"All of it," she breathed. "For being a bitch to you when you first got here, for making your life hell, for not seeing you were just trying to help me, for not seeing what I was doing to you and to myself. The willful ignorance . . ." She shook her head, that silver-blonde hair falling partly over one eye. "For blaming you for my friends seeing me in that state last night. For the posters and Will and Drew and this whole mess. I'm sorry for all of it."

She squared her shoulders and gave me one firm nod, ready to accept whatever I threw at her, however I reacted. So strong even in her humility.

I moved closer and allowed myself a single touch—a brush of my fingers against her temple as I tucked that lock of hair behind her ear—before I forced my hands down to my sides. Just because she was here, just because she was apologizing, didn't mean she wanted more from me.

"I gave as good as I got." My voice was as low as hers but just as decisive. "I goaded you, Donna, and a part of me wanted my life to be hell. I didn't feel like I deserved happiness, friends, light after what I'd done. As for the other shit, I chose to follow you and push you, and I was probably crossing lines and sticking my nose where it didn't belong, and for that I'm sorry too." She shook her head and opened her mouth to object, but I rushed on before she could. "As for Will and Drew and that whole mess—I promise you none of that is your fault. I was getting dragged into that shit before Will realized there was anything between us. That's not on you."

She searched my gaze for a long time, then gave a tiny nod and a barely audible "OK."

"OK." I resisted the urge to pull her against me, hold her, protect her, devour her. There was barely a sliver of moonlight between us, our bodies drifting closer and closer.

"Hendrix?" Those round, perfectly imperfect, mismatched eyes still held me prisoner in my own room.

"Yeah?"

"Thank you. For sticking your nose where it didn't belong. For pushing me. For seeing what was happening when no one else did—when even I didn't let myself see the extent of it."

"I'd do it all again in a heartbeat, take every mean thing you said and did, to make sure you were safe."

"I know." She reached up and finally touched me, gripping my shoulders. "I know . . . I . . ."

My heart beat so fucking hard in my chest I was sure the thudding would wake the neighbors. I dared not speak as she tried to get whatever she was trying to say out. But with a slight shake of her head, she gave up on words altogether.

Instead, she lifted onto her toes and tilted her face up to mine, her eyes already half-closed as I reacted to her—naturally, instinctually. My hands went to her back as I met her halfway in a kiss. Her nose was still cold from being outside so long, but her lips . . . her lips were warm and soft and perfect.

She kissed me with such tenderness—such purposeful, gentle tenderness—that it felt as if this kiss were our first. Despite all the other times we'd kissed, all the other depraved things we'd done to each other.

This moment felt more raw and honest than any of it. The softness of that chaste kiss filled me with such contentment that I would've been happy to simply stand there and hold her—just like that—for the rest of the night.

It was Donna who teased my lips with a hint of her tongue, asking for more. I gave it to her, opening my mouth to hers, kissing her deeper, holding her tighter, my fingers digging into her back.

It was Donna who unzipped my hoodie, who whipped her own off before mashing her lips right back to mine. I helped her get all our clothes off until we were skin-to-skin. She was so hot against me, her body so soft and perfect, my cock in agony where it was pressed between us.

It was Donna who nudged me toward the bed until I was sitting down and she was climbing over me, straddling me. We moaned against each other's lips as our breaths turned to pants, as we caressed and kissed and licked and gripped, moving seamlessly together. So seamlessly I almost forgot to grab a condom before she slid down my length.

All the other times had been rushed, frenzied, as much fighting as it was fucking. But this time, in the quiet darkness of my warm bedroom—this time it was slow, deliberate, *intentional.*

Before, the sex had been about release—hers and mine. About Donna getting that rush of adrenaline. About her easing the insane pressure of constantly being in control by giving up control of her body to me.

Now, as she took her time lowering herself onto me, this was not about control or danger or release. This was Donna showing me with her body what she couldn't seem to say with her words.

She pulled back to look at me as her hips met mine, her knees splayed wide, my hands in her hair, on her ass. I groaned deep in my throat at the sensation of being so completely inside her, so carnally connected.

For a few moments she just sat there, not moving against me as my granite-hard cock twitched inside her warmth.

Breathing hard, she pressed her forehead to mine and finally found her words. "I want this, you, all of you. I want you, Hendrix—in my body, in my life, in my heart. I want . . . more."

I kissed her forehead, her eyes, her cheeks, her nose, which was finally as warm as the rest of her. "I want more too. Everything. Even if I don't deserve it. Even if it makes me selfish."

She took my face in her hands and trailed her thumbs down my cheeks. "You do deserve it. You deserve happiness and light and . . . love. I love you."

An indescribable feeling washed over me—something warm and intense and overwhelming and terrifying all at once. No one had ever said those words to me with such conviction.

"I love you," I told her with just as much certainty.

Only then did she start to move against me. Her core ground against my pelvis, not even bouncing up and down—as if she couldn't stand to not have me inside her for even the fraction of a second it would take to thrust back in.

We stared into each other's eyes as we worshipped at the altar of this crazy, cosmic thing between us. And I watched as the orgasm washed over her face, her legs twitching at my sides, her whole body going tense and then so, so loose. I drank in every second of the ecstasy she was finding with me.

And then I flipped us over and lowered her gently onto the bed, claiming her lips in a kiss. My tongue moved in rhythm with my hips as I pumped in and out and in and out, but it didn't take long. I came inside her, so deep, and moaned into her mouth. She held me close through it, clawing gently at my back, my ass.

After our breathing evened out and we cleaned up in my bathroom, we curled up on my bed with the blanket drawn up to our chins. Outside the window, the light was starting to turn that grayish indigo that signaled a new day.

"It's dawn," she whispered against my arm and placed a little kiss there. Her bare ass was against my crotch, her hot little body pressed to mine. Even our legs were tangled.

"I guess that means you have to go soon." I squeezed a little tighter, not ready for her to run away as she always did.

"Nah." She reached for her phone. "I think I'll stay. The girls can cover for me."

I smiled against the soft hair at the back of her head and was asleep before she even finished writing the text.

For the next few days, we all went back to our lives and pretended that nothing had changed. Everyone acted as though I didn't exist, and I went about my business with my usual disinterested look on my face. It was so fucking hard not to smile though, after what Donna and I had shared, after how we'd managed to come out the other end after all we'd been through. I wanted to grin like a fool. She was as frustrated by it as I was. More than once, she pulled me into an empty classroom for a secret kiss, and on Tuesday night, I got home from the gym to find her in the kitchen with Aunt Hannah, chatting and cooking dinner.

I wanted to forget everything else and just . . . be happy. But I kept it all locked down tight. Seeing Will's smug face at school was enough of a reminder why I needed to bide my time just a little longer.

The school hadn't been able to prove who'd put all the posters up, the cameras having conveniently failed that day, so no one was being punished. But I knew it was him, and he knew I knew. I could see it in his smirk, the way he looked down his nose at me, the taunting glint in his eyes. When I was looking at William Frydenberg was the only time I let my true feelings show—my disgust, my disdain, my rage at who he was and all he represented. I let him see how badly I wanted to beat his ass every time I passed him in the halls. I figured it would only serve to prove I was serious about changing my mind and wanting to get into the ring with him.

I'd texted Shady the day after our little meeting in the woods, telling him I wanted in but only if I could fight Will. Said I had a score to settle. He'd replied with a thumbs-up and nothing more. I resisted the urge to push him, ask for more info, show my impatience.

For now, we had to just sit and wait.

I used the gym to thrash out my frustration. On Wednesday afternoon, I finished a brutal leg session with Turner and hobbled out the back door to find Donna leaning on the wall.

I didn't even say hi. I just checked that no one was around before dropping my gym bag and diving in for a kiss. She laughed against my mouth as I pressed her into the concrete at her back. It was just about dusk, the street lights starting to come on, and I wondered if we could get away with a quickie, if the parking lot was too exposed. My girl would totally be up for it too—she was freaky like that.

"Daaaamn." The sound of Shady's voice was like a bucket of cold water being dumped over our heads. He strutted up to us from the corner of the building and leaned against the wall, grinning. "I might be jealous at this new development if I wasn't sporting a semi. But please, don't let me interrupt—I like to watch anyway."

He bit his lip and scanned Donna's body without a lick of shame.

"Shady." Donna gave him a tight smile. "You know I don't do jealousy."

"Yeah, but you never wore that uniform for me, baby girl. What makes *him* so special?"

We looked at each other and couldn't hold back the genuine smiles. She was special—more precious to me than anything.

"What's up, Shady?" I said, keeping my eyes on Donna. Her arms were wrapped around my neck, her tight little body still flush with mine. I hadn't missed the little flash of excitement in her eyes at Shady's suggestion to watch us. I was pretty open-minded, but I knew they'd slept together on more than one occasion, and I wasn't sure I could control my own jealousy. Not yet. I wanted her all to myself for a while.

"Shit." Some of the teasing tone left Shady's voice as he looked between us. "This is the real deal then? You two are a thing? Didn't see that one coming." Then he grinned. "Nah, I'm fuckin' with ya. Saw this coming a mile away!" He threw his head back and laughed.

Donna finally dropped her arms. I put some distance between us but kept one arm propped on the wall next to her head.

"Stop messing around." Now Donna had gone serious. "What are you doing here?"

"I gotta talk to your man about a dog," he said.

"You can talk in front of Donna. She—"

"No, it's OK." She looked over my shoulder; people were coming out of the gym. "I should go anyway. Call me later."

She gave me a quick peck on the lips and pushed off the wall.

Shady leaned forward and puckered his lips, raising his eyebrows expectantly, but she just flipped him off and sauntered away. I smirked as we both watched her disappear around the corner.

Once she was gone and the people from the gym were in their cars, Shady turned a dead serious expression on me. "What the fuck you doin', man? We both know you have no interest in those fights."

"I told you. I have a score to settle. I'll only come if your people can guarantee Will Frydenberg will be in the ring with me."

"Not my people." He crossed his arms and tipped his head back, watching me for a few moments.

I stared him down, not faltering.

"OK." He gave a disappointed shake of his head, as if he wanted to say more, and turned to leave.

"Shady." He stopped. "Do you go to the fights?"

"Sometimes."

I glanced around the darkening parking lot one more time. He'd looked out for me in his own way, and he'd made it clear he wasn't on board with this fight club bullshit. "If you happen to have other plans for this particular fight . . . that might not be a bad thing."

I raised my eyebrows, hoping he got my gist.

But guys like Shady operated in gray areas, were fluent in ambiguity. He cocked his head to the side, then slowly nodded. "All right."

Without another word, he walked away.

The next day, around lunchtime, I got a text message from an unknown number. It contained an address, the word *tonight*, and nothing more.

CHAPTER TWENTY-NINE

The address was for an abandoned factory in an industrial district about an hour out of town. It was massive, and the adjoining properties were far enough away that no one would hear any noise coming from the squat but sprawling building I'd just pulled up to.

I'd asked Donna to check if Drew had gotten the same message, not daring to piss off the younger Mead sister by contacting him myself. Donna and I had been texting each other freely—it fit with what the Frydenbergs suspected of our relationship anyway—but we dared not discuss the fight or our plan. Donna's text to Drew had been masked as her asking him for the address because I was being stubborn and wouldn't tell her. He was home sick that day, but Donna confirmed he'd received the text too.

As soon as I got word to the others, Harlow sent all the evidence from Joseph's computer in anonymously—directly to a cop Donna knew from the legal center where she used to volunteer, knew wasn't dirty. Harlow had been corresponding with him, though she'd refused to come in and make a statement, and had told him to be ready near the factory that evening.

I got out of the car and walked slowly toward the building. Half the windows were smashed, and weeds grew between the cracks in the concrete. Not a single light was on, either outside or shining from within, but even without light, it was clear there were no other cars parked near me and no other people hanging around. Maybe everyone was already inside. Maybe they were instructed to park at the back.

Still, as I neared the building and looked for a way in, my steps slowed. It was too quiet. Was it possible the fight was set up in some underground area, away from prying eyes and ears? I wasn't sure, but something didn't feel right.

"Right on time, my man!" Shady emerged from the shadows near a side door set deep into the wall. He was in one of his tracksuits, the cocky grin firmly in place.

"Hey, dude." I slapped his hand and thumped his back, looking around. No one—not a single other person—was in sight. "I thought you had other plans."

He shrugged. "They fell through. Couldn't miss your debut in the ring!" He laughed, then turned for the door and gestured for me to follow him. "Everyone parks in the back or down the street. I figured you wouldn't know where to go since it's your first time."

The heavy metal door creaked as he pulled it open, but when we stepped inside the warehouse, I grabbed his shoulder. "Thanks, man, I appreciate it." Then I lowered my voice. "You can go now."

He dropped the bravado to give me a rare serious look. "Nah, I think I'll stay."

Stupid petty criminal. I sighed, but he was already walking away before I could say more. I was trying to save him from getting arrested, and he was sticking by my side out of some misguided sense of loyalty? Fine, his problem. I had to stay focused.

I texted Donna, knowing my phone would probably be taken at any moment.

Heading in now.

Shady led me past rows of dilapidated, rusting machinery and sagging conveyor belts. The rest of the space was bare, covered in dust and grime. Broken windows high above our heads let in beams of weak light as rats scurried in the shadows.

We rounded a corner, and several floodlights set on high stands flared to life. I pulled up short and squinted, my eyes adjusting to the sudden brightness.

Two figures stood in the middle of the starkly lit area. Two men, and no one else.

My whole body tensed, hands curling into fists at my sides. Something had gone very wrong.

The space did indeed look as though it was set up for a fight. A rough circle had been painted on the dirty concrete floor, plenty of space around it, and there was a balcony overhead on one side with what looked like empty offices behind the railing. But clearly, I was the only one who'd come here expecting to see an illegal fight ring.

"Hendrix Hawthorn." The man standing next to Will had the same brown hair, the same build, the same sneering mouth. They even stood in the same pose. Will's dad had his hands in the pockets of his long coat, worn over a suit and tie, while Will's were in the pockets of his Fulton Academy varsity jacket. "I've been told you want to settle a score with my son." A pause, a cold grin. "Have at it."

Will rolled his neck, his full focus on me.

I gritted my teeth and threw a murderous look at Shady.

He just flashed me that stupid grin. "You're a cool dude, but business is business."

That spineless son of a bitch. He retreated to lean against the staircase leading up to the balcony, whipping his phone out as if he was already bored.

"You see, the thing about dealing with criminals is you have to remember they're self-serving at their core," Mr. Frydenberg explained to me as if he were giving a lecture. "They're always going to do what's in their best interest. And Shady here is going to prosper greatly from our new mutually beneficial arrangement."

Shady just gave him a thumbs-up, hardly even raising his eyes from his screen.

"Criminals and businessmen both," I said, rolling my shoulders.

He laughed low. Will took off the varsity jacket and draped it over the railing next to Shady, loosening up too.

I was going to beat his ass into this disgusting concrete until his every breath was a gurgle. His dad looked as if he'd hardly stepped foot on a treadmill in a decade, his gut poking out of his coat—it wouldn't take much to get him on his ass either. Shady would be running by then; that's what rats do. But I'd catch him. I'd chase him down and . . .

And . . .

Austin's face flashed in my mind, his eyes wide but unseeing, blood slowly pooling around his head. For a split second, I was back on that street in New York, once again realizing what I'd done. How irrevocable it was.

I had so much adrenaline pumping through my system, so much rage and outrage, my body practically screamed at me to start throwing punches. But I also felt sick to my stomach. All three of the men standing before me were the lowest kind of trash, but I refused to take another life. I couldn't have that on my conscience. Not again. Not *ever* again.

I forced myself to take a deep breath, flex my fingers and not curl them back into fists. I knew I'd walk away from this broken in more ways than I could count —if I even walked away at all—but my decision was made.

"I'm not going to fight you, Will," I said, proud of how steady and clear my voice sounded. "I was never going to fight you."

"Oh, you're going to fight me." Will sneered, slowly pacing back and forth, closing in like a hyena.

"No, I'm not." I shook my head. "I'm done with that shit. No amount of threats and intimidation were ever going to get me to throw another punch. Sorry you wasted your time putting all those posters up. Hope you didn't get too many paper cuts."

"Stop being a pussy and hit him!" Joseph's voice echoed in the cavernous space. Like a good little boy, Will immediately moved to obey his father.

He sprang forward, throwing a wide right hook. But he wasn't quick enough. I ducked out of the way and backed up, hands raised in front of me. I wasn't going to fight him—but I was going to defend myself as long as I could.

Will growled and came for me again. Football had made him fast, strong—he was relentless. I batted his swings out of the way, dodging and weaving, but eventually I started to get winded.

He pulled back, dancing on his toes, waiting, but his face had lost some of its confidence. If this was for real, if I'd actually stepped into the ring with him, I would've already won—and he knew it.

"Do I have to do everything myself?" Joseph barked and shrugged out of his coat, letting it flop to the filthy ground, before loosening his tie. They both advanced on me. I considered running, but what was the point? They'd catch up —eventually. Even if it wasn't before I reached my car and got away, they'd find me and do what they planned to do. Might as well get it over with.

I tried to get away from them, duck out of their reach, but it was two against one. After some grappling and shoving, Joseph managed to grab my arms and held me by the elbows as I thrashed.

Pain exploded in my skull with Will's first punch, and my eye felt as if it had burst in its socket.

Is this what Austin felt, right before he stopped feeling anything at all? Or was there no pain whatsoever for him?

I saw the next hit coming and tensed, but it still hurt like a motherfucker when Will's fist collided with my core. My insides clenched, and my stomach roiled. I half hoped I'd puke all over him.

Like a little bitch, Will backhanded me, but he was wearing a ring, and it split my bottom lip open. The hit rattled my brain even more after that initial punch. It threw my head to the side, and for a moment, I caught a glimpse of Shady. He was still leaning on the railing, still casually scrolling through his phone. *Unbelievable . . .*

He glanced up and winced, but my full focus was taken up by Will's fist smashing into my ribs. I coughed and wheezed, doubling over as much as possible with his father holding me tightly.

Finally, Will took a few steps back, breathing hard.

I spit blood onto the concrete and fixed him with as firm a look as I could manage through a rapidly swelling eye. "I was never going to fight you," I repeated. "The police are already on their way." I prayed that was true—or at least that they would believe it enough to leave. What if the police came past, saw it was as quiet as I thought when I arrived, and didn't bother to check inside?

Shady's chuckle echoed. Will grinned before stepping a little closer. "We both know the cops aren't coming. And even if they do, what are they gonna find?" He spread his arms wide and looked around. "All I see is a man and his son protecting their property from a known murderer."

"You think you can get one over on me, boy?" Frydenberg's mouth was close to my ear, but he was practically yelling anyway. "I've been in business for years. Been running circles around the police *and* everyone in this town. I have eyes and ears everywhere. You think I don't know about that little weasel Drew? My son has been keeping an eye on him for months. Weak piece of shit. Shady's already taking care of him. I'm going to personally watch the life drain out of your eyes, and then I'm going to feed you to the rats. And that little whore of yours? Well, I guess she's just going to have to forget you ever existed. Just like everyone else."

He talked about business as if what happened here was the same as his stocks and mergers and emails. He insinuated he was having Drew and me killed as if it was just part of a bad day at the office. But when he mentioned Donna, that's when cold, unadulterated rage coursed through me.

I growled, then threw my head back as hard and fast as I could. It hurt like a bitch, another blow to my already aching skull, but the crunch of his nose when I connected was beyond satisfying.

Will's eyes widened and he rushed forward, but it was too late. I'd startled Frydenberg enough to wrench out of his hold and shove him toward his son. They stumbled but quickly righted themselves, both of them watching me with surprise.

I bared my teeth at them like an animal, fists clenched, eyes narrowed. Warm blood was trickling from my split lip down my chin, but I didn't bother to wipe at it. I knew I looked feral. I *felt* feral—I wanted to tear them to pieces with my bare hands for even *mentioning* Donna. But I wasn't going to attack. I wasn't going to be that guy anymore.

"OK. That's enough of that." Shady strode forward casually, clicking his fingers and then slapping his hands, the sharp sound like a punctuation.

"Stay out of this," Frydenberg barked at him.

Shady just cocked his head. "No. And for the record, I don't like people taking credit for my work. You wouldn't know my buddy here was even planning to bring your operation down if it wasn't for me. Your idiot son was ready to fight him at the actual fight night tonight." So there was another location, an actual fight. "I'm the one who got Drew out of the way. Unthankful bitch."

Frydenberg was ready to beat both our asses now, but before he could say anything, I shook my head at Shady and scowled. "I thought you might be a decent guy somewhere underneath all those tracksuits."

He laughed as if I'd made a hilarious joke. "Well, I don't know about that." He moved closer until he was standing shoulder to shoulder with me, facing Will and his dad. "But I did also save your ass."

"What?" the Frydenbergs and I all asked at once, frowning. Senior stepped forward, pointing a finger at Shady as if he were telling off a toddler. "Listen here, you lunatic, I'm—"

Shady cut him off by placing his thumb and forefinger between his lips and letting off a piercing whistle.

"I'd get on your knees, bro," he muttered to me as he did exactly that, putting his hands behind his head while Will and his dad stared in confusion.

Before Shady's first knee hit the concrete, the empty factory exploded in a cacophony of sound. Several heavily armed men poured down those rickety stairs he'd been leaning against, guns pointed, shouting at us all to get down on the ground. More came in through a back door beyond the bright floodlights, and within moments, about a dozen police officers surrounded us.

I took Shady's advice and placed my hands behind my head, cringing against the pain in my torso as I slowly lowered myself to my knees.

Joseph raged, cursed Shady and me to hell, vowed bloody murder. Spit flew from his mouth as he screamed at the police that they had no idea who they were dealing with. Will was as silent as his father was frantic while they cuffed him. When the officers pulled the two of them past us, the look on his face was stoic, but I could've sworn I saw a bit of relief in his lowered gaze.

Once they were out of sight, the three remaining police officers lowered their weapons and approached us, but instead of cuffing us as I thought they might, they helped us to our feet.

A guy with brown eyes and a salt-and-pepper five-o'clock shadow nodded at Shady. "You better hope your info is good. That's a prominent member of Devilbend society we just arrested."

"It's good. And here's junior's phone. I already forwarded the voice recording of senior's little villain rant before you all showed up. You should have enough to charge them both from that alone." He pulled an iPhone out of his pocket and handed it over to the cops, who sealed it in an evidence bag. I glanced at the varsity jacket Will had draped over the railing next to where Shady had been standing.

"You're lucky we got other anonymous tips on both these locations. They were enough to justify a bigger force than we initially planned. A lot of arrests tonight." He grinned, as if he ate arrests for dinner and tonight he was having a feast. Donna and the others were responsible for calling in this address; I wondered who Shady had gotten to report the actual fight.

"We good?" Shady raised his eyebrows.

The cop eyed him up and down. "For now." Then he turned to me. "We'll need to take your statement, but I think an EMT should check you out first. Can you walk, son?"

"Yeah." I gripped my ribs but hobbled out of there on my own two damn feet.

"That was a dumbass thing to do," the cop said to me as he hurried ahead, one hand resting on the butt of his rifle. "Next time you might not get so lucky."

I resisted the urge to give him the finger. All things considered, shit could've gone much, *much* worse. Instead I turned to Shady. "You're an asshole."

He chuckled. "Maybe."

"You couldn't've let me in on your plan?"

"You couldn't've let me in on yours?"

Fair point. "I told you to stay away so you wouldn't get caught up in this shit."

"Yeah, but you know how it is, man. I saw an opportunity, and I took it. Everything worked out." He winked at me.

As we emerged into the night through the same creaky door, I realized Shady was a fucking genius. And I needed to be more careful around him. He'd wanted to be rid of the people running the fights and making his life difficult, and maybe he'd wanted to help me out on some level too, but at the end of the day, he was always going to look out for his best interests first. He hadn't told me jack shit because if the police hadn't shown, he'd still be in with Frydenberg. I had no doubt he would've handed me over if shit hadn't gone to plan. It was a win-win for him.

The area outside the factory was lit up now. A few cop cars and a van had converged near where I'd parked, and several police officers were milling about, talking on their radios, searching the property—doing whatever the fuck it was they did after busting bad guys doing bad shit.

I just wanted to sit down, go to sleep, maybe have Donna run her hands through my hair while I nestled my face into her tits.

As if I'd summoned the little hellion, her pearl-white Beamer came screeching around the corner and pulled to a stop next to my Tesla. She burst out of the car, and several cops tensed.

"Hendrix!" she bellowed as they approached her.

My heart lodged itself in my throat at all those guns pointed at her, but before I could yell, run, do *something*, they realized the little blonde chick in jeans and an oversized hoodie—my hoodie—was not a threat. The cops lowered their guns and just held their arms out instead, trying to herd her back.

"Don't you touch me." She pointed in their faces. "I'll sue the department so fast and so hard none of you will be able to sit for a month."

Despite the fucked-up situation, I chuckled. She was glorious when she was livid, and now that it wasn't directed at me, it was hilarious. *And* she'd cracked an anal joke.

"What is she even doing here?" The plan had been for Harlow to send the address to the cop she'd been emailing as soon as the agreed-upon twenty minutes were up. In the meantime, the others were supposed to make anonymous calls from various public phones—which are not that easy to find anymore

—while Drew headed down to the station to make his statement. Donna's role was to wait for my call and, if I was arrested, come down to save the day with the lawyers the Meads paid an exorbitant amount of money to keep on retainer.

"Apparently Drew didn't head to the station like he was supposed to and wasn't answering his phone. So weird!" Shady grinned. "Then she found out the fight had actually gone down at a completely different spot—man, these rich people gossip when their kids start getting arrested. When she didn't hear from you and couldn't get any information out of the cops, she blew up my phone demanding to know what I knew." He raised his arm to wave at her. "Over here, baby doll! It's OK, guys, that's just my girlfriend!"

Reluctantly, they let her pass, and she jogged over to us.

"You told her to come here?" I gritted my teeth. If she'd gotten here five minutes earlier . . .

"Psh! Naw, man. I got ninety-nine problems. I don't need rich bitch drama on a night like this. Not like she didn't have your last known whereabouts though. Must be true love." He placed both hands over his heart and fluttered his eyelashes at me.

"You fucking prick!" Donna put the momentum of her jog behind a shove to Shady's chest. He actually staggered back but laughed at the same time. Then she noticed me, and those gorgeous mismatched eyes went wide. "Oh, shit. Oh my god, what did they do to you?"

Her hands ghosted over my chest as she scanned my face. I must've looked even worse than I felt, because tears welled in her eyes, and her bottom lip quivered. Donna *never* cried in front of other people.

Keeping one hand braced against my aching ribs, I cupped her cheek with the other and pressed my forehead to hers. "It's OK. I'm OK. I'm still standing."

She just breathed, ragged, trying to get her emotions under control.

"How'd you get here so fast?" I tried to distract her.

"I was parked halfway between here and the nearest police station where I thought they'd take you." She still looked as if she was fighting those tears, as if she was losing.

I quirked up the side of my mouth that wasn't bleeding and tried for humor instead. "You should see the other guy."

"The other guy is just fine." Will's cocky voice made me look up, and Donna froze. A police officer was leading him past us toward the back seat of a cruiser, while his dad was already being assisted into another one next to it.

"Bro, you're in handcuffs." Shady gave him an incredulous look. "You lost."

Before he could reply, Donna turned toward him, putting her back to me. "You're a piece of shit, Will. I hope you and your dad both rot in jail. And Hendrix might be too noble to hit you, but I'm not." Lightning quick, she threw a punch. It was wobbly and off-center, but it still landed, making Will's head snap back a little.

"Ow." He lifted his hands to his face, prodding his nose, then balled them into fists at his chest. "What the fuck, Donna?"

I wrapped my free arm around her middle and pulled her back, wincing through the pain, as another cop rushed over.

"Ma'am, you need to step back." The cop leading Will had let him pause, but now she was holding a hand out. "I'm going to have to place you under—"

Shady stepped forward and threw a punch of his own. His was much more powerful and accurate, and Will cried out in agony as blood started pouring down his face.

The cops rushed in, grabbing Shady and shuffling Will into the cruiser. Donna was forgotten as they roughly cuffed Shady's arms behind his back and arrested him for assault.

Donna and I both raised our eyebrows at him.

"What?" He shrugged and grinned. "I like hitting people. Also, that guy was a dick. And I got a reputation to uphold."

He winked at me as they dragged him away.

One of the cops eyed Donna disapprovingly, her hand hovering over the cuffs at her belt. But then she glanced at me—I made sure to look extra pathetic—and gave us both a warning look before walking off.

Donna turned to me as the two cruisers carrying Will and his dad peeled out of the lot. With a hiss, she held her hand out. "Holy fucking shit, that hurts so much."

I smiled at her, and more blood trickled out of my busted lip. "I hope the pain was worth defending my honor."

Her face was dead serious as she replied, "It was."

An ambulance pulled in, lights flashing but siren off. I slung my free arm around her shoulders and started shuffling toward it. "Let's get that checked out, Rambo."

"Me? You're the one who looks like you went into the ring with Ronda Rousey."

"You know who that is? I'm impressed."

"Don't fucking patronize me, Hendrix."

We bickered all the way to the ambulance. It was the perfect distraction from the pain of every step.

CHAPTER THIRTY

Donna

The weather was warm enough that we could have the windows down as Hendrix drove us to school. With both our sunglasses firmly in place and Post Malone blasting from the speakers, we held hands over the center console. That car practically drove itself anyway.

The girls wanted to give Hendrix this boyfriend moment—driving his girl to school—so they were meeting us there.

I was looking forward to getting back to classes, routine, some semblance of normalcy, but I knew all eyes would be on us instantly, and I wasn't sure I was looking forward to that. We hadn't been to school for about a week with everything going on between our families and the police. Plus, Hendrix had needed time to heal from his injuries.

The EMT and the two separate doctors his aunt had insisted he see all said he was very lucky. Nothing was broken or permanently damaged, but he did have some internal bruising, and his ribs were black and blue. It made me wince every time he took his shirt off. While the bruises did finally seem to be fading, the cut on his lip was going to leave a scar. I'd told him "chicks dig scars" and distracted him with a BJ, and he hadn't seemed too put out by it after that.

His parents hadn't even bothered to fly over to check on their son. I'd overheard a stilted phone conversation with his mom while he was waiting in the hospital to be x-rayed and tested, but he hadn't spoken to his dad once. His parents really were trash, and I was glad he had his aunt. Hannah had been frantic with worry and pissed Hendrix hadn't told her what was going on, but in the end, she admitted she was proud of him—for the way he handled himself and the way he stuck to his values throughout the whole terrible ordeal.

We pulled into the student parking lot at the busiest time. People were arriving, walking up to the entrance, some hanging out and talking—it was still a good twenty minutes until the bell.

The lot was filling fast, but my spot right near the front was empty. Hendrix rolled to a stop and looked at me over the top of his sunglasses, the sun glinting off the frame. A lock of hair fell over his forehead, and I resisted the urge to sweep it back, run my fingers over his scalp, pull him in for a kiss . . .

I rolled my eyes but smiled. "I'll allow it. But only because I'm in the car with you."

He laughed low, the sound sending a shiver down my spine, and pulled into my spot.

Amaya's purple Jag was on one side, and Drew's matte black Audi was on the other. They were all milling around on the path in front of us, chatting, leaning against the hoods of their cars.

Shady's men had released Drew as soon as Will and his dad were taken into custody. Apparently, they'd picked him up on his way to school the morning of the fight and had been the ones replying to anyone who texted his phone. Drew had been nearly out of his mind with worry, but they wouldn't let him leave the suite at the Hilton they'd stashed him in. They'd actually treated him pretty well, hadn't gotten violent—much—and had explained the whole situation before letting him go.

He was so relieved that Will and his dad had been arrested—that his nightmare was over, that we were all OK—he hadn't even reported Shady or pressed charges. I tried not to think about what would've happened to him in the hotel room had things gone sideways and the police never showed up.

The Frydenbergs' arrests had shaken the Devilbend community to its core. No one had suspected Mr. Frydenberg of being involved in anything illegal, let alone the extent of what the police discovered.

His lawyers put up a good fight, but ultimately, the evidence was too damaging. They'd managed to get Will out on parole by arguing he was a victim of his father as much as anyone, but he was being strictly monitored until his trial date.

As we'd hoped, the info Harlow had dug up was enough for the police to launch a massive investigation. Joseph Frydenberg was practically running a crime empire while moving about in California's high circles and pretending to be an upstanding citizen. It appeared he had some legitimate businesses, but he'd also been at the helm of an operation responsible for multiple fight rings across the state, drug dealing, prostitution, all kinds of things.

He might have been able to get away with a slap on the wrist—he was, after all, filthy rich and not above buying his way out—but he'd embarrassed a lot of people in Devilbend who had invested in his business ventures. Not to mention the fact that he'd put so many people in danger, that his thugs had been responsible for the accident that nearly killed Luke and the other guys. The rich and famous of Devilbend were going to make sure he went away for a long time—they were going to ruin him, *bury* him. If he ever got out of jail, he'd never step foot in this town again, let alone do business.

Raine Clayton, the CEO of BestLyf, was denouncing him as vehemently as all the other people who had been at my parents' Christmas party. She'd brushed off questions about his regular sizeable donations, and her PR machine was working in overdrive to squash any suspicion in that area. They'd put out only one statement, making it clear they had no involvement with Joseph Frydenberg past his being a member of the organization, like so many other prominent Americans, and that they'd been unaware of the illegal activity. The press was so preoccupied with all the other constant bombshells surrounding the case, no one hardly looked in BestLyf's direction.

Turner was more pissed than any of us about that. "That is such a load of shit! Those people are evil incarnate and were so involved in this," he'd raged a few days after everything came out. Every time a statement even mentioning BestLyf appeared in the press, he'd lose his shit and go on a tirade about what had happened to his mom and what he and his dad had discovered. He'd only calm down once Mena dragged him out of the room.

It wasn't that I didn't believe Turner. I'd seen Raine and Joseph talking at our party that night, and she gave me weird vibes, but there was no way to prove BestLyf had done anything illegal. The sums Frydenberg had handed over were substantial, but there were no laws against making donations—and both sides claimed that was exactly what they were. The police were attempting to seize some of the money as proceeds of crime, but BestLyf's legal team was wrapping that up in so much litigation it would probably be years before the government got their hands on it—if ever.

"You ready?" Hendrix squeezed my hand as he pushed a button, and all the car windows soundlessly slid up.

I'd let him see my apprehension when he'd picked me up, but I'd had the ride over to steel myself, and I wasn't about to show vulnerability to any of these people.

With him by my side and my girls having my back, it didn't feel so much like a mask anymore. I wasn't hiding. I was just reserving the most private parts of myself—the real parts—for those closest to me.

"Ready." I gave him a genuine smile.

We got out of the car together. Heads turned, whispers sounded, but we ignored it all and just joined our friends.

I gave the girls and Drew a kiss on the cheek each, and Mena started showing us photos of an elaborate makeup look she'd done over the weekend. She was so talented.

Next to us, Drew sat up a little straighter on the hood of his car and nodded to Hendrix. "Welcome back, man."

Hendrix watched him for a beat, and I waited with bated breath. With everything going on, we hadn't really had a chance to talk about Drew, but I knew that whatever my boyfriend decided, there would be no changing his mind.

The side of his mouth quirked, and he held out a fist. "Thanks, man. Good to be back."

They fist-bumped, then did that sideways high five, and I breathed a sigh of relief.

Amaya snorted. "Men."

"I know, right?" I shook my head. It was that easy. No conversations necessary; they were just friends now. Drew asked how Hendrix was healing, Hendrix made out as if he was practically back to normal (lies), and just like that, they launched into a conversation about baseball.

Mena frowned at my sister, who kept glancing over my shoulder. "Why do you keep looking at the front gates?"

Harlow shrugged. "I'm waiting for Mom to pull up. I can hardly believe she let Donna out this morning."

I laughed, but it ended on a groan. "She nearly didn't. She made Hendrix come inside and promise to drive carefully and to text her if we needed anything. I'm so glad Dad had to go on his work trip. I think if they were both home, they would've insisted I take another week off."

Mom and Dad had been . . . hovering. For the first time since I could remember, they were more worried about me than Harlow. Mom was worse than Dad, even coming in to check on me in the middle of the night as if I were a toddler. She'd startled me awake several times.

But they'd both been pissed, *livid*, when they first found out what we'd done —that we hadn't told them the second we found out Will and Drew were involved in something illegal, that we got *ourselves* involved. I knew most of it came from a place of worry for us, so I did my best to remain calm, take the verbal lashing, and act appropriately contrite.

Once they'd calmed down, I did the mature thing and told them everything. I went through every detail of what we found out—glossing over Harlow's potentially illegal methods of getting the information—why we chose not to tell anyone, how the night had played out. They were grudgingly happy Hendrix was willing to go to great lengths to protect me like that but still didn't condone his reckless actions.

I left out my regular visits to Davey's—figured my parents didn't need to know how many guys I'd fucked—but I told them about how I'd been feeling suffocated, pressured, and overwhelmed and that I didn't want to go to law school anymore.

With everything else that had happened, they were hardly even bothered.

"You do whatever you want, go to whatever school you choose, study arts for all I care." Dad waved a dismissive hand, his hair a mess, an empty glass sitting on his desk. "We just want you to be happy and safe."

"You're not mad about all the work I've put in over the years going to waste? All the connections I've made and . . . and . . ."

"Honey." Mom scooted closer to me on the couch, and Dad pushed off his desk and came to sit on my other side. "We're not mad at all. We want you to be successful, but what that looks like is entirely up to you. Above all, we want you to be happy. And safe."

I nodded, a lump forming in my throat. "I just want you to be proud of me, and I feel like I'm failing."

"Donna." Dad took my hand and made me look at him. "We are proud of you. So proud of you. No matter what."

My tears spilled over.

"We love you so much, honey." Mom wrapped me up in a hug.

That was pretty much the end of the conversation. The following week had been focused more on Hendrix's recovery, police statements, and my parents constantly reassuring themselves I was safe and well. They'd been hovering over Harlow and me both, but I was definitely copping more of it after opening up about how I'd been struggling.

I shook my head and pushed the memory away, taking a deep breath of the fresh, sun-soaked spring air. I still got a bit misty thinking about what an emotional roller coaster the past week had been.

Nicola walked past with Luke, and they both smiled at me and waved. I smiled and waved back. A lot of the guys from the football team had been at the fight when the police busted in, and were arrested. Every single one of them had walked away without being charged—thanks to expert lawyers, their parents' influence, and their enthusiasm to testify against the Frydenbergs. Nicola and I had talked, bitched about Will, and we were cool now.

"Let's head in." Amaya picked up her bag, linked arms with Mena, and took the lead. Drew slung an arm over Harlow's shoulders, and they were cracking jokes and messing around before we even reached the front stairs.

Hendrix threaded his fingers through mine and kissed the top of my head as we followed our friends into the school.

People stared and whispered, none of them daring to come up to us and actually ask about what happened, but by now the whole school knew everything that was public knowledge. The stares and whispers were just as much about the fact that I was walking into school hand in hand with the guy they'd all thought I despised just a week ago. I smiled to myself.

At the start of the hallway where all the seniors' lockers were, we pulled up short so we wouldn't collide with Mr. Monroe. He was barreling past—students parting in his wake, some even turning to walk in the opposite direction to avoid him—but he stopped when he spotted us.

"Welcome back, both of you." His lips twitched slightly in what I thought might constitute a smile. He was in a charcoal sweater, the shirt underneath buttoned all the way to his throat.

We mumbled our thanks.

"It's been brought to my attention that you've withdrawn your applications for some of the colleges you applied to," he said, looking right at me.

"Uh . . . yea . . . yes, sir." He was an English teacher and not even *my* English teacher. He must've seen the confusion in my eyes.

"Mrs. Fielding is on leave, and I've been asked to step in and assist for a short time." His lips pressed together slightly—clearly he wasn't thrilled to be helping with careers counseling. "Please come see me if you'd like to discuss options. You too, Mr. Hawthorn."

With another tiny smile, he stalked off again, clutching a pile of papers at his side.

Hendrix and I looked at each other with raised eyebrows, then burst into laughter. It was so good to be back—hanging out with my friends, dealing with Mr. Monroe's moods, getting ready for classes. As much as I'd felt suffocated by some of those same things in the past few months, the familiarity of it all was weirdly bringing me comfort.

The others had already dispersed, so we hurried off to our own lockers. I quickly grabbed my books and rushed over to Hendrix's side just as he closed his.

Pulling his shoulder down, I leaned in to whisper in his ear. "I'm not wearing any underwear."

His eyes squeezed shut, and he groaned low, gripping my hip and moving in close. "Why would you tell me that? I really don't want to spend all day with a semi, Donna."

There was an edge of annoyance in his voice, but his gaze was pure lust.

"Who said anything about all day?" I whispered against his lips. Then, without kissing him, I started to back away. "Meet me at our spot at lunch."

He frowned. With a grin, I turned and rushed off to class, fully aware he had to go in the opposite direction or risk being late.

"What spot?" he called after me. "Donna! What spot?"

I rounded the corner and picked up my pace. He'd figure it out once the lust cleared a little and he could think straight. Now I just had to make sure I made it to the little room at the back of the auditorium before he did.

LIKE YOU SHOULD

CHAPTER ONE

Harlow

The doorbell rang just as I pulled an oversized hoodie over my head. Mom and Dad were out for drinks with friends, and our housekeeper, Magda, was having a long weekend off, so I jammed my bare feet into fluffy slippers and rushed down the sprawling staircase to answer it.

The bell rang again a second before I reached the door. "Yeah, yeah!" I yelled as I pulled the heavy thing open. "Keep your panties on."

My sister's boyfriend, Hendrix, and my cousin's boyfriend, Turner, shouldered their way in as soon as the door cracked open, each carrying a six-pack of beer. I had all the snacks ready to go.

"Hey, Baby Mead." Hendrix flashed me a grin, and I fist-bumped them both.

"Hendrix?" Donna came down the stairs with a frown, her short blonde hair still damp from her shower. My hair was a little darker than her ashy blonde shade, but it was way longer too, hanging to my waist. "I thought we weren't doing anything tonight."

"We're not." He slung an arm over my shoulders. "I'm here to see your sister."

"What?" Donna looked between the three of us. Hendrix and Turner dwarfed me between them. For some reason the women in my family were attracted to ridiculously tall men—or maybe I was just so damn short that everyone felt taller than me.

"Quit teasing." Turner whacked Hendrix on the back of the head. "We're having a gaming night." He grabbed the beer out of Hendrix's hand and headed toward the media room at the back of the house.

"She likes it when I tease," Hendrix called after him, laughing, before looking Donna up and down and biting his bottom lip.

"Ew!" I ducked out from under his arm and rushed after Turner. "At least wait until I'm out of the room before you start foreplay."

I'd never met two people who got under each other's skin more than Donna and Hendrix, but it seemed to work for them. They called each other on their shit as no one else could—and it only made them stronger. They deserved to have that after everything they'd been through.

Hendrix told my sister he'd come and find her later—gag!—and she said she wasn't going to wait up. He caught up to me as I got to the media room.

Turner had already turned on the massive screen and was booting up three separate Xboxes. We had four, plus four PlayStations, and a state-of-the-art sound system. Several deep, comfy couches took up most of the room.

I launched myself onto one and opened a beer as the boys tore into several chip bags. I usually played online with these two morons, but occasionally we got together to mix it up. Turner had been complaining recently about doing nothing but school and work for the past few weeks, so I'd invited them over.

An hour and one six-pack of beer later, we were wrapping up a match of Fortnite. Before we could start the next game, Hendrix shouted, "Toilet break!" and launched himself over the back of the couch. I glared after him. Guys could never last as long as girls. I could sit here or in my computer chair for a solid four hours without a pee break—you just couldn't break the seal; otherwise it was all over, and you'd be peeing every twenty minutes.

Turner stretched his arms over his head and flopped back against the couch, running a hand through his shaggy blond hair. "How was your birthday trip, Harls? Mena said she had an amazing time."

When my parents had asked what I wanted to do for my eighteenth, a party had been tempting, but we'd had so much drama and craziness lately I hadn't really felt like it. So I asked if we could take a trip instead—just my parents and my closest friends. They readily agreed and packed us all off to an exclusive resort in the Maldives for a week. Amaya's Instagram was spammed with postcard-worthy pics of beaches and us four girls, each with #DevilbendDynasty and #GirlsTrip in the caption.

My sister had done the whole big-eighteenth-party thing, with everyone we knew invited. I was content to be with my nearest and dearest while getting a break from winter. Donna was only eleven months older than me, so her party had kind of felt like mine too anyway. Technically, she should've been in the year above, already graduated, based on when our birthdays fell, but we were so close our parents had made sure we stayed together during our schooling. And even though she annoyed me like no one else could sometimes, I was glad they had—Donna was my best friend.

"It was so good." I smiled at Turner. "I'm sorry you guys weren't there for my birthday dinner"—which we'd had at the resort restaurant as the sun set over the turquoise water—"but it was good to get away for a little while. And the warm weather was perfect!"

As if to punctuate my statement, a big gust of wind drew our eyes to the narrow window. There was a storm brewing, and I shivered.

"Well, I can't say I'm not jealous, but at least I got bikini shots out of it."

I smacked him on the arm as he laughed. Mena and Turner were so cute together, and that was the first time they'd been apart since they started dating. It had also been my cousin's first trip out of the country. The rush to get her passport sorted when we realized she didn't have one had been an adventure itself. But as usual, Donna took charge and got it done.

"If the next words out of your mouth include anything remotely resembling spank-bank, I'm going to hit you for real." I pointed a warning finger at him.

He just grinned wider and stuck his tongue out, biting it as if to stop himself saying exactly what I'd just told him not to.

"What's this about spanking?" Hendrix reappeared, plonking down on my other side.

I rolled my eyes. "Don't you start."

My sister and I were close—I knew they got freaky. I knew *all* about Donna's, Amaya's, and Mena's sex lives. I just didn't want to discuss it with their boyfriends. Girl code! Donna wasn't shy about telling her closest friends intimate details. Her days of hiding things from us were over.

I wished I could tell them all my secret too—it was a doozie. But I had to keep this one to myself until I could find a way out of it.

Whenever I found myself in a sticky situation, I thought to myself, *WWDD. What would Donna do?* Donna would do whatever she had to in order to protect those she loved. So that's what I was going to do.

"All right, come on." Turner opened his third beer and gestured to the screen. "Let's go."

I shoveled a handful of Doritos into my mouth with one hand and picked up my custom pink controller with the other.

We spent the next several hours going on missions and shooting virtual enemies while gorging on junk food, talking shit, and taking way too many pee breaks.

It was just after one in the morning when Turner came back from the bathroom yet again. He flopped onto the couch as Hendrix finished his last beer and released a belch that shook the windows almost as badly as the storm raging outside.

"All right, let's hit it!" I brushed Dorito crumbs off my fingers, grabbed my controller, and started the next match. We'd been playing online all night, our friend Drew making up our squad, but he'd bailed before the last game. He told everyone through the headset that some chick was booty-calling him and logged off. So now we had to let internet randoms play with us. The last one hadn't had a microphone and had probably had to endure the three of us flaying each other with insults through their speakers the entire match. Now we had to wait for the game to randomly assign us another player.

The screen loaded, the username popped up, and all the blood drained from my face. The junk food twirled in my stomach as if it were a washing machine.

Ocean1k had been the bane of my existence for nearly a month now. They were good—a much better hacker than I was—but I never expected them to plant themselves into our squad. Technically, anything could be hacked, but this was probably just a coincidence.

I repeated the word in my head over and over. *Coincidence, coincidence, coincidence.* The guys shared quips as the match started, making bets on who would take the first hit, but I had gone completely silent.

All I could do was stare at that name, remembering all the shit I'd had to do since it appeared on my computer screen that night. A Telegram message, a spoofed number—completely untraceable.

Were they taunting me? Trying to prove they could get to me anywhere— even in a game while I had fun with my friends? Surely they had better things to do.

We were in Game Chat mode, and Ocean1k showed an active mic, but when the boys tried to say hi, they didn't respond. My hands tightened around my controller, the pink plastic groaning.

We moved through the match as a team. Ocean1k followed us around but didn't shoot any of the opponents, didn't engage with them or us at all, didn't say a word on the other end of the mic.

"Dude!" Turner yelled. "Pick a gun and shoot something."

"Come on!" Hendrix growled as the safe zone shrank and we ran from the storm. Another squad started attacking, and we frantically bashed the buttons on our controllers, fighting back.

The guys were yelling as usual, talking about strategy and what weapons and ammo they had left. I remained silent, my teeth gritted, listening for any little sound in my headphones.

Ocean1k's avatar just stood there watching, listening, waiting.

It was a *coincidence*.

Fuck this.

I leaned forward and propped my elbows on my knees, my full focus on the screen. My fingers flew on the controller as I turned my avatar and drew a pistol, pointed, and emptied the entirety of my available bullets in Ocean1k's direction.

"Whoa, what the fuck?" Turner glanced at me, then back to the screen, shooting at the enemy.

"Calm down, Baby Mead." Hendrix chuckled and nudged me with his shoulder.

My rage only grew hotter. Hendrix had said my last name. *Idiot!* Not that it mattered. Ocean1k already knew everything about me.

My bullets did nothing, of course, since Ocean1k and I were on the same team. I growled and wrenched my headset off, throwing it and my controller down on the coffee table.

The guys bailed us out of the game. They both dropped their controllers to the table and removed their headsets. I could see them turning to look at me in my periphery, but I couldn't seem to tear my eyes away from the screen.

I couldn't even do anything to Ocean1k in a game. I wished they were dead in real life. I wished I knew who they were so I could destroy them.

"Harls, are you OK?" Turner sounded genuinely worried.

Hendrix gently waved a hand in front of my face, which snapped me out of my rage-filled staring. I looked between my two friends, both wearing matching looks of concern, and flopped back into the cushions with a sigh.

"I'm fine." I tried to take the tension out of my voice. "That guy was just pissing me off."

"That was pretty intense for an internet random pissing you off." Hendrix frowned.

"Yeah, I've never seen you that worked up before." Turner backed him up. "You sure there's nothing else going on?"

"Yeah." I forced a small smile. "I'm just tired." When they both frowned— because I routinely stayed up until dawn—I rushed to add, "I didn't sleep at all last night, and I'm basically running on Doritos and Red Bull. I think it's catching up with me."

"Actually, I worked an eight-hour shift today." Turner worked at a gym downtown, and Saturdays were busy. "I'm beat. Maybe we should just call it a night."

"Suit yourselves." Hendrix shrugged. "I got other ways of keeping myself entertained."

He flashed us a devious grin, and I had no doubt he was heading upstairs to bone my sister. Turner and I both threw empty beer cans and loose Doritos at him as he ran out of the room.

"Magda set up the spare room for you," I told Turner as I switched off the consoles and the TV. It was late, and I didn't want him driving all the way to Devilbend North if he was tired.

"Thanks." He caught my hand as we passed the kitchen. "Harls. You know you can talk to me, right? I'm here for you."

I gave him a genuine smile and a hug. "Thanks. I know."

I left him in the kitchen with his head buried in our massive fridge, then trudged up the stairs, rushing past Donna's room, where disgusting noises already drifted out from under the door.

I had to be more careful. It was stupid—reckless—letting myself get worked up like that over seeing Ocean1k in the game. If I kept it up, someone would notice. I had to keep my shit together until I found a way out of this or figured out what they wanted. Donna's life depended on it.

CHAPTER TWO

Harlow

After I dragged my ass upstairs, I tossed and turned in bed for hours, thinking about Ocean1k—the faceless entity blackmailing me into doing dodgy shit on the internet. I couldn't quite believe I was in this situation, and no matter how many sleepless nights I spent obsessing over it, I still had no way out. I managed to drift off around dawn. Thank god it was Sunday and I could sleep past midday, undisturbed.

An uneventful Sunday was followed by yet another sleepless night.

It took me forever to fall asleep most nights, my brain just refusing to switch off. Some nights it would whirl with whatever I'd been doing on the computer before I went to bed, and some nights I found myself thinking about the vastness of space and meaning of life—you know, regular teenage girl shit. When I did finally manage to fall asleep, I was a light sleeper. I tossed and turned, woke up throughout the night, was disturbed by every little sound. I couldn't remember the last time I'd had a really solid sleep without passing out drunk or getting high. Not that I did that shit much either. I may have been an insomniac, but I wasn't an idiot—I had no interest in developing a substance abuse problem.

Since Ocean1k came into my life via my computer screen, my sleep had gotten even worse. Half the time I didn't even know how I functioned.

The rest of the week passed in routine—school, tennis, homework, struggling to sleep. At least my new "friend" was being quiet.

I hit snooze at least five times on Friday morning, eventually dragging my ass out of bed with fifteen minutes to spare. I'd managed a solid four hours, so I counted it as a win.

No time for a shower, I liberally applied deodorant, tied my hair back into two messy low braids, yanked on my uniform, and rushed down the stairs just as Donna finished her smashed avocado and poached eggs.

"Hey, pumpkin!" Dad flashed me a grin and got back to his stock report on his tablet.

Mom smoothed the top of my hair with a frown. It made absolutely no difference to the mess. "How'd you sleep, honey?"

I grunted something resembling "fine," and Donna swooped in at the perfect moment, insisting we had to leave. Mom gave me a kiss on the cheek, and next thing I knew, I was following my sister into the garage.

"Take the front." She dumped her own bag into the back seat. "Amaya's getting Mena from the bus station."

I gave her the dirtiest look I could muster, but it morphed into a yawn. "I could've slept for another forty-five minutes? Dick move, Donna."

We got into the car, and she started the engine. My cousin Mena attended Fulton Academy with us, but my parents paid her tuition. She lived in a small apartment in Devilbend North—the unsavory side of town—and we picked her up from home or the bus station most mornings.

"It's in the group chat, dickhead." Donna chuckled as she pulled her pearl-white Beamer out of the garage, heading toward the winding road that would take us to the picturesque grounds of one of the most exclusive schools in the country.

I pulled my phone out, and sure enough, there was a whole conversation in our group chat. I vaguely remembered checking the messages after I'd shut myself in my room, but then I'd gotten an idea for how to track Ocean1k, and the contents of the messages hadn't registered at all.

"Sorry," I mumbled and yawned into my shoulder, shuffling farther down into the seat.

"It's OK, Harls." Donna's voice had gone soft—the one reserved only for me in these moments of unspoken understanding. "I have to go in early to deal with a student body thing, but you can nap for half an hour in the car."

She didn't even know for sure what she would do at college anymore, but Donna was still the most organized, punctual, hardworking nerd I knew. Except she wasn't a nerd at all—she was a total badass. She'd planned to go to law school since we were little kids, but a couple of months ago, she had a bit of a mental breakdown and realized she didn't want that at all. Now she was just trying to figure out what to do with the rest of her life—like everyone else her age.

"Thanks, D." I jammed my sunglasses on, rested my head on the side of the car door, and was asleep before we even got to school.

My phone vibrating in my lap startled me awake. I rubbed my sore neck and groaned before picking it up to read the Telegram message.

Ocean1k: Don't make plans tonight. Be ready to work.

I frowned at the screen even as my anxiety spiked.

The first time I'd received a message from Ocean1k was a Tuesday night; I'd been trawling reddit on my computer after having given up any attempt at sleep. A Telegram notification popped up with a new message from an unknown number. That first message was simple but chilling in its accuracy.

Ocean1k : You're the one who exposed Joseph Frydenberg to the police, Harlow Mead. I have another criminal for you to take down. Interested?

I should've trusted my gut—ignored and blocked immediately. But taking down Frydenberg had felt good. He was a prominent member of Devilbend society, a friend of my parents, and I'd helped prove he was running a massive criminal organization. For once, all the time I spent online—creeping around chatrooms and forums, learning code and how computer networks worked, maybe even doing some slightly illegal shit—didn't feel like a waste of time. For the first time, I didn't feel like a dumbass in a world of gifted, intelligent, beautiful people. I had something to contribute.

So I replied. Ocean1k sent me the name and IP address of some Wall Street psycho conning elderly people out of their savings. When I asked why they couldn't do it themselves—they clearly had the skills, considering they'd found me and used an encrypted messaging app and a spoofed number to remain anonymous—they said I had an existing line of communication with a police officer. I'd swapped several emails with someone in the Devilbend PD while sending them the evidence to take down Frydenberg, but I definitely wouldn't have said I trusted the guy; I hadn't even met him. Ocean1k said this case was sensitive, and they didn't want to risk the info slipping through the cracks if it came from an anonymous source.

Like an idiot, I believed them and got sucked into a new puzzle. It only took me one energy-drink-fueled night to get what I needed and send it to my contact. Once again, achieving something positive exhilarated me. Seeing mentions of the case in the news a few days later was the best kind of payoff.

It wasn't worth it.

I should've run from Ocean1k the second they popped up on my screen. Not that it would've mattered. They would've found a way to get to me eventually.

After that first time, they started sending me other leads, never sharing anything about who they were or how they had the information. I was convinced they were someone in the system—a legal assistant, a frustrated cop—someone sick of seeing rich, privileged assholes get away with crimes. I could get behind that.

But then Ocean1k asked me to plant evidence. They demanded I hack into some pharmaceutical rep's computer and make it look as if certain emails had been exchanged, certain files had been created and hidden there, to frame them for insider trading.

My fun playing at vigilante quickly turned into a nightmare—as if I didn't already have enough trouble sleeping. As soon as that message came through, I did what I should've done on that first day. I wiped all my electronics; destroyed my laptop, computer, and phone; and got fresh, air-locked hardware. The very next day I had another message from Ocean1k.

That's when I knew I was dealing with a professional. When they started threatening me, when Donna was brought into the equation, I knew I was dealing with someone dangerous. So I did the awful thing they demanded. I framed an innocent woman.

I'd been obsessively watching the news for mentions of it, but nothing had come up, and I hadn't been contacted by Ocean1k since.

Until now.

A second text came in moments after the first.

Ocean1k: Further instructions coming at 8 p.m.

Then a third, just to drive the point home—a picture, a threat. It was a still shot from a video, prominently featuring my sister. If it got out, she would be devastated. It would ruin her life.

I stared at my phone, wanting to throw it, scream, reach through it and wring this faceless fucker's neck.

A knock at the car window startled me so much I dropped the phone into the footwell.

On the other side of the glass, Mena and Amaya burst into laughter, falling against each other in uncontrollable mirth at my expense.

Deciding the creepy messages from my blackmailer didn't require a response, I retrieved my phone, jammed it into my bag, and got out of the car to glare at my two friends.

"Bitch, stop murdering me with your eyes." Amaya cocked a perfectly outlined eyebrow. "We brought you breakfast."

"And coffee!" Mena held the cup out with a smile. "Sorry we startled you."

"It's OK." I sighed. I could never stay mad at Mena—it was one of her evil superpowers. "Thanks for the coffee and . . ." I held my hand out expectantly.

Amaya flipped her long, shiny black hair over her shoulder before handing over a brown paper bag. "Smoked salmon bagel."

I moaned as the smell hit me. I'd need all the fuel I could get today. "I love you guys."

"We love you too." Mena looped her arm through mine and held my coffee as I devoured the bagel on our way into the school. Amaya just grunted and buried her head in her phone. It was as close to an endearment as I was likely to get from her.

Both of them looked as put together and groomed as my sister had over an hour ago: teal-and-white uniforms pressed, hair styled, makeup expertly applied—in Mena's case, literally. She was so good at makeup she could have easily charged for it. She'd done a full face today, which covered the port-wine-stain birthmark on her right cheek and nose—but she was just as pretty without the makeup. Inside and out.

I threw the empty paper bag from the bagel in the trash and tucked my shirt into my teal tartan skirt, straightened my tie, retied my hair. I did the best I could with what I had to work with; Fulton had a strict uniform code. Apparently, it still wasn't enough though.

"Pull your socks up, Miss Mead." At the sound of Mr. Monroe's voice, I nearly dropped the coffee Mena had just handed back to me. "And do up your top button, and for *god's sake* scrub your nails. *Excellentia, scientia, perseverantia. Excellence* is in the school motto. That includes one's appearance."

"Yes, sir." I pulled my socks up one-handed, and Mena did up my top button, but I scowled at my nails. I had a habit of scribbling on them with highlighters when I was supposed to be studying. They were currently a washed-out neon green. "I'll get to the ladies' room and wash the . . ."

He was already walking away, back stiff, messenger bag crossed over his body, shiny brown shoes clacking on the polished floors as students parted to make way for him.

I gave his back my neon-colored middle finger. What difference did it make what I looked like if I did the work? But my world didn't function that way—Fulton didn't function that way. And I couldn't afford to get any more detentions, warnings, or strikes against me.

"What an asshole." Mena glared at his retreating form. "I don't know why half the girls here have crushes on him. He's so *mean*."

Mr. Monroe was the youngest teacher at Fulton by at least ten years. He'd started here last year, but I'd never had the misfortune of being in his class. He was reportedly a hard-ass, never gave extensions, marked harshly, handed out detentions for the slightest missteps, and never smiled. But the lines under his buttoned-up shirts and sweaters hinted at a lean physique, and his hard hazel eyes contrasted with his black hair and the black-rimmed glasses he wore, and . . . I was spending way too much time thinking about why girls had crushes on him.

"It doesn't matter that he's mean. We're in a privileged, exclusive school,"

Amaya drawled. "Half the student body has daddy issues. Hell, I'd let him bend me over his desk and spank me with his ruler too."

I snorted. Amaya's dry wit never failed to brighten my mood. Mena rolled her eyes, but she chuckled too before giving us each a kiss on the cheek and rushing off to her first class.

Amaya slung an arm around my neck and kissed the side of my head. "You look gorgeous, Harls. Don't let any of these assholes get you down—no matter how hot they are."

"Thanks, Amaya." I smiled at her and sipped my coffee as we headed to our lockers.

Friday mornings were the absolute worst. I had History, Algebra, and Political Studies—all information I'd never use after high school. And why did I need to know how to find the value of x when I had a powerful calculator in my pocket at all times? I was barely passing all those classes, and I was so tired I hardly took anything in all morning.

But at least Mena was in my Algebra class—she struggled as much as I did— and Drew and Amaya sat with me in History. Sometimes we pretended we didn't have phones and sent each other handwritten notes. Donna took AP everything, so we didn't have any classes together.

The afternoon was much easier. During gym class we played tennis on the school's four courts—something I was actually good at. My last class for the day was IT, and I pretty much just slept through it. We were learning about design concepts in relation to graphical user interface—shit I'd taught myself before high school. I'd skimmed through the entire semester's course material in one sitting, breezed through the assessments, and completed the assignments in a fraction of the time it took everyone else. I could've taught this class, but I was just as happy to be acing it. It was the only one.

My afternoon classes were almost enough to make me forget about the messages in my phone—the ones that felt like a bomb I was carrying around in my pocket. But as soon as we got home, I couldn't think about anything else. I was so on edge all evening that my family started asking if I was OK. I told them I was just tired, then went to hide out in my room.

I paced the floor, kicking shoes and empty plates out of the way. The rest of the house was pristine at all times, but I allowed Magda and the cleaners into my room only once a week. I needed my space, my privacy.

At a few minutes past eight, another text came through.

Ocean1k: Be at the alleyway behind the building at 229 Gibson Avenue at 2 a.m. Bring a drive with a trojan.

I slumped onto the edge of my bed, my hand shaking slightly. Yeah, I'd done some dodgy shit from the privacy of my own keyboard, but I'd never broken into someone's house and installed malicious code on their computer.

I blew out a big breath and replied.

Harlow: That's break and enter. I didn't agree to this.
Ocean1k: You'll have assistance. Your contact will be waiting for you in the alley.

Now I was supposed to willingly put myself in a dark alleyway with this nutcase's people? How was this my life?

Harlow: It's too risky. I won't do it.

I sent the message and chewed on my nail, realizing I'd forgotten to scrub the highlighter off them earlier.

The reply was a photo—a threat in HD—and my stomach plummeted. My shoulders slumped, and my eyes squeezed shut. How many times had Donna bailed me out of trouble, protected me?

I had to protect her now. All the previous images of my sister that Ocean1k had sent were a threat to expose her, ruin her. This one was different. It was a photo of her leaving her boyfriend's house just the other day. Someone was actually following her now.

Harlow: Fine. But I don't want to do anything like this again. This is a once-off.

I sent the message and waited. When no reply showed up, I threw my phone onto the bed and dropped my head into my hands.

The next few hours were torture, every possible worst-case scenario running through my mind while I copied a few different versions of the code onto a thumb drive. I did, like, six nervous pees in the space of a few hours, and I wasn't even drinking anything!

With the house silent and asleep, I braided my hair back and put on black yoga pants, a black hoodie, and my black Nikes. I'd worried—maybe even hoped—that someone would bust me on my way out. But the carpets were plush and my steps soundless, and my parents slept in the opposite wing of the house. Donna had managed to sneak out for months without anyone noticing a thing.

I drove my electric-blue Mercedes convertible right out of the garage without incident and headed toward the address in downtown Devilbend. The color of my car wasn't exactly inconspicuous, but it was better than the neon orange I'd initially wanted. *Thank you, Donna, for talking me out of that one.*

I parked two blocks away and walked to the alleyway with my hood up and my head down, trying not to jump at every little sound. My breath misted in the cold night air. A car drove past every once in a while, but this part of the city was mostly residential—and eerily quiet.

At the corner of the alley, I took one last steadying breath, rolled my shoulders back, and did my best to channel my sister's stone-cold confidence as I stepped into the darkness.

My eyes adjusted quickly, and I immediately spotted the man standing next to a fire escape. Like me, he was dressed in all black, a hood over his face.

I approached, and he met me halfway.

"Are you . . . uh . . ." *Damn*! I hadn't thought about how to ask a stranger if he was there to commit a crime with me. "Did Ocean1k send you?"

"Yeah." He sounded irritated—as though he'd rather be anywhere else. There was something strangely familiar about that low, disappointed voice. So much conveyed with one word. "Are you the—"

He cut himself off with a gasp, and I stepped a little closer, frowning. How did I know this guy?

He threw his hood back, and the light from the end of the alley glinted off his glasses. "*You're* the hacker? *Jesus*." He ran a hand through his jet-black hair.

"I don't know that I'd call myself a hacker exactly, but—*holy shit*." My hand went to my mouth as my eyes widened.

Standing before me was Mr. Easton Monroe—Fulton Academy's youngest and surliest teacher.

CHAPTER THREE

Easton

The contact I was supposed to get into the building was a fucking *student*? I'd never had Harlow Mead in my class, but I knew she was the student body president's sister, and I'd heard other teachers mention her from time to time: lots of potential but couldn't focus, great at sports and had a keen interest in tech, but Ms. Murphy, a fellow English teacher, couldn't even get her to read the first few scenes of *The Crucible*.

Harlow was probably too busy with boys and recording TikToks to actually do her homework, spoiled rotten by rich parents, without a worry for her job prospects after school. But regardless of how much she represented everything I hated about the youth of America today, I still couldn't put a teenager in danger like this.

"No. We're not doing this," I hissed, doing my best to put on my teacher voice while speaking quietly.

She snatched the key card out of my hand, moving way faster than I anticipated. "Suit yourself. I'll find my own way in."

When she moved toward the street, I stepped into her path. "Are you insane? *No*. We're *not* doing this."

"Are you *stupid*?" She frowned up at me and cocked her head to the side. "I already said I don't need you. Run along."

She actually shooed me with both hands, as if I were a racoon. The irritation I felt dealing with teenagers on a daily basis washed through me tenfold. I pushed it down and remained calm, blocking her path once again. "Think about this for a second, Harlow."

"Don't." She got right in my space and poked me in the chest, then glanced around the alley. "Don't say my name out here. And I *have* thought about this, dickhead. If you're working with *them*, then this is clearly a test, and I'm not going to fail. If you really are in the same boat as me, they must have something on you that's just as bad as what they're holding over me. Are you willing to risk it? Because I'm not."

Was I willing to risk my brother's life? No. But how was I supposed to risk a student's—even if she had just called me a dickhead? I had to hand it to her; she'd sized up the situation very quickly and made some excellent points. Her problem-solving skills were good, even under stress. And I couldn't exactly let her go in there alone.

"Fuck," I muttered under my breath and snatched the key card back from her, heading toward the street before I could change my mind.

"Did you just cuss, sir?" She gasped, but grinned. "Can't believe you're setting such a bad example for my young, impressionable mind."

This little delinquent was mocking me. And how she could smile in this mess of a pressure cooker was beyond me.

"No more talking until we get inside," I ordered, and she clamped her mouth shut. Ocean1k had said the cameras would be off, but there were still other people in the building. We had to be as silent as possible.

I led Harlow to the back entrance and let us in using the key card I'd stolen from Coach Cooper earlier that day. He lived in this building, but he wouldn't be in his fifth-story apartment. He'd been telling everyone at work—loudly—about the camping trip he was taking his family on this weekend. It wasn't his apartment we were going to illegally enter anyway. We were headed to the penthouse.

I tried to remain light on my feet as we approached the elevators, listening out for any sound, acutely aware of the teenager at my back. What the hell was I *doing*?

The building had a doorman but only during the day, and Ocean1k had assured me the security guy would be in his office in the basement, his monitors blank. But there was no accounting for a resident who might come home late after a night out, or a teenager sneaking out.

The ding of the elevator in the completely empty, totally silent lobby was almost obscene.

We shuffled in, and I scanned the key card and pressed the button. When the doors opened on the top floor, I hesitated. I would do anything to protect Ford, but could I live with the potential consequences of putting another young person in danger to do it?

"Don't bitch out now," Harlow muttered as she stepped into the hallway, not even glancing back. I followed with a sigh.

She went straight to apartment 1502. Presumably Ocean1k had filled her in on where she needed to be as well. There were only two units on this level. Were the neighbors home? I glanced at 1501 and suppressed a shudder. Were they watching us right now through the peephole, calling the cops? Was Ocean1k behind the door?

I forced myself to focus and turned to Harlow. "Before we go in," I whispered, and she looked up at me with her big, round eyes. Her youthful face looked so innocent, her petite frame cloaked in black fabric. "I don't know any more than you do what we're going to find on the other side of that door. So if anything goes wrong—the *slightest* hint of trouble—you run. Do you understand? You run and you don't turn back."

She swallowed, and her eyes darted about the hallway, showing her first signs of trepidation. Then she steeled herself and nodded firmly.

It was a small comfort to know that she'd taken me seriously, that I'd at least made sure to put her safety ahead of mine before taking her into a dangerous situation.

Unwilling to waste any more time, I kneeled in front of the door and pulled out a lock-picking set. The unassuming little pouch had appeared in my mailbox last week, with instructions from Ocean1k arriving just as I opened it. I'd resisted, argued, pointed out that I was a fucking *English teacher* and had no idea how to pick locks.

But then the photos of Ford came in, and I crumbled like ancient ruins. I'd spent every day since watching videos online on how to pick different locks. I'd even gone to the hardware store and purchased a few different ones to practice on.

With a shaky breath, I set to work.

Despite the nerves, it was surprisingly easy. The lock clicked, and the door inched open. Harlow and I shared a loaded look, and then she squared her shoulders and pushed her way inside.

The one positive about breaking into an apartment in a building with security —no security system in the apartment itself. God! When did I start thinking like a petty criminal? *Probably when I started doing petty criminal shit.*

I shut the door behind us as silently as possible, and we paused in the dark entryway. The lights were out, and there wasn't a sound. Ocean1k had assured me no one would be home, but I had no way of confirming that short of calling out "*Hello*" like a bimbo in a crappy slasher flick. I didn't even know whose apartment this was.

But I did know where we needed to go. Turn right, down the hall, last door on the left. I reached out and found Harlow's arm, gripping her wrist and tugging. She followed without protest, the light from under the front door and the small window at the end of the hall barely providing enough light to see by. Her wrist felt light and fragile in my hand, and warmth seeped through the fabric of her hoodie. If anyone even *tried* to hurt her tonight...

At the last door on the left, I took another steadying breath and turned the handle.

The room was as empty and silent as the rest of the apartment. I still didn't dare turn on the lights. A large window on the other side of the room, its curtains half-closed, let in the yellow light of a streetlamp, Illuminating a desk and a computer, bookshelves, a few plush chairs.

Harlow yanked her wrist from my grasp, crossed over to the computer, and pulled the large executive chair up to the desk. I hovered near the door, listening for the slightest hint of movement, as I watched her.

She pulled a thumb drive from her pocket and plugged it in, and the screen came to life. Even after she turned the brightness down, the glow still washed over her face as her fingers flew over the keyboard. She looked intensely focused, her round eyes glued to the monitor.

After barely ten minutes, she packed up as swiftly as she'd set up, returned the monitor to its original brightness level, and even repositioned the keyboard to how she'd found it. Then she turned everything off and rushed back to my side.

We didn't speak at all as we made our way out of the apartment, into the elevator, and toward the same door at the rear of the building. Just as the elevator doors closed behind us, several voices cut through the silence.

My heart jumped into my throat, and every muscle in my body tensed. We were set up. They'd waited for us to finish the deed just so they could bust us. *Shit! Fuck! Fucking shit!*

The sound of voices and laughter mingled with uneven footsteps.

Harlow and I had screeched to a stop right by the door. Through the narrow window, we could see four people coming toward the building, their voices getting louder.

Harlow snatched the key card out of my hand for the second time that night and turned back the way we'd just come. She opened a side door, grabbed the sleeve of my hoodie, and pulled me into the stairwell. My senses returned, and I clicked the door shut just as the voices began to echo inside. Despite the darkness, a narrow window in the door—matching the one we'd just been looking through—allowed in just enough light to expose us if any of the drunk fools looked too closely.

Harlow made to head up the stairs, but I grabbed the back of her sweatshirt and tugged her toward the corner. Unless someone opened the door, we wouldn't be visible from there, but they just might hear the sound of our footfalls echoing on the steps.

I pressed myself against the narrow bit of concrete wall and pulled Harlow in next to me, putting my finger against my lips and bugging my eyes out. She gave a nod, her own eyes wide with fear. They were hazel, like mine. This close to her, I could just make out hints of green at the edges.

There wasn't really room for both of us to back up fully against the wall, so I ended up with a student from my school squeezed tight against my right side. As if this night wasn't batshit enough, I was now close enough to smell the vanilla in her shampoo, to feel her hip against my thigh, to hear the rattle in her throat as she struggled to breathe silently. We were both breathing hard, the adrenaline shooting through our veins, all senses on alert.

And I couldn't seem to banish the thought that her eyes were beautiful . . .

The voices of the drunks came past the door, and I held my breath.

Harlow shivered, a small, involuntary movement I wouldn't have even noticed had she not been plastered against me. I frowned—she couldn't be cold. I was practically panting from how hard my heart was thumping. When she shivered again, I realized she was scared.

For all her bravado and sarcastic digs, she was just a young girl caught in a dangerous situation, and she was *scared*.

My right arm was squished between her and the wall, but I lifted my left and wrapped it around her shoulders. She stiffened for a split second, then lifted her own arms and tucked them into my sides, her fingers digging into the fabric, holding on. I tightened my hold on her shoulders and rubbed gently with my thumb. Her shivering stopped, and her head came to rest on my chest.

I resisted the urge to smell her hair like a creep as I got another whiff of sweet vanilla.

When the elevator dinged and the boisterous voices gave way to silence once more, neither of us moved.

"What have we done?" she whispered into my shoulder, her voice as shaky as her body.

I held her a little tighter. "We did what we had to."

The urge to protect this young, naive girl in my arms was so strong it almost brought me to my knees. I didn't know Harlow Mead, but she didn't deserve this —neither of us did—and I would do everything in my power to keep her safe.

She cleared her throat and backed away, checking through the window, then carefully pulled the door open without looking at me. I followed her into the cold night and back to the alley, where she handed me the key card.

"Did you get what we came for?" I asked, stuffing the card into my pocket. I had to know. I couldn't do that again, couldn't put her through it.

"I got us a way in." She still didn't meet my gaze. "That's all they wanted."

"So, you don't know what they were after?"

She shook her head. "I don't even know whose apartment that was . . . yet."

"Yet?" I stepped closer.

She finally looked at me, rolled her eyes. "I modified the code a little and created a back door for me to peek through. I should have more info soon."

"Is that wise?" I gritted my teeth. She shouldn't be pissing Ocean1k off. There was no telling what they'd do to her.

"I can't keep doing this forever," she snapped. "Information is powerful."

She was looking for answers, a way out. She may have been terrified, but she was brave too, and smart.

"Just . . . be careful."

"Yeah, yeah." She turned and started walking away. I followed.

"I'm serious. We both know these people are dangerous. Please let me know if you're in trouble. I want to help."

"I'll be fine." She stopped a few feet away from the bright main street. "We probably shouldn't walk around downtown together at three in the morning . . . *sir*. People might get the wrong idea."

I narrowed my eyes at her. Brave and intelligent, yes, but also belligerent. No one was around at this hour, but I got her point. Still . . . "Where did you park? I can't let you—"

"I got here on my own just fine, didn't I? Seriously, dude. Go home."

She left without waiting for a response, and I let her. I stood at the corner of the alley and watched her walk away, kept watching until she turned the corner. Then I listened like a hawk, my anxiety ratcheting up, for any sounds of . . . I didn't even know. Distress? Screeching tires? A scream?

I ran the pointer finger of my right hand up the side of my left thumb, then back down the other side, following my fingers up and down until I got to the bottom of my pinkie. It was a breathing technique I'd learned years ago and used to calm myself often. You were supposed to breathe in while moving a finger up, and out while moving down. It wasn't doing much to steady my nerves in that moment.

After a few minutes, I forced myself to turn around and walk the length of the alley to the street on the other side, running over everything in my mind.

I'd been trying to think of a way out of this fucked-up situation since Ocean1k's first message appeared on my phone, accompanied by some disturbing photos and a clear threat. I couldn't see a way out of it—not one that would keep my brother safe. But maybe two heads were better than one. Maybe Harlow and I could find a way out of this nightmare together.

CHAPTER FOUR

Harlow

I used to think all the girls at Fulton Academy with raging lady-boners for Mr. Monroe were idiots. I mean, yeah, objectively he was good-looking or whatever, but his personality was just trash: mean and harsh and without a kind word for anyone. I just couldn't understand why everyone had a crush on him. I put it down to hormones and wanting what they could never have, and didn't bother to think about it much. It wasn't hard—I wasn't in any of his classes and hardly even saw the guy in the halls.

By the time Donna pulled into her spot on Monday morning, I'd thought about Easton Monroe more than all the girls in our school combined. I couldn't *stop* thinking about the fucker. What was his deal? What did Ocean1k have on him? How was he involved? *Could I trust him?* That was the big one. After what I'd learned over the weekend about the person we'd hacked, could I trust Mr. Monroe to actually help me as he said he wanted to? I wasn't entirely sure what he could do, but I *was* entirely sure I couldn't handle this shit on my own. It was too big.

"Need a hand, Harls?" I looked up at the sound of Mena's voice.

"Huh?" They'd all gotten out of the car while I sat there, lost once again in my own head. Mena was leaning into the car, her face inches from mine. She hadn't put on any makeup today, and the port-wine-stain birthmark on her nose and cheek stood out starkly against her pale skin.

She smiled and pointed to my hip. "Is the seat belt stuck or something? You've been fiddling with it for ages."

"Oh." I glanced down at the buckle and undid it. "Nah, I'm good."

"You OK?" Mena asked as we walked over to join Donna and Amaya. "You've been really distracted this morning—more than usual."

"Yeah, I'm fine." I forced myself to smile and make eye contact, but I couldn't hold it for long. I hated lying to my friends. "I just didn't get any sleep last night. My head's all fuzzy."

It wasn't a lie, but it wasn't why I was so distracted.

"Yeah, so's your hair." Donna looked me up and down. I knew it came from a place of concern more than anything, but I couldn't help feeling judged. My sister may have decided halfway through senior year that she didn't want to go to law school anymore, but that hadn't made her any less type-A. She and Amaya stood side by side, both their uniforms, hair, and makeup pristine.

I flipped them off and tucked my shirt into my skirt, straightening out my uniform. "Does anyone have a—"

Donna held a hair tie up under my nose before I could even finish the sentence.

"Thanks," I muttered and swept my hair up into a messy bun. It would have to do.

It was hard not to feel inadequate next to their perfection. Donna was trying out all kinds of new things in her search for what she wanted to do after high school; her determination and drive hadn't just disappeared overnight. She still studied hard, still got perfect grades, still looked perfect every day, was still the most organized, amazing person I knew. And here I was, still needing my big sister to hand me hair ties and talk my teachers out of giving me detentions for being constantly late—to say nothing of my grades. Not even Donna could do much about that. I was a screw-up, no denying it.

Which made it even more important to me that I deal with this clusterfuck I'd found myself in with Ocean1k. I needed to prove to my sister, my friends, and *myself* that I could do this. I didn't need to be managed all the damn time. *I* could be the one protecting *them* every once in a while.

An obnoxiously loud engine roar announced Drew's arrival moments before he pulled into the spot next to Donna, his matte-black Audi stark next to her pearl-white BMW. Hendrix got out of the passenger seat—the two of them joking and laughing about something—then went straight to Donna and gave her a completely inappropriate kiss for this early in the morning. A few months ago, there was no way Donna would've allowed that, no way she would've even been seen speaking to Hendrix in public.

I gagged and turned away.

"Let's get you away from these heathens and inside this fine educational institution, shall we?" Drew draped one arm over my shoulders and the other over Mena's.

I snorted. "Please. You're the worst heathen in this whole town."

"True, true. Speaking of fun things, Mena, when are you going to let me take you out on a date?"

We both groaned, but it was good-natured. This was a long-running joke with Drew and Mena.

"I don't know how many times I have to tell you I have a boyfriend. Turner is your friend, Drew."

"What if we all three of us go? You, me, Harls. I'm happy to share if Turner is."

"Ugh! Pig." She couldn't hide her laughter as she extracted herself from Drew and sped off after Amaya.

"How about you, Harls? You got plans this weekend?" Drew dropped his voice, along with some of the levity.

I looked up into his warm, mischievous eyes and sighed. It was tempting—spending an evening with Drew, letting him help me forget everything that had been going on lately.

Drew had been my first. Not that I subscribed to the social construct of virginity, but I was a teenager and not totally immune to wanting to keep up with my peers. We'd practically grown up with Drew, been friends with him since elementary school, so he'd seemed like a safe choice—good-looking, kind, and respectful, despite his cheeky personality. Good enough for my sixteen-year-old self. After making it clear he wasn't interested in a relationship, he agreed. Unwanted romantic feelings had never become an issue for either of us, but we never really stopped visiting each other's beds either.

I dated and slept with other people, but there was something comforting about Drew, something familiar and safe. I wondered what he got out of it, but never asked. Maybe I was too scared to hear the answer.

"Nah, not this weekend." I didn't actually have anything planned, but for once, I didn't feel like using my friend to distract myself. Maybe I was too stressed to even think about sex.

Drew groaned and rolled his eyes so hard I thought they might get stuck.

I raised a brow at him and laughed. "Dramatic much?"

"When I'm being denied what I want? Always."

"Whatever. You won't have any trouble finding another willing participant."

"Yeah, but that's so much work."

I smacked his shoulder. "You are so spoiled."

Was that why he kept coming back to me? I was a sure, easy thing?

Before I could go down that spiral of self-hatred, Mr. Monroe came striding up the hall and stole my full focus. He was in his usual outfit of perfectly tailored slacks and a sweater with the collar of a shirt visible over the top. I'd never given much thought to what he wore, having never thought about him much at all, but after that weekend I realized I'd never seen him in a short-sleeved shirt, even in summer. I'd never even seen that shirt unbuttoned at the top. Previously, I would've put it down to just another example of how pedantic and tightly wound he was, but I'd glimpsed something when I'd found myself plastered against him in that stairwell. As his warm hand soothed me, my face against his strong chest, I'd noticed some ink peeking out of the top of his T-shirt. What other secrets was he hiding underneath that neat outfit and harsh glare?

I reached into my pocket, but he rushed past before I could snap myself out of my thoughts and grab the piece of paper I had stashed there.

"Come on. Let's get to English." Drew nudged me along. I definitely did *not* look casually over my shoulder and check out how well those tailored pants hugged Mr. Monroe's ass.

The day dragged as I wore a hole in the paper in my pocket. I couldn't seem to stop touching it, couldn't get my mind off how I was going to hand it off. It made it even more difficult to focus in class than usual.

I finally got my chance at lunch. I was standing around with the girls, waiting for Amaya to fix her lipstick in her locker mirror before we went out for food, when I spotted him out of the corner of my eye.

He walked up the hall, his eyes narrowed, students leaping out of his way.

My heartbeat kicked up a notch. Because of what I was about to do, not because I was excited to see him again. That would be ridiculous.

I pulled the paper out of my pocket and took a step back just as he passed, propping my hands on my hips. He had to shift to avoid touching me, but it was close enough.

I dropped the paper, then looked after him before picking it up.

"I think Mr. Monroe dropped this." I let an evil look cross my face as I leaned in to the girls. Slowly, I made a show of starting to unfold it and peek inside.

Just as I'd hoped, Mena snatched it from me with a disapproving look. "Can't you stay out of trouble for five minutes?"

She rushed after Mr. Monroe without waiting for a response, and I laughed along with the other two. I couldn't hear what they said after she caught up and tapped him on the shoulder, but there was no missing the brief flash of confusion in his eyes.

He was smart though, and quick. He glanced over Mena's shoulder and met my gaze—only for the briefest of moments—then took the note and rushed off. I held in the sigh of relief.

"Goodie two-shoes," Amaya teased once Mena rejoined us.

"Teacher's pet," I joined in.

"Whatever. That's why you love me." Mena held her chin up, smug as shit.

"Yes, it is, you little cinnamon roll." Donna looped her arm through Mena's. "Now let's go get food. I'm starving."

The rest of the day was just as uneventful as the first half, but the edge of anticipation didn't abate. I'd managed to get the note to him; now I just hoped he'd actually show up.

I pulled my Merc into a spot at Oak Hill Park five minutes before the time specified in my note, but his Mazda was already there. At least, I hoped it was his car. There wasn't a single other car in the parking area, not a hint of another human being around. Not surprising for midnight on a weeknight, and exactly as I'd planned.

The fur trim of my coat tickled my cheeks as I stepped out and pulled my hood up, but the icy wind still stung. I tried not to look too interested in the other car, on the off chance it wasn't actually him, but I'd barely locked mine before he was getting out too.

He stepped toward me and opened his mouth to speak—to ask what the fuck we were doing in a park in the middle of the night, no doubt—but I cut him off with a firm look and my finger pressed to my lips. Then I put my hand to my ear like a phone. He frowned but, after a moment, pulled his phone out of his back pocket. I motioned for him to leave it in the car, then took off for the looming trees.

Once we reached the start of the hiking path, I turned to face him. "Sorry about all the cloak-and-dagger shit." I kept my voice pitched low—the midnight hour and the stillness of nature seemed to demand it. "Couldn't risk Ocean1k listening in on our conversation."

"Using our phones?" He ran his hand through his hair. It was messy, the neat style he wore to work completely ruined. He still wore the same clothes though, a coat over the top. "They can do that?"

I gave him an incredulous look. "Yeah, man. We're dealing with a hacker with questionable morals and possible criminal intentions. How do you think Siri works? Your phone is always listening."

"That is so creepy." He looked freaked out. He was staring, wide-eyed, into where the hiking path disappeared into the darkness, trees making it impossible for the moonlight to penetrate.

"You all right?" I took a step closer. That seemed to snap him out of his anxiety spiral, and he looked me right in the eye for the first time. He had such expressive eyes once you could see past the cold exterior.

"Yeah. I'm just out of my depth with this shit." He sighed. "How are you? What's going on?"

Was he worried about me? He had no idea how a smart phone worked, but he was worried about *me* in this situation. It would be insulting if it wasn't so adorable.

"I took a peek at the computer we . . . uh . . . *accessed* the other night, and I thought we needed to discuss what I found."

"Are you . . . were you safe?"

"Yeah. I'm as safe as I can be, considering the circumstances, but . . ." I jammed my hands into my pockets and squeezed them into fists. I didn't want to admit how terrified this whole thing made me.

"What did you find?" he asked, and I didn't think I imagined the way his voice softened.

I licked my lips. "The apartment and the computer belong to Judge Graham Keating. The judge appears to have a pretty serious gambling problem, and he's in debt. Like, *a lot* of debt."

Monroe's eyes went wide, and he cursed under his breath. "They're going to blackmail him."

"Yeah, I think so too."

"Fuck," he ground out. I knew exactly how he felt. The frustration, the sense of helplessness, the undercurrent of fear underneath it all.

"I've been thinking about why Ocean1k has been using me—us. They obviously have the skills to do all the things I've done, technologically speaking. They probably could've done it faster. So why bring us into it?"

"Plausible deniability." His shoulders slumped a little. "I've been thinking about that too. If shit hits the fan, we're the ones caught doing illegal things with no way to prove we were coerced."

"Exactly. Plus, the more we do, the more they have to hold over us." I took a deep breath and fiddled with the inside seams of my pockets. I was nervous to ask this, but I still wasn't one-hundred-percent sure I could trust him. "What do they have on you? How did they get to you?"

He obviously didn't have the same worries about trusting me, because he answered right away. "My brother. They . . . he did something and . . . I'm just trying to protect my brother. You?"

It was crazy how similar our situations were. "My sister."

"Donna?"

"Yeah."

The look he gave me could've been mistaken for pity had he not just told me he was in the same situation. We stared at each other for a loaded moment, sharing the pain and worry of the mess we were both in.

"This needs to stop," he finally said.

"That's partly why I called you here. We need to start fighting back."

"How? We don't even know who we're dealing with."

"Exactly. We need to start getting information. Discreetly. Can you talk to your brother? Would he know anything about this judge?" I didn't know how his brother came into it—if he was as innocent and uninvolved as Donna.

"I don't know. Maybe. Now that you've made me paranoid about using my phone, I'm reluctant to contact him. But I'll try. What about your sister?"

I shook my head. "Donna doesn't know anything. But . . . there may be a connection I've been reluctant to explore." The thought had occurred to me as soon as Ocean1k started sending me images of my sister, but I really didn't want to go to the horrible place where my sister had done reckless, dangerous things. Now that it was her life and not just her reputation on the line, I didn't have a choice.

"What is it? Is it dangerous?"

"No." I bit my lip. "Maybe? It should be fine."

"Harlow, please." He held a hand out as if to grab my arm, then snapped it back to his side. "You're helping me with the tech stuff. Let me help you in whatever way I can. There's no point in doing any of this if we don't stay safe."

"I don't know if that's an option anymo—"

A sharp, snapping sound cut through the darkness beyond the trees, and I startled so hard I nearly jumped into the air. With my heart hammering and all senses on alert, I instinctively flashed to Mr. Monroe's side, wrapping his arm in a death grip.

"What was that?" I rushed out, and the words somehow managed to sound both whispered and squeaked.

He extracted a small flashlight from his coat pocket and slowly swept the white beam over the trees around us. Silence and stillness stared back. He clicked the light off. "There's nothing there. Sounded like a twig. It was probably a racoon or something."

"Right. Racoon." I couldn't seem to make my fingers release their grip on him. He felt so strong and steady, while I felt as though I was flailing around all the time.

He paused for a beat, then wrapped his free arm around me, extracted the one I was holding hostage, and banded that one around my back too. I tucked my arms up under my chin and immediately relaxed against him. I didn't know what it was about this stern, complicated man I hardly knew, but he made me feel safe.

"It's OK." His breath tickled the hair on my forehead as he whispered—so close. "It's going to be OK. We'll figure this out."

I tipped my head back to look him in the eyes, the hood of my coat falling off. "Will we?"

"We have to." He said it with such conviction I had no choice but to believe him. But I couldn't seem to force my mouth to form words. All I could do was stare into his eyes as his arms warmed me and his smell reminded me of long summer days on the beach—fresh and warm and happy. Those eyes made me feel as though I was both drowning and saved at the same time.

I wondered what his lips would taste like. Would they be cold from the biting night air? Or would they be as warm as his embrace?

As if he could read my mind, his gaze dropped to my lips and he swallowed, his Adam's apple bobbing. I gasped. *No fucking way.*

I was done lying to myself and pretending I wasn't hot for teacher. I never in a million years expected that teacher might be hot for me too.

CHAPTER FIVE

Easton

Despite the giant puffy coat, Harlow Mead felt small and fragile in my arms. She was terrified. The critter in the woods had startled her, made her jump into my embrace, but the fear in her eyes was bigger, more insurmountable than that. We were dealing with a faceless threat with no apparent way out. It scared me too.

Yet, she was here, in the woods in the middle of the night, trying to find some way out of it. She was damn brave and determined, and I couldn't help but admire that. It wasn't until something else replaced the fear in her gaze, something softer and more intimate, that I realized just how *much* I admired her. Most people went their whole lives without having to handle the kind of pressure she faced. She was fucking amazing. And she fit into my arms so perfectly, and her lips . . .

She's a student!

I didn't examine too closely how hard I had to focus to drop my arms to my sides, take a step back. I just forced my gaze to the darkness beyond the path and cleared my throat.

This was just bonding due to shared trauma. We had no one else to lean on in this situation. Lines had become blurred because of factors out of my control, but it was up to me to make sure boundaries remained intact.

"So . . ." My voice came out strained, and I had to clear my throat again, force myself to square my shoulders and look at her. "What do we do now?"

Idiot! I'd just determined it was my responsibility to maintain boundaries, then I go and defer to her for decision-making. But to be fair, she'd called the meeting, and she had more information than I did.

Harlow crossed her arms and huffed, her breath misting in the frigid air. "We see what we can find out, then we meet up again and . . ." She shrugged. "Brainstorm or something?"

"Right." I sighed. "I'll get some markers. We can do a mind map."

We stared at each other with blank faces for a beat, then cracked grins at the same time, chuckling through the tension.

"We can't keep meeting in the park," I said once the mirth faded. "Aside from the fact that I can't feel my toes, it's too risky. Too open."

"Agreed. Let's try to think of another solution."

"OK. So I'll just wait for your friend to pass me another note?" I raised my brows.

She winced. "Yeah. Sorry. It was the best I could do on short notice. I couldn't risk using technology. Oh, that reminds me." She reached into her pocket and pulled out an older-looking smart phone. "My number is in here. Don't use it to contact anyone else, and don't, under any circumstances, use it to go on the internet or log into any of your accounts."

"Got it." I tucked it into my pocket.

"OK." She looked around and shuffled her feet. "Until the next clandestine meeting, Mr. Monroe."

I cringed on the inside but managed to keep my face neutral. "Until then. Bye, Harlow."

She turned and started walking away, calling over her shoulder, "Bye, Easton."

I watched her until she got into her car and drove away. Then I groaned and tipped my head back. Why did my name sound so good coming out of her mouth?

The stars twinkled above, peeking at me through the branches. They had no answers.

———

On Saturday mornings I woke earlier than I did during the work week so I could be in San Francisco by ten. The little bell over the door dinged as I let myself into Twin Peaks Ink.

"Hey, East." Lori grinned at me from behind the counter. I'd never seen her in anything brighter than dark gray, but she was the bubbliest, most positive person I knew.

"Hey, Lori." I handed her a large coffee and took a sip of mine. "How are you?"

She bounced in her seat before taking a sip and moaning. "I'm good now that I have coffee. I love you."

I just smiled and headed to my station.

Twin Peaks Ink was housed in an old converted tobacco shop—flooded with light—and had four full-time artists. Massive prints of the different artists' work hung on the exposed brick walls.

Since I had a full-time job teaching and only came in on Saturdays, I was booked out nine months in advance. Tattooing was something I was actually good at.

I'd graduated high school at sixteen, finished my teaching degree, with honors, at twenty. My parents had pushed me to continue studying, maybe get a doctorate or two, but despite my love for *reading* literature, I'd had enough of studying it. I insisted I needed practical teaching experience and, after only a few years, landed a permanent position at Fulton Academy—one of the best schools in the country. It had the added bonus of being located on the opposite side of the country from where my parents lived and worked . . . and studied and worked and studied. *Lived* was probably a bit of an exaggeration for how they . . . existed.

Nothing was above the pursuit of knowledge for them—not even their sons.

I'd been painting and drawing since I was a little kid, but it wasn't until age eleven, when my uncle Joe took me with him when he was getting a tattoo, that I fell in love with ink.

Uncle Joe was the black sheep of the family. The Monroes did not get tattoos and wear ripped jeans and graphic T-shirts—kind of like the one I had on right now. My brother Ford was a bit of a black sheep as well.

I'd tried to get in contact with him several times after Harlow and I met in the woods, but all my calls and messages went unanswered other than a simple "I'm alive, we'll talk later." I couldn't exactly come out and tell him why I needed to speak with him, considering the whole bugged-phones-and-hackers situation, and I didn't dare use my new secret phone. I was stuck waiting for him to get back to me.

At least spending the day tattooing would be a good distraction. Nothing like the buzz of a needle and a killer design to take my mind off everything else.

"Your first client is here." Lori popped her head around the corner, her coffee clutched to her chest.

"Thanks." I flashed her a smile as I set up my station. "Just give me five and send her in."

"Uh-huh." She hummed around a sip. "Hey, when are you going to quit your stuffy teacher job and tattoo full time?"

Cass, the owner of the shop, strolled past just at that moment. "I'd like to know that too. You know you have a spot here whenever you want it. Clients practically gag for your tats."

"I know. Thanks." I looked away and smiled. Someone asked me this exact question every damn Saturday, and I knew Cass was serious about giving me a permanent spot in her shop. I just couldn't do it.

My mother taught linguistics at Harvard. My father was the head of the literature department and had a doctorate in nineteenth-century British literature. Both my father's siblings were educators—my aunt the dean of some stuffy boarding school in Upstate New York; my uncle a behaviorist who'd devised new learning theory for late-elementary education, which was being rolled out in Scandinavian countries. He *taught teachers*! Their parents had both been highly respected educators with long successful careers. The Monroes had been teachers for generations—as far back as Robert Francis Monroe, who had established his English village's first school sometime in the 1700s.

At twenty-three I was the youngest teacher at Fulton. I enjoyed having some distance from my parents and loved my independence, but after teaching high school for a few years, I'd often wondered if I would've been better off continuing to study. Perhaps my own work ethic and upbringing colored my opinions, but I'd never encountered a more apathetic group of individuals than the obscenely privileged Fulton student body. Yes, there were exceptions—truly bright, driven students who took their education seriously. But the rest of them were more interested in who was kissing whom on Instagram than they were in securing their futures. Their parents could buy them spots at college, so why bother? It infuriated me.

But then Saturdays rolled around, and I drove to Twin Peaks Ink to spend the day creating art, and everything felt right with the world again. I'd been teaching myself about art and tattooing since that day my uncle took me into my first shop—without my parents' knowledge, of course. Tattoos were for thugs and criminals, not their educated, respectable son. Every spare second I had between studying to become a teacher, I spent learning how to tattoo. By the time I moved to California, I'd gotten pretty good and had a decent following on social media.

Lori led my first client over to my station, and I gave her a genuine smile. She wanted a literary tattoo—my specialty—and I got to work, the buzz of the machine and the easy conversation with my bookish client making all my troubles fall away.

Three tattoos and nine hours later, my back was stiff as I drove home, but I smiled to myself the whole way—relaxed despite the ton of pressure looming over my head.

I went to the fridge and opened a beer, taking a long, satisfying pull. In moments like this I wondered why I didn't just quit. Fuck my parents and teaching and everything else. But then that little voice—the one that sounded suspiciously like my father—would pipe up and remind me of all the hard work I'd put in, all the years I'd spent busting my ass to achieve what I had. Did I really want to throw all that away? Maybe working with underprivileged kids would be more rewarding? Maybe younger education was more my jam? Or a life in academia?

I wasn't a quitter, and I felt as if I'd be giving up on something I'd worked hard for if I quit now.

Plus, there was my brother to think of.

Much like me, Ford wasn't that enthusiastic about becoming a teacher, but unlike me, he refused to squeeze himself into that rigid mold my parents had so graciously provided. He hadn't graduated anything early and only just managed to scrape up enough passing grades to finish high school. He did, however, build his first computer at age twelve and constantly had his nose in a screen.

Even though I sometimes felt that I was letting my parents down, at least by following their path for me, I could divert their attention away from my brother. They'd pulled some favors to get him into the University of Washington in Seattle, but they were kidding themselves if they thought he'd ever end up teaching.

I checked my phone for the millionth time that week as I took another sip of beer. I still hadn't heard back from him, and I was beginning to worry.

I'd just started typing out another text message—I couldn't help myself—when a knock sounded at the door. The number of people who'd knocked on my door could be counted on one hand, and one of them had been a wrong-apartment-number situation. I didn't really . . . socialize.

Phone and beer abandoned on the counter, I cautiously approached the door, trying to make my steps soundless. The myriad terrible possibilities flashed through my mind too fast to process as my heart started to hammer in my chest. What if Ocean1k had decided I was no longer useful and had sent someone to get rid of me? Was that the level of criminal we were dealing with here?

The knock came again when I was a few feet from the door, an edge of impatience to the *tap-tap-tap*. I forced myself to lean forward and look through the peephole.

My eyes widened, and relief washed over me with such force I nearly lost my footing. I fumbled with the locks and wrenched the door open.

Before I could say a word, my little brother rushed past me and slammed the door shut. "Took you long enough. What, were you jerking off or something?"

I just stared at him in disbelief as he dropped his duffel to the floor and turned to face me. He was in jeans and a plain black sweater. We were the same height—although Ford had a slighter, leaner build—and had the same black hair, but his was grown out past his ears and messy. I hadn't seen him in months, but my lips quirked into a smile when I saw we'd happened to pick out the exact same glasses. He looked weary, worried. I knew the feeling. My smile fell, and I turned to bolt the door.

Then I pulled my little brother into a hug.

Our biggest problem during his last visit, nearly a year ago, was that our parents had found out he hadn't been going to any of his college classes even though they'd been paying for it. They were furious, but to be fair, he'd been telling them from day one he didn't want to go to college. When they sent him to Seattle, he'd gotten enrolled, settled into student accommodation, and immediately started looking for a job. He landed a position with a cybersecurity company within a few weeks.

Mom and Dad could rage and argue all they wanted, but Ford was an adult and had already moved into his own place. There was nothing they could do.

Dealing with that mess had been stressful, but it didn't have anything on our current situation. A few months ago, a girl he'd met in the student residence had come to him, begging for his help with a piece-of-shit ex who was posting revenge porn of her all over the internet. Within an hour Ford had taken all the images down, hacked into the guy's computer, transferred the entirety of his bank account to a women's shelter, and wiped it clean. Only a few days later, he'd started getting threatening messages from Ocean1k—blackmailing him over the incident—and the chick had disappeared. Not long after, I received a message from our new internet friend too. Apparently, Ford had told them to go get fucked. He was willing to go to prison and ruin his career to avoid being controlled by someone else. But the threats to his *life* came to me.

I rang my little brother as soon as I got that first message. I almost ignored it, wrote it off as some prank or scam, but the image that accompanied the graphic threat of violence was clearly Ford, coming out of his apartment building. After swearing profusely, he told me the whole sordid story, his voice wavering as he said how sorry he was that I'd been dragged into it.

We'd both been doing whatever Ocean1k asked ever since.

Their first demand of me had been that I volunteer to fill the careers counselor role while Mrs. Fielding was on leave. I did as I was told, but there had been no mention of it since from Ocean1k—while I suffered through even more interactions with teenagers than what I could handle already. It had probably just been a test to make sure I would do as told. I'd been ordered to pick up and deliver three separate packages on different occasions. I didn't dare look inside them, didn't research the addresses for more info, and wore gloves while doing it. I'd found some comfort in ignorance, telling myself it wasn't necessarily illegal. But when the order to steal a coworker's key card had come through, any illusion that my life wasn't screwed disappeared. From there, it was a slippery slope to learning how to pick locks and breaking into a judge's apartment with a student.

Ford was forced to do hacker things I didn't understand, followed around by faceless men and not permitted to leave Seattle. Until now.

He held me as tightly as I held him, but after a few moments he pushed me away. "All right already. I'm fine, East."

"Are you?" I looked him up and down.

"Yeah. Just sick of the meathead they had following me around twenty-four seven."

"Jesus." I leaned on the counter, and my abandoned beer caught my attention. I snagged it and downed the rest in one go.

"Rough day?" Ford leaned on the counter next to me and crossed his arms.

"Rough couple of months, asshole." I went to the fridge and got another two beers, handed my brother one. "You have no idea how fucking worried I was about you."

"Yeah?" He raised his eyebrows as he took a swig. "Is that why you decided to break into a penthouse apartment? Blow some steam off?"

I gave him a sharp look. "How do you know about that?"

He pulled his phone out and showed me the screen. Staring back at me was a photo of me on my knees in front of apartment 1502, picking the lock. Harlow stood next to me, looking over her shoulder toward the elevators. She looked cute in her black getup. I nearly smiled, then realized the implications of Ford having that photo and cursed worse than I ever had in my life.

"You done?" Ford asked when my tirade ended, an irritated edge entering his tone. "What the fuck were you thinking?"

"I was thinking my little brother might get killed if I didn't," I shot back and slammed my beer bottle on the counter.

He slammed his down next to mine and got in my face, but the energy drained out of him just as fast as it had risen, and he backed off with a sigh, shoulders slumped. "Yeah, well, silver lining—now that they have *your* future to hold over *my* head, I don't have a stalker anymore and I can come for a visit. Yay."

"This is so fucked up." I wanted to scream. I had no idea how any of us were going to crawl out from under this. We just seemed to be digging ourselves in deeper. "Wait. Aren't you worried about, like, listening devices or whatever?"

Ford shrugged. "We're not talking about anything they don't already know. And now that they have us both by the balls, I highly doubt they'd bother keeping tabs on us that closely."

"Yeah, I guess."

"Also, I have an audio jammer in my bag." He grinned, then got serious again. "Easton, if this gets out, you could be arrested, convicted. This could ruin your life. You won't be allowed to teach again."

"Maybe that wouldn't be such a bad thing. Teenagers are all dumb, depraved, and disappointing."

Ford snorted. "Loving the teaching life then?"

"Yeah, it's really rewarding," I deadpanned and took another swig.

"Who's the chick in the photo?"

"She's . . ." I sighed, suddenly completely exhausted. "I need a shower. Order a pizza. Let's talk after we eat."

I didn't wait for a response before walking off toward the bathroom. The hot water released some of the tension in my neck, and I was tempted to stay in there longer, really let the bathroom steam up. Maybe the steam would get so thick it would swallow me whole and I could cease to exist. That would solve all my problems. But I was actually really happy to see my brother again—safe and still giving me attitude. So I got out and dried off quickly, itching to ask him a million questions.

When I opened the bathroom door, the steam hardly had a chance to billow out into the hallway before Ford shuffled past me and shut the door in my face. "Pizza's on the way," he called just before the water started up again.

I'd barely pulled on a pair of sweats when someone knocked. Assuming it was the pizza guy, I opened the door without checking the peephole, but the person on the other side made me freeze.

I blinked at Harlow Mead. Standing at my door. On a Saturday night.

Harlow blinked at my bare chest, looking about as stunned as I felt.

CHAPTER SIX

Harlow

The door swung open, and everything I'd planned to say just kind of evaporated. *Poofed* out of my brain by the magnificent tattooed man I found before me. Did I knock on the wrong door? I looked up and into Easton's familiar frowning face, his hazel eyes framed by his black glasses. Nope, definitely the right door.

"Holy shit." My wide eyes took in the tight muscles of his chest, shoulders, arms. I didn't even know where to start with exploring the amazing art on his body. Tattoos covered his right arm from the wrist all the way over his shoulder and chest, the designs reaching across to his left side. His left arm was bare except for some text I couldn't make out on the inside of his bicep. The ink was vibrant, colorful, intricate. I could spend hours staring at it. In my current state I managed to make out some kind of thorny vine dipping down under his pants, but then my brain short-circuited again.

He had on gray sweatpants and nothing else—judging by the outline between his legs, not even underwear. But the sight of his bare feet, so masculine with the tendons and the neat toes and the little bit of hair near the ankle, seemed the most outrageous for some reason. I was standing there looking at Mr. Monroe's feet. Like . . . *what?*

"What are you doing here?" he gritted out as he leaned forward, bringing his chest mere inches from my face. Any normal person would've leaned back to give him space. Not me. I just stood there, frozen, and blinked as his clean, warm smell hit the back of my nose. He glanced up and down the hallway before he pulled me inside, closed the door, and turned both locks, even fastening the chain for good measure.

I finally managed to get my brain to start sending words to my mouth. "I was not expecting this." I chuckled, somewhere between dazed and confused.

"Expecting what? How do you even know where I live?" he demanded, crossing his arms over his chest, making his biceps bulge.

It was a battle to tear my gaze away and look at his face, but I managed it. "Was not expecting there to be ink underneath all those button-ups and sweaters, and your address is in Ms. Perry's contacts info on her personal computer." I shrugged.

He sighed, but then another Easton Monroe walked out of a hallway, and my brain short-circuited again. This one was in tight briefs, a towel hanging around his shoulders as he used one corner to dry his hair, but the eyes, the face, the amazing body, even the glasses were the same.

"You're not pizza." He frowned at me.

I looked from one to the other. Then I squeezed my eyes shut and shook my head before having another look. It had finally happened—I'd completely lost my shit.

"Easton." I held my arms out, feeling as though I might fall over. "I don't feel so good. I'm seeing double."

He reached out immediately and took me by the elbows. "You're not seeing double. That's my brother, Ford."

"Oh." I nodded, suddenly feeling much better, though still reluctant to step away from the shirtless man holding on to me.

"You think I look like this douchebag?" The more naked one scoffed, and Easton rolled his eyes, his lips twitching with a held-back smile. "I take offense to that."

When my feet felt solid under me again, I raised an eyebrow and looked the brother up and down, taking my time, then I gave Easton the same treatment. He seemed to realize how close he was and dropped his arms, clearing his throat as he took a step back.

"Nah, you're right," I said. "Now that I've had a closer look, he's clearly the better-looking one, and his ink is way better than yours."

Ford threw his head back and laughed. "Well, East is the one who put this ink on my body so—" He cut himself off and stepped closer. "You're the chick from the photo."

Before I had a chance to ask if he was saying *Mr. Monroe* had a talent for tattooing, or what photo he was talking about, a knock sounded at the door.

The brothers shared a loaded look, and Easton's jaw clenched. He grabbed my wrist and dragged me to the hallway, shoving me behind him as Ford went to the door to check the peephole.

Ford's shoulders relaxed. "It's just the pizza."

But Easton's whole body remained rigid. He even reached behind him to grip my hip, as though to make sure I wouldn't jump out and wave my arms around at the pizza guy. I couldn't really see much around Easton's broad shoulders, but I registered the sound of the door opening, Ford saying something about keeping the change.

My heart had leapt into my throat when they reacted to the knock as though it was an explicit death threat. But now that it was clear there was no danger, it was beating fast for a whole other reason. Easton Monroe was once again inches from me, shirtless, and this time with his hand on my hip. He had ink on his back too, but I couldn't focus on it. I couldn't stop staring at the slope of his back, the way it moved with every breath, the dip in his spine. I was so close I could smell his body wash and that warm, manly scent. I had a sudden urge to lick the spot between his shoulder blades. It was *right there*—all it would take was for me to just barely lean forward. I bet he tasted as good as he smelled.

"Bro, chill." Ford's voice snapped me out of it a split second before my lips connected with Easton's back. "He's gone. Door's locked."

I released a heavy breath, and he shivered. Then he cleared his throat and rolled his shoulders. Once again, instead of moving away like a normal person, I let his back brush the tip of my nose. I wanted so badly to close my eyes and nuzzle into the warmth, wrap my arms around his middle. But he took a miniscule step forward.

"Right," he said, his hand still on my hip. I couldn't move, didn't want to. He squeezed lightly, then released me and took several steps away before turning around.

Ford stood just to his left, the open pizza box in one hand, his eyes darting between Easton and me. I rubbed my hands on my jeans, then pulled the sleeves of my sweatshirt down over my thumbs, suddenly feeling all kinds of observed and awkward.

"Harlow, did you seriously hack the headmistress's computer to find my address?" Easton asked.

I raised my eyebrows and smirked.

"Never mind." He waved his hand at me. "I don't want to know."

"Wait," Ford mumbled around a bite of pizza before taking a big swallow. "Your B and E partner is a hacker?" He looked way too amused by this.

"No." I shook my head. "And how do you know about that?"

"She's a student at Fulton, but not *my* student. I don't teach her myself."

"Semantics." Ford shrugged and grinned, taking another massive bite.

Easton gave him a dirty look. "Can you please put some damn clothes on?"

Ford held the pizza box out to the side and looked down at himself, as though he'd just remembered he was in nothing but very tight underwear and a towel. "You first." He smirked.

The disgruntled look remained on Easton's face as he stepped over to a closet next to the kitchen, which revealed a washer and dryer. He grabbed a T-shirt off the top of an overflowing laundry basket and pulled it over his head. I watched his abdominals shift and flex with the movement.

Ford chuckled, and I glanced up just in time to catch his knowing look as he passed me on his way into the hall. Easton snatched the pizza box from him just before he disappeared.

"Don't let the schoolgirl eat any of my pizza, bro!" he called.

"It's covered in pineapple. It won't be an issue," I threw over my shoulder.

Easton paused with a bit of pineapple at his lips, and our eyes met just as he popped it into his mouth and licked his thumb and finger clean. I stared. I stared just as I had at his abs a moment earlier, just as I had at his tats. I was doing a lot of staring lately.

I forced myself to remember why I'd come over in the first place, but all I could see was the tip of his tongue as it darted out to lick his thumb, the hint of a V leading below the waist of his sweats, all that ink . . .

He dropped the pizza box on the counter and rubbed his right eye, knocking his glasses off-kilter.

"Did you really do Ford's tattoos?" I asked. It wasn't even remotely what I'd come over to talk about, but I'd been thrown a lot of surprises in a short period of time, so whatever!

"Yeah." He righted his glasses and gave me a small smile. "I tattoo on the weekends."

"I didn't mean what I said earlier." I moved forward and leaned my hip on the counter. "I was just teasing. They're actually really beautiful."

"Thanks." This time his smile was more genuine, bigger.

"Who did yours?" I tilted my head slightly, looking at his covered right arm in more detail. Maple leaves in different sizes drifted down his skin as though they were floating down from a tree, but each one had a different image inside it—a cityscape here, a realistic puppy there, a classic skull and roses. The maple leaf shape tied it all together but allowed for multiple styles, colors, and subjects. It all worked beautifully.

"A few different artists. People I learned from or whose work I admire."

I wanted to ask him more about it; I wanted to run my hands all over the designs, get up close and really study them. But then Ford came back into the kitchen, wedged himself between us, and grabbed another slice of pizza. He looked from his brother to me, amused.

I sat on one of the stools at the counter, opposite Easton, and Ford leaned on the end.

"OK, out with it. How'd you two end up breaking and entering together?" he demanded around a big mouthful of pizza.

"Ocean1k." Easton and I sighed at the same time.

"They sent me a photo of you sleeping in your bed, a gun pointed at you, after I tried to refuse," Easton said, sounding miserable. "They sent instructions on how to pick locks and gave me an address and a time, told me I had to steal a coworker's key card to get myself and a hacker into the building. You can only imagine my horror when Harlow showed up."

"Fuck," Ford muttered. "I knew they were following me, making sure I wouldn't leave town, threatening my life, blah blah. But I had no idea they were letting themselves into my apartment."

"You always did sleep like the dead," Easton said.

"I'm really sorry, bro. I'm so sorry you got dragged into this shit."

"It's not your fault. You were dragged into it too."

They shared a look—that look only siblings can exchange—full of a lifetime of moments, inside jokes, and being there for each other. It reminded me of Donna. I wished I had my sister with me.

"How about you, schoolgirl?" Ford nodded at me. "How'd you get into this mess?"

"I have a sister who would do anything to protect me. Now it's my turn to protect her." That's why I couldn't have her here with me. I had to remember why I was doing all this. I had to be the strong one for a change.

"Well, shit, I know what I did to get on their blackmail list, but what did your sister do?"

"Nothing." I shrugged and pressed my lips together. "Nothing illegal. She's not involved in this at all. She just . . . she went through something recently. Went off the rails a little. She used to go to this shitty bar and . . . do things. There were cameras. The video could ruin her future. That's how it started anyway—still shots from the footage. But recently they've been sending me photos of her at the gym, with her boyfriend, leaving school. The message is clear—they can get to her whenever they want—but they still spelled it out in the texts. Nothing motivates quite like a threat against the life of someone you love."

Ford's and Easton's eyebrows rose, and I was once again struck by how similar they looked. But not enough to distract me.

"Do not judge my sister." I pointed a finger at each of them. "You have no idea who she is and what she went through."

They both backed up, hands held up defensively.

"No judgment here. Just surprise." Easton smiled at me. His smiles were so rare I forgave him immediately.

"Moving on." Ford threw the last pizza crust back into the box and stood up straight. "You're a hacker? Talk me through what you did after breaking into a penthouse apartment."

"I'm not really a hacker." I rolled my eyes, pulling my sleeves over my hands. "I just like computers and code and stuff. Anyway, it was just a backdoor trojan. We were in and out within ten minutes."

He flashed me a grin. "If it walks like a hacker and quacks like a hacker . . ."

We spent the next hour talking tech, comparing computers and security measures, going over everything Ocean1k had made us all do.

Easton made tea while Ford and I talked firewalls and hardware, and we all ended up sitting around his little circular dining table. Despite the fucked-up situation, it was actually kind of . . . cozy? I felt comfortable with them, and though I'd never admit it—lest his head swell to the point of exploding—I actually admired Ford and his skills. We veered off topic for a while as I asked him about his cybersecurity job, and he told me about the girl from his brief stint at college whom he'd helped—illegally. I admired that too.

Ford questioned me just as much and seemed impressed by the knowledge and capability I had with computers "at my age." I let the age dig slide, since the praise seemed genuine.

At a natural lull in the conversation, I finished the rest of my tea and set the mug on the table.

Ford leaned back and somberly looked at us both in turn. "I don't know if you two have discussed this, but I think Ocean1k might be connected to BestLyf, if not directly doing their bidding."

I slumped back in my chair. "Yeah, me too."

Easton frowned. "That professional-development company? *What?*"

"Yeah." I nodded. "A few things have happened over the last year or so that, combined with what's going on now . . . I didn't want to believe it, but I think you're right."

Between Turner's conviction that BestLyf was an evil cult responsible for his mom's death, Donna and Hendrix uncovering a whole crime empire run by a prominent BestLyf member, and the kind of shit I was being blackmailed into doing—I couldn't ignore my suspicions any longer.

"What you've both told me, and what I've had to do for them," Ford explained, "most of it benefits BestLyf in some way—if not directly, then one of their members. And the things I *haven't* been able to tie to them yet . . . give it some time, and I'm sure they will eventually."

"So, what you're saying is we're not dealing with a single deranged hacker?" Easton ran a hand through his hair, messing it all up. I liked it like that. It fit him better than the smooth, neat style he wore to work. "We're dealing with a national organization with countless powerful people involved."

"Yep." Ford popped the *p*.

"OK. That's . . . not great." Easton nodded slowly. "But three heads are better than one. So what can we do about it?"

"Oh!" I sat up straight. "That's actually why I came over. I have an idea that could provide a lead. It's just a little risky."

CHAPTER SEVEN

Harlow arrived a solid twenty minutes later than planned. I'd been sitting in my car for a good forty waiting for her.

I'd shown up early to make sure I didn't miss her—and just to get a look at the place. It was an absolute dump. Shitty neighborhood, chain-link fence, drab brick building. The only thing that even marked it as a bar was the neon sign above the door that read *Davey's*. That and the cliché big, mean guy at the door and the steady stream of rough people walking through it. Not many had walked out yet, but it was still early.

The longer I sat there and watched the bikers, prostitutes, and derelicts make their way inside, the more uneasy I became about the idea of Harlow going in there alone. My hand squeezed the steering wheel so hard it made a squeak.

The petite blonde who jumped out of the expensive blue car in the row behind me wore painted-on black pants and a top that was little more than a scrap of fabric—exposing her abdomen, her cleavage, and her entire back. She looked different out of her regular baggy hoodies and jeans, or her school uniform, but it was definitely Harlow. If I wasn't so worried about her getting hurt the minute she stepped foot inside that shithole, I would've been worried about her freezing to death.

She walked to the end of the row of parked cars, out of the sight of my rearview. No way was I letting her go in there alone; I didn't care what we agreed to. I got out of the car and spotted her heading toward the building, but instead of walking up to the entrance, she veered off to the side and disappeared around a corner.

I jogged to catch up, my shoulders tensing at the darkness of the alley.

As soon as I stepped around the corner, I came to a skidding stop. Harlow stood right in front of me, arms crossed—I dug my nails into my palms with the effort of not looking at how it pushed her boobs up. She didn't seem at all surprised to see me. If anything, she looked pissed.

"We agreed you'd stay in the car," she gritted out.

"Yeah, well, that was before I got a look at the place. *Jesus*, Harlow." I crossed my arms too and frowned at her.

The bravado drained from her features. "I don't know how the hell Donna came here all those times on her own, without anyone even knowing where she was."

I didn't know what to say to that. From what little she'd mentioned, her sister had gone through some hard things. But I knew the fiercely protective feelings siblings had for each other.

"WWDD," Harlow murmured.

"What?"

"What would Donna do?" She stared off to the side, thinking, and I realized that as protective as Harlow felt of her sister, she looked up to her a lot.

"Let's just go. We'll figure something else out."

"No." She shook her head, the steel back in her spine. "Donna would figure it out, take charge. Look, I concede that this is a dangerous place, and feminism aside, I would feel safer if you went in with me. But keep your distance. I don't wanna spook the guy or raise any suspicions."

I chewed on my bottom lip and thought of Ford. We literally didn't have any other leads. "Fine. But any sign of trouble, and we leave immediately."

"Fair." She nodded.

I turned to head toward the entrance, ready to get this shit over with, but Harlow stopped me by grabbing my elbow.

"What?"

"You need to at least *try* to look . . ." She waved her hand around.

"What?" I raised an eyebrow. "Like a criminal?"

She chuckled. "Just, like, a little tougher? Roll up your sleeves so your tats show."

I gave her a withering look but did as she asked, pushing up the sleeves of my plain black long-sleeved T-shirt. I had black ripped jeans and boots on. Nothing particularly proper or eye-catching. Wasn't the whole point for me to disappear into the background?

Harlow placed one hand on my shoulder, her shiny black nail polish glinting in the dim light, and lifted up onto her toes. I froze as I found myself staring right down her top. She stuck the fingers of her free hand in my hair and mussed it up, completely ruining the careful styling I'd done earlier. Just as her sweet vanilla scent hit my nose, she backed away and gave me a quick scan.

"That'll do. Let's go. Just don't talk much, and try not to smile. Pretend you're at school."

I scowled, the thought of that infuriating place filled with hormonal, irrational children nearly making me recoil.

"Perfect." Harlow patted me on the shoulder and breezed past me, swinging her hips. I tried—I *really* did—not to look at her ass, but my eyes went straight to the perfect, toned curve of it. Those pants were so tight I was pretty sure she didn't have on any underwear. I mentally slapped myself for even going there and followed after her.

A couple of people were hanging around the front of the building, smoking— by the smell of it, not just cigarettes. Harlow strolled past them and right up to the bouncer, who looked as if he could eat her whole in one swallow.

I tried to hang back, but the sheer size of him and the leering looks from the smokers made me get closer—close enough to hear everything.

"Hello." She gave him a bright, cheery smile and tried to skip right past, but he held out a meaty hand and stopped her. My fists clenched, but he dropped his arm and I made myself take a deep breath.

"Nice try." He gave her a condescending smirk. "But unless you can show me an ID, you need to beat it, sweetheart."

Harlow's sunny smile turned a little darker, her eyes calculating.

"OK." She reached into the tiny bag across her body and pulled something out, but her hand stayed wrapped around it. Then she leaned in just a little, as if to tell Burly a secret. "I think you know my sister, Donna. She used to come here a lot. A little taller than me, short blonde hair, drop-dead gorgeous?"

Burly tipped his head back and watched her, not giving anything away.

Undeterred, Harlow kept speaking. "I'll take that as a yes. Donna's pretty unforgettable. Anyway, I'm after the same arrangement. Here's my ID."

She held out a hundred-dollar bill, folded twice and pinched between her first two fingers.

One side of Burly's mouth twitched in an almost smile as he watched her in silence. Then he grabbed the money with his meaty hand and tipped his head to the door.

"Excellent." Harlow beamed, the sunshine smile back, then reached into her bag again and brought out a fifty, holding it the same way. "For your trouble."

Burly went to snatch it, but she flicked it out of reach lightning fast. "And a little information?"

He huffed and folded his arms. "What?"

"I just want to know if Shady's here."

"Why?" He sat up a little straighter.

Harlow bit her lip and smiled, looking up at him through her eyelashes. "I just want to talk to him."

Clever girl. The implication was there and not even remotely threatening or suspicious. I bit my tongue to keep myself from smiling.

"I've seen him piss in the men's room. It's not even that big." Burly rolled his eyes and held his hand out. "Yeah, he's here."

Without wasting any more time, Harlow handed over the cash and headed right into the seediest bar I'd come across.

I flashed my ID at the bouncer—who barely even glanced at it or me, too busy pocketing his cash—and followed close behind.

Once we entered the main room, Harlow strutted right through the middle, shoulders back, hips swinging, as though she owned the place. I slunk off to the side and toward the bar, keeping to the shadows while doing my best not to actually touch the wall or anything else in this place.

Keeping an eye on Harlow through the crowd wasn't easy—she was short, and the place was pretty packed—but I could just make her out as she stopped in the middle of the room and started dancing. I guessed it was a good place to start looking for this Shady guy. What kind of a name was that? This would definitely end in disaster. Either at the hands of this Shady character or one of the grown-ass men eyeing the petite blonde as if they wanted to eat her.

I crossed my arms, embracing the surly persona she wanted me to adopt, not even trying to hide my scowl.

"Hey, pretty boy, you gonna order or what?"

I turned my head to find a bartender with dreadlocks halfway down her back, half-heartedly wiping the bar. I hadn't even realized I'd made it all the way to the bar; I'd been so focused on watching Harlow. Managing to keep a look of disgust off my face, I ordered a bourbon.

Several guys circled Harlow on the dance floor as she spun and weaved around them, throwing coy looks and shakes of her head, making it clear she wanted to dance alone. I didn't like the way some of them were closing in.

The bar chick dropped a glass in front of me, and I slapped a twenty next to it, barely looking. "Keep the change." My eyes tracked Harlow as I brought the glass to my lips. The bourbon was *terrible*, and I had to force myself to swallow instead of spraying it all over the bearded biker dude standing next to me. I scowled at the horrid excuse for bourbon and contemplated just drinking it anyway. I needed something to get me through the insanity that was currently my life.

"She's underage." The bar chick with the dreads was back.

"Huh?" I glanced at her and back to the dance floor.

"You're a generous tipper, so I'm just doing you a solid," she said. "The blonde that looks like she doesn't belong here—the one you've been staring at? Jailbait. Trust me, I know her sister."

She knew Donna? How often did that girl come here? So damn dangerous. I was beginning to realize the Mead sisters were a handful.

"Yeah, I know." I rubbed the bridge of my nose and readjusted my glasses. I'd taken a peek at Harlow's file at work. She was eighteen, so not technically jailbait—unless you factored in the whole *I'm a teacher* thing.

Bar chick nodded and looked me up and down. "Good. Glad she's at least got someone looking out for her. But watch yourself. Half the people in here are packing."

"Of course they are." I downed the terrible bourbon and ordered another.

She brought it quickly, and I gave her another twenty, if for no other reason than that she seemed like the only decent human in this dump.

When I turned back to the dance floor, I couldn't spot Harlow. My heart rate kicked up a notch, and my back snapped straight as I scanned the dark mass of bodies moving together to the beat.

After a few panicked moments, I caught a glimpse of shiny blonde hair. Her long ponytail swooped through the air as she spun around and danced. I leaned to the side to see her better, nearly burying my nose in some woman's wrinkly cleavage.

A guy who looked like trouble was trying to dance with Harlow. He had on a denim jacket and looked about twice her age, and he was *persistent*. She ducked away several times and even shook her head, holding her hand out and saying something, but he just said something back and grabbed her waist. Harlow pushed against his shoulders. I cursed under my breath, downed the second shitty bourbon, and rushed through the crowd.

I reached them just as she managed to push out of his grasp. Her back collided with my front, and I stuck my arm out over her shoulder to stop him from advancing on her any farther. He stumbled once his chest hit my hand, then shot me a sneer at the same time Harlow tipped her head back to see my face. Once she realized it was me and not another creep, she relaxed against me. I kept my stare fixed on the misogynistic piece of shit who looked as if he was seconds away from pulling a knife or a gun.

I'd been in my fair share of fights as a teenager, I kept fit, but I was not an idiot. I knew I couldn't take this guy. He probably killed people for fun. And he probably had a whole group of his jerk-off buddies around here somewhere. Not gonna lie—I was scared, but I stood my ground for the fragile girl who was way out of her depth, no matter how confident she sounded.

"I told you I had a boyfriend," Harlow yelled over the loud music.

He bared his teeth at her and tensed. I grabbed her hips, ready to shove her out of the way once fists started flying. But the asshole decided we weren't worth it.

"Fucking cocktease," he spat and disappeared into the crowd.

The relief that flooded through me nearly made my knees buckle. I released a massive breath and dropped my head to speak into Harlow's ear. "I think I just nearly died."

She laughed. *Fucking laughed.* I was starting to worry she might be a little unhinged. Why did that make me amused at the same time though?

"I put my life on the line, and you're laughing?" I couldn't hide the smile in my voice. The adrenaline was making me a little giddy.

She turned, her ponytail flicking out at the sudden movement, and wrapped her arms around my neck. My arms encircled her reflexively.

"Thank you for defending my honor," she said so close to my ear that I could feel her warm breath.

Any words I might have said flitted out of my mind, and I held her close as I scanned the crowd, making sure that douchebag wasn't coming back.

"You were supposed to stay out of sight." Again with her warm breath at my ear. I nearly shivered. I needed to put a stop to this, put some distance between us.

"Unless you were in danger," I countered and left my traitor hands right where they were.

"OK, fair enough. But now several guys think you're the boyfriend I mentioned to get rid of them so . . . you'd better sell it." She pulled back to give me an innocent smile and started swaying from side to side. My body followed hers without my mind really making any decisions.

"We've been here, like, twenty minutes." I frowned. "How many guys have hit on you already?"

She just shrugged and gave me a coy smile.

She's a student! Some still-functioning part of my brain managed to break through the fog of this night, which had started to feel like a fever dream. I shouldn't be dancing with her like this. She shouldn't even be in a bar in the first place. I needed to be the adult and put boundaries back up with this girl.

But with her soft body against mine; with my hands on her hips, feeling her curves; with her breasts pressed up against my chest—it was getting harder and harder not to think of Harlow Mead as a *woman*. A smart, determined, stunning woman I couldn't seem to take my hands off of.

CHAPTER EIGHT

Harlow

The minute I stepped into Davey's, I felt out of my depth. But I just reminded myself Donna would've taken it in stride, so that was what I did. I squared my shoulders, lifted my chin, and strutted my way into the crowd. I could feel eyes on me the entire time—leery, dangerous eyes. They were impossible to ignore, but I pretended to anyway. I felt like a juicy steak floating past a pack of hungry, drooling wolves.

But now that Easton's arms were around me—his firm, strong body against mine—I felt infinitely calmer. Not that I'd admit it to him, but I was glad he'd intervened, glad he was here. And as we stared at each other, I couldn't even feel those dangerous eyes on me, as if he'd wrapped us up in our own little bubble.

I could see the doubt in his eyes though, the real world—where he was a teacher and I was a student—threatening to burst this bubble. So I made myself remember why we were here in the first place.

"Dance in circles with me so I can try to spot our friend," I told him and looked over his shoulder. He hesitated, his hands flexing and then relaxing against my back, but he started to move.

He was stiff at first, clearly trying to keep some semblance of distance between us as we swayed. I really did scan the crowd. I looked at the people on the dance floor, the ones at the bar, the groups playing pool in the back of the room. I couldn't spot him, but the crowd was thick.

On our third rotation, my eyes snagged on a familiar face, but it definitely wasn't Shady. The tall girl had brown hair with highlights halfway down her back, and she wore a short skirt and off-the-shoulder top. And I had no clue why she looked familiar. Was my mind playing tricks on me? Was I so desperately looking to spot a particular someone that my mind just decided this girl was it, because she reminded me of someone I'd seen on TV or at a party or something? But then she glanced in my direction, and when our eyes met, I *knew* she knew me too. I frowned, still unable to place her. She frowned too, but hers was more hostile.

Easton turned me, and I lost sight of her. When I moved my head to the other side of his, she'd disappeared.

"Did you spot him?" he asked.

"Nah. Just someone I thought I knew."

"It's getting really crowded. Maybe we should get off the dance floor and check out some of those dark corners."

"Yeah." I nodded my head, but neither of us moved. Our feet kept shuffling, our hips kept swaying. His hands remained on my waist, mine on his shoulders. If anything, we drew closer.

I looked into his eyes, framed by those sexy black glasses, and couldn't seem to break my gaze. For once, he wasn't pushing me away. In that moment we weren't a teacher and a student, in a place we didn't belong, doing what we shouldn't be. We were a man and a woman, dancing close, falling into each other.

I let myself get lost in his eyes, his touch, the beat of the music. He seemed to do the same. He relaxed, his movements becoming more fluid. His knee was suddenly between my legs, our hips flush, his hands trailing liquid heat over my lower back and between my shoulder blades. I wrapped my arms around his neck and tried to remember how to keep breathing. We were both nearly panting— with need? With the mere closeness? I had no idea, but if he'd dragged me back to his car in that moment, I would've been ready to get naked with him. Judging by the hardness pressing against my hip, he felt the same.

The pull between us was beyond magnetic, and I didn't even remotely want to stop it. Our faces got so close that our breath mingled. His had a tinge of alcohol on it. When our noses brushed, it felt more intimate than if he'd grabbed my ass with both hands.

Emboldened, I tilted my head and moved my lips toward his—an invitation and a suggestion in one. He responded by meeting me halfway. My entire body felt awash in sensation, but my full focus was on my lips, and his, and the fraction of an inch between them. Then—*contact*. Our lips brushed with the lightest of touches. I didn't pucker mine, didn't try to push forward to make it an actual kiss. I was content to let it happen in its own time, to ride this wave of inevitability until it became a force of nature to be reckoned with.

The kiss never eventuated, never got past that tantalizing brush of lips, because he pulled back. He screwed his eyes shut and tilted his head away from mine, his hands falling to my hips.

I slid my hands down his chest and then let them drop to my sides. Easton was gone and Mr. Monroe was back.

The feelings writhing inside me were crushing. I had been so convinced he reciprocated what I felt for him, but in that moment, I wondered if it really was one-sided. Was I a stupid schoolgirl with a crush?

No! Fuck that! I felt his desire pressing against me; I saw the longing in his eyes. I wasn't deluded. He wanted me—but he was still a teacher and I was still a student, so of course he struggled with the boundaries that had been blurred. Both by the circumstances we found ourselves in and by what we felt for each other. Whatever. Now wasn't the time for this anyway.

He took a deep breath and opened his eyes, but before he could lower them to look at me, I stepped away. His hands dropped from my hips, the last bit of contact gone, and I looked over his shoulder with a carefully blank face.

He leaned in close enough that I could hear him over the music, but was very careful not to actually touch me. "Harlow, we—"

I cut him off with a sharp hand gesture and frowned, focusing on a dark corner near the bar. A couple of drunks shifted out of the way, and my suspicion was confirmed. Shady sat on a stool at a high bar table. His tracksuit had drawn my attention—bright yellow with black stripes down the arms and legs. Other dudes in tracksuits and scantily clad women crowded in around him.

"There," I told Easton, glancing at him briefly. "Let's go."

I didn't wait for a response—just marched through the crowd.

Everyone at the table turned to stare at me. I glanced around at them and smiled, hoping it didn't look too much like a grimace. Then I put my focus on the sole reason we were here. "Hey, Shady."

He quirked one side of his mouth into an amused smirk and looked me up and down.

"Step off, bitch." One of the women at the table got to her feet and sneered.

Easton moved to my side and angled his shoulder in front of me. My insides melted momentarily at his protectiveness, but I wasn't about to get distracted when I was clearly being threatened.

Correction—*we* were being threatened. Because as soon as Easton moved, three guys in tracksuits puffed out their chests and moved in; they stopped just in front of Shady, throwing him the occasional glance, as if waiting for a command like good little boys.

"Okaaay." I slowly moved out from behind Easton until we stood shoulder to shoulder. "We come in peace." I held my hands out and chuckled, but no one else found the joke funny.

Shady leaned his forearms on the table and took a sip of his drink. "Who are you, baby doll? And more importantly, how do you know who I am?"

I ignored the sexist nickname. "I'm Harlow. Donna's little sister. We've met briefly once or twice."

He squinted at me, then broke into a grin. "Oh yeah! What's a princess like you doing in a place like this?"

I propped my hands on my hips. "Did you ever ask my sister that?" I hated how people constantly assumed I was some naive, sheltered little girl.

"Quite a few times, actually. Always got a rise out of her, just like that." He pointed at my defensive posture and chuckled before taking another sip. "The sex was better when she was pissed off."

I made a grossed-out face, and Easton huffed next to me.

"That why you're here, cutie? You want a piece?" He grabbed his junk under the table and kissed the air in my direction.

The glaring from his female companions intensified.

"We should go," Easton ground out, and I batted him away.

"As tempting as that is"—I gave him a sarcastic smile—"no. I just want to talk. Privately." I glanced around at all his . . . er . . . hangers-on? Crew? Squad?

His face went serious, suddenly all business. "About?"

"I'll tell you—in private." I could practically hear Easton yelling at me in his head: *Stop antagonizing the dangerous criminal!*

"Who's he?" Shady tipped his chin in Easton's direction.

"A friend."

"We just want to talk," Easton added. "That's all."

Shady considered us for a moment, then turned his head a fraction of an inch to the side and nodded. The tracksuit brigade backed off, slinking away to their dark corners but staying close. The glaring women walked off too, still glaring. I couldn't blame them, I guess—I'd just ruined their party. Shady grabbed one of them by the arm, a blonde with legs for days, and whispered something in her ear. As she turned to leave, he smacked her on the ass.

I held back an eye roll. It was all so cliché.

She walked up to Easton. "I have to search you," she said with a smile, looking a little too pleased about it.

Seriously? I raised my eyebrows at Shady, but he just sat there, sipping his drink.

Easton sighed and held his arms out at the sides. The blonde took her time running her hands all over him—even over his toned, exposed forearms, where there was clearly nothing to hide. She took extra time around his ass and crotch, copping a good feel as he stared into space, a muscle ticking in his jaw.

I clenched my hands at my sides to stop myself from attacking her like a rabid monkey.

After an obnoxiously long time, she gave Shady a nod and disappeared into the crowd.

"Don't feel the need to search me?" I asked innocently. Easton growled next to me—a warning to *please. Stop. Antagonizing. The. Dangerous. Criminal.*

"Baby girl, if you're hiding a weapon in *that* outfit, I'd like to see you remove it." He laughed, and I rolled my eyes. He had a point. The pants were Donna's, and while I was a little shorter than my sister, I had a bigger ass, so they were tight as fuck. And the top . . . well, everywhere Easton had touched me on the dance floor had been skin-to-skin.

I pushed that out of my mind and took a seat on one of the bar stools. Easton took the other.

Shady looked between the two of us leisurely. He clearly wasn't going to speak first. Fair enough—I was the one who'd demanded this talk—but the way he just watched us was unsettling.

Doing my best to sit up straight and sound as confident as Donna would've, I laced my fingers on the table and looked him in the eyes. "I'd like you to get me into whichever room in this place contains the security system."

"What makes you think there is a security system?" He was all business. No teasing remarks or lewd looks.

"There's a camera at the front door, one behind the bar, and one at the back door in the alleyway. I haven't spotted the others yet, but I'm sure they're there."

"There's another back that way." Easton gestured to a hallway leading away from the bathrooms.

"What makes you think they're not just for show? This is a pretty shitty bar."

"I know they're not for show." I didn't elaborate. We both knew the cameras worked. I had video of my sister from the one in the back alley to prove it.

Shady smiled for a moment, amused. "What makes you think I can get you access? I don't own the joint."

"No, but you do a lot of business here, and I have a feeling you can get pretty much anything you want." I leaned forward on the table and raised my eyebrows. No harm in stroking his ego a little bit.

He smiled again, his full focus on me. "OK, dollface, say, hypothetically, I can get you in—what's in it for me?"

Shit! Did I think he'd just help us out of the goodness of his heart? I was such a *moron.*

Easton jumped in. "Hypothetically, what would you like?"

Shady grinned, the serious business face giving way to something mischievous and a little dangerous, then he looked directly at my tits.

"Not that," Easton and I said at the same time.

"Look, you want money?" I asked. "I've got money. How much?" Money talked. Didn't matter if you were in a boardroom with people in thousand-dollar outfits or in a dive bar with a guy in a tracksuit. *Money talked.*

"I got plenty of money." He waved that away but didn't say anything else. I began to get the feeling he was playing with us, amusing himself by making us sweat.

"It's for Donna," I blurted. I was taking a massive risk, showing my hand like this, but he seemed ready to laugh us out of the room at any moment. "You helped her and Hendrix once before. I know you and Hendrix are friends. If any part of you cares about my sister at all, please help us."

"Donna in some kind of trouble?" he asked.

Easton squeezed my knee under the table—a warning not to give too much away.

"I'm trying to make sure she isn't," I said.

Shady gave me a long hard look. "Tell you what, I'll get you access, and in exchange you can owe me a favor. You're handy with computers. I could use that."

My shoulders slumped, and I sighed. I felt so defeated, so fucking stuck. The only way to get myself out of a shitty situation was to get myself into another shitty situation? Kind of poetic in a depressing way.

Easton got to his feet and placed a warm, gentle hand on my back. "Let's go. We'll find another way."

But there was no other way. We had no other leads on Ocean1k and no way to confirm our suspicions about BestLyf. Even if I ended up being used in the same way by Shady, at least he wouldn't bring Donna into it. My sister and Easton's brother would be safe.

I looked at Shady, resigned. "You take us there now, tonight, and you answer any questions we may have. In exchange, I do *one* tech-related favor for you. This does not make me your hacker slave for life."

"Harlow!" Easton dropped his hand from my back, warning, pleading.

"Deal." Shady nodded.

I had no guarantees he would stick to it, but I had no other choice. "Deal."

"Goddamnit, Harlow," Easton muttered. "You're gonna be the death of me."

"No, I won't." I fixed him with a serious look. "But our anonymous friend just might be."

Not wasting any time, Shady got to his feet and gestured for us to follow.

He swaggered to the end of the bar and said something to a guy with face tats, and they both looked in our direction and laughed. Then the guy reached into his pocket and handed something to Shady. I didn't even want to know what they'd said.

It didn't matter, because he led us straight down that corridor, fist-bumping a bouncer near the bathrooms as we waltzed right past. Apparently Face-Tats had given Shady keys, because he used one to unlock the last door on the left. Once the three of us were inside, he closed it.

The music from the bar was muted in the small, windowless room. A stack of boxes and a metal cabinet sat on one side, with the surveillance system on the other. My first glance at it made me so disappointed I almost turned right around and walked out, but I took a closer look anyway.

A beat-up black PC and a few hard drives rested on the table next to a monitor, its four-way split screen showing the locations we'd mentioned. No internet connection. I got down on my knees to look under the table, behind the setup. Not even a port to connect to the internet. No sign of a router.

I'd tried to access this security system countless times since I received my first video of my sister banging some biker. I'd suspected this would be what I'd find —I mean, Davey's didn't even have a website or a Facebook page—but the confirmation was still disappointing.

"Shit." I leaned on the table.

"What is it?" Easton asked. He was sounding more and more worried. He really didn't want to be here. I didn't either.

"This is a really old-school setup. No internet connection. Which is why I couldn't find a way in remotely to try to get some clues for how Oce—" I glanced at Shady over my shoulder. "How our *friend* got the footage. But it looks like it's just recorded onto hard drives. Anyone could've taken it, copied it."

Easton cursed under his breath, then turned to Shady. "Who has access to this room?"

"The staff." He held the keys up and jingled them. "Anyone who has a set of these. I don't work here though, so I don't know everything."

"Do you know who owns the place?" I asked.

"Dude named . . . uh . . ." He snapped his fingers, frowning at the beige carpet, then looked up and pointed at me. "Calvin Clayton. But he's never here. Chick with the dreads—Bea—she manages the bar. A dude named Tricksy runs the *other* aspect of the business." Shady winked, clearly referring to whatever illegal activity he was profiting from. I didn't want any details.

But I did want to know more about the owner. His last name had sent a chill trickling down my spine, but I deliberately avoided looking at Easton, my expression carefully neutral.

"Know anything else about the owner?" Easton beat me to the question.

"Naw, man. I only met him once—boring business type, average height, average hair, average personality. I came here during the day to discuss something with Tricksy, and Clayton happened to be here. Only reason I even know his name is because I had one of my guys tail him and dig up some info. But he really didn't get much else." Shady shrugged.

"Harlow." Easton's voice was soft, and when I looked at him, so were his eyes. "Let's go."

I sighed and nodded. We both knew this was a bust.

As we walked back out into the main bar area, Shady came up behind me and spoke into my ear. "I'll be in touch, baby girl." He swaggered away without waiting for a response.

A warm hand wrapped around mine, and I looked down to see Easton's strong masculine fingers holding my hand firmly. He was already moving through the crowd, pulling me along to the exit.

When we emerged into the crisp night, he didn't let go—and neither did I. He made me feel tethered when all I wanted was to let myself float away into despair and defeat.

We were no closer to finding out Ocean1k's identity, but I had managed to get myself in debt to *another* dangerous person for the effort. In the end, all we'd gained was the name of the man who owned Davey's: Calvin Clayton. And even though it seemed like too much of a coincidence to ignore, I had no idea what to do with the fact that he shared a last name with Raine Clayton—owner and CEO of BestLyf.

Easton and I walked hand in hand all the way to my car. When he finally let go, I wrapped my arms around my middle, wishing for an oversized hoodie.

"It was a good idea," he said, voice low. "We'll think of something else."

I gave him a weak smile. Talking was impossible when I was trying so hard not to cry.

He pulled me into a tight hug, and I rested my head on his chest. A few tears escaped, seeping into his shirt, as I relaxed against him. It was better than any hoodie I owned.

CHAPTER NINE

Harlow

As soon as I woke up the next morning and saw the time, I jumped out of bed and ran into the casual living area on the second floor. It was ten past eleven, and I didn't want to miss anything.

Magda had the ironing board set up, a pile of wrinkled clothes in a basket next to her, and the TV was showing our favorite telenovela.

"What did I miss?" I launched myself over the back of the couch.

She grabbed a shirt and spread it out on the board. "Rodrigo just found out that the father of Consuela's baby is his evil twin."

"Ah shit! I missed it!" I punched a pillow next to me.

"No, no." Magda waved at me dismissively. "Just crazy eyes staring so far and some mean word from Rodrigo. I think."

Magda's native tongue was Polish, her second language English. Neither of us knew enough Spanish to really understand what the characters said, but this late Saturday morning telenovela had turned into a ritual of sorts. Magda would set up the ironing, her crochet, or some other repetitive task, and I'd crawl out of bed just before the show started. A bowl of cereal always waited for me on the coffee table, and I ate while we watched together.

The characters started raising their voices and speaking faster as the music intensified, and then Consuela slapped Rodrigo. Magda and I gasped. Magda propped the iron on the board and lowered herself onto the couch next to me, our eyes glued to the TV as the slap was replayed several times from different angles and in slow-mo.

During the last commercial break, Mom and Donna came up the stairs, all in white, fresh from a round of tennis. My sister disappeared into her room, but Mom came over and kissed the top of my head from behind the couch.

"What have you got planned for the rest of the day?" she asked.

"Not sure yet." I kept one eye on the screen. I didn't want to miss the end—the cliff-hangers were epic!

"OK, well, make sure you get some study in. We've got to get that GPA up." Her tone was cheery, but the room suddenly became very tense. I kept my eyes trained on the TV, but I no longer saw what was on it.

"Yep, I will," I said, hoping she'd just go away.

"It's not too late to get a tutor, you know. We can have someone here next week, honey."

"I know. It's OK. I'll be fine." I didn't want a tutor because I didn't want to study. I sucked at it. I sucked at pretty much everything school related. I hated feeling like an idiot, and I wasn't entirely sure I wanted to keep feeling that way for another several years at college.

Mom didn't say anything more. She just gave me a kiss and left the room.

Magda got up and fluffed another shirt onto the ironing board.

As soon as Mom disappeared, Donna came out of her room and took Mom's spot, leaning on the back of the couch. "I'll help you with your English assignment this afternoon. You can do this, Harls. I know you can."

"Thanks." I gave her a smile, and she left. I appreciated my sister's confidence in me, but I really *couldn't* do this. With my embarrassing GPA, I'd be lucky to get into a community college at this stage. I just wanted this year to end so the failure could be over and I could figure something else out. The constant uphill battle was exhausting.

The telenovela had ended. I'd missed the cliff-hanger. I sighed and let my head roll back against the couch.

My phone vibrated next to me. When I glanced at the screen, my heartbeat jumped and my teeth clenched. It was a message from Ocean1k. I didn't even want to look at it.

I grabbed my phone and got to my feet—better to read this in the privacy of my room.

"Harlow." Magda's accent always sounded more pronounced when she said my name, dropping the *w* and making the *o* sound soft.

"Yeah?" I looked up to find her watching me with a frown. Magda just knew things sometimes. Maybe it was the wisdom of old age, or maybe she was a nosy gossip, but I felt as if she saw right through me to all the heavy shit weighing me down on a sunny Saturday. I fought hard to keep my eyes from filling with tears, swallowed the lump in my throat. But Magda knew. She always knew.

She held her arms out, and I stepped into one of her warm hugs. They were few and far between. She was a busy woman and not overly emotional, but when her arms enveloped me and squeezed me against her big, soft bosom, it comforted me beyond words.

"Everything will be OK in end, beautiful girl. If is not OK, is not end," she said to the top of my head, gave me one last squeeze, and turned back to the ironing.

"Thanks, Magda." I wiped a stray tear and dragged my feet back to my bedroom.

The room was still dark, bright sunshine just peeking through the corners of the blinds, as I flopped back onto my unmade bed. I stared at the ceiling and forced myself to think about the videos I'd watched about hummingbirds at three in the morning when I couldn't sleep. They were the only bird that could fly backward.

Eventually the intense urge to cry subsided, but the crushing weight of hopelessness stayed. I had a feeling that wasn't going anywhere, possibly for the rest of my life.

I picked up my phone and read the message from Ocean1k. Another hacking demand. With a sigh, I let the hand with the phone fall back to the mattress while I dragged my other hand down my face.

I didn't argue. Didn't obsess about what they wanted with this new information. Didn't give them a chance to send more threats, another picture of my sister they shouldn't have or a photo of me breaking into the home of a judge. I just replied that I was doing it, sat at my computer, and got started.

Why stress about it when I clearly couldn't do anything about it? I told myself I was practicing radical acceptance—getting my Buddhist on. But it wasn't acceptance. It was defeat. All I could do at this point was hope this ended someday. Until then, if I had to suffer, at least I could keep my family safe.

It took me a couple of hours to do what they requested—gain access to an IP address in Bulgaria, copy the contents of the hard drive, and send it on to them. After that I got in the shower and thought some more about hummingbirds. There wasn't a whole lot in the shower to distract oneself from depressing, dejected thoughts.

When I stepped out of the bathroom—my hair leaving wet patches on my blue hoodie dress—my room was bathed in light. Magda had opened the blinds and started changing the sheets.

Donna popped her head in. "Hey. We're in my room. Come on."

"We?"

"Yeah, the girls came over so we could all study."

I grabbed my books and laptop and followed her across the hall.

"Hey! We've been waiting for you to get out of the shower." Mena gave me a kiss and hug hello, then started taking books out of her bag.

"You mean you've been procrastinating." I raised an eyebrow.

"Yep." Amaya gave me a kiss and hug too. "It's fucking Saturday. Who wants to study?" She joined Mena on Donna's bed and took her phone out.

"Why did you even come?" Donna shook her head as I pulled a chair up to sit next to her at the desk.

Amaya shrugged. "I wanted to hang with you guys."

"Did you even bring books?" I asked.

"I finished all my homework last night."

We all looked at her and frowned. Amaya was smart, but she wasn't Donna's level of intense when it came to schoolwork.

She didn't look up from her phone as she explained. "Mom had a date, and I needed something more than Netflix to focus on."

My stomach sank. Amaya's mom was . . . complicated. She went a little crazy sometimes and drank too much or did too many drugs and would have all kinds of people at the house. Amaya ended up parenting her own mother a lot of the time. She'd messaged the group chat last night, asking us to hang out, but Donna was at Hendrix's and Mena was working and I was at a dive bar with our teacher —not that I'd told them.

"Why didn't you say something in your message?" Mena put her hand on Amaya's arm.

Amaya looked up at us all, brows furrowed. "It's fine. It was just the one guy, and I locked my door. It was pretty tame as far as Mom's benders go. I wouldn't expect you to leave work just to hang out with me."

"Yeah, but I would've," Mena said. "If you need me, I'll always be there."

"Yeah, and I would've ditched Hendrix in a heartbeat," Donna added.

"I'm sorry you were alone last night." I couldn't add that I would've changed my plans for her, because what I'd been doing last night was just as important, and they couldn't know.

"Can we just drop it?" Amaya rolled her eyes. "I'm fine. Let's go to the mall or something."

"I really have to study." Mena groaned. "Psych is kicking my ass, and I really don't want to fail."

"All right, fine." Amaya turned to face her, legs crossed. "I'll quiz you."

Donna had done most of her homework too, so she mostly helped me with my English essay—which felt like pulling teeth. I didn't care about the book we were studying, hadn't even read the whole thing, and considering what I was dealing with on the Ocean1k front, it just didn't seem important. I managed to get something resembling a coherent essay together with a lot of help from my sister, and by the end, it felt as if I'd run a marathon.

"Just read over it a few more times and maybe add a quote here." Donna pointed to a paragraph in the middle. "And I think you're good to hand it in."

She gave me an encouraging smile. Amaya and Mena had already abandoned studying. They were lying on the bed, heads together, as Mena showed Amaya her most recent makeup creations.

"Yep. OK." I closed the books, knowing I wouldn't touch that essay or even think about it again before turning it in. But my sister did genuinely care, so I gave her a genuine smile. "Thanks, Donna."

Donna got up and stretched, arms over her head. That got the other two moving too, and we all ended up on Donna's balcony, sitting around on the comfy outdoor couches. Amaya lit a cigarette. The afternoon sun shone in the clear early-spring sky, but the breeze still had an icy chill that made me pull my hood up.

"I need some advice." Mena cleared her throat and started to blush.

I leaned forward. "This should be good if you're blushing like that."

Donna smacked my arm. "What's up?"

Amaya took a leisurely drag of her cigarette and cocked her head, her long black hair practically sparkling in the sun.

"OK. So, um . . ." Mena took a deep breath and made herself look at us properly. "I need some practical advice about . . . er . . . anal."

Amaya blew out her smoke quickly and sat up straight. "Is that motherfucker pressuring you to do it up the ass? I swear to god . . ." She folded her arms and took another angry puff.

"No, no, no." Mena waved her down. "We haven't even discussed it. It's me. I want to try it."

Amaya glared at her for a moment, then relaxed into her seat again. "OK, go on."

I couldn't hold it in any longer. I let out a massive laugh, and the others joined in. Even Mena giggled through admonishing me.

"It's not funny!" She leaned over Donna to smack me. Why was everyone smacking me today?

"OK, OK." Donna got her giggles under control and rested one elbow on the back of the couch, crossing her legs. "First things first. Lube. The ass, unlike the vag, does not self-lubricate—so you want to get yourself a good-quality water-based lube."

Amaya nodded along sagely. I tucked my legs under me. I didn't have any practical experience with this, but you never knew—so I paid attention.

"Now, you want to work your way up to it," Donna continued. "We'll get you some butt plugs. You need to get used to the sensation of having something up there before you go putting full-sized dicks in . . ."

For a little while—as we sat around laughing and talking about anal sex, Mena's blush gradually disappearing—I managed to forget about Ocean1k and the threats and Easton Monroe and how fucked up my life was. For a little while, I was just a young woman hanging out with her girls, talking and joking and being . . . *normal*.

But I'd never been normal. Not really. Between my total inability to grasp anything at school, the insomnia, and the weird niche things I was into, sometimes I wondered if I really fit in with my friends. Maybe they just tolerated me because I was Donna's sister.

Then one of them would say something or do something to make me feel loved and special, and I'd put those thoughts aside.

As the conversation turned from anal to sex in general, I found myself getting more and more quiet. Donna was crazy about Hendrix. Mena and Turner would get married—no question. Amaya complained about how guys our age were too immature.

I had a guy I wanted to talk to my friends about. A guy who was smart and creative and protective of me and looked fucking hot in a shirt and tie but also in loose sweats. I wanted to tell them I was falling for him so hard I'd stopped hooking up with Drew. I was pretty sure he liked me back, but I was too nervous to make a move—there was too much at stake. I wanted to ask them for advice.

But I couldn't.

He was our teacher, and we were both being blackmailed by some douchebag who was probably connected to a multibillion-dollar corporation, and bringing them into it would just put them in danger.

How long could I live like this? Hiding major parts of my life from those closest to me, constantly on edge, with no idea what my future would look like because I couldn't be certain it wouldn't end with me in prison—or dead?

I wanted to protect my sister, keep her safe as she'd always kept me safe. But in the process, I'd created a massive divide between myself and my loved ones.

What was even the point of any of this? This wasn't a life.

CHAPTER TEN

Easton

I slammed my car door a little too hard, then looked around Fulton's parking lot to make sure no one had noticed. My foul mood hadn't eased up at all since the visit to Davey's a few days ago. Getting a hint of hope and then having it wrenched out of your grasp was soul crushing.

Even tattooing over the weekend hadn't pulled me out of this pit of despair. I'd done a full color peony with a ladybug on the petals for a twentysomething. It was her first tattoo, and she asked me out at the end. I'd hardly spoken to her and completely missed any signs of her being into me.

There was something about tattoos; the artists got hit on a lot. I almost always said no. That time I actually considered it—not because I found the girl particularly attractive but because I needed a distraction . . . with someone my age.

Maybe peony chick wouldn't have minded being a distraction for me, but it didn't feel right to use her like that. Especially since I knew I'd spend our time together thinking about someone else. Someone I definitely should not be thinking about at all, *whatsoever*.

As much time as I'd spent in the last few days wallowing in hopelessness over the Davey's dead end, I'd spent just as much thinking about Harlow Mead in those painted-on pants.

Just being in that bar with her would land me in big trouble with the school and the board of education. When you factored in how close we were dancing, her body rubbing all over mine, the fact that I had a hard-on half the night . . . If I'd heard of a teacher behaving like that with a student, I would've reported him to the police too.

The problem was that I was getting to know her. If it had been just physical, a sign of me having gone too long without getting laid, I could've simply picked up a chick or said yes to one at Twin Peaks Ink and scratched that itch. But it wasn't about my physical needs; it was about our connection. The more time we spent together, the more I learned how resourceful and determined she was, how deeply she cared about her sister and friends. I thought of her less as a Fulton student—an ignorant, shallow, frustrating walking hormone—and more as a person. A *woman*, with a woman's body, whom I could relate to and understand and admire.

She had curves in all the right places, and her skin was so soft as I ran my palms up her back while we danced. She smelled amazing—sweet vanilla and just so . . . *female*.

I paused outside the doors to the school and rubbed my eyes. I could not be thinking like that about a student as I walked into work. Or *ever* really.

With a sigh, I readjusted my glasses, preparing myself for another day of dealing with several hundred teenagers. One of the hormones on legs rushed past me, nearly knocking me over as I headed up to my office.

"No running in the halls!" I called after him and gritted my teeth.

It was bad enough dealing with these little shits on a regular day, but now I had to do it with the knowledge that there was no way out of my shitty situation with Ocean1k. Maybe that was the reason for my inappropriate feelings toward Harlow—I needed something to hold on to, some sense of fun or excitement to cling to in my life.

No. I couldn't think like that. I was *not* developing feelings for a student. This was just a temporary mental dysfunction. The result of extreme stress. Undoubtedly there was a perfectly reasonable psychological explanation.

I needed a damn vacation.

To get myself through the day, I focused on the syllabus and avoided calling on students, assigning more independent study. I just wasn't in the mood to listen to their pedestrian, unoriginal thoughts that they all had the arrogance to think they'd come up with first. Oh, you think *The Great Gatsby* is a critique of the American dream? *Really*? No shit.

I should've used the quiet time to do some grading or lesson planning, or to keep an eye on the students. But I couldn't even dredge up enough fucks to give when I saw Nicola on her phone or Tess and Donnie whispering to each other. My mind was on the weekend, on Harlow and Ocean1k and my brother.

I'd told him everything about Davey's as soon as I got home that night, glossing over the parts where I had to beat guys off Harlow and dance with her.

Usually he'd give me all kinds of shit when a woman was involved, but he only asked questions about the security system and Shady.

Sadly, I didn't have much to tell him. Instead I started asking him questions—desperately grasping at straws, hoping for another lead.

Do you remember anything, anything at all, that we could use? Did the chick from college ever say anything about where she was from? Are you sure you didn't get a look at her license plate?

We'd been through all this before—he'd told me all the details when I called him after I received that first threatening message—but he answered all my questions anyway. At first he was patient, but as I got more agitated, he got more frustrated.

"Don't you think I would've already done everything I could to get us out of this if I had any more information?" he finally snapped, throwing his hands up.

I deflated and dragged a hand down my face. "Yes, of course. I'm sorry. I just feel so . . ."

"Defeated." He gave my shoulder a squeeze. "Me too, man."

We'd gone to bed after that, not much left to say.

The sense of defeat stayed with me and was still present as I dragged myself through Monday. After my morning classes I went out and got myself a burrito, eating it in the car for some peace and quiet. When I got back to Fulton, half of me hoped to spot Harlow as I dodged students in the busy halls. I wanted to see her, check her eyes for a hint of how she was feeling, even though I had a pretty good idea already. The other half of me wanted to avoid her at all costs. She was another reminder of how stuck I was, and another complication.

"Hey, Monroe!" Coach Cooper's booming voice made me pull up just before I walked straight into him. He was in a Fulton tracksuit, whistle hanging around his neck, and grinned at me widely.

"Hey, Dale." I gave him a polite smile and stuffed my hands into my pockets. We'd stopped just outside the main office, near the reception area.

"Hey, thanks for picking up my key card last week, man. Saved me fifty bucks having to have it replaced."

"Yeah, no problem." I was dying on the inside. *Dying!* That was the key card I'd stolen and used to break into a judge's apartment with a student.

"Where'd you find it? Linda was a bit vague on the details." He crossed his big arms over his chest and tilted his head.

"In the parking lot. I think we parked next to each other that day maybe?" *Dying!* But I did my best to keep my expression casual, my breathing even. I hated lying. Maybe that was why pretending to like teaching was killing me slowly from the inside. Every damn day was a lie.

"So weird." He shook his head. "I never even took my wallet out of my pocket. I have no idea how it fell out."

"Yeah . . . weird." I didn't offer anything else.

"Anyway!" He smacked me on the shoulder. "Glad one of us was paying attention that day! Hey, we should go get some beers sometime soon. I have this poker game with some buddies once a month. You should . . ."

Coach Cooper's chatter faded into the background as my eyes zeroed in on something on the wall. Even my anxiety about the key card melted away when I read the poster. It was for a fundraising and networking event that Fulton Academy was holding in conjunction with the Devilbend Legal Association. Judge Keating was the guest of honor and would be giving a speech.

Maybe we still had a chance at undoing some of the shitty stuff we'd been forced to do.

"Yeah, that sounds good." I cut across whatever Dale was saying. "I gotta do something before my next class. I'll see you around!"

"No problem! See you around, Monroe."

I probably would not see him around. He spent most of his time in the gym or out on the field. I hadn't seen him since the day I'd stolen the key card.

I walked over to the reception area. Linda, the head receptionist, was on the phone, but one of the other admin staff—a young woman with her brown hair up in a ponytail—approached the desk.

"Hi. Are there any tickets to this still available?" I pointed to the poster.

"Yes, I think so." She smiled and tapped at the keyboard. "Easton Monroe, right?"

I nodded. "I'm sorry. What was your name?"

"Irene. It's OK. Fulton is massive. I'm still struggling to remember everyone's names. Yep! About a dozen tickets left." She looked up from the screen. "You teach English though, right? Why the interest in a law event?"

"Uh . . . I don't . . . I just want to support the . . ." I glanced at the poster. "Devilbend Community Legal Center. And to be honest, I moved here nearly a year ago, and I still don't really know anyone. I figure it'll be a good way to hang out with some of the faculty. Something to do on a Saturday night."

"Oh, I moved here about six months ago too. Coming from a small town, sometimes I still feel like I need a map to this place." She leaned forward on the counter and gave me a more-than-friendly smile. Understated makeup highlighted her eyes, and she wore a pencil skirt and a sweater with tiny strawberries embroidered around the collar. Despite the cutesy detail, the outfit accentuated her curves. If my life were normal, I might've even asked her out.

Just before I made a disinterested comment and hurried her along, I thought about it for a second. I had no plan to speak of at this stage—just a vague sense that if I could get close to the judge, I could speak to him and do . . . something. But Irene was right—it was a little odd for me to be going to an event like this.

"Hey, would you be interested in going with me?" I smiled back at her. Perhaps a date would make it less suspicious.

She looked down shyly, grinning, then gave me a nod.

"In that case, I'll take two tickets."

"Great." She struggled to make eye contact as she took my credit card and got two tickets out of a drawer for me. I already felt bad for using her and vowed not to lead her on after the event.

"Should I pick you up? What's your address?" I asked.

"Oh, I volunteered to help with the setup. I'll just meet you there."

"Sounds good." The next logical thing to do would be to get her number, but the bell rang, and I had to rush to avoid being late for my next class.

I had to force my fingers to loosen from around my phone as I speed-walked across the school. In that moment when I'd reached for it to grab Irene's number, all I'd really wanted to do was text Harlow.

I wanted to tell her about the event, talk about what we could do with this opportunity. Mostly I wanted to wipe that hopeless, defeated look off her face—the one I'd seen when we left Davey's. The same feeling that had been weighing me down for days.

I had to remind myself that I couldn't use my actual phone to contact her, that the secure one she'd given me was in an inside pocket of my satchel, and that it should only be used with the utmost discretion.

The last of the students darted into the classroom just before I did. Resigned, I forced the urge to contact her down and started the lesson, counting down the minutes until I could leave for the day and message her from my car.

CHAPTER ELEVEN

Being the daughter of rich and prominent people meant I'd known how to strut in a pair of heels since I was fifteen. That didn't mean I liked it though. I wore sneakers as much as possible and only put on heels for any stuffy events my parents dragged me to—or if the girls wanted to get dressed up and go dancing.

The silver pumps on my feet fit perfectly and were as comfortable as heels could be, but I still wished for my Adidas as I made my way to the entrance of The Bend—Devilbend's premier function venue. It was about half an hour into the hills, nestled into the trees on the side of a cliff that overlooked the city and the natural California landscape beyond.

The shoes had a matching silver clutch, tucked under my arm, and I wore a black A-line number with infinite layers of tulle that I'd bought for some party last year. I liked bright, fun colors, but the simple dress was more appropriate for a fundraiser with the legal crowd. I'd had to get *myself* ready for this—neither Mena nor a professional stylist had been available to do my hair and makeup—so I'd kept it simple, leaving my hair out to cascade down my back in soft waves.

The decision to come to the fundraiser had been last minute, and I'd pulled this look together before sneaking down the stairs. Luckily, Donna and Hendrix were wrapped up in each other, making out on the couch while the TV provided the only light.

When Easton had texted me on Monday after school, my first gut reaction was to smile at the sight of the notification. I got something that felt like that butterflies-in-my-gut feeling girls talked about when they really, really liked a guy. I'd liked guys before, but not like this. None of them had given me butterflies.

Then when I read his news about the judge attending the event, the heaviness that had been hanging over me lifted a little. Hope swooped in to help with the weight of the despair.

We spent the rest of the week texting, planning, and debating the best approach. He had no idea what we could achieve by speaking to the judge, but we agreed we couldn't miss this opportunity to *try*.

We considered blackmailing him with his gambling debt, getting him to go to the police, but we dismissed that quickly. We didn't even know if Ocean1k was using the info we'd stolen to manipulate the judge yet; plus, if we did it that way, we'd be no better than Ocean1k.

We debated whether to tell Judge Keating that we'd broken into his house, but decided against that too. No point in getting ourselves in more trouble by admitting our crime to a *judge*.

In the end, we decided to keep it simple and just try to undo what evil we'd helped create—or prevent it from happening in the first place.

"How do we get him alone though?" Easton had asked while we texted late on Wednesday night.

> *Harlow: I don't know. We'll have to play it by ear.*
> *Easton: Maybe we shouldn't be seen talking to him at all.*
> *Harlow: Are you saying you wanna bail?*
> *Easton: No! I'm just saying . . . maybe we should be more discreet.*
> *Harlow: How??*
> *Easton: Perhaps we could pass the esteemed judge a note.*
> *Harlow: OMFG! Shut up!*
> *Easton: Perhaps one of the wait staff could be tipped off to hand it to him on the sly.*
> *Harlow: You're never going to let me live that down, are you?*
> *Easton: Nope! :D*

The grin on my face was so huge my cheeks started to hurt.

> *Easton: Seriously. I don't think we should both talk to him. We shouldn't risk being seen together. Who knows where Ocean1k has eyes and ears?*
> *Harlow: Good point. I think you should do it.*
> *Easton: Me? Why?*
> *Harlow: It's your genius plan! Also he's an old white man. He'll take one look at me and give me a condescending pat on the head before he laughs me out of the room. You're a teacher at the best school in the US, and you're a dude. He'll take you more seriously.*
> *Easton: You think I'll be taken more seriously because of what's between my legs?*

Harlow: Hey, man, I don't make the rules. Patriarchy does.
Easton: Good point . . .

The question of who would talk to the judge was a moot point anyway, because when I went to buy a ticket, they were all sold out. Easton said it was probably better if I stayed away, but it killed me that I couldn't be there to help—the way he'd helped me at Davey's.

Also, I really wanted to see him in a suit.

Our chats grew longer and longer every day, even once we'd figured out the plan. We talked about everything—music, movies, books (that one was one-sided, as I didn't really read much, but I loved it when he nerded out over his faves). I asked him about tattooing, and he asked me about coding and tech ("that computer stuff"). We talked about our siblings and families, about how we were feeling with the whole Ocean1k situation. He understood me in a way no one else could—and not just when it came to the creepy stalker controlling us both. Whenever I tried to explain something or tell him how I felt about a topic, his immediate comprehension felt validating in a way I couldn't even describe.

By the end of the week, we were even talking during school hours, although we both knew it was risky. Barely an hour went by without us having something to say to each other. Good thing I usually spent a lot of time with my face in my phone anyway, or my friends would've thought I'd lost it.

He was the first person I spoke to when I woke up, and the last one before I attempted sleep. A few times I'd drifted off in the middle of typing out a response and woke up to several confused *"hello? You there?"* texts.

We hadn't spoken face-to-face since Davey's, and we purposely avoided eye contact on the few occasions our paths crossed at school, but I felt closer to Easton Monroe than anyone else in my life. I wondered if he felt the same way.

But now wasn't the time to worry about that. I had to focus. And I had to find some way to let Easton know I was here.

I handed my ticket to the lady at the entrance and went into the crowded event space. The sprawling room was softly lit, allowing the twinkling lights of the town below—visible through the wall of windows—to add to the ambiance. The dim lighting, along with the fact that I'd arrived about an hour after the event started, allowed me to slip in unnoticed. Everyone was already in conversations, on their second drinks.

I kept to the edges of the crowd and looked for Easton or the judge.

I'd spotted the tickets for the fundraiser on my dad's desk only that morning. When I went in to see if he was up for a round of tennis, he'd told me that sounded great, finished off the email he was writing, and then started asking me about my classes. Both my parents were pushing me to get a tutor, worried about my prospects after high school.

I avoided his gaze and tried to end the conversation as quickly as possible, fiddling with the papers on his desk. The tickets peeked out when I shifted a book about economics or something just as dull.

"Are you and Mom going to this tonight?" I held up the tickets and tried not to sound too interested. Thankfully, he seemed to assume I just wanted to stop talking about my grades.

He sighed but, after a moment, decided to drop it. "No. I purchased those a few months ago. I was planning to attend with your sister, but since she no longer wishes to pursue a career in law . . ." He grabbed them out of my hand and dropped them into the trash can next to his desk.

After tennis I snuck into Dad's office and plucked one of the tickets out of the trash. I'd messaged Easton several times to let him know, but I never got a response. I knew he spent Saturdays tattooing and would have to rush to get to the fundraiser on time, so I didn't think anything of it.

"Miss Mead?" I froze at the sound of my name, then turned in the direction of the voice, trying not to look as guilty as I felt.

"Ms. Murphy! Hello." I smiled politely at my English teacher. She was in a dark green taffeta gown, standing with several other impeccably dressed women. I'd already spotted several other Fulton teachers and a few students, but no one I was friends with. More than half the crowd were people I didn't know. I had a feeling Donna would've been able to name each one.

WWDD.

At the thought of my sister, I relaxed my shoulders and plastered a polite, slightly bored smile on my face. Donna would turn on the charm and act as though she was exactly where she belonged.

"I'm surprised to see you here, Harlow," Ms. Murphy said, a hint of confusion and worry in her gaze. "You're not interested in pursuing law, are you?"

I could see why she was worried—no way was I smart enough to get into law school.

"Oh no." I channeled my sister and my mother and chuckled lightly, waving the comment away. "I'm just here with a friend."

The relief at not having to sit me down and explain my limitations was palpable in Ms. Murphy's laugh and the gulp of champagne she took.

"Mead . . ." One of the other women tapped her champagne flute with a ringed finger, making a tinkling sound, as she regarded me with a cocked head. "I do believe I was at a Christmas party at your parents' home this past holiday season. Do you have a sister? I distinctly remember a beautiful, bright young Mead lady with a keen interest in the law."

"Yes, that would be my sister, Donna." I had no idea who the woman in the asymmetrical black-and-white gown was. Donna had covered for me and the girls the night of that party, staying behind to mingle while Mena, Amaya, and I stole a bottle of champagne from the kitchen and hid out in my room.

"Harlow, this is Raine Clayton, the CEO and owner of BestLyf, and this is . . ."

Ms. Murphy started to introduce the other ladies with her, but I didn't hear anything after learning I was face-to-face with Raine Clayton. All my energy went into keeping a neutral, polite look on my face while I screamed on the inside.

Did she know Ocean1k? Were they acting on her direct orders? Did Raine know who I was and what I was doing?

I mentally talked myself off the ledge. This might not have anything to do with BestLyf after all. It was just a theory I had . . . that Easton agreed with, and that Ford was convinced was true. Maybe Raine herself didn't know anything about the illegal activities. BestLyf was a massive corporation; she couldn't possibly be across every aspect of it.

I still felt as if she was dissecting me, though, as she looked at me. As if she could see right through me and knew exactly why I was there. Was that a little smirk as she took a sip of her champagne?

Fuck, I was losing it.

"Yes, I remember Donna now." Raine nodded. "Very driven, an exceptional young woman."

Unlike me. I just smiled and nodded.

"Is she here?" Raine looked around.

"No. Donna has realized that pursuing a career in the legal field is not what she truly wants to do," I explained.

"Oh?" Raine raised one eyebrow, and several of the other women looked just as interested. They kept throwing her glances, as though waiting for cues on how to react, what to do, what to *think.* "And what has she decided to pursue instead?"

"She's currently exploring her options." I kept it vague. Raine was giving me the creeps. I didn't want her knowing anything about me or my family.

"Well, I'm positive she'll excel at any endeavor she chooses to put her mind to. We have a youth program at BestLyf that could help her figure out her true potential. She'd be an ideal candidate."

I didn't know what it was about me that screamed "underachiever," but Raine Clayton, Ms. Murphy, and pretty much everyone I came into contact with seemed to pick up on it. The invitation to this fancy program wasn't extended to me. It didn't matter. Over my dead body was I letting Donna, or any of my friends, get anywhere near this woman.

"Good evening, ladies!" Coach Cooper barged his way into the group—his voice, demeanor, and pretty much everything about him way too loud for this sophisticated crowd. I was glad for the distraction though.

I glanced over Raine's shoulder, smiling at nothing. "Excuse me. I see my friend looking for me. It was a pleasure to meet you all."

They all murmured pleasantries, and Raine said, "Do let your sister know she has a spot in the program if she wants it."

"I'll be sure to do that. Thank you," I hurriedly answered as I walked away. "Over my decomposing body," I murmured under my breath.

Once I was no longer in their line of sight, I heaved a sigh and rolled my shoulders before scanning the room. Still no sign of Judge Keating, but there had to be three hundred people present—it might take a while to find him.

I did spot Easton though, and once again, I had to school my features into an impassive mask while my insides writhed.

He was on the dance floor with some woman in an electric-blue dress, her hair up in an elegant twist. Her hands rested on his shoulders; his on her hips.

Such intense jealousy shot through me I almost punctured my clutch with my nails. It took an insane amount of effort to keep a bored look on my face, let alone stop myself from marching over there to demand what the *fuck* was *happening* here. But we weren't together. I wasn't even sure he felt the same way about me as I did about him.

Easton looked up, and our eyes met briefly through the crowd. Then he looked past me, swaying the woman in his arms in a circle. He would've looked completely normal to anyone else, but I saw the little twitch in his jaw, the slight frown behind his glasses.

The woman turned her head, and I recognized Irene from the front office at school. Did they just bump into each other here? Were they on a date? Did she ask him to dance or did he ask her?

I couldn't watch his hands all over another woman when I knew what they felt like on my own skin. I walked over to the bar.

It took a while for the crowd around it to clear and one of the bartenders to come to me. I so badly wanted to ask for a shot of tequila or four. But I had to remember where I was. I had to be a good girl.

"An orange juice, please," I said.

He nodded and poured the juice. Just as he delivered it to me, Easton appeared at my side.

I didn't need to look to know it was him. I could *smell* him, his masculine, clean scent. I could *feel* him, his presence drawing some subconscious, physiological attention from deep within my body.

I looked anyway.

Why did he have to look so amazing in his suit? Completely unfair. It was slate gray, the shirt crisp white. His perfectly styled hair and a gray bowtie with blue polka dots completed his neat look.

The bowtie matched her dress.

"I thought you couldn't come," he said, keeping his eyes on the busy bar staff.

I took a sip of my juice. It tasted bitter. "My dad got tickets months ago. I only found them this morning. Looks like you found someone else to spend the night with anyway."

Ugh! I sounded jealous, and I hated it. He looked so calm and put together and just . . . *fucking perfect*. And I was a jealous schoolgirl with an old dress and unrealistic expectations.

"You know we—" He cut himself off as the bartender delivered his beer, then he waited until no one was paying attention to us. "You know we couldn't have spent tonight together. This isn't some party. We're trying to accomplish something here."

I took another sip of my bitterness—and the juice. He was right. I was being petty, but I'd been surprised too. By the sight of him dancing with another woman and by the strength of my reaction to it.

After a moment, he sighed. "Irene sold me the tickets. I figured since I have no interest in legal studies and hardly know anyone here, coming with a date would be less suspicious. Why didn't you tell me you were coming?"

"I sent you several messages. Why didn't you tell me you were bringing a date?" I shot back.

"Crap. I was so busy at the shop today I didn't get a chance to check either phone. Figured you'd contact Ford if there was any emergency. I'm sorry."

It didn't escape me that he'd avoided my question. But I'd also had a few moments to calm down, to remind myself why I'd come in the first place. I shoved all my annoying feelings to the back of my mind, promising to overthink them later. We'd been standing at the bar a little too long already.

"I'm sorry," I rushed out. "Let's just get this done. I'm here now, so what can I do to help?"

"Let me know if you spot him. I haven't seen him yet."

I nodded and downed the rest of my juice.

"Also," he added, "when I manage to pull him aside, maybe keep an eye on Irene? Stop her from coming to find me."

"Got it." I turned to leave.

"Harlow," he whisper-shouted, and I paused with my back to him, pretending to fiddle with something in my clutch.

"I'm glad you're here," he said under his breath as he breezed past me, then disappeared into the crowd.

I resisted the urge to close my eyes and inhale deeply, let his essence wash over me.

Instead I went the opposite way, searching for the judge.

I spotted him just a few minutes later, chatting by the stage with the headmistress of Fulton Academy, the head of our legal studies department, and a few other people I didn't recognize. Keeping the judge in the corner of my eye, I searched for Easton. I just hadn't figured out how to tell him where to look.

Just as I spotted him in the crowd, almost all the way across the room, the music cut out and the headmistress cleared her throat into a microphone on stage, harnessing everyone's attention. I cursed under my breath. With everyone now silent and still, moving about the room would be nearly impossible.

At least I could still keep an eye on Keating; the man was climbing onto the stage to a round of applause.

The next twenty minutes, while the judge delivered his speech, were torture. He was a barrel-chested, overweight man with receding gray hair, and he clearly liked the sound of his own voice, because he took his time, pausing way too long for people to politely laugh at his jokes.

I didn't hear a single word. I was too busy trying not to fidget while resisting the urge to glance at Easton every few seconds.

When the judge finally finished, there was a raucous round of applause, the music kicked back up, and everyone started moving again. The speech must have been about as rousing as I thought, because several people crowded the bar. A group converged on Judge Keating near the edge of the stage, grappling for his attention.

Now wasn't the time to try to drag him off, but I moved closer to wait for his hangers-on to leave. I was so focused on not letting him out of my sight that I wasn't paying enough attention.

"Harls?" Drew appeared in front of me, blocking my path and my view. He had on a black suit, but he'd drawn the line at a tie and wore the crisp white shirt with the top few buttons open. He was no more a formalwear kind of guy than I was a heels kind of girl. He *definitely* wasn't a legal center fundraiser kind of guy.

I stepped to the side so I could see the judge and frowned at my friend. "What are you doing here?"

He chuckled and shoved one hand into a pocket. "My dad is dating some lawyer. He insisted I come, even though they've both ignored me since we got here." He rolled his eyes.

Drew's dad was an asshole, and once he decided something . . . well, Drew learned at a very young age not to argue with his father.

"Right . . ." I lost focus, watching Keating disappear down the hall toward the restrooms. I needed to find Easton. Now would be a great time to pull the judge aside. I looked around and spotted him heading for the same hallway, just in time.

"Harlow." Drew leaned down and demanded my attention.

"Sorry, what?" I glanced at him but kept one eye on Easton and that hallway.

"What's up with you? What are you even doing here?"

Shit. I had to deal with Drew properly.

Instead of answering, I asked him, "Is anyone else here? Anyone we're friends with?"

"Huh? No. A couple kids from school, but no one we hang with."

"OK, good. That's . . ." I trailed off as I caught sight of Easton and the judge slipping out onto a side balcony. " . . . Excellent," I finished with a grin.

"What the fu—" Drew started to turn, following my line of sight, but I grabbed his arm.

"Drew." I stepped in close.

He looked at me, wide-eyed.

"Drew, listen. You can't tell anyone you saw me here, OK?"

"Why?" His eyes narrowed. "You in some kinda trouble, Harls?"

"No. Maybe? Look, I'm trying not to be, OK? I don't have time to explain right now. I . . . I'm trying to do a good thing. I just . . . I need you to trust me." I stared at him, hoping my intense gaze conveyed how serious this was, even if my intense words hadn't.

Drew stared me down for a few moments. But we'd known each other since we were kids. He knew I wasn't fucking around.

"OK." He finally nodded.

"And I need your help."

The request might have been pushing my luck, but he agreed immediately.

"Can you please try to find Irene from the front office at school? Don't approach her or anything unless she tries to leave. If she tries to exit this room, stall her."

"What? Why?"

"No questions," I snapped. I was getting antsy. I couldn't spot Irene from where we were, and Easton needed as much uninterrupted time as I could get him. "Are you helping or not? I have to go."

Drew gave me a puzzled look but nodded. I squeezed his arm, and we took off in opposite directions.

I spotted Irene by the bar, talking to a few of the ladies from the admin team. She looked engrossed in the conversation, but she could decide to go looking for her date at any moment.

I hung around and kept one eye on her and one on the balcony door. Drew had planted himself on the other side of the bar, casual as ever, a big grin on his face, seemingly chatting some girl up.

Barely a few minutes later, Judge Keating came back into the function room. The look on his face was grave, tinged with anger. A few people tried to flag him down, but he beelined for the exit, ignoring them all.

I glanced at the balcony door, then at the judge's retreating back. Why hadn't Easton come back? Was he in trouble?

He was a big boy; I had to trust he could handle himself. I took off after the judge.

Judge Keating reached the bottom of the stairs just as I got about halfway down. Praying I was far enough away from the entrance that no one would hear me shout, I called his name.

He turned in a huff, his mouth open—ready to tell me to fuck off, probably— but I cut off whatever he'd been about to say. "Fight for the things that you care about, but do it in a way that will lead others to join you."

Donna had kept a poster with those words above her desk since our first day of high school. I'd memorized it over the years, and judging by the way Keating stopped and stared at me, it was a good thing my study mind wasn't completely useless.

"Please, sir. *Please*. Do the right thing." I slowly descended the rest of the stairs as I spoke, putting all my desperation and earnestness into my words.

He didn't say anything. He just watched me for another moment, then turned and walked away. He looked tired.

As the judge disappeared down the path toward the parking lot, I wrapped my arms around myself, sighed, and turned my face to the sky. Out of the corner of my eye, up on the edge of the balcony, movement caught my attention.

I looked over and immediately recognized Easton's silhouette, leaning on the railing.

A second set of stairs rose up the side of the building, hugging the breath-taking cliffs below on its way up to the balcony. I started climbing.

The stars were much brighter out here in the hills; I hoped their glow had given us a little bit of luck.

CHAPTER TWELVE

Easton

It was a clear night. Devilbend glittered in the distance below, but it didn't have anything on the stars above. The night sky was resplendent, shining down on us all through the crisp night air.

The cold of the sleek iron railing bit into my forearms, but I couldn't find it in me to move—just as the glorious night sky could no longer hold my attention, despite the fact that my face was turned up to it.

My focus was on Harlow.

Her slow approaching steps sounded like inevitability. What was done was done, and an odd kind of calm had spread through me after Judge Keating left. No point in worrying about what was to come. I was beginning to accept just how little control I had over anything.

She came to stand next to me, hands on the railing, and glanced around at the empty balcony. It curved around the modern building, covering the length of the wall of glass that faced the city. The night was cold enough that only the occasional smoker had come out, and they stayed grouped around the chairs and tables (and ashtrays) near the opposite end. Here, nothing but a set of stairs and concrete was at our backs—the building's curve hiding us from view.

Once Harlow saw we were as safe as we could get, she turned her eyes up to the sky too. "How did it go?" she asked, her voice soft.

I sighed and stared at my hands. I moved the tip of my finger up and down the fingers of my other hand reflexively. I was doing the breathing technique out of habit more than anything; I felt strangely calm.

"OK, I think," I finally answered. "He didn't immediately admit to everything and join the take-Ocean1k-down crew or anything. But he didn't deny it either."

I'd approached Judge Keating just as he left the bathroom, and told him I needed to speak to him about an extremely sensitive, urgent matter. By some miracle, that was enough to convince him, and he followed me out to the same spot where I now stood with Harlow.

I hadn't wasted time or minced words with the judge. I just got right to the point.

"I know you have a gambling problem, sir," I said. "And I know it's cost you almost everything you own."

His eyes narrowed and his chest puffed out as he took a small step away from me. "Who are you? What the hell is this?"

"Please, Your Honor." I held a placating hand out to him and hoped the respectful title would keep him listening. "I just want to warn you. That's all. I'm not the only one who has this information, and I believe the other party means to use it to blackmail you—if they haven't already."

"What other party?" he spat. "How do I know it's not you who intends to blackmail me?"

"Because I would've done so already. I simply mean to warn you. Maybe save you from my own fate."

When he just stared at me, his frown deepening, I elaborated. "I'm being blackmailed myself. And I don't know who it is, though I have my suspicions. I only know them as Ocean1k."

The judge had an excellent poker face—I supposed it came with his line of work—so I wasn't entirely sure if I imagined the little spark of recognition. "And what would you have me do? Since you seem to have all the answers."

"Come clean. Step down. Take away their power. If the truth is out, they can't use it against you."

"You don't know what you're asking," he hissed.

"I can't imagine," I rushed to agree. "But what's the alternative? They coerce you to make an unjust ruling, and when the truth comes out—because it *always does*—your entire career is tarnished, every case you presided over put into question. How many murderers and rapists would suddenly be able to appeal their sentences, their guilty verdicts?"

I paused to let that sink in. "All I'm asking you—a man who has dedicated his life to justice—is to consider what is right, what is righteous, what harm you would do if you allowed this to happen."

He stared at me, his mouth slowly lifting into a sneer. Without another word, he shook his head and stormed back toward the function room, bumping me as he passed.

I thought maybe he would go get security, or even insist they call the police. Part of me had kind of hoped he would. At least then it would have been over.

I gave Harlow the CliffsNotes version of my talk with Judge Keating. Then I glanced in the direction of the stairs, at the spot where Keating had stopped and Harlow had delivered her profound words like a one-two punch. I'd set him up, and she'd knocked him out. It felt good to have her standing with me.

"I guess we've done all we can," she said. "The rest is out of our control."

"Yeah." I smiled at her words—so similar to what I was thinking. "I didn't know you were a fan of the Notorious RBG."

She chuckled. "My sister had a poster of that quote up in her room for years. It just kind of got stuck in there."

"Well, I'm glad it did. It was the perfect thing to say."

She smiled and looked up to the sky again. "I'm sorry I showed up without you knowing. I didn't mean to make you more nervous."

"You have nothing to apologize for." I straightened and turned toward her, one hand on the railing next to hers. "I overreacted. I was just on edge. I'm glad you're here."

She nodded but didn't look at me. The other part of that conversation we'd had at the bar hung in the chilly air between us.

Without overthinking it, I decided to address it. "I'm sorry I didn't tell you Irene and I were coming here together."

She turned to face me, surprise lighting up her eyes before they quickly turned searching. Then she shivered. Goosebumps appeared all over her arms as she wrapped them around herself, and I realized that while I was wearing a suit, she was in a strapless dress, probably freezing her ass off.

I rubbed her arms up and down.

It was inappropriate. She was still a student; I was still a teacher. There was a room full of people *right there*. Irene was probably looking for me.

But I didn't care about Irene. She'd been flirting and trying to dance closer to me all night, and I'd spent half my time looking for the judge and the other half trying to put distance between us. I hoped she'd get the hint eventually, but I couldn't think about that now—not when Harlow was shaking and all I wanted to do was pull her against me. Because I *did* care about Harlow. I cared too much.

"Why didn't you tell me about Irene?" she asked, her voice nearly a whisper.

My hands paused on her arms. I'd brought it up, so I couldn't blame her for asking, but I hadn't allowed myself to think about why I'd kept that from her. I'd only come with Irene to give myself better cover for being here. There was nothing else to it. I supposed that was the crux of the matter—I didn't want Harlow to think there was something to it.

The implications of that were sobering, but I couldn't lie to her face.

I just couldn't quite bring myself to say it either—not when it didn't make sense in my own head yet.

"You know why," I whispered back. I knew she'd heard me, because we'd moved into each other's space as though it was second nature. I hadn't even noticed it happen, but now all she had to do was unwrap her arms from around herself, and they were at my waist.

"Why?" she pushed, her voice shaky.

Maybe it was the sense of calm, of inevitability, that had settled around us; maybe it was the fact that a growing part of me just wanted to let it all collapse in on itself. But this time, I didn't resist Harlow Mead. I didn't think about why I shouldn't, why it was wrong, what the consequences would be.

Her sweet vanilla scent was intoxicating, her shoulders warm and delicate under my hands, and the stars above would keep on shining bright for millennia regardless of what I did next.

So I kissed her.

I leaned into the moment, leaned into what I knew was wrong but felt *so fucking right* to every fiber of my being. I leaned in, and I pressed my lips to hers. My arms wrapped around her, holding her as closely as I needed to until she felt real. Until this moment felt real.

Her fingers dug into my back, creeping up under the jacket, and I threaded my hand into her hair. It was so soft, decadent, sinfully smooth.

Her tongue swiped along my bottom lip, and the kiss intensified. I sighed. She groaned. Our tongues moved against each other as we held on and stroked and licked and gripped and *drowned in the moment.*

A door opened, letting the sounds of the ongoing party drift out and mingle with the night.

We stopped kissing and stared at each other, wide-eyed, but her hands remained around me, and mine remained tangled in her hair. Reality was crashing down around us, as heavy and inevitable as the stars above, yet we couldn't—wouldn't—let go.

The door closed with a soft click, and several voices carried across to us— chatting, laughter, a lighter flicking.

"Holy shit," Harlow breathed, panting. The kiss had been intense. I'd never experienced anything like it—never allowed myself to get so lost in another person.

"Yeah," I croaked, my voice unsteady.

Her gaze darted behind me, the interruption registering, and her hands slid out from under my suit.

"*Holy shit.*" She still whispered, but this time the two words held a very differ- ent, much more panicked meaning.

I stroked her cheek one last time with my thumb and dropped my arms to my sides, stepping back. The air that was suddenly between us felt much more frigid than it had just moments ago.

Harlow turned and rushed down the stairs. She did it on her toes, keeping the killer heels from making any sound, but she still moved impressively fast, her fluffy skirt bouncing, her long hair flowing out behind her. I watched her until she disappeared down the path toward the parking area.

I always seemed to be watching her walk away. I didn't like it.

After a deep steadying breath, I straightened my clothes and wiped my mouth, just in case there was lipstick. My stomach dropped, and I felt sick.

Not for kissing her. I couldn't find it in me to feel bad about it, even though I knew I should. It was the secrecy—the way she had to run away when she realized someone might see us together—that made me want to lean over the railing and vomit.

I made myself push it all out of my mind and walk back toward the balcony doors. Irene walked out before I reached the doorway.

"There you are!" She beamed at me and stepped in close.

"Here I am." I did my best to smile, but it felt as though Harlow had taken all my joy with her when she ran into the night. "Shall we get another drink?"

"Actually"—she pulled on my elbow, stopping me midstride—"can we stay out here for a bit? I just managed to extract myself from a conversation with one of the students, and I don't want to get cornered again. He was weirdly intense."

I managed a little chuckle. "Someone has a crush?"

We wandered away from the smokers to stand by the railing, looking out at the view. I wished Harlow was still here—it felt wrong to be taking this magical scene in with someone else.

Irene scoffed. "On me? Highly unlikely. He's probably on drugs or something."

I turned to look at her, frowning. She was facing straight ahead but didn't seem to be taking in the glittery lights at all. Her eyes darted about, and she looked uncomfortable.

My evening with her had been . . . all right. I'd been distracted all night, of course, but she was a decent dancer, had told me a little about her family and hometown and how she always felt as though she didn't quite belong there. She'd asked me questions about myself and seemed genuinely interested.

So why couldn't I stop thinking about the high school student whose kiss I could still taste on my lips?

I felt like shit for crossing that boundary, I felt like shit for wanting to do it again, and I felt like shit for doing it while supposedly on a date with another woman.

I didn't know why Irene had such low confidence, and I definitely didn't want to add to it by leading her on, but I had to say something.

"I think you'll find that a lot of boys at Fulton are harboring secret crushes on you. Don't sell yourself short, Irene."

She looked at me with a little surprise in her wide eyes. When she leaned in, it was clear she was about to try to kiss me.

I turned for the door and held my hand out. "Let's have one more drink and a last dance before the night ends."

I could do without the dancing. I just knew I'd spend the whole time wishing it was a certain blonde turning in my arms. But I really needed the drink—for exactly the same reason.

CHAPTER THIRTEEN

Harlow

For once I wasn't dragging my feet when I walked into school on Monday. I'd gotten up early enough to do my hair and have breakfast. I hadn't heard from Ocean1k in nearly a week, we were hopefully undoing the situation with Judge Keating, and *Easton Monroe had fucking kissed me.*

I smiled every time I thought about it.

"Are you on something?" Amaya looped her arm through mine.

"What?" I laughed. "No."

She pursed her lips and looked at me suspiciously. "Are you sure? You usually don't say two words to us before school starts, and you definitely don't smile on Mondays. Something's up."

"I just slept well last night. That's all." I gave her arm a squeeze and leaned in to whisper, "But if I decide to take illicit substances during school hours, I'll be sure to let you know."

She laughed and thankfully dropped it.

An arm looped around my waist, and I turned to see Drew had joined us.

Shit! Drew! In all the excitement and emotions, I'd completely forgotten I needed to do damage control.

"Mind if I cut in?" He acted normal, flashing us his grin—the one that always seemed to imply a double entendre for no reason whatsoever.

Amaya's grip on my arm tightened. "Fuck off. She's mine."

Drew swooped down, picked me up, and swung me over his shoulder. I made a surprised high-pitched sound and scrambled to hold on to my backpack.

"Hey! Bring that back!" Amaya called after us as Drew carried me off down the hall.

"No!" he boomed back.

He didn't set me down until we reached an alcove under the main staircase. I righted my skirt and looked up into his very serious face. His arms were crossed menacingly over his chest, but it wasn't *at* me—it was *for* me. My friend was worried.

"OK, so . . . you seem upset," I hedged.

"Start talking, Harls. What the fuck was that on Saturday night?"

I cringed. "I can't tell you. I'm sorry."

"That's bullshit." He pointed at my chest. "I spent a good fifteen minutes talking to Irene about football while she tried to get away from me. At one point I had to physically step in front of her and reenact a catch so she wouldn't leave. She thinks I'm a fucking psycho now! Then when I went looking for you, you'd bailed! Now, I did all that because you're my friend and I love you, but I know you're in some kind of trouble, and I think I deserve an explanation."

Dammit, he did deserve one. I just couldn't give it to him. He might end up pissed at me, but telling him everything would just put him in danger.

"I'm sorry, Drew." I rubbed one of his extremely tense biceps.

After a moment, he uncrossed his arms with a resigned huff.

"Thank you so much," I went on. "You have no idea how grateful I am that you had my back. And you do one-hundred-percent deserve an explanation and my undying gratitude and, like, a mountain of triple-choc cookies."

He quirked one side of his mouth in an almost smile. They were his favorite.

"The thing is . . . I still can't really tell you."

"Why?" he gritted out.

"It's not just my story to tell." That was technically the truth. Easton and Ford were involved too.

"You're trying to protect someone?"

"Yes." *My sister, you, everyone around me.*

"Who?"

I shook my head. "I can't . . ."

"Goddammit, Harlow." He ran his fingers through his hair. "How much danger are you in? Please tell me something."

"It's better if you don't know."

"Do the girls know?"

"No. And you can't say anything." I got in his face a little, hoping to convey how serious I was.

"Maybe . . . shit. Maybe you should tell Donna. I don't know what this is about, but she'll know what to do. Donna can—"

"Donna is not my keeper." I loved my sister, and I wasn't embarrassed to admit I looked up to her. But I wasn't an infant or incapable of making my own decisions. Sometimes, I got a little frustrated at how easily people dismissed me. "It may come as a shock, but I am capable of taking care of myself."

"Of course you are." Now it was me crossing my arms and him rubbing them to calm me. "I didn't mean it like that. I just meant that if you won't talk to me about it, maybe you can talk to one of the girls. For support or whatever. I'm just worried about you, boo."

In that moment, Easton walked past. My eyes were drawn to him before I even knew why. He was in his school "uniform" of pressed slacks, shirt, and sweater, his messenger bag crossed over his body.

I looked over Drew's shoulder. Easton glanced at us, his eyes taking in our serious expressions, Drew's hands on me. In the space of a blink, he looked away and kept walking, but I could see that little tic in his jaw.

I hadn't spoken to him the day before. The kiss had been unexpected—more than welcome, but definitely unexpected—just like the longing in his gaze and the pain in his admission before he took me into his arms and made the whole world fall away.

I'd never been kissed like that. I'd kissed plenty of guys, but no one had made me feel like *that*. My lips tingled for hours after; not even weed could calm my mind and make everything fade away the way he had.

It was confusing in the best and worst ways. Where did this leave us? He'd always maintained a careful distance with me, but I'd felt something the entire time. Now I knew for sure he'd felt it too. But he was still a teacher, and we still had Ocean1k to contend with.

Maybe I hadn't texted him because I didn't know what to say.

As I stood in that alcove with Drew, I admitted to myself I was avoiding the issue. I'd wanted to just bask in the feeling he'd left in my chest and ignore all the crap stacked against us. But then he hadn't contacted me either, so maybe he was avoiding it too.

"Harlow?" Drew frowned, and I made myself focus.

"Drew." I took his hands and looked at him with as much conviction as I could muster. "If you care about me, if you love me like you say and want what's best for me, then please—I need you to trust me and keep this to yourself. I know it's unfair of me to ask you to keep this secret when I haven't even told you what it is. But I'm asking. Just let me figure this out. I just need some time."

The bell rang then, and I used it as an excuse to end this painful conversation. With one last pleading look, I left Drew alone in the alcove. I couldn't control what he did next; I just hoped I'd convinced him.

I didn't see Easton for the rest of the day, and I didn't message him either. What would I tell him? That Drew was just a friend, although we had been having regular sex until recently? But that hadn't happened since . . . what? Since

I got a crush on the incorrigible Mr. Monroe? Easton and I weren't even in a relationship. Would he even care? And then we'd *definitely* have to discuss the kiss, because that was why my relationship with Drew was relevant.

I gave up and spent the evening, and half the night, going down a research rabbit hole on the Unified Extensible Firmware Interface.

Easton didn't contact me either, and for the rest of the week, I didn't so much as spot him at the opposite end of a hallway at school. I was pretty positive he was avoiding me. At least Drew kept his mouth shut. He wouldn't stop throwing me meaningful looks, but he kept quiet.

That Saturday night, Amaya's mom was away, so we all went over to her house to hang out. A few cocktails in, I decided I'd had enough and finally messaged Easton.

Harlow: Are we OK?

The others were chatting and laughing around the firepit. Turner fell off his chair, making everyone laugh way more than it was actually funny.

Easton's reply came immediately.

Easton: Yes. Of course.

Then the three little bubbles appeared, indicating he was writing a message. Then they stopped and reappeared several times.

My heartbeat kicked up a notch, and I chewed on my bottom lip. What was he struggling so much to say?

Finally, he sent it.

Easton: I've just been trying to process everything. And I've been on edge waiting for any judge-related news. And I wasn't sure if you wanted to hear from me. I didn't mean to freeze you out. I'm sorry.

I rolled my eyes.

Harlow: I'm sorry too. I thought you didn't want to hear from me either.
   Easton: This is an unusual situation.
   Harlow: To put it mildly.

I hesitated, but the alcohol in my system gave me the reckless drive to just type and send the next bit.

Harlow: I've missed you.
   Easton: I've missed you too.

His response made me smile, and I decided to leave it at that for now. There was still so much left unsaid between us, but I wanted to see his face, hear his voice when we addressed the kiss. Or we could just go on ignoring it. I was fine with that too—as long as he kept kissing me.

News of the judge didn't come for nearly another week.

Easton and I had gone back to texting every day, talking about anything and everything while decidedly *not* mentioning the kiss. But we had started flirting more. It was subtle—an emoji here, a suggestive joke there—but I practically lived online. I was of the tech generation, born with a device in my chubby little hands. I knew digital flirting when I saw it.

Late on Friday afternoon, I had yet to change out of my uniform as I lay on my bed, scrolling through the AITA subreddit, when a notification came through. I'd put the judge's name, along with a handful of other carefully chosen keywords, on alerts.

I sat up and clicked through to an article on a reputable national news site: *Breaking. Judge Graham Keating steps down amid blackmail scandal. More details to follow.*

He was actually doing it.

I literally whooped as I got to my feet and ran to my wardrobe for some jeans and a baggy hoodie. Then I rushed down the stairs, barely containing my grin. I couldn't quite believe it, but several news sites were reporting it, so it had to be true.

I couldn't wait to tell Easton. I could've just texted him, but I wanted to see the look on his face when he found out. We fought back and it *worked*!

The front door swung open just before I reached it, and Donna and Hendrix came inside, laughing about something. Hendrix gave me a wave and a "hey" as he toed off his shoes.

"You going out?" Donna asked.

"Yeah. I won't be home for dinner. Can you let Mom and Dad know?"

"I think they're at some function in the city."

"Oh, OK, sweet! Bye!"

"Hey! Wait!" She grabbed my backpack, and I reluctantly turned back to face them. The need to get to Easton was making me bounce on my toes.

"Wassup?"

"You gonna be late?" Donna asked. "I was just about to text the others and invite them over. Turner has the night off. I thought we could all hang out."

"Ah, shit. Sorry, this was already planned. I'm catching up with my computer nerds." I had to tell her it was someone she didn't know all that well. Drew couldn't cover for me tonight if he was at my house.

"You gonna be doing molly?" She lowered her voice so Magda wouldn't hear. "Call me if you need a lift or anything."

"Yeah, I'd be happy to carry you to the car anytime." Hendrix grinned and flexed his bicep. I rolled my eyes. He was referring to the Halloween party a few months ago when Amaya and I got a little . . . *happy* . . . and Hendrix had to help Donna wrangle us into the car. The guys who organized that party were the ones I was supposedly hanging out with tonight. When they weren't coding into the wee hours of the morning, they went to raves and did drugs. Sometimes I joined them.

"Nah. It's more of a 'Red Bull and pizza in the glow of several computer screens' kind of night," I reassured them. "I'll bail early and come hang with you guys."

"All right. Have fun. Love you." Donna waved me off.

Hendrix pulled me in for a one-armed hug and kissed my cheek. "Bye, Baby Mead. Be safe."

"Yes, Dad." I frowned at him and shook my head.

He turned to my sister and grinned, his eyes practically sparkling.

She stared at him for a beat, incredulous, then crossed her arms. "No."

"Oh, come on. We'd make adorable babies."

"What the fuck is wrong with you? We're in high school!"

They started climbing the stairs.

"Obviously I don't mean right now. But eventually, *someday*, I'd like to put a baby in you. I love you. Fucking sue me!"

"The only thing you're putting inside of me in the near future is going to be wrapped in latex, Hendrix Hawthorn."

They bickered all the way up the stairs but were laughing and joking by the time they walked out of view. I smiled after them. This was exactly why I hadn't told Donna about Ocean1k and the threats. After going through so much, she was finally happy. She'd taken care of me so many times. It was my turn to keep her safe.

But first—celebration!

I let the grin take over my face as I rushed to my car.

My knee bounced with impatience at every red light on the way. When I finally got to Easton's building, several people were going in and out—getting home from work or heading out for dinners and drinks—but I hardly paid attention to the other three people in the elevator as I mashed the button.

Another guy got out on the same floor, and I made myself walk slowly, letting him go around a corner before I sped to Easton's door. I was excited, but I wasn't a complete dumbass—I didn't want anyone seeing me go into his apartment.

I knocked, fast and insistent, and the door opened quickly.

"What's wrong?" he asked in place of a greeting, scanning me for signs of distress.

"We did it!" I practically bounced into the apartment and pushed him backward to close the door.

"Did what?" His hand covered mine on his abs, and my fingers dug lightly into the soft cotton of his T-shirt, feeling the hard muscle beneath. My heart was already beating fast from excitement, but now it had another reason to. I was touching him; he was holding my hand.

I forced myself to focus. "Judge Keating has resigned. It's all over the news. The story just broke a couple hours ago."

"What?" His eyes widened and he nearly smiled, but he was too wary to let himself be happy just yet. "Are you serious?"

"Yes!" I nodded vigorously. "I'll show you."

I swung my backpack off, but he grabbed it and dropped it to the ground before I could reach for my phone. His arms wrapped around me tightly and lifted me clean off the floor. I held on to him and laughed, giddy, feeling as if I were flying, feeling better than I had in a long time.

"Holy shit!" He laughed too, the joyous sound reverberating through his chest and into mine. "Oh my god, I can't believe it."

He spun me around, my feet flying out, my hair flicking to one side with the sudden movement.

Then, as if we'd somehow agreed on it, we both fell silent and still. I felt him swallow and resisted the urge to wrap my legs around his hips. I didn't get the chance anyway. His strong arms slowly lowered me until my toes touched the ground, but he held on, still hugging me.

I'd hold on to him for as long as he held on to me. I'd never pulled away from him. It was always him pulling away.

But not this time. This time he held me a little tighter as he moved his head, his cheek scraping slightly against mine, the corner of his lips right next to mine.

Emboldened by what had happened when he last looked at me like that—on a terrace with the stars shining bright—I tilted my head and closed the distance. His lips were so soft, his tongue warm as it traced my bottom lip. I opened for him, and then we were really making out.

He shuffled me backward until my back hit the wall, and I threaded my hand through his hair. We were all hot breath and roaming hands. My nose bumped against his glasses, but he didn't even notice, and I didn't care. Because *he was kissing me again*, and nothing else mattered.

There was only his mouth devouring mine, the taut muscles of his back shifting under my hand, the hard evidence of his arousal trapped between our aching bodies.

Someone knocked at the door, and we sprang apart as though we'd been busted having sex at school or something, both of us breathing hard.

The knock came again—loud, impatient.

Easton righted his glasses and tiptoed over. His whole body tensed as he looked through the peephole, and when he pulled away to look at me, his eyes were full of panic.

"It's Coach Cooper," he hissed in a frantic whisper.

"Monroe!" Coach Cooper's unmistakable booming voice came from the other side of the door, accompanied by more knocking. "Open up. I know you're in there!"

"Fuck!" I mouthed.

"Hide." He pointed down the short hallway.

I grabbed my backpack and rushed off as silently as I could. As soon as I slipped behind the nearest door, I heard the distinctive sound of the front door latch opening and some muffled words from Easton.

"Not a fan of knocking?" The voice behind me yanked my focus away from whatever was happening at the front door.

Apparently, I'd decided to hide in Ford's room. He cocked an eyebrow as he removed his hand from his pants, not bothering to turn off the porn playing on his laptop.

"Ugh! Gross!" I looked away and lowered my bag next to the door, leaning my ear against it to listen.

Ford got off the bed and came to stand right behind me, copying my ear-to-the-door pose. "Hey," he whispered, "you're acting more batshit than usual. Wassup?"

"The coach from my school just showed up at your front door."

"Oh. Shit."

"Yeah, shit. Now shut up. I'm trying to listen."

CHAPTER FOURTEEN

Easton

I took a calming breath that didn't calm me at all, and opened the door.

"Dale, hey. What's going on?" I did my best to sound casual, mildly surprised—not absolutely terrified and completely guilty.

Coach Cooper stood in the hallway in jeans and a bomber jacket, hands on hips and mouth in a thin line. He just stared at me from under his red baseball cap, not saying anything.

After a few awkward moments, I had to fill the silence. "Uh. You all right, man? What . . . I mean, how do you know where I live?"

"You had a few of the faculty over for drinks when you first started at Fulton," he said, still glaring.

"OK, then—"

"Please tell me you do not have Harlow Mead in your apartment right now, Easton."

My jaw dropped, and I gaped at him. I hadn't expected him to just straight-up accuse me of exactly what I was doing like that. But I should've known—Cooper was a pretty direct guy. My mouth couldn't seem to form words. I hadn't planned for this, hadn't thought about what I'd say if he came right out and asked.

I must've looked as guilty as I felt.

"Goddammit, Monroe." He slapped the door open and shoved past me into my apartment. As he peered into the kitchen and living room, I closed the front door.

"Look, uh, where is this coming from?" I prodded, trying to figure out how much he already knew.

"I saw her come in here, so don't even try to deny it." He came to stand right in front of me. "I was on my way to a poker night with some buddies. One of 'em lives upstairs. I saw her come out of the elevator, and I watched her go right to your door and breeze on inside like she lives here. Please tell me there is a reasonable explanation for this. Where is she? The longer you hide, the worse this looks."

Before I could formulate a response, Ford's door opened. Laughter flowed out of his room just before Ford and Harlow came tumbling out together. He was behind her, one hand on her hip and the other up her sweatshirt, tickling her, exposing her belly button. She was laughing hysterically, trying to bat him away as they shuffled toward us. They were completely wrapped up in each other, not paying us any attention. They looked like . . . a couple.

My hands tightened into fists, and I ground my teeth together. What the fuck was he doing touching my girl like that? I loved my brother, but I was seconds away from pummeling him. And why did Harlow look as if she was exactly where she wanted to be—where she *should* be—in his arms? Younger and freer than my own. More appropriate than my own.

Harlow looked up first, her eyes going straight to Coach Cooper and widening almost comically. She stopped wriggling and slapped at Ford until he looked up.

He frowned at Coach, then down at Harlow. "What is it, babe?"

Babe? *Babe??* What the actual . . .

Then my jealous rage lifted enough for me to remember Dale Cooper was standing right next to me, and my brother and my . . . Harlow had come up with the perfect move to make this situation look as innocent as possible.

Harlow cleared her throat and pulled her sleeves over her hands. "Hi, Coach Cooper."

Ford draped an arm over her shoulders and gave Coach a little wave.

I forced a calm expression onto my face and stuffed my hands into my pockets. "Cooper, this is Ford, my little brother."

Coach propped his hands on his hips and frowned, looking from the happy couple to me and back again. "Right, so . . . " He gestured between Harlow and Ford with an upturned palm, then glanced at me.

I raised my eyebrows and gave him a thin-lipped smile, and he released a massive breath.

"Oh man, what a relief!" He chuckled. "Why didn't you just say so in the first place?"

"You kind of didn't give me a chance." I forced a chuckle of my own. "And I was pretty surprised to see you."

"Coach Cooper, am I in trouble?" Harlow asked in a small, vulnerable voice that almost made me burst out laughing.

"No, not at all," he quickly reassured her. "I just had to make sure you were safe."

She nodded and leaned farther into my brother.

"Is my brother in trouble?" Ford asked.

"No, son." Cooper shook his head, then turned to me. "But why'd you keep it a secret?"

Now it was my turn to lie convincingly. "I didn't. Just never came up. I'm not really into gossiping about who the students are dating." I added a derisive scoff to really sell it, and he bought it, laughing along.

"All right, all right. I'll get out of your hair." He was already moving toward the door. After inviting me to join his poker game upstairs, he left.

I locked the door and turned around. We all held still, waiting for a few moments to make sure he was gone. Then I collapsed against the door with my hands on my knees. "Holy shit."

Harlow shoved out of Ford's embrace with a disgusted look on her face—which I felt happier to see than I wanted to admit. "I feel dirty."

"Whatever. You love it." Ford winked at her and went to the fridge, not looking even remotely disturbed by the near miss.

"That was too close." I stood up straight and ran both hands through my hair. "Harlow, you can't just keep coming here. It's too dangerous."

"Why?" Ford took a massive gulp of milk right out of the carton. "She's got the perfect reason now." He wiggled his eyebrows at me, then at her, then drank more milk while lifting his T-shirt and gyrating his hips.

Harlow scowled at him. I marched over and slapped his hand away from his T-shirt, then turned to face Harlow.

"Stop." She held both hands out, and I snapped my mouth shut. "Can we please, *please*, just celebrate a win first? Let's give ourselves a second to enjoy this. Then we can get back to the angst and the crippling panic over everything else."

I sighed but couldn't hold back a smile. "So, Judge Keating actually did it, huh?"

She grinned. "Yeah. Because of us. For once, we actually stopped those bastards from accomplishing what they tried to use us for."

"Go team!" Ford whooped as he returned the almost empty carton to the fridge, then burped loudly. "So, did he come clean about his debts? The blackmail?"

"I don't know," Harlow said. "The news reports I read didn't have much detail —they were just breaking the story. I think we'll get more info over the next few days."

Ford took his phone out and tapped at it.

"I'm proud of you," I told Harlow, and she beamed. I couldn't believe she thought she was dumb. She was the most resourceful, determined, clever woman I knew. She'd done this. I may have played a small part in speaking with the judge, but none of this would've been possible if she hadn't gotten the information we needed.

"Oh, hey!" Ford rushed into the living room and grabbed the remote. "Apparently the dishonorable judge is going to hold a press conference any minute now."

Harlow and I followed him to the couch as he put the TV on a news channel. Harlow sat in the middle, and as we settled in, she shifted closer to me—her thigh against mine, her arm pressed against mine. So close. I wanted to put my arm around her and draw her even closer—but I knew I should put some distance between us.

God, I'd fucking kissed her just moments ago! *Again*. I'd been so caught up in the rush of excitement at her news, in her big smile and bouncing energy, in *her*. It felt so damn right holding her in my arms, breathing in her smell, tasting her soft lips.

But I knew it was wrong. I was the teacher and she was the student, and this couldn't happen as long as I was a teacher and she was a student.

But when I lay awake at night—worrying about Ocean1k and BestLyf, thinking about Harlow—I allowed my mind to consider what-ifs. The end of the school year wasn't that far away. She was a senior. I wasn't that attached to Fulton as an employer; I wasn't sure I wanted to be a teacher anymore at all. In another six months, if we lived through this, maybe . . .

The maybes made me smile in the dark like a teenage boy with his first crush.

I was stuck. Stuck between *knowing* it was wrong and *feeling* it was right— between wanting to draw her into my lap on the couch and knowing I should just go sit in the armchair. In the end I didn't do either. I stayed where I was, my body hyperaware of every single spot it connected with hers.

The presenter on the TV announced they had some breaking news and then cut to a live feed of the press conference. All three of us leaned forward. Cameras flashed and the room went quiet as a somber-looking Judge Graham Keating stepped up to a small podium.

"Good evening, ladies and gentlemen," he began. "As you all know, I have made the difficult decision to step down from my position as district judge of the United States District Court for the Northern District of California."

He talked about his career briefly and what it meant to him, then dropped the bombshell of his gambling addiction. The reporters started flashing their cameras again and firing off questions. The judge took it all in stride, gesturing for them to calm down.

"I will do my best to answer questions at the end. Please allow me to finish."

Once he had the room quiet again, he continued. He chose his words carefully, being very specific in what he said and what he left out—as any person with decades in the legal field would. He talked about his family and expressed deep regret for the hurt he had caused, then circled back to his position as a judge. Without saying whether he had made any rulings after being blackmailed, he made it clear blackmail attempts had been made.

The room once again erupted in a furor, cameras going off, reporters shouting questions about specific cases.

The judge waited again for quiet.

"I have just one last thing to say." He cleared his throat. "To the party who encouraged me to do the right thing and come forward, thank you. You know who you are, and despite my initial resistance . . ."

I frowned and leaned my elbows on my knees. He'd been *very* precise with his choice of words throughout, and the way he spoke now . . . it felt intentional. Like more than an acknowledgement.

The reporters launched into questions when he finished, but I'd stopped paying attention. I was staring at Keating's face, my mind whirring. There had definitely been a pattern in what he'd said and the way he'd said it.

"Easton?" Harlow's hand on my shoulder made me realize she and Ford had been speaking. I hadn't heard any of it, too focused on what felt like a word on the tip of my tongue.

Ford leaned around her to stare at me.

Still half in my own head, I opened my mouth, then closed it. Then I snapped my fingers at Ford and mimed writing with my hands. He rushed to the table near the front door and passed me a notepad and pen.

"Are you OK?" Harlow asked, then turned to Ford. "Is he OK?"

"He's fine. He's just trying to puzzle something out. He'll be normal again once it's out of his head. Or as normal as East's ever been."

I frowned at the blank piece of paper, then looked back up at them. "I need to hear it again. Is there a replay?"

"It's still going but . . ." Harlow tapped furiously at her phone as Ford muted the TV. "Here. This website has it from the start."

She handed me the phone. I pressed play, put it on the coffee table, and focused on the notepad and the judge's words.

Once he started the last part of his speech—the one about deciding to go public and doing the right thing—certain words started to jump out at me. I wrote them all down.

Party.

Education.

Schooling.

Faculty.

Class.

The video ended, and I stared at the words on the page.

"I think the judge is trying to give us a message," I said with a tentative smile.

"What do you mean?" Harlow glanced at the notepad.

"The speech pattern and the choice of words—it was different from the rest of what he said. I think he's trying to point us in Ocean1k's direction."

"Are you sure the message is for you?" Ford asked.

I shrugged. "No. I could be misinterpreting it. But he said, 'To the party who encouraged me to do the right thing . . .' The *party*, not the person—which would've made much more sense as a word choice in this context. I think he's referring to the party when we talked." I held up the notepad. "When you consider all these other words—all in place of synonyms that would've made more sense . . ."

"He's saying Ocean1k is someone at Fulton," Harlow said. "Faculty . . . a teacher?"

"Maybe. But it could be anyone. He could've just inserted *faculty* as a word for us to pick up on."

"Hold up." Ford rubbed his chin. "He could be alluding to the college where he lectures, his alma mater, his kids' school. It could be anywhere."

"It's the only lead we have." I sighed. "It makes sense to check out Fulton first, then maybe the other schools Keating has connections with. Is there any hacking mojo you two can do to figure this out?"

Ford groaned, and Harlow snorted. "Hacking mojo."

"Yeah, old man, we can try a few things." Ford got to his feet.

Harlow cleared the dining table while Ford brought out his laptop and her backpack. They set up next to each other, fingers flying across screens as they seemingly spoke in another language. The only words I understood were basic English ones like "How about . . ." and "What if we . . ." and "The school is probably . . ." The rest went way over my head.

I stood next to the table, feeling utterly useless and more than a little jealous of this complex thing my brother shared with Harlow. This was a huge part of her life, and I had no idea how to even talk to her about it.

I shook myself out of it and leaned on the table. "Guys, is there anything I can do to help?"

"Get us some pizza," Ford said, not taking his eyes off the screen.

"And Red Bull." Harlow's eyes stayed glued to her screen too. "It might be a long night."

"And M&Ms," Ford added, then at the same time, they said, "Peanut butter."

They grinned at each other and fist-bumped before focusing back on their laptops.

I shoved the jealousy down again. It was an ugly emotion, and I didn't like feeling it—especially when it came to the two people I cared about most.

I grabbed my keys and headed out for supplies. If that was all I was good for during this part, I would do a damn good job of it.

CHAPTER FIFTEEN

Harlow

Ford started snoring sometime after midnight, sprawled on the other side of the couch, head thrown back, mouth hanging open. Not that it mattered—I couldn't sleep anyway. I tucked a throw blanket over him, checked the script we had running, and yawned so wide my jaw clicked.

We'd debated how to go about gaining access to the school network. Fulton actually had decent security, but it wasn't *that* good. In the end, we decided to keep it simple and brute-force our way in. While we waited for the script to run, we'd discussed how to even look for signs of Ocean1k when we didn't have much more than a hunch to go on.

They were good. They would've covered their tracks, would probably avoid using the school computers. But everyone makes mistakes, and we figured the best place to start would be the firewall logs. So, while the brute-force script did its thing, we wrote another script to run once we got access. We'd finished over an hour ago. Now there was nothing to do but wait.

A soft ping went off—a message notification on Ford's computer. He'd been messaging with someone on and off all night, occasionally smiling at the screen. I knew that look. It was the same look I gave my phone when I was talking to Easton. Ford was digitally flirting.

Deciding not to invade his privacy, I hauled myself off the couch and padded on bare feet into the kitchen, pulling the sleeves of my hoodie over my hands and the hem over my butt. I'd ditched the jeans after Easton went to bed. They cut into my waist, and the hoodie covered my boy shorts anyway.

Just as I shuffled up to the fridge, Easton appeared out of the hallway. We both paused and took each other in, his eyes lingering on my bare legs, mine devouring his chest—the ink, the dips and curves of his muscles, the light hair over his pecs. He was in nothing but light lounge pants hanging low on his hips. I'd forgotten what I came into the kitchen for, but now I was desperate for a glass of water.

Neither of us turned the light on. The moon shone in through the window over the sink, casting everything in a silvery, muted glow between the shadows.

I opened the cupboard closest to me, looking for glasses, but it contained only food, cans, cereal boxes. I moved to the next one, but then the tap came on. He was there, filling a tall glass. I sidled up next to him, and he handed the water to me before getting some for himself. We drank deeply, staring at each other over the rims. The cool water washed down my fevered insides, but I was still thirsty when I finished. Parched for a man I couldn't have.

He took the glass from me and placed both in the sink, then leaned heavily on the edge, dropping his head. He looked . . . defeated.

"Everything just keeps getting more complicated," he whispered, and I moved closer, drawn in by his hushed tone and his melancholy. "I feel like every move I make, every decision, is the wrong one and just makes everything worse. I feel like . . . I'm not sure there's a way out of this, and I don't know how to keep you safe. How to keep Ford safe. I . . ." He shook his head and sighed, the muscles in his back tensing and relaxing with the movement.

He was just as worried and stressed about this situation as I was. But where I felt we were in this together, trying to figure it out *together*, apparently he felt it was his responsibility to take care of us. I didn't know why he put that burden on himself, but I couldn't just stand there and watch him suffer. The need to comfort him was impossible to resist.

I placed a palm between his shoulder blades. He tensed, the muscles under my hand going hard and unyielding, but after a moment he relaxed, and I took that as a sign. Dragging my hand slowly down his back, I stepped in closer behind him. The urge to just stand there and run my hands over his back until I memorized every bump and smooth surface, every detail of the tattoos there, was strong. But I resisted. Slowly, cautiously, I wrapped my arms around his waist and pressed my front to his back.

We'd hugged before; he'd held me when I was scared, in rushed, surprised moments. Never like this. Never with so little clothing between us. I allowed my forehead to rest on his spine and breathed him in. So warm, so strong yet so fragile in my embrace. He smelled like sleeping in on a Sunday morning—warm and fresh and something distinctly Easton. With a sigh, he relaxed further, and my arms tightened around him.

After a few blissful moments, his hand landed on my forearm, and he wrapped his fingers around it. "Harlow . . ." His voice was low, strained, but I could feel my name in his chest as he breathed the syllables. "We can't . . . this is so wrong."

"But why does it feel so good?" He shivered slightly when my own whispered words flittered over his bare back.

"I don't know." His answer came out more like a plea. For what? Strength to stop? The will to keep going?

He hadn't thrown me off or run away from me, the way he usually did. He'd even inadvertently admitted that having my arms around him felt good. My heart started to race, and I moved forward the fraction of an inch necessary to bring my lips into contact with his back, to place a gentle, lingering kiss there.

He shuddered again, so I kissed him again, a little firmer. My boobs pressed against him, my body trying to get closer without me even meaning to. He caressed my arm once, twice. Then he gripped my wrists and pulled my arms apart, stepping out of them.

I took one stunned step back.

"I'm your teacher." He scrubbed a hand down his face as he turned toward me. "You shouldn't even be in my house."

"You're not my teacher. You just happen to teach at my school."

"I'm older and in a position of power. I have a duty of care. It's still wrong."

"I'm eighteen. I'm an adult, and there's barely five years between us."

"This crazy, stressful situation has forced us to be close, lean on each other. You should be free—be with someone like Drew." He was practically pleading with me, but when he said Drew's name, his teeth clenched. I remembered how his jaw had ticked when he passed by us in that alcove under the stairs.

"That's why you wouldn't talk to me for a week?" My hands tightened into fists. Stupid, stubborn man. "Because you think I want to be with Drew?"

He didn't say anything. Just stared at me, his eyes narrowing.

I threw my hands up and let them flop to my sides. "I'm not with him. I don't want to be. He's just a friend. I want . . ." *you.* It was on the tip of my tongue, but I couldn't bring myself to say it when he was looking at me with so much disapproval in his eyes.

"I'm a teacher. You're a student." This time his voice had an edge of frustration to it. It felt as if he was talking down to me, and I *fucking hated* it. I was pretty sure I was falling in love with Easton Monroe, but I wasn't about to stand there and beg him to love me back like some desperate teenage girl. Even if I was exactly that.

"I'm not an idiot," I gritted out. "I know what the laws are. I know what you stand to lose if anyone finds out. But I see the way you look at me, I feel the way you hold me, and I know you feel it too. And who I want to be with is not up to you. It's up to *me.* You don't have to return my feelings, but you don't get to tell me I can't have them. So don't use your teacher voice on me like you're explaining uniform regulations to a simpleton. I may be failing most of my classes, but *I'm not a fucking idiot.*"

Tears choked me, pressing behind my eyes, threatening to betray just how hurt I was. I turned to storm away—to find my pants and leave—but Easton shot forward and grabbed my wrist. He swung me back around and pulled me into a fierce hug, one arm around my waist and the other around my neck. I held him just as tightly; I didn't want to, but my body couldn't resist his. My eyes drifted closed as I breathed him in, his chest heaving under my cheek, and a few tears spilled over.

He ran a hand through my hair, then pulled back just enough to press his forehead to mine. I kept my eyes closed. I couldn't look at him, couldn't stand not knowing what I'd see in his eyes. He wiped the tears off my right cheek with his thumb.

"You are not an idiot, Harlow." His words mingled with my panting breath. We were so close. "You are my weakness and my strength."

And then he kissed me, and my eyes flew open to look into his stormy ones. The kiss was firm, determined, his hands clutching me as though I might do exactly what he'd told me to do—leave.

As our bodies responded to each other, the kiss deepened naturally, his tongue swiping against mine. A low moan sounded at the back of his throat, part pained, part pure ecstasy. His eyes closed as he lost himself in the moment, the sensation, and I let myself get lost in him too.

We shuffled until my hips hit the edge of the counter, and then he picked me up and sat me on the edge, never breaking the kiss for a second. I wrapped my legs around him and rolled my hips. He was hard as steel, and it felt *so fucking good*.

Eventually he pulled his lips away from mine, dragging them down my jaw and over to my neck. I tilted my head to give him access as he pulled my hoodie aside as far as it would go. My hands slid down the rigid planes of his back all the way to his pants, and I started to tuck my fingers under the waistband, ready to grab his bare ass, aching to feel the muscles contracting and relaxing as his hips rolled against mine.

A beeping sound from the living room cut through the silence. It wasn't even that loud or particularly shrill, but in the dark, quiet apartment it may as well have been a siren. I gasped and we pulled apart, staring at each other, panting.

"Harlow!" Ford called from the living room.

Easton's eyes widened, and he took a shaky step away from me, running his fingers through his hair.

"Harlow! We're in," Ford shouted again.

"Fuck," I muttered and jumped down from the counter, pushing past Easton and rushing into the living area. My entire lower half was throbbing, my underwear soaked. All I wanted was to turn around and go back to him, keep doing what we were doing until we were both naked and he was inside me. But I couldn't do that with his brother a few feet away, our hope for freedom at his fingertips.

Ford was bent over his laptop, his face illuminated by the glow as his fingers flew over the keyboard. I sat down next to him, the two of us practically cheek-to-cheek as we both stared at the screen. He was already looking for the firewall logs.

The couch dipped on my other side, and Easton leaned in too, squishing me between them. Suddenly I found it hard to breathe. My mind may have been focused on the computer, but my body was still in the kitchen, wondering why the fuck it was no closer to release.

I sat up straight, forcing Easton to make room for me.

"What are we looking at?" Easton asked as Ford found the logs, then ran the script to search for infrequently occurring ports.

It probably looked like gibberish to him, but to me and Ford, the activity on the screen made perfect sense. If Ocean1k had used a school computer at any point, we figured there would be some evidence of that. They would use proxies to hide what they were doing—both Ford and I would've done the same—and that would show up in the logs.

We checked the past month. It only took a few minutes, and there it was. That rush of excitement—the euphoric feeling of getting code to work and getting the exact result you were aiming for—coursed through me and made me grin.

"This, my inferior and worse-looking brother, is exactly what we were hoping to find." Ford ran both hands down his face, smiling.

I leaned forward and took over. My fingers flew over the keyboard, my eyes tracking the screen as I looked for the MAC address responsible for the infrequently occurring ports. And there it was, the six sets of two characters separated by dashes, indicating a specific computer in the school. Next, I looked for a record of which MAC addresses corresponded to which computers in which locations in the buildings.

I dug deeper, looking through names assigned to workstations and rosters. "It's a workstation in . . . the gym?"

"The gym?" Easton scratched his head. "That's where all the PE teachers' offices are, I think."

"It's one of the eight workstations in that part of the school. Just looking for the name now . . . oh shit."

Easton and Ford leaned in to look at the name on the screen.

"Dale Cooper is Ocean1k?" Easton's voice went high. "Friendly, clueless Coach Cooper who was in my apartment earlier?"

"Maybe." I flopped back against the couch. I had no idea how to feel about this.

"Anyone could be a hacker, bro," Ford said. "You never know what people are doing in their private lives. Anyway, it may not even be him."

"What do you mean?" Easton pointed at the name on the screen.

"I mean that, yes, that computer is assigned as his workstation, but it's entirely possible someone else used it when he was at lunch or out sick or whatever. It could still be someone else. This could be completely unrelated to Ocean1k and our situation."

"That's true." Easton nodded. "Why have me steal his own key card off him? Why barge in here like he was legitimately worried about a student? He has a wife and kids. Why would he be doing this?"

He made some good points, but my gut said we were on the right track. It all lined up too well for it to be coincidence. "It's actually kind of genius in an evil way, if you think about it. He acts dumb about the key card for plausible deniability; comes here to try to get more dirt on us maybe? Catch us in the act. He was at the fundraiser. Maybe he saw us together and wanted . . . uh." I cut myself off and glanced at Ford before coming out and saying we'd kissed.

The jerk was fighting a smile. I gave him a sweet one of my own and asked, "Hey, Ford, who's been DMing you all night?"

His smug smile fell, and he looked away. Easton got us back on topic, discussing the possibility that Coach Cooper was Ocean1k.

We must've spent a good hour talking about different possible scenarios and arguing about what to do next. But we were all exhausted, so instead of getting more energized as we spoke, we all melted into the couch. We slouched, legs on the coffee table, heads lolling on cushions as our words began to slur and the gaps between sentences lengthened.

The laptops had been closed, and the only light came from the TV—infomercials on mute.

Ford yawned. "I gotta get some sleep. Let's talk about this when we can think straight. Use protection, you two." He managed a teasing grin before dragging his feet to his bedroom.

Easton and I both gave him the finger. I just couldn't muster the energy for a witty comeback.

"Sorry," Easton said around a yawn. "My little bro is a bit of an . . ." He trailed off and sighed, his eyes heavy.

"Sack of shit?" I supplied helpfully.

He nodded.

"You should get some sleep too. Go to bed." I gave him a half-hearted nudge.

He shook his head and wrapped an arm around my shoulders, sliding down to one side of the couch and taking me with him. "Nah. I wanna stay here with you." His eyes were closed as he said it. He was practically asleep.

I leaned my head on his shoulder, and his arm around me tightened. I knew I should get up and go home, or at least find somewhere else to sleep. But despite the heated words we'd shared in the kitchen earlier, despite the fact that he kept trying to put distance between us, I didn't want to be anywhere other than right where I was—in his arms. I didn't have the energy to pretend otherwise.

I'll just have a little snooze, and then I'll head home, I told myself as I pulled a throw blanket over us. I fell into a deep sleep after that. I hadn't fallen asleep that easily or slept that peacefully since I was a child.

CHAPTER SIXTEEN

Easton

An irritating sound was trying to drag me from sleep—some kind of crispy grating that made me groan and shift slightly. I didn't want to wake up. I was warm and comfortable and Harlow's hair smelled amazing. Her body tangled up with mine felt amazing. I smiled and held her a little tighter.

Then, despite how badly I didn't want consciousness to invade and ruin everything, my eyes flew open. Harlow shifted against me, disturbed by my movement.

The irritating crunching sound came again, and I frowned, looking around.

"Morning!" Ford stood grinning at the end of the couch, a bowl of cereal in his hands.

Fuck. I dragged a hand down my face. Obviously, we'd fallen asleep on the couch, and judging by the brightness of the room, we'd stayed there for quite some time.

Harlow rubbed her eyes and stretched. Her legs tugged the blanket down, revealing her exposed stomach where the hoodie had ridden up. "Oh man. What time is it?" she half mumbled and snuggled into me, wrapping an arm around my waist. She still hadn't opened her eyes.

"It's nearly eleven, sleeping beauty." Ford took another obnoxiously loud mouthful of cereal.

Harlow shot up, propping herself up on one hand. But she wasn't embarrassed or panicked that my little shit brother had caught us in such a compromising position.

"Are you serious?" She gaped at him. "It's *eleven*?" She reached over me to grab her phone off the coffee table, and her breasts pressed into my belly. I gritted my teeth, trying to focus on anything but how fucking soft they felt.

Ford burst out laughing, a bit of milk dribbling down his chin. I glared at him, then gently tugged Harlow's hoodie back into place.

At the touch, she looked at me and smiled. "I can't remember the last time I slept so long. Or so soundly."

I frowned. "It's understandable that with everything going on, your sleep would suffer."

"Yeah." She bit her bottom lip. "I've had insomnia since before all this shit, but the recent stress definitely hasn't been helping."

"I'm sorry. That sucks." I absentmindedly dragged my fingertips up and down her arm, and for a moment, we just stared at each other. It was so . . . comfortable. Everything about being around her was comfortable—the conversations, the silences, the touches and looks and . . . feelings. Way too comfortable.

"If you two are gonna bang again, can you at least go into another room?" Ford said.

"You're such a fucking creep." Harlow threw a cushion at him, and he laughed as he dodged it.

After Harlow and I took turns in the bathroom, we congregated in the kitchen. Ford had actually made himself useful for once and cooked bacon and eggs. The toast was a little burned, but I appreciated the effort.

Once we finished stuffing our faces, we sat around the little dining table and drank coffee. Harlow took hers with three sugars and just a splash of cream. I found myself filing that information away, as if I'd have use for it again in the near future.

I resisted rolling my eyes at myself and instead started the conversation. "So, do we have enough to go to the police?"

They both shook their heads.

"Nope," Ford said. "The logs by themselves aren't enough to prove anything. Could someone be logging in with Coach's details?"

Harlow swung her head from side to side and pursed her lips. "It's possible but not very likely. The logs indicate long periods of that username being on that computer. I'm, like, ninety-seven percent sure it's him."

"We need to eliminate that three percent. We need to do this once and do it right. Not to mention we don't know if we can trust the police," Ford said.

I reeled back in surprise. "What do you mean? Why can't we trust the police?"

"This is Devilbend. BestLyf's HQ is here. If they're willing to blackmail a judge, it's not exactly a stretch to assume they have some dirty cops in their pockets," Harlow explained.

"Shit." I deflated, resting my elbows on the table and taking another miserable sip of my coffee. Why did this constantly feel like two steps forward and one step back?

"Let's just focus on one issue at a time." Harlow squeezed my hand. "We need to confirm it's him, and we need to get evidence. We need access to either his computers or his phone."

Ford nodded and sighed, as though he'd been thinking the same thing but didn't like it. "Ocean1k's fucking good though. Won't be easy."

"OK, well"—I sat up—"we're at school five days a week. I'm sure we can find a way to hack his computer or whatever."

Again, both Ford and Harlow shook their heads; I felt as if I was contributing nothing to the conversation.

"Ocean1k's not stupid enough to leave anything incriminating on a work computer," Ford said. "We'd need to get access to their personal computer— likely at their home."

"Great. More break and enter." I rolled my eyes.

"Yeah, I'd rather avoid that too. I prefer to commit my crimes remotely with an internet connection," Harlow quipped.

"His phone then," Ford said.

Harlow nodded. "Right. We start keeping an eye on him as much as we can, track his movements, try to see where he keeps his phone. In the meantime, we have to go on like nothing's changed, pretend we know nothing."

"I don't know how the hell I'll be able to look at him without showing my hatred on my face," I gritted out.

"You have to." Harlow finished off her coffee. "We all have to. Or this was for nothing."

For a while we all just sat around lost in our own thoughts, which were probably all along the lines of *This is such a load of shit.*

Harlow sighed and slumped back in her chair. "As if school wasn't miserable enough as it is."

"We'll get through this." I gave her an encouraging smile.

"I hope so. Everything other than the lunch period sucks major balls. I'm failing everything, and the only reason I even remotely still look forward to it is because I get to see my friends every day. That and the cafeteria does amazing fries."

"So quit." Ford collected our empty mugs.

I shot him a disapproving frown, but he ignored me and leaned on the sink.

Harlow smiled wryly. "Trust me, I've thought about it. But what would I do? And I don't know how my parents would take it, and . . . I just don't need any more stress right now."

"I can help you get your grades up," I said, and she gave me a thin smile. My heart sank. Why did it feel as if I'd said the exact worst thing I could possibly have said?

"Bro, it sounds like she enjoys going to school about as much as you enjoy teaching. Harls, baby. I could get you a job."

"Really?" She got up and stood at the counter.

I folded my arms. I didn't like that my brother had the answers she wanted when I didn't. Or maybe it was just easier to focus on that little pang of jealousy than to acknowledge the other thoughts that flitted through my mind at the idea of Harlow quitting school. If she wasn't a student anymore and I wasn't a teacher . . . she was eighteen; we were consenting adults.

Maybe there could be cause for me to know how she takes her coffee in the morning.

An image of me bringing her a cup as she stirred awake in my bed, my sheets wrapped around her hips, flashed in my mind. I yearned for it so painfully that I had to stop myself from trying to convince her to quit school myself.

"You've got some serious skills." Ford shrugged. "I could put in a good word with my boss. You'd need some training, and it would be an entry-level wage, but you could totally work in cybersecurity."

"Without a high school diploma or a college degree?" Harlow sounded hesitant but hopeful.

Ford pointed at himself and grinned. "College dropout. Most tech companies care much more about your experience than the fancy pieces of paper you happen to have."

They chatted about it while I forced myself to remain silent, fearful of arguing too hard for either side. Then Harlow's phone went off.

"Shit. I gotta get home before anyone gets too suspicious. I ditched my friends last night." Within moments, she gathered her things and disappeared with a quick goodbye.

"You know." Ford drew out that last word, and I raised an eyebrow. "If she was no longer a student at Fulton and you were no longer a teacher . . ."

"I know." I groaned and dropped my forehead on the table with a thump.

Ford just laughed.

"You're such an asshole." My words were muffled by the tabletop, but judging by the renewed laughter, he heard me just fine.

My game plan on Monday was to avoid Dale as much as possible. I needed a bit of time to acclimate to this new information before I started stalking him to find a way to steal his phone. *When did this become my life?*

I went straight up the back stairs to my office and settled in at my desk. There was still half an hour before the first period, and I planned to go through emails.

I'd only managed to reply to two emails before someone knocked at my door and stepped inside.

"Knock knock."

Irene's voice made me pause, fingers hovering over the keyboard. I forced a neutral, polite smile onto my face before I looked up. "Good morning."

She smiled at me sweetly.

"You're in early." She walked up to my desk, and I leaned back in my chair, trying to make it look casual and not send her any mixed signals. "I was just going to drop this by, but now I get to see you. Lucky me."

"Yep. Lucky." My smile felt tight. "What is it?"

"Oh!" She pulled a cardboard box out from under her arm. "No idea. It was delivered to the school for the careers advisor." She dropped the box on the desk and leaned over it, flashing me her cleavage. "How was your weekend?"

I made a point of not looking at her tits and did my breathing exercise, my finger tracing a path up and down the fingers of my other hand. It didn't do much to calm me.

"It was good. Nothing special. I hung out with my brother." *And found out who was blackmailing me.*

"That's nice. Are you two close? Do you have any other siblings?"

She was being friendly, as she'd been at the fundraiser, but I was too on edge about Cooper. "Irene, I'm so sorry, but I'm really behind on my emails, and I want to knock some more out before my first class."

"Say no more." She straightened. "You can tell me more about your family over coffee some time."

"That sounds great. Have a good day." Hopefully, if I dodged her messages and avoided making plans, she'd get the hint.

"You too!" she called and closed the door behind her.

My phone vibrated with a text just as I opened the package she'd dropped off. The box was filled with brochures for a youth program at BestLyf. I nearly threw the whole damn thing across the room, then checked my phone—with the sinking feeling I already knew who it was.

Sure enough, a message from Ocean1k popped up on the screen.

Ocean1k: Start handing the brochures out to students. Anyone is good, but find a way to recruit these specific individuals.

They listed about a dozen names, kids of some of the most prominent and influential people in Devilbend. Business people, politicians, celebrities. Interestingly, neither of the Mead sisters was on the list, despite their parents being very rich and connected.

Easton: So you're admitting that you work for BestLyf then?

Ocean1k: Just do what you're told.

Easton: This is beyond unethical. These are kids!

Ocean1k: Get off your high horse, Mr. Monroe. They're only kids when it suits you.

I frowned, momentarily confused by the message, but then an image came through. It was a perfectly framed nighttime shot, the glass railing reflecting the lights of Devilbend below. But the focus was me and Harlow—kissing. Wrapped up in each other. Holding each other as though we were one another's oxygen supply and we were a thousand feet below the surface.

I simultaneously wanted to throw my phone across the room and print the image out so I could frame it.

It was taken from below, probably from the bushes that lined the path near the edge of the cliff. Where was Coach Cooper during this time? I'd hardly even bothered to notice he was there that night. Was it possible he wasn't working alone? Now that he'd all but confirmed his involvement with BestLyf, there was no telling what kind of resources he had at his disposal.

The bell sounded, and I gathered my things. I needed to get to my first class and teach freshmen American literature. Joy. There was no time to dwell on the panic and despair. I had to pretend everything was fine. I'd been doing that for much longer than I cared to admit, so it shouldn't be that hard. Except I was reaching my limit.

No further messages came in from Ocean1k—he knew he had me.

Two steps forward and *two* steps back.

Despite my decision to avoid Dale until I could think his name without scowling, he found me anyway. I just wanted one day to get my shit together, so despite the fact that our paths hardly ever crossed at work, I'd gone off campus for lunch. I'd never seen anyone from Fulton at the little vegetarian café I sometimes went to, but as I finished my meal, in strolled Dale fucking Cooper.

I lowered the last spoonful of vegetable tagine back to the bowl and picked up my novel, forcing my face not to show my hate for the man stepping up to the counter and ordering a protein shake in an obnoxiously loud voice. I prayed he wouldn't notice me, but the place was tiny.

"Hey! Monroe!" He made his way over and took a seat in the chair opposite.

I gritted my teeth and forced a surprised smile onto my face before lowering my book. "Dale. Hello."

"Nice place, huh?" He looked around as if it were his café and he was proudly showing it off.

"Yep. They do a great veggie lasagne." *Please, for the love of god, just leave before I stab you in the eye with this fork.*

"Didn't even know it was here until one of the boys on the football team told me about it." He laughed, startling the woman at the table next to us. "I'm no vegetarian"—he made a disgusted face—"but I'm trying out this whole plant protein thing."

"Right." I nodded with a tight smile, fiddling with the fork.

"Man, that was crazy the other night at your place." He leaned in and lowered his voice. My hand on the fork stilled, and I looked him dead in the eyes. "If you knew the crazy shit that was running through my mind. You have no idea how relieved I am there's a reasonable explanation."

He'd followed me here to taunt me about Harlow. He fucking *knew*—he'd just sent me a photo of us kissing earlier that day. He just wanted to torture me about it.

I'm doing what you asked. Just leave me the fuck alone. It was on the tip of my tongue. I was ready to drop the bullshit and let my frustration out.

But I thought of Harlow and Ford. We needed proof.

"Me too," I said instead, leaning back and managing a smile.

His order was called then, and he left just as abruptly as he'd arrived.

"I'll be seeing you, Monroe." He pointed and winked at me, as if we shared a secret.

It took me the rest of my lunch time to calm down enough so I could head back to work and pretend it was another boring Monday.

CHAPTER SEVENTEEN

Dodgeball was for commoners. At Fulton Academy we did equestrian for physical education.

Sports were the only subjects I ever got decent grades in, so I actually enjoyed this part of my day. The sun streamed in through the open stable doors as I climbed onto Harriet—a Friesian. Like the rest of the class, I'd geared up in a full riding outfit and helmet and saddled the horse myself. It was part of the lesson. Now we got to go outside and ride them.

I smiled at Amaya sitting on the horse next to me, her long hair braided down her back. She looked like royalty.

"I wish I could take a selfie of us right now." She grinned. "It's rare to catch you smiling at school."

I just laughed and patted Harriet's neck. That was another reason I'd come to love equestrian so damn much—no phones allowed. We weren't supposed to have them during regular classes either, but for equestrian it was a very strict rule. For the hour and a half I spent with horses, I could pretend Ocean1k didn't exist.

"OK, class. Everyone ready?" Mrs. Hartel raised her voice. She was a retired Olympic gold medalist and only taught this one class at Fulton. "Let's head out."

She led the way outside, riding her own Arabian, and the students followed.

As Amaya and I exited the stables, I turned my face up to the sun. It was warm and the air smelled sweet—summer was on the way.

The professional-grade equestrian field stretched out behind the football field and tennis courts, hugging the far end of Fulton Academy's property. Wilderness spread into the rolling hills beyond. This hardly even felt like being at school.

A whistle sounded in the distance, drawing my attention to the football field, where Coach Cooper was running a junior class through drills. I clenched my teeth, and the day suddenly felt a little less bright. I was fully prepared to do whatever it took to get Cooper's phone, to take him down, but I hadn't prepared myself for how I'd feel the first time I saw him after learning who he really was —allegedly.

I forced myself to turn away and immediately spotted Easton at the fence near the entrance. The sight of him always made something warm and indescribably happy bloom in my chest, but what was he doing out here? Maybe taking a walk on a break? Many people liked to walk the paths between the courts and the stables—it was a beautiful and relatively quiet part of the school grounds.

Then I caught sight of the person beside him, and I ground my already clenched teeth.

Harriet whinnied and shifted under me.

Irene was talking to Easton openly and casually—just standing there in the bright sunlight, chatting away without a worry for what people might think. They both laughed, and she leaned forward, resting her hand on his arm.

It wasn't fair. Little petty thoughts started pecking away at my already frayed nerves.

Maybe he wanted someone older, more mature—like Irene. Maybe he'd asked her out on a date because he actually wanted to, not just as a cover. Maybe he was just pretending to care about me until this Ocean1k crap was over and he could be with her.

In the distance, Coach blew his whistle again. The shrill sound made something inside me crack. I wanted to pull the damn thing from his mouth and strangle him with it, maybe shove the whistle down his throat for good measure.

Instead, I tugged the reins and turned Harriet toward the fence, then leaned forward and moved her into a gallop. Easton and Irene both took a step back as I approached, their eyes going wide. I must've looked as if I was about to jump the fence into them.

At the last moment, I turned Harriet to run along the perimeter of the fence. As I slowed the horse down and gave her a pat, I glanced behind me.

Dust still billowed from Harriet's sudden change in direction, and Irene seemed to have caught the brunt of it. She was spluttering and brushing at her ridiculous pink cardigan.

It may have been childish and impulsive, but fuck did it make me feel better. I allowed myself a full grin as I turned back to join the rest of my class.

"Burr under your saddle, Miss Mead?" Mrs. Hartel gave me a disapproving look, but I could hear some amusement in her voice.

"Sorry, ma'am." I smiled. "Harriet just got excited to be out of the stables and wanted a quick run."

That was horseshit, and we all knew it. Harriet was a placid animal and not at all hard to control. Thankfully, Mrs. Hartel decided to let it go.

I glanced over at Amaya, and she gave me a look: *What the fuck was that, you fruit loop?*

I smirked at her and shook my head: *Never mind, I'm good.*

She raised an eyebrow: *We're going to talk about this later.*

After that I focused on the lesson as we practiced various maneuvers. For the last ten minutes, Mrs. Hartel allowed us free riding time, and I loosened Harriet's reins, letting her wander to the back fence while I enjoyed the sun on my shoulders and spoke gibberish to her.

Amaya's horse was a little more difficult to control and kept trying to hang out with his bestie—the horse our friend Nicola was riding. By the time she managed to get him to cooperate and head in my direction, determination in her gaze, class had already ended.

She tried to corner me in the changing room, but I waved it off and cracked a joke about what a stuck-up grump Mr. Monroe was (while laughing on the inside because I knew he really wasn't like that at all), and she dropped it. We didn't have time to chat anyway. The stables were a good distance from the main building, and we had to rush to get to our next classes.

My last class for the day was English, but I had to drop my riding gear at my locker and grab my books first. My phone vibrated with a text just as I closed the locker. It was Ocean1k, because of course it was.

I gritted my teeth as I read it.

Ocean1k: I know your dirty little secret. You think you're fooling me, but you're not.

I looked up and down the hall with panicked eyes.

Empty.

Maybe our little show at Easton's apartment hadn't fooled him. Weird how he happened to be in his building just as I got there.

Before I could panic any more or reply, another message came in.

Ocean1k: The honorable judge was important to us. You'll regret meddling.

I couldn't help the sigh of relief. They didn't know about us—they were just pissed we'd stopped them from exploiting a judge.

"*I have no idea what you're talking about,*" I typed out as I ran to English.

About five minutes late, I finally burst into the classroom—and froze.

Everyone turned to look at me, including Easton, who stood at the front of the room, an open book in one hand and his other stuffed into a pocket. Damn, he looked good in his tailored pants and neat sweater, those hard eyes watching me over the rim of his glasses.

I shook myself out of it and looked around. Had I run into the wrong classroom? But no, there was my free seat next to Drew in the middle row.

"Nice of you to join us, Miss Mead," Easton said in a firm, disapproving voice. You'd think we didn't know each other at all and I was just another frustrating student he had to deal with. I reminded myself that was *good*. He needed to pretend everything was normal, and I should do the same.

I cleared my throat and smoothed my uniform, still a bit out of breath. "Sorry I'm late, sir. I had to rush here from equestrian."

He sighed and looked down at his book. "As I just told the rest of your class, who bothered to show up on time, Ms. Murphy is out sick, and I'm substituting for her today."

I rushed to my seat and pulled my books out of my bag as Mr. Serious Teacher got right into the lesson.

Everyone in the class sat a little straighter than usual. Ms. Murphy knew how to manage a rowdy class, but she wasn't a total hard-ass and actually made the classes somewhat enjoyable—at least for those with an interest in English. But everyone here had either been taught by Mr. Monroe or knew his reputation, and they were on their absolute best behavior.

Other than Drew, of course, who never seemed to be affected by anything anywhere. I knew him and knew it wasn't true, but he was exceptionally good at putting up that devil-may-care mask, a joke always at the tip of his tongue.

He slouched in his chair, one leg bent under it and the other stretched out in front of him. As I scrambled to find the page we were supposed to be on, Drew draped an arm over the back of my seat.

It wasn't something I was unused to. He did it all the time; I hardly even noticed it anymore. But with Easton in the room, I was suddenly *very* aware of Drew's arm at my back, at how *familiar* the gesture was.

Trying not to stare at him directly, I looked to Easton for any hint of a response. He droned on about something I would've hardly paid attention to anyway. With him in the room and Drew's arm burning the backs of my shoulders, I didn't have a clue what the lesson was about.

Easton seemed not to notice or care, his attention split between the book in his hand and the whiteboard. He only occasionally glanced up at the students, and never in my direction. I knew it was petty, but I wanted him to be just as jealous as I'd been when I saw him at the fence with Irene.

Drew leaned in, keeping his eyes on the front of the room, and whispered, "What's up with you, Harls? You OK?"

"I'm fine," I muttered back. "What do you mean?"

"You're ridiculously tense. I don't think I've ever seen you sit so straight."

I was saved from having to come up with an excuse when Easton started strolling down the aisle, reading from the book. He pulled up next to my desk, finished the sentence, and snapped the book closed. Half the class jumped in their seats from the sharp sound.

"Mr. Ingram." Easton turned to Drew on my other side, not even glancing at me. "Sit up straight and pay attention. You are in class, not in a party about to pass the blunt."

No one else dared to laugh, but I couldn't hold back the snort as Drew reluctantly removed his arm from my chair and sat up. "Yes, sir."

"Something funny, Miss Mead?" Easton's gaze locked on to mine, and I had to look away or I'd laugh again—or let all the feelings I had churning in my gut show in my eyes.

"No, sir. Just a scratch in my throat." I coughed for good measure.

After a loaded silence, Easton continued the lesson, and Drew and I shared a *holy shit* look.

The most excruciating, awkward lesson in the history of high school continued, and by the time the bell rang, my neck ached with tension. I purposely dawdled while getting my things together as Drew waited impatiently on the other side of the desks. It was the end of the school day, and everyone was rushing to get to their lockers and out of here. I surreptitiously placed a pen on the seat and headed toward the door with Drew.

"Oh shit." I pulled up short just as we reached the door, looking through my stuff and checking the pocket on my skirt. "I think I left my fave pen behind."

Drew groaned.

"Just go." I rolled my eyes and shoved him toward the door, and he rushed away with a grin. By the time I retrieved my pen, all the students had left the room, and Easton had packed up, swinging his messenger bag over his shoulder.

"That was the most awkward forty-five minutes of my life." I kept my voice low.

He came to stand in front of me and dragged a hand down his face. "Tell me about it."

"You kept your cool like a pro, except for that whole 'sit up straight, Mr. Ingram' bit," I imitated his voice.

"Oh, you can talk, Miss Blazing Saddles," he shot back, stuffing his hands into his pockets. "What the hell was that?"

"I just . . ." I lowered my voice even more. I could admit to myself that I'd been jealous, but it was hard to say it to him.

"I nearly had a heart attack. Irene was on the verge of tears, she was so rattled."

I lowered my head. It had felt good at the time, but now I felt bad. None of this was her fault.

Easton sighed. "I know it must've been hard for you to see him for the first time, but you can't go taking it out on nice office ladies."

Of course he knew seeing Coach would've upset me. Easton was attentive and caring like that. I wasn't kidding myself—he definitely realized jealousy had played a part too, but I was grateful he didn't bring it up. I cleared my throat. "What were you guys doing there anyway?"

He rubbed the bridge of his nose and readjusted his glasses. "I was going for a walk. She just appeared out of nowhere for small talk. She's been doing that all day—popping up."

"Right . . ." He seemed a bit irritated, and I couldn't help myself. "And you're not pleased about that?"

"No." His lips quirked, an almost smile. "She's a lovely person and I don't want to be rude, but I don't want to lead her on."

I was a total and complete moron who'd let her jealousy completely take over. I reminded myself of all the looks, the touches, the heated moments we'd shared. You couldn't fake that kind of connection.

Easton glanced at the door behind me and spoke before I could apologize for being an immature idiot. "Listen, we have a problem."

"What now?" I didn't even want to know.

"I got a package and a message from our *friends* this morning. They want me to start recruiting students into the BestLyf youth program."

"Not that surprising. They made you take the careers role for a reason, and we've suspected BestLyf from the start."

"Yeah. The problem is . . ." He sighed, his shoulders dropping. "He has a photo of us."

"What? What photo?" All the possibilities ran through my mind as the blood drained from my face.

"A photo from the fundraiser, on the balcony, just before you left." We were at school. He couldn't exactly say out loud that it was photographic evidence of us kissing.

The rage that flared in my chest scorched me in its intensity. That was our first kiss, a moment I'd played over and over in my mind, a moment I cherished. And now it was tarnished, made into something shameful and dirty—fodder for threats.

"That motherfucking cu—"

"Harlow!" Easton hissed, grabbing me by the wrist before I could run out of the room, right to the gym, and hurl myself at that horrid man. "This is exactly why I didn't message you and tell you this morning."

I breathed hard, my hands in fists. His grip didn't loosen until I took a deliberate deep breath. Then he slowly released me, our fingers brushing for a brief forbidden moment of tenderness.

"We can't be impulsive." His tone was gentler, both pleading and encouraging somehow. "This changes nothing. We still can't prove anything. We still need to stick to the plan."

I nodded, then frowned and shook my head. "This changes everything. Even if we do get proof, we can't go to the police. Your career will be ruined. Your life will be ruined."

"Fuck my career. *This changes nothing.* We stay the course." He didn't seem half as worried as I was about this.

But I didn't have time to argue. A group of students came past the classroom door, laughing and talking on their way out of the school, and we both remembered where we were.

"Shit. We're going to talk more about this later." I pointed at him and started to back toward the door.

He smiled and stuffed his hands in his pockets again. "There are things far more important to me, far more precious, than my career. Go."

As I turned to leave, I couldn't help feeling as though those important, precious things he was referring to might just be . . . me.

CHAPTER EIGHTEEN

Harlow

Mom and Auntie Eleanor had just walked off to look at handbags in the back of the store when I felt my phone vibrate in my back pocket.

I pulled it out and nearly choked on my sip of iced coffee: it was a message from Ocean1k. Why did I still have such strong reactions to them contacting me? It had been a shitty but regular part of my life for months now. You'd think I'd be used to it.

I checked that Donna and Mena were occupied—Donna was trying on her fifth pair of heels—and read the message.

Ocean1k: Check your coat pocket.

A chill ran down my spine, and I instinctively looked around. People walked past on the street outside, the shop assistants bustled about, the moms were still holding up handbags, and Donna posed in front of the mirror while Mena told her what she thought. Everything was normal. I didn't know what I'd expected exactly. Someone in a trench coat leaning around a corner and staring at me while twirling a moustache?

I put my drink down next to a glittery pair of flats and reached into my pocket tentatively. Why did I feel as though something was about to bite my fingers off? After a moment, I frowned and dug around in there properly. Nothing but a tissue. I stuck my hand in the other pocket, half expecting to find it empty too, but my fingers wrapped around something small and light. It felt as if it was made of paper, or maybe wrapped in it.

Another message came in:

Ocean1k: I need you to deliver it.

I sighed and replied.

Harlow: Where?

The response was an address in the city, several blocks away, but the last sentence made me panic.

Ocean1k: By 3:45 p.m. Hand it to the man wearing a pink polka-dot tie and bowler hat.

What? What the fuck was a bowler hat? I double-checked the address. It was just far enough away that you could justify driving, but whether it would get you there faster than going on foot was another question. Hoofing it allowed me more control. And I needed to get moving if I had any chance of getting there in time.

"Girls," I whisper-yelled, keeping an eye on the moms. Looked like Mom was trying to talk Auntie Eleanor into letting her buy the handbag for her. Donna and Mena turned to face me, and I leaned in so no one would hear us. "I have to go. Can you cover for me?"

"What? Where?" Donna crossed her arms.

"Are you OK?" Mena asked.

"I just need to do something. For a friend. They need my help. I'll meet you guys back at the apartment in time for dinner. *Please.*"

"Fine." Donna nodded. I could see the "but" on the tip of her tongue, but I didn't wait to hear it. I turned around and rushed out of the store.

I ran as fast as I could without barreling into someone. Around the corner, across the street—watch out for the cable car! I checked the map on my phone constantly so I wouldn't get lost. After rounding another corner, I paused and groaned. The hill was so steep it practically looked vertical.

I started to climb. By the time I got to the top and turned the next corner, my thighs were burning.

This was the street. Three minutes until my deadline. I ran once again, looking for the street number. It came up on me suddenly, and I skidded to a stop in front of a tall modern building, red sculptures of the numbers sitting in the window next to the revolving door.

People were walking in and out, rushing past on the sidewalk. I ran my hands through my hair, breathing hard, and turned slowly in a circle.

"Polka dots. Bowler hat," I mumbled to myself as I scanned the street. I didn't see anyone that might match that description.

Just as I was about to google what exactly a bowler hat looked like, a man wearing a gray coat and pink polka-dot tie came out of the building. He paused and put a black hat with a small rim onto his bald head.

I reached into my pocket and went up to him. "Excuse me."

"Yes." He gave me a polite, questioning look.

"Um . . ." What was I supposed to say? "I was told to deliver this to you."

I held out the . . . whatever it was . . . and he took it, frowning slightly. Tucking a newspaper under his arm, he unwrapped the brown paper to reveal . . . a Chapstick? *A motherfucking Chapstick?*

The man threw his head back and laughed, the hat nearly falling off. "Ah, good one."

I stared at him, dumbfounded. What the hell was this?

His smile faltered. "Are you not . . . one of my followers?"

"What? No, I was told to deliver this to you. What is this?"

"Oh. I have a vlog about corporate office life. It has a very healthy following." I didn't see how that was possible, but OK. "The Chapstick is kind of an ongoing joke. This must be from one of my viewers."

When I continued to stare at him, uncomprehending, he cleared his throat and reached into his pocket. "Here's your tip. Thanks," he said and walked away.

I balled the bills up in my fist and walked in the opposite direction.

Several blocks down, I spotted a bench around the corner and sat down on it heavily. The street went all the way to the water, a steep drop. Alcatraz was just visible, the bay shining in the afternoon sunlight around it. But I hardly looked.

I pulled my phone out and messaged Ocean1k.

Harlow: Why?

All their other demands had clearly related to an agenda I didn't have enough knowledge to comprehend. It may not have been obvious to me at the time, but all those hacks I did, every errand, had gotten Ocean1k access to some information, some network, some person they hadn't had before.

This time—delivering this little package and nearly having a stress-induced heart attack in the process—was different. They didn't benefit from this at all. That man wouldn't give me any clues even if I interrogated him as though he were a prisoner on Guantanamo. Because he didn't know anything. His identity, this stupid prank, it was all public knowledge if you were inclined to look.

This felt . . . *personal.*

My phone buzzed in my hand.

Ocean1k: Because I can.

The cruel words confirmed what I pretty much already knew. Ocean1k had sent me on this errand just to fuck with me, to hold their power over me. Maybe even to punish me for thwarting whatever plan they had for Judge Keating.

I'd wondered if BestLyf was maybe blackmailing Coach Cooper, using his family to make him make us do things. But after today . . . there was no point to this other than to be cruel.

I put my phone away and tried really hard not to cry.

My lower lip trembled anyway. My throat got tight. Silent tears streaked down both cheeks.

I'd felt manipulated and threatened since the first time Ocean1k made their intentions clear, but as I sat on that bench, tears soaking into the collar of my shirt, I felt utterly *crushed*.

A sob tore from my throat, and I squeezed my eyes shut so tightly I saw stars.

Wiping my cheeks with my hands, I looked down the street at the water. I needed something else to focus on. Something besides the appeal of just stepping out in front of a cable car so this would all just end.

A shop front on the opposite corner caught my attention. Something seemed familiar about it. Twin Peaks Ink. Where had I heard that?

Wiping at my cheeks again, I got to my feet.

That was where Easton tattooed on the weekends. Today was Saturday. He was probably in there right now.

The urge to go to him pulled at me so forcefully I actually stumbled forward a step. I wanted to tell him what just happened, see his kind eyes and feel his warm embrace. I wanted to relax against him and let him make me feel safe again.

I knew it was dangerous, that we needed to avoid being in the same place, especially in public. But I didn't give a shit. I craved him so much in that moment I couldn't stop myself from making my way over.

Several people came out onto the street as I approached—three men and a woman, all tattooed and pierced and beautiful in that forbidden way. The woman was gorgeous, with deep purple hair and a bright smile. I ducked my head, feeling inadequate, and waited for them to walk on before I opened the door and stepped into the tattoo shop.

Easton stood next to the counter, his messenger bag slung over his shoulder, keys in hand. He blinked once, as if he couldn't quite believe his eyes.

"I'm sorry. We're about to close up." I hadn't even noticed the woman behind the counter until she spoke. She gave me a polite smile. "The best way to book an appointment is online, sweetheart. We can match you with an artist."

"I . . ." My voice came out croaky, and I had to clear my throat while sniffling. I looked at Easton, my eyes filling with tears again.

I didn't know if it was the moisture in my eyes or the waver in my voice, but he finally snapped out of it.

"You go, Cass." He flashed the lady a quick smile and dropped his bag and keys on the counter. "I'll lock up."

"Are you sure?" She looked between us.

"Yeah. I know her. It's all good."

After a long pause, Cass finally shrugged and gathered her things. She gave Easton one last questioning look on her way out, but he stuffed his hands in his pockets and smiled. He looked so relaxed and unaffected I almost believed he didn't care I was standing there at all.

The little bell above the door tinkled as Cass walked out. As soon as she left, Easton dropped the calm act and rushed toward me, his eyes wide and searching. He wrapped me up in his arms, and I buried my face in his chest as another weak sob tore from me.

"What happened?" He held me tightly, rocking us from side to side. I opened my mouth and tried to answer, but my throat was too tight, my spirit too broken. All I could seem to do was hold on to him and soak his T-shirt with my misery.

After a few long moments, my breathing started to even out, the clamping sensation around my throat easing. Easton guided me to a black leather couch, then quickly locked the front door and flipped the sign from Open to Closed.

"Harlow, you're scaring me. Please tell me what's wrong." He took a seat beside me, his voice quiet, pleading.

I cleared my throat and leaned into him. "I got a text from Ocean1k."

"OK . . ." That wasn't unusual.

I told him what had happened over the course of the last hour—had it only been an hour?—forcing the words out and holding back more tears. He handed me tissues, and I cleaned my face as I spoke. By the end of it, I felt angry more than anything. The anger gave me strength, banishing the tears, and I held on to it.

"It was just so unnecessarily cruel," I gritted out as Easton rubbed my back. "Not that all the other shit wasn't cruel, but all the other times had a purpose. We had to gain access to something, get some kind of information—there was a clear reason for it. But this . . ." I shook my head. "It was purely to torture me. And I didn't even question it!"

I got to my feet and started pacing. "I've become so accustomed to the threats —against Donna, against you, against me—that I just jumped to do what was demanded. I'm such an idiot!"

"No, you're not." Easton got to his feet and placed his hands on my shoulders, forcing me to stop moving. "You're resourceful and bright, and you have a mind of your own, and you care fiercely for those you love, and you are so fucking smart."

"Whatever," I mumbled. I was not smart, but I appreciated all the other nice things he'd said about me. That fluttery-stomach feeling started to push all the anger and despair to the side, and I wrapped my arms around his middle.

He kissed the top of my head and leaned his chin on the spot. "I wonder what's changed," he said, almost absentmindedly.

"Huh?" I pulled back to look at him.

"With Ocean1k. Like you said, this doesn't follow the pattern. Plus, I still haven't received any threats or admonishments for interfering with the judge, and they clearly know we were both there."

I'd received threats and taunts almost on the daily—even when they didn't have something they wanted me to hack.

"I don't know." I shrugged, drained.

But no—I refused to let that dick in a tracksuit ruin my day. I'd been having a great time with my family, and now I was with Easton in his happy place, surrounded by the most gorgeous tattoo art I'd ever seen. Massive framed pieces by all the artists lined the walls of the studio. Now that I'd gotten the emotional breakdown out of my system, I could really appreciate their beauty.

"Give me a tattoo," I said, staring at a framed black-and-gray piece on the opposite wall. It depicted a striking woman's face, turned up, her eyeliner continuing down one cheek and swirling under her mouth to create a whimsical pattern. Somehow, I knew it was his.

He followed my gaze to the frame, then looked at me again, running both hands through his hair. "I don't know, Harlow."

"Why not? I'm eighteen. It's perfectly legal." I pulled my phone out and checked the time. "I have a few hours before I have to get back to my family for dinner."

"Are you sure you even want one? Do you know what you want? This feels impulsive."

"Of course it's impulsive, but don't you think it's kind of . . . I don't know, the universe telling us something that I happened to fall apart right outside your tattoo shop? And yes, I've wanted one for ages. I can't think of a better artist to give me one—or one I trust more with my body."

His eyes narrowed a little, something different—heavy—entering his gaze.

I batted my lashes, maybe laying it on a little thick. "Do you think you can squeeze me in?"

He sighed and smiled, and I knew I had him. "OK, fine, but only because you asked so nicely."

I clapped and jumped up and down with excitement. I'd been expecting him to say no. "Let me just freshen up quickly. Is there a bathroom?"

He pointed to a door in the back. "Yeah, through there, past the kitchenette."

In the bathroom, I washed the tears off my face and ran my fingers through my hair, which had gotten hella tangled from running at full speed through the city. When it came to what tattoo I wanted, I realized I just wanted one Easton had done. I trusted him. No matter what happened, I'd have his art on me for the rest of my life.

CHAPTER NINETEEN

Easton

After putting so much time and effort into keeping some distance between us, I was literally about to have my hands on Harlow for an extended period of time. She would sit on the tattoo bed, and I would mark her permanently with my art.

The idea pleased me in some perverse way. Some dark, primal part of me I tried to ignore *really* liked that she'd be laid out in front of me while I put my mark on her with careful, painful passes of the needle. It was beautiful and brutal at the same time, and I was anticipating it way too much.

I set up my station while she was in the bathroom, making sure everything was sterile and ready to go.

This was wrong—just like all the other secret time we'd spent together, just like every touch and every kiss and every deep, dark, yearning feeling I'd ever had for her. But at the very least, this was legal. I was a professional tattoo artist, and she was not a minor. We were in a tattoo shop, not hiding in a dark classroom at school. Never mind that the shop was closed and no one else was here and no one knew she was with me. Those were just pesky details.

I knew I should've been stronger, firmer in saying no. She was making a rash decision in a vulnerable state of mind, and I didn't want her to regret it. But I also knew Harlow. I knew her a lot better than any teacher had any business knowing a student. I knew she could be spontaneous, she hungered for new experiences, and once her mind was made up, there was no changing it.

Maybe I was just making excuses, trying to justify doing something I knew I shouldn't. But I couldn't say no to her after holding her sobbing in my arms. When she walked through that door looking absolutely devastated, I wanted to find who did this to her, wrap my hands around their neck, and watch the life fade from their eyes.

But of course, I couldn't do anything to Ocean1k just yet. We had to bide our time, wait until we had the evidence. I couldn't defend Harlow, couldn't keep her safe from our demon. But I could make her feel better.

Fuck it.

We'd been through so much; we deserved a little fun.

She came out of the back room clutching her coat to her front, and my gaze dropped to her bare feet and legs as she padded across the concrete floor. The coat hit just above her knees, and as she walked, it gave me a flash of bare thigh.

By the time she stood before me, I knew where this was going. I let out a big breath and clenched my jaw.

"Harlow." Her name came out sounding more like a plea than the warning I intended.

"You're an artist, Easton," she said, her voice pitched low. "An incredibly talented one. And I'm honored to have your art on me. I want whatever you want to give me."

I couldn't help hearing a double meaning in her words. My breathing suddenly grew shallower, and I had to force my throat to work so I could speak. "And where would you like your tattoo?"

"Wherever you want to put it." She pulled her coat apart, and my worst fear and darkest hope were confirmed—she was completely nude.

I released a shaky breath; my brain felt like static. No words, no thoughts. All the blood drained down to my crotch, and I started to get hard.

"You're the artist. I'm your canvas." Harlow gave me one last look full of trust and determination, then lifted her hands to her face. She had a piece of fabric in one hand—a scarf or something—and tied it over her eyes.

I looked to the ceiling and, even though I was far from a pious man, prayed for strength.

After several moments standing there, fighting my baser instincts, I managed to regain some logical thought and cleared my throat. "Harlow, are you absolutely sure you want to do this? It's OK if you don't." I had to make sure.

"I'm positive." She smiled and tilted her chin up slightly. I had to admire her confidence. So many women were self-conscious about their bodies, especially young women. Yet she trusted me enough not only to let me tattoo whatever the fuck I wanted, but to stand in front of me, completely naked, blindfolded . . . *vulnerable.*

She was making herself vulnerable to me, and just as I'd heard double meaning in her words earlier, I knew this vulnerability involved more than her body.

The sense of responsibility and pride that came with that realization sobered me up some, and I made myself assess my "canvas," looking at her not just as the drop-dead gorgeous woman I couldn't wait to get under me but as someone deserving of my best work.

I stepped to her side and lifted her right arm with a gentle hand on her wrist. At that first contact she gasped, then visibly calmed herself.

I gave her a moment, then dragged the fingers of my free hand from her wrist all the way up to her shoulder, slowly stepping around until I stood behind her. She had perfect skin. Soft, supple, unblemished . . . virgin skin.

Releasing her arm, I kept my fingers at her shoulder to maintain contact. Her hair cascaded down her back, all the way to her waist. It gleamed in the low light of the room, and I remembered how good it had felt threaded through my fingers the night we first kissed.

As I ran my hands through it again, it proved to be just as soft and silky as I remembered. When my fingers reached her neck, I moved her hair over her shoulder, exposing her back.

Her delicate shoulders, the curve of her spine, her ass. *My god*, her ass! It was fucking perfect. I wanted to pull her back against me, grind my thickening cock against her softness.

Instead, I swept the fingertips of one hand down her spine, right down the middle, all the way to the top of her ass. I didn't dare go any lower. She wouldn't be getting a tattoo if I gave in to that impulse.

Goosebumps rose on her skin at my touch, and her shoulders moved up and down slightly as her breathing became more labored. I steeled myself before inching my hand back up, over her shoulder, and moving to stand in front of her.

She'd stood in front of me when she dropped her coat, but I'd deliberately tried not to look, to focus on what she wanted and needed from me in the moment. Now, as I brushed my fingers just above her breasts, I *had* to look. I had to look closely—for best tattoo placement, of course.

She was breathing through her mouth, her plump lips slightly parted. I could feel her warm breath on my wrist as I passed it back across her collarbones.

My middle finger caressed that little dip right at the base of her throat, eliciting more goosebumps across her skin. When I saw her nipples harden, I had to stifle a moan. I stared at them in a way I wouldn't have dared had she not been blindfolded. I was greedy in my observation, claiming every inch of skin with my eyes. The way her breasts rose and fell with her every breath mesmerized me.

Acutely aware of our limited time, I dragged my hand down her front, between her breasts, over her belly button . . .

Could she be as turned on as I was? All I had to do to find out was let my fingers travel a little farther down. Would she be as painfully wet as I was now hard, my cock practically twitching against my jeans?

When I reached the spot just above where her light pubic hair started, I had to pause and force myself to focus again.

The whole time I'd been touching her, some part of my brain had actually remembered I was supposed to be giving her a tattoo, had assessed her skin through the lens of an artist and not just a horny, morally corrupt man. That part of my brain saved me just before I ruined us both.

I knew exactly what I wanted to tattoo on her and where I wanted to put it.

By this point, Harlow was practically panting, and I was breathing pretty hard myself. I moved my hand to her hip and pressed my palm to it, forcing my words out on a whisper. "How about here?"

She swallowed, her throat bobbing, and nodded, apparently as incapable of forming words as I was.

I took her hands in mine and walked backward toward my station, then leaned down and picked her up, one arm under her knees, the other at her back. Instinctively, she wrapped her arms around my neck. She was so light, so fragile —the moment her bare body pressed against my fully clothed one, it struck me once again how vulnerable she was.

It took me a few moments to convince my arms to set her down on the table. She caressed my jaw as she released me, making me want to lean down . . .

Focus, Easton!

I had to physically turn away from her to get my shit together. Her coat lay in a pile on the floor, and I picked it up and draped it over her.

"So you don't get cold," I said. *And also so I don't forget how to tattoo.*

"Thanks." She smiled and pulled it up to her neck.

I draped the coat so it would expose her hip and positioned her on her side, then put my gloves on and got to work. After cleaning the area, I roughly sketched out what I planned to do with a marker, poured the ink into pots, fit the best needle for the job, and leaned over her.

I buzzed the tattoo gun a few times so she wouldn't be startled by the sound. "I'm going to start now, OK? It might hurt—everyone handles it differently. So if you need me to stop, just say so."

"Got it." She nodded, not looking even remotely nervous.

I got right up close to her hip and started tattooing. She tensed briefly but didn't jump or jerk or cry out. After a few minutes, she started to relax, her muscles loosening.

"How are you doing?" I asked as I dipped the needle into the ink.

"Good."

I grinned. "Don't be brave. I've seen grown men cry from certain tattoos."

"Yeah, well, grown men are pussies."

I laughed. "Seriously, though. I need to know how you're feeling."

"I'm totally fine, Easton," she assured me. "It doesn't hurt nearly as much as I thought it would. It was startling at the start, but now it's just, like . . . I dunno. An intense kind of humming sensation?"

I grinned again. My girl was taking her first tat like a champ, because *of course* she was.

The routine of tattooing helped get my mind out of the gutter, and eventually we fell into easy conversation, avoiding difficult and depressing topics—like what sent her running here in tears. I was getting close to finishing when the conversation reached a lull.

"Can I ask you a question?" Something had been bothering me for a while.

"Sure."

"Why do you always refer to yourself as stupid?"

Silence. I glanced up at her; her mouth had pressed into a thin line.

"I've heard you say it a few times now," I elaborated. "That you're a dumbass or not smart like your sister and stuff like that. It just makes me sad to think you're putting yourself down like that in your own mind."

After another silence, she sighed. The coat shifted a little, moved by her fidgeting hands beneath. "I'm failing pretty much every class. The only things I'm even remotely good at are computers and sports. I'm pretty sure I'm not going to be able to graduate. I hate reading books, math makes me feel like that GIF of the confused woman while equations drift past her head, and science . . . science makes my head hurt. I've accepted it, but sometimes I do wish I was smarter, like my friends."

I paused my tattooing to look up at her. The blindfold covered her face, but she still looked so incredibly sad. I hated that she felt inadequate in any way.

I put the needle back to her skin to do the finishing touches. The buzz of the gun filled the space around us, and I purposely waited a beat. I wanted what I said next to make an impact.

"There's this quote. It's often attributed to Einstein, but I'm not sure he actually said it. It doesn't really matter. The sentiment is the important part, and it goes something like this: 'Every person has the potential to be a genius, but if you judge a fish by its ability to climb a tree, it's always going to think it's an idiot.'"

I completed the final stroke of the tattoo and let the last buzz of the gun fade out around us.

"Don't feel like you have to climb trees, Harlow. You're already fucking brilliant at swimming upstream."

I left it at that, letting her come to her own conclusions. She remained silent and still as I cleaned the excess ink off her skin and removed my gloves.

"Do you want to look at it before I wrap it?" I leaned on the bed next to her.

"Yes." She grinned and wriggled her arms out from under the coat to remove her blindfold. Her big doe eyes opened and looked at me, and suddenly I found myself unable to look away. She was so damn beautiful.

After a beat, I shook myself and started moving back to let her sit up, but her hand shot out and gripped my forearm.

"Easton. Thank you." She rose up onto her elbows, holding the coat to her chest with one hand. She wasn't just talking about the tattoo.

"You're amazing," I told her and let her see it in my gaze.

She tilted her face up, I leaned down farther, and then we were kissing.

As her arms wrapped around my neck, the coat fell to her lap, exposing her breasts. I had to grip the edge of the bed above her head, fingers digging into the leather, to stop myself from going right for her boobs like a teenage boy. She pulled me down until she was flat on her back again, and I groaned.

Her hands started moving—feeling my arms and shoulders, running through my hair, dipping under my T-shirt, dangerously close to the front of my pants and the raging boner contained within. In response I kissed her jaw, down her neck, licked those collarbones I'd been staring at earlier. Her back arched.

"Touch me, Easton." The words rushed out of her hot little mouth on a groan.

I pulled back and stared at her, panting, acutely aware that I had no idea how experienced she was. I couldn't just . . . fuck her on my tattoo bed. But I couldn't resist her either. I didn't know how to anymore, didn't want to try. She was so incredibly sexy lying there, her eyes hooded, in the place where I felt most like myself.

My resolve cracked.

I grabbed the coat and threw it off to the side, then dragged my eyes down her body, taking in every curve and dip. I wanted to taste her pert nipples, feel the flesh on my tongue. So I leaned down and took one into my mouth.

Harlow moaned, her hands flying to the back of my head to hold me in place. I kneaded her other breast with my free hand, running my thumb over the nipple.

Moving up her breast, over her chest, and up her neck, I licked and kissed and sucked along the way. At last my mouth found hers in a messy, intense kiss—all tongues and deep strokes and *oh my god I feel like I'm floating and falling at the same time.*

I kept one hand next to her head for balance and slid the other down her body, over the dip of her waist, to grab the meaty flesh of her ass.

Then I pulled back. I wanted to watch her face for this part.

Forcing myself to slow down a little, I deliberately dragged my fingers over the top of her thigh. She spread her legs and gasped, once again telling me to touch her, speaking only with her body. I glided the backs of my knuckles halfway down the inside of her thigh, my fingertips back up the other thigh . . .

And then I was running my fingers through her warm arousal. I groaned and cursed under my breath.

Harlow closed her eyes, her lips parted, her body practically trembling with anticipation. I wanted to give her what she wanted, what she needed. I wanted to give her the world. But for now, pleasure would have to do.

I pushed one finger inside, and she moaned, the sound going right to my groin. She was so wet, so tight, so warm. I couldn't wait to feel her on my cock.

I leaned down and licked her lips as I pulled my finger out, then pushed back in, deeper. Her mouth opened on another moan, her tongue brushing mine.

The distinctive sound of a key in the door made me freeze. Harlow fluttered her eyes open, confused.

When the little bell over the door jingled, it finally registered that we were about to have company. Moving faster than I ever had in my entire life, I pulled Harlow up into a sitting position and turned to face the door, blocking her with my body as best I could.

Cass walked inside, digging through her handbag as I surreptitiously wiped Harlow's arousal off on my jeans. She briefly glanced up from her bag on the way to the reception desk. "You still here? I forgot my fucking tablet. Again. I got all the way home, was halfway through . . ."

She trailed off and examined me properly. I had to have looked as awkward as I felt. My entire body was in a full cringe. Harlow had plastered herself to my back, her legs tucked under her but clearly visible next to me. I wasn't wide enough to completely hide her, but I hid the important bits, doing my best to protect her.

"Well, shit," Cass said, blinking slowly.

I cleared my throat. "I know how unprofessional this is. I'm sorry. It won't happen again."

She threw her head back and burst out laughing. "You think you're the first tattoo artist to get it on after doing a piece on someone? Honestly, I'm glad to see you having some fun, East. Hey there, mystery woman."

Harlow stuck a hand up over my shoulder and waved but kept her forehead pressed to my back.

Cass reached under the counter and grabbed her tablet. "All righty then. You kids just make sure to disinfect any surfaces you bang on before you leave. Have fun. Byeeee!" She closed the door and locked it behind her.

I released a massive breath, my body sagging, and Harlow peeled herself away from me. When I turned, she had her face in her hands and was shaking.

Panicked, I grabbed her shoulders, but when she lowered her hands, I could see she was just laughing. The giggles had a slightly manic edge to them, but seeing mirth in her eyes gave me so much relief I didn't even care.

Hilarity bubbled up in my chest too, and then we were both losing it. Our loud, unabashed laughter filled the studio as we let all that tension go, leaning on each other and wiping tears away. A few times we tried to stop, but then we'd make eye contact and lose it all over again. By the time the laughter actually started to die down, my belly was pleasantly sore.

Harlow took a deep breath and shook her head, smiling at me. God, she was beautiful—flushed from laughing and the other things we'd been doing before.

"I better get going." She jumped down from the bench.

"Wait." I grabbed her waist. "I need to wrap your tattoo."

"Oh! I haven't even looked at it!" Her eyes widened, and she walked over to the full-length mirror on the other side of the bench. She stared at her reflection for several long moments as I grabbed the Saniderm.

When she looked back at me, her eyes glistened with tears. "It's perfect. I love it so much. Thank you."

I smiled and cupped her cheek, leaning in for a soft kiss. It was so tempting to deepen it, get her back on that bench and finish what I started, but I had to let her go. For now.

I pulled away and covered the tattoo with the clear tattoo bandage, going over aftercare instructions. Once I finished, she gave me another kiss and sauntered away, her arms stretched over her head, her hair cascading down her back, her ass . . . oh, that perfect ass. I marveled at how she managed to captivate me with her whole being.

By the time I had everything tidied up and wiped down, she'd come back out of the bathroom, fully clothed.

She shrugged her coat on, slipped her phone into her pocket—after checking the time and cringing—then looked around for anything else she might've forgotten. I knew she had to go, but I needed to keep her with me, just for a few moments more.

She'd been so vulnerable with me, so open about what she wanted on so many levels. She'd been brave through this whole ordeal, and now it was my turn. If she could be that vulnerable with me, that trusting, then I owed it to her to show some vulnerability too.

"Harlow." I took her hands and rubbed the backs of them with my thumbs. "I know you have to go, but . . . I need to tell you something."

"What is it?" She squeezed my hands, a bit of trepidation entering her eyes. Every time we'd had to tell each other something, it had been something crushing, scary, and demoralizing. I didn't want that anxiety marring this moment. So instead of working up to it, I just . . . jumped.

"I'm falling in love with you." I didn't add any buts, left all the obstacles out of it—she knew them all. This was about setting all that bullshit aside and being real—even if just for this one perfect, private moment.

She wrapped her arms around my waist and leaned in.

"I'm falling in love with you too," she whispered against my lips and kissed me. Every ounce of what she felt, she poured into that kiss, and I returned it, opening myself up to her in every way.

I pulled back and stroked her cheek with my thumb. "This isn't easy for me to say. I've spent my whole life hiding my true feelings and dreams from my parents; I've spent so much of our time together fighting my true feelings for you. And since I'm putting it all out there, deep down, I was worried your feelings would fade, that this was a fleeting infatuation for you, intensified by the situation we're in."

"Easton . . ." She loosened her grip, went to pull away from me, but I held on to her. I'd never let her go again without a fight.

"No, listen. I know you now—I know you don't do anything by halves. It takes immense strength to be vulnerable with someone like you have been with me. I want to be strong too. This is me being vulnerable with you. I don't want to pretend anymore. I promise you, I'm going to do everything in my power to give us a fighting chance. If that's something you want, I'm going to fight to the death to give you that choice." So many of our choices had been taken from us lately. I wanted her to have this one. I wanted her to choose me, because I'd already chosen her. I was only just allowing myself to own it.

"We'll figure it out. Together," she replied, and then she really did have to go.

I stood alone in the silent studio for a long time after she left. It felt damn good to lean into the things I really wanted in life, but fuck, it terrified me—especially when the stakes were so impossibly high.

CHAPTER TWENTY

Harlow

Agust of wind sent the rain flying sideways to pelt the dining room windows. Despite the wild weather outside, the house was warm and bright as we sat around one end of our massive dining table, eating dinner as a family.

It didn't happen as often as it used to when Donna and I were little. Sometimes Dad was out of town or Mom had a meeting with a client, and Donna had been spending more of her evenings with Hendrix. But on this particular Thursday, we'd all managed to be home, and Magda had made chicken schnitzels, mashed potatoes, and steamed veg—one of my fave meals. My mood couldn't have been better.

Hendrix and my dad were talking about electric cars or something. After an initial period of distrust and hostility, they'd soon realized they got along pretty great.

My mom was reminiscing about last weekend's shopping trip. "I can't believe I managed to get your aunt to let me buy that bag for her." She smiled. Some old, complicated tension existed between my mom and her sister—something about an inheritance my aunt refused to touch—but they'd been getting along better and better since Mena started going to Fulton Academy with us.

"It probably helped that you got the same one in red," Donna said.

"I never say no to a gorgeous handbag. It's just a bonus that it was for a good cause this time." She popped a green bean into her mouth, then nudged my elbow. "I would've got you something too, sweetheart, if you hadn't disappeared on us."

I'd stuffed my mouth so full that one of my cheeks puffed out. I couldn't reply if I wanted to.

My sister came to my rescue. "The dinner was fun after. We should remember that restaurant."

I swallowed my giant mouthful and nodded. "Yeah, the fondant I had for dessert was amazing."

My enthusiasm was genuine—the fondant really had been incredible. Almost as good as having Easton's hands on me.

I smiled—a private, unavoidable smile I couldn't hold back whenever I thought about our time together in his tattoo studio. He was falling in love with me! I could hardly believe he felt as strongly about me as I did him.

I'd practically walked on clouds back to our apartment that evening. I'd felt crazy wound up, my body still aching for him, but the declaration that came instead of me . . . well, me coming—was totally worth it.

He was falling in love with me!

The sting of my new tattoo on my hip was the sweetest pain. Every time my clothes brushed against the spot, I remembered how he'd bared his soul to me. Anytime I looked at it in the mirror, I couldn't help smiling. He'd poured his feelings out on my skin before he'd even spoken the words.

The image depicted a tree and a fish, done in a restrained style with flowing lines, the two opposing images intertwined with grace. I'd asked him about it after and found out the tree was a maple sapling, the fish a betta fish. It was a reference to the conversation we'd had while he worked on it, but it was so much more. I kept finding new symbolism every time I thought about it.

It was him telling me he believed in me.

It was a homage to embracing your individuality.

It was about growth and beauty.

It was even a subtle representation of him—the tree on my skin a match to the leaves on his.

The girls had naturally descended on me as soon as I got back. They'd told our moms I'd rushed off to help a friend in trouble; Mom and Auntie Eleanor asked after my friend but didn't seem to be suspicious otherwise. My sister and cousin, however . . .

That was the only sour part of the evening—having to keep my joy from them. In the end, I sucked at keeping it hidden and ended up having to tell them *something*. Just a little morsel of truth.

"Look"—I waved them and their sharp eyes down—"I really did have to help someone out who was in some trouble." Technically that was true, but the person in trouble had been me. "But then after, I bumped into this guy I've kind of been seeing and . . ."

I didn't even get to finish my sentence before they practically tackled me to the bed, bursting with questions. Amaya got put on a video call, and I managed to convince them that it was too new and too uncertain. That I wasn't ready to share details just yet.

I pledged not to make a liar of myself in this case. I would tell my friends about Easton Monroe. Eventually.

"No phones at the dinner table." Dad's firm voice snapped me back to the present. He was frowning at Donna, who had her face in her phone, but I could see the smile fighting to break through. Both my parents often checked messages and took calls in the middle of dinner. We tried to eat around the same time when we were all home, but they weren't militant about it.

Instead of replying to my father, Donna looked at me with a worried expression.

Immediately, my mind went to the worst-case scenario. Ocean1k had contacted her, dragging her into blackmail. They'd sent her photos of me and Easton. Maybe they would send everyone I loved messages describing in vivid detail how they were going to kill me, just to prolong the cruelty.

"What is it?" I gripped the edge of the table, ready to run for some reason. Fight-or-flight instinct could be so weird sometimes, but you try explaining to your primitive brain there's no tiger to escape from right now.

"Mena," my sister said.

Relief flooded through me, only to immediately be replaced by worry for my cousin. I reached into my pocket but remembered I'd left my phone in my room.

"What's happened?" Mom asked, she and Dad both wearing serious expressions now. Everyone's cutlery lay abandoned on the table next to half-eaten meals.

"A friend of hers from work has been killed. Maybe murdered," Donna said, and my mom gasped. Hendrix wrapped an arm around Donna's shoulders, but she didn't lean into him.

"We need to go see her. Sorry, guys." My sister and I both jumped out of our seats before she'd even finished speaking.

"I'll come with you." Hendrix got to his feet. As I ran upstairs to grab a warmer hoodie and my phone, I heard my sister telling him to stay, that we needed some girl time. My mom had already called up our aunt before we even reached the garage.

Amaya's purple Jag pulled up at the end of the driveway just as we came through the gate. She jumped out and rushed through the rain to get into the back seat of Donna's BMW.

"Fucking hell," she cursed and did up her belt. My sister took off, driving as fast as she dared in the rain.

"Should we stop for supplies?" I suggested as we passed through Devilbend's downtown. "Ice cream, junk food, and shit."

"Tequila," Amaya added.

"Let's just get to her. We can order anything she wants to be delivered," Donna said.

We rode in silence the rest of the way.

The rain had let up a little by the time we parked at Mena's building. We still rushed to the entrance, eager to wrap her up in our support.

Uncle Brad answered the door. Mena sat on the couch, her mom holding her hand. She wasn't crying, but she looked as though she had been, her eyes red and swollen.

"Hey," she said, her voice so small.

I held my arms out. She got up and walked into them, and I hugged her so, so tightly. Amaya joined us on one side and Donna on the other, and we just stood there for a while, hugging, holding her. She started to cry again but then pulled back, making us all back up and give her some space.

After taking a shaky breath, she turned to her parents. "We're gonna hang out in my room for a bit, OK?"

"Sure, honey." Her mom smiled. "You want me to bring you some food or anything?"

"No, that's OK. I just need a distraction," Mena said, and I took her hand. She squeezed it hard and started walking down the hall.

"Thank you, girls, for coming over," Uncle Brad said, and Donna stayed behind to briefly talk to them.

As we filed into Mena's tiny bedroom, Donna rushed to catch up to us and closed the door. It was a tight squeeze. With Mena's single bed, her desk and chair, and all her makeup piled on a rickety table in the corner, we could barely find any floor space, but we all piled onto her bed, surrounding her.

"What happened?" Amaya asked.

Mena sighed. "I don't know if you guys remember Chelsea? She used to work at Leah's Diner with me, but she quit not long before I started at Fulton. I didn't really get why she was leaving a steady job when she'd just broken up with her boyfriend, but she had been talking about moving to the city, so . . ." She shrugged and fiddled with the tissue in her hand.

"We were friends. Or at least, I thought we were. We talked a lot when we were working together, and we really got along. I tried to keep in touch with her after she left, but I never managed to find a time to see her in person, and eventually the messages stopped. I figured she'd just started her new life and maybe we weren't as close as I thought. She'd probably just seen me as a coworker and not a friend. She never even told me where she was living or working or anything, come to think of it. I kept thinking I'd get all the details when I saw her, but . . ."

Her eyes filled with tears, and her voice wavered. We waited patiently for her to calm herself.

Mena had struggled with self-confidence for years. She'd been bullied at her old school, and none of us even knew about it. Even though she was doing much better since transferring to Fulton, she'd admitted that she sometimes felt as though she didn't fit in with us—that we meant more to her than she did to us. She always underestimated how much people cared about her.

"Anyway." Mena cleared her throat and wiped her eyes again, her smudged makeup revealing a bit of her birthmark. "A cop showed up at the diner just after my shift started. He's the one who told us she'd been found dead. He didn't go into much detail, but her body was found in the woods, way off a hiking track. I don't know how. They're treating it as a murder. He was asking a lot of questions about her ex."

"It's usually the ex," Amaya said. "Or the current partner. Men make me sick."

Mena shook her head. "I don't think it was him. I mean, it could've been, but she got in so deep with BestLyf after doing all these accelerated courses with them. Apparently, her parents hadn't even heard from her in weeks. I don't know. I hate to fuel Turner's conspiracy theories, but something's not right with that organization."

"I think Turner might be right," I said before I could stop myself, but the others didn't disagree. They didn't so much as raise an eyebrow. "Between what happened to Turner's mom, all that mess with Hendrix and Will's dad, and now this . . . it's too weird." Not to mention someone who'd pretty much admitted to working with BestLyf was blackmailing me.

Maybe it was time to mention that.

As the girls chatted—about Chelsea and then other things to distract Mena— I tried to think through my rising panic.

When I received that first threatening message from Ocean1k, that first picture of my sister, I just wanted to protect her as she'd protected me so many times. And when the threats escalated, I got scared. I felt as if the only way to prevent something horrible from happening was to keep doing what they told me —in secret. If I told Donna, she'd want to protect me, and I was petrified I'd get her killed. Then Easton Monroe got involved, making everything so much more complicated. Suddenly I was hiding not only the blackmail and the threats but an illicit relationship with a teacher. I'd spent more than a little time worrying about how my friends would take that news. Now that Ocean1k had started using that very relationship against us . . . I was just in too deep.

By the time I found myself sitting in Mena's room, comforting her about her friend who had probably been killed by the same people blackmailing me, I'd been lying for *so long*, about so many things, I didn't even know where to start untangling it.

It shamed me to admit that part of my reluctance to tell my friends hadn't just been protectiveness of Donna. I also wanted to prove to myself I didn't need her. Donna had fought so many of my battles since we were little that I'd begun to resent it. For once, I wanted to deal with my own mess. Why I picked the most high-stakes, dangerous mess I'd ever been in to prove my independence was beyond me.

The time had come to accept I couldn't handle it on my own. Yes, I had Easton and Ford, but we still hadn't gotten very far, and the secrets took a toll on all of us.

It had been over a week since we hacked into the school network and found out Coach Cooper was probably Ocean1k. While Ford and Easton had hardly heard from Ocean1k during that time—apart from Easton being told to recruit students into the youth program—I was now apparently his main target. I'd received incessant taunting messages, graphic accounts of what he was going to do to my sister. I'd had to do a "job" for him every night, including a few pointless ones like the Chapstick. What little sleep I'd managed to get in the past had completely vanished, all my time taken up by Ocean1k's bullshit. Only adrenaline and sheer force of will kept me going.

In the meantime, we'd been watching Coach as much as possible. Ford had been watching his apartment building—in case we had to resort to breaking and entering again—while Easton and I kept an eye on him at school. Coach Cooper was unpredictable, running PE lessons indoors and outdoors, in and out of his office irregularly, just as likely to go off campus for lunch as he was to skip it altogether. He always seemed to have his cell with him though, like everyone else in the entire world.

I didn't want to run to my big sister to solve my problems, but this had gone way beyond that. All my old justifications for keeping secret after secret didn't seem that convincing anymore. Not when the gravity of the situation settled around me in Mena's tiny bedroom.

A woman had died. I was pretty sure the same organization blackmailing and threatening both me and those I loved was to blame. What I'd been doing so far to fight them, to try to get myself out of this, wasn't working.

Donna needed to know what was happening. My friends deserved my honesty. I needed their help, their support, their advice, but most of all, it was now abundantly clear that the only way to protect them was to tell them the truth.

The threat was too unpredictable, too monolithic for me to monitor on my own.

I had to come clean to the girls.

CHAPTER TWENTY-ONE

Harlow

It took me a couple days to work up the courage. By Wednesday, Easton was done with gentle support and sent me a message to just suck it up and do it.

That evening, I got so in my own head, wrapped up in worrying about how they would react, I almost missed Amaya and Mena arriving. I heard Magda's voice, then two sets of footsteps on the stairs, and it finally registered in my brain. I stuck my head out my bedroom door just as Donna came out of her room with a frown.

"What are you two doing here?" she asked.

I'd messaged them to come over. This was not a conversation for the group chat—this needed face-to-face action. But I'd left Donna out of it because I knew she'd demand to know the reason and would drag it out of me before the others came over. I really didn't want to go through this twice, so . . .

"Are you OK?" Mena asked as they reached the top of the stairs.

"Harlow messaged us," Amaya said, and they all glanced at where nothing but my head stuck out of my door.

"I'm fine." Donna's frown deepened. "What's this about, Harlow?"

With a sigh, I pulled my door open and gestured for them to come in. They filed into my room and perched on the side of my bed in a neat little row, watching me expectantly.

I closed and locked my door and turned to face them—and my stomach *kept* turning. Over and over, making me feel sick with nerves. But I had to get this out in the open. Donna at the very least had a right to know her life was being threatened.

But as I looked at them watching me, concern and confusion in their eyes, I just couldn't find my voice. I started pacing, chewing on my thumbnail, and searched for the right words to start. But my mind was racing so fast I couldn't latch on to a single one.

My phone vibrated in my hand, and I looked at it reflexively. Another message calling my sister a whore and threatening sexual violence, accompanied by a photo of her at Davey's. There wasn't even a hacking demand—just torment for the hell of it.

Donna broke the silence. "Is this going to take much longer? I'm going to be late for my pottery class." Pottery was her hobby of the moment, the latest in her fevered search for something to devote all her energy to now that law was no longer in her future.

"Right." I nodded. I was so fucking tired. "I have something to tell you guys. Something . . . *shit*!" I threaded my fingers through my hair and tried to take a deep breath.

"Harlow, you're starting to freak me out." Mena's voice was soft.

"Just spit it out. Whatever it is, we've got you, girl." Amaya sounded as firm and strong as Mena had gentle. But it was my sister who finally got me to start talking.

"Harlow." She fixed me with a worried look and grabbed my hand as I paced past her for the millionth time. "Tell us."

I looked at them, then let it all spill out. "OK, I'm gonna tell you some stuff. It's . . . well, it's pretty bad. But I need you to just listen, OK? Just let me talk until it's all out, and then you can ask questions and yell at me and . . . I dunno, fucking disown me or whatever."

When they all stared at me, expressionless, I propped my hands on my hips and stared them down. "*OK*? I need some kind of agreement here."

They nodded and mumbled, confused.

So I told them. All of it. The blackmail, the photos, Ocean1k, BestLyf, right down to Easton and me and the whole fucked-up situation. *Everything*. By the end of it I was breathing hard, my palms sweaty, and I had a strong urge to just run out of the room and hide.

Mena gaped at me, wide-eyed, her mouth hanging open. Donna had dropped her head into her hands about halfway through and just stayed in that position, her elbows on her knees. Amaya wore a blank expression, her arms crossed over her chest. When I made eye contact with her, she raised a questioning eyebrow.

I nodded. "I'm done."

She got to her feet and looked at me, then at the two on the bed, her lips pursed. "What the fuck is it with you bitches and keeping secrets?" she yelled, making me take an actual step back. That run-and-hide plan was looking better and better.

Mena finally snapped her mouth shut, and my sister lifted her head and frowned at Amaya.

"This one doesn't bother to tell us she's being fucking *tortured* at school"—Amaya pointed at Mena, then at Donna—"meanwhile this one is living a whole other slutty life, on the verge of a *mental breakdown*, for fuck knows how long. And you!" She jabbed a finger at my face and laughed darkly. "*You.* Does Devilbend Dynasty mean nothing to any of you? Is it just a fun hashtag to use on Insta? Am I the only one who actually takes this friendship seriously? I trust you all with my life and . . . and you all *lie*. What the fuck?!"

Amaya pinched the bridge of her nose and refused to look at any of us. I'd expected to be blasted, but I definitely hadn't thought things would go like this. Still, I realized this was just Amaya's way of expressing her fear and hurt. Because I knew her. And loved her. Because Devilbend Dynasty meant as much to me as it did to her.

I stepped forward, took her hand, and squeezed hard. She squeezed back.

"I'm sorry," I told her, then looked at my sister and cousin. "I'm sorry. I fucked up." I swallowed my pride, literally—the big lump in my throat making it hard to get the words out. "I need help."

"This is really serious, Harlow." Donna got to her feet too, Mena right behind her. We all bunched close together, and just like that, we were back to the issue at hand.

"I can't believe Coach Cooper is some evil hacker person." Mena shook her head.

"I can't believe you're fucking Mr. Monroe." Amaya grabbed her head and mimicked an explosion. "Like, *holy shit!*"

"We're not fucking," I said. "Yet."

Amaya snorted a laugh, and Mena shook her head again. But Donna pressed her lips together.

"Harls." My sister's voice was serious, concerned. "Is he pressuring you? Making you do things you don't want to?"

"What?" I reeled back and almost laughed, but I reminded myself how this might look to people who didn't know the whole situation. There was a reason why teachers dating students was completely unethical, not to mention illegal. "No. Donna, I swear it's not like that. I didn't even like him when I realized he was involved. But then we started spending all this time together, and . . . he's really smart, and caring, and talented, and I just . . . fell for him."

Donna still looked skeptical. Mena chewed the side of her lip, unsure, but Amaya was smirking, already on board this new ship.

"He resisted it for ages, but I could tell he felt the same way. He did the right thing, you guys. He tried to put distance between us. I didn't. In the end, we just

. . . we couldn't deny our attraction anymore. With the constant threat looming over our heads, life's too short, ya know?"

Mena had hearts in her eyes now, but Donna still looked unconvinced.

"Anyway, this is totally beside the point," I said. "I just told you your life is being threatened, and you're worried about my nonexistent innocence."

Donna waved that away. "I could get hit by a bus tomorrow. If they really wanted me dead, I'd be dead. I think they're bluffing. I think you should stop doing what they're asking. It's not worth it."

"You think they're . . ." I blinked, stunned. "You know what happened to Turner's family, what you and Hendrix were dragged into a few months ago. Chelsea just showed up *murdered*. The organization behind it all is making threats against you, and you think they're *bluffing*?"

"What would be the point in killing me? It's more effort than it's worth and would draw attention. The *threat* of it is much more useful to them to keep you doing what you're doing."

"Why aren't you taking this seriously?"

"I am." My sister rubbed my arm. "But do you really think they'd waste resources on offing a high school senior over a noncompliant hacker? If we notice anyone following us or something feels off, we can always get private security. You know Dad would jump at the idea without even asking questions."

Our dad had wanted to get us a bodyguard each when we turned twelve and started leaving the house alone. He could be a little overprotective. Thankfully Mom put the brakes on that, but Donna was right. We had resources at our disposal too.

"Can we do that now? Just in case?" I asked.

Donna shrugged. "I don't think it's necessary."

"You're being kind of blasé about this, D," Amaya said.

"Thank you!" I threw my hands up.

"I don't mean to be. Look, I know this is serious, but I don't want to overreact. We'll tell the guys, of course, and we should probably avoid going anywhere on our own, but I'm guessing you have some kind of plan for sorting this out?" Donna raised her eyebrows.

"Well, yeah, but . . ."

"Great!" My sister smiled. "You can tell me about it after my pottery class."

"You're still going to that?" Amaya sounded as outraged as I felt.

Donna shrugged. "I went through a lot recently. I nearly destroyed myself and Hendrix trying to live my life like I *thought* I should. I'm not about to start holding back from making myself happy now because of some sociopathic asshole."

She had a point but . . . "What about the videos of you at Davey's? Even if you don't think the death threats are real, I've seen those videos with my own eyes—which I now want to gouge out, by the way. They could definitely release those."

"Let them." Donna's voice was all defiance. "I will not be shamed or judged for my sexual appetites and preferences."

"I appreciate your feminism and 'I'm going to live my life' attitude," Mena spoke up, "but, you guys, maybe we should tell our parents about this. Or call the cops or something. This is really serious."

"No parents and no cops," I said firmly. "We need evidence first. If we tell Mom and Dad, they'll go straight to the police, and then who knows how BestLyf will retaliate? Against Donna, against Easton and his brother, maybe even against you guys. I can't trust the police yet. Everyone can be bought."

"Fuck, you sound even more paranoid than usual," Amaya said.

"Yeah, well, it's been a crazy couple of months. And is it really paranoia if they actually *are* watching you?"

"Fair point."

"I agree. No parents," Donna said. "Yet. But I really do think you should stop giving them what they want. Call their bluff. And I really need to get going to my pottery class."

"Again with the fucking pottery class." Amaya rolled her eyes, but Donna had already pulled the door open. I shared a look with the others, and we all followed her down the stairs and into the garage.

"What are you doing?" Donna frowned at us as she unlocked her car.

"We're going with you." I pulled the passenger door open. "You just agreed we shouldn't go places alone. You're going to give me a damn heart attack, Donna. I have been dying with worry for you over the last few months, and you just ... don't give a shit."

Donna watched me for a moment, then sighed and got into the car, followed by the rest of us. I didn't know you could put a seat belt on angrily, but that was what I did.

No one spoke until she pulled out of our driveway and headed toward Devilbend.

"I'm sorry if it seems like I'm not taking this seriously," my sister finally said, keeping her eyes on the road. "I am. I just refuse to let anyone dictate how I live my life. And I hate that you're going through exactly that. And I hate that you didn't think you could come to me with this. I would've helped you, Harls."

"I know." I leaned my head on the window. "I just wanted you to be happy. I wanted to protect *you* for once. I wanted to clean up my own mess."

"It's not your mess," Amaya piped in from the back. "That dick did this."

"Yeah, and even if it was, we'll always be here for you." Mena reached out from the back seat to grip my shoulder.

I had to clear my throat and take a deep breath to keep the tears at bay. "Thank you. I love you all. But I can't just stop doing what Ocean1k says. They have too much on me. Even if you think they're bluffing about threats against you, Donna, they have proof of me doing so much illegal shit. And it's not just my life on the line. This affects Easton too. They have a picture of us . . . kissing."

The three of them cursed profusely at the same time.

"All right then, what's the plan?" Donna had gone into organization mode; she was dangerous when she got like this.

I ran them through the plan we'd vaguely figured out, answered their questions, and told them how little luck we'd had getting to Coach's devices. By the time we arrived at the pottery studio, they were completely up to date and on board to help, determined to find a way to get this done.

We all ended up taking the pottery class together—luckily, they had spots for us—and while Donna took it seriously, the rest of us just made a mess and had fun. I could hardly believe how much better I felt now that I'd told my girls about it all. Just knowing that they knew what I was going through, that they were ready to support me . . . I felt more grounded, more confident, more hopeful.

We were actually laughing as we walked out of the studio at the end of the class. Donna had managed to create a perfectly symmetrical little vase by the end of it—she was too good at everything. The rest of us had ended up with blobs vaguely resembling bowls.

"Shit, Turner is going to have a field day with this." Mena groaned. With no one around on the street as we made our way to Donna's car, the conversation turned back to my recent revelations.

"Is there any way you can *not* tell him?" Amaya winced, picking out a bit of clay that had splatted into her glorious long hair. "Because you're right, he's going to flip his shit."

"No. He should know." Mena sighed.

Turner went into a rage anytime BestLyf was so much as mentioned. Recent events would confirm all his worst suspicions.

"Just try to make sure he doesn't do anything stupid and expose us," I insisted. "I'll talk to him too."

Before anyone could say anything else, a figure stepped out in front of us.

"Ladies." A baseball cap low on Shady's head cast his face in shadow, even as dusk stole more light away by the second, but his voice and the tracksuit were unmissable.

"Shady?" Donna stepped forward and crossed her arms. "You know most people just send a message when they want to talk."

"You're lookin' fine." He stepped up to her and grinned. "But you're not the sister I'm after today. Hey, baby girl." He tipped his head at me.

I rolled my eyes and gave him a lazy wave.

Donna frowned at me over her shoulder. "What could you possibly want with my sister?"

I wanted to know the same thing.

"We got some business." He stepped to the side and opened the back door of his black SUV, the interior light making his white tracksuit glow. "Let's go for a ride. I'm calling in my favor."

Why now? I had the shittiest luck lately. "Can't this wait?" I almost pleaded.

"Nope. Let's go." Shady jerked his chin at the car.

"What deal?" Donna demanded, now addressing me. "What the hell is this? What did you do?"

I cringed. "Shady got us access to the security system so I could try to find out who got the footage of you, but it was a bust. In exchange, I promised him one favor."

Donna dragged her hand down her face.

"I ain't even gonna make you do any illegal shit. All you gotta do is come for a drive and talk to someone. But I'm a busy man, and I'm running out of patience, so get in the fucking car." His voice took on a bit of a growl, and I remembered that for all his comical appearance and attitude, he was a dangerous man, nick-named Shady for a reason.

CHAPTER TWENTY-TWO

Harlow

Donna calmly walked up to Shady. "No way in hell am I letting my little sister get in a car with you. I'm coming with."

"So are we." Amaya locked elbows with me, and on my other side, Mena crossed her arms and nodded.

"Ah, come on." Shady smirked. "I don't bite."

"I know for a fact you do," Donna countered.

"Ew." I shook my friends off and walked over. "I've seen footage of you two fucking—I really don't need reminders of it. Let's just get this over with." I really appreciated my friends backing me up, but I needed to get Shady off my back. I couldn't afford any more distractions.

Shady threw his head back and laughed. "I like her."

Donna wouldn't drop the issue though, so after some bickering, two disgruntled criminals vacated the vehicle. I found myself in the middle of the back seat, Amaya and Mena on either side of me, with Donna riding shotgun as Shady drove.

During the tense, nearly forty-minute drive, we all fired questions at Shady. What did he want me to do? Who was it he wanted me to talk to? Where were we going? But apparently, now that he had me in a car moving too fast for me to jump out, he didn't feel inclined to answer. The only time he spoke, it was completely unrelated to the current situation.

"How's Hendy doing?" he asked, keeping his eyes on the road.

Donna turned to him and pursed her lips. "If you answered any of his calls or messages, maybe you'd know how he was doing."

"Yeah. I've been busy." Shady scratched his chin.

Donna huffed and went back to staring out the window.

The rest of the drive passed in silence, and eventually, Shady pulled into the parking lot of what appeared to be a club. It was on the opposite side of Devilbend to Davey's and looked a little nicer—but not by much.

This early in the evening, the parking lot was mostly empty, but Shady drove around the building and parked in a reserved spot right by a back entrance. As we exited the car, the unassuming door swung open, held by a chick with a high ponytail and dark makeup.

"Boss." She nodded as Shady passed. If the fact that he was bringing underage girls into a club bothered her at all, she didn't show it. Amaya even still had her school uniform on. She and my sister strutted in behind Shady with their shoulders back, noses in the air, as if they had every right to be there.

I didn't feel nearly as confident, all caught up in what the fuck waited for me in there, but I did my best to look as sure of myself as my friends did. Mena looped an arm through mine, giving me support I hadn't realized I needed so badly.

I turned my head to smile at her, but she was looking at the chick holding the door open.

"Your winged liner is impeccable." Mena stared at her, and the chick smiled for the first time.

"Thanks."

"What brand do you use?"

They chatted as we passed through a corridor and weaved our way through the main club area—definitely nicer than Davey's. It had booths at one end, a proper dance floor, a DJ setup, and floors that weren't sticky. A real classy joint, this one.

Shady led us into another hallway, this one faintly lit and decorated like the main room. There were four doors—we stopped at the first.

He placed his hand on the knob and fixed me with a look. "They only asked to speak with you, baby girl."

Donna responded before I could. "No. We all go in or we all leave."

"Whatever." Shady looked *so done* with this whole thing.

As soon as he opened the door, I rushed past the others to lead the way through. I appreciated my friends being here with me, but this was my mess, and I wanted to meet it head-on.

"What the fuck?" I stopped so suddenly Donna nearly crashed into me.

Changing neon lights lit a small, relatively clean room, just big enough for a leather couch, a chair, and a small side table. I was confused about the room's purpose for a moment, but then I spotted the mirrors lining one wall and the pole in the corner.

The three people who'd clearly been waiting for us looked as surprised as I was pissed.

"What the hell is this, Shady?" Donna demanded.

"Absolutely fucking not." Amaya cut her hand through the air. "We're leaving."

Shady didn't say anything. Neither did Mena. She just stared at the people who had made her life hell at her old school. The people who had told her to kill herself. The people who had hurt her over and over again. Or two of them, anyway. The third was Donna's ex.

William Frydenberg had nearly beat Hendrix to death, with the help of his piece-of-shit father, just before we exposed his dad as a criminal. He wasn't supposed to step foot in Devilbend—there were restraining orders—which was probably why we had to drive forty minutes out here. Will stood next to the couch with his arms crossed over his peacoat, looking every bit the privileged fuckboy he was.

He turned to Shady. "You were only supposed to bring Harlow."

Shady shrugged. "You never specified who *not* to bring. We're square now, you and me. We're done."

He had his serious face on, the one that radiated danger. Will looked as if he wanted to argue, but instead he nodded.

Jayden Burrows stepped forward, his skinny jeans and long hoodie much more casual than Will's look. He'd lost that cocky smirk he'd worn last time I saw him though. The girls and I closed ranks in front of Mena. I was prepared to go fully feral to stop him from touching her. The shit he and his friends had put her through would haunt her for the rest of her life. She was still in therapy for it.

He stopped and held his hands out. "We just want to talk. It's important. And private." He threw Shady a look. "Can we have the room for a while?"

"Nah, I think I'll stay." Shady leaned back against the wall.

"This doesn't concern you," Will gritted out. Looked as though he still hadn't gotten his temper in check.

Shady remained unfazed. He just lifted the front of his shirt, pulled out the gun tucked into his pants, and let it hang in front of him, both hands folded over it casually.

Everyone in the room tensed. The problem with Shady was that you never knew what his game was. He could've been throwing his weight around to protect us, but just as likely we were all in danger of a bullet to the head if he didn't like what he heard. Or maybe he just wanted to mess with us.

"Fuck this. We're leaving," Amaya said again, turning for the door.

The third person—a girl our age I was struggling to place—finally spoke up.

"Mena, please. We don't want any trouble. Just hear us out. We're trying to do the right thing here."

She was in jeans and a white sweatshirt, tall, pretty.

I cursed under my breath as I recognized her. She was the girl I'd seen at Davey's that night—the one who seemed vaguely familiar. I hadn't given her any thought since, too preoccupied with everything else. Kelsey had been part of the group of girls bullying Mena but had backed off when Donna threatened her with something—something she still hadn't told us about.

I turned to look at Mena. Donna and Amaya were already at the door, but Mena hadn't moved, her eyes on the three assholes in front of us. I'd expected her to be scared, emotional, cowering. But she looked confident and calm as she stood there, staring them down. She looked fucking *strong*.

Mena folded her hands in front of her, similar to how Shady held his gun. "Let's hear them out." Her voice was steady, almost bored.

I nearly grinned, pride swelling in my chest. She wasn't letting anything get her down anymore.

Donna came up beside her and leaned in. "Are you sure?"

Mena gave her a small smile. "I'm sure. They went to a lot of trouble, and there's nothing they can do to us now—not without much worse consequences. They must have a damn good reason for orchestrating this."

Amaya sighed and crossed her arms, one hip popped.

Donna nodded. "Say what you came to say."

"I saw you at Davey's that night." Kelsey looked right at me. "I thought it was a little odd, and I asked Shady about it. He told me what you were doing in that back room."

I flashed Shady an annoyed frown, but he didn't look even remotely contrite.

"I told the others"—she gestured vaguely to Jayden and Will—"and we thought we should warn you."

"How the hell do you three even know each other?" Mena asked. Jayden and Kelsey went to her old school in Devilbend North—an underfunded public school in a bad neighborhood. Will had attended Fulton Academy with us until recently.

"Jayden's dad used to work for BestLyf. Our dads kind of knew each other, and we crossed paths at company picnics." Will's voice contained a good dose of derision, and I had a feeling "company picnics" was code for something else. "We know you're trying to get info or whatever. Fight back against the big evil corporation. We just wanted to warn you. You need to stop. Now. Before someone who's *really* dangerous notices."

"You're threatening us?" Donna sounded amused, and I knew her well enough to know that was dangerous in itself. "Last I checked, both your dads were in prison, and neither one of you was permitted to step foot in Devilbend."

Will's lips thinned. He looked as if he wanted to start arguing, but Kelsey jumped in first. "No. We're not threatening you. We're warning you."

"Why? Why would any of you give a shit?" Donna countered.

Kelsey swallowed and looked at Mena. "Because we're trying to do better. Be better than our parents."

All four of us snorted or rolled our eyes.

"I know you think we're evil, horrible people. But we're trying to be better. I want to be better. We asked to see only you, Harlow"—her eyes flashed to me, then back to Mena—"because we didn't want to upset Mena. But since you're here, I'm sorry. I am so sorry for all we put you through. For all the horrible, mean, disgusting things I did to you."

Mena's face didn't give anything away, her posture still rigid, her hands still folded, but her breathing grew heavier.

"We could've been friends, you and I," Jayden said. "We were briefly. I wonder if anything would've turned out differently—if I would've turned out differently—if I wasn't so fucking stupid. I'm sorry I abandoned you. I'm sorry for all the shit I put you through. I'm sorry I wasn't strong enough to know that power and popularity are worthless if you hate who you become in order to have it."

Were these assholes serious? *The nerve!*

"Is that it?" Amaya shrugged. "A pointless warning and empty apologies? Message received. Let's go."

"Whatever it is you're doing, *stop*." Will looked at us each in turn. Was he going to apologize too? But no, Will may have been with the "sorry gang," but he was still the same cold asshole. "You have no idea who you're dealing with. There is no fighting back. I know you think you run this town, Donna, but this is not something you can solve with rumors and threats." He turned to me. "Or amateur hacking and sleuthing."

I raised my eyebrows. "You have no idea what you're talking about."

"No, *you* have no idea." His voice rose. "You're trying to stop a speeding train by standing in front of it and holding your hands out. You're going to get squished like bugs."

"And you'll ruin what they're trying to—" A whack in the stomach from Kelsey cut off Jayden's outburst. She and Will both glared at him.

"Ruin what?" Donna demanded. "Who's *they*?"

"Never mind that," Will gritted out. "We're trying to help you. For once in your life, just do as you're told."

Now all of us raised our eyebrows, indignant. If there was a surefire way to make us do something, it was to order us not to. That was one thing my girls and I had in common—one way we were always in sync.

"So, you drag us here, make demands, but you won't share any information?" Mena cocked her head. "Kelsey, what are you even doing here? You testified against the others. We were done."

"I have a debt to pay. It didn't feel right not doing anything when I saw Harlow at Davey's."

"What does that even mean?" I threw my hands up, frustrated.

Kelsey fixed Donna with a confused look. "You didn't tell them?"

When we first found out Mena was being bullied, Donna got all our friends to turn up at Mena's school and pretty much threatened and intimidated the culprits into leaving Mena alone. She had something on all of them, some way to poke at their vulnerabilities, their families. But whatever she whispered in Kelsey's ear that day was scary enough to send the mean girl running. Donna had never told us what it was.

"Secrets only have power while they remain secret" was my sister's answer at the time, but I never thought much about it. Now that I was carrying so many heavy, crushing secrets myself, the words hit me in the chest with the weight of their meaning.

Kelsey sighed and dropped onto the arm of the couch. "My mom was never very smart—never able to keep a job longer than six months, always forgetting to pay the utilities . . . just a mess. A couple of years ago she went to this free seminar with a friend, run by BestLyf, and she got addicted or something. She went to all the free ones, then she started going to the paid ones, but by that time she didn't have a job because she'd missed so many shifts to go to seminars and trainings, group events, volunteering . . . whatever. It took over her whole life. She borrowed a lot of money from bad people, but eventually they cut her off. When she couldn't afford to pay for any more courses, BestLyf dropped her, all her new friends abandoned her. She was broken, completely defeated. They'd decided she was useless, and she believed them.

"But there was still debt to pay. A lot of debt. She started stripping in a couple of clubs to pay it off, then eventually that turned into hooking. That's what Donna found out. That my mother was a whore. I was so worried about my reputation, about the one last bit of normalcy I had—my friends and school—I would've done anything to keep that secret. But it doesn't matter anymore. I dropped out of school. I don't have friends."

I almost didn't want to ask—I was actually beginning to feel sorry for her—but I had to know. "Why?"

"My mom died. An overdose with one of her clients. Except she'd never touched drugs. She made a lot of mistakes, but she never did drugs."

Kelsey's nostrils flared, and a cold chill ran down my spine. But why would BestLyf bother killing a woman who was no longer any kind of threat to them?

"My little brothers are in foster care, and I can't get them back until I can get a steady job and an apartment," Kelsey went on. "But I can't do that while I have my mom's debt to pay. Shady bought all my debt. He's the only one I owe now, so at least I don't have to . . . Point is—whatever you think you're going to achieve, the price is too high if you fail."

"And you will fail," Will said, punctuating Kelsey's story.

I sighed. Even if I did, reluctantly, believe Kelsey, they weren't giving us any information. And despite their warnings, we couldn't just stop trying to take Ocean1k down. I couldn't live like this. Easton couldn't either.

"Warning received," Donna said, finality in her tone. "Now here's one from us. Stay out of Devilbend like you're supposed to. Don't contact us. Leave us alone."

Will smiled sadly and shook his head. "I've already told you, D, there's nothing you can do to hurt me, nothing you can do to me that's worse than what my sperm donor has already done."

With those chilling words hanging in the air, Mena was the first to turn and head for the door. Donna, Amaya, and I silently filed out after her, Shady following us.

We made our way through the slightly busier club and back out into the fresh night air. I took several deep gulps of it, still processing that oppressive, intense, completely unexpected conversation.

"Joey will drive you back." Shady tapped something into his phone, already turning to leave.

I grabbed him by the elbow. "Whatever favor I owed you has been paid."

He eyed my hand on his elbow, then looked at me with narrowed eyes before nodding once. "We're good."

I dropped my hand, and Donna appeared at my side. "Shady."

His eyes softened a bit when he looked at her, and I wondered if this degenerate was actually capable of genuine feelings.

"Can we trust them?" she asked, and my mouth dropped open. Donna wanted Shady's opinion? "Do you know anything? What they were referring to when they wouldn't answer our questions? If you ever really gave a shit about Hendrix, or me, please..."

Please? I could count on one hand the number of times my sister had said please in a non-sarcastic way to someone other than family or one of the girls.

"I don't know," Shady said, then clamped his mouth shut, a muscle ticking in his cheek. He looked troubled and more than a little unhappy.

Donna sighed and nodded.

A guy in jeans and a baggy sweatsuit jacket came out through the same door, nodded to Shady, and got behind the wheel of the same SUV we'd arrived in. As soon as he appeared, Shady dropped any hint of uncertainty or worry from his expression—a neutral mask falling over it all.

Then he was gone, and we were getting into the car, and my mind just kept whirling through the silent ride back.

Despite all the surprises and disturbing information we'd just learned, it was my sister's comment about the power of secrets that I couldn't seem to stop mulling over.

CHAPTER TWENTY-THREE

Easton

Donna Mead walked into my office with a disturbingly even expression on her face. That girl would've made a brilliant lawyer. But I guess she wanted to be a lawyer about as much as I wanted to be a teacher. She was smarter than me too—got out before it was too late.

"Miss Mead." I smiled and gestured to the chair across from my desk. "How are you?"

She sat down, but her posture remained rigid, her legs crossed, her eyes—so much like Harlow's—staring me down. When she didn't say anything, I figured I might as well begin.

"Now, I know you've recently made a change in your plans for college education. Do you know what you'd like to do after high school? Are there any schools I can recommend? Any particular—"

"Let's cut the bullshit."

I raised my eyebrows. "Excuse me?"

"I know you're fucking my sister, you pervert." Her voice didn't rise, but just a hint of disgust and derision appeared in her sneer, aimed directly at me.

I resisted the urge to clear my throat or fidget. I simply stared her down and tried to get the conversation back on track. "We're here to discuss your future, Donna. Now, as I was saying—"

"What about Harlow's future? What happens to her when she gets too old for you and you move on to some poor fourteen-year-old because grown women can't get you off? What happens to my sister's future when you get locked up for molesting minors? She seems to think she's in love with you, but this is *wrong*. You're taking advantage of her, and I'm not just going to sit here and let you ruin her life. You won't be able to get a job cleaning toilets when I'm done with you."

I leaned back and rested my elbows on the armrests. I wanted to smile at her; I admired how intensely protective Donna was of her sister. "Are you done?" I asked instead, managing to keep a straight face.

"No." She crossed her arms. So fierce. "Harlow is kind and sweet and smart. I know she doesn't get good grades, but she's smarter than you and me combined—people just don't see it. She has a family and friends who love her like crazy, and we . . . I'm not going to let you ruin her life. You don't deserve her. So do us all a favor and quit while you can. Pack your shit and leave and never look back. I suggest Canada—you wouldn't last in Mexico."

This time I couldn't stop my lips from quirking into a small smile. "I tendered my resignation two weeks ago."

She hadn't expected that. Her arms dropped, and her brow furrowed in confusion the tiniest bit. "What?"

"My last day is next Friday. I quit as soon as I realized I was falling for your sister. Because you're right—it is wrong for me to be a teacher and be with her. We've crossed way too many lines already, but I don't want to feel dirty or wrong for loving her. I don't want her to feel like she has to keep secrets from her loved ones. So I quit. Because it was the right move for me. Because I agree—I *don't* deserve her. But I'm going to spend my life trying my goddamn best to make her happy and keep her safe. If she'll let me."

I leaned forward and fixed her with a firm look. "And if you think your sister is still a kid, you don't know her as well as you think. She's an incredible, brave, determined woman, and she'll never be too old for me because I intend to grow old with her."

"So you're going to quit your job at one of the top schools in the country, ruin your career, and then eventually resent her for it? Does Harlow know you've quit?"

"I haven't told her yet, because I'm not just doing it for her. This isn't what I want to do with my life. Having Harlow around, going through this situation with her, has only just made me admit it to myself. Life's too short to spend in a job that makes you miserable. I think you might understand what that feels like."

Donna watched me with calculating eyes. I meant every word. Hopefully I could build a bridge with Harlow's family eventually, because I did want them—her—in my life.

"OK." Donna finally nodded. It looked as though it pained her to concede anything . . . *ever*. "Yeah, I do get that. And my sister really cares for you, so . . . I don't know. Don't fuck it up. Don't hurt her."

"Or you'll hurt me." I smiled. "I don't doubt it. And for what it's worth, I think it took a lot of courage to be honest about the fact that you don't want to go into law. It's the kind of backbone I wish I'd had when I was your age and my parents were pushing me into teaching."

"Thanks." That got a small smile from her. Then her face turned stern again. "Seriously, though, don't hurt my sister."

"I promise you—the only person trying to hurt her is Ocean1k. And I'm going to do everything in my power to stop them."

"*We* will. Harlow is not alone in this anymore. I mean, I know she had you and everything, but now she has us too. We're going to help bring Ocean1k down. No one messes with Devilbend Dynasty."

I had no idea what Devilbend Dynasty was, but I didn't doubt for a second she and her friends would do whatever it took to get Harlow out of this crazy blackmail mess. "Thank you, Donna. Now, should we use what time we have left to discuss your plans for after high school?"

We spent the rest of the appointment exploring options for Donna's future—as intended—discussing fields of study, colleges, gap years, and international programs. She still hadn't decided on a clear path, but I had no doubt she would succeed in whatever she chose to devote herself to. And hopefully I'd at least helped her think some of it through.

By the time she left my office, the hostility she'd walked in with had vanished, and I tentatively hoped I'd managed to get Donna Mead on my side. No small feat.

Not five minutes later, another Mead sister walked through the door.

"Hi, Mr. Monroe, do you have a moment?" she asked, slightly louder than usual, no doubt for the benefit of the people walking past.

"Sure. What can I help you with, Miss Mead?" I fought the smile trying to break through. Any time I laid eyes on her, I wanted to grin and scoop her into my arms.

"Thank you, sir." She shut the door and came to stand in front of my desk. "I bumped into Donna just now and wanted to make sure you weren't bleeding out on the floor or something."

"Your sister is very protective of you." I chuckled. "But it's fine. We talked. No blood was shed. I think I may have even won her over."

Harlow raised her eyebrows. "I'm impressed."

"Listen, I know this isn't the best time for this, but I have to tell you something." I glanced at the closed door. No one could hear us, but the door was glass, next to a window. If anyone happened to walk past, this couldn't look like anything more than a conversation between a careers counselor and a student.

"I quit my job," I said.

She smiled, then frowned. "I don't want you to do that for me."

"I'm not. I promise." I gripped the armrests of my chair to stop myself from getting up and wrapping her in a hug. "I gave my notice two weeks ago. I realized

I was having real feelings for you, and it made me question a lot of things. Mostly it made me realize I didn't want to live my life according to what other people wanted. I want to tattoo, and I'm good at it. I love it. And I'm a shitty teacher."

She laughed and shook her head. "You said it, not me. I'm happy for you. If you're doing it for yourself, I'm really happy."

"I am. But I won't lie. The fact that it makes it easier for us to be together is a massive bonus."

She smirked. "Mr. Monroe, that is a rather inappropriate thing to say to a student."

"No one can hear us, Miss Mead. So long as we don't give anything away with our body language or faces . . ."

I trailed off, realizing what a colossal mistake I'd made as Harlow's lips curved slowly into the most wicked grin I'd ever seen.

"Well, that's true." She rolled her shoulders back, clasped her hands behind her back, and stood straight like a good girl. "And we're not stupid or reckless. As much as we might want . . . to do things, we wouldn't make such a silly mistake as to do them on school grounds."

I narrowed my eyes and pursed my lips, silently warning her, but a part of me wanted to know exactly what . . . *things* she was talking about. "Of course not. You should get to your next class."

"Oh, absolutely." She nodded with an innocent look on her face. "Just one last thing."

She looked me dead in the eyes. *Shit.*

"If we were a bit more stupid and reckless, I just want you to know that I'd check there was no one coming past the door, then I'd duck under your desk."

Her eyes flicked to the very desk, then looked up at me through her lashes. I shifted in my chair, my pants suddenly feeling tighter.

"You're doing a great job keeping a straight face now," she went on, "but I wonder if you could manage it as I unhooked your belt, pulled your zipper down, and reached into your pants to stroke you."

My heart started to hammer, my hard-on almost painful. I had to clench my teeth to stop myself from opening my mouth to pant like a dog.

"Then I'd take your cock out and wrap my lips around it." She licked those plump lips, making me wonder how exactly that would feel. "I'd suck you down as far as possible. I wouldn't tease you. I have to get to class, and you probably have a million things to do—there's no time for teasing. I'd make quick work of it, licking and sucking until you came down my throat. And I'd swallow it all up—to make sure I didn't leave a mess, of course."

I reached up to rub my chin, covering my mouth so I could release a shuddering breath. "Fucking hell, Harlow." I groaned behind my hand.

"Anyway, I'd better get to class." With a bright smile, she practically skipped to the door. "Thanks for listening, Mr. Monroe," she threw over her shoulder.

And then she was gone, leaving me in my office chair with a raging boner, wondering how the fuck that had escalated so fast.

Through pure luck I didn't have a class to teach that period and managed to force myself to focus on grading sophomore papers—a proven boner killer.

Neither my dick nor I were particularly happy about it, but I got through most of the rest of the day without seeing Harlow again. Until the second to last period, that is. Ms. Murphy had called out sick once again, and I had to substitute.

The last time I'd had to teach this class and pretend I didn't know Harlow from the rest of these miscreants, it was torture. The jealousy that came up when Drew Ingram had his arm around her almost drove me to complete distraction.

It hadn't been that long since then, but a lot had happened, a lot had changed. And there was Harlow, who'd only just hours earlier said the dirtiest things to me, sitting in her seat and pointedly not looking my way. And there was Drew, sitting next to her and openly glaring at me. I supposed he knew, then. Harlow had said she'd told her friends. I couldn't blame her. I couldn't blame him either, especially if they had history. I just hoped he wouldn't blow it for us by doing something stupid—like punching my lights out in the middle of class.

Teaching this class last time had been hard. This time was almost impossible.

I forced myself to focus on the lesson, one step at a time, and made a conscious effort not to look in their direction. It was the only way to keep a straight face. At some point, out of the corner of my eye, I saw Harlow lean over and whisper something harshly in Drew's ear. His glaring eased up after that, and miraculously, we got through the rest of the lesson without incident.

The bell rang, and all the students scrambled to rush for the door, throwing me wary glances, as if I might start breathing fire at any moment. Granted, I was a little more temperamental than usual.

As everyone filed out, I couldn't help myself. I needed to talk to her.

"Miss Mead, a word, please," I called from behind my desk.

Drew's lips thinned, his expression stormy as he looked between us, as if he were preparing to throw my girl over his shoulder and make a run for it.

Harlow waited for the others to disappear before shoving Drew in the chest. "Stop. You're being ridiculous. I'll talk to you later. Go."

He sighed and gave me one last glare—a warning. "Call me after school or I'm coming to find you, Harls."

"All right. Go." She shooed him, and he finally left.

She came back to stand in front of my desk, much as she had in my office earlier. With the door at the other end of the room, no one could see us in here, let alone hear us. But anyone could pop their head in through the open door, so I still kept my voice low.

"Is Drew going to be a problem?" I asked.

Harlow sighed. "No. I just need to talk to him again. He's just . . . being an idiot. We've known each other since we were kids. He's protective."

"Will he tell anyone?"

"No. The only people other than my girlfriends who know are Drew, Hendrix, and Mena's boyfriend, Turner. We're all really close, and it's not going to go past that. We've all been affected by BestLyf in one way or another. They want to help us end this."

I nodded slowly. If she trusted them, I did too. We'd already been over this on the phone. Before I could stop myself, I asked the question I really wanted answered.

"Is this jealousy?"

She cringed, and my heart felt as if a mousetrap had suddenly closed on it—the sudden pain in my chest almost left me breathless.

"I don't think it's jealousy," she said. "Drew and I used to . . . hook up. It was never anything serious. Just physical. And I haven't been with him like that for months."

Some of the tightness eased. I didn't like thinking about her with another guy, but I liked very much that she hadn't been with him since we started . . . I didn't even know what to call it. *Dating* wasn't the right word at all.

"OK. Thanks for telling me." I started packing my things into my messenger bag.

"How painful was it to choke that out?" She chuckled. "You're cute when you're jealous."

I froze and looked at her over the rim of my glasses. She was teasing me? That little . . . I laced my fingers and placed my forearms on the desk, cocking my head slightly. "That's not a very appropriate way to speak to a teacher, Miss Mead."

She grinned, then folded her hands in front of her. "Sorry, Mr. Monroe. Are you going to punish me now?"

As she bit her bottom lip, the erection I'd been fighting all day returned with a vengeance.

If I had to walk out of here uncomfortable and aching, then so did she.

"Not in the way you'd like me to, I'm sure." I let my voice drop a little lower. "As you pointed out earlier today, we're both too smart and cautious to risk getting caught doing something . . . *indecent*. But if we *were* reckless, I'd make you go close that door, then walk back and sit on this desk right in front of me."

Her eyes widened in surprise, but her lips parted too. I was getting to her.

I resisted the urge to smile or wonder if her panties were getting wet yet.

"Easton, what are you doing?" she whispered.

"Like I said—nothing. But if I wasn't so cautious, I'd feel the weight of your breasts in my hands, bury my face in your cleavage as you sat on this desk. I'd drag my hands down your sides, then up under your skirt."

She swallowed and shuddered lightly. I allowed myself a little smile.

"Then I'd push your panties to the side to see how wet you were for me. Are you wet for me, Harlow?"

"Fuck. Yes," she breathed, wringing her hands where they were still clasped in front of her.

"I'd pull those panties off and have a quick taste while I was down there, but it would be silly to take too long and risk getting caught. So I'd undo my belt and pull my pants down just enough, drag you to the edge of the desk . . ." I flattened my hands on the desk and leaned back in the chair, doing my best to look casual in case anyone happened to walk in. "And I'd fuck you, right here, with all those people just on the other side of the door."

"I'd have to bite your neck to be quiet," she said, her voice strained.

"Oh, I wouldn't let you come." I smirked. "Don't forget we were discussing a punishment."

"You are just as awful as all your students say."

I gave her one last heated look, then got back to packing my things. "You're dismissed, Miss Mead."

"You are such an asshole." She laughed lightly, then turned around and walked out.

I finished putting my things away and pulled out my phone. For the second time that day, I needed to give myself time to calm down so I wouldn't walk through school pitching a tent.

As fun as it was teasing each other, I really couldn't wait to get Harlow into bed, and now I knew she wanted it just as badly as I did. I ached for her, and not just physically. I wanted to wake up with her in my arms, have breakfast together, do corny couple shit like go to a farmer's market or something.

I just wanted to *be* with her.

I opened the calendar on my phone, wanting to count out the few remaining days before my last day as a teacher, before my freedom. Something caught my eye amid all the appointments and reminders. I expanded the planner for next Friday and read over the item under the "Last day in hell" note again.

We still had the issue of Ocean1k to deal with. I was pretty sure I'd found a way for us to get what we needed, but Harlow and I couldn't do it alone. It would have to be a team effort. And it was risky, but fuck it. What did I have to lose?

Swinging my bag over my shoulder, I strolled out of the classroom, a slight smile on my face.

CHAPTER TWENTY-FOUR

Harlow

The first two periods went by in a blur. I never managed to focus well in class anyway, but that day it was next to impossible. I didn't take any notes, hardly heard what the teachers said. Mena and Hendrix both had to nudge me a few times in my social studies class to remind me to at least pretend to pay attention.

After all this time—the secrets and lies and feeling helpless at the mercy of a heartless hacker—it came down to this. By the end of the day, it would all be over one way or another. We'd done everything we could to plan it out, everyone knew exactly what they had to do, but so much was still out of our control. This could very well end in violence.

The bell rang, and I sprang to my feet, drawing a few weird looks from my classmates and the teacher. Mena and Hendrix packed up on either side of me.

"Breathe, Harls," Mena whispered in my ear. "We got this."

I forced myself to take slow, measured breaths, and we made our way out with the rest of the class.

Hendrix draped an arm around my shoulders and leaned in, his voice low. "You need to get your shit together, Baby Mead. It's just another day. If you don't look cool, everything else falls apart."

He was right. If Coach Cooper noticed me acting jumpy, he'd get suspicious immediately, and then who knew what would happen?

"How?" I whined. I couldn't *not* think about all the ways in which this could go horribly wrong.

"You take all those wriggly feelings writhing around inside, and you squeeze them into a tight little ball, and you shove them deep, deep down until they can't be seen or heard. And you put your mask on and put on the show of your goddamn life so the rest of us can do what needs to be done."

"That sounds healthy." I rolled my eyes.

Hendrix grinned. "Never said it was healthy, but it works. You can let it all out later. Right now, you strut down this hallway like you fucking own it and it's just another day in your privileged, sheltered little life."

"No one fucks with Devilbend Dynasty." Mena's voice was so steady it actually gave me confidence. I hated having to ask my friends to put themselves at risk, but her words reminded me I would do the same thing for each of them, and more.

I forced the nerves and worries aside, taking Hendrix's advice, and let my lips curve into a subtle smile that made me feel as if I were made of steel. I'd need to be if anything went wrong today.

Mena stopped, and we did too, Hendrix dropping his arm.

"Hold my books for a sec." Mena handed me her books and pencil case, then crouched down, fiddling with her perfectly tied shoe.

Hendrix looked around casually, checking for any teachers, then tapped his foot—the signal that she was good to go. She stood and, after giving me one last firm look, quickly disappeared into the girls' bathroom next to us.

Hendrix and I kept walking.

I went to my locker and deposited our books, then followed the rest of the student body and most of the faculty into the auditorium for assembly. It was crowded and loud and took forever to seat everyone—as usual.

Donna and Amaya were sitting near the front with Drew, Nicola, Luke, and a few other people we hung out with. Hendrix and I shuffled into the row behind them, and Donna tipped her head back so he could give her an upside-down kiss.

Easton stood near the stage, waving kids into seats with a bored expression on his face. I looked down and smiled—I knew for a fact he was dying on the inside just as much as I was.

We'd worked together over the past week to iron out the details of this plan, but he'd come up with the idea to strike during assembly. More than once during the week, though, he'd had second thoughts and tried to put a stop to it, to find a way to pull it off without my friends.

We hadn't seen each other outside of school at all and only spoke on the phone, trying to lie low and minimize any potential extra trouble. It was infuriating. Anytime I'd seen him in the halls over the last week, my fingers literally twitched with the need to touch him, lick him.

The dirty, bordering-on-phone-sex conversations we'd been having didn't help.

The last few students took their seats, and Headmistress Perry stepped up to the lectern. My heart kicked up a notch as she gestured for silence and the several hundred people in the room stopped talking. I forced myself to breathe steadily and slumped down in my seat. Casting my eyes around the auditorium, I spotted Coach near the main doors.

He had on his Fulton Academy tracksuit. As I watched, he tucked his cell into the pocket of the jacket.

I glanced at Hendrix. He didn't return my look but, after a moment, leaned in and whispered very quietly, "I see it."

Ms. Perry had barely gotten through her first sentence when my phone vibrated. I knew the others would've received the same message in our group chat, but as planned, no one checked their phones. It would've looked weird if we all peered into our laps at the same time.

I leaned my head on my hand and glanced down as I unlocked my screen.

About five minutes ago, Donna had sent a GIF of runners crouched at the starting line. *Ready*. Below that, Ford had just sent a GIF of a blindfolded woman walking into a wall. Fulton's surveillance cameras were down.

Here we go . . .

The fire alarm blared, startling half the students in their seats. The teachers shared confused looks but gathered themselves quickly. This was not a drill.

"Everybody remain calm and follow instructions out to the emergency area in an orderly manner," Ms. Perry said firmly through the microphone, then moved off the stage. Everyone got to their feet as teachers started ushering hundreds of scared, excited kids out the main doors.

Coach left the room before we managed to, getting caught up in the crowd. I hoped he wasn't going back to his desk or about to disappear.

When I finally did make it to the hall, I spotted him halfway to the school's main entrance, helping guide students out. Easton stood across from him, closer to the door. Coach had a severe look on his face, lips pursed, as he started to scan the crowd. Just before his eyes landed on me, I looked away and looped my arm casually through Donna's, laughing as though my sister had said something funny. Nothing to see here.

At the sound of my laugh, Drew picked Luke up in a fireman's hold and started barreling through the students, shouting, "I got you, bro! You're not turning into a kebab on my watch!"

Several kids laughed, but the teachers were not amused, chastising the two boys and reminding them to exit in an orderly fashion. While all eyes turned to them, Amaya gave my hand a quick squeeze and ducked down an empty hallway, going to hide behind the first set of lockers. I held my breath for a moment, but no one seemed to notice.

Hendrix broke away from us and rushed after Drew and Luke. "Hey! Who's gonna carry me out like a damsel?" he yelled after them, drawing even more attention. As he reached Coach Cooper, he pretended to look in the opposite direction and slammed right into him. He spun quickly and righted them both, muttering apologies, and then rushed on after his friends.

The look on Coach's face was murderous, but I didn't dare look directly at him. I forced air into my lungs when he stayed put instead of chasing the boys down. I pressed my palm to my pocket, waiting to see if it vibrated. If Hendrix hadn't managed to lift his phone, one of us would have to try again.

Nothing.

I waited until we were a little farther down the hall before checking it for good measure. No new messages.

But then my phone vibrated in my hand.

My heart dropped. Donna and I shared a brief worried look, and I quickly unlocked my screen—and breathed a massive sigh of relief. The message was from Amaya. She'd sent a GIF of a fuel gauge, the arrow pointing to empty. There was nothing to be found in Coach's office.

After she'd slipped away, Amaya had made her way to Coach Cooper's office to check his desk. She'd volunteered for this part of the plan because she said she had plenty of experience sneaking around—thanks to her mom constantly bringing men into the house. Plus, she had more confidence and self-assurance than anyone I knew; I had no doubt that if she got caught, she'd have no problem making up an excuse without looking guilty.

Easton had tried to insist he do this part; as a teacher, he was less likely to raise suspicion if someone happened to see him there. But we all agreed he needed to stay in plain view. Just as I did. Coach had to be able to see us both, or he'd get suspicious.

As Donna and I reached the front doors, Mena came walking up from around the corner, ready to slip back into the crowd. Mr. Kirke started to turn his head, and she froze, eyes widening. She had nowhere to hide.

"Mr. Kirke." Donna's commanding voice carried over the chatter of everyone else around us. "Is this a drill? Because we had one just last month, and it's terribly disruptive, especially for the seniors. As student body president—"

"Please keep moving, Miss Mead. You'll be updated with the rest of the students."

Mena rejoined the throng and moved up next to us, unnoticed.

I took her hand in mine. "You good?"

"Yep!" She smiled, then lowered her voice. "That was the funnest thing I've ever done."

I laughed and shook my head. "You need to get out more."

Mena had insisted she be the one to pull the fire alarm. She'd never done something "bad" before and had jumped at the opportunity.

The emergency meeting point was the gently rolling, manicured patch of grass next to the student parking lot, the front iron fence closing it in. By the time we reached the fence, the others were already there, leaning back against it, looking as if they were modeling for a Hugo Boss ad—draped over each other, sunglasses on, smugly beautiful.

They looked relaxed, but we all knew this short window of time was critical.

Drew wolf-whistled obnoxiously loudly and made some kind of crass joke about Mena, me, and a threesome.

Moments later, Turner came walking up the street in a hoodie, headphones swinging around his neck. Fulton was pretty far out of town and on a massive piece of land. The road outside the main entrance didn't get that much foot traffic, but a small strip of stores was fifteen minutes up the hill, so it wasn't that out of the ordinary.

Turner had ditched school to help with this part. None of us so much as glanced at him as he approached. Donna leaned back against Hendrix, her shoulder flush with Drew's next to her, their bodies blocking Hendrix's arm from view. I wanted to look over, make sure it went smoothly, but I forced my gaze elsewhere, flicked Mena's hair, tried to look casual. A few seconds later, Turner had disappeared around the bend.

Hendrix caught my eye and winked. He'd managed to pass the cell to Turner, who was now taking it to Ford in a parked car around the corner, laptop ready.

Arms wrapped around me from behind, and I jumped, then laughed when I realized they belonged to Amaya. "Fuck! You gave me a heart attack. You're like a ninja."

"A sexy ninja." She flipped her hair over my shoulder and snapped a few selfies of us, posting one to IG—#devilbenddynasty #firedrill #toohottohandle

"No issues?" I asked, voice low. After snooping around Coach's desk, Amaya had planned to sneak down the side of the gym and slip into the crowd through the parking lot. It left her exposed as she walked past the cars, but I hadn't noticed her, and it seemed no one else had either.

"Easy peasy, lemon squeezy." She grinned.

"Who's squeezing what now?" Drew called. "I want in on that."

The wail of sirens floated on the breeze, and I cursed under my breath. The fire department had already arrived. Never underestimate the power of several hundred children of the rich and powerful being in danger.

Ford needed time to crack into the cell and copy all the contents. He was good, but so was Ocean1k, and Kaye had no idea what kind of security he'd be up against or how long it would take.

The staff would arrange us into year levels to do a head count while the fire department inspected the school. Once the teachers called us to line up, we'd have to move away from the fence, and Turner would have no way of handing the phone back.

Two fire trucks pulled through the ornate front gates and came to a stop in front of the school, then about a dozen fire fighters in full gear rushed inside. A shrill whistle sounded, and the teachers started gesturing for everyone to be quiet.

I glanced over Hendrix's shoulder, but still no sign of Turner. *Shitshitshit!*

Panicked, my eyes went straight to Easton.

CHAPTER TWENTY-FIVE

Easton

Just as Mrs. Shepard—one of our fire wardens—blew the whistle, Harlow's wide eyes flew to mine. I ignored the pang of perverse pleasure at the fact she instinctively turned to me when she was worried, and made my eyes scan over her and her friends like the rest of the students.

I had no way of knowing if the plan so far had gone smoothly. The group chat messages only went to my burner phone, and I couldn't risk whipping out a completely different phone in front of all these people—in front of who we suspected was Ocean1k. Having to sit back and hope for the best infuriated me.

I had no doubt Ford could do what needed to be done; I trusted that Harlow's friends loved her fiercely and would do anything necessary to keep her safe. But this was my mess, Harlow's mess. It just didn't feel right having other people clean it up for us.

When the idea for using the assembly as a distraction came to me, I definitely didn't envision letting others take all the risks. But after several arguments and extensive planning, I had to concede it was the smartest way to go. If Harlow and I were in sight of Cooper the whole time and acting as if nothing was wrong, he'd be much less likely to get suspicious.

Still fucking killed me to just stand there, hands in pockets, a neutral mask in place.

Harlow's worried look clued me in that something had gone awry. I'd never met Mena's boyfriend, Turner, but I'd seen some guy in a hoodie walk past the fence; no one had come back the same way yet. Now Ella had started to get all the students lined up so we could do a head count, and Harlow was panicking. Didn't take a genius to figure out they needed more time.

Thinking quickly, I walked over to Ella Shepard just as she loudly blew the whistle again. Getting a couple hundred hormonal adolescents to pay attention during an exciting situation was a nightmare.

I cringed at the shrill sound, and she looked at me, her deep frown lifting a little. "Sorry, Easton, didn't see you there."

"That's all good. I just had a thought—about the head count."

"Yeah." She was only half paying attention, her gaze on the teachers trying to round everyone up.

"I know that in the drills we get the students to separate into their year levels pretty much as they come out onto the meeting spot, but that's because we lead them out of their classrooms, already with their peers. We've just come out of the auditorium—they're all mixed up and can hardly contain themselves."

"Yeah, it's a damn mess," she muttered, propping her hands on her hips.

"So instead of trying to wrangle them all at once, why don't we separate out all the freshmen first, then the sophomores, and so on. The younger ones are harder to wrangle—better if we work together."

She tilted her head from side to side, considering it. I glanced over the crowd. They were quieting down, starting to pay attention.

"Our fire-safety procedure doesn't follow that method," she said.

I shrugged, already trying to think of some other way to delay this. "Just a suggestion."

"It's a good one." She nodded.

I smiled and walked off to help as she updated the staff on the adjusted plan. Then she got out the megaphone and informed the students of what needed to happen next, instructing all the freshmen to make their way to the side of the field farthest from the fence.

I didn't dare look in Harlow's direction. All I could do was hope I'd given the others some breathing room.

By the time we had all the juniors lined up, Turner still hadn't come past the fence, and I had no idea what else I could do to buy more time.

Maybe I could fake a fainting? Or a seizure or something?

"All right, seniors!" Ella shouted through the megaphone.

The senior students started to move, as sluggish as teens always were.

Just as I'd decided to fake the symptoms of a burst appendix, a guy in a T-shirt came skateboarding along the road. I couldn't help glancing over. When I saw Harlow and her friends move away from the fence to line up with their classmates, I released a tense breath through my nose.

Most of the other students had been counted by the time we got to the seniors, and about five minutes after everyone had been accounted for, the firemen came streaming out of the building. Ella went to meet with the one heading in our direction, Headmistress Perry joining her.

After a few moments, Ella came back and spoke with a few of us teachers in a low tone. "We can start heading back in. Looks like it was a dumb prank. Headmistress is going to talk to the fire department, but she wants everyone back in the auditorium."

I nodded and moved off, passing the message on to a few other teachers as Ella got on the megaphone to tell the students.

As the students streamed back into the building, dragging their feet, not ready for this unplanned break to end, I looked over at Dale. He stood a few feet to my right, frowning. Was he just put out by the fire alarm? Or did he know his phone was missing? He looked in my direction, scowl deepening, and I looked away.

"Come on! Keep it moving!" I raised my voice, not speaking to anyone in particular.

The commotion of the fire alarm had acted as a pretty good distraction, but now a lot of people were reaching for their phones, bored while waiting for the crowd to move, or checking in with people at home. It was only a matter of time before he noticed his cell missing, if he hadn't already.

I caught sight of Harlow moving toward the front doors, her arm interlocked with Amaya's. All her friends were with her, none of them even glancing in my direction.

We'd aimed for Harlow's friends to slip the phone back before Cooper noticed it missing. But none of them had even come close to where we were standing.

Shit! What the hell was I supposed to do now?

To my utter shock, Dale reached into the pocket of his tracksuit pants and pulled out his phone, checking it as he kept one eye on the students. How in the actual fuck had they managed that? Cooper was on the other side of the field when the seniors started lining up. He'd moved next to me when all the students were instructed to head back inside. Harlow and her friends had been nowhere near him this whole time.

"Don't rat me out, man." He chuckled, voice low, before putting his phone back into his pocket.

I realized I'd been frowning at his phone and wiped the expression off my face, replacing it with a smile.

"I was just checking the score of a soccer match in France. I got some money riding on it." He gave me a wink, as if we were buddies sharing a harmless secret.

"Right. Yeah." I tried to look friendly. Was this some kind of mind game? Or was he really oblivious to what we were doing?

"Excuse me, Coach Cooper?" A freshman boy with curly brown hair and skinny arms walked up to Cooper and held out a cell phone. "I think someone dropped this. It was in the grass over there."

"OK. Thanks, Ben." Cooper patted him on the shoulder, and Ben ran off. "That's weird." He huffed a laugh and showed me the smartphone. "That's the second time someone's handed in this same lost phone. I must've dropped it earlier."

Oh god . . .

I glimpsed Donna just before she stepped through the main entrance, right as Ben caught up to her. She beamed at him, wrapped an arm around his shoulders, and kissed him on the cheek.

Oh no . . .

We'd pulled the plan off perfectly. Cooper's phone was lifted, copied, and returned without so much as a hint of him being suspicious of us. But it was all for nothing. It was the wrong phone, and we were back to square one.

It was difficult to swallow past the tightness in my throat—the mix of dread and frustration. I somehow managed to keep a neutral look on my face while wanting to tackle the asshole standing next to me, take his phone, and run for the gates like a maniac.

"Easton?" Irene appeared on my other side, pulling me from my rage fantasy. She wore an A-line skirt and a peach cardigan, her hair in a bouncy ponytail, and she looked *pissed*. "I can't find my cell. I think someone stole it."

"Stole it?" I raised my eyebrows. I'd never seen the sweet, quiet woman look murderous. It took me a moment to shake off the shock of constant surprises. "You sure you didn't lose it? When's the last time you remember having it?"

Her anger melted at my genuine concern, and she propped her hands on her hips and looked down, thinking. "I had it with me at my desk, then we all made our way to the assembly . . ."

As Irene retraced her steps, my mind connected the dots to the realization that had me reeling just moments earlier.

"Oh! Wait a sec." I snapped my fingers and turned to the man I despised more than anyone on the planet. "Dale? You still have that lost cell?"

"Yeah." He pulled it out of his jacket pocket.

Irene stepped around me and breathed a sigh of relief. "Thank god. My whole life is on that thing."

Coach handed it over, and she tucked the phone into her pocket.

"Thank you, Easton." She had that look in her eyes again—the same hopeful one she'd had on the terrace the night of the fundraiser.

I smiled, doing my best not to show anything other than polite friendliness as I withered on the inside.

I was glad Irene had gotten her phone back, but I was pretty pissed that all Ford had managed to copy would be pictures of cats and bookmarked cardigan sales, maybe some freaky porn if we were lucky.

What a joke.

CHAPTER TWENTY-SIX

Harlow

Everyone piled back into the auditorium. I sat with my friends, trying to act normal, wondering if they were bursting to jump up and down and scream as much as I was.

"I am deeply disappointed," Headmistress Perry said from the stage after all the students had retaken their seats. She enunciated each word, leaning into the mic so her voice reverberated through the room. "The fire department has informed me there was no sign of a fire anywhere in the building, and the fire alarm in the east hallway was pulled by someone without reason. We will find out who it was. If you know who it was and you don't come forward by the end of the day, your punishment will be as severe as that of the person who pulled the alarm."

Ms. Perry continued with her finger-wagging speech, but we knew she was wrong. They'd never find out who pulled that alarm. Ford had turned all the cameras off, and none of us would blab. We had too much riding on this. When you believed that strongly in something, had that much conviction the end goal was worth it, you'd bend all the rules necessary to make it happen.

Maybe that was why Coach Cooper did all these horrible things. Did he just believe so much in whatever bullshit BestLyf had fed him that he was willing to ruin people's lives for it, put them in danger?

But even if he was sick in the head, he was dangerous, and this needed to stop before someone I loved got seriously hurt.

Donna gently placed her hand over mine, and I realized I'd balled both my hands into tight fists in my lap. I flexed my fingers and took a deep breath—I really needed to keep my shit together.

WWDD.

My fierce sister would roll her shoulders back, strut through the day as if nothing had happened, and keep everyone else in line too. Because secrets had power, and this one could be our salvation. If she could do it, so could I. If all my friends were willing to risk themselves for me, then I could hold my head high and protect us from any suspicion.

Once Ms. Perry had finished her lectures and threats, the rest of the assembly went ahead as originally planned, only shorter and more to the point. None of the student clubs performed, only the most relevant information was announced, and at the very end, Ms. Perry officially thanked Easton for his hard work at the school and said goodbye. When she instructed the students to give Mr. Monroe a round of applause, the noise became almost deafening. People whooped and cheered.

I threw my head back and laughed. They weren't so much applauding him as a teacher—they were celebrating his departure.

Easton tried to keep his glare in place, but I saw a grin split his face just before he turned away.

The rest of the day passed as uneventfully as I possibly could've hoped: We went to lunch. Drew cracked inappropriate jokes. Nicola babbled about how her mom had gotten her onto the set of some blockbuster she was starring in. We went to our last few classes and didn't even mention our semi-successful heist to each other.

I was hyperaware of my phone in my pocket, constantly waiting for it to vibrate with a message from Ford. Supposedly he'd gone straight home to start combing through the copied contents of the cell, but it had been hours, and we still hadn't heard anything. I was beginning to get a little nervous.

"Can you drop me off downtown, please?" I asked as soon as the girls and I all piled into the car.

"Is that wise in the middle of the afternoon? What if you're being watched?" Donna started the car and took off.

"Mr. Monroe might not even be home by the time you get there," Mena said.

"I know. But Ford will be. I need to know what he's managed to find. He's not replying to any messages, and I can't take this anymore." He hadn't even seen the messages in the group chat.

Amaya glanced back at me from the passenger seat. "What if something happened to him?"

"I was trying not to go there." My forehead dropped against the seat in front of me. The worry that he'd gotten into some kind of trouble had been gnawing at me for hours, but I'd done my best to focus on my annoyance that he hadn't been in touch—instead of those other, terrifying thoughts.

"We'll all go," Donna said in her in-charge voice and turned toward the center of Devilbend. I knew there was no point arguing once she'd made a decision. At least I wouldn't have to deal with whatever was coming alone.

We found a parking spot two blocks away from Easton's building and walked up the street, keeping an eye out for anything suspicious. Thankfully, we made it into the building and up to his floor without incident.

I rushed to his door and knocked. Then I banged. Then I banged and kicked incessantly as panic rose up inside me.

Donna and Amaya had to pull me back. I was making so much noise.

"Maybe he went out to get a snack or something?" Mena didn't sound even remotely confident in her own suggestion.

The lock on the door clicked, and it swung open.

Ford stood on the other side in sweatpants and a faded green T-shirt, his hair sticking up all over the place, one hand holding a bowl of cereal. He rubbed his eye with the heel of his free hand. "Hey."

"Hey?" I gaped at him. "Hey?!"

The girls shuffled us all inside and closed the door before I started yelling at this stupid idiot.

"Why are you always eating cereal?" I raged at him, and his eyes widened, glancing at the bowl. "It's four in the afternoon. What the hell is wrong with you?"

He scooped up a spoonful and spoke around the food, a bit of milk escaping from one corner of his mouth. "I get the feeling this isn't about cereal."

I smacked the bowl out of his hand. It clattered to the ground, milk and cereal splashing everywhere, but miraculously the dish didn't smash on the tiles.

"Jesus! What the f—"

"Why haven't you replied?" I cut him off. "We thought something had happened to you. I've been out of my mind all afternoon wondering if we got anything off the cell."

"What?" He scratched his head and pulled out his phone. "I sent a text in the group . . . oh . . ." He cringed. "I thought I sent it but I didn't. Oops."

All four of us laid into him then, berating him about all the text messages and the suspense and how thoughtless he was being.

"I'm sorry!" he yelled, cutting his hands through the air. "Fuck! I thought I sent it. I put my phone away and took a nap."

"I was so worried, you douche." My voice wavered, and I was horrified to feel my eyes getting misty. Without thinking too hard about it, I wrapped my arms around his waist. This jerk constantly stirred shit, but he'd somehow managed to weasel his way into my heart. "I'm glad you're not dead or kidnapped or whatever."

"Uh-huh." He rubbed my back, hugging me just as tightly. "Whatever. You love me. I'm telling Easton."

I pulled out of his grasp and whacked him on the arm. We did a little wrestle thing, swiping at each other's heads, until he pinned my back to his front, his arms banded around me.

"Hey! I'm Ford," he said to the others. I rolled my eyes at the sly grin in his voice.

The girls introduced themselves.

"Boyfriend, boyfriend, single." I pointed at them each in turn.

Amaya crossed her arms and smirked. I could just imagine the kind of look he was giving her. I couldn't blame him—she was stunning.

"And not interested." She smiled wider. How the hell did she make a smile look sarcastic? It was a gift.

The front door opened, and Easton let himself in. He took in the room and frowned. "Um . . . what?"

"Hey, bro!" Ford moved his arms up around my shoulders and leaned his chin on my head.

Easton's eyes narrowed. The girls all struggled to hide their amusement at his jealousy. I elbowed Ford, but he kept me in his clutches.

"What the hell is happening here? Why aren't you answering your phone?" Easton dropped his bag on the dining table and propped his hands on his hips.

"Haven't checked my phone. I've been busy with these fine ladies." I could hear the grin in Ford's voice. I elbowed him harder and this time got an *oof* out of him, but his damn stomach actually hurt my elbow.

Easton whacked Ford on the back of the head, and he finally released me.

"Oh my god!" Donna lifted her arms and let them flop to her sides. "Does no one else want to know what was on that damn phone?"

"Yeah." Easton looked so dejected as he rubbed his eye under the glasses. "I'm guessing it's a whole lot of nothing. I didn't want to risk messaging you all in the group chat, but we got the wrong phone."

My heart sank even as confusion set in. Hendrix had definitely stolen Coach's phone.

"What are you talking about, bro?" Ford leaned on the counter as I took Easton's hand. "We got him. The threatening messages on Telegram, the blackmail, the illegal shit he was doing at school, communication between him and whoever was giving orders. We got everything. This is definitely Ocean1k."

Everyone in the room breathed a massive sigh of relief. Mena actually leaned on her knees, while Amaya whipped her phone out, already letting the others know.

My heart soared just as quickly as it had plummeted earlier, but Easton didn't look excited at all. He looked pale.

"Wait!" Easton raised his voice, and everyone fell silent. "You're positive the device you copied is Ocean1k's?"

"Yeah." Ford shrugged. "It's all right there. There's no doubt."

Easton rubbed his hand over his mouth, then let it drop to his side. "Then Cooper isn't Ocean1k. Irene Richards is."

"*What?*" the girls and I said at the same time.

"After you got Ben to hand the phone back, Dale said it was the second time that day it had been handed in. His phone was in his pants pocket the whole time. You lifted the wrong device. Irene claimed it right in front of me. It's her. Has to be."

"That actually makes more sense." Ford looked disturbed, the teasing lightness gone from his tone.

"What do you mean?" I asked.

"Just some of the other stuff I found on there. Makes more sense it's a woman." He waved it away. I was itching to comb through it all myself.

"Wait." My head was hurting. It didn't add up. "What about the firewall logs? All the anomalies were on Cooper's computer, using his login."

"She could've snuck in there, learned his password?" Easton shrugged. "Anytime he's teaching a class, he's away from his desk."

"OK, but all the other PE teachers' desks are in that same area. Plus, you said you found her right after I left the night of the fundraiser. There's no way she could've taken that photo of us."

"They could be working together." Ford dragged a hand down his face. He looked as if he hated saying it as much as I hated hearing it. "Ocean1k could be more than one person."

I cursed under my breath.

"That's a possibility." Easton sounded almost upbeat. "Regardless, we have proof. Something concrete that ties to Irene Richards. Who knows what else that will lead us to? This is a win, guys."

Mena shook her head in disbelief. "Irene from the front office is a crazy hacker?"

I didn't feel so bad about charging her with a horse anymore, or having all those jealousy-induced violent thoughts toward her.

"This is insane." Donna looked just as surprised.

"No one is who they appear to be at first." Amaya shrugged, already rolling with the revelation.

"Well, we may have lifted the wrong phone, but it was a damn lucky thing we did," Ford said.

"I trudged home deflated, ready to break it to everyone we'd screwed up, but I'd call this a success!" Easton tugged on my hand, pulled me against him, and kissed me. Right there in front of his brother and my sister and my friends, he kissed me as though I'd just given him the best news of his life.

I was giddy. After hiding my feelings for so long, it felt good to be relatively comfortable in our affection. Not to mention the massive weight that had just been lifted off my shoulders.

"This is so weird," Amaya said, reminding me not to take the kiss further—like to his bedroom.

"Right?" Mena added. "Harlow is kissing Mr. Monroe. Like . . . what?"

Easton and I separated and faced them, but he took my hand again, not embarrassed or cautious anymore.

"I'd prefer it if you called me Easton from now on." He smiled at my friends. "I'm not your teacher anymore. I'm not going to be anyone's teacher anymore."

"Yeah, whatever, Easton." My sister waved dismissively. "Just rein in the PDA."

"What do we do now?" Mena asked.

"Can we just send it to the media or something?" Amaya asked.

"Definitely cops over media." Ford winked at her, and she rolled her eyes. "We just need to be careful about it. We need to find someone we can trust."

After some back and forth about how we'd go about doing that, we agreed to figure it out after dinner, and the girls left. Ford cleaned up the milky mess on the floor and left not long after that too, saying something about a milkshake. Judging by the shifty look on his face, I was pretty sure *milkshake* was code for something else.

And then Easton and I were alone.

We grinned, our arms winding around each other.

"Is this really over?" he asked.

"Nearly." I leaned my head on his shoulder. I wanted to go through what Ford had found on the phone, check it all out myself, then start brainstorming how to find a cop we could trust with the information. But right now, in Easton's arms, there was something else I wanted to do even more.

"I can't wait to put this behind us." I tilted my head up and kissed the side of his neck. "But for tonight, let's celebrate. We actually pulled this insane plan off."

His throat moved under my lips as he spoke. "How would you like to celebrate?"

I kissed him again, dragging my lips up to his ear, and whispered, "Take me to your room and I'll show you."

His lips met mine—his tongue invaded my mouth as I felt him harden between us. He spun us around and walked me backward through the door, never breaking the kiss, the two of us devouring each other.

I pulled away only when the backs of my knees hit the bed. I'd looked forward to this moment for so long; right then I couldn't care less what his bedroom looked like. All my focus stayed locked on the incredible, talented, caring man I felt so lucky to be with.

I yanked his sweater off, leaving his glasses askew on his face, and he tossed them onto a side table before pulling my teal Fulton Academy sweater off too. Breathing hard, we made a start on each other's shirt buttons. My fingers fumbled—this was taking too long.

With a frustrated huff, I gave up and just pulled his shirt over his head instead. He had to unbutton the sleeves to get it all the way off, and I removed my own shirt while he did so. The feral heat in his gaze as he watched me—so unexpected from thoughtful, measured Easton Monroe—made my breath catch in my throat, and liquid heat pooled at the base of my spine.

His hands went to my waist, his thumbs grazing my ribs as he started kissing me again. But before he could lower me to the bed, I stepped around him and pushed him down so he was sitting on the edge. His focus moved to the part of me now in front of his face, and he brought his hands up to my breasts and licked my cleavage.

I moaned and grabbed his shoulders, toed my shoes off, straddled his lap. As he kissed and nipped his way up to my neck, his hands slipped under my uniform skirt to grip my ass. I ground against his erection; he rolled his hips, fingers digging into my flesh.

"God, I can't wait to be inside you," he breathed, his voice low.

I leaned against him until he lowered his back onto the bed. The blue-and-white sheets that lay crumpled beneath us smelled like him.

When he tugged on my underwear, I shifted down, out of his reach. We'd waited for so long, and the urge to just crash into him and do it fast and frantic almost overwhelmed me. But I wanted to take my time, really savor the moment.

I dropped to my knees between his legs and undid his belt, then the single button and zipper on his slacks. His defined chest rose and fell as he watched me. All that glorious skin and beautiful ink . . . I reached up to touch it, then dragged my hands down his chest and abs, enjoying the feel of his smooth muscles.

When I got to the waistband of his pants, I tugged. He wiggled his hips to help, and I pulled the slacks down to his ankles, removed them along with his shoes and socks. Then I ran my hands up his calves, over his knees. The coarse dark hair under my palms contrasted with how smooth and warm his chest had felt just moments earlier.

He dropped his head back and closed his eyes—his jaw looked sharper from this angle.

My pressure increased as I massaged up his thighs, rubbing my thumbs dangerously close to the bulge in his briefs. I took my time, kissing, caressing, teasing, but never touching him where I wanted to the most.

"Harlow . . ." My name on his lips was part moan, part reproach.

I bit my lip to keep from grinning and pulled his underwear off. His cock was long and smooth, and it had the slightest kink near the top, which made it oddly endearing for some reason. I rubbed my thighs together as I gave it a soft stroke.

It was hot and smooth, so soft and impossibly hard at the same time. I couldn't wait to have it inside me.

I let him feel my breath on the tip, my hair tickling his thighs, but I pointedly avoided touching it. Once again, I kissed and licked and teased, paying attention to all the areas his underwear had been covering.

He was panting now, and his length twitched every time my mouth got close or my hair swept over it.

With a sharp exhale, he lifted his head to look at me. I held his gaze as I gripped him at the base, opened my mouth, and wrapped my lips around him. His mouth parted on a soft moan, and he tangled his fingers in the sheets, his head falling back.

In contrast to how I'd been teasing him, I sucked him down as far as he could go and started pumping my head up and down. I kept my pressure firm, scraped my teeth, swirled my tongue around the head. I used every damn trick I knew as Easton panted and moaned under me. His abdominal muscles contracted with the effort not to twitch his hips too much. One hand ran gently through my hair, and he propped himself up on an elbow to stare at what I was doing to him.

When he cursed under his breath, I knew he was getting close.

With one last slow stroke, I removed my mouth and hands. He groaned and flopped back onto the bed, digging the heels of his hands into his eyes.

I smiled to myself and moved up his body, resuming my earlier slow pace. Every kiss, lick, and scrape of my teeth had him shivering beneath me—until finally I hovered over him, my knees on either side of his hips.

He grasped my waist, then palmed my breasts, caressing them through the lace of my bra. I sucked on his neck as my hand trailed down his chest, down his stomach, all the way to his cock—hot beneath my fingers and slick with my saliva.

With a groan, Easton pushed against my shoulders until we were looking at each other. "Harlow, I can't take this anymore. Please."

His voice was desperate and hoarse. I'd teased him mercilessly, but he deserved it.

I sat up and ground myself against his hardness. "I'm just paying you back for how long you made me wait—for how long I pined for you thinking it was one-sided."

His hands tightened around my hips, and his eyes narrowed. "You've been torturing me to get back at me? You little . . ."

I rolled my hips again, pleasure shooting through my core at the friction. "What are you gonna do about it, Mr. Monroe? I didn't hear you compl—"

My words died in my throat, replaced with a surprised yelp as Easton shot up unexpectedly, wrapped his arms around me, and flipped us over. I suddenly found myself on my back, my heart hammering with excitement.

"I'm going to punish you, you naughty girl. I told you I'm not Mr. Monroe anymore," he practically growled as he gripped my chin and turned my face up. Easton kissed me, his lips rough, his hand holding my head in place. I squirmed beneath him, seeking more of that delicious friction, but he shifted his weight to trap my hips.

When he pulled back, that feral look had returned to his gaze, but it was more amused now, more calculating, and I knew I was in trouble.

CHAPTER TWENTY-SEVEN

I was completely naked, and Harlow had only removed her shirt and shoes. Time to remedy that. I couldn't believe that cute little devil had been teasing me on purpose. Not that I minded too much. It felt so indescribably good to have her hands on me. Her mouth, her body. I became so lost in her I hardly even cared what she did to me as long as she kept touching me, as long as she stayed with me.

But two could play at this game, and now that I knew what the game was, she was about to find out just how impeccable my self-control could be. Never underestimate someone who has to keep his eye rolls in check every damn day.

Keeping her pinned to the bed with my hips while she did all she could to wriggle and writhe under me felt so damn satisfying. It also tested my restraint. She'd brought me to the edge of climax two, maybe three times already, and the urge to just pull her panties aside and sink into her was . . . *fuck*, it was strong.

With a deep, calming breath, I started with her mouth. I licked each lip in turn, then kissed the corners, then nipped her bottom lip before sucking it. She panted and kept trying to kiss me, darting her tongue out to taste me, but I denied her as she'd been denying me. Instead I moved to her neck, across her collarbones, dipping down into her cleavage.

Her hands roamed my back, neck, hair, as if she couldn't quite decide which part of me she wanted to touch, while I concentrated on her breasts. I avoided the nipple, running my thumbs along the undersides of soft, pliant flesh, teasing with my tongue at the edge of the lace.

I sat her up before reaching behind her to unclasp the bra, keeping eye contact. She bit her bottom lip as I slowly slid the straps down her shoulders and arms, then threw the bra over the edge of the bed.

Harlow's fingers trailed down my chest toward my erection. It almost pained me to stop her—I craved that release so badly—but I gripped her wrist and pushed her back onto the mattress. Her glorious, perky tits bounced as she landed on her back, and I couldn't resist them any longer. I dove down and sucked one nipple into my mouth, kneading the other mound with my hand.

She moaned and arched her back, her fingers threading into my hair, trying to keep me there. I moved on to the other peak and got another moan when I gave it a gentle bite. The raw sound of her moaning sent jolts of something heady and possessive through my body—all the way to my dick. I would never get tired of that sound.

She started rolling her hips, seeking friction, and that's when I pulled back.

"Ugh!" She frowned at me, but it wasn't all frustration. "I don't think I've ever been that close to orgasm just from someone sucking my nipples."

I couldn't help the satisfied grin from splitting my face. Part of me wanted to get back down there and see if I could get her over the edge with just my mouth on her chest. But I wanted to be buried deep inside her when she came, and I was going to make her beg for it before then.

So I sat back on my heels and took hold of her left ankle, then propped her foot on my chest. After pulling the knee-high sock off, I caressed her leg from the ankle to her shin, across her knee, and up her thigh. My hand disappeared under her skirt, and I had to steel my resolve.

The image of her splayed out on my bed, topless, her eyes hungry, my hand up her skirt, was beyond the most erotic thing I'd ever seen.

I ran my fingers over the edge of her panties, just teasing at the crease of her thigh. Then I dragged my fingers back down and returned her leg to the bed.

I repeated the process with her other leg—removing the sock, fondling her smooth skin, teasing under her skirt before pulling back. With a gentle grip, I pushed her knees apart until her legs were open wide for me.

Supporting myself on one arm, I moved to hover over her so I could watch her beautiful face as my other hand made its way back up her skirt.

She licked her lips and tried to lift up to kiss me, but I moved out of the way with a smile. "Hold still."

She looked as if she might argue for a second, but when I caressed her pussy over her underwear, her eyes grew hooded, any notion of arguing gone. Instead, she stroked my arms and chest as I rubbed her most sensitive area. Her panties were damp, and she was so hot under my touch, burning up under my fingers.

I nudged the fabric to the side and slipped my fingers up and down her slick folds. *Fuck*, she felt good—so smooth and warm and wet for me. My dick twitched, demanding to be inside that heavenly heat, but I resisted.

Instead, I pushed two fingers inside and drank in the sight of Harlow closing her eyes and arching her back in pleasure. I couldn't resist the temptation of her perfect breasts, the nipples hard, so I leaned my head down and licked one before sucking it into my mouth. Harlow dug her fingers into my shoulders as she writhed under me, riding my hand while I sucked on her tits. I didn't stop her from moving, didn't tease. I pumped my fingers inside her and gave her breasts the same treatment that had nearly sent her over the edge earlier.

It didn't take long for her to get close to that edge again.

"Oh shit," she breathed, moaning at every stroke of my fingers. She was seconds away from climax.

I sat back, removing my mouth and my fingers. For a moment she continued to move, seeking her release, as though her body hadn't quite caught up to the fact that the pleasure had disappeared. Then she opened her eyes and stared at me, incredulous.

"Nooo," she whined and gave me a dirty look.

I leaned over her again, careful to keep my dick away, and kissed her gently. Her plump lips responded to mine immediately, and I let myself enjoy the sensual kiss.

"Don't worry, beautiful. I'm going to take care of you," I whispered against her lips. *Eventually*, I added silently and had to duck my head to hide my smile.

I lowered my weight over her and slid down her body, dragging my skin against her sensitive nipples, until I was settled between her legs. This time, when I reached under her skirt, I pulled her underwear down and got rid of it. Her knees parted, falling to the bed on either side of me in invitation. I gladly accepted and got to teasing her again. I had to make sure she wouldn't come as soon as I got my mouth on her.

I licked and sucked the supple flesh on the inside of her thighs, kissed the sensitive area at the creases. I paid detailed attention to every part of her lower body except the warm wet center of it all, where she wanted to be touched the most.

"Easton, come *on*," she panted, releasing an adorable little growl at the end.

"What do you want?" I asked, looking at her lasciviously as I darted my tongue out and gave her clit a quick lick.

She gasped. "*That*. More of that. Lick me, touch me, fuck me, just . . . argh!"

I couldn't say no to that. I shoved the skirt up around her waist, fit my hands under her ass, and finally licked her where I'd been wanting to for weeks—since the days I was still trying not to fantasize about her in the shower.

I moaned against her slick lips. She was so wet, her pussy practically throbbing with need as I explored it with my tongue, my lips, even my teeth. Her musky, erotic scent wrapped around me and heightened the experience.

Harlow rolled her hips in rhythm with my mouth, once again chasing her release, as her hands threaded through my hair. I kept the pace steady and looked up her body. Her breasts were squished together by her arms, her smooth stomach rolling, her head thrown back. She was so damn beautiful . . . and about to come on my face.

The sounds she made were addictive. I wanted to keep licking her all night so I could listen to the raw pleasure coming out of her throat.

But just as her thighs started to quiver, I sat up. She lifted her head to look at me, fire in her gaze for more than one reason.

"You have got to be fucking kidding me." She balled her hands into fists and pounded the bed.

I considered going one more round, edging her just one last time before I let us both find ecstasy. But I wanted to make her happy more than I wanted anything else in my life. That, and my hard-on had begun to border on painful. Taking this any further would just be torture for both of us.

As Harlow panted on my bed, her shiny hair a mess around her gorgeous face, I unbuttoned her skirt and slid it down her legs. She watched as I grabbed a condom from my bedside drawer and put it on, then lay down next to her.

We pulled each other close, hands roaming over skin, legs tangling, breath mingling. Our bodies gravitated closer until the space between us completely disappeared. Every inch of my body pressed against hers as our lips met in a deep, all-consuming kiss.

All I felt, saw, heard, and tasted was *Harlow*. The woman I loved, in my bed, in my arms, in my very being.

I reached between us and positioned my cock at her entrance. She hooked her leg over my hip, we shifted just that little bit, and then I was sliding into her and it was *the greatest feeling I'd ever experienced*.

After all the turmoil and waiting, after all the teasing, there was no longer any holding back, no more fighting for control. We were just *together*, and it felt so right.

As my hips met hers and I was fully inside her, we both moaned. Our arms were wrapped around each other, our breathing in sync, and it felt as though our souls touched.

I kissed her again, our tongues moving in languorous strokes in rhythm with our hips. Both of us were so turned on, so ready for this, it didn't take long before we both started thrusting harder, faster, seeking more, deeper, higher.

I rolled onto my back and took her with me. She propped her hands on my shoulders and adjusted her legs, and then I was in even deeper.

"Oh god, you feel so good." I groaned as she lifted herself up, then slammed her hips down again.

"So deep," she panted as her pussy stroked up my cock and then dropped down hard on it. "Feels so good, Easton. You feel so *fucking good* inside me."

She widened her knees even more, taking me as deep as I could go, and started grinding her hips to get the friction she needed.

"That's it, ride me." I rolled my hips in rhythm with hers, my hands on her ass, encouraging her to fuck me as hard as she needed. She wouldn't let me deny her another orgasm, and I didn't care to try. I wanted to see her come apart on top of me.

Deep, carnal sounds slipped past her lips as her eyes fluttered closed and her nails dug into my shoulders. Her pussy pulsed around my cock, and she threw her head back when she came, her beautiful body shaking with little tremors of pleasure as she moaned and *moaned*.

Watching Harlow come on my cock was a religious experience. She looked ethereal, glowing in her pleasure, and I couldn't tear my eyes away.

When she collapsed on my chest—breathing hard, her thighs still shaking—I caressed her body and continued to roll my hips under her. I was so close, and my body screamed for release.

After a few moments, Harlow started to move once more, gyrating her hips as she kissed my neck and shoulder. I wrapped my arms around her, then flipped us over again, following the momentum straight into a fast, deep rhythm.

My hair fell into my eyes, and she raked her fingers through it before pulling me down for a messy kiss. She felt so damn amazing, her heat and her body and her hands on me. She was soaking wet from her own climax.

Heat tingled through my body, gathering in my groin, and I had to break the kiss so I could moan and pant like an animal as I fucked her harder.

"Come inside me," she demanded.

I groaned loudly, my whole body going taut with the best damn orgasm of my life. For a moment, I actually saw stars, and when they disappeared, there was Harlow's smile, her hazel eyes sparkling.

I kissed every inch of her face before reluctantly pulling out of her. Then we just looked at each other. Without restraint or worry or apprehension, we stared at each other openly and lovingly.

"I love you so much," she whispered.

"I love you more than I can express," I told her.

After, we cleaned up in my bathroom and went in search of food. Ford still hadn't returned, so Harlow and I sat at my little dining table—her in nothing but one of my T-shirts, me in just my sweatpants—and ate Chinese leftovers and the last of Ford's cookies-and-cream ice cream.

Leaving the mess on the table, we headed back into the bathroom to shower. *Together.* We kept catching each other looking and smiling—not in an awkward way. Was this true happiness? Just being with the most important person in your life?

We couldn't keep our hands off each other in the shower, but it was small and cramped, so I lifted her onto the counter next to the sink and we made wet, sudsy love again before we rinsed off.

Then *again* after we got into my bed and talked for a few hours.

I knew we still had some tough obstacles ahead of us, but as Harlow drifted off in my arms, I wanted to focus on how damn happy I was. Just for a little while.

CHAPTER TWENTY-EIGHT

Easton

The next morning Harlow sat at my dining table, her eyes glued to her laptop. Ford had sent her access to the files from Irene's phone.

We'd slept wrapped up in each other until midmorning, and she looked more well-rested than I'd ever seen her. After checking in with her sister, she hadn't moved while I cleaned up our mess from dinner and made breakfast.

The bacon was sizzling in the pan as I set a cup of coffee in front of her.

"This fucking bitch . . ." Harlow muttered, and I smiled as I went back to the stove. She'd been murmuring similar things every time she discovered some new encrypted message and who knew what else. I didn't even want to know. I just wanted to hand it all over so this could end.

But I enjoyed having her there with me, listening to her mutter curses while I thought about how much I'd love to make her breakfast every damn day for the rest of my life.

Half her coffee was gone by the time I placed a plate of bacon and eggs next to it, just a few minutes later. I slowly pushed the laptop closed. She followed the movement, tilting her head to the side and shifting down to see the screen, then realized what I was doing.

"Hey!" She gave me a reproachful look and pushed the screen back up.

"Eat." I pointed at the plate. "Or the computer gets it."

She gasped and wrapped the laptop up in a protective hug. "You wouldn't dare."

"Try me."

She grumbled and started eating, one eye still on the screen, but I didn't miss the smile pulling at her lips. I grabbed a paperback I'd halfway finished, and we ate in comfortable silence, our feet tangling under the table.

My phone rang, the vibrations on the table startling me. Harlow didn't even blink, still engrossed in the info on her computer.

The incoming call was from my parents, and I decided to silence it. I didn't want to ruin this perfect morning with yet another pointless argument.

I'd told them I'd quit teaching a couple of days earlier. They'd called immediately to demand answers and to threaten to put their foot down, as if I were a child and they had any say in what I did with my life. They couldn't cope with the fact that I'd defied them, let alone that I'd secretly learned how to tattoo and planned to do it full time. I'd never argued like that with my parents, but I was not backing down. Enough was enough. The call had ended abruptly with all of us upset and angry. I hadn't spoken to them since then, although they kept trying to call and message. I needed some time.

"Shit." This time Harlow's tone held genuine alarm instead of the incredulity she'd been cursing with all morning.

I set my book down. "What is it?"

Her eyes flew across the screen, and then she looked at me. "Where's Ford?"

"I'm not sure. I don't think he's been home yet."

Harlow shot to her feet and rushed into his bedroom, calling his name. I stood up too, but she raced back into the kitchen before I could follow her.

"Harlow, what is happening? You're scaring me."

"I might've found something. I'm not sure but . . . just call your brother. *Now*."

I didn't argue. I just grabbed my phone and called Ford.

It rang once, twice. On the third ring, it connected.

"Finally!" a female voice said. "Do you care so little for your brother that you only just noticed he was missing?"

I stared at Harlow, her presence the only thing that kept the panic cresting in my chest from dragging me under. "Irene?"

"Oh, cut the bullshit, Easton. I know you know who I am, and I know what you did yesterday. That was a very stupid thing to do. I have your brother. Get your ass to Fulton now before *I* do something stupid."

"Wait!" I pulled at my hair in desperation. "What have you done to him? I want to speak to him!"

"East!" My brother sounded as if he was halfway across a room—a big echoey one. "Don't listen to her. Stay away!"

Harlow ran down the hall.

"Do not contact the police. And bring your little whore. Don't make me wait." Irene hung up, and I nearly hurled the phone across the room.

Harlow came running back with her own phone in hand. She dialed 911, but I snatched the phone from her before she could put the call through.

"She said no cops." I ran into my room and pulled on the first T-shirt I saw and a pair of sneakers. "And I thought you said we didn't know who we could trust in the police."

"Yeah, but I thought it was worth the gamble, reporting a kidnapping anonymously." She didn't bother to take off my T-shirt that hung loosely off her frame —she just pulled on her skirt and jammed her shoes on without socks, then tied her hair up in a loose bun as we rushed out the door.

At the elevators, I jabbed at the button impatiently.

"You sure you don't want to call the cops?" she asked. "We'll deal with whatever consequences come from that later."

"I'm sure." The elevator doors opened, and I attacked the button for the ground floor the moment we stepped inside. "She has my brother, and I have no idea what she's capable of. I don't want to take the chance." With only six floors remaining, I turned to her. "I want you to stay here, OK? Or go home."

"What? No." She folded her arms.

"Harlow, I can't stand the thought of you in danger, the thought of losing you." My voice broke, and I had to force steel down my spine. Now was not the time to fall apart. "I just found you."

"And I'm supposed to just sit at home and deal with the thought of losing *you*? No. Fuck that. If you leave me behind, I'm calling the cops. I'm not letting you go there alone."

I didn't have the energy or the mental space to argue with her. I was pretty sure Irene meant Harlow when she'd said to "bring your little whore." Would Ford be in more danger if I showed up without her? How was I supposed to choose between my brother and the woman I loved?

Not that Harlow was giving me much of a choice anyway. She didn't even hesitate when we stepped out of the elevator.

Out on the street, I grabbed her hand and pulled her to the left, toward where I'd parked. We rounded the corner at a run, weaving around Saturday morning shoppers and the brunch crowd.

As soon as we piled into my car, I took off so fast the tires screeched, startling me. I'd always been a cautious driver. I'd never done a screech in my life.

"Easton. Seat belt," Harlow ordered as she buckled her own. I fumbled with it, and she held the wheel steady as I clicked the belt into place.

Once we'd left the busy downtown area behind and were on the main road to Fulton, breaking speed limits, I started connecting dots. "What the fuck is going on? What did you find?"

"Messages. It looks like Irene has been talking to Ford under an alias, pretending to be into him. Or maybe she wasn't pretending. I don't know. That bitch seems crazier by the minute."

"She was catfishing my brother? That's the chick he's been talking to online? What? Why?" It didn't make sense. She already had dirt on both of us; we were doing exactly as instructed. Why go to the extra effort?

"I don't know." Harlow sighed. "For the fun of it? I don't think we're dealing with a rational person here."

"He must've seen the messages and put it together yesterday. Why didn't he tell me? *Oh god*, how long has she had him?" I gripped the steering wheel so hard my knuckles turned white, taking the windy road at nearly double the limit.

"Maybe he only worked it out this morning. We don't know anything yet." She put her hand on my knee and rubbed my leg. "But we won't be able to do anything about it if we crash and die on the way."

I eased off the gas and muttered an apology. I was losing my damn mind. Thank god Harlow was here.

We pulled into the long drive at Fulton, but the gates were closed. I cursed and punched the steering wheel. Of course it was locked up! It was a Saturday.

My phone vibrated in the cup holder, and I grabbed it. I read the text message from Ford's number out loud. "Old art building. You have five minutes."

"Turn the car around. Go back the way we just came, and turn left." Harlow kept her voice even, and I did as she asked, white-knuckling the steering wheel so my hands wouldn't shake. She navigated us down a long, empty road—Fulton Academy on one side and a field with horses on the other. Right at the end of the property, she had me turn down some back road, and we parked in a patch of gravel at the dead end of another empty, tree-lined lane.

Harlow got out of the car. "I don't think security patrols the grounds this far out."

"Where are we?" I asked as she led the way through some bushes to a low wire fence.

"The back corner of Fulton's property. The fencing at the front and down the sides of the property is high, and the wrought-iron spikes may be pretty, but they're sharp. But the back property line is the original fence from when this was a farm, before Fulton purchased it. Replacing this fence is in next year's budget."

I decided not to question how she knew all that. Instead, I once again thanked my lucky stars she was with me, then followed her over the drooping wire that barely reached my thighs.

The fence stood at the bottom of a sloping hill covered in tall grass, the roof of the main building just visible in the distance. Harlow veered to the left and up the hill, toward an aging barn.

"This used to be the old art building—before the east wing was built about fifteen years ago. No one comes here anymore except to get high and hook up." She kept her voice low. The barn doors were closed, but a chain and padlock lay on the ground next to them, gleaming in the brilliant sunshine.

I lengthened my steps and put myself in front. "Stay behind me. First sign of trouble, you bolt."

She nodded, wide eyes betraying her first hint of fear. It made me want to throw her over my shoulder and run far away from whatever waited on the other side of that door, but she nudged me forward before I could give in to the impulse. She was so fucking brave. I had no idea what I'd done to deserve her.

The big door made a clattering noise as it slid on its tracks. So much for a stealthy entry.

"Oh, good!" Irene called from somewhere within the building. "You brought your little slut with you."

My eyes took a few moments to adjust to the dusty darkness, but once they did, I pushed Harlow farther behind me.

Irene stood at the other end of the building, facing us, holding a gun. I didn't know what I'd expected, but I was an idiot for agreeing to come here. I was especially an idiot to bring Harlow.

As panic threatened to overwhelm me again, I scanned the area for signs of Ford. Dust floated through beams of light that cut in through the high windows, and paint- and clay-stained tables sat against the walls, old art supplies and damaged easels cluttering the space between.

"Let's just stay calm," I called out. My voice sounded much more level than I felt.

Irene laughed and raised the gun. My breath froze in my throat despite the warm weather, and Harlow gasped behind me.

"I'm calm!" Irene yelled, sounding anything but. "And I'm done playing games. Come here. Now!"

"OK." I held my hands out in a placating gesture. "It's just kind of hard to come any closer when you're pointing a gun at me, Irene."

She swung the gun to her right, keeping her focus on us. "I said now."

My eyes followed the gun, and there was my brother, on the ground, handcuffed to one of the heavy benches.

"Ford!" I took a step forward, then looked over my shoulder. "Stay back," I whispered to Harlow. For once she didn't argue and just nodded.

I kept walking, keeping an eye on Irene and my brother.

Ford sat slumped against the table leg, his legs crossed, but looked unhurt—just tired and wary. "I told you not to come. This is my mess."

"Oh, please. As if I wasn't going to come."

"You're always protecting me, cleaning up after me. I wanted to protect *you* for once. And I fucked that up too."

"I'm your big brother. It's my job."

"Yeah, well, we're both adults and—"

"Hello!" Irene cut him off. "Lady with a gun here. I don't give a shit about your little sibling moment. And *you!*" She swung the gun around and pointed it at Harlow. "Who said you could stay there? *Come here.*"

"Hey, hey! Everything is fine. We're doing what you asked." I stepped to the side, between the woman I loved and the gun barrel.

Ford lifted himself onto his knees and tried to get her attention too. "Leave her out of it. Just point the gun back at me. Over here, you nutcase!"

Irene swung the gun back to Ford, and I didn't know if that was better or worse. I felt as though my heart were being torn in two even as it beat out of my chest with stress.

"I don't give a shit about you!" Irene shouted. "You've served your purpose."

Harlow appeared next to me and took my hand. We held on to each other as though our lives depended on it—it certainly felt as if they did.

"Irene," Harlow called in a soft, calm voice. "Look. We're here. We've done everything you asked." We were barely six feet away from her now, with Ford about the same distance away on her right, creating the most fucked-up triangle I'd ever seen. "How about you put down the gun and just tell us what this is about. What do you want?"

Irene lowered the gun and looked at Harlow. When she spoke again, her voice was a complete contrast to her previous outbursts—calm and calculating.

"I want you to die."

CHAPTER TWENTY-NINE

Harlow

*M*e? She wanted *me* to die? *This bitch* . . .

"Uh . . ." I looked at Easton, then at Ford, then back at the lunatic with the gun who'd just announced she wished for my death.

Waves of something unpleasant washed through my body—panic? Terror? Probably both. My breathing became erratic, and my mouth grew suddenly dry. I couldn't have forced words out even if I knew what to say.

Easton's fingers around my hand tightened almost painfully, and he tried to tug me behind him, but Irene shouted again.

"No! *Don't* try to protect her! You're making it worse." Tears started falling down her red cheeks. "Why? Why her? She's just a spoiled brat with mediocre tech skills."

Mediocre? Even in my terrified state, some part of me managed to be insulted. I was damn good, thank you very much.

Ford jumped to my defense. "She's much more than mediocre, and you know it. She's going to be better than you and me both one day."

Aww! That might have been the sweetest thing he'd ever said about me.

"Shut up!" Irene screeched. She lifted both hands to the sides of her head and growled. All three of us watched the gun pressed to her temple with trepidation. Bits of tangled hair stuck out of her ponytail, and her peach cardigan was askew, one white bra strap showing. She still had on the same clothes as yesterday. Had she gone to bed at all?

"I'm good. I'm smart," she muttered to herself, then raised her voice. "If she's so fucking good, then how did I manage to get to her, huh? How did I manage to get to you all?" She swung the gun around as she gestured, no longer pointing it at anyone, as if she'd forgotten she was even holding it. "I had you all doing exactly what I wanted for months, and none of you had any clue it was me. When you didn't reply to my messages last night, lover boy"—she rolled her eyes at Ford—"I knew something was off. *I knew.* I figured it out all by myself. I didn't even need their help. I don't need them anymore. *Screw* them."

She was crying again. Obviously, she did still need them, whoever they were. I wasn't about to ask.

"I'm not an idiot. I knew you'd stolen my phone and hacked it. *I knew.* I'm smart." She spoke in an almost childish tone, as if trying to convince her parents she was a good girl.

"You are." Easton was using his teacher voice but with a soft, cajoling timbre to it. "You're so smart, Irene. You did it all yourself. Coach Cooper was useless, wasn't he?"

Even with a gun in play, Easton was trying to confirm the facts of who was involved.

Irene laughed, a grating, disturbing laugh that echoed in the large space. "Cooper is a moron. You know he doesn't even lock his screen when he leaves his desk? It took one conversation about football and a box of homemade protein balls, and he thought we were besties."

She'd had a reason to pop into his office whenever she wanted. She was downright devious.

"Very smart, Irene." Easton nodded. "I knew you'd figure it out. I kept thinking, *Any second now, she's going to see, and she'll be mad at me.*" He canted his head to the side and gave her a sad look, almost like a puppy in trouble. "Please don't be mad at me, Irene."

She stared at him, mesmerized, her eyebrows arched, mouth slightly open.

"Please don't be mad at us," Easton said.

The dreamy look on Irene's face evaporated, and she narrowed her eyes at Easton as if he were an idiot. "Us? *Us, us, us, us.*" She sounded more and more unhinged every time the single syllable came out of her mouth. "They don't care about you. Not like I do. They don't *know* you like I do."

Ford was his brother, and I had the man inside me hours ago, but sure, she knew him better. The fear kept me from rolling my eyes.

"At first, I was just doing my duty. I was being good and contributing. You had to be made to do the things they needed, and I could make you. I was so good at making you." She talked about the months of threats and blackmail as if it were just another recurring task on her to-do. "But then I saw you were different. You're different, like me, Easton. I could see it in your eyes that night at the fundraiser. We understood each other. I was going to make you free. I was nearly there. You'd quit your job, and I told them they didn't need you anymore. We were free. I had it all planned out, but . . ." Her bottom lip quivered before she gritted her teeth and glared at me.

Oh shit. I leaned back involuntarily.

"But then *she* tricked you. She seduced you and made you turn away from me. And now she's ruined everything."

"Irene. Irene, look at me." Easton drew her attention away from me. The devotion in her eyes when she looked at him was fucking terrifying. "I'm here. I'm doing what you asked. But I love my brother, so please don't hurt him. How . . ." He licked his lips, and I could tell he was struggling to keep calm. "How are we supposed to have a future together if you hurt my brother?"

"I . . . I . . . I'm not going to hurt Ford." She looked confused, glancing between the two brothers. Neither Ford nor I dared even breathe. The only person not making her fly into a rage was Easton, and he'd deliberately left me out of the narrative.

With Ford tied up and an unhinged person still brandishing a gun, I just didn't know how we were going to get out of this situation.

"Good. That's good. Thank you, Irene," Easton said. "My brother is very important to me. I knew you'd understand."

"I understand." She nodded, but then her eyes drifted down to where we still held hands, and her bottom lip started to tremble again. She tightened her grip on the gun.

All that time I spent yearning for him, convinced I was in love and we could never be together, didn't even compare to how hard it was to loosen my fingers and let his hand go in that moment.

But we did it—together. We let go to keep each other safe.

"I did what you asked." Easton immediately pulled her attention back to himself. "I came when you called. Everything is out in the open now. So what am I doing here, Irene? What happens now?"

"I'm . . . I don't . . ." She looked confused. "We were supposed to . . . but then . . ."

She took a step forward, and I reflexively stepped back. Every muscle in Easton's body tensed. I had no idea how he managed to keep himself from backing away from that lunatic, but he did, and she remained focused on him.

"Everything's falling apart. It wasn't supposed to happen like this." Irene looked like a lost little girl. "What do I do, Easton?"

Easton's shoulders relaxed the tiniest bit. Ford was watching with just as much trepidation as me, but judging by the hint of hope in his eyes, we'd come to the same conclusion. Easton could talk her down. If the two of us just kept our mouths shut, we might all be able to walk out of here.

"It's OK. I'm here now." I could hear the smile in his voice. "Everything will be fine. We'll figure it out. How about we start with a hug, hmm? A hug always makes me feel better."

She nodded, smiling at him as if he was her whole world.

"Can you put the gun down first, Irene?" Easton asked gently. "We don't want any accidents, do we?"

She nodded again and glanced down at the weapon, adjusting her grip on it. Ford and I shared a wide-eyed look. I didn't move a muscle, chanting *I'm invisible, I'm invisible* in my head.

A thud sounded on my right—something connecting with the wooden wall of the old barn. We all turned our heads to look, and then a rustling in the grass made my stomach plummet.

We almost had her.

Irene turned an enraged look on us and raised the gun.

"It's probably just an animal," Easton rushed out. "Something rummaging in the tall grass."

But the rustling came again, this time sounding very much like footsteps, and then the unmistakable sound of low voices.

Someone was here.

"I told you to come alone!" Irene was back to screaming.

"We did," Easton said, panicked. "I did. I promise. I don't know who—"

"Shut up! Shut up! Shut up! *Shut up!* This is all your fault!"

The gun swung in my direction, and all the air was squeezed out of my lungs.

Several things happened in the next few moments, all in a rush of overwhelming sights, sounds, and emotions my brain had no chance of processing.

The gun went off—a loud *BOOM* in the cavernous barn.

At the same time, Easton moved faster than I could even comprehend. Suddenly he was in front of me, his back to me, arms thrown wide.

Ford shouted expletives, yelling for Irene to point the gun at him.

A loud thud came from the right, and a small side door I hadn't noticed before flew open, throwing more sunshine across the dusty floor as Hendrix and Turner burst into the room.

By the time I'd gasped in surprise and blinked, it had all happened.

The boys went for Irene, but Easton blocked my view. His hands went to the sides of my face, and his eyes searched mine.

"Are you OK? Are you OK? *Oh god*, are you OK?" he breathed in rapid fire.

I mentally scanned my body as Easton crowded me in, squishing my arms between us. Other than the tension in every muscle, I couldn't register any pain. "I'm fine. I'm not hurt."

He squeezed his eyes tight and took a shaky breath. "I love you so much."

"I love you." I kissed him even as his lips continued to mouth the words like a prayer. Then I wedged my arms out from between us and wrapped them around his waist. We held each other as he continued to tell me he loved me again and again.

Over his shoulder I saw Irene facedown on the ground, staring at us and sobbing, her shirt torn at the waist. Hendrix crouched by her, and Turner stood on the other side, watching everything like a sentinel.

Amaya was kneeling next to Ford, picking the lock on the handcuffs while he stared at us, wide-eyed. I frowned. Why did he still look terrified? I glanced over to the side door. Donna and Mena stood side by side, so close they looked as if they were leaning on each other, both of them watching us intently.

Mena clutched her cell phone. When she spoke, her hollow voice carried through the large space. "Police and ambulance are on the way."

Donna had one hand wrapped around her middle, the other loosely holding her throat. I'd never seen my sister look so *disturbed*.

Easton stopped repeating his declarations of love, and his arms loosened around me, one of them dropping to his side. His other hand grasped at my borrowed T-shirt. I pulled back to look at him and got distracted by how sticky the shirt felt. Frowning, I glanced down and gasped.

I was covered in blood—the front of the T-shirt soaked in crimson. My head felt as if it were swimming, but I didn't feel pain. When I stuck my hand up under the fabric, my fingers glided through the warm blood but encountered only smooth skin.

"You're OK." Easton's voice sounded weak.

Blood covered his shirt too—which had a hole in it, on his left side, just below his ribs. In fact, blood was still gushing from the spot.

No.

I looked up into his pale face, realization washing over me: the bullet meant for *me* was in *him*.

Tears blurred my vision, and I blinked them away rapidly. He gave me a small, sad smile, as if to say *sorry* and *not sorry* and *goodbye* all at the same time.

"No." The single word came out on a sob.

Easton's eyes rolled, then focused on me once more as he swayed in place. I wrapped my arms around him, but he was too heavy for my small frame to hold up.

"Easton!" Ford yelled. Amaya had finally unlocked the handcuffs, and Ford wrenched his arms apart and shot toward us. Several other sets of footsteps joined his, and then we were surrounded.

Ford and the girls helped me lower Easton to the ground.

"Fuck!" I cried as my knees hit the floor. "What do I do? What do I do?" I looked around at my friends desperately.

Amaya covered her mouth with her hands. "Oh my god."

"There's so much blood." Mena pinched her lips together as if she might vomit.

Ford was crying, looking as lost as I felt.

"We need to stem the bleeding." Donna pulled her sleeves up and pointed at Ford. "Give me your hoodie."

Ford wrenched it off and handed it over. Donna bundled it up, then pressed it against the wound.

"It says here that you need to put a lot of pressure on it. Put your knee into it if you have to." Amaya had her face in her phone, scrolling frantically. "The most important thing is to try to stop the bleeding. We need to check for an exit wound."

"There's no exit wound." Ford shook his head. "He wasn't bleeding from the back. Here, let me." He nudged Donna out of the way and leaned his full weight into the wadded-up hoodie.

Easton moaned in pain, drawing another sob from me. I took his hand and brushed his hair back from his forehead. My fingers left a macabre trail of blood.

This was so fucked up.

"Turner." My sister got to her feet, finally looking like the in-charge boss bitch she was. It was a small comfort. "Run up to the school, find someone, bring a first-aid kit."

He nodded and took off, sprinting out the door.

"Hendrix, don't let her move." Donna sneered at Irene. "Sit on her if you have to."

"She's not going anywhere." Hendrix crossed his arms.

Irene sobbed louder, staring at the object of her obsession. I moved to Easton's other side to block her view of his face. She didn't deserve to look at him. She didn't even deserve to breathe the same air.

"Mena, go out to the back road and wait for the ambulance so they know where to go. Amaya, call them again. Tell them the situation is much worse than we thought. Tell them whatever you have to so they get here *now*."

Amaya was already dialing, Mena heading for the exit.

Donna said something else, then Ford said something. Amaya used her no-bullshit tone on the phone.

I didn't register any of it, focusing fully on the man I loved. I stared into his eyes and thought about all the time we'd spent together, all the good things, how he made me feel. Anything to not think about how much blood . . . I didn't want him to see the fear in my eyes.

I didn't want to say any empty platitudes either. I was done lying—especially to him.

I just stroked his hair and willed him to stay with me. He stared back into my face, his gaze going in and out of focus as he struggled to breathe.

Eventually the distant sound of sirens cut into my consciousness, and I whipped my head up, listening harder. Help was coming—help was here.

Please, god, don't let it end like this.

When I looked back down, Easton's eyes were closed.

CHAPTER THIRTY

Harlow

The few minutes after the gun went off felt like the blink of an eye.

Everything that happened between Easton closing his eyes and me getting to the hospital felt like an *eternity*—but I only remember bits of it.

The sirens getting louder.

The barn suddenly swarming with uniformed people.

Paramedics working on Easton as someone pulled me away from him.

Police officers leading a handcuffed, screaming Irene out.

Paramedics carrying the stretcher while I stumbled through the tall grass after them.

Ford jumping in the back of the ambulance before it sped off.

The girls shuffling me into Donna's car.

I must've asked how they knew where we were, because I remember Donna explaining that Turner saw Easton and me running down the street like lunatics as he got off his shift at the gym. He called the others and followed us at a distance, worried something had happened.

Then I was in a hospital waiting room, staring at Ford in one of the chairs, his head in his hands. I sat down next to him and leaned my head back against the wall.

"Why didn't you tell us when you realized it was her?" My voice sounded and felt raw. Had I been screaming?

"I was embarrassed," Ford told the floor between his feet. "I work in cybersecurity, and I got catfished, for fuck's sake. Seems ridiculous now, but I was ashamed. I felt responsible. I walked around the city until after midnight, ignoring constant texts from her. We talked every night. Isn't that nuts? I still feel like she knows me better than anyone." He sounded bitter.

I rubbed his shoulder. "It could've happened to anyone. There's no firewall against human emotions. That's one vulnerability that can always be exploited."

He dragged his hands down his face and sat up, taking my hand. "I was just so angry and, in a sick way, mourning the loss of this person who wasn't real, and . . . I really wasn't thinking straight. When she messaged asking to meet up . . . we'd been talking about meeting up for a few weeks now. I thought I'd go there, confront her, maybe . . . I don't know what I thought I'd do. I wasn't expecting her to have a gun."

I sighed, and we both stared at the opposite wall in silence.

"If he doesn't make it, it'll be my fault," he finally said. "I let my ego get in the way and made it possible for her to lure him there in the first place."

I scoffed. "I'm the one who insisted on going with him. She wouldn't have even fired the gun if I wasn't there. I knew I should've just called the police."

Amaya appeared in front of us, frowning, arms crossed. "Call me crazy, but I think the only person at fault here is the nutcase that shot him. Get your heads out of your asses."

"Yes, ma'am," Ford and I said at the same time.

Donna joined us, putting her phone away. "Mom and Dad will be here any minute. I think it would be better if they didn't see you covered in blood as soon as they walk in."

"Oh shit." Ford winced. "I'd better call my parents."

I glanced down. I'd forgotten all about the blood. I looked like an extra from a slasher flick. With a sigh, I got to my feet and followed my sister into the nearest bathroom, Mena and Amaya following behind with supplies.

The girls helped me peel off the blood-soaked T-shirt and my school skirt—both of which went into the trash, ruined. After that I cleaned up in the sink, trying not to cry as I wiped off the blood with a hand towel Mena had gotten from the nurses. She'd found me a pair of scrubs too, and despite being flimsy, the turquoise pants and T-shirt fit well enough. Amaya brushed out my hair and braided it all the way down my back, and Donna even had some deodorant and makeup remover wipes and mouthwash.

By the end of it all, I felt more human.

As the girls cleaned up our mess, my phone vibrated on the counter. It was a message from Shady.

Shady: Hopkins is clean.

I frowned and put it in my pocket. I really didn't have the energy for his bullshit.

Mena wrapped her arm around my waist as we left the bathroom. "You doing OK?"

"No." I chuckled darkly. "But I can handle it now that you girls are here."

She smiled, then suddenly backed away with wide eyes when my mom appeared in front of us.

"Harlow!" Mom pulled me into her arms and squeezed. "Oh my god! Are you OK? What happened? Someone *shot* at you? *Oh my god!*"

I cringed as she practically shouted into my ear. Then Dad was there too, wrapping his arms around us both and rocking us from side to side.

"Guys. Can't breathe." I tried to wiggle out of their hold, but they didn't let up. After a beat, I realized I was glad. I actually really needed a hug from my parents right now.

When I started to cry again, the two of them finally pulled back, but they continued to caress my head and rub my arms.

"Sit down, sweetheart." Dad led me to the seats by the wall. I sat next to Ford again, and Donna took a seat on my other side.

"I swear . . ." Mom shook her head. "Between the two of you, I'm going to have a heart attack and die of worry before either of you gives me a grandchild."

"What happened?" Dad crouched down, one hand on my knee, and looked up at me with worried eyes. "Your sister said you got in some trouble and there's a teacher involved and someone got shot. Do we need to speak with the police? Should I call our lawyer?"

"The police were at the scene," Donna answered for me. "They took Irene into custody already. It was a bit hectic earlier, and then we all came to the hospital because of Easton, but I'm sure they'll want to get statements from us all soon."

"Irene? Isn't that the lady from the front office at your school?" Mom asked.

I had to clear my throat. "Yes. She was the . . . uh . . . she's the one . . ."

Donna squeezed my hand. "She's the one who shot Easton. She seems to be mentally disturbed or something."

I nodded. What would I do without my sister?

"Who's Easton?" Mom asked.

"Easton is my brother." Ford lifted a hand in an awkward wave.

"And who are you?" Mom looked him up and down, her protective mother face on.

"I'm Ford Monroe, ma'am. Nice to meet you."

I'd never heard Ford sound so polite. It almost made me laugh. Almost.

"Monroe?" Dad got to his feet. "Isn't that the English teacher who just left Fulton Academy?"

"Yes." Ford and I nodded at the same time, although neither of us elaborated. Ford clearly wasn't about to tell my parents that his big bro was banging me. And neither was I. I couldn't have that conversation now—not with Easton in an operating room fighting for his life. But Mom and Dad were already looking between us with worry and suspicion; they knew something was up.

"I'm calling our lawyer," Dad announced and walked to a quiet corner.

"Daddy, I don't think that will be necessary." Donna jumped to her feet and followed him.

I rubbed my forehead and sighed. Everything was just so fucked up.

"Harlow, honey." Mom leaned down, one hand on my shoulder. "Let's go—"

"Ford Monroe?" a surgeon in scrubs called out, cutting her off.

Ford and I jumped up and rushed toward him, and the others all crowded around us.

"I'm Ford." Ford rubbed his palms on his jeans.

"Is everyone else family?" the doctor asked.

Ford waved him off. "I'm Easton's brother, but I want everyone here. Please tell us . . ." His voice broke, and I took his hand.

The doctor smiled faintly and nodded.

I felt as though I was about to pass out.

Please, please, please . . .

"Your brother is out of surgery and doing well," the doctor said, and I cried out with relief, tears tracking down my face. Everyone else audibly sighed as the tension melted off their faces.

The doctor kept speaking: "He lost a lot of blood. The bullet nicked his small intestine and got lodged in the back of his rib, but it miraculously didn't hit any other major organs. We removed the bullet and repaired the damage. He's had several blood transfusions and will probably need another one. He's going to be weak and in a lot of pain for a while, but we expect him to make a full recovery."

"Thank you, doctor." Ford's hands shook as much as his voice. "Can we see him?"

"You're welcome," the doctor replied. "And yes, you can see him. But immediate family only at this stage."

"No. Why?" I demanded rudely.

"It's hospital policy when there's a violent crime involved. A police officer will be present in the room at all times. Once Easton's awake and we've assessed his mental capacity, he must give us permission to allow others into his room."

"I'll come update you as soon as possible." Ford pulled me into a quick hug.

"No. Stay with him." I nudged him toward the doctor, who was already turning away. "I don't want him to wake up alone."

Ford nodded and jogged after the doctor. I wanted to follow, tackle anyone who got in my way and handcuff myself to Easton's bed. My whole body ached to go to him.

But instead, I turned to face my friends and family.

They were all looking at me, Mom and Dad with more and more confusion.

Turner wrapped a comforting arm around my shoulders, holding hands with Mena on my other side.

"Harlow, what is going on here?" Dad asked in his low, demanding voice—the one he used on tough business calls and when Donna and I were in trouble. Mom had that look on her face that said she wasn't leaving until I spilled.

"Easton . . . uh . . ." I had to take a deep breath. Where to start?

Donna stepped forward, ready to stand up for me, protect me, as always. "Easton Monroe has—"

I cut her off with a firm grip on her forearm. She looked at me quizzically, and I smiled and shook my head. I had to do this myself. If I wanted my parents to ever take me seriously, see my relationship with Easton as an adult one, I had to face this like an adult.

I lifted my chin and made sure my voice came out even. "He was shot protecting me. Irene was aiming that gun at me, ready to shoot me, kill me, do whatever her messed-up mind told her needed to be done. Easton put himself in the path of a bullet for me. He probably saved my life."

Mom and Dad looked shocked, horrified, and scared all at once. I'd figured pointing out that Easton had taken a bullet for me would be a good place to start, and it seemed I was right.

"Why would he do that?" Mom asked softly, but the tightening around her eyes suggested she already knew.

Here goes nothing. "Because he loves me. And I love him."

Dad pinched the bridge of his nose and sighed deeply. Mom pressed her lips together. I shrugged Turner's arm off and prepared myself for the shitstorm my parents were about to unleash.

I was *exhausted* and really didn't want to deal with this, but Easton had put his life on the line to protect me. Now it was my turn to fight for him.

"Excuse me." A man in a suit interrupted before my parents could start freaking out. "I'm looking for Ford Monroe and Harlow Mead."

My dad stepped forward. "Ford is with his brother, who just came out of surgery. What is this about?"

The man was of average height and build, somewhere in his midthirties or forties, with light brown hair and light stubble. He wore a plain white shirt under his black suit, and no tie. An altogether unremarkable person. Forgettable. And after my dad artfully avoided pointing me out, he looked over his shoulder directly at me.

"Harlow Mead?"

Shit. I glanced around at the others for help, but they looked as clueless as I did.

"My name is Detective Hopkins," he went on. "I'd like to ask you some questions."

"Absolutely not," my father cut in, standing to his full height. Mom stepped in front of me protectively.

Donna crossed her arms. "My sister has a right to have a lawyer present while speaking with law enforcement."

"Our lawyer is already on the way," Dad said. "You can wait if you want to."

"Harlow," Hopkins called, sounding professionally detached. "You can talk to me now, or I can have you placed under arrest and we can have a recorded conversation down at the local station. We both know it's only a matter of time."

My family all started arguing with him. "How dare he" this, and "our lawyers" that.

Standing behind them, I felt so small.

I was the baby of the family, even though Donna was only eleven months older, and they'd always treated me with extra coddling. I'd let them. My parents were so smart, powerful, and well-connected, and Donna . . . Donna was who I wanted to be when I grew up, even while we both grew together. I couldn't count the number of times I'd wished I had her confidence and intellect.

But a lot had happened over the past year, and I was realizing everyone had flaws, and nothing was as it seemed. I'd had to deal with so much recently, and I may have screwed a lot of it up, but I did learn I could handle things on my own when I had to.

Hopkins . . .

Shady's random text from earlier popped into my head like a notification going off. I pulled it out and read it again, then shoved past my family to stand in front of the detective.

They all fell into stunned silence.

"What did you say your name was?" I asked.

"Detective Mark Hopkins," he replied with a tight smile and showed me his credentials. He was losing patience with my family, and I didn't blame him.

Maybe I couldn't trust Shady—you never knew his real motives—but my gut and logic told me that he wouldn't go out of his way to hurt me, that for whatever reason, he wanted BestLyf brought down too.

Time for me to start acting like the adult I wanted to be, to take charge of my own life, to stop wondering what *Donna* would do, and act on what *Harlow* knew was right.

"I'll speak with you." I nodded, and his politely professional smile turned more genuine.

My family immediately piped up with outrage. I spun around and faced them with my shoulders back and my head high. When I showed Donna the text from Shady, she backed off right away.

"I'm eighteen," I said to my parents. "I know you want to protect me, and I love you for it, but I am legally an adult, and I'm choosing to speak with Detective Hopkins now. I need you to trust that I know this situation better than anyone here, and I know what the best course of action is. If you can't get on board with that, please leave, and I'll see you at home later."

I didn't wait for a response. I just turned around and left my stunned parents and my proudly smiling sister standing there.

"Let's step outside," I said to Detective Hopkins, and we walked through a side door into a courtyard.

The sunny weather had persisted, and the early afternoon sun bathed the tree-lined courtyard in warm, bright light. Hopkins and I sat on a bench under the shade of a tree. Other than a couple of nurses having their lunch several yards away, we were alone.

"I'll get right to the point, Miss Mead." Hopkins propped one elbow on the back of the bench and looked directly into my eyes. "The local law enforcement has filled me in on what happened this morning, but they seem rather baffled as to why an admin from Fulton Academy shot a teacher who just quit the same school and why several students were involved. They have yet to get everyone's statements, but they'll likely remain confused, as those statements will now be taken by my team. This situation will be handled by the Federal Bureau of Investigation."

I did my best to appear calm and mature, but that made me raise my eyebrows. When he'd introduced himself as a detective, I just assumed he worked for DPD. He was with the FBI? My exhausted and food-deprived brain raced. This was either a good thing or a very bad thing.

"We have interviewed Irene Richards. There will be a much longer, more thorough interview, but her initial comments were strongly focused on yourself and Mr. Monroe. We'll want to speak with him, of course, but seeing as he's still unconscious . . ." He canted his head to the side. "We will also be speaking with everyone else who was present, but I wanted to start with you. I believe you're more involved in this than any of your friends."

He raised his brows and gave me an expectant look.

I just stared back at him, waiting for an actual question.

After a few moments, he sighed. "I thought you were going to cooperate."

"I am," I rushed out, then made myself speak in a more measured tone. "I want to. I want to do the right thing, but . . ." *Fuck it.* "I'm scared. I don't know what Irene told you, and I'm not entirely sure I can trust you."

He stared at me for a beat, a contemplative look on his face, then nodded. "Ms. Richards has made some serious allegations against you and suggested she has proof. However, I suspect there is much more to this situation. We've been watching her for some time. I just want your side of the story."

I slid my hand into the pocket of my borrowed pants and rubbed the USB with my thumb. The first thing I'd done that morning was make several copies of the information Ford had gotten. I'd kept one on me the whole time. Now I seriously contemplated giving it to the detective.

He'd shown me I could trust him by trusting me with some information—that Irene had thrown some accusations at me and maybe even Easton.

We needed to get this evidence into the hands of law enforcement, who could actually do something about it.

Shady said Hopkins was trustworthy—or something like it.

Hopkins had gotten down here pretty fast, and his team had taken over the investigation within hours. I couldn't help but assume they were investigating BestLyf, or at least someone connected to it.

It was still a risk, but my gut told me this was my best option.

I pulled the USB out of my pocket and fiddled with it while I spoke. "Irene has been blackmailing myself and Easton and Ford Monroe for several months. I've lived in constant fear, and I've done things I'm not proud of lately. But I did them to protect people I love."

Now it was him watching me with a carefully neutral look, not saying anything.

"Yesterday, we came into possession of the contents of Irene's personal mobile phone." I lifted the USB. "This contains proof that she blackmailed not just us but several other people. There is proof of stalking, extortion, and threats of violence. There is also proof of her connections to several other high-ranking BestLyf members, as well as instructions from another person regarding some of what she put us through."

We had no idea who that other person might be. It was just a number, no name, and no chitchat—only instructions and confirmations. For all we knew, it was just Irene messaging herself. But maybe the FBI had the resources to find out for sure.

Hopkins glanced at the USB, and I caught the briefest flash of intense interest. "And how did you come into possession of this information?"

"By chance." I gave him a tight smile. I wasn't about to implicate myself.

His lips quirked. "If it contains what you say it does, then you won't be in any trouble, Harlow."

He held his hand out. I was suddenly Harlow and not Miss Mead.

I twirled the USB in my fingers. "I'll gladly hand this over to you, but I need some assurances first."

He dropped his hand. "Like what?"

"This information will prove we were coerced into any illegal shit we did, but I want immunity for Ford, Easton, and myself for anything related to this whole mess of a situation."

"Done."

"I want it in writing."

"Of course."

"Additionally . . ." *How to phrase this?* "I don't know what kind of accusations

Irene has made against Easton, but even if they're not directly related to this situation, I want them to go away."

He watched me for a second. "You're referring to the accusations that he engaged in a relationship with a student."

"I am."

"I have no interest in pursuing that. My team is focused on much bigger fish."

"All the same, someone else might be. Detective, I am eighteen, Easton has quit teaching. We are nothing more than consenting adults starting a relationship. I'd like to hand this drive over to you, safe in the knowledge that we can get on with our lives without fear of unjustified prosecution. I'm asking you to *make* this of interest to you."

"All right, fine." He sighed.

"One last thing."

"Yes?" He sounded amused.

"There are several copies of this information in existence, held by a few select people." Not yet, but I would make sure they were by the end of the day. "If you prove that I shouldn't have trusted you, and you're in fact working for BestLyf, I'm going to use this information and all the connections and influence my family has to bring it down on your head like a ton of bricks."

Maybe it wasn't a good idea to threaten an FBI agent, but he still looked amused, even a little impressed. "I assure you our goals are aligned, and they are something I've been working toward for several years."

He looked serious, intense, and I got the distinct impression this was more than just a job to him. He glanced over my shoulder and got to his feet, buttoned the suit jacket, and held his hand out.

"Our time is up, Miss Mead. I'll be in touch once the paperwork is drawn up later today. We will have to speak with Ford and Easton separately, of course, but assuming all your demands are in line, there shouldn't be any issues. Thank you for your time."

I shook his hand, and we turned to head back inside just as Dad came marching through the door with Mr. Walsh, our family lawyer, on his heels.

"Excuse me!" Walsh called. "I am Miss Mead's counsel, and whatever she said to you was under duress and will not—"

The detective just ignored him and walked past, disappearing inside.

"What did he want?" Dad asked, concerned.

"Whatever he made you say, we can undo it." Walsh nodded decisively.

I rolled my eyes and stepped back inside, where everyone was waiting. "There's nothing to be undone. We made a deal. I won't be in any trouble or be charged with anything."

"Did you get a recording of him saying that? It needs to be in writing." Walsh shook his head.

"He's bringing the necessary paperwork later today."

They both stared at me, a little stunned, and then Dad smiled and stuffed his hands into his pockets. "That's my girl."

"I'd like to look over any paperwork before you sign it," Walsh said.

"Sure." I shrugged. If Dad wanted to pay him an obscene hourly rate to double-check everything, who was I to say no?

"Harlow?" Ford rounded the corner.

My heart plummeted as all the blood drained from my face. I rushed to him, tears already welling. "What happened?"

"No, no." He smiled and grabbed my shoulders. "Everything's OK. East is awake."

"Oh." I felt lightheaded from the intense panic and sudden relief washing through me in rapid succession. "That was fast."

"Yeah. It's not unheard of, but the doc says he did wake up sooner than most people do from that sedative. Anyway, he wants to see you." Ford chuckled. "He's *demanding* to see you. Refuses to even answer the doctors and nurses about how he's feeling until they let you into his room."

I laughed and followed Ford. Everything else could wait. The man I loved was safe and awake, and he wanted to see me more than anything. Nothing could keep me from him now.

CHAPTER THIRTY-ONE

Harlow

My alarm went off, and for the first time in I didn't even know how long, I was already awake. I reached over and silenced it, then cuddled my pillow and looked out my bedroom window. Patches of blue sky had already started to peek through the soft gray cloud cover. It was going to be a glorious day.

I sighed—a happy, content sigh, not a sad, overwhelmed one. I'd slept well for three nights in a row, and for the first time since I started high school, I felt *rested*. I guess putting my big girl panties on had really helped relieve stress.

Speaking of panties . . . I rushed through my bathroom routine and got dressed in ripped jeans and a light neon-pink sweater.

My phone vibrated on my bedside table, and a pang of anxiety shot through my chest. Reminding myself Irene couldn't hurt anyone ever again, I checked it. It was just an Instagram notification. Amaya had tagged me in a throwback post—a pic of us at the beach last summer.

I felt better than I had in years, but it had only been a week since the whole Ocean1k situation blew up. It would take time for me to process all that shit.

But not today. Today was a good day.

I didn't even yawn as I skipped down the stairs. No shuffling feet and heavy eyelids, just a rumbling, ravenous tummy.

"Morning!" I beamed at my parents and took a seat opposite Mom in the breakfast nook.

They both lowered their devices and stared at me, stunned. It was the first time I'd come down to breakfast before Donna, *ever*.

I just widened my smile and reached for the toast.

"My sunshine girl." Magda came out of the kitchen and brushed my hair off my shoulder. "Good morning. I get you coffee?"

"Actually, I'll just have OJ. Thanks!" I grabbed the jug of freshly squeezed juice as my parents continued to stare. Magda cleared Dad's dirty plate and left.

Mom was the first to recover. She cleared her throat and took a sip of her latte. "Now that you don't have to go to school, you're up on time?" Sarcasm rode her tone, but I caught the twitch in the corner of her mouth.

Dad sighed and picked his tablet back up. He still hadn't come to terms with my decision to quit school with just a few months left. Both my parents had been beside themselves when I laid that one on them.

After spending the rest of that day at Easton's bedside in the hospital, I got home in the early evening, ignored everyone except Magda and the bowl of stew she had waiting for me, and fell into bed.

Detective Hopkins hadn't managed to get the paperwork ready that same day —I guess the FBI lawyers weren't as efficient as ours. He showed up at our front door at eight the next morning. Mr. Walsh was already there, having his third coffee with Dad.

We went over the documents together, but even I could see they were fair and clear. He'd put in everything he promised. I handed over the USB, and the detective went on his way.

After Walsh left too, Mom and Dad laid into me about Easton. *What did he do to you? Did he hurt you? Did he pressure you? You don't have to protect him. He's never going to teach again when we're done with him!*

"He doesn't want to!" I got to my feet and leaned on the back of the chair across the table from my parents. "He quit. Not just Fulton. He's done with teaching. He *literally* took a bullet for me. Lay off!"

As they sat there looking appropriately conflicted, I took a breath and composed myself. I didn't want to say this next bit in an immature way. Being adult and shit was totally my new jam.

"And I'm quitting too. I'm not going back to school."

"What?" they both burst out, Evil Easton completely forgotten.

I was proud of how calm I remained through the whole conversation that followed. I'd made up my mind—this was the right decision for me. My parents made every attempt to convince me otherwise, but I had a rational, measured answer to each of their objections.

When they argued a good education was important for my future, I pointed out I'd barely passed the previous years and would probably fail anyway.

When they argued I needed a high school diploma to get into college, I said I had no interest in going.

When they smugly asked what I thought I would do for work, I told them I planned to go into IT, had already researched online courses and areas of specialization.

They didn't even let me finish before Dad moved on to threats. When he threatened to kick me out if I didn't complete high school, Mom threw him a reproachful look, and I told him I already had a job lined up and had no problem looking for my own place.

Eventually, they had to concede that I'd really given my plans some thought. The heavy, twisty feeling inside me began to ease, and we managed to have a proper, honest conversation. I didn't back down on what I wanted—what I thought was best for *me*—but they did raise some concerns and set down some rules for moving forward.

The girls were sad we wouldn't be finishing the year together, but they supported my decision. I didn't want to miss out on spending time with them either—graduation, prom, the last few months before all our lives changed. But the amount of stress, pressure, and existential anxiety school caused me just wasn't worth it anymore. They understood that.

And judging by my parents' reactions to my new positive attitude, I had hope they would understand it soon too.

I was spreading butter and jam on my third piece of toast by the time Donna showed up. She was in her uniform, pristine as always, her short hair smooth and shiny. When she spotted me, she paused halfway to the table.

"What the f—"

"Language," Mom cut her off with a narrow-eyed look.

Donna shook herself out of it and sat down next to me.

"Morning." I smiled at my sister, taking a big crunchy bite of toast.

She watched me for a beat, noting my clear eyes, my brushed hair, my relaxed shoulders.

"Morning," she said softly and gave my arm a squeeze just as Magda placed her poached eggs and avocado in front of her. "You're ruining the routine, Harlow. How are we supposed to bitch about you if you get up in time for breakfast?" Smirking, she heaved a dramatic sigh.

"Donna!" Mom abandoned her phone and leaned forward. "Harlow, honey, we do not—"

"I know, Mom," I cut her off, laughing.

"Don't worry," Dad piped in, his eyes still on his tablet. "It won't last. She's only up so early because *that man* is getting out of the hospital today."

No one said anything, and I lowered the last corner of my toast to the plate, my appetite suddenly gone.

My parents were really struggling with how my relationship with Easton had started. I knew it had more to do with wanting to protect me or whatever, but combined with their misgivings about my quitting school . . . I hated feeling as though I was letting them down. I was *so sick* of letting everyone down—including myself.

All I could do now was continue to make good choices—prove to them I wasn't a baby that needed taking care of all the time.

"I've organized a town car," Mom said casually, ignoring Dad's shitty attitude. "To take you to the hospital and then take Easton home."

Dad scowled at her.

"Wow. Thanks, Mom," I said, touched and surprised.

"It's the least we could do. The man did throw himself in front of a bullet for my precious girl." Mom took a sip of her latte, her eyes pointedly avoiding Dad.

Dad looked appropriately guilty and went back to ignoring everyone.

He kept oscillating between passive-aggressive comments about "that man" and deeply conflicted gratitude for the fact Easton had saved my life. Mom was clearly getting over it faster. That gave me hope this could work out without anyone getting shot again.

They just had to get to know him, and I knew they'd love him. Hopefully the weekly dinners would help and not escalate the situation further.

My parents had agreed not to go after Easton for "having a relationship with a student" and all that bullshit on two conditions. First, we had to all have dinner together once per week. Second, I would remain living at home for at least one more year. That was an easy one. I could find my own place if I had to, but I wasn't really ready to move out and be away from my family yet.

Donna gave everyone kisses and rushed off to pick up Amaya and Mena for school. Mom took a call from a client and walked off toward her office. I downed the rest of my juice and rushed to get up too. The air always hung heavy these days when I was alone with Dad, and I didn't want it to ruin this day.

"Harlow." His soft, tired voice pulled me up short. He was looking right at me, his tablet abandoned, both hands on the table.

"Yes, Daddy." I squared my shoulders. I knew I'd always be his baby, but I was determined to start acting like an adult.

"I'm proud of you," he said with warmth in his eyes.

Something squeezed my chest, and I had to take a moment before I could reply. "Thanks, Dad."

"I just want you to know that. You made a well-thought-out plan and some tough, mature decisions, and you're sticking to it. I may not agree with them, but I'm proud of the young woman you've turned into. And I am grateful to Easton. I just need some time to get used to the idea. It's not easy on any of us. This has been a trying year."

"I know." It had been a fucked-up year, to say the least. I guess I hadn't really appreciated the toll it had taken on our parents. "But we'll be OK, you'll see. I love you, Dad."

"I love you too." He gave me a genuine smile. "Now go. I can hear your car pulling up."

I didn't hesitate, turning on my heel and heading for the front door with a grin.

I spent the entire drive to the hospital smiling at my phone. When I first decided to quit school, I'd been worried about missing out, getting more distant from the girls. But they'd vowed to keep me in the loop for the last few months of the school year, and our group chat was *lit*. All week, they'd been sending me selfies with the whole gang, surreptitious pics in the middle of their classes, updates on all the gossip.

That morning, it was all about our friends Nicola and Donnie.

Amaya: OMFG. Nic and Donnie have broken up . . . again.

Harlow: Again???

Mena: What is that, the third time this year?

Amaya: More like the third time this month.

Harlow: LOL!

Donna: They'll be back together by Monday. I'm more interested in the new guy.

Harlow: New guy?? What?

Mena: I know, right? I thought it was weird for me to start a few weeks after the school year began. Haha!

Donna: And we all thought it was weird when Hendrix showed up halfway through. This guy wins.

Amaya: So weird.

Harlow: Do we have any more info? Who is he?

Donna: Nope. I'm working on it. It's his first day. Drew saw him before we got here.

Mena: Let's just stay away from this one, OK? New guys seem to bring trouble at this school.

Amaya: I'm telling Hendrix you said that!

Mena: Go ahead! He is trouble.

Harlow: Agreed. No more BS this year. I can't handle it.

Amaya: What if he's hot though . . .

*Mena: *groans*

Harlow: I need pics!

Amaya: I'll get you several angles by the end of the day.

Donna started typing out a response, but the car pulled up at the hospital, and I put my phone away. I'd get back to them later.

I took the now familiar path to Easton's room, waving to the nurses at the station closest. I'd been there every day.

Easton was sitting on his bed when I let myself in, his legs hanging off the side as he gingerly pulled on a hoodie.

"Easton!" I rushed forward to help him with the second sleeve.

"I'm fine." He chuckled. "Just have to do things a bit slower."

I nearly launched into a lecture about how decidedly not fine he was, but then he kissed me on the cheek, and I forgot all about it. Stepping between his knees, I wrapped my arms gently around his shoulders.

He gripped my hips and pulled me in closer. His eyes were bright and happy, and any time he looked at me with intensity like that, I found it hard to focus on anything else. Our relationship may have started out in a weird and crazy way, and we may have only been together a few weeks, but facing death had a way of sharpening how you looked at the world. I loved him so much, and I refused to let a day pass without making sure he knew it.

"I love you so much," I whispered. Before he could respond, I pressed my lips to his in a gentle, languid kiss. It didn't take long for the kiss to intensify, our tongues stroking, hands groping.

He leaned back and pushed me away by the hips.

"I love you too." He licked his lips and smiled. "And I can't wait to get you home. But if we keep doing that, I won't be able to walk out of here without scandalizing sweet old Nurse Jane."

I laughed and stepped back, forcing myself not to look at the erection obvious in the outline of his gray sweats. Fucking gray sweats . . .

"Actually, you have to be wheeled out, so you're good, bro." Ford pushed a wheelchair into the room and grinned.

I couldn't even be mad at him for the invasion of privacy. He'd been at the hospital with Easton as much as I had, and he'd gotten me an interview with his boss. Which I'd aced. I was starting in two weeks—after I had some time off to relax and take care of Easton while he recovered.

"You're the worst nursemaid ever." Easton rolled his eyes.

"Just wait until you see the matching outfits I got for me and Harls to wear while we tend to your injuries." Ford wiggled his eyebrows.

Easton and I shared a look, and I knew we were thinking the same thing. The "outfits" probably came from some kinky website, and while the thought of me in one was a massive turn on, the thought of Ford in one was downright preposterous.

"I managed to keep Mom and Dad away from the hospital," Ford continued, "but they're insisting on meeting us at home with lunch." He shrugged, and Easton gave a resigned nod.

I bit the inside of my cheek, doing my best to hide my nerves. I was going to meet his parents. After Ford had called them from the hospital, they'd flown down the following day—the first flight they could find. So at least they genuinely seemed to love their sons, even if they did have a kind of messed-up way of showing it. They'd been by his bedside every day, like me, but we hadn't crossed paths.

"All right, let's get you out of here." A doctor walked in to go over the final paperwork, Easton's medication, and strict instructions for rest and checkups.

I sent the girls a selfie of the three of us in the elevator as we headed down. Outside, the black town car waited at the curb, the driver holding the door open. Bright sunlight had beaten its way through the dense clouds, and I put my sunglasses on and smiled as Easton took my hand.

It was a good day, and we'd deal with all the bad ones together.

LIKE YOU KNOW

PROLOGUE

The splash of crimson all but glowed against the white beading of my designer dress. If I weren't standing in a dark alley, staring in disbelief at the bleeding uniformed policeman on the ground, I would've thought it was an edgy fashion statement about privilege in America.

The policeman groaned and screwed up his eyes in pain, his hands pressed to his hip where he'd been shot.

I'd been standing so close to someone when they got shot that their blood splattered on my dress.

I started to shake. Why was I shaking? It was a warm night; summer was practically here.

The sharp screech of tires rounding the corner cut through the night and my shock. I let out a pained, desperate cry and started to go after them. That couldn't be the last time I saw her.

"Amaya!" Jet's voice stopped me in my tracks. "Stay with me."

He was crouching by the officer's prone form, holding his shirt over the bullet wound as the poor man writhed in pain.

"They're gone." His tone softened, and his dark eyes turned gentle. "I need your help. I need your help with this. Please."

I didn't want to help Jet. I wanted to run. But he had a point—there was no sense in running after a speeding car, and the man on the ground was in real trouble. His arms hung limp beside him, and he'd gone really pale.

I dropped to my knees next to them, and Jet took charge, guiding my hands to take over from his and press into the wound. The shirt was soaked, and my fingers felt disgusting in the warm, slippery blood.

It was kind of fucked up that I already knew what to do in case of a shooting —that this wasn't my first.

"We need to call 911." My voice shook.

But I had no idea where my phone was, and I needed both hands to lean all my body weight into the bullet wound. Jet would have to call.

I looked in his direction, but he'd already turned away, giving me his back.

He was going to leave me here, elbow deep in a dying man's blood. I just knew it.

CHAPTER ONE

It was a bright, sunny Monday the first time I laid eyes on Jet. I'd been hearing whispers about him all day. Fulton Academy wasn't a massive school—exorbitant fees made it out of reach for many. Most of us seniors knew one another, and I made it my business to know the latest gossip. Since before school even started that day, I'd been hearing about the new guy. His name was Jet, and he was hot. That was about the extent of it.

I was a sucker for a mystery. That was the only reason I looked up when I noticed someone unfamiliar walk by.

The final bell had rung ten minutes ago, and I was the first one out. I'd been leaning on the hood of my purple Jaguar F-Type, waiting for the girls, sunglasses on, enjoying the sun on my face as I read a romance novel on my phone. He came striding past, curious looks and secrets trailing in his wake.

He wasn't even carrying a backpack. He had his left hand in his pocket, and his right gripped a helmet and a leather jacket. No one had picked up that the new guy rode a motorcycle? At least they'd gotten one thing right. He was hot.

His hair was shorn close to his head, and he had a body I could only describe as "solid." Not super tall or overweight, but the fit of his school uniform hinted at strength. Despite the helmet and leather, or maybe *because* of it, he looked innocent. He had a round face that somehow fit with a square jaw and full lips. Kind of a baby face.

When he glanced over, he caught my gaze and flashed a lopsided grin. He even had dimples. I nearly smiled back, nearly gave in to the giddy, amused feeling in my chest. He was a walking list of contradictions, and that intrigued me.

I held it back though, dropping my gaze back to my screen as if I hadn't even noticed him. Better to keep a distance from people until you could figure them out. Less chance of giving them power over you. Out of the corner of my eye, I caught how his grin widened before he turned away.

I tried to go back to my book. The main characters were arguing, and I could tell they were about to have rage-sex. But even enemies-to-lovers couldn't get me to focus. I bookmarked my spot and navigated out of the app.

A motorbike engine came to life somewhere behind me. It had to be Jet. No one else at Fulton rode a motorbike—they all preferred luxury cars to show off their privilege. Not that I could judge anyone, considering the car I was sitting on.

Everyone looked in his direction, the girls and some of the boys practically drooling at the prospect of a mysterious new student who was a bit of a bad boy. If romance novels had taught me anything, it was that bad boys rode motorbikes and would break your heart.

Once again, I refused to look, but resisting the urge to turn around was almost painful. So I compromised with myself, opening the selfie camera and striking a pose. I took several shots but didn't even look at myself. I was watching the bad boy in the background as he zipped up his leather jacket and glanced around before securing his helmet.

As he rode off, the engine making an obscene amount of noise in the tranquil grounds of the school, I lowered my phone and flicked through the photos. I zoomed in on him over my shoulder. In one pic, it looked as if he was staring right at me. I zoomed in even more. Was he smiling again? But the image was too fuzzy this zoomed in. I pulled it back a bit. His ass looked great in the gray slacks of the Fulton uniform.

I bit my lip, shamelessly perving on photos I'd taken secretly like a grade-A creep.

"Whatcha doin'?"

I jumped and nearly dropped my phone. Mena was suddenly by my side, perched on the car and leaning in to look at my screen. She laughed as I fumbled and shoved the phone into my pocket.

"Bitch, you gave me a heart attack!" I shoved her shoulder, then pulled her in for a side-hug.

"I called your name, like, three times." She laughed, her pale blue eyes sparkling. She'd done her eye makeup perfectly, making them pop even more, but she'd left the foundation and cover-up off today. Her port-wine stain birthmark was clearly visible on her nose and cheek. She was beautiful, regardless of whether she wore makeup or not.

I slid my sunglasses on. "I was just trying to get info on the new guy. No one seems to have any dirt on him."

"By staring at a picture of him?" Mena gave me a teasing look.

"Research?" I shrugged, and we both chuckled. She'd seen me checking his ass out like a stalker. If it were anyone else, I would've been embarrassed.

Hendrix and Donna walked up, hands clasped, both their bags over Hendrix's shoulder. He dropped them both onto the ground as they stopped in front of us.

"How much longer?" he groaned.

Mena checked the countdown timer on her phone. We all had the same one. "Thirteen days, sixteen hours, forty-nine minutes."

Hendrix groaned again, and Donna pulled her own phone out. "Is that it? I was hoping to squeeze in a few more practice exams, but with tennis and pottery …"

The only thing Donna loved more than overachieving was Hendrix. Which was a good thing, because he helped her stay balanced. Her tendency to be extremely hard on herself had come to a head a few months ago, with some messy consequences.

"I'm sure you can find a corner to do some study while we're away, babe." Hendrix was only half teasing.

"I wonder if the resort has a business center," Donna mused.

"No!" I slapped at her phone, and she twisted out of my reach with a frown. "No studying on spring break."

In the past, we'd usually spent spring break hanging out by the pool, shopping in San Francisco, going to parties, and relaxing. But this was our senior year, and we'd decided to take a trip—one last Devilbend Dynasty party before we had to take exams and think about our futures. We were heading to the Bahamas on a private plane, courtesy of our friend Nicola. Most of our parents could've afforded to do the same, but Nicola's mom was a movie star and felt as if she had something to prove to the old-money crowd of Devilbend. No one was complaining though.

"Come on, babe." Hendrix picked the bags up again and headed for his Tesla, parked two spots down. "I wanna hit the gym. Turner's meeting me there."

Turner was Mena's boyfriend and worked at the gym. He went to a different school.

"You coming with us?" Donna asked Mena.

"I can drive you," I offered. I really didn't want to go home yet.

We said our goodbyes, and Mena jumped into the car with me.

"You can just drop me off at the bus station if you want," she said as I backed out of the spot.

"I don't mind driving you home." I shrugged, pulling up behind a Maserati and waiting to turn out of the school gates.

Mena gave my knee a squeeze but didn't say what we were both thinking. I kept nothing from my friends; they knew exactly what my mom was like. But Mena knew I didn't want to talk about it all the damn time either. Like the caring friend she was, she cranked up the music instead, and we jammed to Doja Cat all the way across town to Devilbend North.

I pulled up outside her apartment building and turned the music down. Mena lived in the bad part of Devilbend, in an apartment complex that had several entrances and thousands of people living on top of one another. The elevators were out of order half the time, the pavement cracked. Donna and Harlow were her cousins, and after we'd all found out she was being horrifically bullied at her old school, her aunt and uncle decided to pay for her to attend Fulton Academy with us. Best silver lining ever. I loved having her around every day. She reminded me not to be such a bitch all the time, and I had a feeling I reminded her not to take people's shit.

"You wanna come in for a bit?" Mena asked. "I have to get ready for work soon, but we could do homework for half an hour or just hang out."

"It's all good." I gave her a smile. "Go have a nap before you have to be on your feet for four hours straight." She worked at a diner, and while I'd never had a job myself, I knew how hard Mena worked, how precious her time was in between all her commitments.

"OK, well, make sure—" The roar of an engine cut Mena off mid-sentence. We both looked to the right and watched the new guy come tearing around the corner and into the parking lot of the building. He parked his motorbike, took the helmet off, and pulled his phone out, tapping away at it while still astride the bike.

"What the hell is he doing here?" I mumbled.

"People do live here, you know." Mena chuckled.

I gave her a withering look before turning back to Jet. "Do you think he lives here? Or is he visiting someone?"

"Dunno. Does it matter?"

"Not really, I guess . . ." It bugged me that no one had any good goss on this guy. And I couldn't stop wondering what it would be like to be on that danger rocket with him as he took that corner a little too fast, my arms holding on tight. He got off the bike and started walking toward the building entrance next to Mena's.

My friend gave me a kiss on the cheek and opened her door to leave.

"Wait." I grabbed her arm.

"What?"

"Follow him," I blurted. "See where he goes, what he's doing here."

"What?" Mena gave me an amused look. "What has gotten into you? No. I have shit to do. If you want to stalk some poor guy, do it yourself."

"I thought you loved me," I joked, pouting.

"With all my heart. Which is why I can tell you that you're acting batshit crazy. I have to go. I'll see you tomorrow."

I gave her a wave and watched her disappear into her building. After another few minutes of looking at the entry next to hers, seriously considering taking a casual walk past there, I decided to put the guy out of my mind. He would've been long gone anyway, so it wouldn't have achieved anything.

I started my car and drove away. It wasn't even four yet, and I really didn't want to go home, so I headed for the hills. The winding road up was fun to navigate, and the concentration required to do it safely kept my mind off my mom.

I turned onto an unmarked side street. It looked more like a paved driveway, so if you didn't know to look for it, you'd miss it, which meant I was on my own when I rolled to a stop at the lookout. I lowered the windows all the way and killed the engine, then took a deep breath and let the sweeping view soothe me.

The edges of Devilbend were visible below, but straight ahead it was hills and valleys, and in the distance, San Francisco looked like a tiny model of a city. On really clear days, like today, you could even make out the hint of water glistening beyond.

I sat in my car and just stared, trying to focus on the clear blue sky and the vastness of it all. I was just one tiny human, barely a speck of dust in the universe. My problems were insignificant in the grand scheme of things. But that didn't stop my chest from tightening when I thought about going home. It didn't stop the empty feeling in my stomach when I thought about messaging one of my friends, then decided against it, convinced they all had better things to do.

Having had enough of my own damn thoughts, I grabbed my phone. I had some stupid number of Instagram notifications. Going through them all would be a good distraction, but I didn't know any of those people, and I couldn't be bothered. Instead, I navigated to the reading app and lost myself in a book.

I'd gotten through more than half of it by the time dusk began to settle around me. The view had changed significantly, the sky a moody blend of colors as the setting sun painted the landscape a soft, warm orange.

I snapped a few pics for Instagram, got out of the car and took some selfies, then drove back down the windy road and reluctantly went home.

I wondered if my mom would be home or not. I'd had to endure her having parties and men over since I was eleven—since not long after my dad died. But this past year or so, she must've noticed I could take care of myself. She didn't need to pretend to parent, so she'd been going out more. Sometimes for days at a time. Wherever she went, she made sure to pay the bills, because the utilities stayed on and the cleaners kept showing up. I just never knew anymore if she'd be home when I got there.

It was almost worse than assuming I'd walk into chaos. At least then I'd know what to expect.

The garage door lowered slowly, and I sat watching it in the dark. Mom's Bentley was in the garage, but that didn't mean anything. It had been there the past two nights, and she still hadn't been home. Eventually, I got hungry and made my way inside, wondering if the Thai place would judge me if I ordered the same meal for the third night in a row.

But my thoughts evaporated when I walked into a lit-up house. The smell of cooking food came from the kitchen, and the sound of voices wafted to me on the aroma. At least there was no music blasting.

I rolled my eyes and followed my nose and ears. The urge to just go upstairs and lock myself in my room was strong, but better to know what I was dealing with.

"There's my beautiful girl." Mom beamed at me from behind the counter. It was always my *beautiful* girl. Never my *smart* girl, or my *brave* girl, or my *strong* girl. Was she cooking? But no, she was uncorking a bottle of wine. It made a pop, and then she poured two glasses.

A man stood at the stove, his back to me. He was average height with brown hair, wearing gray slacks and a white shirt with the sleeves rolled up. At the sound of my mom's voice, he looked over his shoulder and smiled. I didn't recognize him. I rarely recognized them. It was worse when I did, because then I'd find myself face-to-face with the father of a school friend or the guy who'd served us at the mechanic or some C-grade actor she'd met through Nicola's mom.

"Hey, Mom. Haven't seen you in a few days. Good to know you're alive."

She laughed before taking a sip of wine. "Of course I'm alive, silly! Come meet my friend." She waved me over enthusiastically as her "friend" turned off the stove and started plating up what looked like pasta.

I moved forward but kept the island between us, eyeing them both warily.

"Sweetie, this is Cal. He's cooking us dinner." She bugged her eyes out and grinned, as if the idea of a man doing something for her was revolutionary. "Cal, this is my beautiful daughter, Amaya Ann."

"Cooking us dinner?" I crossed my arms over my chest.

"Well, of course!" Mom sipped her wine.

"I've heard so much about you, Amaya," Cal said, all friendly and shit. "It's a pleasure to meet you."

"Let's sit at the dining table." Mom grabbed her bowl of pasta and sauntered over to the table that had not been used for dining in I didn't even know how long.

"Yes, let's." Cal smiled. "Can I get you something to drink?"

This motherfucker—literally—was offering me a drink in my own damn house.

"No thanks." I gave him a tight smile, then turned to my mom. I'd seen enough. "You should've checked in at some point over the past three days. Then you would've known that I was busy tonight." I grabbed the bowl of pasta. I was hungry and not about to say no to a home-cooked meal.

Without another word, I made my way upstairs to lock myself in my room, eat alone, and read until I couldn't keep my eyes open.

CHAPTER TWO

The next day, I didn't so much as catch a glimpse of Jet until lunch. I had just packed my books into my locker, and when I closed the door, I found him casually leaning on the locker behind it, hands in pockets, the tie of his school uniform askew.

He'd clearly been hoping to startle me, sneaking up like that. I didn't give him the satisfaction. Instead, I looked past him as if he weren't there and made to turn away.

"Amaya, right?" He flashed an amused grin. He had dimples. He had that baby face that made him look as if he was too young to be a senior and that tight body that suggested he was too old to be in high school.

I sighed and decided to indulge my curiosity. "Yeah?"

"Do you make it a habit to stalk all your classmates? Or am I a special case?"

"I have absolutely zero idea what you're talking about, and the fucks I have to give are in the negative." Had he seen me parked at Mena's building? He hadn't even glanced in our direction.

"The F-Type has a custom exhaust system with valve control, twenty-inch gloss black wheels, and probably a whole lot of other custom mods I couldn't see from a distance. It's one of my dream cars. I'd recognize it anywhere, even without the purple custom paint job. You drive a distinctive car, especially for that neighborhood. What were you doing there?"

"That's none of your business, but rest assured it had nothing to do with you." I crossed my arms. Who did he think he was, accusing me of stalking? Never mind that I'd been on the verge of doing exactly that.

He dropped the teasing smile and stood up to his full height. He wasn't that much taller than me, but he had strong shoulders and really good posture. Still, I refused to be cowed by any man.

"If you want to know something about me, just ask," he said matter-of-factly. "I don't appreciate being spied on any more than I'm sure you would."

I snorted. "You wish. I was dropping off a friend who lives there, OK? And I've had enough of this."

I turned and walked toward the cafeteria.

He caught up to me in a matter of a few paces, his gait easy, relaxed. "So . . . I may have jumped the gun a bit there." He rubbed the back of his head.

"Whatever. I'm used to men assuming the world revolves around them."

He laughed, and it was such a free, genuine sound it almost made me crack a smile. "We started off on the wrong foot."

I gave him a withering look.

"And that's my fault," he rushed to add. "So can we start again?"

Before I could respond, he jumped in front of me, blocking my way just feet from the cafeteria and my sushi lunch. "Hi. I'm Jet. What's your name?"

He held his hand out, smiling at me like an eager puppy.

"What kind of name is that? Were your parents aircraft enthusiasts or something?"

"Actually, my mom was an *NCIS* enthusiast. Full name is Jethro." He chuckled as if he'd just told a great joke.

"What?" I had no idea what this weirdo was saying.

"Never mind." He waved it away and stuck his hand out farther.

I was so damn hungry I just chose the path of least resistance: I took his hand and shook it. It was warm, his grip firm but gentle. I left my hand in his a moment longer than necessary as a sudden urge to lean forward and hug him over-whelmed me. I wondered if his hugs were as comforting as his handshakes.

"There. We're good. Now, I'm going to eat." I shook myself out of it and walked away, avoiding eye contact. I got my sushi and an iced tea, so wrapped up in trying to figure out what the hell had come over me that I didn't notice him following until I walked up to our table.

My friends were already there, joking, eating, a spare seat saved for me next to Donna. They threw curious glances over my shoulder, and only then did I realize Jet was still with me, holding a tray piled high with food. All kinds of food that didn't go together. Pasta and fries next to a sandwich and stir-fry and sushi and a burrito bowl. No way in hell could he eat all that on his own.

"What the hell are you doing?" I asked, not sure if I was referring to his disgusting lunch or the fact that he was still following me around.

"We're friends now." He shrugged. "I'm joining you for lunch."

"No, we're not, and no, you're not." I frowned as I took my seat. My friends had all gone silent, watching the exchange.

"Oh, come on." He smiled and pulled over a spare chair. It made an obnoxious scraping sound as he wedged it between Nicola and Drew. "I'm new here. I don't know anyone. Introduce me to your friends."

I rolled my eyes. "Jethro, these are my friends. Friends, this is some asshole that's decided to follow me around."

I then promptly started eating my sushi, my other hand checking my phone as I ignored him.

He was ballsy, I had to give him that. People didn't just *invite themselves* to our table. It wasn't some pretentious rule or anything, but a lot of the other students were too intimidated to approach us. Jet was new though; he probably hadn't figured that out yet, and my standoffish attitude hadn't put him off. He was either that confident or stupid.

He didn't strike me as stupid though . . .

My friends were much more welcoming, apparently charmed by his easy attitude and dimpled smiles.

"Hey, bro!" Drew clapped him on the back. "I'm Drew. Welcome to Fulton Academy. And don't worry about Amaya—the fact that she's calling you an asshole is practically an endearment. She must like you."

"I do not," I stated calmly, keeping my eyes on my phone.

A few people around the table laughed, and everyone pretty much got back to their lunches and conversations. It didn't take long for Nicola to start flirting with Jet while Donnie threw them glares from the other side of the table. Those two had been on again/off again since junior year. They were currently off again as of yesterday.

In record time, Nicola threw her hair over her shoulder and asked Jet out on a date. I nearly rolled my eyes. Everyone at that table knew damn well she'd be back with Donnie within the next week and she was using Jet to make him jealous.

"Someone should tell him," Donna whispered in my ear, chuckling with amusement. "Poor guy."

"Not it," I rushed to say. "I have a feeling he can handle himself anyway. Plus, more fun for us this way." I grinned at her, letting an edge of mischief enter my gaze, and we laughed.

"What are you two laughing about?" Mena leaned around Hendrix to ask.

"Tell you later," Donna said and changed topics.

I glanced at Jet and Nicola, still flirting, heads bent together as they planned their date. I had a sudden urge to get to my feet and tell him it wasn't going to go anywhere with Nic. I wanted to call everyone out on their bullshit almost daily. But I kept my mouth shut. It was more powerful to know things about people than to expose them.

He glanced at me, and our eyes connected across the table for a fraction of a second. And for that fraction of a second, I almost felt as if he knew what I was thinking. There was definitely intelligence in that gaze, an understanding that spoke to life experience. Jet had been through some shit. It was that same restrained look I saw every day in the mirror.

I picked my phone back up. I absorbed not a single word of the page I'd tried to read several times now, too distracted by the new guy who was still too much of a mystery for comfort. Instead, I texted Harlow.

A: New guy update. He's pushy and annoyingly confident. Straight-up followed me to lunch today and just sat with us.

Her response was immediate.

H: The audacity!
  A: I know right?! He's currently in the process of planning a hot date with Nic.
  H: Baahaha! Someone should tell him.
  A: He'll figure it out soon enough.

I snapped a pic of them surreptitiously, *just* tilting my phone to get the right angle while still pretending to type. I was a master of the low-key snap. I sent it to Harlow, hoping I wasn't interrupting her time with Easton too much.

Harlow was Donna's sister and had decided to quit school just last week. What was it with people leaving and arriving with barely a few months left in the year? Very inconvenient for me. But Harlow had a good reason. She'd never been any good at school and only managed to scrape by with the help of her crazy-smart sister and her crazy-influential parents. After being blackmailed and going through hell, she'd decided life was too short and got herself a job in tech—one thing she was exceptional at.

Maybe I should ask her to dig up some info on Jet. Because I couldn't think of a reasonable explanation for him starting at Fulton this close to the end of the year.

H: Oh damnnnnn! New guy is HOT!
  A: I'm telling Mr. Monroe you're perving on other guys while he's incapacitated.
  H: His name is Easton. He's not a teacher anymore!

Harlow was in a serious relationship with Easton—who used to teach at Fulton. He'd been shit at it, so it was a good thing he quit anyway.

A: The man took a bullet for you and this is how you treat him?
  H: Shut up. Why are you deflecting?
  A: What? LOL! I'm not.
  H: Yes you are!
  H: OMG! You have the hots for new guy!!!

A: I do not. He's not my type at all.
H: We all know you don't have a type.

She wasn't wrong. There wasn't a particular look I was attracted to. I'd never been in a serious relationship, but I'd casually dated and hooked up with all kinds of guys and girls. From ripped fitness influencers I met on Instagram to shy nerdy girls. I went for personality and energy more than anything else. I liked interesting people—but I also tended to lose interest pretty fast.

A new text notification popped up. Harlow had texted our group chat, and it wasn't long before Donna and Mena were throwing me secret looks as they all teased me about my "crush."

Please. I didn't have crushes. I had fascinations. And the jury was still out on whether Jet would be one of them.

CHAPTER THREE

Jet and Nicola went on their date that weekend, immortalized in several pictures posted to social media. As predicted by literally everyone, it didn't go anywhere. By Wednesday of the following week, she was back with Donnie.

"You know, sometimes guys just need to see what they've lost before they can appreciate what they had," Nic told me wisely in English. We had seats in the back, and Ms. Murphy was pretty easygoing as long as we did the work, so most of the class chatted while pulling quotes to memorize for essays. "And I kid you not, Donnie was at my front door waiting for me when I got back from my date with Jet."

"Mm-hmm." I nodded. We'd all heard some version of this story countless times. The date pics had clearly been a strategy to get this exact result. Those two were addicted to the drama and heartbreak and emotional reunions of their push-and-pull relationship.

We couldn't be more different. When I was done with someone, I was *done*.

"Not that Jet isn't great. We're just not right for each other. And honestly, I was probably not in the right headspace for dating so soon after my breakup. But Jet was *so* sweet. He was super understanding, and he still made sure I had a good time. He's so easy to talk to. And he's funny! And you know, I feel bad about how things went down between us, so I told him—I said I'll set you up with someone. But he already has another date lined up with Tess! That's exactly who I was going to set him up with too. He's totally fine, which makes me feel better because . . ."

Nicola droned on through the rest of class, with very minimal input from me. She told me in detail why Jet and Tess would make the perfect couple and about what a gentleman he was on their date and how he hadn't even tried to kiss her. She was convinced he was being sensitive to her situation with Donnie. I was pretty sure he just hadn't been able to find a break in her constant talking.

As I headed to equestrian, I wondered why he hadn't asked me out. Why Tess? Not that I'd have said yes. Although I might have—just to dig underneath that layer of unaffected casual cool and figure out what his deal was.

But as I passed through the hall where all the senior lockers were, I saw him walking by with Sara. They were clearly flirting. So was he going out with Tess or Sara?

I momentarily dropped my guard and frowned. Jet caught my eye over Sara's head and winked.

I shot off a few texts as I got into my horse-riding gear. Harlow had been in this class with me, and I found myself checking the door to the locker room, waiting for her to walk through it, before I remembered she'd quit. I missed the little troublemaker already.

Riding Harriet—Harlow's favorite horse before she went and abandoned me —and running through drills and tricks in the sunshine and fresh air for a double period helped get my mind off everything. When I checked my phone after, I had the answers I wanted.

A few junior girls had found out the gossip for me. Turned out Tess had asked Jet out and not the other way around. But apparently Sara had been planning to, and her friend got in first. They both liked him, and it seemed to be putting a wedge in their friendship.

I snorted and finished changing. Whatever happened to girl code? I would never ever let a man come between me and my girls. No dick on the planet was worth risking that.

Speaking of girls, I smiled with my whole face—and maybe even a little bit with that thing in my chest that occasionally pumped emotion through my body —when I spotted Mena and Donna making their way to lunch. I sped up to catch them and wrapped my arms around their necks.

I was feeling extra grateful for my friends. We'd been through a mountain of shit together.

They greeted me warmly, and we walked into the cafeteria with our arms around each other. Nicola and Donnie were making out at our table. Drew and Hendrix were in fits of laughter over what almost certainly was a dirty joke.

Jet was not there. Before I could stop myself, I scanned the room.

Even with every single person in the cafeteria wearing the exact same uniform, I spotted Jet easily. There was just something about his confident energy. He was sitting backward on a chair with the lacrosse team, having a quiet conversation with Oliver.

Once again, I wondered what his deal was.

He'd sat with us a few times during lunch, but he'd also sat with pretty much everyone else in the senior class. I'd even seen him sipping on a smoothie with the cheerleading team after practice the other day.

It was as if he purposely didn't fit anywhere yet slotted in seamlessly everywhere. I grudgingly admired him for it. High school had been nearly four years of figuring out who we were and where we belonged. To actively go against that was either deranged or genius. Especially in a place like Fulton Academy where everyone was *someone* or the child of *someone*.

I did my best to put him out of my mind for the rest of the day, focusing on my friends and my classes. Donna dropped Mena off at the bus station, so I pulled out of the parking lot on my own, my gaze snagging on the infuriatingly confusing new guy as he swung his leg over his bike.

He had a good ass. I had to hand it to him.

I thought about taking my homework to the library or the lookout and doing it in the car, but I decided to go straight home. I needed space to lay out all my books and notes to finish off an assignment.

When I walked into the house and heard voices coming from the living area, I sighed but wasn't surprised.

Mom had been home for the longest stretch in over a year. But so had Cal. Every single night, for a week straight, I'd come home to the two of them in the living area talking, or in the kitchen cooking, or in the media room watching an old movie. It was so fucking domesticated it made me feel sick. It was fake fake fake! Vivian Ellis didn't have a domestic, parental bone in her body, and Cal wouldn't be the first or the last asshole to try to play the husband role to get to her money.

She can pretend with him but can't even try to pretend with her own daughter? I thought bitterly as I followed the sound of chatter and laughter, my teeth clenching harder with each step.

The two of them sat on the veranda off the living room, the bifold doors open all the way, the sky sickeningly blue beyond. Lounging on designer outdoor furniture, cocktails in hand, they were the picture of laidback #CoupleGoals. More like #LiesAndDenial

I did not want to talk to either of them. I could hardly even stand to look at them. But I was never the sneaking type, and I refused to pretend I didn't exist in my own home, so I didn't give a shit about the sound my keys made as they hit the counter. I didn't rush to get away from them or stay silent. I took my time pouring myself a glass of icy water and chugging it down.

Staying hydrated was the key to good skin, and I had been slacking on my H_2O intake today. Mom came flitting into the room just as I slammed my empty glass down on the counter.

"There's my beautiful girl." She beamed at me, pouring herself another cocktail from the pre-loaded shaker. "Where have you been all day? It's so nice out."

"At school." I let the contempt I felt show in my expression.

"Oh right, of course." She waved me off, ignoring the WTF look I gave her. "We're going out to dinner tonight. Cal booked us a table at that nice place on the top floor of that tall building downtown. It's not for a few hours yet though, so come sit. Have a cocktail with us. Tell us about what boy has your attention." She wiggled her eyebrows.

"Can't. Busy." I turned on my heel and walked off. I would rather have ripped out my own nails than spend an entire night with that excuse for a mother and her creepy boyfriend. To think I'd spent weeks hoping she'd just come home. It was worse having her here, with him. Dealing with her every damn day just shoved in my face that I had no one to rely on. It was easier to pretend when she wasn't here.

I guessed we both liked to pretend—apples and trees. I may not have fallen that far from the shit-show tree that birthed me, but I was determined to roll as far away as I could.

"Amaya Ann Ellis-Lahari." Mom's angry tone made me pause a few steps up the stairs, and I turned to face her, eyebrows raised. "You come back down here this instant."

"Or what?" I scoffed. What was she going to do? Bend me over her knee for a spanking? I'd like to see her try.

Cal walked up to join her, a worried expression on his stupid face.

"Don't take that tone with me. I am your mother, and you will show me the respect I deserve." She was nearly shaking with frustration. Cal gently wrapped an arm around her shoulders, and some of the tension actually left her body.

"Are you?" I cocked my head. "You sure don't act like it. You haven't even tried to pretend you're my mother since Dad—" I cut myself off. Nothing could make me cry at the drop of a hat like talking, *thinking*, about my father. And I refused to cry in front of them. "Ugh. Not worth it." I started climbing the stairs again.

"Don't you walk away from me!" Vivian screamed after me.

I flipped her off over my shoulder, not even looking back. If she didn't want me walking away from her, she shouldn't have done the same to me over and over.

I heard Cal's deep voice speaking low and calm but didn't try to work out what he was saying. I resisted the urge to slam my door so hard it would bring the house down, closing and locking it instead. Good thing I did too, because barely a moment later, footsteps thudded on the stairs and my door handle jiggled.

"Open this door!" Mom pounded on it.

I ground my teeth, rushing into my walk-in and changing into activewear. I really didn't want to go out the window, but I would if I had to.

Cal's irritatingly calm voice said something to Mom as I gathered my shit and slung my gym bag over my shoulder.

A soft knock sounded on my door, then Cal spoke to me. "Amaya? Could you please open the door? Your mom has gone downstairs to cool off. I'd just like to have a word with you."

He'd like to have a word with me? Fuck that. And fuck going out the window. Fuck them both!

I marched to my door, unlocked it, and opened it. Cal stepped out of my way reflexively as I barreled through, giving him my back as I made sure to lock my door from the outside.

"Listen, I know that you and your mother—"

"You don't know shit, Cal." Without waiting for a response, I jogged down the stairs, snatched my keys, and peeled out of there, my tires giving a little screech as I took off out of the garage.

I drove straight to the gym, forcing deep breaths down my throat the whole way so I wouldn't crash and die from rage-driving. Once I parked, I leaned against the car and lit a cigarette, hoping the death stick would calm my nerves, but I only got halfway through. It was doing nothing to stop the frustrated energy coursing through me, so I put it out and headed inside. I needed to thrash this out on some gym equipment. Then I'd call the girls and bitch about it. Then I'd have some ice cream, and everything would be right with the world again.

I spotted Jet on the bench press as soon as I walked in, and I sighed, pinching the bridge of my nose. Either this would make my night a hell of a lot worse, or it would be just the distraction I needed.

Half an hour into my workout, I still wasn't doing any better. If anything, I was even more frustrated, because Jet followed me around the gym like a bad smell. I'd changed machines three times, going from the treadmill to the cross trainer to the rowing machine without completing any semblance of a proper set.

"Hey, Turner." I abandoned the rowing machine and darted up to grab Mena's boyfriend as he passed. He'd been moving about the equipment with a spray bottle and a cloth, wiping everything down between answering the phone at the front desk.

"Wassup?" He spun the spray bottle on his finger like a gun.

"Can you kick that creep out or something?" I huffed, glaring in Jet's direction.

Turner followed my gaze. "Jet?"

"Yes. Jethro," I gritted out. "He's been following me around since I got here."

"Amaya, you're the one that's used half the machines since you arrived. He's stayed in the weights section this whole time."

"Yeah, well . . . ," I spluttered. Technically he was right, but I'd made eye contact with Jet several times, and no matter which machine I was on, he seemed to be positioned so he could see me. "He's just . . . he's . . . he's looking at me too much. It's distracting."

Turner raised his brows and pointedly looked over his shoulder. "He's not even facing you."

He wasn't, dammit! He was doing lunges with a weight in each hand. His shorts tightened around his ass with every lunge in the most delicious yet infuriating way.

"It's … he's …" I sighed. "His very existence is an affront."

"Okaaay …" Turner frowned. "Are you all right?"

"I'm fine." I did my best not to let it come out snappy as I rubbed my temples. He was going to push me for more—he didn't believe me, I could tell. But then his coworker called him over to the reception area. Turner reluctantly rushed off, saying he'd be back as soon as he could.

There was nothing between me and Jet now, nothing to distract me from his inconvenient presence. He'd finished his lunges and shook his arms out, took a drink from his water bottle. Then he removed his sweaty T-shirt.

I barely resisted the urge to roll my eyes. Who did he think he was to just take his clothing off like that in public? The nerve of this guy, showing off his—admittedly pretty tight—body. I mean, his back was so damn smooth and defined it was downright … insulting!

And because he was clearly an asshole, he jumped up, grabbed the pole above his head, and started doing pull-ups. *Pull-ups*! The audacity! I mean, how was I supposed to focus on my own workout when he was over there, clenching every muscle in his back and arms and shoulders? His movements were smooth and practiced, his feet crossed at the ankles, his flesh dancing under all that smooth skin.

He finished a set and jumped down, making me realize I'd been staring at him this entire time—like the creep I'd accused him of being. With a huff, I sat my butt back down on the rowing machine, determined to focus.

Jet did a few stretches, checked his phone, then glanced at me over his shoulder. I caught his smirk just as he turned away. Why was he getting under my skin so badly? That little satisfied smirk made me grind my teeth.

When he jumped up onto the bar again, he didn't do another normal set of pull-ups. Instead, he lifted his legs so they were straight out in front of him—as if he were sitting down. Then he started pulling himself up and down again. He was clearly showing off.

Before I knew what I was doing, I'd jumped to my feet and marched over. I stopped in front of him and off to the side and … got completely distracted by his abs. I mean, there were *eight* of them, and each one popped out with the effort required to hold his legs up like that. It must've hurt, but he just powered through it with barely an occasional grunt. His front was just as defined as his back, and this close, I could see the veins bulging on his arms. All of it glistened with a sheen of sweat.

He chuckled, the cocky sound grating on my nerves and pulling my attention to his face. I followed his amused expression with my eyes as it moved up and down slowly.

"You're disrupting my workout," I stated, lifting my chin haughtily. "Please leave."

Jet paused at the top of the bar, his arms holding him in place, his legs not even shaking a little.

"Hey. Amaya, right? From school?" he said with a slight tilt of his head.

"Hey, Jethro." As if he didn't remember who I was. I didn't look that different out of my school uniform with my hair up in a braid. Did I? I resisted the urge to adjust my leggings a little higher over my belly. "Stop playing dumb and leave me alone."

"*You* came over to *me*." He lowered his body and dropped from the bar.

"Yes, because I can't fucking focus."

"I was here first, which I know you noticed, and I haven't come near you or said a single thing to you."

"Yeah, well, you keep looking at me. It's disturbing."

"No more than you're looking at me." He flashed me a grin. Jerk. He had a point, but I wasn't about to tell him that. "And I don't know what you're complaining about. It's taken your mind off whatever had you in such a foul mood when you got here."

Whatever snarky response had been on the tip of my tongue fizzled out. I was stunned he'd noticed I was upset in the first place. I was even more stunned to realize he was totally right—I hadn't thought about the shit show at home for a good half hour. I may have redirected my ire at him, but I had stopped obsessing.

"Your face will freeze like that if the wind changes," Jet teased before taking a drink from his bottle.

I snapped my mouth shut and glared at him. He wasn't even remotely bothered by it.

"Come on." He tugged on my hand and immediately released it as he walked past. "Let's see if we can get you to stay on the same machine for longer than five minutes. I need to do cardio anyway."

Like hell he needed to do cardio. I'd never seen someone so fit, and I spent a lot of time in gyms. I still found myself following him over to the treadmills though, my thumb rubbing the spot on my fingers he'd touched. So weird.

Wordlessly, we got started on treadmills next to each other. They faced the windows, and I watched the people of Devilbend walking past on the street, on their way home from work or taking their dogs for a walk. The view and the steady repetition of putting one foot in front of the other were no different from when I'd first arrived. But something about having another person next to me, matching my pace, had the effect I'd been hoping for when I came here. My mind settled, my legs started to feel a pleasant burn, and my lungs and heart worked harder—I felt more in my body and not so much all up in my ugly emotions.

Jet didn't try to make conversation. He just jogged alongside me, his eyes trained forward. I snuck a look at his treadmill and confirmed my suspicion that he'd set his to the exact same speed as mine. It should've been distracting having him right there, shirtless, all that smooth muscle moving rhythmically. But it wasn't. If anything it was . . . comforting. There was something disarming about this guy, and that in itself should've worried me. But in that moment, I was just glad he was there, that he wasn't being an asshole like I'd been to him, that I didn't have to be alone.

"Wanna tell me about it?" he asked. "Or should we just crank up the speed and sweat it out?"

Reflexively, I reached for the controls. There were exactly three people on this planet I let myself be vulnerable with. It did not feel safe to talk about private shit with anyone else. Except . . .

I let my hand fall to my side, keeping the same manageable pace, and wondered why I actually did kind of want to vent to Jet.

It's not him. It's just that I want to vent, period. He just happens to be here, I told myself.

It was a load of crap. Turner stood right by the reception desk, and I knew and trusted him way more than this virtual stranger. But it had been a weird evening, and I found myself leaning into the instinct to talk to Jet.

"My dad is dead, my mom is the definition of flighty, and this new guy she's dating just won't go away," I blurted, severely simplifying all the shit pissing me off.

"Is this boyfriend hurting you? Or her?" Jet's voice was serious and low, and he looked right at me for the first time since we got on the treadmills. The sudden intensity took me a little aback.

"What? No. He's just around all the fucking time, and my mom expects me to play house with them all of a sudden when she hasn't been anything resembling a mother for years."

"Right." He stayed silent for a few moments, but I could feel him holding back whatever he wanted to say.

"Anyway, she lost her shit at me tonight because I refuse to play the good little daughter. Then the boyfriend tried to step in and talk to me like a father figure." I rolled my eyes so hard I nearly lost my balance on the treadmill. "I just had to get out of there for a while."

"Sounds frustrating."

"It is."

After another stretch of silence, he glanced at me again. "I'm sorry about your dad. Did he pass recently?"

"No, it was six years ago. Thanks." And that was about when I hit my limit for talking about my feelings. *Ugh!* I definitely wasn't getting into my dead daddy issues in the gym with some new guy I knew nothing about. "Anyway, I'm fine now. And you owe me some answers."

"I do?" He chuckled, but he was smart enough not to push me.

"Yep. I just spilled some really personal shit. I think it's only fair that you tell me about yourself too."

"I mean, I did pull you out of your funk, so I think we're even." A teasing smile pulled at his lips.

"I don't know what you're talking about. I had a momentary lapse of sanity and said things to you I hardly even talk to my friends about. Now it's your turn. I need something to hold over you so you won't go around telling people I have emotions and shit."

"I won't tell anyone what we talked about, Amaya. No mutually assured destruction necessary." He had that serious tone in his voice again, and I didn't like it. It made me feel awkward and kind of itchy.

"What's your deal, Jethro?" I forged on with the lighter topics—or at least ones not focused on me. "Why'd you transfer to Fulton so late in the year?"

"I got a scholarship." He shrugged. That explained the living situation but not the late admission.

"They hand out scholarships with barely two months left in the year? *Senior* year, no less?"

"I think we both know Fulton Academy doesn't hand out much of anything," he grumbled.

"True. So what's your deal then?"

"I had to move. They agreed to let me start now."

"Your parents got a new job or something? Why'd you have to move?" And why Devilbend North of all the shitty neighborhoods in the country?

"No, my parents are . . . they're not in the picture."

Oh, now this was getting interesting. "Siblings?"

"Only child."

"Same. So you're staying with a relative or something?" Did his parents both die suddenly? He had that look in his eyes—that look that people got when they'd seen some shit. I hoped I wasn't bringing up something painful.

"Nope." Despite the short answer, he didn't seem offended by my questions. Could be just a defense mechanism . . .

"Look, I'm sorry if I hit on a touchy subject. If your parents are—"

He cut me off with a loud laugh. "My parents aren't dead. They're just . . . not currently parenting."

"Yikes. Yeah, OK, say no more. I get it." My one remaining parent hadn't been parenting for some time. I guessed it was even tougher when you didn't have the kind of money we had. Mom may not have been around much, but the fridge was always full and the house was always clean.

"Are we done with the interrogation?" he teased. "Because I got shit to do."

"No, actually." I grabbed on to the safety bar and jumped to the sides of the treadmill so I could look at him properly without risking a face-plant. "Now that I know I'm not being a bitch by making you talk about your dead parents, I'd like an answer to my original question."

He grinned without looking at me, still maintaining a steady jog. I forced my eyes to stay trained on the side of his head instead of wandering down all that sculpted muscle and sweaty skin.

"If you must know"—he was actually starting to sound a little winded after all that exercise—"I was supposed to finish my senior year last year. But, ya know, life got in the way and that never happened. So then I tried a few times to get my shit together this year but . . . yeah, life. To cut a long story short, I managed to get myself a scholarship at Fulton—for next year. But because I'm eighteen, I've aged out of the system, so to keep receiving benefits, I have to be in school. Fulton agreed to let me start now so I wouldn't end up homeless." He powered down the treadmill and stepped off, turning to face me. "You seem to be back to your demanding, abrupt self, so I'm going to get on with my evening now. See you tomorrow."

With one last dimpled grin, he turned and walked into the men's locker room, grabbing his stuff on the way.

I stared after him, slightly stunned, my treadmill still whirring under me. I didn't know jack shit about the system and benefits and homelessness, but I felt as if I knew a bit more about the real Jethro Collins now. He hadn't been dealt an easy life, yet he still walked around with a smile and a positive attitude every day. He still took the time to make me feel better when his problems made mine pale in comparison.

I admired him. And he probably thought I was a spoiled rich girl who had no idea how good she had it.

The next day at school, he sat with us at lunch again. He just waltzed up, and my friends made room for him as if he'd been a permanent fixture of the group for years. It irritated me, and I buried my face in the book I was reading. But it also made me feel . . . some kind of way to have him close by. I worried he'd tell people about the personal shit I'd shared with him at the gym, but I also wanted to go sit closer to him at the same time—I craved more of that calming, grounding energy he seemed to have.

It confused me and I didn't like it. He never even mentioned seeing me at the gym though. He kept my confidence. The few times I glanced up from my phone, he caught my eye, and for a split second, everything around me slowed to a crawl. It was as if he held me in his calm, steady gaze, telling me with nothing more than a glance that he remembered, that he cared, that he had me.

It was weird feeling like I could actually trust this relative stranger with my feelings. It was weird I even wanted to. I wanted to tell him about how my mom pretended nothing had happened when I got home. I wanted to tell him how Cal still being there made me want to punch a wall. I even wanted to tell him about my dad. Listening to Drew and Nicola and the others gossip about people at school, and even their parents, I wanted to pull him aside and tell him which parts were true and which were just sensational gossip. I wanted to ask him things too—to know him. More intrusive questions hovered on the tip of my tongue, but I held them in.

Because they were also talking about the gossip surrounding Jet and his apparently very active dating life. He'd taken half a dozen girls out on dates since he started at Fulton. They all had nothing but nice things to say about him, but not a single one had scored a second date.

He was a player—even though that didn't exactly fit with the parts of him I'd gotten to know so far—and I was not interested in that mess. I refused to follow in my mother's footsteps and choose shitty men. Not that I thought Jet was a shitty man, but he wasn't denying going on all those dates either. Nothing made fucking sense.

I left lunch early, over not being able to focus on my book because I couldn't stop obsessing over a guy. How cliché!

But there was no avoiding him now—not when he felt like a puzzle to solve.

That weekend, the sisters and I went to the diner where Mena worked, to get burgers and keep her company during her break. Jet was there in a booth at the back, bent over some notebooks and his phone. He waved to us but didn't come over. I kept my butt planted on the cheap vinyl seat, fighting the urge to go over there and snoop.

When I went to the mall to pick up shampoo, I spotted him in the food court with some guys from the lacrosse team.

He was even in my yoga class on Sunday morning! And he was surprisingly flexible for someone who could do that many pull-ups with ease. I lost my balance several times, while out of the corner of my eye, I could see him holding a perfect tree pose without so much as a wobble.

I rushed out at the end of the class, avoiding him as I had been since that night at the gym. This had to stop. If I couldn't figure out why he had me off-kilter every time I saw him, I'd just have to fuck him out of my system and be done with it.

The upcoming spring break trip couldn't come soon enough. I needed a break from him so I could *think*.

CHAPTER FOUR

I saw the car pull up from my bedroom window and grinned. My friends jumped out before the driver could come around to open the door for them. It was not normal to be this excited before eight in the morning, but here we were. I'd been packed and ready for half an hour already, waiting for my ride to the airport. My bags lay at the bottom of the stairs, my shoes were on, and I'd been sitting in the window scrolling social media to kill time. I put my cigarette out half-smoked and closed the window, did one last scan of my room to make sure I hadn't forgotten anything, then rushed down the stairs and opened the door.

"Heeey!" Donna, Harlow, and Mena all singsonged at once, throwing their arms out. They were in shorts and T-shirts and had their sunglasses on. It was going to be a glorious Cali day, not a cloud in the sky. The view from the plane would be spectacular.

I whooped and put on my own shades. "Let's get this show on the road!"

I waved the driver through, and he carried my bags to the car while I hugged my besties. Mena was literally bouncing with excitement.

"Amaya? What's all this racket so early in the morning?"

My mother's voice knocked the smile clean off my face, and I glanced at the sky. It was just as bright and cloudless as it had been a moment ago. Apparently the gloom was all in my head.

"Good morning, Mrs. Ellis," Harlow and Donna said in perfectly polite synchronicity.

". . . Mrs. Ellis." Mena was only a beat behind.

"Oh, hello, girls! How lovely to see you!"

I turned to watch Vivian walk down the stairs and nearly fell onto my ass from shock. She was actually dressed, her hair brushed and makeup done. She didn't even look hungover.

The gloom darkened when Cal appeared behind her, coming down the stairs as he adjusted his tie.

"What fun things are you up to today?" Mom asked my friends. "Shopping trip to the city? Maybe I'll join you!"

Oh god, no!

"We're going on a trip, Mom," I rushed out. "It's spring break."

"I wasn't aware of any trip," she said while giving my friends air kisses. "Isn't the school supposed to notify the parents of these things?"

"The school does. You're just never around to see it," I gritted out. "This isn't a school trip. It's spring break. A bunch of us just organized to go together."

"Where?" Mom smoothed a hand down my hair, and I flinched out of her reach with a huff.

"We're flying to the Bahamas," Donna interjected, picking up on my rising irritation.

"On a private jet!" Mena added, eyes so wide I worried they might fall right out of her head. Her excitement was infectious, and I couldn't help the small smile that quirked my lips. It died just as fast when my mother turned a stern look at me.

"Amaya Ann, you can't just leave the country whenever you feel like it without even telling me," she chided as if she cared.

"Why? You do. All the fucking time." I folded my arms.

Cal placed his hands on my mother's shoulders, and whatever bullshit she was about to spit at me died on her lips.

"Take three deep breaths, love," he whispered in her ear. "Just like we talked about."

I resisted the urge to gag as she did exactly as he'd ordered, but I saw my opening. "OK, bye!" I called, shuffling the girls out and following after them.

"Amaya!" Mom snapped and grabbed my wrist. I spun around and wrenched it out of her grip.

"You don't get to ghost me for my entire childhood, then decide to have an opinion on what I do with my life!" I shouted, surprising everyone with my outburst.

Mom's wide eyes narrowed as the shock quickly gave way to anger. Cal squeezed her shoulders, and she pressed her lips together so hard they went white.

"Amaya is a smart, responsible young woman," Cal said, and I gave him a WTF look. "I'm sure she's going to be perfectly safe with her smart, responsible friends."

I mean, one of them did have a secret double life for a while, another frequently did illegal shit online, and the third once joined her boyfriend in a confrontation with the man who killed his mother, but . . . yeah, I was totally safe with them. I trusted my Devilbend Dynasty girls with my life.

"Perhaps if you could give your mother the details of where you're staying and check in when you get there, it would give her peace of mind. We can discuss anything else after." The last part was directed more at Mom, and I didn't know what this "we" was. I had no intention of discussing anything with her—I sure as shit wasn't going to discuss it with *him*. But I was over this whole conversation and wanted to get the fuck out of there already.

"Sure. Whatever. I'll text you the details from the car. We have to go now," I said.

Donna stepped forward and held out a card. "This is the resort we're staying at, and my number is on the back too—just in case."

Her type-A shit was irritating sometimes, but I loved her for it anyway. Because of moments like these. Getting what she wanted (or had been convinced she wanted) totally defused my mom's anger.

"Thank you, Donna." She gave my bestie a warm smile. "You girls be safe and have fun."

I was walking away before she even finished the sentence, and I reached the car before the others.

"I love you, Amaya!" she called after me.

I ignored her, climbing into the car and bouncing my knee. The girls piled in behind me, and I didn't relax until we were through my front gates and on the road toward the airport.

Mena took my hand and gave it a gentle squeeze. "Are you OK?"

My friends were all wearing concerned expressions.

"Yeah, I'm fine." I squeezed Mena's hand back and then released it. "Just another day with Vivian Ellis as my mother. Let's talk about something else."

I really didn't want parental bullshit ruining our trip before it had even begun.

There was a tense moment of silence, and I could tell they wanted to push the issue, talk it out and sync periods or some shit. But I was not in the mood.

"So"—Harlow kicked off her sneakers and crossed her legs up on the seat —"Mena, how's your butthole doing?"

We all burst out laughing, and the tension of the past fifteen minutes started to leave my body. Trust Harlow to take the conversation in a completely unex- pected direction.

"Seriously? What the fuck kind of question is that?" Donna smacked her sister on the arm, even as she laughed along.

"What?" Harlow swatted her back between giggles. "She's the one who wanted advice on anal. I'm just checking in."

"Oh god!" Mena dropped her red face into her hands. "Do you seriously want an update, because we did actually buy some toys, and, uh . . ." She peeked at us from between her fingers.

"Yes!" all three of us yelled at once.

Harlow's phone vibrated in her hand, and a rare serious expression washed over her face, cutting off Mena's butt-sex story before it even started.

"Hello?" She answered it immediately, then listened to whatever the person on the other end said.

"What? How?" She gave us a wide-eyed look, and my stomach bottomed out.

The call barely lasted five minutes, but it had those of us not clued in to the other side of it on the edge of our seats. All we caught from Harlow's end was the occasional, agitated "OK" and "what?" and "why?"

"Yes, yes, I promise to behave, Detective Hopkins." Harlow rolled her eyes, said goodbye, and hung up. "Well, shit." She sighed, then looked up at us. "Irene is dead."

"What?" Donna gasped.

"Oh my god." Mena flopped back against her seat.

I just gritted my teeth, waiting for the rest of the bad news.

"Apparently, she killed herself in her cell last night."

"Apparently?" I prompted.

"Yeah, that's what Hopkins said, but come on." She scoffed. "She has enough eye-witness evidence and digital proof to take down several high-profile members of BestLyf, if not the entire organization, and just as the authorities start building their case and questioning her, she offs herself? Please."

The implication sat heavy between us. No one needed to voice it. We all knew what this meant. BestLyf had managed to murder Irene in prison and make it look like a suicide to protect themselves.

"What did Hopkins want?" Donna always asked the practical questions. "I know he has to notify you because you're a victim of the crimes she's charged with, but what else did he have to say?"

"He was basically telling me to heel." Harlow shrugged.

"What do you mean?" Mena asked, her eyes still wide.

"He did this whole spiel about how there was so much happening behind the scenes that I was unaware of, that I needed to keep my hacker nose out of official police business, blah blah blah."

"Maybe you should," I said.

"What?" Harlow looked at me as if I'd just kicked her kitten.

"All I'm saying is, there's a reason they kept Irene's arrest and her involvement with BestLyf hush-hush. Whatever they're doing—"

"Whatever they're doing isn't fucking working." She cut me off.

"And what? You think you're gonna get your hacker crew together and solve this for them? Come on, Harlow. Look how that ended last time—Easton got fucking shot."

"I know Easton got fucking shot!" she yelled. "I was there, Amaya! And it's not like I decided to start digging around for shits and giggles. I was being blackmailed!"

"I know that!" I forced myself to take a deep breath and speak in a calmer tone. "I know that. I'm not saying any of it was your fault, but you were in some deep shit. I just . . . I can't lose you. Any of you."

Mena's eyes were watery, and Donna pursed her lips. She'd stayed uncharacteristically quiet during our argument.

"No one's losing anyone," she declared as if calling an end to a board meeting. "And we're not going to let this evil corporation keep ruining people's lives. We've all been affected by it."

Harlow threw me a smug smile, but it turned into an eye roll as Donna kept speaking.

"But Amaya has a point. We need to be careful. Safe. We just got this information about Irene, and realistically, we can't do much about it until we have more details—if we can do anything at all. So for this trip, let's just . . . fuck, let's just *chill*. I need a break from all this life-or-death bullshit. Senior year is stressful enough."

"Agreed." I nodded and gave Harlow a nudge with my shoulder. "Love you."

"Love you too," she mumbled.

"I need a drink," Mena declared, releasing a breath. "With a little umbrella in it. Do you think they'll let us drink at the resort?"

The conversation turned to lighter topics, and I wondered if the driver would notice if I cracked a window and lit a cigarette. But we were turning into the gates of the airport and driving over the tarmac before I could dig the packet out of my bag.

The car drove right up to the side of the small jet, and the driver came around to open the door for us.

"Fashionably late, as always!" Nicola called from the bottom of the stairs leading up to the plane, but she was grinning.

"You know us, darling! We like to make an entrance," Donna joked. I jammed my sunglasses on to hide my eye roll. Sure, that was why we were late. Not because my psycho mother delayed us with her tantrum.

Our friends—about twenty of us—were all mingling around the bottom of the stairs, greeting each other and chatting while our luggage was loaded. I took my cigarettes out but was thwarted yet again by a stern man in a neon orange vest. There was strictly no smoking on the tarmac. Fair enough, I supposed—all that jet-fuel . . .

We boarded the plane, and almost every seat on the small jet ended up occupied. I settled into my seat and closed my eyes, resting my head back and listening to the sounds of seat belts clicking and my friends chatting excitedly.

This vacation was exactly what I needed. A break from studying stress. A break from Mom's bullshit. A break from the insanity of having a cult in our hometown. A break from everything.

The engines started up, but when I opened my eyes, the door was still open. Nicola stood next to it, speaking with a woman in a smart uniform and a nametag.

What now? I frowned. If this trip got canceled, I was marching my ass to the commercial terminal and buying a ticket on the next flight out of here. I didn't even care where to—I was leaving.

Footsteps sounded on the metal stairs, and the reason for the delay entered the plane to a chorus of cheers and applause.

Jet held his arms up over his head, hands in fists in a kind of victory pose, grinning at all my friends. Then he hugged Nic, and they both went to find seats as the flight attendant closed the door.

Dammit! Too late to get off the plane.

I turned my face to the window as he passed my seat, but not before I caught the little wink he sent my way.

This was supposed to be a trip to escape all the stress of my life for a while— literal escapism. Yet here was this guy who seemed able to see right through me, coming along to make sure I couldn't enjoy it.

Fucking perfect.

CHAPTER FIVE

He was stealing my damn friends! I glared at Jet over the top of my phone—where the screen was stuck on the same page I'd been rereading for the past half hour.

Jet was a few rows down, sitting with Hendrix and Drew. Donna sat perched on Hendrix's lap, and Mena had wandered over to them too. I couldn't blame her. I'd whipped my phone out to read before we even took off, and Harlow was engrossed in something on her computer screen, her bright pink headphones firmly in place. I really hoped she wasn't doing exactly what we'd agreed not to do in the car, but no one could really tell Harlow what to do.

". . . flew through the air, and landed right in my lap!" Jet's voice rose over the hum of the engines as he finished telling some story. Apparently, it was hilarious, because my friends all lost it.

I wanted to stuff something into his mouth so he'd shut up. But I also really wanted to hear the funny story. I thought about just getting up and joining them, but then I realized I was staring at Jet's crotch. He'd gestured to his lap as he delivered the punch line, and my eyes had gone straight to the area.

I shot my gaze back up and caught him glancing at me as he listened to something Mena said. The moment our eyes met, he gave me a knowing smirk and adjusted his position in his seat, making sure to thrust his pelvis up as he did so.

That smug, infuriating jerk!

"Ugh!" I slammed my phone down on the seat next to me and got to my feet. Harlow looked up and frowned at me, but I waved her off and made my way to the bathroom.

I didn't really need to go, but I needed some space and privacy to get my shit together. I knew he wasn't really stealing my friends—my girls and I were solid. Chicks before dicks and all that. Jet's presence still felt like an intrusion though.

The whole point of the trip was to get away from our responsibilities and worries, and I couldn't do that with him around. He made me want to ask him questions, to get to know him more (*ugh!*), and to tell him things about myself. Like in the gym that night. It had been so easy to talk to him about real shit, shit I hardly talked to anyone about. It was disconcerting to feel so out of control with another person—to feel so seen by someone I hardly knew.

How was I supposed to relax on the beach and forget all my worries when I had to be vigilant around that asshole?

I leaned on the little sink and stared myself down in the mirror.

"You are not letting one arrogant, admittedly hot guy with a frustratingly good ass ruin your spring break," I told myself with a firm look. "You're better than that, Amaya."

I refused to be this affected by a guy. I'd just avoid him as much as possible. It was a big resort and there were a lot of us. How hard could it be to keep my distance?

But we weren't on a tropical island resort yet. We were in a very expensive tin can speeding through the air, and when I stepped out of the bathroom, Jet was right there in front of me.

"You've been in there for a while. You all right?" he asked in a low voice. He kept his posture casual, but he was so close in the tight space next to the bathroom door I could smell him. A fresh smell, unfussy and masculine—just soap and aftershave that hinted at bergamot but crisp. I could feel the heat of his chest, inches from mine.

The urge to scowl and tell him to fuck off was strong, but I gave him a tight smile instead.

"Fine." I hoped the one-word response came off as dismissive as I'd intended. I moved to squeeze past. And because the universe hated me, we hit some turbulence at that exact moment.

The plane lurched to one side, making me stumble back against the wall. Jet stumbled too but managed to avoid crushing me by throwing a hand out against the wall next to my head. His other hand went to my arm, gripping firmly.

"Shit. You all right?" he asked, eyes slightly wide.

"Would you stop asking me that?" I shook his hand off. The plane lurched again, this time in the other direction. Jet's back hit the opposite wall, and I tumbled right against his chest. His hands went to my waist, and I was thankful for the contact this time. With his feet set wide, he stayed steady through the turbulence and kept me on my feet too.

As the shaking eased up, he licked his lips and looked down at me. I bit down on my tongue to keep it in my mouth, stop it from mirroring his.

"Are you—"

"Nope!" I clapped a hand over his mouth. "Do not ask me if I'm all right again."

The seat belt sign came on with a ding, and the captain made a quick announcement that we were moving through an uneven patch but it was nothing serious.

Jet smiled under my hand, and his dark eyes sparkled with mischief. For a second I thought it was better that I couldn't see his lips. But it was so much worse. I could *feel* them. They were soft and warm under my palm, and I could feel them move as he smiled. I could feel them as they parted slightly and the tip of his tongue darted out to lick my palm.

The simple yet unexpected sensation shot up my arm and made the back of my head feel tingly.

I removed my hand and pushed myself upright. His hands stayed on my waist.

"Gross," I whispered and mentally slapped myself. Why was I whispering as if we were sharing a moment? This was like a meet-cute from one of my romance novels.

"We'd better get buckled in," Jet said, but his hands stayed on my waist, and neither of us moved.

The plane jostled under our feet again, literally shaking us out of our cliché staring moment. We stumbled to the nearest empty seats, which just so happened to be next to each other.

What the hell was wrong with me? If this was how I was acting before the plane even landed, how was I going to avoid him for the whole trip? At least the bathroom was at the back of the plane and no one had seen my moment of temporary insanity.

Harlow lifted herself as high as the seat belt would allow and looked over the back of the seat. When she spotted me, she mouthed *OK?* I gave her a reassuring nod and smiled back. She turned to face the front again just as the plane dipped, making everyone shout in surprise or laugh nervously.

I tightened my seat belt a little and wished I hadn't left my phone in the other seat. I'd been through worse turbulence—what bothered me more was that I didn't have anything to distract me from the guy sitting beside me. I did my best to ignore him, but it was next to impossible. He was inches away, his elbow brushing mine with every tremor, his hand gripping the armrest between us.

He had nice hands—strong and thick and . . . his knuckles were white, and his nails dug into the leather of the armrest.

Was carefree, cocky, cool-as-a-cuke Jet scared of a little turbulence?

A wicked smile pulled at my lips. I was going to have fun teasing him. But when I looked up at his face, my stupid conscience kicked in. His eyes were closed, his head back against the seat, his whole body so tense it looked as if he were in an electric chair rather than a soft seat in a private jet.

Instead of having my teasing fun, I placed my hand gently over his. His eyes flew open, and he gave me a deer-in-headlights look.

"You're going to punch a hole in the leather if you don't ease up." I squeezed his hand a little. It flexed under mine, then relaxed, but still held on to the armrest.

"Thanks. I definitely can't afford to pay Nicola to have it repaired." His attempt at a smile looked more like a grimace.

"She wouldn't care." I waved it off. "Are you seriously this scared of flying?"

"Not flying, no. It's the turbulence. I haven't taken many flights, and this is the first time I've experienced turbulence. It's . . . unnerving. Like, it just really makes you aware of the fact that you're hurtling through the sky in a metal tube."

"You seemed fine before, when it first started." I clasped his hand a little tighter, wordlessly reminding him to ease up on the leather once more. Every time we lurched, his grip would tighten up again.

"Yeah, well, I was distracted," he said as he finally let go of the armrest completely—only to turn his hand and grip mine instead.

Now I was the one distracted.

"Do you want to hear a secret?" I blurted out.

"I love secrets." He turned his head in my direction, and I angled to face him more.

"Nicola's mom is having an affair with her driver." I kept my voice low, even though no one could've heard me over the sound of the engines.

Jet blinked, and one corner of his mouth quirked up. "That . . . was not what I was expecting."

We both chuckled, then he asked, "Are you going to tell her?"

"Oh, she already knows. She doesn't like her mom's third husband, so she doesn't give a shit, but it would cause a massive scandal if it got out."

"Right, because she's a movie star and all that."

"Yep. And the husband is a producer. Very high-profile divorce if it comes to that."

"Yeah, I can see that." He nodded sagely, then bugged his eyes out. "Scandalous."

"I know, right?" I rolled my eyes.

"I thought you were about to tell me one of *your* secrets." He stared at me with those eyes that made me feel naked—and not in a good way.

I leaned back slightly. "I don't give up my secrets so easily, but I can tell you one about Luke."

The turbulence only lasted another ten minutes, but Jet relaxed way before that as I chatted about Devilbend gossip. His eyes lost that panicked quality, and his hand no longer gripped mine as if it were the only thing keeping him from plummeting to his death. In fact, his thumb started to rub circles on the back of my hand while we talked. And I let him. It felt good.

The conversation naturally shifted to other topics, and I stayed sitting next to Jet long after the seat belt sign turned off. Once again, he'd lulled me into a sense of security. Maybe he was using some kind of magic to make me keep talking.

I just couldn't figure him out, and that bugged me.

At a lull in the conversation, I studied his profile. The deep set of his eyes made them look even darker, and his jawline was sharper from the side, dulling that baby face he had front-on.

"I don't get you," I said before I'd even decided to say anything.

"What is there to get?" He shrugged and flashed me a smile.

"That's just it, I don't know. You know all our secrets . . ."

"Because you just spilled them all!"

". . . but we hardly know anything about you."

"What do you want to know?" He looked like an open book, with his expression calm if a bit amused, his body relaxed and angled toward me.

I had a feeling he really would honestly answer any question I asked in that moment.

"What's with all the dates?" *That* was the question my stupid brain decided to throw out first? I mentally dragged a hand down my face.

Jet looked as if he was fighting a smile. "You want me to explain the concept of dating? Surely you've been on a date before?"

"Shut up, smartass!" I whacked him in the shoulder—his very solid, sculpted shoulder. "You know what I mean. Why are you taking all these girls out but then never on a second date? They all gush about how wonderful you are." I pretended to faint. "How you're a perfect gentleman, and so attentive, yet none of them seem to be mad about not getting a second date. You're obviously not just trying to get laid—the whole school would know you were a man-whore by now if you were. So what's your deal? What's the agenda?"

"Agenda?"

"Everyone has an agenda."

He frowned slightly, not liking or maybe not agreeing with what I'd said. "Maybe I'm just looking for a girlfriend. That's what dates are for."

I narrowed my eyes at him. "Maybe. But I don't think so."

He stared me down for a while, and I held his gaze. I'd never backed down from anyone, and I wasn't going to now.

"Smart and beautiful," he murmured. "You're dangerous, Amaya Ann."

I was taken aback, not expecting the sudden compliment. And what exactly had he meant by "dangerous"?

"Hey, you two!" Nicola appeared, leaning her elbows on the backs of the seats in front of us. "That turbulence was crazy!"

"Yeah, I nearly fell on my ass!" I laughed.

"I caught her though," Jet added. "Saved that ass."

"Of course you did!" She winked at him.

"Don't wink at him when he's saying things about my ass!" I pointed a finger at her, but she just laughed.

The last few hours of the flight were pretty chill. Everyone moved about the plane, changing seats and chatting, but most people congregated around the middle, which was set up like a living room with two long rows of couchlike seats facing each other. I tried to go back to my spot next to Harlow and read, but I couldn't concentrate, so I drifted over to the main group.

Nicola and a few of the others started talking about BestLyf, and not in the way the girls and I talked about it. They were all part of this youth program and raved about how much they were getting out of it, the people they got to work with, and some bullshit about elevating the different realms of their beings into perfect alignment so they could float above everyone else in their smug superiority. OK, maybe I added that last bit myself, but they sounded pretentious as fuck while having no idea how brainwashed they were becoming.

The last thing I wanted was to think about that mess, so I joined another conversation. I didn't really care about the specifics of what they were saying, but Jet definitely seemed to. He looked genuinely interested as he asked them questions about the program and the people involved and the kinds of things they did there.

I hoped he wasn't looking to join. He'd be sorely disappointed when he was knocked back—not because he wasn't intelligent or talented enough but because he wasn't rich or influential enough. Oh, yeah! Plus, the fact that it was a fucking cult.

I wanted to drag him away from them and tell him to stay clear of it, protect him from all the crap BestLyf had put us through. Looking out the window at the crystal blue water below, I added that to my growing list of bullshit to deal with after the trip.

CHAPTER SIX

The sun felt wonderful on my skin, and the gentle sound of waves crashing on the beach was almost enough to lull me to sleep. I didn't even know what time it was—long enough after breakfast to feel settled on the beach, but not close enough to lunch to really feel hungry. I didn't care. We were about halfway through the trip, and time had ceased to have any meaning.

We spent the nights partying or just chilling by the pool, and we spent the days island hopping, snorkeling, and just chilling on the beach. There was a lot of chilling. Exactly what we all needed.

"Do you think they're having sex out there?" Mena cocked her head and lowered her sunglasses a fraction. She was on the lounger to my left.

"Gross!" Harlow gagged on the lounger to my right. There was an empty one next to her. Donna and Hendrix had gone for a swim in the crystal-clear water some time ago. We could see them way out in the distance. They'd been . . . *hugging* in the same spot for a while.

"Yeah, they're definitely having sex out there." I chuckled.

Harlow gagged again. "Can you stop! I want to go for a dip soon and now I can't."

"Sure you can. They're miles away," Mena argued.

"No, I can't! They're in the same body of water. I don't want to be swimming in their juices!"

"Whose juices are we swimming in?" Drew leaned on the back of my lounger and grinned before exaggeratedly licking his lips. "I fucking love juice."

I tipped my head back and gave him a sweet smile. "Hendrix's."

The girls burst out laughing as Drew's face fell. Then he raised his eyebrows and tilted his head as though actually considering it.

The three of them started cracking dirty jokes and teasing each other until Drew picked Mena up off her lounger and ran for the water, Harlow chasing after them.

I reached for the packet of smokes on the little table next to me and lit one, watching my friends frolic in the water. The long drag I took made me feel light-headed for a moment. I'd been smoking way less since we arrived, and this was my first one for the day. I guessed the stress-free environment was good from my health or some shit.

A wave of melancholy washed over me, tinged with loneliness. It was an odd feeling to have in paradise, surrounded by my closest friends. Irrational. I knew I could get to my feet, walk down to the water, and be welcomed with open arms. I knew my girls had my back no matter what, but . . . sometimes I felt as though I didn't matter. As if I could get up from this lounger and walk off into the sunset and no one would notice.

OK, that was dramatic. Of course my friends would notice if I just disappeared, but they'd get over it eventually. No one in my life would be so devastated that they'd struggle to go on without me.

I hadn't bothered checking in with Mom when we landed. She'd probably forgotten where I was as soon as the car had turned out of our driveway. I hadn't heard anything from her, no missed calls or messages demanding to know I was OK.

My friends were the closest thing I had to family. But Donna and Harlow were sisters and Mena was their cousin. They actually were family. I'd always be the extra. I knew they didn't see me like that, not really, but I couldn't help wishing I was tied to them by blood too. I wanted that irrefutable connection they had to each other.

I took another drag of my cigarette. I didn't want to be thinking about this shit. Didn't want to be feeling . . . *things*.

I grabbed my phone, put the cigarette out after one last puff, and snapped a photo of the paradise before me, making sure to position my legs just so and get them into the shot. Ignoring the countless notifications, I posted it. My followers loved the vacay posts, probably because of all the bikini shots. Two separate swimwear companies had already reached out to me, offering to pay me to wear their stuff. I couldn't be bothered dealing with any of it until we got home. Instead, I opened my reading app and lost myself in an epic romantic fantasy.

It did the trick getting my mind off everything, and an hour flew past before I realized. My friends had been in and out of the water, chatting and messing around while I was absorbed in my book. Now most of the girls were lined up on the sand tanning, and some of the guys were in the shallow water throwing a ball around.

I got to my feet, pulled my bikini wedgie out of my ass, and wandered down to the water. I was sweaty and overheated from sitting in the sun for so long, but the ocean in the Bahamas always felt perfect. The softest sand ever squished between my toes as I stepped into the refreshing waves.

I'd waded up to my thighs when one of the guys threw the ball too wide and it landed with a splat right next to me. In the next moment, Luke and Jet both leaped for it, jostling and flailing all over the place, splashing the shit out of me.

I squealed, the shock of the water enough to startle me despite its mild temperature.

Luke and Jet turned wide eyes to me, the ball bobbing between them. Then they both burst out laughing.

"Fucking hell, Amaya! I thought you were dying!" Luke said through chuckles.

I huffed and leaned back into the water. "You startled me!"

Jet smacked Luke in the junk. "What he means is, we didn't mean to get in your way. Sorry."

I'd managed to avoid Jet on the trip so far . . . sort of. We spent most of our time as a group, so it wasn't too difficult to keep at least three people between us at all times. We hadn't had any "alone time," and I'd hardly had to speak to him directly at all.

His presence was still distracting though. I was constantly aware of him—talking to all my friends, roughhousing with the guys, having long conversations with the girls, going for runs on the beach while most of us were still in bed. And he was goddamn shirtless most of the time! All that toned muscle and tanned skin constantly in my face. He seemed to always be around whenever I got to a spicy part in my book. Which frustrated me in a whole other way.

I wasn't so stubborn that I couldn't admit the dude was insanely hot. But I was my mother's daughter and determined not to make her mistakes. I refused to chase men. Especially ones that dated so much and always managed to avoid sharing anything about themselves in any detail.

But I couldn't avoid noticing him—especially in this setting.

Most of the time his eyes looked so dark I'd thought they were black. But in the bright sunshine and the turquoise water all around him, I could see streaks of warm, rich brown. It was kind of mesmerizing.

I tipped my head back to wet my hair (and avoid licking him with my hungry eyes).

"Whatever." I waved them off as I got to my feet. "I'm all wet now anyway."

Jet cleared his throat and looked to the side, his lips pressed tightly together. Luke's shoulders shook and his face went red with the effort to hold back his own laughter.

I rolled my eyes. "Grow up."

They both lost it, the laughs busting out.

"Are we playing ball?" Drew called from behind them. "Or are you two just going to stand around and listen to Amaya talk about how wet she is?"

Trust Drew to take a double entendre and ride it even harder—pun totally intended. I flipped him off as Luke scooped the ball up and turned back toward the guys.

"Second option!" Jet called and threw me a heated look. "Every damn time."

Before I could process or respond, his eyes widened as if he hadn't meant to say that out loud—or at all. He turned and splashed past Luke in an awkward water run. Was he flirting? Or running away from me?

I raced after them and jumped onto Luke's back. With the element of surprise on my side, I wrestled the ball out of his grip but also managed to send us both splashing into the water.

I joined the guys for a while, trying to keep up with them. They tossed me around almost as much as the ball and lifted me into the air to make catches when someone threw it extra high. It was good exercise—and a good distraction from Jet and his perplexing behavior.

My mood had significantly lifted by evening. The melancholy I'd been feeling earlier completely vanished, chased away by the sun, sand, and splashing around with my friends. I wasn't even bothered by hanging around Jet all day.

A smug little voice in the back of my head suggested it was probably *because* I'd been hanging around Jet that my mood had lifted. That it was because he'd shared his fries with me at lunch, because he'd made me laugh when he cracked a joke about Nicola and Donnie looking as if they were on the verge of another breakup. That it was because he'd picked me up and thrown me around in the water more than any of the others—and I liked it. I'd stayed in the sun without reapplying sunscreen way longer than I would've at any other time. I liked his hands on me. A little too much.

"You ready?" Harlow asked, dropping her headphones on the bed before slipping her flip-flops on. She couldn't exactly have brought her ex-teacher boyfriend on our spring break trip. Turner didn't really know the rest of our group, so he hadn't joined Mena. And I was single, so the three of us were sharing a room. We were having a barbecue and a bonfire on the beach tonight. Mena had already headed down there.

"You go ahead," I called over my shoulder. "I'll catch up."

I put my focus back on getting my winged liner to match on both sides.

Harlow's grinning face appeared above mine in the mirror. "Why are you putting makeup on?"

I'd hardly worn any since we arrived. It was too hot and humid and messy with all the sand and constant layers of sunscreen.

"I just feel like it." I shrugged but narrowed my eyes at her.

She hummed, tapping her chin and squinting at me suspiciously.

"What?"

"I don't suppose you might be making an extra effort for a certain someone who you spent half the day splashing around with? Maybe someone named after an extremely fast aircraft?"

I burst out laughing at her dig at Jet's name but still waved her off. "As if. I'm not going to change any part of myself for any guy. I wear makeup because I want to."

"Naturally." Harlow dropped her hands on my shoulders. "I'm just saying—it would be OK if you wanted him to notice you. You deserve to be happy, Amaya. With or without a man."

I blinked at my friend in the mirror, the eyeliner hovering in front of my face.

Had I really felt as though I didn't belong with my girls? I swallowed around the lump in my throat and forced the emotion down. I didn't want to ruin my makeup. I also was really shit at talking about emotional crap. I blamed my two absent parents.

But of course, Harlow knew that.

"I'll see you out there." She gave my shoulders a squeeze and kissed me on the top of my head. "Love you."

"Love you," I whispered into the mirror, but she was already out the door.

I pushed the tricky thoughts and feelings away and finished my makeup. Halfway to the door, I caught a glimpse of myself in the mirror and decided I looked hot. My long, straight black hair was half up, my simple white slip dress fit me perfectly, and the eyeliner was precisely even on both sides. I could count on one hand the number of times I'd managed that feat on the first try.

I meandered up the path from our room, taking my time and enjoying the moment of peace in the dusk. All the rooms were set among lush, tropical gardens, connected to the communal parts of the resort by artfully manicured walkways. Cicadas sang loudly as rich colors shifted in the sky above.

My phone vibrated in the little crochet bag crossed over my body. A treacherous part of me immediately thought it might be Mom remembering she had a daughter that needed to be checked on, and my stupid excited hand reached for it immediately.

Of course, it wasn't her. My heart sank a little at the realization, but I opened the DMs responsible for the notification anyway.

I replied to a few messages, reported and deleted a dick pic, and scanned through the comments of my latest post as I walked. Habit made me turn left at the end of the path, toward the resort restaurants. I was halfway to our usual dinner spot before I remembered we were all meeting at the beach for the barbecue. Tucking my phone away, I decided to cut through past another row of rooms rather than go all the way around.

A distinctly male voice mingled with the ever-present buzz of the cicadas just before I rounded the bend in the path. It definitely sounded like Jet, but I couldn't make out exactly what he was saying over the noise of the insects.

I slowed my steps and peeked around a palm tree. He stood in front of the door to one of the rooms, his phone held to his ear. He was facing away from me, so I moseyed a little closer. It wasn't my fault he wasn't paying attention. I just happened to be coming past here, and if he wanted to keep his conversation private, he should've taken the call inside.

Not that I could hear much anyway.

". . . that's enough yet," he said, sounding more serious than I'd ever heard him. He listened to whatever the other person was saying for a few seconds. "Yes, if I can find a way to access the . . ."

The stupid cicadas got louder, and I missed the end of what he said. What was enough? What was he trying to find access to?

I was barely a few feet away from him when he hung up and tucked the phone into his pocket. He leaned sideways, planting one foot in the garden bed. He looked as if he was inspecting the window. Had he locked himself out of his room?

I glanced at the number on the door—308—and frowned. I could've sworn he was bunking with Drew in 312.

Stopping next to him, I crossed my arms. "What the fuck are you doing?"

CHAPTER SEVEN

He looked over his shoulder, not at all startled by my presence, and held his finger to his lips. I raised a brow as he hunched over and reached for the window.

Was this guy seriously trying to break into someone's room? And who the fuck did he think he was, shushing me?

Before I could tell him off, he straightened and stepped out of the garden bed, his hands cupped in front of himself as if he was holding water.

"Check it out!" He grinned, stepping closer.

I leaned forward and rolled my eyes. "Seriously? Jet, those things are everywhere."

A little gecko rested in his hands. He stared at it as if it were some mystical creature no one had ever laid eyes on.

"Yeah, I know." He shrugged. "This is my first time out of the country, if you don't count that unfortunate trip to Mexico. I've never seen one up close. I've been trying to catch one since we got here."

Well, shit. Now I felt like a privileged bitch, and a judgmental one at that. I shouldn't have assumed he was being shifty, trying to break into someone's room.

I shuffled closer, and our arms brushed as we gazed at the little lizard darting around on Jet's palms.

"Cute little guy," I said softly.

Jet lifted his gaze to mine, and I realized how close we were. The cicadas continued to trill, and the last rays of sunlight disappeared as we stood there, staring into each other's eyes. Subconsciously, I licked my lips, and Jet's gaze shot to my mouth. I started to lean in and—

The gecko leaped out of Jet's hands, the sudden movement startling us both. He stepped away as the little creature scuttled into the garden and disappeared under the foliage.

Jet cleared his throat. "Shall we? I'm starving."

He started walking before I could reply. I fell into step with him, willing my heart to stop hammering as we walked the rest of the way to the beach in silence.

Thankfully, the staff started serving food just as we arrived, and I grabbed a seat among my friends while everyone was distracted. The last thing I needed was for Harlow to tease me about showing up with Jet. Especially since my heart was still beating that little bit harder after our near-kiss.

"Holy shit, this is amazing!" Hendrix announced between heaping mouthfuls of barbecued lobster and conch. A chorus of agreement went up from everyone at the long table that had been set up in the sand for us. It was piled high with fresh seafood and sides of all kinds, while a bartender mixed tropical cocktails at a makeshift bar off to the side. The legal drinking age in the Bahamas was eighteen, but no one gave a shit that some of us hadn't had that birthday yet.

The jovial mood only continued to get more fun as the night wore on. Jet was seated at the other end of the table with Drew and some of the other boys, and I irritatingly couldn't stop glancing in that direction through dinner.

"Damn, you got it bad," Harlow said, keeping her voice low. I shot her a warning look and glanced around to make sure no one had heard.

Donna leaned across the table. "I don't think I've ever seen you this into someone. Ever."

I took another glance up and down the table, but the only other person listening in was Mena. She had her chin propped on her hand as she stared at me with love-heart eyes and an excited grin.

"You bitches better drop this right now," I said in a low, even tone as I lifted my mojito to my lips. "I have a reputation to uphold."

That got some laughs out of them, but they dropped it, thankfully. I forced myself to keep my eyes away from the guy at the end of the table while I finished off my drink.

Everyone was half-drunk by the time they brought out dessert and cheese platters, and the roaring bonfire gave everything a warm glow. Someone turned the volume up on the music, and a few of the girls started dancing around the fire.

The night was still, the sky clear, the stars shining bright beyond the tall flames licking up at the sky. The sound of waves softly lapping at the sand was only just audible under the music. There was something electric in the air.

When the staff had cleared the tables and left us to our own devices, leaving only the bartender, Nicola announced she had enough molly to get us all fucked up three times over. I knew we'd flown in a private plane, but bringing that amount of drugs internationally was still ballsy as fuck.

At least half the group decided to partake. Hendrix and Donna, who'd been making out on the cushions by the fire for a good half hour, declined and left—probably to go have kinky sex in their room. To my surprise, Mena decided to try some.

"I've never done drugs." She shrugged, but I could see the nervousness in her eyes. "Seems like as good a night to try as any."

"You don't have to if you don't want to." I lit a cigarette and leaned back in the sand. "I'm not having any. Because I don't feel like it. Don't let these assholes peer-pressure you."

She gave me a kiss on the cheek. "They're not. I'm curious."

"All right." Harlow sighed and got to her feet, holding her hands out for Mena. "Let's get you high. I'll take care of you."

Mena giggled, and they headed for Nicola hand in hand.

I stuck with mojitos and danced a bit with the others, keeping an eye on Mena. She was totally fine though, marveling at the sand and the water with the most wonderous smile I'd ever seen on anyone's face. And Harlow followed her around like the good friend she was.

I'd managed to stay distracted enough not to look for Jet the whole night, only catching glimpses of him here and there. And he was staying away from me. Was that on purpose? Did I intimidate him? Or maybe I was the one who was intimidated. Because the girls were right—no guy had ever had this effect on me before.

With the fire dying and everyone either gone back to their rooms or enjoying the tail end of their trip by staring at the stars, I decided to go for a stroll before bed.

Leaving my shoes and bag behind, I made my way down to the ocean. The warm water lapped at my feet as my toes dug into the wet sand. A bright waning gibbous moon reflected off the waves and, away from the fire's glow, cast everything around me in silvery, shadowy grays.

It was beautiful, and kind of soothing.

I'd nearly reached the end of the beach, some rocks creating a natural end point with what must've been staff quarters beyond, when I realized I wasn't alone. There was someone sitting in the sand, looking out over the water.

The strong shoulders and closely cropped hair told me it was probably a man, and I paused. If it was one of the staff, I didn't want to bother them during their time off. And regardless, alarm bells went off in the back of my mind just from being in a dark, secluded place with a male I didn't know.

Just as I was about to turn around and walk a little faster back to my room, the man on the beach tilted his face up to the sky. The moonlight illuminated Jet's features, and the tension in my body seeped out of me.

He didn't look in my direction, but surely he knew I was there. Even as I moved forward—my feet carrying me to him without me really making the deci-sion—he still remained staring at the moon as if it had all the answers.

I wished I knew what the questions were.

It wasn't until I'd sat down next to him that I wondered if maybe he wanted to be alone. Why else wander out here in the middle of the night?

"Are you stalking me, princess?" he asked, his voice low, his gaze still refusing to meet mine.

"Not this shit again." I sighed dramatically. He quirked his lips in a barely there smile, the dimple making a brief appearance before it was gone.

We fell into silence for a while, nothing but the light of the moon and the sound of gentle waves between us.

"Did you have any of Nicola's treats?" I asked. Maybe that explained why he was so mesmerized by the sky.

He chuckled. "Nah. Not really my jam."

I nodded, secretly satisfied I'd chosen not to partake tonight. I didn't want him to judge me, or think less of me.

"You?" he asked, flicking me the first look since I'd joined him.

I shook my head no, and he nodded.

The several cocktails I'd had were quickly draining out of my system, so I wasn't so drunk I'd make reckless choices—just buzzed enough to do something a bit out of character. I'd never made the first move with a guy, but the liquid courage made me feel as if maybe I should. Maybe this time. Maybe this guy.

"Jet?" I had no idea why I whispered, but he heard me just fine.

I tucked one leg under me and turned to face him. He leaned back on one hand, angling his body a bit more toward mine. He looked at me with an open expression, waiting patiently.

"Earlier." I licked my lips and forced myself to at least appear confident, even if I didn't feel it one bit on the inside. "Before the barbecue. We had a moment, right? I didn't imagine that."

His eyes softened slightly, but he held very still before answering. "Yeah, we had a moment."

"I think I'd like to have another moment, with you. One that doesn't get inter-rupted." My heart beat so fast I was sure the sound of it was drowning out the waves. Nervous but exhilarated, I slowly leaned forward.

Jet's lips parted on an exhale, and his gaze flicked down to my mouth. He leaned in too. Our lips were barely an inch apart, my eyes were drifting closed, my skin tingled with anticipation, and—

He pulled away.

With a sigh, Jet turned his head to the side and leaned back. His hand gripped my upper arm, as if he had to physically hold me back from trying to jump him.

"W-what . . . ," I stammered, genuinely confused. He was into me; we had a connection. I could see in his eyes that he wanted to kiss me just as badly.

"We . . . I . . . I can't . . ." He seemed to be struggling as much as I was to form a complete sentence. He removed his hand from my arm as if I'd burned him and flashed me a wide-eyed look.

"Fuck," he muttered as he scrambled to his feet. Dragging a hand down his face, he walked away from me.

I was confused, hurt, embarrassed—all the emotions. And that asshole had scampered away before the anger set in and gave me back my words.

I wanted to storm after him, give him a piece of my mind. But I stayed put. No point making my humiliation even worse by causing a scene in the middle of the night. At least this way, Jet and I would be the only ones who knew what a fool I'd made of myself.

Angry tears tracked down my face as I sat there in the sand and my own misery. There was a reason I hadn't had a proper relationship, never made the first move. There was a reason everyone thought I was a cold, heartless bitch. Because when you cracked your chest open and let someone take a peek at your heart, they'd just reach in and crush it the first chance they got.

They'd leave the vulnerable organ bleeding silver in the moonlight and run away as if you didn't matter.

The angry tears turned into sad, miserable, self-pity tears. Thank God this had happened in such a secluded part of the island.

I stayed in that spot until my tears dried up. I stayed there until the light of the moon gave way to the brilliant colors of the sunrise.

It all still looked gray to me though.

CHAPTER EIGHT

The weather matched my mood when we landed in San Francisco: rainy and miserable. I wasn't the only subdued one as we filed off the private plane. The shitty weather and the post-vacay blues had set in for the whole group.

Maybe my bad attitude was rubbing off on them too, although I'd kept mostly to myself for the last few days of the trip. I'd let myself get drawn in by a piece-of-shit man and I'd gotten hurt. I had only myself to blame. Which was why I was reluctant to talk to anyone about it, or let my misery ruin everyone else's good time.

My girls had noticed my shift in mood right away, but when I made it clear I didn't want to discuss it, they'd dropped it. I knew it wasn't over, that they were worried and would likely bring it up again after giving me some space, but I wasn't ready to admit my humiliation just yet. It was still too raw.

The rest of our group didn't notice anything until probably the last day. I couldn't blame them—we were all there to have fun, and there were plenty of activities and distractions. But by the time we left, Nicola and Drew had both pulled me aside to ask if I was all right, and the others threw me looks the entire flight. They'd picked up on the tension, and it probably hadn't escaped anyone's notice that I refused to speak to Jet. I left every room/conversation/activity as soon as he appeared and didn't make any excuses.

They could all speculate as much as they wanted. I didn't give a fuck.

"Ugh! Can't believe I have to be at work tomorrow morning." Mena groaned. She'd gotten a great tan.

Sometimes I wished I could just give her some of my money, but I knew that would be patronizing. I really admired her. She'd been through a lot of shit.

"School on Monday," Hendrix added to the list of things we had to look forward to. I'd never seen him so miserable. Even when he thought he'd lost Donna.

"Not for me!" Harlow was the only one with pep in her step. She was about to start her new job with some tech company, and she probably couldn't wait to see her boyfriend—and screw his brains out.

The limo pulled up then, and the boys helped the driver with our luggage as we all piled in.

By the time we reached Devilbend, the sun had come out. Unfortunately, it did nothing to chase away the dark and stormy clouds in my own head.

The Mead sisters were the only ones left in the car when we reached my place. Everyone else had been dropped off on our way. As the driver started getting my luggage out, I found myself still sitting in the limo, staring at my front door. Despite how miserable and angry I'd been for the last few days of the trip, it still seemed preferable to going home. Would Mom even be there? Would she notice I was back? She seemed to have forgotten I'd ever left. Or existed at all.

Donna squeezed my knee, snapping me out of my staring contest with my house.

"Come over if you want," she said, her voice sympathetic. "I'm just going to watch movies and do a face mask."

"Thanks, D." I mustered up a smile for her. The girls knew all about what a nightmare of a mother I had. "I'll see what the situation is inside."

"Love you." Harlow pulled me into a tight hug, and Donna piled on too. I held them firmly for a long moment, then extracted myself with a sigh.

The driver carried my bags inside, I waved the girls off as he drove away, and then I was alone.

The house was empty. It had that stillness I'd become all too accustomed to. I wasn't sure if I was relieved or disappointed. Probably a bit of both.

Putting an audiobook on, I decided to distract myself with some self-care and spent the rest of the day taking a bath, putting a hair mask in my hair, exfoliating and soaking and moisturizing. I booked a nail appointment too, as my nails were looking a bit ratty after all that frolicking in the sand.

I headed downstairs in the evening, wondering if my empty stomach had the patience to wait for takeout to be delivered.

"Come on, fridge, do me a solid," I mumbled to myself as I opened the refrigerator. To my utter astonishment, it was stocked—and not just with the basics. This was next level. There were half a dozen bottles of coconut water lined up neatly on the top shelf, cold cuts, fresh vegetables in the crisper, at least four different types of cheese, and containers of what looked like leftovers.

I lifted the lids on a few of the tubs. "Don't suppose any of you contain mac and cheese?"

"Nope, but I'd be happy to make you some," a male voice answered.

I literally jumped. The contents of the fridge door rattled with how hard I slammed it shut.

"Jesus! Fuck!" I pressed a hand to my chest, willing my heart to stop trying to bust out of my rib cage as I glared at Cal. "You scared the crap out of me!"

"Sorry, sorry!" He held his hands out and winced, backing up a step. "I didn't mean to, I swear."

"What the fuck are you doing here? Where's my mom?"

"She's in a meeting that's running late." He frowned slightly as he moved into the kitchen, grabbed a pot and macaroni from the pantry, and dug around in the fridge.

I watched him, noting how comfortable he was in my kitchen, how he knew where everything was.

"You're persistent, I'll give you that," I said as I perched on a stool, putting the island between us.

"What do you mean?" He stayed focused on the cheese he was grating.

"No man has hung around this long. Either Mom gets bored with them, or they decide her bullshit isn't worth the money she comes with. No one has lasted longer than two weeks."

He leveled a disapproving look at me, but I was only stating the truth. Not my fault if he couldn't handle it.

"That's probably because none of them bothered to get to know her. Not really. Your mother is—"

"Save it." I cut him off. "Don't waste your time trying to convince me that you think she's the greatest thing since sliced bread. Vivian doesn't put much stock in my opinion on anything, let alone the men she's fucking. She hardly even remembers she has a daughter most of the time."

He was at the stove with his back to me, but I saw how his shoulders slumped with his sigh. He didn't speak as he served me up a steaming bowl of fresh, home-made mac and cheese.

"I understand why you're wary, Amaya." He slid a fork across the island to me. "I get why you might feel like you need to scare me off, or maybe you're testing me. I don't know."

"You don't know shit, Bob." I flashed him a saccharine smile, deliberately getting his name wrong, before scooping some cheesy pasta into my mouth. Dammit! It was actually really good—creamy and rich, with a slight biteyness from the aged cheddar he'd added.

He ignored my bratty retort. "But I love your mother. Trust me when I say that neither of us expected this, but we genuinely care for each other. I have my own money, so I'm not after hers. I have no ulterior motives. I just want to make her happy." He shrugged. "And I want to get to know you. You're important to her, so you're important to me."

"She's got a funny way of showing it," I grumbled. I didn't know how to take what he was saying. He seemed genuine, but I didn't have much experience with genuine, so maybe he was totally bullshitting me. Lacking the energy to try to puzzle it out, I made my way over to the pantry to distract myself. The mac and cheese tasted amazing, but it was missing something—some other element from when I used to have it as a kid.

I found turmeric and chili powder and sprinkled some into the bowl just as the click of heels on marble announced my mother's arrival. She breezed into the room with a bright smile, then froze when she spotted me.

I stirred the spices into my meal and took a tentative bite. Close, but something was still missing. Maybe it needed more turmeric. I reached for the small jar of the yellow stuff, but suddenly Mom was there, moving it out of my reach.

I frowned up at her, but she'd already turned her back to me as she poked around in the pantry. She emerged a second later, came to my side of the island, and added some cumin to my bowl.

"Turmeric, cumin, and chili," she said as she stirred it in and held a forkful up to my mouth. Confused as fuck, I took the bite.

Holy shit! That's it! I bugged my eyes out at my mom as I chewed and slumped in my seat. She gave me a warm smile and ran her hand through my hair. The look on her face, the affection—it felt real.

The attention from my mom and the flavor on my tongue made me feel like a little girl again.

"Sri Lankan mac and cheese," she murmured, her smile turning melancholy. "It was your favorite when you were little. It was your dad's favorite too. He used to make it all the time."

I'd gotten through half the bowl, but the last bite caught against a lump in my throat.

Memories came flooding back. My dad in the kitchen, turmeric stains on the counters, his eyes shining with so much love. She hadn't so much as mentioned him since . . . I couldn't even remember when. I could hardly believe she'd brought him up at all.

I took a shuddering breath, my vision turning blurry.

"I'm such a terrible cook." Mom chuckled, wiping some moisture from under her own eyes. "I always was. But now that Cal is moving in, he can make it for you whenever you want."

Too much.

It was too much.

The memories of my dad. The first real connection my mom and I had shared in years. Cal was moving in? What the fuck was happening?

I shot to my feet, the stool scraping on the floor, and shoved the bowl away. It slid all the way across the island, and Cal caught it before it fell off. He was looking at me with something resembling sympathy. Or maybe it was pity.

It was all *too much.*

Swiping at my tears angrily, I rushed up the stairs.

"Amaya!" Mom called after me, the usual angry, disapproving tone missing from her voice. Another thing to be confused and overwhelmed with.

I locked myself in my room before she could catch up with me.

CHAPTER NINE

For the next two weeks I went into full denial mode. I was practically Cleopatra—that's how well acquainted I became with that particular river in Egypt.

I went to the gym in the mornings, when Jet wasn't there, and even started taking my yoga classes in the mornings too. It had the added bonus of getting me out of the house early enough to avoid my mom and Cal.

Fucking Cal. He was around all the damn time. At least Jet was easy enough to avoid at school, seeing as how he worked just as hard to stay away from me. If I walked into the cafeteria to find him sitting with our friends, I went off campus to eat. If he walked in last, he'd sit with someone else. He was friends with half the school anyway.

Our friends had noticed the tension between us and how determinedly we were avoiding each other, but neither of us was saying shit about it, so the rumor mill had gone into a frenzy.

I knew I could talk to the girls about the Jet thing and about the shit at home, but then I'd have to acknowledge all the shit I was dealing with and . . . yeah, Cleopatra. So I avoided them a bit too, only hanging out in bigger groups. I buried myself in my books, my social media following, and my exercise. I even studied more than usual, which was probably a good thing considering our exams were fast approaching.

It was a Friday afternoon when it all came crashing down around me.

I'd been making sure to come home late enough that Mom and Cal were in the living room at the back of the house and unable to corner me before I could make it to my room. There'd been no more mac and cheese, but a plate of something homemade waited for me on the stove every day. Without fail. Even if they weren't home when I got in, the food would be there.

More often than not, I'd eat it, scowling at the delicious food the entire time, resenting the person who'd prepared it and the person who'd brought him into my life. Mom must've been telling Cal what my fave dishes were, because he was making them all. Spicy noodle soup, baked rice with chicken, sloppy joes (don't judge me! It was another childhood fave). I was honestly impressed she even remembered.

She'd tried to talk to me several times. Sometimes through the door of my room, sometimes trying to catch me as I passed through the house. She'd even called and texted me. She hadn't yelled or raged or done any of her usual bullshit at all. I brushed her off every time. All I'd wanted since Dad died was my mother's attention, and she'd chosen to shower it on me when I wanted it least.

That Friday, I drove straight home from school—rather than spend the afternoon doing literally anything else, as usual. I pulled up outside our house, parking crookedly.

There was a moving van in the driveway and two dudes carrying boxes into my home.

"What the fuck is happening?" I demanded, bursting through the open front door.

Mom and Cal stood side by side at the kitchen island, chopping, matching glasses of wine in front of them. My mother was in the kitchen. *Chopping*.

"Amaya." She blinked, clearly surprised to see me, then gave me a small nervous smile. "You're home."

"What the fuck is happening?" I repeated, enunciating each word.

Mom frowned, probably at the cursing, and it was Cal who answered.

"I'm moving in. I sold all my furniture, so it's mostly just clothes and personal items, a few sentimental pieces. Nothing much will change. I know this is your home, and I want to—"

"You didn't think to ask me if I was OK with some random dude moving into my house?" I cut him off deliberately, practically shaking with rage.

"I told you two weeks ago Calvin would be moving in. I admit, I could've done that more tactfully, but—"

"It's like I don't even exist to you!" I screeched at her. "You clearly wish I wasn't around, cramping your style, so why didn't you just move in with him? It's not like you've been here half the time anyway. This is *my* home!"

A brief flash of hurt passed over Mom's face, but it quickly disappeared as she ground her teeth.

"I've been trying to talk to you for two damn weeks, Amaya Ann. What am I supposed to do? The world doesn't revolve around you, you know!" Her tone had gone screechy too. I knew she'd been waiting in there somewhere—my selfish, quick-to-anger mother.

I scoffed and shook my head as I backed out of the kitchen. Upstairs, I grabbed my gym bag and a change of clothes, then stormed right back out the front door, past the pile of boxes in the foyer and the stunned moving guys.

The tires squealed as I tore out of there, speeding all the way to the gym.

I found a spot in the back lot and grabbed my bag. As I got out of my car, the back door of the gym opened and Jet came out. His head was down as he held his cell phone to his ear and walked a few paces.

Great. Fucking fantastic. Just what I needed now on top of everything else.

I didn't even entertain the idea of getting back in the car and leaving. He was not going to keep me from my exercise. I chose to ignore the little feeling deep in my gut that told me I was staying not out of stubbornness but because I was secretly happy to see him.

Shoulders back, I marched across the lot, doing my best not to glance in his direction.

It was a bit irritating he hadn't noticed me yet, but the person on the other end of that call was not sharing happy news.

Jet looked . . . well, not as pissed off as I felt, but I'd never seen him look even remotely angry. I couldn't help peeking over as I got closer, fascinated with the way his brows furrowed in a deep frown, the way his jaw worked as he listened, how the tension in his shoulders made them look even harder and more defined than usual. And he hadn't even had his workout yet—his tank was completely dry.

"Yes, of course I understand that." He pinched the bridge of his nose. "You try not getting emotionally—"

He cut himself off as soon as he spotted me. I gave him a flat look and opened the door to the gym. I badly wanted to eavesdrop and try to figure out who he was talking to and what about. But I wouldn't hear anything interesting now that he knew he had an audience.

"I have to go," I heard him mutter as the door started to swing shut behind me. "Yes, sir."

He stopped the door before it slammed shut and jogged to catch up to me.

"Amaya, hey," he called, and I turned to face him just before I reached the locker rooms.

"Hey," I said, voice emotionless. "Listen, can we not do this today?"

He frowned, concern entering his gaze as he scanned me. I resisted the urge to fidget with the hem of my T-shirt. I was still in my Fulton uniform and really wanted to just get into my gym gear.

"What's wrong?" he asked and moved closer.

I stepped to the side, avoiding what I knew would be a comforting touch on my arm. He stuffed his hands into his pockets.

"This is exactly what I'm talking about. I've had a really shitty day, and you

. . ." I huffed. "You just seem to always find some way to get me to talk about it, and I really, really don't want to today. So please, let's not."

He took a few steps back and leaned against the opposite wall, then watched me in silence for a beat. He was giving me physical space, and I had a feeling he was trying to give me emotional space too.

A sweaty middle-aged man came past clutching a towel and a water bottle, interrupting our eye contact for a split second before disappearing into the men's locker room.

"Do you ever just . . . wish you could be someone else?" Jet asked.

I cocked my head to the side. I'd been expecting him to push me to talk, or to drag me to the treadmills like last time. I hadn't expected this random question, and I found myself actually thinking about it.

Did I wish I could be someone who wasn't constantly fighting with her mother and hadn't lost her father when she was eleven? Did I wish I could have normal teenage worries—like homework and boys and whether I was pretty enough—instead of having those worries *and* the insanity of a cult in my town and best friends whose lives were periodically in danger?

"I mean, yeah, sometimes. Doesn't everyone?" I shrugged.

He smiled, but it lacked his usual enthusiastic positivity. "No, I don't think everyone does."

"Do you?" I threw the question back at him.

He nodded slowly and sighed. Then he pushed off the wall, some of that signature energy returning. "Let's do it."

"What?"

"Let's go be someone else," he said, as if it were obvious and I was the slow one in this conversation.

"Jet, what the fuck are you talking about?" I groaned.

"Just for the afternoon." He took my hands and leaned in, looking me right in the eye. "Let's go somewhere that's not here and pretend to be people we're not. Say yes!"

It was sad how tempting that sounded. I looked down one side of the hallway, then the other. Was I actually considering this?

"Fuck it, OK, whatever." I rolled my eyes, but something like excitement started to stir in my belly. "But if you turn out to be some psycho axe murderer, I'm going to kill you. Slowly."

"You're so violent." He chuckled before ducking into the locker room to get his bag. He reappeared before I could change my mind, grabbed me by the wrist, and pulled me out the door. I let him. I was pretending to be someone else, after all.

"Your ride or mine?" he asked as the door swung closed behind us. "Or should we really lean into this 'being other people' thing and take public transport?"

"Ew!" I scrunched my face up. "Let's not take this too far. Where are we even going?"

"Wherever the road takes us."

"Fine, you can drive then, since this whole ridiculous idea was yours."

Without answering me, he changed directions, and we stopped next to his bike near the entrance to the parking lot.

"Ugh! I forgot about the crotch rocket," I said.

He threw his head back and laughed, pulling a helmet out of his bag and another one out of the compartment under the seat. He held one out to me, and I stared at it without taking it.

"Never mind. I'll drive." I started to turn, but Jet always knew what to say to make me pause.

"Don't tell me you're scared." He laughed. "Have you never been on a motor-bike before?"

"No, I haven't, and no, I'm not scared." I crossed my arms. I was kind of scared, to be honest.

Jet dropped the teasing smile and held the helmet out to me again. "I'll keep you safe, Amaya, I promise."

Despite my better judgment, I quickly braided my hair and took the helmet. I was someone else today—not some girl afraid of getting on a bike with a boy.

Jet stuffed our bags into the compartment, put his own helmet on, then helped me with mine. It was heavy and tight on my head, but he assured me it was meant to feel like that. Once he'd finished fiddling with the strap under my chin, he smacked the top of my helmet and swung his leg over the seat.

Without thinking about it too hard, I got on behind him.

"Hold on tight." He pulled my arms around his waist, forcing my body flush with his. "If you need me to stop, tap my shoulder."

I couldn't force my throat to spit out a response. In the next second, he started the engine with a roar, and I couldn't have been heard over it anyway.

We took off, Jet navigating the streets of downtown Devilbend, the traffic forcing us to go slow. After a few minutes, I started to feel more comfortable. This wasn't so bad. There was no reason for me to be hugging him so tightly, really. I tried to put some distance between us, sitting up a bit straighter and peeling my legs away from his.

But then we finally got out of the city and onto a highway, and Jet *took off*.

The engine roared beneath us, and the wind whipped past as I released a high-pitched sound of surprise and fear. He probably hadn't heard me over the noise, but I didn't really care. I was too focused on holding on for dear life.

Any semblance of distance I'd tried to put between us vanished—left behind at the start of the highway, alongside my stomach. My front was flush with his back, my arms locked around his waist, my legs plastered to his. I could feel every shift of his thigh muscles, every flex and release of his back and abs. His body heat and the firmness of his frame against mine were comforting.

As my breathing started to settle and my stomach caught up with the rest of my body, I realized I had my eyes closed. I forced them open and gasped at how quickly the trees were flying past. We were going at an obscene speed! Or did it just feel faster without the illusion of safety provided by car doors and seats and a roof?

I didn't dare turn enough to look behind, but we weren't gaining on the car ahead of us, so I figured Jet was sticking to the speed limit.

Eventually, fear gave way to exhilaration, and I started to really enjoy the ride. The noise made conversation impossible, but there was something calming about that. We were moving in the same direction, together, just occupying the same space without filling it with awkward words. Between that and the wind tugging at our clothes, the trees occasionally giving way to a view of the valley below, I found myself feeling profoundly . . . free.

I even loosened my death grip on Jet—not to force distance between us but simply because my body relaxed into the rhythm of the ride. I even let myself acknowledge and enjoy the way his body felt against mine.

Between the feelings of freedom and the feelings stirring between my legs, I wasn't paying any attention to where we were going. We could've been riding for twenty minutes or two hours. I had no idea. All I knew was the feel of him pressed against me, the shift of his body as he controlled the bike, the lashing of the wind and roaring of the engine.

Everything else fell away, and for a little while, I didn't have a care in the world.

And then we pulled onto a quieter street, somewhere totally unfamiliar. Jet took a few turns and parked at the edge of a strip mall.

"Where are we?" I asked once he killed the engine. The shopfronts didn't give any clues.

I struggled to get the helmet off as much as I'd struggled to get it on, so we got off the bike and Jet helped me with it.

"Does it matter?" He gave me a dimpled smile as he put my helmet away.

"It does if you're about to murder me and bury my body behind that Wendy's." I nodded toward the first store on the strip. The signage was faded, the door rusted in the bottom corner.

"That sounds like a very Amaya thing to say." Jet shook his head in disappointment.

"Right. Forgot we were playing this stupid game." I put on a plastic smile. "Oh my gosh, Jethro! I can't wait to see what you have planned!"

He chuckled and took my hand, pulling me along. I followed willingly, matching his pace up the sidewalk.

Unfortunately it wasn't a long walk. In the middle of the strip mall, the biggest storefront belonged to a thrift store. We paused at the entrance to let an elderly man with a cane exit, and then Jet dragged me inside.

It smelled musty—like a closet full of clothes that hadn't been worn in a decade. I supposed it was exactly that. Racks and racks of clothing that hadn't been worn in years. At the back of the store was a section with some furniture and housewares, sad-looking toys, and faded paperbacks.

I raised an eyebrow at Jet. He was already looking at me, trying to stifle a laugh.

"This is a thrift store." He leaned in and spoke low. "All the items in here—"

"I know what a thrift store is, asshole." I cut him off with a smack to his stomach. The back of my hand stung for a second—it felt as if I'd whacked a brick wall.

I'd been to plenty of thrift stores—usually in the city. It was amazing the kind of things people threw out. You could find some real fashion treasures if you were willing to dig through the literal mountains of polyester trash.

"Let me guess." I turned to face him. "You're going to find the ugliest outfit you can for me, and I'm going to find the ugliest outfit I can for you, and then—"

"Nope!" He gave me a self-satisfied grin. "I'd never try to tell you who you should be or how you should dress. This is about being whoever the fuck we want to be. Pick your own outfit, beautiful. Just make sure it's one *Amaya* wouldn't go for."

With that, he walked off, strolling down an aisle packed with men's pants.

For lack of anything better to do, and secretly excited to get into this weird little exercise, I headed for the ladies' section.

Before I knew it, a half hour had passed, and I had about a dozen items slung over my arm—half of them quirky, fun finds I could actually work into my wardrobe. I even had a whole series of posts planned for Instagram. One of my finds was a vintage nineties Diesel denim skirt. There was no label on it, and it was creased in all the wrong places, but I knew Diesel when I saw it.

The other half of the items were things I'd never wear in my regular life.

I flicked hangers from one side to the other swiftly, going through the last rack of dresses. Most of them were hideous.

"I swear it wasn't me." Jet popped up on the other side of the rack, startling me. He was wearing a golf hat that had seen better days, and his own pile of clothing hung over his arm.

"What?" I snapped, pressing my hand to my chest in a vain effort to get my heart to stop hammering. That seemed to be a losing battle whenever Jethro Collins was around.

"The look on your face." He pulled his lips into an almost snarl—apparently an imitation of my expression. "You look like you've just walked into a fart cloud. Just saying it wasn't me."

I forced my features into a blank mask, embarrassed he'd caught me letting my thoughts show.

Jet's teasing smile faltered. "Hey, no, don't do that," he said softly, leaning his forearms on the rack between us. "I thought you knew by now you can't hide from me."

Yeah, that's what I was afraid of.

"I was offended by the horrendous scraps of fabric that pass for clothing in this place," I said, ignoring his statement.

He chose to ignore mine too. "I like it when you let your emotions show on your face, Amaya. It's beautiful."

The words hung between us among the musty secondhand clothing as we shared a loaded look. A look almost as intense as the one we'd shared on the beach that night—when I'd been convinced he felt the same way. When I went in for a kiss and he rejected me.

I forced myself to look away and started flicking hangers again, not really seeing any of the dresses whipping past.

Jet ducked down, shoved the clothing apart, and crouched through it so he was on my side of the rack. I couldn't help the chuckle that bubbled up.

"Are you ready to go try our new personalities on?" He flashed me an easy grin, dimples popping, eyes sparkling.

I shrugged, grateful for the switch in mood. "Sure. Let's do it."

He moved past me toward the changing rooms.

As I passed the end of the rack, a swath of floral print caught my eye. I grabbed the dress without even looking at it properly and rushed to catch up with Jet.

We spent the next half hour trying on increasingly ridiculous combinations of the clothes we'd picked out, making sure to step out at the same time. We laughed and teased each other and made way too much noise for the two elderly ladies manning the register.

The best moment was when we both emerged dressed as old people, matching without even trying. I had a calf-length wool skirt on, paired with a crocheted cardigan, pearls, and a bag with a snap closure. Jet shuffled out from behind the curtain wearing pants three sizes too big and cinched so high with a belt they practically reached his armpits. He'd paired them with a tweed coat and fedora and came out leaning heavily on a cane.

When we saw each other, we collapsed into uncontrollable laughter before standing in the mirror side by side to admire our matching looks. He talked about his time in 'Nam. I offered to make sandwiches before we went to church. We linked arms like an old married couple and pretended to worry about our sixteen grandchildren and the state of youth these days.

We kept it light and fun, but just before we went back to change again, I caught his eye in the mirror and wondered if he was thinking the same thing— how easy and natural this felt. I hoped I'd find someone to grow old with one day. Someone who made me laugh and forget my worries as well as Jet did.

In the dressing room, I put my final item on—the dress I'd grabbed at the last second. It was a strappy sundress with big flowers all over it in shades of pink. It hit the floor even with my shoes on but fit OK otherwise. There was nothing particularly outrageous about it—just a floral-print dress. I wore dresses all the time. I wore pink too. But the particular style, the fact it was some no-name brand, the general vibe of it just wasn't me. Did I wish it was me? I didn't know, but I liked pretending I was the kind of girl who would wear this dress. The kind of girl who didn't care about labels and felt as loose and free as the skirt swinging around my feet.

I took my hair out of the braid, letting it hang loose down my back, and stepped out.

Jet stepped out a moment later, and we silently took each other in. He'd chosen a preppy outfit—pleated shorts, a polo shirt, even a sweater over his shoulders with the arms looped together on his chest. The pastel blue of the shirt contrasted with his near-black eyes. It gave him a dark edge, despite the baby face. The look suited him. I could totally picture him on a sailboat with a Rolex on his wrist. But then, Jet looked good in everything.

"I love it when you let your hair out," he said, stepping closer. He stuffed one hand into his pocket and grabbed a strand of my hair with the other, fiddling with it gently.

"Oh, thanks, I . . ." I was about to tell him it needed a wash and was all frizzy from the braid and helmet, that I usually wouldn't be caught dead with my hair looking like this. But then I remembered the game we were playing and forced all that down. The girl who wore no-name-brand floral dresses with sneakers didn't care that deeply about her hair. "Thank you."

I left it at that and ducked my head to hide my smile. Apparently floral dress girl was also fucking coy.

"You look great too." I smoothed out the collar of his shirt. "The old-money, Ivy League look suits you."

He shrugged, letting go of my hair. "I'm not going to be in your world very long, but when in Rome and all that . . ."

With a grin, he spun on the spot, leaving one hand in his pocket. Of course his ass looked good in a smelly pair of secondhand shorts.

We kept the outfits on as we went to the counter and paid for them. As I laid out the handful of other items I'd decided to buy, I wondered about Jet's choice of words, his choice of outfit. He wasn't going to be in my world for very long. He was on scholarship and would only be at Fulton for one more year, but did he *want* to be in my world? Was he referring to the bubble of privilege I'd grown up in, or was he talking about being in *my* bubble specifically?

"You hungry?" He pulled me out of my thoughts as we exited the store, an ugly plastic bag stuffed with clothes hanging over my arm. "There's a pizza place at the end of the strip mall there. Or we can drive to someplace else?"

"Pizza sounds good." I took off up the street, not quite ready to be so close to him on the bike after the confusing thoughts I'd just been thinking.

We got a giant slice and a soda each and took them to a picnic table in a grassy area behind the row of stores. We ate in comfortable silence, then joked about some of the more horrible clothes we'd tried on. The hum of traffic in the background mingled with birdsong, and the air was warm. Summer was just around the corner, and I leaned back on my hands, enjoying the easy moment.

It didn't last long. Jet's attempts at distraction were valiant, but I couldn't force the complicated thoughts from my mind in every in-between moment of stillness. I could feel him watching me, but he stayed true to his word and didn't try to make me talk.

For the first time since we'd met, I offered up the information. "My mom's new boyfriend is moving into my house. I came home from school to a van in the driveway and moving boxes everywhere."

Jet rested his elbows on his knees, his legs propped up on the bench seat. "You don't like him? Do you not feel safe with him around?"

"It's not that." I shook my head. "He doesn't give me the creeps at all, actually, unlike most of Mom's previous men. Not like that anyway."

"Abuse can look like a lot of different things."

"I'm not being abused," I rushed out, a little irritated. "Unless you count the years of neglect from my mother."

"I do," he responded immediately, but I ignored him.

"It's just that they didn't even give me a chance to say no. I mean, shouldn't I get a say in who lives in my fucking house?"

"Of course you should."

"I just don't understand what the hell is happening, you know? Like, Mom's suddenly around all the damn time, and it's kind of suffocating, even though I don't really feel like she's there for me. Like, I don't really have a mother back because *he's* around all the fucking time too. And I'll straight-up murder you if you repeat this to anyone, but I actually think he might be a decent guy. Like, he's good for her or something. But . . . I don't know. It feels like everything is changing around me and I don't have anything solid to hold on to, ya know? Like nothing is certain, and that's fucking terrifying."

I took a deep breath and dug my nails into the dirty wood of the table.

"Yeah, I know how that feels. Change can be scary."

"Oh god." I sat up and ran my hands through my messy, frizzy hair. "You must think I'm such a drama queen. You don't have either of your parents, and you live in a shitty apartment on your own, and here I am complaining about my mom being around more and feeling like my literal mansion is not big enough to give me space from her boyfriend."

"Did you say my apartment was shitty?" Jet chuckled. "You've never seen it. How'd you know it was shitty?"

I looked up at him with wide eyes, mortified. "Oh crap, I'm so sorry. It was just . . . I was just trying to say . . ."

He cut me off by getting to his feet and coming to stand in front of me. "Amaya, it's OK. I'm just teasing. I know you didn't mean it like that. I don't think you're a drama queen. And I can totally see why your situation at home has you upset. Please don't pile guilt on top of it all. Just because other people have problems that may seem bigger than yours doesn't make your problems any easier to deal with, or any less valid."

I looked up at him, tears stinging the backs of my eyes, everything from the past few weeks spilling over. Last time, I'd made myself hold the tears back until he was gone. This time, they tracked down my face as he stood close enough to taste them.

That time I'd been crying over him; this time I was crying for a whole bunch of other reasons. That was how I justified it to myself.

Something cracked in his expression, and he looked pained at the evidence of my own pain. He gently cupped my face with both hands, wiping the salty moisture off my cheeks with his thumbs. The tenderness in his touch, the broken expression on his face, made me cry harder.

He pulled me into his chest. One arm banded around my waist, and the other gripped the back of my neck, his fingers tangling with my hair. I held on to him so tightly my hands ached, and I let go completely in his warm embrace. Just for a few indulgent moments. His strong arms, his firm chest—he made me feel safe.

Even though he'd been the one who made me cry last time. How fucked up was that?

The thought was sobering, making it easier to stem the flow of tears and lean back. I still struggled to fully pull away from him though, and my fingers clung to the front of his new, old shirt.

"Why . . ." I started to ask what I'd been dying to know for weeks. Why had he not kissed me? Why was no one good enough for him? Why was *I* not good enough?

But I stopped myself before the rest of the words tumbled past my trembling lips. I forced a deep breath into my lungs and made myself release my grip on his shirt.

"Why what?" He tilted his head to the side, trying to catch my gaze.

I couldn't help it; I looked into his eyes.

He saw it right away. As if the image of that beach at night, of our lips nearly crashing together like the waves on the sand, was reflected in the depths of my irises. His expression hardened, something like regret flashing across his features before he took a tiny step back.

I wrapped my arms around my middle. I couldn't take another blow to my softest parts.

"Take me home, Jet." I was so fucking tired.

CHAPTER TEN

Freshmen scurried out of my way as I marched through Fulton Academy after the end-of-day bell. They always scurried, but I was in a particularly shitty mood, so they scurried particularly well.

I didn't let any of it show on my face as I headed for the library, forcing my shoulders back and striding as if I owned the place. Which, to be fair, most of these freshmen would tell you I did.

The library doors were in sight ahead when the one asshole who never scurried from me came around the corner.

"Hey, Amaya." Jet walked directly toward me.

"Jethro." I barely spared him a glance as I walked past—or tried to. He stepped sideways and blocked me, forcing me to come to a stop a few feet away from the library.

"Amaya, can we please talk?" He leaned in and kept his voice lowered.

"About what?" It had been three days since our impromptu thrift shop adventure. I'd ignored just about everyone for the weekend, but come Monday, he'd spent all day trying to talk to me. I'd managed to dodge him so far, but he had that determined look on his face. As if he was ready to throw me over his shoulder and tie me up until I agreed to speak to him.

"About the other day. I feel like we left things unfinished. You wanted to go home, and I wasn't going to keep you somewhere you didn't want to be, but I don't think our conversation is quite over."

"It's over. Trust me."

"I just . . . I've been worried about you." He swallowed hard, his Adam's apple bobbing. For the first time since we'd met, he looked uncertain—maybe even nervous.

"Look, I appreciate you getting my mind off shit on Friday, but I shouldn't have unloaded on you like that." He shook his head, but I forged on. "You're not interested in me. I get it. But I'm not interested in being just your friend, so we have nothing to talk about anymore. You don't get to be worried. I have my girl-friends to be there for me, to worry about me, to talk to. You're off the hook, OK?"

He stared at me with an indecipherable look on his face. I could tell he wanted to say something, a lot of things, but he couldn't seem to find the words.

"Speaking of friends, I'm meeting mine in the library to study, and I'm late." I gave him a firm look. After a long moment, his shoulders dropped in defeat, and he stepped aside.

"See ya, Amaya." He sounded sad, and as I passed, his fingers brushed against mine. I forced my hand to grip the strap of my bag so it wouldn't grab on to him and never let go.

"Goodbye, Jet." I said it softly, more for myself than him, but I had a feeling he heard it anyway.

I found the girls and Hendrix at a table in the back of the library. They'd set up right next to a window, away from all the shelves. Weaving through the desks in the study area—half of which were full with other seniors studying for exams—I made my way over.

They all gave me halfhearted waves of acknowledgment, already buried in books and flash cards. Donna was methodically crosschecking some English notes against the relevant reading. Mena had that deer-in-the-headlights look as she switched between her math and political science notes every few seconds. Hendrix's head was in his hands as he stared at a blank page on the table before him.

If I was going to be miserable, at least I'd be in good company. Dropping my bag, I flopped into the last free chair. I reached down to grab my books, but I just slumped against the back of the chair instead.

Exams were fast approaching and I'd come here fully prepared to study. But . . . *ugh*! This was all Jet's fault.

Mena's hand covered mine on the table, and I looked up to find she'd aban-doned her frantic attempts at study to instead study me. Across from us, Donna sat up and looked at me too. Hendrix was still stuck in whatever depth of despair that blank sheet of paper had him trapped in.

"What?" I frowned.

"You look sad," Mena said, sounding sad herself.

Hendrix looked up from his existential crisis, and then all three of them were watching me with worried expressions. Mena didn't resist when I pulled my hand out from under hers, but Donna never let anyone get away with shit.

"A, you've been off for weeks and you won't talk to us. We're seriously getting worried here. Please . . ." I could count on one hand the number of times I'd seen Donna Mead lost for words.

"We just love you and we want to be here for you. That's all," Mena practically pleaded.

"Others are starting to notice too," Hendrix added. Damn him! He knew I hated having people up in my business, that it would bother me more than anything to know they were talking shit about me.

I opened my mouth to . . . say something, and I just made a weird strangled sound before closing it again.

Shit. Fuck! I could feel all the pent-up emotions building up, literally choking me to the point I couldn't speak. In school, with half our year sitting all around us, dammit! I glanced around the library and then at my friends.

I must've looked like a caged animal. I wanted to talk to them, I did, but there was so much shit to let out it was clogging the way.

But my friends knew me—like, *really* knew me. Donna and Mena packed their books up right away. Hendrix frowned and hesitantly started grabbing his stuff too.

Donna placed a hand on his shoulder. "We need some girl time. You need to stay here and actually study."

"Harlow will meet us downtown," Mena announced, tucking her phone away and zipping up her bag.

Looking disappointed, Hendrix slouched back into his seat and took out a book with actual words on it.

"Whatever it is, Amaya, we got your back," he said, and I gave him a genuine smile. Then Donna gave him a big, sloppy, totally-inappropriate-for-the-school-library kiss, and we turned to leave.

"How the fuck am I supposed to focus on equations with a raging boner?" Hendrix grumbled as we left, making us and a few others nearby laugh.

Twenty minutes later, we were settled in the courtyard of our favorite smoothie place in Devilbend, four large cups with straws sitting on the table between me and my very attentive friends.

They all had expectant looks on their faces. It was a little unnerving being stared at, and I found myself leaning back in my chair.

Harlow grabbed her drink and slurped the chocolate-peanut-butter smoothie while narrowing her eyes at me.

"Bitch. Start talking." Donna was done handling me with kid gloves and was back to her straightforward, demanding self.

Weirdly, it made me feel better. It was comforting in that way familiar things were.

"My mom's latest man-thing is moving into my house, and the strange thing is they both seem actually serious about it and are acting vaguely like adults, and it's bringing up all kinds of feelings." I gagged. "Like, about my dad, and about my mom too, and for some infuriating reason, I find it really easy to talk about all this shit to Jethro fucking Collins, and I think I really fucking like him, which is super inconvenient because he clearly does not like me back, because we had a moment on spring break and we nearly kissed, but he practically recoiled from me and ran away, and then the other day when I was upset about the douchebag invading my home, he went out of his way to cheer me up—like, boyfriend level of effort—and that's two times now that I felt things for him but it didn't go anywhere, and I'm fucking humiliated and pissed off, because I still fucking like him."

I sucked in a deep breath, then released it with a huff before reaching for my green goddess smoothie. I took big gulps while looking between my friends, waiting for their reactions to the pile of emotional shit I'd just dumped on them.

All three wore matching wide-eyed looks.

Harlow was the first to speak, giving me a smug little smile. "I knew you had a thing for him."

I flipped her off.

"You guys nearly kissed?" Mena looked as though she wanted to smile at the romance of it all, but the rest of the heavy crap was weighing it down.

"Your mom is in a stable relationship?" Donna sounded as if she wanted proof that would stand up in a court of law. I didn't blame her. I wouldn't have believed it either if I hadn't seen it with my own eyes.

"Yep." I didn't know which of them I was responding to. "So, yeah. The past few weeks have been . . ."

"Overwhelming?" Mena suggested.

"A clusterfuck?" Harlow added.

"Bullshit." Donna frowned.

"All of the above." I nodded.

"Why didn't you tell us any of this?" Mena asked.

I shrugged and fidgeted with my straw. "The thing with Jet happened on our vacation, and I didn't want to bring the mood down. And also I was embarrassed. Then after, I was determined to just ignore him until he went away since nothing is ever going to happen between us. And the shit with my mom . . . I honestly didn't even know where to start. I still don't really know how I feel about it all."

For the next hour, we sat around that little table in the quirky courtyard of a juice place, and I poured it all out for my friends. They listened and asked questions and offered unwavering support as I worked through my feelings.

I had the best friends. They didn't judge me or rush me, but they called me out on my crap too. It was exactly what I needed, and I felt so much better after letting it all out.

Yes, the situation at home was still upsetting and overwhelming. And yes, I was still confused and embarrassed about the crap with Jet. But at least I didn't have to deal with it all on my own.

The girls made me realize I needed to talk to my mom. Properly talk to her, without getting into a fight, and tell her how I felt about everything. I also probably needed to talk to a therapist, maybe with my mom there too. I wasn't quite ready for either of those things, but I promised my girls I'd keep thinking about it, and I'd at least try to talk to my mom soon in a mature way.

When it came to Jet, the unanimous decision was that he was dead to us.

"Want me to look into him?" Harlow asked, glancing around the busy courtyard. She meant by using less-than-legal hacking ways. "I might find something we can use."

I wasn't sure I wanted to hurt or embarrass Jet. I just wanted him to stop doing the same to me.

"Nah." I shook my head. "I don't want to waste any more energy on him."

"Good." Mena nodded and crossed her arms. "As a very good friend of mine once wisely told me—he should be ride-or-die. He didn't ride, so he should die. Literally."

"I believe I said figuratively." I chuckled. "And this is a completely different situation."

"Yeah, well, I mean *literally*."

"OK, murder fairy. Let's tone down the violent tendencies, shall we?" I patted her on the arm.

"He's going to regret ever coming to Fulton Academy. There might only be a few weeks left in the year, but that's plenty of time to make his life hell." Donna slurped the last dregs of her smoothie aggressively, probably already plotting Jet's demise in detail.

"Donna, stand down." I gave her a firm look, then threw the same look at the other two. "Everyone stand down. Please. It's not like we were together and he cheated or something. He never made me any promises. We haven't even fucking kissed. He just doesn't like me. It might hurt, but it's not a crime."

"It should be. You're fucking fabulous," Mena grumbled.

"Fine. No absolute destruction. But only because you asked," Donna conceded.

"All right, I gotta get some more work done before I head to Easton's for dinner." Harlow got to her feet, and we followed suit. It didn't escape my notice that she hadn't agreed not to look into Jet on the dark web or whatever, but there was no arguing with her when she got a digital mission in her head.

We chatted about her new job on the way out. She was really enjoying the flexible hours and doing something she was genuinely good at. After years of feeling like a failure at school and life, she seemed happy, and that made me happy.

"Let's take a photo!" Mena whipped her phone out, and the three of them shoved me into the middle and hugged the breath out of me. "Everyone say, 'Amaya is a bad bitch'!"

"Amaya is a bad bitch!" the three of them chanted as I laughed and Mena snapped multiple pictures. She posted one with the same caption and #besties.

She'd caught me mid-laugh with my friends' love surrounding me, and I made a mental note to get it printed and framed.

When I got home, the house was empty. Not for the first time, I didn't know whether to be relieved or disappointed.

I headed to the fridge for a snack and paused with my hand on the handle. There was a thick piece of paper with silver embellishments stuck to the door with a magnet. The word *BestLyf* caught my attention, and I forgot all about the snack as I snatched the paper off the fridge.

In raised cursive script, the invitation was addressed to my mom. Raine Clayton was throwing a fundraiser, sponsored by BestLyf, at her private residence. I didn't even read what cause they were raising funds for or any of the other details on the invite. As soon as I saw my mom's name in the same vicinity as Raine Clayton's, I started to hyperventilate.

CHAPTER ELEVEN

I didn't want my mother anywhere near Raine fucking Clayton or anything remotely related to BestLyf. Why was she even invited to this party? What was the point of it?

I tried calling her several times, but she didn't answer. It wasn't unusual for her, but it was extra irritating when I actually wanted to talk to her.

The worst thing was I *knew* this would turn into a fight. I'd just vowed to try to talk to my mom calmly and rationally, like an adult, but there was no way that "hey, don't go to this party, because I can't tell you why, but you have to promise not to go" wouldn't turn into a screaming match.

After pacing the kitchen for a good twenty minutes, I decided to go for a run. Hopefully she'd be home by the time I got back and I'd be calmer from the endorphins.

I changed into running gear, put my earbuds in, and jogged up our ridiculous driveway. Barely half a mile in, I started to get cramps. I ran all the time, I was fit, and these were definitely not the kind of cramps one got from too much cardio.

Stopping with my hands on my hips, I glared at my uterus. "Really? Now?"

As if she were answering me with attitude, I felt that telltale sensation of the first bit of blood leaking out and stiffened, squeezing my thighs together.

Muttering under my breath, I made my way home. Even after I showered, took a couple of Advil, and accepted that the universe hated me for some reason, Mom was still not home.

I tried her phone one more time, then grudgingly gave in and called Cal. Mom had put his number in my phone weeks ago before I could snatch it back, for "emergencies."

He picked up on the second ring. "Hello?"

"Cal, it's Amaya. Is Mom with you? Do you know when she'll be home?"

"Not right this second. Is everything OK?"

"Yeah, fine. Do you know where she is?"

"We're both in the city. She's having drinks with friends while I take care of some work matters. We were planning to spend the night here. Do you need us to come home?"

I hesitated. "No, that's OK. I'll talk to her when you get back."

"Are you sure?"

"Yeah, it's fine." The party wasn't for a few weeks yet. I had time to talk her out of it.

I hung up after quickly thanking him.

It annoyed me that he'd been so . . . accommodating. I had a feeling he would've actually found Mom and come home if I'd said I wanted them to, and that bothered me. I didn't want to like him. I didn't want to admit he was good for her.

I hated him for being the one to convince her to get her shit together. Why couldn't she have done it for me?

Suddenly, the house I'd wanted all to myself felt too empty. Without any plan, I grabbed my keys and headed out.

My first instinct was to head to the Meads' place, but I needed to get out of this neighborhood. I thought about going to my lookout, but I was in a state and didn't want to navigate those tight turns in the dark.

Frustration steadily rising, I decided to head downtown and get some dinner, but somehow I found myself at Mena's apartment building instead. Yes. Fine. Good. I'd go up and hang with her for a while, maybe see if she wanted to go get ice cream with me or something.

But a few steps from Mena's entrance to the building, my feet turned and marched over to the next entrance instead. Jet's address was in the secret spreadsheet the girls and I kept. It contained the names, occupations, and addresses of people we knew, along with any other information we had. Knowledge was power, and information was currency. Next thing I knew, I was in the elevator, smacking the button for Jet's floor. The doors opened before I had time to come to my senses, and I rushed to his apartment and banged on the door.

When it didn't immediately open, I banged on it harder, even adding a kick for good measure.

Then it dawned on me that I had no idea if he lived alone or if someone was sleeping.

"Fuck!" I whisper-shouted, feeling like a total fool. I'd already turned to get out of there when the door opened with a squeak that echoed in the hallway.

"Amaya?" Jet frowned at me through the gap. He slammed the door closed, making me jump, then a metal chain jiggled against the wood, and he opened the door fully. "What are you doing here? You all right?"

"No, I'm not fucking all right! I—ugh!" I huffed. "Never mind. I shouldn't have come here."

He grabbed my wrist before I had a chance to run away. He was shirtless and barefoot, wearing only that pair of beach shorts I'd seen him wear repeatedly in the Bahamas. I hated that I knew how good his ass looked in those shorts, even as I fought the urge to tell him to turn around so I could have a look.

Was I panting before I realized he was half-naked? Probably. I'd practically run here I'd been working myself up so much in the car.

"What happened?" he asked, his thumb caressing my wrist.

"Nothing happened." I half-heartedly tried to twist out of his grip. "I'm just over everything. I feel like I'm drowning half the time, and just as I manage to catch a breath, some other bullshit comes up to push my head under the water. Between Mom and school and this BestLyf—" I cut myself off. Better not to go into detail about all that.

"What about BestLyf?" He frowned. I didn't blame him for being confused. I was a total rambling mess.

"Never mind. I'm sorry for just showing up like this." I glanced behind him, mortified that someone may have overheard all that.

Jet chuckled. "There's no one else here."

I clung onto the change in topic. "Where is . . . uh, who lives here with you?"

"Nobody." He shrugged. "I live by myself."

"What?" I blinked, not following. "How? Is that even allowed?"

"I'm not a minor and . . ." He sighed. "It's a long story."

"Tell me? I need the distraction." I slid my wrist out of his grip enough to take his hand with mine.

"Maybe someday." He smiled sadly and looked away.

"Are you embarrassed? I would never judge you." I seemed like a total bitch to most people, but I thought Jet knew me well enough to know who I was underneath it.

"No, I'm not embarrassed. I just can't . . . it'll change things and I . . . can't talk about it yet."

"OK," I said softly. I knew what it felt like to not want to open all your deepest wounds. Vulnerability was fucking scary.

"You wanna grab something to eat and tell me what's brought you here all worked up?" He gave me that dimpled smile, paired with that deep look in his eyes. He was clearly deflecting, but I was stubborn. If he wasn't going to open up, I wasn't either. And anyway, wasn't I mad at him? There was a reason I'd refused to speak to him for days.

I dropped his hand, irritation flaring up inside me again. God, my fuse was short tonight.

I'd started paying more attention to our surroundings as we spoke, and my brain finally registered what I was seeing in the apartment behind him.

"Jet, what the fuck is that?" I pointed at the coffee table.

He glanced over his shoulder, then turned back with a completely neutral look on his face. "A gun," he said matter-of-factly.

A dirty rag was spread out on the surface of the table. A handgun, along with a few other metal things I had no names for, sat on it.

"What are you doing with a gun?" I hissed.

"Cleaning it."

"Why do you even have that thing?" Didn't he know how often the police came looking for someone in this part of town, how quickly Fulton Academy would cancel his scholarship and dump his ass if he was caught doing anything remotely illegal?

"I have my reasons." He leaned on the door frame, blocking my view of the weapon.

I opened my mouth to argue but snapped it closed. I had enough shit to worry about. I'd reached my threshold.

"You know what? Whatever." I held my hands up and took a step back. "I shouldn't have come here in the first place. I'm gonna go."

"No, Amaya, wait. Let's head out and talk somewhere else. Just let me put a shirt on."

"Why? So you can drag more of the most personal things in my life out of me while not telling me shit about yourself?" My voice rose along with my ire. "So I can feel close to you and then you can reject me again? I am so sick of this shit, Jet!" OK, I was pretty much shouting, and I needed to get the fuck out of there before people started coming out of their apartments—or before the tears pushing at the backs of my eyes spilled over.

"Amaya." He said my name softly, pleadingly. My heart tugged against my chest, wanting me to fall into his arms. But no. I took another step back and shook my head.

"No, Jet. I hate that I came here. I hate that you always have a way to make me feel better about my fucked-up life. And I hate that I keep letting you hurt me. Do not follow me."

I turned on my heel and rushed toward the elevators as the tears trickled down my cheeks.

I heard Jet curse behind me before his door slammed shut.

Part of me had been hoping he would chase after me, pull me into his arms, and make it all better. I hated that part as much as I hated that he'd slammed his door on me instead.

I turned the corner and bashed the elevator call button repeatedly. It didn't sound like the thing was moving, so either someone was holding it up on another floor or it had broken down like the one in Mena's part of the building often did.

With a growl of frustration, I pushed the door to the stairs open and started heading down, desperate to get to my car and far away from here.

I was so wrapped up in my own emotional mess I didn't even hear the group of people climbing up until we were practically on top of each other. A loud laugh followed by indistinct chatter clued me in moments before we crossed paths on a landing.

Three men in their midtwenties stumbled toward me, eyes glassy and limbs loose. The one in front spotted me first and slapped at the other two until I had the full attention of all three of them. I tried to rush past, but they stood practically shoulder to shoulder, blocking the stairs.

"You're pretty when you cry," the one in front said. "You must be an absolute knockout when you're happy."

"Yeah, come on, sweetheart," one of the others slurred. "Give us a pretty smile."

"I dunno," the third one chimed in, "I kind of like it when their makeup is all messed up and running down their cheeks."

He leered at me as the others laughed.

"Excuse me, I'm running late." I tried to push past again, my tears drying up as a chill of fear skittered down my spine.

They didn't budge, and the one in front grabbed my arm.

"Hey, we're trying to have a conversation here," he snapped.

"And I'm not interested." I set my shoulders and fixed him with a hard look. "Now take your dirty fucking hand off me before I scream so loud half the building comes running."

They all stared at me for a beat, then burst out laughing.

"Folks know to mind their own damn business in this neighborhood, princess," Douchebag 2 said. "Scream all you want. No one's coming to save you."

Adrenaline pumped through my veins at the implication. Flight wasn't an option—they were blocking the stairs—and I was not a freeze kind of girl, so I guessed I'd go down fighting. Because they would have to kill me before I let myself get raped.

I brought my knee up, aiming for Douchebag 1's balls, but he dropped his grip on my arm and twisted out of the way. I shoved him, hoping he'd break his neck on the stairs. Then I turned to run up the way I'd come. They were drunk and I ran nearly every day. Maybe I could outrun them long enough to make it back to Jet's door.

Douchebag 1 stumbled and nearly met the fate I'd hoped for, but his buddies caught him. Douchebag 3 was tall and threw out a long arm, catching my hoodie over the railing and thwarting my escape attempt.

Panic shot through me, and I did scream—a piercing sound that echoed off the concrete walls. I thrashed and kicked, shouting profanities at them between banshee screeches.

Only seconds passed between me shoving the first guy and the three of them crowding me into the corner.

A clanging sound of metal on metal made us all look up. There was Jet, standing a few steps above us, leaning casually on the railing. I'd never been so happy to see someone in my entire life.

"Boys." He flashed them his easy, dimpled grin. "You're keeping half the building up with all this noise. Is there a problem?"

"Nothing that's any of your business, kid. Get lost." Douchebag 2 turned to face Jet and pulled a knife out.

My panic tripled at the sight of the weapon.

Jet sighed and raised his right hand, the one gripping a gleaming gun. He rested it on his left forearm, still leaning on the handrail.

"Yeah, see, the thing is, she is my business." He nodded at me. "And if you don't get your hands off her immediately, I'm going to get really fucking pissed off." He dropped the easy smile and stared them down.

"Bullshit she is," Douchebag 1 spat but released his hold on me anyway.

Jet took the safety off slowly, deliberately, his expression not cracking. It was unnerving how calm he was—how comfortable he was pointing that gun at people.

The Douchebags must've come to the same conclusion, because they tucked away their silly knife and their stupid attitudes and backed away. Jet waited until they were out of sight before he moved toward me.

"Joke's on them for bringing a knife to a gun fight," I quipped, but there was no humor in it, and to my horror, my chuckles turned into sobs.

Next thing I knew, my face was pressed to Jet's chest—covered in a T-shirt now—and his arm wrapped around my back to keep me from sliding to the dirty floor. I held on to him, fighting to get my shit together as the adrenaline exited my body as violently as it had invaded it.

After a while, the sobs stopped and the tears dried up, but I couldn't seem to pull away from his comforting embrace. His hand on my back rubbed soothing circles, while his other hand still gripped the gun by his side.

I lifted my head as a horrible thought struck me. "What if they come back? With more people and guns and stuff?"

Jet wiped a stray tear off my cheek, his eyes scanning me. "They won't come back. I'll keep you safe," he declared. I believed him. "Did they hurt you?"

I shook my head, perversely pleased at the way his jaw had ticked and his eyes had flashed with menace when he voiced his concern.

"Good." He took a small step back. "Let's get out of here. It smells like piss."

I managed a laugh that didn't collapse into sobs again. It really did smell awful, and my skin was starting to crawl—especially on my back where I'd been leaning against the wall.

He took my hand as we descended the stairs, and I held on to it tightly.

"Did you put your gun back together before coming after me?" I asked, the barrier between my brain and my mouth severely compromised. I immediately felt like an idiot for even assuming he'd been coming after me at all. Maybe he'd just decided to go out.

"No. This is a different gun," he said softly, managing to keep his voice from echoing off the walls.

I gave him a wide-eyed look. "How many guns do you have?"

"A few." He smirked, refusing to meet my eyes.

By the time we reached the ground floor and exited the building, I felt more like myself. Meaning I was pissed off at the audacity of those jerks for trying to attack me like that, and I was back to being frustrated and confused by Jet.

The parking lot was empty, but I didn't miss the way Jet scanned it repeatedly before tucking the gun into the waistband of his shorts and hiding it under his T-shirt.

"Want me to drive you home?" he asked as we reached my car. "Or somewhere else? I don't want you driving in this state."

"What state?" I crossed my arms and gave him a challenging look.

"There she is." He grinned at me.

"Who?" I cocked an eyebrow.

"The strong, beautiful, infuriating woman I've come to . . . know."

Was that really how he saw me? That wasn't a casual kind of thing to say about someone—*to their face*. If he thought so highly of me, why did he keep me at arm's length?

Ugh! I did not have the emotional bandwidth to go down that track again.

A familiar figure caught my attention, and I frowned as two men came around the corner of the building. Jet followed my gaze, and we just stood there watching for a few moments.

"What is it?" he asked.

"I know that guy. That's Shady . . . er . . . I don't know his last name. Actually, I don't think that's his first name either." There was no missing the red tracksuit the man always wore. For someone who ran a criminal empire, and probably needed to stay under the radar, he sure did wear a lot of bright clothing.

"Shady, eh? How do you know him?" There was an edge to Jet's question, and his jaw tightened, but I didn't have time to worry about that, because I realized I knew the other guy too.

"Actually, I know both of them. The other one, in the suit with the neat brown hair—that's my mom's boyfriend." What the fuck was he doing talking to Shady? What the fuck was he doing in Devilbend North when he'd just told me on the phone half an hour ago that he was in San Francisco with my mom?

"That's the guy who's moved into your place?" Again Jet sounded a little intense. Was he being protective? He'd certainly protected me tonight.

Shady made his way to a dark SUV that took off right away. Cal walked off in the opposite direction and disappeared around the corner. I returned my attention to my protector.

"Would you really have shot them if they didn't leave?" I was morbidly curious. His bluff had worked like a charm, but how much of a bluff was it? "Is that thing even loaded?"

He watched me intently for a beat, some kind of inner conflict clear in his eyes. Then he slowly pulled the gun out and held it between us. Releasing the clip, he showed me it was fully loaded before tucking it away.

"I would've blown every one of their brains out over those piss-stained stairs and not given it another thought." He looked me right in the eye as he said it, his gaze full of calm conviction.

CHAPTER TWELVE

I was the baby of my friend group. The last one to turn eighteen. And I used it as an excuse to throw the most epic party of the year.

The girls and I arrived in a limo about an hour after it started. I liked to make an entrance, and I was indulging all my whims on this glorious Saturday night. The weather was warm, my makeup flawless, my friends in a good mood, and in a few short hours, I'd officially be an adult. Nothing could ruin this night for me.

"To Amaya!" Harlow held up her champagne flute and we toasted, finishing off the last of the bottle we'd shared on the drive over. The driver opened the door for us, and we made our way up to my party.

The elevator opened on the rooftop of the tallest building in Devilbend, and as we stepped out, everyone cheered. I flipped my sleek ponytail over my shoulder and smiled widely before moving into the crowd to say hi to everyone.

During the day, the roof was reserved for residents of the high-rise's top few floors, but at night it became a venue for hire. A pool hung over the edge of the building, and there was a covered bar, a dance floor, and seating areas. Pearl- and champagne-colored balloon arches and cascading balloon installations decorated the whole area, along with carefully placed lighting. It looked as if the rooftop was dripping in giant glowing bubbles, and it was filled with a hundred of my closest friends.

"Happy birthday, sexy!" Drew darted up to scoop me off the floor in a massive hug.

I laughed and swatted him as he set me down. "Watch the Prada!" I chided, smoothing the green silk and making sure it still looked good on my ass. The minidress had a plunging neckline that made my small boobs look great. "Thank you, Drew."

"Let's get you a drink." He looped my hand through his arm and started leading me toward the bar, but I pulled out of his grip.

"I have a few more people to say hi to. Can you get me a champagne?"

"Anything for the birthday girl!"

I made my way through the crowd until I found my besties again. They were standing near the railing with their men, the stunning view of Devilbend behind them. They looked amazing. All of them. They looked happy.

I was happy for them, but a pang of something else stabbed at me too. It wasn't jealousy exactly. I didn't begrudge my friends their happiness—they deserved it after everything we'd been through. It was just . . . well, didn't I deserve it too? I wanted what they had.

The girls had gotten ready with me at the Meads' place, but I hadn't seen the guys yet. Hendrix came up first to give me a hug and a happy birthday. Turner was right behind him with a warm hug and warmer wishes.

Harlow's boyfriend, Easton, looked awkward as he stepped forward next. He gave me a chaste kiss on the cheek, then quickly backed off with a murmured birthday wish. Harlow took his hand and squeezed it, beaming up at him.

Was it weird to have my former English teacher at my birthday party? A little, but it helped that he wasn't in one of his uptight suits, instead sporting a more casual shirt with the sleeves rolled up to expose his tattoos.

"How's it feel being at a party with your students, Easton?" Turner asked. He was the most casual with Easton, as he went to another school and had only ever met him as Harlow's boyfriend.

"Well, my eye is twitching a little at all the underage drinking." He chuckled. "But it's not too bad. They're not my students anymore."

"Got you a GlenDronach." Easton's brother, Ford, joined us and handed him a glass with amber liquid in it. His own drink was some kind of orange fruity cocktail with a pineapple garnish and an umbrella. "Hey, birthday girl!"

He dashed forward as soon as he spotted me, and the hug he gave lasted longer than any hug with a guy you weren't even really friends with should last. He pressed his whole body flush with mine and whispered "happy birthday" into my ear.

"Thanks, Ford." I gave him a smile as I pulled away. Reluctantly, he let me go.

"Save me a dance?" He flashed me that flirtatious smile before wrapping his lips around the colorful paper straw in his drink. It wasn't the first time Ford had flirted with me. I'd only met him a few times, and he'd managed to come onto me during most of them.

My initial knee-jerk reaction was to turn my nose up and tell him "you wish"—like I had all the other times. But I wondered if maybe I should dance with him, let him flirt, flirt a little back.

Because the person I actually wanted to do all those things with wasn't here.

Jet had ghosted me after that frightening incident at his apartment building.

His violent words, on reflection, had been a bit disturbing. But the neglected, abandoned, sad girl inside me perversely reveled in how fiercely he'd been ready to protect me.

A week had passed since then, and he'd almost dropped off the face of the earth. He'd been at school on Monday and Tuesday—I'd seen him rushing through the halls—but he hadn't been at lunch, and I could've sworn he was avoiding me. Then he didn't even show up at school for the rest of the week. Nicola told me he was out sick, but I didn't believe that for one second.

I still texted him to say I'd heard he was sick and hoped he was OK. Then I texted him to say thank you for stepping in with those creeps again. Then I invited him to my birthday party. He ignored all my messages, but I knew he was talking to Drew (he'd mentioned as much at lunch on Friday), so I wasn't worried about him. I was pissed.

By the end of the day on Friday, I sent him one last text, telling him he was *un*invited from my party and from my life in general.

"You know what? I'm in a good mood, so sure, I'll dance with you." I gave Ford an easy smile, and he winked at me. Winked! This guy . . .

The girls gave me knowing looks but didn't say anything. They were determined to make this night fun and carefree for me, but they knew everything. Since that day at the juice bar when I'd told them what a mess my life was, I'd been keeping them updated.

They were appropriately reproachful when I told them I'd gone to his apartment, totally horrified when I told them about being attacked, then grudgingly forgiving when I told them Jet had come to my rescue. Plus, Harlow had dug further into him, even though I'd told her to leave it, because of course she had. She'd decided he was a walking red flag because he had barely any online presence. His school records were sparse, and even her shadiest contacts couldn't dig up anything about his parents or his life before coming to Devilbend.

It was a little odd, but whatever. I was never speaking to him again anyway. I'd flirt with Ford, maybe hook up with him for a bit of birthday fun, and forget all about *Jethro*.

"You better not be giving away dances to any of these inferior peasants!" Drew appeared and handed me my champagne before slinging an arm around my neck. "Your ass is mine tonight, A."

"I belong to no man. Especially not tonight." I cocked an eyebrow at him and took a delicate sip of my drink.

Maybe I could hook up with Drew. He was always up for some fun. Plus, he was a genuinely good friend and wouldn't hurt me. Maybe I could talk Drew and Ford into some group fun. It was my birthday, after all.

"Come on, let's dance!" Donna pulled me out of my dirty fantasies just before

I let my mind acknowledge that I'd rather have one night with Jet than multiple nights with any number of dudes I didn't feel as strongly about.

We made our way to the dance floor area near the pool, where I greeted some more friends and let the music chase my thoughts away. For the next several hours, I danced, drank expensive champagne, ate the best hors d'oeuvres money could buy, talked to my friends, and forgot about all my worries.

Donna made a speech with assistance from Harlow and even Mena—though her cheeks went so red it was visible under her makeup. They almost made me cry. Then a giant cake was brought out. Donna demanded no one sing "Happy Birthday" until the clock struck midnight, since it was technically my actual birthday tomorrow. She was going to make us do a countdown as if it were New Year's Eve. It was ridiculously over the top, and I loved it!

The cake was cut up and distributed, and we got back to dancing. They were playing all my favorite songs.

"I believe I was promised a dance," a deep, teasing voice said behind me, and I turned to find a smiling Ford. He lifted his eyebrows and held his hands out in something between an invitation and a request.

With a carefree laugh, I stepped into him and draped one arm over his shoulder. He gripped my hips, and we started swaying to the music. Between the alcohol, the attention from all my friends, and the thumping bass, I was riding an almost euphoric high.

Ford's body moved incrementally closer to mine, and I leaned into him until we were chest to chest. One of his hands went to my lower back just as the music changed to some nasty song that was impossible not to grind your hips to. He was a surprisingly good dancer and we moved in sync, our hips rolling.

He held my gaze as he started to lean in for a kiss.

Jet's stupid face flashed in my mind, and for a split second I wished it was him about to kiss me. But I shoved the errant thought away and forced myself to focus on my cute, *interested* dance partner.

His nose brushed mine, but before our lips met, another body appeared at my back. I gasped and giggled—I was definitely getting drunk if I was giggling. Ford lifted his head and threw a crooked grin over my shoulder, not put out at all by the interruption.

I looked back to see who was holding my waist and crowding me in.

Drew's eyes were a bit glazed over but still glinted with his signature mischief.

"Birthday girl sandwich!" he called out, and as if they'd been friends for years, the two guys high-fived.

"Am I the meat in this sandwich?" I asked.

"Wait, I don't wanna be bread," Ford complained. "Bread is boring."

"I've got all the meat you need, birthday girl." Drew plastered his chest to my back, and we all laughed as we somehow managed to find the beat again. Our hips swayed in rhythm, and I started to get that heavy, pressured feeling low in my belly.

Maybe some three-way fun was actually in the cards for tonight. If one guy couldn't drive Jet from my mind, surely two would.

I don't know what made me glance in the direction of the elevators, but it was as if my thoughts had summoned him. Jethro Collins stepped out onto the rooftop in blue slacks and a white shirt right when I'd devised a multi-penis plan to forget him. His eyes scanned the crowd for barely a second before they found mine.

Instead of holding his gaze, I rested my head on Drew's shoulder and raked my fingers through Ford's hair. If I said I wasn't putting on a show to make Jet jealous, I'd be lying.

Drew drifted off and started dancing with others after a short time, but Ford got that intense look in his eyes as soon as we were alone again. When I glanced back toward the elevator, Jet was gone.

I really, really wanted to crane my neck to find where he was, if he was still looking my way, if he appeared jealous. But I forced myself to keep dancing—even though I was hardly aware of Ford and his roaming hands anymore.

As it turned out, Jet was like the devil. I'd thought of him and he appeared, right by my side.

"Hey, can I cut in?" Jet's jaw was hard, his brilliant eyes narrowed.

CHAPTER THIRTEEN

Ford, cocky bastard that he was, looked Jet up and down and held me even closer. His hand splayed over my belly possessively.

"No. Fuck off," he said with a little smirk, his gaze glued to mine.

"Wasn't asking you," Jet said, his voice deceptively calm. He had that look in his eyes—the one he'd had when he confronted those douchebags in his building, the one that promised violence. Was he jealous?

"No. Fuck off." I lifted my chin haughtily as I repeated Ford's words. Where did he get off acting all jealous and entitled when he'd rejected me more times than my ego cared to admit?

"Amaya." Jet sighed. "Can we just—"

"She said no, dude." Ford twisted a little, putting himself between us. "Back off."

I stumbled but caught myself on Ford's shoulder.

"I don't know who you *think* you are, but trust me, you don't want to mess with me." Jet cracked his neck with a sharp cant of his head, his mouth pulling up into a mocking grin.

I was inclined to agree. Everyone thought Jet was this fun, friendly, nice guy, but I'd seen another side of him. He was dangerous.

We'd started to draw a crowd. I mean, it was a party, so there was already a crowd, but we were drawing all their attention. A few people even had their cell phones out, hoping to capture some drama on video.

"Oh, you wanna go?" Ford threw his head back and laughed. "Let's go, pretty boy."

He dropped his grip on me as the two of them faced off.

They were acting like Neanderthals. At my fucking birthday party. The audacity of these testosterone-fueled muscle bags.

Neither of them was even looking at me. Did they even remember why they'd started this bullshit in the first place?

I caught Donna's eye from across the crowd. The others were nowhere to be seen, but she was saying something to Easton while keeping her focus on me. Ford's brother pinched the bridge of his nose.

I gave Donna a smirk and an eye roll. *Men.*

She returned my smirk, amusement in her gaze. *Can't wait to see you put them in their place.*

The two idiots were still bickering, chests puffed, really in each other's faces.

I moved to stand at their sides and folded my hands behind me. When I leaned forward, bringing my face close to theirs, they both stopped what they were doing and gave me frowns. As though I was the one acting weird.

"Is this the part where you kiss?" I asked, looking between them. A couple people chuckled.

Ford leaned back and grinned. "I'm up for it, if that's what you're into."

Jet's expression was the complete opposite—all serious and intense—his full focus on me. "I'm only interested in kissing one person here."

What? "What?" I huffed. "Seriously? It's my fucking birthday, Jet. I refuse to deal with your bullshit on my damn birthday!"

More people looked our way, ironically because of me and my raised voice. As usual, this asshole was getting under my skin.

"Can we please go somewhere quiet and talk?" he asked, voice low, as he stepped in close.

I moved back to regain my distance and folded my arms over my chest.

"No. Fuck you!" I didn't bother to keep my voice down. "I'm not leaving my birthday party to have you—I'm not doing this, Jet. I'm having a fun night, and that's the end of that."

A cheer went up from my friends and acquaintances, and a few people I'd never seen in my life, backing me in my quest for a fun time.

"You." I pointed at Ford. "Go get me a drink." My buzz was wearing off.

"And you." I pointed at Jet. "Go away."

Ford headed toward the bar, laughing as he went, but Jet was not as good at taking directions.

"I'm not leaving until I give the birthday girl a kiss," Jet said, his expression no longer so serious but still kind of intense. Those damn dimples came out as he stepped closer again. This time, I didn't move away.

I pursed my lips as I tipped my head back. I'd had more than a few people cower under my bitch-face. It made me feel strong, and I refused to be anything other than the badass bitch I wanted to be in this moment. Jet had made me feel like shit one too many times. He'd rejected me and humiliated me one too many times. I refused to let him make me think he wanted me before he inevitably changed his mind at the last possible second. Not in front of all these people. Not on my fucking birthday.

"If you insist." I gave him a mocking smile. "You can kiss my foot."

He could either do exactly that or turn around and leave. I was fine with either option.

He narrowed his eyes at me, but his smile didn't seem forced—he looked amused. Keeping his gaze locked on mine, he took a step back. A pang of disappointment shot through my chest, but I didn't let it show. I wanted him to leave, and he was leaving. What did I expect?

To my utter surprise, he didn't turn on his heel and bail. He lowered himself to one knee and leaned forward to wrap a hand around my calf.

His warm hand on my bare leg steadied me when I felt ready to fall on my face from shock. Still, I kept my bitchy look firmly in place. I wasn't paying attention to anyone else. All the people and the music and everything else faded into the background as my focus zeroed in on his touch. He tightened his grip and nudged my leg gently, and I let him guide my heeled foot to rest on his knee.

He kept his eyes on mine as long as he could as he placed a kiss on the top of my foot. I couldn't hold back a small gasp as his pillow-soft lips connected with my skin. He'd actually fucking done it. His lips lingered on my foot for a brief moment before he looked back up at me. His thumb caressed my calf, sending tingles up my leg.

"I'll happily kiss any part of your body if you'll let me, Amaya," he said, his words only for me. Still, everyone heard, and I became aware of all the people around us, watching and making all kinds of amused sounds.

I sighed dramatically and rolled my eyes. "Don't push your luck." My foot dropped back to the floor, and I waved my arm dismissively in his general direction. "I suppose you can stay."

He caught my hand and kissed the back of it as he got to his feet. A massive grin split his face. "Thank you."

"I don't know why you look so damn happy. I'm still mad at you."

"I know."

The grin didn't even falter as he stepped in closer. A crowd favorite came on, and someone turned the volume up.

"Well, now that I've successfully cut in, dance with me?" He held his hand out like a gentleman and everything.

"Bold of you to even ask, to be honest." I raised a brow.

He shrugged. "I'm feelin' plucky."

I knew I probably shouldn't, not after the way he'd treated me, but it was my birthday and I really wanted to dance with Jet.

He flashed a grin, those dimples popping, when he saw the acquiescence in my expression. Before I'd even said anything, he placed his hands on my waist, and I slowly reached up to rest mine on his shoulders.

"I never stood a chance, did I?"

I turned to find Ford watching us with my champagne in his hand.

I opened my mouth and closed it, like a moron. I didn't know what to say. Jet's grip on my waist tightened slightly, but he was smart enough to keep his mouth shut.

Ford sighed dramatically and downed half of my champagne before giving me a confident smile. "It's all good. Gimme a call when it doesn't work out and you're ready to level up from high school boys."

Sipping more champagne, he stepped back and disappeared into the crowd. He didn't seem all that hurt, and his cocky attitude made me feel not so bad after all.

"Amaya." Jet drew my body closer, holding me tighter as the music changed to something with a more sultry, sexy tempo. "About this past week—"

"No." I covered his mouth with my hand. "I don't want to hear it. I really don't even want to think about it tonight, Jet. You've been a colossal jerk to me, but for some fucked-up reason, I'm still glad you're here. So I'm going to let myself enjoy this for tonight. But come tomorrow, I'm done. You don't want me? Fine. I don't want to play these games. So just stay away from me for the last few weeks of school, and we never have to see each other again."

We turned slowly around the dance floor, our bodies in sync with each other and the music. I liked the feeling of his strong shoulders under my touch, and I ran my hands over the muscle there.

Jet flattened his palm on my lower back, making me reflexively arch into him. With his free hand, he gripped my wrist and removed my hand from his mouth. He planted a gentle kiss on my palm, then placed my hand over his heart and held it there.

"I don't want to never see you again. I don't want to play games either. I like you, Amaya. A lot."

"You've got a funny way of showing it," I muttered.

"I know. I'm sorry. You don't want to get into any of that stuff tonight, and that's fair. I'm going to respect your wishes, but I am sorry."

I watched him for a few moments as we swayed, mulling over the sincerity in his gaze, acutely aware of every spot our bodies touched.

Was it a little convenient that he wanted to honor my wishes by not getting into explaining himself? Maybe. But he was openly telling me he liked me, pulling me closer instead of pushing me away. He'd literally gotten on his knees and kissed my feet in front of everyone.

Whatever. I'd overthink it all tomorrow when it wasn't my birthday party and I wasn't half-drunk.

"You're sorry, huh?" I threaded my fingers together behind his neck and took the lead in our dance.

"Absolutely." He nodded.

"So you've had a change of heart?"

"For sure."

"And you don't care if everyone sees that you're into me?"

"Nope." His eyes sparkled with amusement. He was enjoying this.

"So, if I tried to kiss you this time . . ." I leaned in, my murmured words just for him. "You'd let me?"

"I'd get on my knees again and beg if it would get me another chance to kiss you, and do it right this time."

Aww! That was kind of sweet. I almost felt bad for what I was about to do. But I'd already made up my mind, and I could be stubborn like that sometimes.

"Good to know." I spoke the words millimeters from his mouth, my lips barely brushing his. His eyes started to close, and I made my move.

I took a quick, sure step backward, planted my hands on his chest, and in one swift move shoved him right into the pool.

He hadn't even noticed me maneuvering us toward the edge as we danced, and the shocked look on his face as he went sailing backward toward the water was priceless. Totally worth another missed opportunity to finally kiss him.

I laughed out loud. I laughed with my whole body, throwing my head back and not giving a shit what I would look like if someone happened to snap a picture. Everyone around us laughed and cheered too as Jet emerged from the water half glaring and half chuckling. Those who hadn't seen what happened moved closer, drawn by the sudden sound of splashing water and whooping people.

When Jet stood, I realized my mistake. The water of the pool reached to just below his chest, and if he looked hot in a dress shirt, he was positively irresistible with it soaking wet and plastered to his body. Droplets of water trickled down his face and neck. It was like a scene from one of my romance novels, and I was so here for it.

Suddenly the music cut off, and my girls came rushing toward me through the tight crowd. For a second, I panicked, wondering what the hell was wrong, but then I realized they looked excited and happy. Donna raised a microphone as they reached my side.

"Everyone, shut up," she demanded, her voice amplified. "Only fifteen seconds to go until my girl is eighteen!"

She checked the phone that Mena held up for her, then started the countdown from ten. Everyone joined in, and a rooftop full of drunk, happy people rang in my birthday like it was 1999.

Jet joined in, grinning up at me as he swiped the water off his face and waded to the edge of the pool. Everyone was still cheering like crazy when the DJ started up the music again with a banger.

The atmosphere was electric!

Electricity and water didn't mix, but Jet looked too good to resist, all wet for me as he was.

I kicked my shoes off, dropped my purse next to them, and launched myself into the pool yelling, "Happy birthday to meeeee!"

I didn't even care about the designer dress or my makeup getting ruined as I let myself sink to the bottom. Kicking up to the surface, I laughed as I brushed water out of my face.

Others joined in, shucking pieces of clothing or jumping in fully dressed. And then half my friends were in the pool, and suddenly it was a pool party.

The warm water felt wonderful against my skin—refreshing after all the dancing and drinking—and it sobered me up quite a bit too. So I can't blame what happened next on the alcohol. It was all me. Well, me and Jet.

I lost track of him with everyone jumping into the pool, but he found me. A strong arm wrapped around my middle from behind, and I turned to face him.

"There's no getting away from me now, unless you plan on throwing me off the building," he joked, pulling me in closer.

"Just shut up and kiss me before I change my mind." I draped my arms around his neck but waited for him to lean in. I'd done enough chasing with this guy. If he wanted me, he'd have to come and get me.

And he did. Confidently, he captured my lips with his, and I could've sworn a round of fireworks went off. The party, the music, all the people splashing around us faded away. There was just Jethro's lips on mine, Jethro's arms holding me close, Jethro's tongue swiping at my mouth, pleading and demanding more all at once.

I opened for him, and our tongues danced. Everything seemed heightened, my skin hyperaware of everywhere we touched, of how the water itself seemed to flow around us as though trying to push us closer. My legs circled his waist, and he gripped my thighs as we kissed for what felt like hours and barely a few seconds at the same time.

This was the best birthday ever!

CHAPTER FOURTEEN

This was the worst birthday ever.

I rolled over and groaned. My stomach seemed to keep rolling long after the rest of my body was still. I pulled the covers over my head to hide from the light, but I had to tug them back off immediately when I started to gag from the smell of my own breath.

After Jet and I finished making out in the pool, I got very drunk. To be fair, I wasn't the only one, and it was my birthday, but I had only vague memories of Hendrix and Jet trying to wrangle us girls into a waiting car. I had no idea where the other boys had ended up, nor how we'd managed to get out of the car and into my house.

Did I puke at some point? Was that why my breath was so horrible? Come to think of it, we all might have puked, other than Donna. She had the alcohol tolerance of a large middle-aged man who'd been working a physical job and drinking a six-pack every day for two decades.

I cracked an eye open and saw my bestie in the bed next to me, her short blonde hair fanning out over her face as she snored.

Someone farted—loudly. A snort-laugh came from the direction of the daybed in the opposite corner of my room, and I lifted my head to find Mena propped up on some pillows, scrolling through her phone.

"Morning," I croaked, my voice sounding as horrible as my breath smelled.

"Morning, birthday girl." She smiled at me, then burped and looked as if she might follow through for a moment.

When I was sure she wasn't going to hurl again, I asked, "Where's Harlow?"

The younger Mead sister had passed out on the other side of me, but it was definitely just me and Donna in the bed now.

Mena pointed to the corner between my desk and a window. I rolled over, and there she was—rolled up into a ball, tucked in among my oversized cushions, sleeping in my reading nook as she drooled on my throw blanket.

"Ugh! I feel like shit." I groaned as I flopped back against the pillows. The bounce woke Donna, and she made one, loud snore as she jerked up in bed.

"I'm up!" She rubbed her eyes, then frowned. "What?"

Mena chuckled again. I smiled, scared that laughing would cause too much movement in my gut.

"We should get something greasy into our stomachs." I yawned.

Donna reached for her phone to check the time. "Breakfast burritos will be here in twenty."

"How?" I gaped at her.

"I ordered them last night and scheduled delivery."

"I love you."

"Of course you do. I'm fucking fabulous."

She really was fucking fabulous—even with her mascara smeared down one cheek and her hair so messy I wasn't sure it could be saved. But, hey, if anyone could rock a shaved head, it was Donna Mead.

Twenty minutes later, the four of us stumbled down the stairs, our faces clean and our teeth brushed but our insides still feeling like sewage. The doorbell rang, our breakfast arriving at just the right time.

Harlow had yet to communicate with anything more than a grunt, but she rushed to the door before the rest of us and yanked the paper bag out of the delivery driver's hands. I gave the stunned guy a tip and closed the door before following the girls into the living room.

"There you are, sleepy head!" Mom came bouncing in from the patio in activewear and a light sheen of sweat. Was she exercising? On a Sunday? Before . . . I checked my phone. To be fair, it was half past eleven, but time meant nothing to this woman.

"Morning." My voice sounded marginally better.

Honestly, it surprised me more that she was actually home on my birthday. She'd missed the last two. I'd woken up to an empty house on my sixteenth and seventeenth birthdays and had received over-the-top gifts several weeks later—out of guilt that she'd forgotten.

"Oh, hey, girls!" She smiled brightly at my friends as she grabbed a water out of the fridge. "I was just thinking about going up to wake you."

The girls all greeted her as politely as their hangovers would allow, and we settled into the couches in the adjoining living room. Harlow's breakfast burrito was nearly half gone by the time the rest of us unwrapped ours.

Mom meandered into the living room and perched on the arm of the couch next to me. Cal walked into the kitchen, talking on his phone as he rummaged in the cupboard. He was in shorts and a T-shirt, barefoot and comfortable—as if he lived here. Because he fucking did.

I ignored him. It was easy to do since I felt pleasantly surprised my mom was actually here. She really did seem to be changing her life. I mean, she was exercising and drinking water! I had to admit there were a lot of positive signs. So I let myself hope she'd remembered her only child was eighteen today, that maybe she'd already gotten me a gift and had wanted to wake me up to give it to me.

"So, what's on the agenda for today?" Mom asked the room.

I shrugged. "Nothing. We're all pretty—" I stopped myself from saying *hungover*, not in the mood for a fight. "Tired. It was a late night."

"Mm-hmm. Tired. Right." Mom glared at us each in turn but with a teasing smile on her face. The woman could write a book on hangovers, so it was probably naive to think she wouldn't know. We all chuckled a little, Mom included. I was relieved she wasn't mad about it, that I could actually have a moment of lightness with my mother.

"So, what did you girls get up to last night that's got you so tired?" she asked.

"Uh, there was a party," Mena answered while I had a mouthful of burrito. Harlow had finished hers and fallen right back to sleep on the other end of the couch.

"Ooh, a party! I hope it was worth the hangover. What was the occasion?"

No one answered on my behalf that time, shooting me subtle looks as they busied their mouths with breakfast. I swallowed my bite with some difficulty. My throat was suddenly tight, and all the food in my stomach felt heavy.

"Mom." I set the remainder of my burrito down and faced her, forcing myself to be calm. There was no way she'd forgotten. Again. *No way.* "It was my party. I threw it."

"You did?" Her brows furrowed slightly, but she still smiled at me in curiosity. "Where? Why not do it here? There's plenty of room."

"Why were you coming to wake me up? Or asking what I was up to today?" Un-fucking-believable.

She shrugged. "Just have nothing much on today. Cal and I are planning to go to lunch, so I was going to ask if you wanted to join us. Maybe we could do some shopping after."

"What day is it?" I got to my feet even though I was exhausted—spent right down to my bones. I just couldn't be sitting when she admitted it. I needed to be standing.

"Uh . . . Sunday? What's gotten into you?" She looked very confused now, and she got to her feet too, crossing her arms over her chest.

"What is today?" I gritted out, digging my nails into the palms of my hands. "The date."

The volume of my voice startled Harlow awake, but I was hardly aware of my friends—awkwardly watching this shit show with front-row seats.

"I don't know, Amaya. What . . ." She huffed. "Like, May . . ."

"May eleventh." Cal appeared next to her, inserting himself into the situation, as usual. Apparently he'd finished with his call.

"Right. May eleventh." Mom nodded and leaned into him. It was almost comical seeing her expression change as the lightbulb went off in her brain. Her shoulders stiffened, and she looked at me, horrified. At least she had the courtesy to feel embarrassed.

"And why might this date be important to me?" I asked with sarcastic pleasantness, grinding my molars.

"Oh, Amaya." Mom's eyes got watery. "It's . . . your . . ."

"It's my fucking birthday!" I yelled into her face, perversely satisfied when she flinched. "I am your only child. You are my only parent. And you've forgotten my birthday for the third year in a row. What the fuck kind of mother are you?"

"I'm sorry. My sweet girl, I am so——"

"Oh, shut up!" I cut her off. "I don't believe you."

Cal rubbed her back soothingly, but they both looked remorseful, or something like it.

"I'm sorry too," he said. "I didn't know it was today, but I should've made an effort. We'll do something special——"

"Fuck off, Cal!" I cut him off too. "No one asked you. You're not my father and you never will be. Because he's gone. The only good parent I ever had is fucking dead, and I'm stuck with *you*." I pointed at my mother with a scowl. "I wish it was you who'd died and not him."

My mother gasped and her tears spilled over. Cal looked shocked.

I didn't care. I turned away from them all and rushed up to my room, locked the door, and dived back under the covers. Maybe if I just slept some more, I'd wake up and realize this had all been some horrible nightmare.

Donna had the only other key to my room. She must've walked home to get it, because it was some time—and several rounds of knocking and calling through the door from both my friends and my mother—before I heard the door open.

My girls climbed into bed with me and just held me while I cried.

Worst birthday ever.

CHAPTER FIFTEEN

The Fulton Academy parking lot was empty, the hot afternoon sun baking the concrete under our feet. Trevor, the security guard, had been happy to take the three neatly folded hundred-dollar bills to let us in on a Saturday. He hovered around the front doors, making sure we stayed in the parking lot as agreed, but other than that, Jet and I were alone.

"Oh my god, it's so heavy." I tensed all my muscles, trying to stay upright. My hands ached from how hard I gripped the handlebars.

"It's OK, just find your balance. I got you, beautiful," Jet encouraged me.

Once I was sure I wouldn't face-plant and take his motorbike with me, I nodded.

It had been a week since my birthday. A whole week of feeling hurt and avoiding my mother. I'd spent this morning studying with the girls, but then the sisters had some tennis thing to get to and Mena had a shift at the diner, so I'd called my . . . er . . . Jet. I'd called Jet.

We hadn't had that conversation yet, so I didn't feel right calling him my boyfriend. But neither of us was seeing other people, and he wasn't shy about holding my hand or kissing me at school, so whatever. Labels were so 2013.

Jet and I had lunch at Mena's diner, and then I managed to talk him into teaching me how to ride a motorbike. Which was how I now found myself at school on a Saturday afternoon with my butt on the bike and my toes touching the ground on either side, trying my hardest not to fall before we even started.

I squeezed everything in an attempt to stay upright as my right leg started to jiggle from the strain. Jet's hands were there, steadying me before I could even ask. Holding the handlebars and the back of the seat, he kept the massive thing under me stable, and I took a breath to release my tension.

"You good?" he asked, but I was too distracted by the muscles and veins popping out on his forearm, by all that tanned skin stretched over strong muscle. I wanted to feel his big hands gripping my thighs just like that.

"Amaya?" He leaned in close with a little smile. "You wanna learn how to do this or just keep eye-fucking my arms? Because you didn't need to waste all that money bribing Trevor for that—we could've just gone to the gym."

"Shut up." I chuckled. "I can do both."

"No, you can't. You need to focus."

"Yeah, yeah. OK, let me try the balance thing again." I flapped my hands at him to back up, but he leaned in instead. With one smooth move, he swung his leg over the back and settled himself behind me.

"Let's go over some basics first." He placed my hands firmly on the handles and pointed to things as he explained. I didn't know how he expected me to focus with his insanely hot body pressed up against mine and both his forearms doing their sexy dance right in front of my face.

Somehow, I managed though.

He ran through how to work the throttle, the brake, changing gears, and all the other knobs and levers—the basics of taking off and stopping. He had me repeat back to him all the functions of the controls, then he checked the helmet was on tightly, zipped his leather jacket up to my chin, and got off the back. I pressed my toes into the ground, making sure to keep the heavy machine upright.

"OK, start her up." Jet crossed his arms, making his chest and biceps bulge. I swear he was doing it on purpose at this stage. I turned the little key, and the engine under me rumbled to life. I grinned, feeling accomplished already, even though I hadn't even done anything yet.

"Now, you're going to powerwalk it first, like I showed you. Then lift your feet when you feel balanced, and you're going to go to the other end of the lot." He pointed to the far side, where the grass sloped down toward the tennis courts. "And then you're going to stop and plant your feet once more. Got it?"

"Got it." I fixed my gaze on my target. Without waiting for any more instructions, or giving myself time to freak out, I revved the engine and slowly released the clutch. The motorbike lurched forward, and I screamed and jammed the brake on.

Jet was there instantly, grabbing the handlebars, balancing me, and fighting a laugh. I smacked him, but he gave me a few more tips and I tried again. And again, and again.

An hour later I was drenched in sweat under the heavy leather jacket, but I could take off, drive to the other side of the lot, and come to a stop. I couldn't turn yet, but we decided to work on that some other time.

We sat in the shade of a tree and passed a bottle of water between us to cool down.

"You did great. I'm proud of you." Jet slung an arm around my neck and planted a kiss on my temple.

I shoved him back. "Don't! I'm all sweaty and gross!"

"I don't care!" With a laugh, he jostled me onto my back in the grass, then rubbed his cheeks all over my face and hairline while I squirmed and screamed and laughed all at once.

When he finally relented, we just stared up at the canopy of the tree, our fingers tangling between us as we caught our breath.

"Thanks for teaching me how to ride a crotch rocket," I said. "It was good to keep my mind occupied with something other than study."

"Anytime," he said. Then after a long pause: "Things still tense at your place? Have you spoken to your mom yet?"

"Yes, they are, and no, I haven't."

Mom had spent every day since my birthday trying to make up for forgetting my birthday. A new gift appeared in front of my door every morning, one of my favorite meals waited for me in the kitchen every night, and in between, she was pretty much love-bombing me. She called and texted all the time with apologies and compliments and declarations of love. All the gifts sat in the hallway outside my door unopened, all the meals went uneaten, and I hadn't replied to a single message.

She and Cal were constantly home now too. She was *always* there, trying to talk to me, trying to be a mother all of a sudden. I just pretended they didn't exist. I could see it getting to her, the frustration building behind the niceties. It was only a matter of time before she blew up at me, and then shit would go back to normal.

"How long are you planning to freeze her out?" Jet asked. His tone was casual, but I knew he wanted me to make up with my mom. I'd shut him down hard the first and only time he'd tried to argue I should talk to her, but he kept nudging me on it. He knew everything that had happened. I wasn't sure why he was so invested, but I had a feeling it had to do with his own absent parents.

"Well, *she* froze *me* out from the moment Dad died so . . . like, seven years, give or take." I shrugged and sat up.

He placed a gentle hand on my back. "I just hate seeing you hurting. That's the only reason I want you to talk to her."

I nodded but didn't reply.

After another long silence during which I locked all that emotion crap down, I turned to face him.

"Let's go for a drive. I have a spot I want to show you." I stood up and pulled on his arm, ready for another distraction.

We got back on the motorbike, Jet driving this time. I hugged him close and leaned into the bends in the road as we headed up the hill. I navigated by pointing. We flew past the concealed turnoff and had to double back, but then we rode up the bumpy dirt road to the lookout.

"Wow!" Jet took a deep breath as we walked closer to the edge of the cliff, hand in hand. It was the kind of lung-expanding, life-affirming breath you couldn't avoid taking when coming face-to-face with a spectacular view.

There wasn't a single cloud in the sky, and the blue stretched out before us infinitely, the California landscape and Devilbend baking in the sun below.

"Absolutely stunning." Jet wrapped an arm around my middle and pulled me close.

"If you crack a joke about how the view is all right too, I'm going to dick-punch you," I warned.

His shoulders shook as he laughed. "I thought you liked all that romantic stuff from your books."

"You know what's romantic? Finding a unique way to express your feelings that's specific to the person you're with. You know what's not romantic? Clichés."

"Personalize the compliments. Got it."

I turned to face him and wrapped my arms around his neck. "Your eyes are practically sparkling. It's fucking enchanting, since they're so dark most of the time."

"Thanks?" He struggled to keep the mirth off his face, his dimples flashing.

I wanted to reply with something witty and flirty, but I was genuinely mesmerized by his eyes. The clear blue sky and the bright sunshine made them look amazing—as if I could dive into their sparkling depths and all my worries would be soothed away.

I lifted onto my tippy toes and kissed him instead. He held me a little tighter as we kissed languidly, getting lost in each other.

It didn't take long for a tingle to build between my legs, that warm, pressured feeling of arousal. I hadn't hooked up with anyone since before our spring break trip, probably longer, and I was horny AF. And despite my valiant efforts, Jet just wasn't getting into my pants.

To be fair, we hadn't had many opportunities to really make magic happen, but the few times we had been alone long enough, he'd stopped before things got to third base. He insisted he wanted to take things slow. I would've started to feel rejected all over again if I couldn't feel the rock-hard evidence of his arousal anytime I so much as brushed against him. He clearly wanted me, and he wasn't shy about showing me care and affection in a nonsexual way.

So I did my best to respect his boundaries and not pressure him, but man, I was starting to get serious blueballitis here. There were only so many nights in a row a girl could get off with her own hand before she needed someone else's touch.

Just the thought of Jet's touch between my legs kicked my arousal up another few notches. I moaned lightly into his mouth and rolled my hips against his. His hands tightened on my back and then dropped to my hips.

As predicted, he broke the kiss and pressed his forehead against mine, both of us breathing hard.

"We should slow down," he whispered.

"Why?" I breathed.

"Anyone could come up that road at any second."

"No one ever comes up here," I argued.

"Still . . ."

I shook my head a little to clear it and leaned back to look at him properly. "Do you . . . not want to?"

"Of course I want to," he declared with so much conviction it took me a little aback. "I want you so badly it's scary, Amaya."

I bit my lip and smiled. "OK, well, I want you too. So why do you keep pulling back? Are you scared? Have you never . . ."

"Hah!" He threw his head back and laughed. "It's not that. I'm . . ." He rubbed the back of his head, looking embarrassed for a moment. "I'm more experienced than I care to admit."

"OK . . ." I waited for him to elaborate. I didn't really care that he'd been with others before—so had I. Jealousy was such a pointless emotion.

"I just don't want to move too fast. I don't want you to feel pressured or . . . anything."

"Wait." I chuckled. "Do you think I'm a virgin?"

"I don't mean to assume anything but . . ."

Now it was my turn to throw my head back and laugh. "First of all, virginity is a bullshit, patriarchal social construct. Second, I'm plenty experienced too, so when I say I want you inside me, I mean it."

Jet watched me with a mixture of emotions on his face—surprise, amusement, admiration maybe? And something really tender I could've easily interpreted as love if I wanted to.

"Noted," he finally responded.

"Come on." I pulled him over to the motorbike, then gestured for him to get on.

"Where are we off to now, princess?" he asked as he swung his leg over.

In answer, I settled myself in front of him, facing him.

He caressed the exposed skin below the hem of my hiked-up skirt. "We're not having sex in a public place in broad daylight. I'm not comfortable with that."

"Noted," I parroted his own sentiment before leaning in for a kiss. I wanted to fuck him right on the back of the motorbike, but we could work up to that. That didn't mean we couldn't fool around a bit though.

I had my back to my favorite view in all of Devilbend, and I didn't even care.

Because in front of me, between my legs, was something that interested me even more.

Jet didn't seem all that impressed with the sprawling landscape or the setting sun anymore either. He only had eyes for me. There was something really addicting about that.

He'd dated practically half the girls at school since he arrived, but none of them had held his interest long enough to even get a kiss. Then he went and practically claimed me in front of everyone and looked at me like *that*. Who wouldn't be intoxicated?

"What's going on in that complicated head of yours?" he asked, the dimples barely flashing with a soft smile.

"Just thinking about you," I said, then nearly reared back in surprise at my own honesty. I hadn't even hesitated. There were exactly three people I was ever that candid with. I guessed now it was four.

"Yeah?" The dimples deepened. "What about me?"

I pulled back slightly, but I didn't have much room, and his grip on my waist tightened. I didn't want to stroke his ego, but I also didn't want to close up completely. I kind of liked being more vulnerable with him. A little. Just dipping my toe in the vulnerability river. The water was nice.

"Those damn dimples, for one." I leaned in and licked the left one, making him chuckle. "And those eyes."

"What about my eyes?"

They see so much—even things I don't want others to see.

"They're pretty." I smirked, wanting to keep it light.

"Pretty." He raised his eyebrows.

"And your thighs." I ran my hands up the solid muscle to his hips. "I love the way they look, spread like this. It's so . . . masculine."

"Mm-hmm." He watched me intently, his thumbs dipping under my shirt to rub at the skin above my waistband.

"And your ass." I reached around to grab it. "You have a great ass. Especially when you're riding."

His hands dropped to my own butt, and with a sure squeeze, he yanked me closer. We ended up chest to chest, my core firmly against his rapidly growing erection. Reluctantly, I released his ass and wrapped my arms around his neck for balance.

"Keep going," he murmured against my lips.

"Talking time is over." My voice was breathy as I closed the minuscule distance and kissed him hard.

Our conversation earlier had cleared the air and apparently lifted some mental block for him. Because he wasn't holding back anymore. There was no hesitation in the way he kissed me—he was letting go, and I wanted all he had to give.

When I moaned into his mouth and ground myself against him this time, he didn't break the kiss or push me away—he drew me in closer. His fingers dug into the hair at the back of my scalp, and he used the leverage to tilt my head a little more, giving his mouth greater access to mine. He devoured me. His tongue, his lips, even his teeth. He was hands-down the best kisser I'd ever had.

His hips started to jerk under me, matching my movements and giving me more of the friction I craved. It was sweet torture. I was exactly where I wanted to be, but it wasn't enough. I didn't think I'd ever get enough of Jet.

My body became a ball of sensation, heat coursing through me. My pussy clenched around nothing as I shamelessly rubbed myself against him. I was definitely soaking through my underwear, probably making a mess on his jeans, and I didn't even care.

I could feel an orgasm building as we clawed at each other as though possessed, but I just couldn't get there. The pleasure was heady, every nerve in my body on the precipice, but I couldn't get over that edge.

I broke our kiss, panting, and groaned. The sound was something between sexy and frustrated.

"What's wrong?" Jet's husky voice, even deeper than usual, made me shiver. Or maybe it was his swollen mouth trailing kisses down my neck as his hand on my ass encouraged me to keep grinding against him.

"Nothing. Everything is very, very right." I swallowed and gasped as he found that sensitive spot at the curve of my neck and sucked. "It's just . . . uh . . ."

He pulled back to look at me, his eyes hooded with desire, his chest rising and falling with labored breaths.

"What is it, Amaya?" Some of the lust fog in his gaze cleared, and I hated it. I wanted to stay in this bubble of hormones and pheromones forever, drunk on each other.

"I just, uh, need more. To get there." I gave him a meaningful look, and he smirked, immediately catching on to what I was saying.

"I told you I'm not going to fuck you here," he said, and I couldn't stop my shoulders from slumping dramatically. I may have even stuck my bottom lip out in a full-on pout. "But I can make you feel good in a thousand different ways without even taking my pants off."

I stared at him, my mouth falling open as I trembled a little. Was the sun setting? It could've been rising on the next day for all I cared.

"Tell me what you need, beautiful." He swiped his thumb over my bottom lip, dragging it down slightly, and I reflexively darted my tongue out to lick it. I wanted to lick every inch of this guy. And I always got what I wanted.

But right now, I wanted to come. "Touch me. Make me come."

With my permission and my demand, Jet gripped my waist and kissed me savagely. He encouraged my hips to keep rolling against his hard length as he dipped his hands under my shirt. There was no hesitancy or uncertainty in his touch; he just went for it, cupping my tits and giving them a light squeeze.

For a split second, I was self-conscious about my meager B cups, wondering if he would be satisfied with them. But then he groaned into my mouth, his kisses became sloppier, and I realized he didn't care. Guys never cared about the size of your boobs, really. They were just happy to be touching boobs.

Moving one hand to my back, he quickly discovered the bralette I was wearing didn't have a clasp, so he just pulled the flimsy lace aside and started playing with my nipples. It was just the right amount of pain as he pinched lightly, then the perfect amount of pressure as he cupped them and massaged again.

It was driving me wild, but it still wasn't enough.

"Jet." I licked his lips, panting. "I need more. *Touch me.*" I gripped his wrist and guided his hand between my legs. "Touch me here."

He didn't respond. There were no more words between us—just panting breaths and moans as he gave me what I needed.

His hand dipped under my skirt, his strong fingers caressing my thigh. Every pass of his touch moved higher until his thumb skimmed the edge of my under-wear. Then he pressed that thumb right at my entrance and rubbed it up to my clit, making me gasp.

"Jesus . . ." He swallowed, then shuddered lightly. "So . . . fuck . . . wet . . ."

It wasn't anywhere near a complete sentence, but I knew what he was saying. He could feel that I'd soaked through my underwear, and he liked it. A lot.

He wriggled his thumb under the sodden fabric and repeated the same caress from my dripping entrance to my clit. With nothing between me and his touch, the sensation was a thousand times more intense. I could feel just how wet I was, his touch gliding over my engorged flesh. After all that buildup, I was so close, but he wasn't done teasing me, exploring me.

He grazed my opening, glided up and down my lips, and flicked my clit with light movements.

I cried out and bucked my hips, but the touch vanished just as suddenly as it had appeared. I whined and frowned at him, but he wasn't looking at me. His head was hanging, his gaze fixed on the spot where his hand disappeared up my skirt.

I reached down and yanked the hem back so we'd both have a better view.

He took my lead and extracted his other hand from under my shirt. As I leaned back slightly to give him more room, he shoved the gusset of my panties to the side. I was completely exposed to him and the warm breeze, which only served to ratchet up my excitement.

He started rubbing my clit more firmly and consistently, and that breathless, rising tide began to course through me.

Shifting slightly, he brought two fingers to my entrance, but the way he had to lean to get the angle right jostled the motorbike and made me feel as if I might topple off. I startled and grabbed on to his shoulders.

We shared an amused look, and he encouraged me to lean back again. I found a good grip on the handlebars behind me, and his thick, strong fingers got back to work.

His hands grasped my upper thighs as one thumb circled my clit and the other did the same at my entrance. My arousal was dripping down between my ass cheeks, probably making a mess on the leather seat, but I didn't give a shit.

I rolled my hips, wordlessly asking for more. The thumb working my most sensitive spot circled a little harder, while his other thumb pressed at my entrance in a kind of pulsing rhythm. It was a new sensation for me—like the pressure just before a cock or finger pushed inside. Torturous but addictive, and I fucking loved it.

I started making incoherent sounds, moans, and gasps. My hips rutted against his touch, seeking more, more, more. I grabbed his arm with one hand and braced myself with the other. His bicep was like stone, even as the muscles in his arms shifted under my touch with what he was doing to me.

The thumb at my clit had found the exact rhythm and pressure I liked best, and Jet didn't change a single, minuscule thing about it. But the other thumb, the one at my entrance, dipped inside. It was the tiniest intrusion, but after so much teasing, it made me throw my head back and moan.

He took the hint, pushing his finger in as far as it would go. He found a good, firm rhythm there too, his hands working in harmony and . . .

I shattered. Pleasure coursed through my body, spreading from my pulsating cunt in electric waves. I felt it at the tips of my toes, the ends of my fingers, the top of my head. The moan I released was long, almost keening, all the ecstasy pouring out of me in that one carnal sound.

Jet slowed his movements, helping me come down from the orgasm gently. When I tried to sit up and my legs and arms wobbled like jelly, he enfolded me in his arms and drew me up against his chest.

I wrapped my arms around his neck and nuzzled against him, feeling sated and safe.

CHAPTER SIXTEEN

My head was still in the clouds when Jet pulled into my driveway. I hadn't been able to wipe the smile off my face, and with the helmet hiding it, I didn't bother to try.

He kissed me long and hard after I got off the bike. It didn't even occur to me to worry about helmet hair. That was how wrapped up I was in him.

"Let me know when you have the house to yourself," he whispered against my mouth, then gave my bottom lip a teasing nip.

"It's a big house." I chuckled. "I'm sure we can find privacy if we really want it. You could come in now . . ."

I took half a step back, tugging on his collar. He may have made me come only an hour earlier, but I was ready for more already. And he hadn't allowed me to return the favor.

He groaned. "I can't. I have to go do some shit."

"What shit?" I pouted.

"Boring adult shit."

"You're an adult?" I bugged my eyes out.

"I'm over eighteen, aren't I?" He raised an eyebrow.

I gasped. "Oh my god! *I'm* an adult."

With one last kiss, I peeled myself away from him and watched his ass as he rode down the driveway and out of view.

I was still thinking about that ass as I let myself into the house. But then my bubble popped.

My mother was sitting on the stairs, hands clasped between her knees, as if she was waiting for me. She looked up at the sound of the door. I couldn't remember ever seeing such a calm, serious look on her face—a face free of makeup. She actually looked like an adult.

I had a thousand questions and snarky remarks on my tongue, but I honestly could not be bothered. I just wanted to go to my room and think about Jet until the light, warm feeling in my chest returned—even just a little.

I started up the stairs, pointedly ignoring her. The staircase could have easily fit four people standing shoulder to shoulder, so it was easy to keep my hand on the banister as I passed, my gaze forward.

"Your father used to ride a motorcycle," she said when I was a few stairs above her.

The mention of my dad made me halt, every fiber of my being unable to walk away from anything to do with the parent I missed most.

"Did you know that?" she went on. "He had it when we met in college. Used to take me on dates on the back of it. I felt like such a rebel, riding around with him, knowing very well my parents would disapprove."

I gripped the banister harder, my knuckles turning white as the metal warmed under my palm.

I looked over my shoulder and glared at her. "What are you doing?"

She was staring up at me, a million different emotions in her clear eyes. The one I could make out clearly was resolve. Whatever this was, my mother was on a mission.

It made me deeply uncomfortable.

I still couldn't walk away. When was the last time she'd even mentioned Dad, not in response to something I'd said—and sober?

She'd been sober for weeks, I realized. Obviously, I'd been avoiding her and what's-his-face like the plague, but every time I'd bumped into her in the house, she'd been sober.

"Something I should've done a long time ago. Something I should've been doing all along." She smiled sadly.

"What the fuck are you talking about, Vivian?" I crossed my arms but turned to face her despite myself.

"I'm making sure you know your father."

What? My breathing sped up as I glanced up the stairs. Half of me wanted to run away from whatever this bizarre conversation was, and the other half wanted to stay, hear more, ask a million questions.

As if she could sense my instinct to bolt, Mom kept talking. "When your dad died, it broke me. He was the love of my life, and I literally didn't know how to exist without him. But that's not an excuse for how horribly I've failed you as a mother. I have not been here—physically or any other way. I know that. And I am so very deeply sorry, Amaya."

I gaped at her, my brain struggling to process what I was hearing. In total shock, I flopped down on the stairs. She was actually admitting it? She was sorry? *What?*

Mom scooted her butt up two steps so she was sitting next to me. "You've grown into an amazing, capable, smart young woman, and I missed it. Parents say that all the time—blink and you'll miss them growing up—but I really did miss it all. And I can't tell you how much I regret that. I regret so many things, especially not talking about your father. I see a lot of him in you, and I should've kept his memory alive. I should've been here to talk about him and show you pictures and tell you stories. Instead, I . . ."

She trailed off, and I forced the lump in my throat down before speaking. "Instead, you were off self-medicating and pretending like it had never happened. Pretending you didn't have a daughter."

"You're right." She nodded, resigned. "You reminded me so much of him. You still do."

"And that makes it OK? How is that my fault?" I could feel the anger rising along with my tone. This was it—she'd yell at me, and we'd end up in a pointless fight like usual. At least it was familiar territory.

Except she didn't yell. She wiped at the moisture under her eyes and spoke in a calm, if strained, voice. "It's not. It's not. I'm just trying to be honest with you, Amaya. And to apologize. I'm sorry."

"You think that's going to fix everything?" I gripped the step on either side of my hips. "You can't just say 'oops! I fucked up for seven years straight. My bad!' and expect everything to be OK."

"Of course not." Once again, she didn't let her anger rise to meet mine. It stumped me—again. "I know an apology is not going to fix all the pain I've caused you, all the damage I've done to our relationship. Maybe nothing will, but as long as I'm breathing, I'm going to show you with my actions and my words that I'm serious. I want to repair our relationship, and I'm going to be here. I'm going to keep trying, keep showing you as long as I live. And I know those are just words too, that it's going to take time for you to start to believe me, but I'm going to prove it to you. I love you, Amaya, and I want to be in your life."

What the fuck was I supposed to do with that? How dare she spring this emotional clusterfuck on me when I was mad at her? Although I'd been mad at her for years now, so maybe that was neither here nor there.

I stared at the grain in the wooden step beneath my feet. This was exactly what I'd wanted to hear from her since . . . I didn't even know when. It had been years. But I was too jaded—I couldn't trust her.

But I wanted this so badly. I hated to admit it, even to myself, but I wanted my mom.

"I can't pretend like none of it ever happened," I told the wood grain, my voice low. Out of the corner of my eye, I could see her nodding. "And I'm not ready to forgive you. I don't know if I'll ever be." More nodding and a stuttering inhale from my mom that made my own throat tighten. "But I've wanted to hear you say some of this stuff for a long time. I'm just not sure if I can trust you yet."

For a few long moments, we sat in silence.

I sighed. "I am sorry I said I wished you'd died instead of Dad though. That was harsh."

She chuckled—a watery, emotional release of tension—and I finally looked into her eyes.

"Way harsh," she agreed. "But I probably deserved it."

I shrugged, not disagreeing. Still, wishing death on someone was pretty fucked up, and if I was being honest, it had been playing on my mind.

"Can we have dinner together?" she asked tentatively. "If you don't have plans. We can just get takeout, nothing fancy. And I'll send Cal out for the night. I don't want to force him on you, and I'm sorry about how that situation has gone down too."

I rolled my eyes. "He can have greasy burgers with us if it's not below his high standards. It's fine."

"Great!" My mom beamed. I hadn't seen her look so happy since I was in elementary school.

"What's brought on this sudden change?" I had to ask. "You get a personality transplant or something?"

She laughed. "It may seem sudden to you, but I've been working hard to change things for months now. It's not an easy road, but I found something that helps to smooth it out. It's how I met Cal, actually. I know he seems like he came out of nowhere too, but we've actually known each other for over a year."

"OK." I was starting to feel drained from the heaviness of the conversation.

We stood at the same time.

"I'm going to take a shower." Before I could think about it too much, I leaned forward and gave my mom a quick hug. I ran up the stairs and into my room without looking at her. Without letting her see the tears on my own face.

CHAPTER SEVENTEEN

I leaned forward to take a sip of my green goddess smoothie, doing my best to keep my hands steady for the nail tech.

"What shape did you say you'd like?" She glanced up at me as she finished cleaning up my cuticles.

"Coffin, please." I gave her a smile, not even bothered that I'd had to repeat myself. I was in an unusually good mood, and nothing could ruin it.

I'd taken my last final exam the day before, prom was tomorrow night, and there had been no drama with Mom. I felt lighter than I had in ages.

Donna sat to my right, Mena on her other side, as we all got our nails done for prom. Harlow hated having any length on her nails and wasn't going to prom, but she didn't want to miss out, so she was hanging out in a spare chair between me and Donna.

"I can't believe you and Jet still haven't boned." Harlow shook her head, rehashing a conversation from last night.

I wanted to smack her, but my hands were otherwise occupied, so I settled for glaring. "We've only been together for a few weeks."

"Never stopped you before," Donna added helpfully.

"True," I mumbled. "Honestly, between exams and my mother being an actual parent, we've hardly had any time together lately."

"I'm so happy I didn't have to do the exams." Harlow stretched her arms over her head with a blissful expression on her face. "Best decision I ever made, quitting school."

"So, things are still good with your mom?" Mena asked me.

"Yeah." I smiled to myself. "For now."

I'd told the girls about Mom's bombshell apology and how things had been progressing since then. They were as shocked but tentatively happy as I was. As good as things were now, it had only been a few weeks, and I couldn't let myself trust it completely yet. Still, the hope grew with every day. My mom and I had been having dinner together almost every night, we hadn't gotten into any fights, and she was asking me about everyday shit and listening as if she really cared. Cal was growing on me more and more too. He treated my mom well, and he had his own money, so I knew he wasn't using her.

"Hey, what did you guys put for question eight on the statistics paper?" Donna asked, chewing her bottom lip.

Harlow, Mena, and I all groaned. Donna hadn't been as unburdened by the end of exams as the rest of us. She couldn't seem to stop questioning her answers.

"Shut up, Donna," Harlow whined in that way only a sister could. "As if you won't have the best results of the entire graduating class."

"You shut up." Donna jerked her head to the side to glare at her sister, earning a disapproving look from her nail tech.

"I couldn't tell you a single thing that happened within the walls of Fulton Academy over the past four years, let alone a specific question on an exam. I've blocked it all out," I declared.

"I'm sure you aced it, Donna." Mena gave her a sweet smile. "You have nothing to stress about. I'll be happy to get average grades. It's been a hell of a year."

We all nodded and fell into silence. Between the kidnapping, roofie-ing, blackmail, fight clubs, and shootings, it had certainly been a doozie. Someone needed to write a book about this batshit year we'd had. It would make a great romantic suspense.

The conversation turned to lighter topics, and we went out for lunch after. It ended up being a perfect day with my #DevilbendDynasty girls, and I was walking on air when I got home later that afternoon.

There didn't seem to be anyone around downstairs, but when I headed up, I could hear faint music coming from Mom's side of the house. I dumped my purse and a few shopping bags in my room and wandered over.

Briefly, I second-guessed the decision—what if they were having an afternoon delight? Gross! But I glimpsed the wide-open door to Mom's bedroom, and her voice floated down the hall singing along to "Total Eclipse of the Heart," totally off-key. Confident I wasn't about to get an eyeful of Cal's bare ass—or worse—I walked into my mom's room.

I knocked softly on the doorframe and leaned on the wall.

Mom turned to face me, a dress on a hanger in each hand, and beamed.

"Amaya! Thank God you're here. I need help deciding on a gown. My boobs look great in this one." She held up a sparkly red number, then switched to the other dress—a lacy blue one. "But this one brings out the color in my eyes, I think. But then, I was thinking . . ." She mumbled something I couldn't hear as she skipped over to her bed. It was covered in dresses every color of the rainbow, making it impossible to see what the sheets even looked like underneath.

I shoved some of the dresses aside so I could sit. I used to hang out in my parents' bedroom all the time as a kid. I loved jumping on their big bed, or sitting in the middle and watching Mom get ready for some fancy event. She'd let me play dress-up sometimes, and Dad would come in wearing his tux and dance with me, my feet on the tops of his, before they went out. I hadn't been in this room in years. It was a little strange to think about—a room in my house I'd avoided for that long.

"What's this for?" I asked.

"A party tomorrow night. It's black tie."

"Not buying a new gown for it?" She usually did. Vivian was never seen in the same outfit twice.

She shrugged and dug around in the pile. "My wardrobe feels like a boutique anyway, so I figured I'd pick one I already have. But now I'm having so much trouble deciding . . ." She propped her hands on her hips. "Maybe I should just go out and get something new. Wanna go shopping?"

I laughed. "I'm sure we can find something."

We started going through the dresses together. I ended up in a vintage eighties number with massive shoulders while Mom tried on dress after dress. Some of them didn't fit anymore and some were too dated, but we found a few options that we had fun styling with the accessories she had.

A shimmery silver fabric near the corner of the bed caught my eye, and I dug it out.

"Oh, that one's too short for black tie." Mom waved it off.

I held it up, inspecting it. It was strapless with a corseted top and looked as if it would hit about mid-thigh. The fabric was stunning, the shape perfect for Mom's delicate shoulders. She was right though; it was too short for black tie.

"I have an idea." I jumped up and went to her wardrobe, digging through her clothes until I found what I was looking for. I handed the silver dress and the other item I'd found to my mom and ordered her to put them on. She gave me a skeptical look but started to remove the dress she was currently in.

I ran to my room and grabbed a clutch I knew would be perfect.

By the time I came back, Mom had the silver dress on and was stepping into the midnight-blue tulle A-line skirt I'd pulled out. The skirt was knee-length.

"I don't think this works, baby." Mom frowned down at herself.

I held up a finger and went in search of the perfect shoes and accessories. With everything gathered, I turned Mom's back to the mirror and dropped to my knees. I pulled the skirt down and tucked it in under the hem of the dress, then gestured for Mom to try on a pair of silver heels. After she put in some earrings and I secured her necklace, I swiveled her to face the mirror.

She gasped and turned a shocked look at me. I grinned at her in the mirror, satisfied with myself.

With the midnight-blue skirt tucked underneath the silver dress, it suddenly looked like a fit-and-flare floor-length gown. The silver shoes with jeweled detail matched the silver of the dress and went great with the jeweled blue clutch I'd grabbed. A sapphire choker and earrings completed the look.

"I can sew the skirt onto the bottom of the dress," I explained as I gathered her hair up. "It won't take me long. But I think you should wear your hair—"

I lost my grip on her locks as she turned to pull me into a hug. "It's perfect!" She bounced on her toes for a moment, then held me out at arm's length and looked at me as if she'd just made some amazing discovery. She'd been doing that a lot lately—gaping at me as if she couldn't quite believe what I'd turned into. "I'm so proud of you, Amaya. You're amazing."

"Thanks, Mom." I ducked my head and started tidying up some of the mess we'd made. Her affection still made me uncomfortable, but at least I wasn't running out of the room anymore. Progress, or whatever.

"Are you going to do fashion design at college? Or something else?" Mom asked, taking everything off and placing it in a neat pile.

I shrugged. "Not sure yet. I've applied to a bunch of colleges but . . ."

"What?" she prodded as she pulled on yoga pants and a T-shirt.

"I'm thinking about taking a gap year."

"Oh?" She started putting the dresses back on their hangers. We floated around each other, keeping our hands busy while I mustered up the courage to say what I wanted to say.

Fuck it. "I think I want to travel for a while first."

"That's a great idea!"

"I want to spend some time in Sri Lanka. Do you think Uncle Inesh and Aunt Ravima would want to see me?"

Mom paused with her back to me, her hands on the hanger she'd just returned to its spot on the rod.

After a moment, she took a breath and turned to face me with a brittle smile. "I think they'd be beyond ecstatic to see you, baby. They can show you where your dad grew up, tell you things about him that I don't know—his childhood and stuff."

"Yeah?" I didn't know what I'd expected, but relief flooded through me at her positive, if strained, response. I really wanted to get in touch with my Sri Lankan roots. My father's parents had passed away before I was born, we'd lost touch with his family after he died, and I had no idea about his culture. But something deep inside me craved to know more. I felt as if I could know him better through learning about his heritage.

"Of course. It's my fault you don't have a relationship with them. I'll reach out and talk to them."

"Thanks, Mom." I gave her a hug and let her hold on for a long time. I could tell it was hard for her to talk about this—about *him*—but she was making an effort for me, and I really appreciated it.

CHAPTER EIGHTEEN

I didn't realize until the next day what I'd helped my mom prepare for. The girls and I had plans to get ready for prom together at Donna's place. We had someone coming to do our hair and makeup, and the boys would come pick us up in a limo.

I had all my things ready to go in a duffel, and I went to the fridge to grab a kombucha before leaving. Cold drink in hand, I shut the fridge door and came face-to-face with the invite to Raine Clayton's party.

"Fuck." I snatched the invite off the fridge and double-checked the date. It was definitely tonight. I tried to tell myself that maybe they were going to something else, that I shouldn't let my worry get out of hand, but I didn't want my mom anywhere near the culty weirdos of BestLyf. All previous experience pointed to the organization being seriously dangerous.

Kombucha forgotten on the counter, I headed back upstairs. I had to know.

"Mom!" I called as I took the stairs two at a time.

"In the sitting room," she called back, and I rushed past her bedroom to the cozy lounge area. She and Cal sat in armchairs facing the massive window, cups of tea in hand. "Did you forget something?"

They both turned to face me. I'd already said goodbye and made plans for them to pop over to the Meads' on their way out so they could see us all ready for prom.

"Is this where you're going tonight?" I thrust the invite at them. Mom frowned down at it, and Cal took the thick piece of impending doom from my outstretched hand.

"Yeah. Why?" Mom leaned on the arm of the chair to face me more fully.

"Please don't." I could hear the desperation in my voice.

She took my hand. "I promise I won't forget to stop by the Meads' to take pictures, baby. We're planning to be late to the party."

I kneeled down next to her chair. "It's not that. I just . . . these are bad people. I'm worried. Please just skip this one."

Mom and Cal shared a look that I was too frazzled to decipher. Were they just concerned about my weird behavior? Or was it something more?

"Holy shit," I breathed out as I sat back on my heels. So very many things were clicking into place at the same time, and the weight of it all nearly crushed me.

She said she'd been working on herself for over a year. She'd been going to "meetings" even though she didn't work. Just yesterday she'd told me that was how she met Cal—through whatever this journey of self-improvement was.

"It's just a party, sweetheart. There's nothing to worry about." Mom tried to calm me down, but I could hear the concern in her voice. I was just as concerned about her, and I had better reason to be.

All the horrible shit that had been happening—all of it tied to BestLyf—flashed through my mind like a waking nightmare. And it jogged my memory of something else. It had been a traumatic night, and I'd forgotten about it, but I'd seen Cal talking to Shady in Devilbend North that night. Shady definitely had his finger in multiple BestLyf pies.

"You dragged her into this," I said, getting to my feet. I needed to be higher than him.

Cal remained seated, slowly placing his mug on the side table. "No, I didn't. We met through BestLyf, but only after Vivian had been attending the seminars for some time. I swear to you, I had nothing to do with recruiting her."

"I don't believe you." I didn't know what to believe.

"Amaya." Mom got to her feet and took my hands in hers. "One of my friends took me to my first BestLyf seminar. Not Calvin. I wouldn't have even gone if I wasn't wasted when she dragged me there. Now, I won't lie and say I wasn't sucked in—I was. They're very persuasive. I spent a lot of money on their seminars and courses, started to get a bit obsessed with passing up to the next level. But Cal helped me realize what was really important." She threw him a warm smile—a look that lingered—and I realized my mom was falling in love with this man. If she wasn't in love already.

That was a whole Pandora's box of mixed feelings I wasn't ready to open.

"We both came to realize that BestLyf is not for us," Cal agreed but didn't elaborate.

I looked between them. "What do you mean?"

"It's . . ." Mom sighed and glanced at Cal again. "Look, we can talk about it some other time, OK? You're going to be late for your hair and makeup."

"Fuck the hair and makeup, Mom! I don't want you involved with these people."

"I'm not." She squeezed my hands for emphasis. "I promise. I'm glad I went, because it was helpful initially, and it led me to meeting Calvin, but I'm done with it."

"Then why are you going to Raine's party?"

"A lot of important people will be there. Raine is very well connected—even with people not part of BestLyf. Calvin and I are planning to start a business, and this party is a great opportunity to network."

"You're starting a business?" Maybe some of those meetings actually were business related. My mother was making my head spin with all these surprises. But I started to feel better about the whole situation. She didn't seem to be sucked into a cult. She was happier and healthier than I'd seen her since before Dad died. Maybe I was overreacting.

"Yes. I'll tell you all about it tomorrow. I promise. Now, go get ready for prom." She nudged me toward the door. I looked between her and Cal, chewing on my bottom lip.

"I won't let anything happen to your mom, Amaya," Cal said with a serious expression. I supposed he wanted to reassure me too, and he had been consistent so far.

"OK, fine," I relented. They would be in a room full of the most prominent members of Devilbend society. What was the worst that could happen? Still . . . "Can you please check in with me during the night? Just so I'm not worrying."

"If it'll get you to go and enjoy your prom, fine, I'll send you a few texts." Mom rolled her eyes.

"Every half hour," I demanded.

She pursed her lips. "Every hour."

"On the hour." I raised a brow.

"Deal."

"Deal."

Then she literally herded me out of the room, and I headed out with a smile on my face.

Mom would be fine. And I would have fun tonight. I fucking deserved it.

CHAPTER NINETEEN

While most girls liked to match their dress to their date's tie, my girls and I picked our outfits to match one another. This plan had been in the works for months—well before Harlow dropped out—so she joined us in getting ready too. Even though she wasn't going to prom. Easton was taking her out on an elaborate date to some fine dining place so the outfit wouldn't go to waste.

She was in a mini dress with a sweetheart neckline and a sheer layer that fell to the ground, her hair in a high, sleek ponytail. The dress was a rich royal blue, and she wore hot pink heels and accessories with it. We'd all agreed on royal blue as our theme color. It matched all our complexions and was easy to individualize.

Donna wore a dramatic fit-and-flare with a black leather corseted top. She was leaning into her Dark Donna vibes with smoky eye makeup and killer heels.

Mena had gone full ballgown after saying, "Fuck it! How many opportunities are we going to get to wear a completely over-the-top princess dress?" It had a cream silk bodice and silk flowers around the bottom hem with layers and layers of tulle.

I'd gone for a solid royal-blue halter-neck gown with a slit and detailed white beading around the waist. I loved how well we matched while still expressing our individual flair.

We took a bunch of pictures on our phones, gushing about how amazing we all looked, before we headed downstairs.

The boys had arrived to pick us up, and my mom and Cal stood with the girls' parents, chatting and waiting for us to make our grand entrance. Even Easton was there to pick up Harlow. He stood at the complete opposite end of the foyer from her dad, looking constipated. But his eyes practically turned into hearts when he caught sight of Harlow leading the way down the curved staircase.

Hendrix looked Donna up and down as if studying the dress and figuring out the fastest way to get it off her. He was lucky all eyes were on us, multiple cameras going off.

Turner was the first to step forward, taking Mena's hand and placing a gentlemanly kiss on the back as she reached the bottom of the staircase. His thoughts were just as dirty as Hendrix's—he just hid it better.

Everything became background noise when I caught Jet's eyes. He looked ridiculously hot. I loved him in jeans and his leather jacket, could hardly keep my eyes off him in shorts at the gym, but I'd never seen him in formalwear. He was in a gray suit, his tie perfectly matched to the blue of my dress. All the guys had royal-blue ties on, indulging us girls and our matching-outfits vision.

"Wow," he mouthed as he watched me. His eyes practically sparkled, taking in all the details. If I was the kind of girl that blushed, my cheeks would've been red as a fire truck. I still couldn't hold back the little grin that tugged at the corners of my mouth.

The boys stepped forward with boxes that they opened to reveal three unique corsages. We'd all hated the idea of a traditional corsage—it would've completely clashed with the style of my dress—so we'd opted for ring corsages. Jet slid the delicate arrangement of little flowers onto my finger.

The parents all oohed and aahed, taking more photos.

Harlow and Easton used the distraction to have a chaste kiss.

"Can I meet the boy who has my daughter smiling so wide?" Mom gripped my elbow and looked between Jet and me with a smile.

"Sure! Mom, this is Jethro. Jet, my mom."

"It's a pleasure to meet you, Mrs. Ellis-Lahari." Jet took Mom's hand in a polite shake and turned on the charm. "I can see where Amaya gets her beauty from."

Mom threw her head back and laughed. "Yes, well, she gets her stubbornness from me too, so good luck with that." She didn't even bother to correct him on her last name. She was an Ellis, and I'd gotten both my parents' last names.

"She knows her mind. I love that about her." And just like that, he had my mom in his pocket and me falling a little harder for him.

"Mom, you look amazing." I took a step back to take her in. I'd sewn the skirt on the night before, and she had on the outfit I'd put together for her.

"Thanks to you." She beamed at me before taking a spin.

Mom introduced Cal, who shook Jet's hand and gave him a cold greeting before moving away to talk to Donna and Harlow's dad. I frowned, wondering what was up his ass all of a sudden, but Jet didn't seem to notice.

After approximately sixteen hours of cameras and phones in our faces, the parents finally waved us off, and we piled into a limo after saying bye to Harlow and Easton.

As soon as the car was moving up the drive, Hendrix turned to Donna. "Your tits look *amazing*!" He released something between a groan and a whine, and we all busted out laughing.

"How long have you been holding that in?" Turner teased as he popped the cork on a bottle of champagne.

"Since they started bouncing down the stairs." Hendrix adjusted his junk and stared at Donna's boobs, getting his fill now that the parents weren't around.

"Excuse you, we did not bounce." Mena crossed her arms. "We floated down the stairs like ladies."

"Yeah, I'm pretty sure he's referring to Donna's boobs," I said before taking a sip of champagne.

We laughed and joked all the way to Fulton Academy. The school could more than afford to hire out a venue for the prom, but why bother when we had a ballroom already? Because no one at our school would be seen dead wearing designer formalwear inside a high school gym.

Nicola squealed when she saw us and gushed about our matching dresses. We joined our friends at our table, and not long after, I felt my phone vibrate. It was one minute past the hour, and there was a message from Mom.

She'd sent a selfie, a spacious powder room in the background. I smiled and sent one back.

The night seemed to be going by in a flash. Everyone was in a good mood, there was no drama, Mom kept checking in as promised. There was food and (spiked) punch, Headmistress Perry gave a speech, and we danced.

When a slow song came on, Jet pulled me into his arms. I wrapped my arms around his shoulders and gave in to the cliché prom moment as we swayed from side to side.

"You are so damn beautiful." He looked me right in the eyes as he said it, drawing me a little closer.

"Thank you," I whispered and rested my cheek on his shoulder. I was responding to his compliment, but I was thankful for so much more. He'd been there for me when I hadn't even realized I needed him. He made me feel safe. I was thankful for *him*.

The official prom ended not long after, but in true Devilbend fashion, the party was set to go on. Nicola was hosting an afterparty at her place—a penthouse apartment in the tallest building in Devilbend.

We all piled into the limo once more, a little more disheveled than we'd arrived but in high spirits. Drew and a few of the football team guys joined us for the ride, so the car was rowdy.

It still didn't stop Donna and Hendrix from making out as if no one was there. Mena and Turner were giggling about something, their heads together.

I pressed my body against Jet's side, and he gripped my thigh.

"I miss you," I breathed against his ear, then gave it a little nibble. His chest rose with a deep breath.

"I'm right here, beautiful." He turned to capture my lips in a soft, lingering kiss.

"I know, but . . ." I sighed. I saw him every day at school, but everything had been so hectic with exams and my mom that we'd hardly had any time together. I was so ready to get into his pants. "My mom and Cal are still at that party, which means the house is empty."

"Hmmm?" He flashed me a little smirk.

"Do you want to just ditch the party and go back to my place?"

"Nobody's ditching anything!" Hendrix shouted before Jet could reply. We'd come to a stop, and everyone was getting out of the limo. Hendrix wrapped an arm around Jet's neck and practically dragged him out onto the street.

I threw Donna an unimpressed look. "You couldn't distract him with your tits for just a few minutes longer?"

She just shrugged. "Come in and have a few drinks with us before you bail to get laid."

"Yeah, come on, Amaya. You can get dick anytime. Prom only happens once." Mena held her hand out to me.

With a sigh and an eye roll, I let her pull me out of the car.

We went up to Nicola's, where the party was already pumping. Every time a new group of people came through the door, everyone would cheer and hoot as if celebrating some epic win. I supposed we were. We'd survived high school—that was something to celebrate.

I had a few drinks and hung out with my friends, but once everyone was distracted, I went looking for Jet.

I found him in the far, shadowed corner of the balcony with his phone pressed to his ear. He frowned and murmured something to whoever was on the other end before noticing me meandering toward him.

He held his arm out, and I settled into his side.

"OK. I gotta go. Bye." He hung up and planted a kiss on my forehead.

"Everything all right? Who was that?"

"Yeah . . ." He looked uncertain for a second but shook it off. "Nothing that can't wait until tomorrow. Look what I found." He gave me a cheeky look, glanced behind us at the raging party, then pulled open a sliding door and tugged me into a dark room.

I giggled, feeling a little naughty that we'd entered a room that looked off-limits. "What is this place?" I could just make out a desk, a couch, shelves filled with books and knickknacks.

"I think it's Nicola's mom's office." Jet shrugged. "The door is locked, but they must've forgotten the one to the balcony." He flicked the lock. "But that's locked now too."

I launched myself at him. All I'd wanted all night was to be alone with him, and now that I finally was, I wouldn't hold back.

He grunted as I collided with his chest, but recovered quickly to wrap me in his arms. I kissed him hard, my tongue demanding that we go deeper. He obliged with enthusiasm, our mouths devouring. He'd lost his suit jacket and tie somewhere already, and I started attacking his buttons. I stepped out of my shoes and dropped my clutch as we shuffled toward the couch.

With a shove from me, Jet fell onto the cushions, and I didn't waste any time hitching up my dress to straddle him. He was hard already, and I ground my core against his erection, finally, *finally* getting the kind of attention I'd wanted all night—all week, if I was being honest.

"Fuck, I am so horny," I groaned as I rolled my hips and rubbed against him harder.

He replied with a deep moan from the back of his throat, his mouth busy at my neck.

"Please tell me you have a condom." My voice was breathy.

Jet lifted his hot mouth from my neck and gripped my hips. "Shit." He sounded pained.

"Dammit, Jethro!" I slapped his shoulder . . . then groped it. He was so solid and strong, and his muscles practically danced under my touch.

"I didn't think I'd need one."

"Neither did I." I hadn't been expecting to find a secret dark corner of privacy. "Stay right there. Donna and Hendrix will have some for sure. Or I'll just raid the bathroom. I mean, it's a party full of horny, drunk teenagers in a movie star's penthouse—I'm sure I can find a few spare rubbers."

I moved to stand as I spoke, but Jet grabbed my wrist. "Don't go," he whined.

"Jet, I may be horny and embracing all the prom night clichés, but I refuse to add teen pregnancy to the list."

"That's not what I meant." He pulled me back down into his lap. "Let's just slip out of the party. No one will notice now. You think your house is still empty?"

"Yeah, probably . . ." I grinned and leaned down to kiss him again. His hands cupped my breasts, and our hips began rocking once more as we started to get carried away. But then it occurred to me that I hadn't checked my phone in a while.

I sat up, glancing around for my clutch.

"What's wrong?" Jet asked, his eyes glued to where his fingers slowly teased the front of my dress down.

"Nothing, I just . . . can't stop thinking about my mom." I twisted the other way, struggling to see in the dark.

Beneath me, Jet froze and pointedly pulled my dress back up over my boobs. "Uh . . . what?" He chuckled.

I laughed and scrambled off his lap. "She promised to check in, and I'm just a little worried . . ." I spotted my bag and picked it up, digging inside for my phone.

It was thirty-eight minutes past midnight, and the last check-in text I'd received was at eleven. I had three missed calls, but they were all from Harlow. Ignoring the calls, I quickly texted my mom.

I chewed on my lip as I stared at the screen, waiting for a reply. She'd just forgotten. It was getting late. Maybe they'd already gone home and fallen asleep.

Jet appeared at my back, startling me. I'd been so focused on my phone I hadn't even heard him get up.

"Hey," he whispered gently, rubbing my shoulders. "What's going on?"

"My mom is at this party, and she hasn't checked in like she promised. I'm just a little worried."

"Why? She's with the Calvin guy, right? It's just a party."

My phone rang, but it was Harlow again. I sent it to voice mail, not wanting to miss my mom's reply. Harlow was probably drunk and calling to tell me how much she loved me.

"It's at this evil woman's house, and there's a cult and shit . . ." I waved a hand over my shoulder. "It's a long story."

Jet just kept massaging my shoulders. He probably thought I was some crazy conspiracy theorist.

A text came in, but the relief had barely washed through me before worry pushed it right away. It wasn't from my mom. It was from Harlow.

"God, she's persistent tonight," I mumbled as I opened it.

H: Call me back ASAP! I couldn't sleep so I started looking at pics online from that party. And then something in my memory clicked so I looked it up. The guy your mom is with— his name is Calvin CLAYTON. He's Raine's son!

An image came through underneath the text—a posed picture of a younger Cal with Raine. It looked like a newspaper clipping, with a caption naming them as mother and son.

"Oh my god." Panic had me breathing hard as I shoved my feet into my shoes and ran for the door.

Jet was hot on my heels, asking worried and confused questions.

I dialed Mom's number as I fumbled with the locked door. With steady hands, Jet moved me aside and unlocked it, and I rushed out into the hallway. Thankfully, the office was near the front door and I wouldn't have to shove my way through the party.

The call went to voice mail. I redialed the number as I jabbed repeatedly at the elevator button. The doors finally opened just as the call went to voice mail again.

"Fuck!" I yelled at the ceiling before continuing to blow up Mom's phone.

"Amaya, you're freaking me out here." Despite his words, Jet sounded pretty calm, if deadly serious.

"Harlow just texted. Calvin is Raine's son."

"OK." Jet nodded, as if waiting for more.

"Raine runs BestLyf. She's a dangerous person, and that whole organization is fucked up! And he's her son!" The slow elevator and constant unanswered calls were getting to me—I felt frantic. "I just need to know she's safe."

Jet pulled me into a tight hug, and instantly I calmed down a little. "Everything is going to be fine. Where's this party? Let's go there and check on your mom."

I released a shaky breath of relief. He wasn't getting irritated or treating me as though I was losing it—even though I kind of was. He was going to come with me and help. "It's only two blocks away."

The elevator doors opened, and we rushed out onto the street.

CHAPTER TWENTY

Even though Mom had calmed my fears about the party, I'd still figured out where Raine's building was and how to get there from school and from Nicola's. So I didn't waste time looking it up—I just ran. I cursed the Louboutins on my feet but didn't bother taking them off. I spent more time in heels than I did barefoot; removing them wouldn't make me any faster.

As we turned the corner—the building entrance just a few feet away—my phone rang.

"Mom!" I yelled into it as soon as I accepted the call, coming to a stop.

"Amaya?" She sounded as panicked as I felt. "What's wrong? What happened?"

"Are you OK?" I was panting, and even Jet was breathing a little heavier next to me as he rubbed my back.

"Am I OK? I have, like, a thousand missed calls from you! What is going on?" The party noise in the background lowered significantly. She must've just stepped into a quiet room, but she was definitely still at Raine's.

"Can you please come downstairs?"

"Downstairs? Are you here?"

"Yes. I'm outside the building. Can you come out, please?"

"I'm on my way. Don't move." She hung up before I could insist she stay on the line. I went to call her back but decided against it. I didn't want to delay her for even a second.

I paced the sidewalk, my feet beginning to throb now that I'd stopped running and my body was catching up. I ignored them. Jet said something in soothing tones, but I ignored that too. I ignored everything and just paced while I watched the entrance to the building.

After what felt like hours of torture—but was probably merely a few minutes—Mom rushed through the brightly lit lobby and out onto the street, her eyes searching.

We ran into each other's arms. She squeezed me so tightly it almost hurt, but I finally felt as though I could breathe.

"You're scaring me, sweetheart," she said as she finally pulled back, scanning my face. "What's happened?"

"You didn't check in," I croaked, and it sounded pathetic. I sounded like an irrational child.

Mom blinked slowly, then sighed. "Seriously, Amaya Ann? I was having fun at a party. I am sorry I forgot to text you. But holy shit, you just gave me a heart attack." She turned to Jet. "Why didn't you stop her from coming all the way down here?"

He glanced between us, looking like a deer in headlights.

"It's not just that." I drew her attention back to me. "It's Calvin. I just found out and then you weren't answering and I panicked."

She frowned in confusion. "What about Calvin?"

"He's not who you think he is, Mom."

"What?"

"He's Raine Clayton's son." I dropped the bombshell, but it didn't seem to hit its mark.

"Yeah, I know . . ." Mom's frown deepened. Shit, maybe she didn't fully appreciate the danger she was in, or maybe they had her brainwashed—my worst fucking nightmare.

"Viv?" someone called from behind me. "Is that you?"

Mom stepped around me, putting on her people-pleasing smile as she looked down the alleyway that ran down the side of the building.

"Ella? Nessa?" she called to the two women waving at her. "I didn't see you upstairs."

"Oh, we just got here! Come have a drink with us," the second one called, gesturing for Mom to come join them.

"I'm just talking to my daughter. I'll be up soon." Mom turned to face me, effectively dismissing her two drinking-buddy friends.

Whatever she'd been about to say was cut off by the screech of tires.

I turned just in time to see two men step out of an average-looking white SUV right across the alley. I'd barely had a chance to process the situation when an arm wrapped around my middle and yanked me backward.

I screamed.

The shrill sound cut through the warm night, echoing off the buildings.

Two men had my mom by the arms, and as I watched in horror, they shoved her roughly into the back seat of the car.

I screamed again, clawing at the arms keeping me prisoner—keeping me from my mom.

"Let the girl go!" a male voice shouted. A uniformed cop ran toward us from the same corner we'd rounded just minutes earlier. He had his gun drawn and pointed in my direction.

Immediately, I was released. I stumbled slightly as I shouted and pointed at the car. I didn't even know what I was saying, but I needed him to save my mom.

Mom started screaming at the same time, the sound muffled from inside the SUV.

The cop turned his gun in that direction. "Step out of the vehicle, now!" he shouted to the two men inside. Of course, they didn't. They took off, and the policeman fired, taking out a taillight.

One of the men leaned out of the SUV's window, and someone yanked me into the air and spun me around on the spot. Only as the sound of several gunshots rent the air did I realize it was Jet holding me. It had been him all along. He'd grabbed me out of the way when those men snatched my mom, and then he'd shielded me against the wall of the building when they fired at us.

Just as suddenly, his weight disappeared. I pushed off the wall, shaking.

Tires screeched again, and I cried out.

They had my mom!

I took a few running steps after the car, but it was pointless. They were gone. My mom was gone.

"Amaya!" Jet's voice stopped me in my tracks, and I turned around. "Stay with me."

He was crouching by the officer's prone form, holding his dress shirt over the bullet wound as the poor man writhed in pain.

"They're gone." His eyes turned soft as mine narrowed. "I need your help, beautiful. I need your help with this. Please."

I didn't want to help Jet. I wanted to run after my mom. But I couldn't possibly catch a speeding car, and the man on the ground was in real trouble. His arms hung limp beside him, and he'd gone really pale.

I stumbled over and dropped to my knees next to them. Jet took charge, guiding my hands to take over from his and press into the wound. The shirt was soaked, and my fingers felt disgusting in the warm, slippery blood.

"We need to call 911." My voice shook.

But I had no idea where my phone was, and I needed both hands to lean all my body weight into the bullet wound. Jet would have to call.

I looked in his direction, but he was already getting to his feet as he pulled the cop's walkie-talkie off his shoulder.

What the fuck was he doing?

He was going to leave me here, elbow deep in a dying man's blood. Just like everyone else. Everyone left me.

"Officer down!" Jet barked into the walkie as his eyes bored into mine. "Corner of Second and Willow. Two armed perpetrators in a white Toyota RAV4 driving south on Park." He rattled off the license plate number, staring me down as the truth came crashing down around me.

CHAPTER TWENTY-ONE

I'd been scrubbing my hands at the station's bathroom sink for a solid ten minutes, but I just couldn't get the blood out from under my nails. I needed a nail brush to really get under there, and even then . . . I blew out a breath and leaned against the porcelain, the water still running.

Who was I kidding? I was going to have to get a manicure, a whole new set. The thought had barely entered my mind before guilt hit me like a punch in the gut. Avoiding my own reflection in the dirty mirror, I squirted more soap into my hands and started lathering again.

A man had nearly died, and here I was worried about my manicure. I was disgusted with myself.

I scrubbed harder, digging under my nails with my other nails.

Jet placed a gentle hand on my shoulder—barely a soft graze—but I startled anyway.

"Hey," he whispered, dragging his hand down my back.

I shook him off. "I need to wash my hands."

He sighed, then shifted until his front was at my back, his arms coming around me.

"You've been washing your hands for ten minutes. Enough." He said it in a gentle, coaxing tone, but his hands closed around my wrists, and he rinsed my hands for me.

I pushed away from the sink, fully intending to wrench out of his grip, scream at him, kick, punch, *something*. But once I was leaning back into him, all the fight drained out of me, and to my horror, my vision blurred with tears.

Don't cry. Don't cry. Don't cry.

Jet shut the water off and ripped a good chunk of paper towel from the dispenser. The brown paper felt rough against my hands, but he was gentle, patting them dry gingerly, even getting between my fingers.

He dropped the wadded-up towel in the sink, then gripped my shoulders and turned me to face him.

"Amaya," he whispered. So much emotion filled his voice, regret and conviction somehow riding the three syllables of my name.

"Don't," I rushed out. Fucking great. Now my voice was shaky too. I cleared my throat and tried again. "Just don't ask me if I'm OK. I fucking hate it when people ask that. Shit's fucked up. No need to pretend otherwise."

He rubbed my arms up and down, shoulder to elbow, and pulled me in for a hug.

I was too weak to resist. I told myself I'd react the same way if it were anyone else offering me a hug after this nightmare of a night, but that wasn't true. Despite the fact I now knew Jet had been lying to me about many things, I still felt comforted by him—his fresh smell, his sure arms around me, his firm chest under my cheek, his breath fanning the top of my head.

He'd put on a blue T-shirt with the police logo on it. His dress shirt would be totally ruined from all the blood.

I wrapped my arms around his middle and let him hold me, because it was what I needed in that moment. His strength grounded me; my breathing matched to his until the infuriating urge to cry subsided. I refused to shed tears during the conversation we were about to have.

"We don't have to talk about what went down tonight if you don't want to," he said, his arms still tight around my back. "But we do need to talk about what you learned because of it. About who I am."

My time to pull myself together was up. Because he was right—no way in hell was I leaving before I got some answers.

I extracted myself from his embrace and leaned back against the sink. With no idea where to start, I just stared at him. He was the one who had been lying to me from the first time I laid eyes on him—he could explain himself.

He licked his lips and straightened his spine. "I'm an officer with SFPD."

I rolled my eyes. No shit.

"I've been a beat cop since I graduated from the academy, but last year I applied for a spot on a task force, and I got it. It didn't take long for the task force to turn into something much bigger than anticipated. Suddenly, I was in a job that required secrecy, and most of the people I was working with were feds. I mostly just pushed papers, did grunt work for the detectives, but I was happy to be involved."

"I don't need your life story. How the fuck did you end up at my school?" I was being a total bitch, but I'd had one hell of a night, and I felt betrayed. I just wanted to know what was going on.

Jet narrowed his eyes—just slightly, just enough to tell me he wasn't going to take my shit. That was why I liked him so much in the first place.

"Amaya, you need to understand that it's not like I set out to fall for you and deceive you. I was doing my job. I'm telling you way more than I have to, because I want you to know me. I want to be real with you."

He was falling for me? I crossed my arms and chewed on the inside of my cheek. I refused to melt into him before he finished explaining himself. I wasn't about to let him hurt me again if I could avoid it.

Jet dragged a hand down his face and powered on. "A couple of months ago, my superior officers offered me an undercover gig. Some shit had gone down at a private school in Devilbend, and they wanted to see if they could get more info."

"Irene Richards," I said. That whole situation with Harlow and Easton and all the blackmail and threats was insane. It had solidified for us how sinister and dangerous BestLyf was. But then Irene conveniently died in jail before they could get more information from her, and we had to just go on with our lives, keeping our mouths shut and hoping the police did something about it. I guessed this was it.

Jet stared blankly at me, then, reluctantly, gave me a tiny nod.

"I'm guessing one of your superior officers is Detective Hopkins? You're on the BestLyf task force."

He sighed. "There's only so much I can tell you."

It was as good as a confirmation. What the hell else could possibly be happening at Fulton that they decided to set up a *21 Jump Street* situation?

"Anyway, they offered me the chance at a promotion. They said it wasn't an ideal situation due to my lack of experience, but they needed to move on it soon —before the school year ended—and I was the only one who could pass as a teenager." He grimaced, not too happy about his youthful appearance, but I could see why they chose him. As much as I'd questioned his scholarship and transfer so late in the year, I never thought he could be *that* much older than us. He had that round baby face with the dimples and the full, pouty lips.

"So why did they stick you in Devilbend North if you're supposed to be getting in with the rich and famous?" I asked.

"We came up with the scholarship story because I needed to be at Fulton and hanging around you guys, but I couldn't have anyone too interested in me."

"Like the kind of people interested in kids of the rich and famous." If BestLyf dug too deeply because he seemed like a good recruit, his cover would be blown.

"Beauty and brains." He grinned at me, letting those dimples come out to play.

"Don't." I pointed a finger at him. "Do not flirt with me right now. I'm so mad at you."

His grin fell, the serious face replacing it. "Fair enough. There's really not much more I can tell you, but considering what you witnessed, I was given permission to at least clue you in on the basics. Keeping that in mind, do you have any questions?"

I had so many important, relevant questions, but instead I blurted out the first thing that occurred to me. "Wait a minute. Is this why you wouldn't touch me with a ten-foot pole until my birthday?"

He rubbed the back of his neck, looking sheepish. "The age of consent in the state of California is eighteen. It would've been fine if I was actually your age but . . ."

"How old are you?" Oh, Jesus, Allah, and Buddha, had I been getting it on with some middle-aged man?

"I'm twenty-five." Jet pulled his wallet out and showed me his ID. It proved his age, the date right there under his name—Jethro Collin Burns.

"Well, at least your first name is actually Jethro."

"I really am sorry I lied to you." He stuffed his hands into his pockets. "But I was just doing my job. I didn't come into this looking for a relationship."

I stared at him, feeling myself harden inside and out, prepared for the blow. My voice was even, almost monotone, when I spoke. "Right. So this was just part of your cover then. At least I know where I stand now."

Walk away! I screamed at myself in my head, but my feet didn't obey before his hands were on me again.

"Amaya, no." He gripped my shoulders and looked me right in the eyes. "I never intended to get personally involved with anyone, but I did. I was stunned by your beauty as soon as I saw you, and every time we interacted, I knew I was in more and more trouble because I can't get you out of my fucking mind. It was killing me to lie to you. Please, please . . ." His voice shook as he pulled me against his chest.

God dammit but I believed him. I returned his embrace and let myself melt into him again. He had no logical motive to try to manipulate me by declaring his feelings, not now that I knew everything.

"So, what now?" I mumbled into his chest.

"I still have a job to do," he said against my hair. "And to be able to do it effectively, I need you to keep what you learned to yourself."

I stiffened against him, my mind racing. I hadn't really thought about it yet, but of course I was going to tell my friends. My mother had been abducted, I'd been through something traumatic, and all our worst fears about BestLyf were confirmed. They had a right to know the gravity of the situation. There was no way to keep Jet's true identity out of it.

"I have to tell a few friends, Jet. They need to know. And I need them."

He held me out at arm's length and sighed, his face full of disappointment. "I can't let you do that."

"Let me?" I shrugged his hands off. I wasn't sure how much more of this roller coaster I could handle.

"You know what I mean. We can't risk my identity and purpose at Fulton getting out. I'm so close to getting the info we need. And I'm not saying you can't ever tell your friends about us, about it all. Just not yet. I want to be with you, Amaya, more than anything I've ever wanted in my life. After this is all over—"

"I have no one." I cut him off. "Do you understand what you're asking? Those girls are my family. My mom . . ." I clenched my teeth and shoved the overwhelming emotions down. I refused to cry. I'd been a fool to let my guard down with him moments earlier. I wouldn't make that mistake again.

"You're not alone, beautiful. You have me." He moved forward as though to pull me into another embrace. I stepped aside and gave him a hard look.

"No, I don't. You just said it—you want to be together once this is all over. How am I supposed to believe you're not just telling me bullshit so I'll keep my mouth shut?"

He pressed his lips together. I could see frustration rising to meet my defensiveness. I didn't give a shit.

"Come on," he said. "You know that's not what this is. I want to be with you, but I can't risk years of work and the resources of an entire task force, the opportunity to take down some seriously bad people, on some teenage gossip."

I reeled back, momentarily shocked at his dismissive tone. He had no idea what we'd been through because of BestLyf. How dare he insinuate I was being immature or unreasonable after the night I'd had?

The outrage simmering in my veins gave me the strength I needed. I was done with this conversation, this night, and quite possibly, this man.

I stepped up to him and rolled my shoulders back. "Fuck. You," I said in an even, firm tone. Then I walked past him and out of the bathroom.

"Amaya! Wait!" he called after me as I stomped through the station and outside.

I pulled my phone out and swiped away the dozens of missed calls and text messages from my friends. I paused with my thumb over the ride-share app. I needed to get the fuck out of here, but at this time of night, it could take a while to get a ride. Plus, I really didn't want to get into a car with a stranger while my clothes were covered in drying blood.

Chewing on my lip, I glanced behind me. The station was lit up, everything clearly visible through the glass doors. Jet stood a few feet away, speaking to an older man. He kept glancing at me, as if I'd vanish if he didn't keep me in sight. Maybe I would. Maybe it would be better if I did.

The older man started walking away, and Jet threw me one more look, loaded with longing and unspoken things, then reluctantly turned to follow.

I paced the area in front of the door and called Donna.

We never called one another unless it was an emergency. If I'd been woken at two in the morning by a phone call from any of the girls, I'd immediately know it was serious.

Donna picked up on the first ring.

"Amaya? What's wrong?" She sounded a bit winded.

"Hey, D. I need a lift. Can you pick me up?"

"Where are you?"

"Police station downtown."

"I'm on my way."

Just like that. No questions asked.

The roads were dead at this time of night, and I had to pace the entry for only about ten minutes before a pearlescent white BMW pulled up out front. I jogged down the stairs as Donna got out of the car and gawked at me over the top of it.

"Holy fuck, Amaya, what—"

"I need to get out of here. Drive. Please." I cut her off, stopping her from coming around the car and wasting time. She got back behind the wheel and took off as soon as my door closed.

I leaned my head against the seat and squeezed my eyes shut, taking a deep breath. Donna drove in silence for a few minutes, but I couldn't blame her when she started to push for answers.

"You don't have to talk about it right now." Her usually sure, firm voice was soft in the dark car. "But I need you to tell me if you're hurt, at least."

I opened my eyes to see her dividing her attention between the road and my bloodied prom dress.

"Physically or . . ." I waved my hand, looking for the right word. "Existentially?"

"Both?"

"The blood is not mine." I dug around in the glove compartment for the packet of cigarettes I had stashed there. Now that I felt safe, calm, I needed something to occupy my mind so I wouldn't think about all the blood, my mom . . .

"OK." Donna nodded and literally bit her tongue. It was killing her not to grill me for details. It actually made me smile a tiny bit as I lit a cigarette and lowered the window halfway.

Donna wouldn't usually let me smoke in her car, but even she could tell this was a special circumstance.

I pulled deep on the cigarette, feeling the smoke burn my lungs, then held it in for a second before blowing it out the window. The massive drag made me feel slightly lightheaded. Or maybe that was the shock setting in.

"I'm sorry for waking you." I took another drag, staring out the window at the trees flying by as we neared our neighborhood. "Thank you for coming to get me."

"Always," Donna said without a beat of hesitation. "You'd do the same for me."

I nodded. No doubt. I'd drop everything for my three closest friends without a second thought. They were my family. After tonight, maybe the only family I had left.

The next drag was harder to force past the lump in my throat.

"You didn't wake me up anyway," my best friend said, and I remembered that everyone had been at Nicola's afterparty.

"Shit, should you even be driving?" I knew for a fact she'd been drinking at the party.

"It's fine. I haven't had anything to drink for hours. I'm sober as fuck."

Hours. It had been hours since my mom was kidnapped. She could be anywhere by now.

CHAPTER TWENTY-TWO

Dawn was breaking as we pulled into the Meads' driveway. Everything had that muted bluish tinge to it—a new day around the corner.

I didn't want it to be a new day. I had no fucking clue what to do now, and every bit lighter that it got, the more stark that reality became.

Donna and I walked into the house through the side door to the garage—only to find a crowd of people waiting for us.

"What the fu . . ." I trailed off to swallow the lump in my throat. Harlow and Mena immediately stood from where they'd been sitting together at the bottom of the stairs. I'd known they'd be here—we'd planned to all spend the night—but I hadn't expected the others.

Hendrix was leaning on the banister, Turner was sitting on the stairs behind Mena, and Drew sat in the accent chair in the corner. Even Easton was there, still in his nice slacks and shirt. The others had changed into casual clothes, but they all looked exhausted. The girls still had their makeup on.

"Jesus, guys. You have no chill," Donna grumbled.

"Yeah, well, you're the one who wouldn't let us come with you to pick her up." Mena huffed.

"Like you had any chill when you were playing dictator and telling us all what to do earlier?" Harlow raised a brow.

The two girls went to pull me into a hug, but I took a step back, acutely aware of the drying blood all over me.

That was when they saw it too. Harlow gasped and Mena's eyes filled with tears.

"It's not her blood," Donna said softly.

"What are you talking about? Why's everyone here?" I asked.

"We've all been out looking for you, A." Drew slumped forward to rest his elbows on his knees.

"You have?" I gaped at them as the girls decided they didn't give a shit about the blood and pulled me into a hug anyway. I extracted myself quickly. It was hard to fight the emotions welling up when they were hugging me like that.

"Nicola saw you running out of the party looking panicked with Jet chasing after you," Hendrix explained. "And no one could get a hold of you for hours. We were worried."

"Oh." I didn't know what to do with this. They'd all been so worried that they ran around town looking for me. And now these amazing people were all here, making sure I was OK after a sleepless night.

I took a shuddering breath, struggling again to keep my emotions under control.

"Where's Jet?" Donna asked, her expression not giving anything away.

"At the police station still, I assume," I said.

There was a loaded pause, and a few of my friends couldn't help looking at the blood all over me.

Easton broke the silence, surprising me with his question and his deathly calm tone. "Did he hurt you?"

I shook my head but had to take a moment before answering. Because he had hurt me, just not in the way they were concerned about. "No. He saved me. But he lied . . ."

"Lied about what, hon?" Mena asked gently.

"Uh . . ." I suddenly felt so fucking overwhelmed. I looked around wide-eyed at the people who cared about me most, and stuttered. I didn't want to say it. If I didn't say it, I could pretend for just a little while longer that none of it had happened.

My gaze met Turner's and stuck. Whatever he saw in my eyes made him sit up straight.

"This has something to do with BestLyf." It was a statement, his voice certain.

I nodded, and he got to his feet to stand before me.

I kept my eyes on his. I couldn't look at anyone else—they wouldn't really understand. But Turner would. He'd lived this nightmare already.

"They took my mom," I wailed, and the emotional dam finally broke. I caught a glimpse of Turner's devastated expression before my vision blurred, and he pulled me into a fierce hug.

***

I woke up the next morning with a start, the horrible events of the previous night rushing through me as violently as wakefulness. I couldn't even have that second of disorientation where your brain takes a moment to catch up.

"You're OK. You're OK." Mena rubbed my shoulder, sitting down next to me on the couch. "You're at Donna and Harlow's. You're safe."

I drew my knees up to my chest as my heart rate slowed down. I must've fallen asleep on the couch after telling my friends all the gory details of my eventful evening. Fuck Jet for telling me to keep my mouth shut. My friends and I had been in too many situations where secrets blew up in our faces. I may not have been the most intelligent one in our friend group, but I was smart enough to learn from mistakes. I'd told them everything.

Afterward, I'd scrubbed my face and put on borrowed sweats, but I couldn't even remember drifting off. I must've just crashed once the adrenaline vacated my body.

They hadn't left me all alone though. There was an extra pillow and blanket on the sectional where Mena must've slept. Turner was in one of the armchairs. He didn't look as if he'd slept at all.

"Hey, Amaya." The girls' mom walked into the living room with a sad expression on her face.

"Good morning, Emily. Thanks for letting me crash."

"Of course. You know you're always welcome." She sat on my other side and brushed my tangled hair over one shoulder. Such a motherly gesture. I sat up and stretched so I wouldn't cry. "The girls told me what happened. Sweetheart, I'm so sorry."

All I could do was nod and frown down at my lap. What the hell was I supposed to do now?

"I want you to come stay with us a while, all right? And I won't take no for an answer. I don't want you alone in that big house. Especially not now."

I nodded again and managed a croaky "thank you."

"Are you hungry? Magda is nearly finished getting breakfast ready."

The Meads' housekeeper put on an epic breakfast spread, but I wasn't sure I could eat anything. "Maybe just some coffee to start?"

"Sure. You take your time and come get some when you're ready." With that, she left, passing Donna and Harlow on her way out.

"We didn't tell her about Jet," Harlow rushed out as soon as her mom was out of earshot. "Just about how . . . yeah . . . what happened with your mom."

"It's OK." I sighed. "I don't give a shit about keeping his secrets anyway. He can stick them up his tight ass."

"There's my girl." Donna grinned at me.

Turner got to his feet and stretched. "I gotta go home and shower. Get some sleep. I've got a shift tonight."

"Thanks for staying. You didn't have to do that," I told him honestly. I was surprised he'd stayed, but I appreciated it more than I knew how to express. Drew and Easton had left before I got into the details. Hendrix had stayed and was probably still snoring in Donna's bed.

"It was nothing." He shrugged, and Mena walked him out.

I took some time to clean up and head into the breakfast area off the kitchen. Richard Mead had joined the rest of his family, and Hendrix looked as if he'd just dragged his ass down the stairs, while Magda bustled around making sure everyone had what they needed. She placed a steaming mug of coffee in front of me before I even had to ask for it.

"Thank you." I smiled up at her, and she gave me one of her stoic Magda looks and a firm squeeze of my shoulder. I sipped my coffee in silence and watched them all eat as a family.

Would I ever have a family? Or was I doomed to walk through life alone? My dad died when I was a kid, and my mom may as well have died the same day—that was how absent she'd been in my life. Then when it seemed as if she might finally get her shit together, she was taken. And the guy I was falling for wasn't even who he said he was.

Was it me? Was I the problem?

Thank fuck for my best friends. They were the only constant in my life. The only people I could truly rely on.

"I'm gonna head back to my place," I announced, getting to my feet. I appreciated them more than they'd ever know, but seeing them all just . . . *be* together was starting to get overwhelming.

Seven frowns were aimed my way, but it was Richard who spoke. "I insist that you stay with us, Amaya. We want to support you. We want you here."

I gave him a brittle smile. "I know. I will. I just want to go pack some things and . . ." I cleared my throat. "Honestly, I just need a bit of time alone."

Thankfully, no one insisted they come with me, but Donna did drive me home. It may have technically been next door, but both our properties were huge, and it would've taken me a good twenty minutes on foot.

The house was deathly silent when I let myself in. Maybe I was just being dramatic, but it felt empty—barren—in a way it never had. Not even when Mom would disappear on days-long benders.

Two champagne flutes rested on the console table in the foyer, a small bit of flat champagne still sitting at the bottom of one. Mom and Calvin must've had a drink before leaving last night. The other glass had her favorite shade of pink lipstick on the rim.

I picked it up and stared at the imprint of her lips on the glass.

Then I threw it against the wall with a pained, frustrated growl. It shattered, the jagged pieces tinkling on the marble floor.

Everything about this was *total fucking bullshit*. Angry tears stabbed at my eyes as I jogged up the stairs. It was so unfair.

Movement out of the corner of my eye made me freeze at the top of the staircase. I swiped away my tears so I could see properly and nearly called out.

Don't be a fucking horror movie bimbo, Amaya.

Whatever had moved was in the general area of my mom's bedroom. And I knew for a fact she wasn't in there. The smart thing to do would be to go downstairs and get the hell out of this house. I'd come back with someone later—maybe a whole group of someones. Hell, I could get Drew and the entire football team down here if I really wanted to.

But before I could do exactly that, a head peeked out from behind the door to Mom's bedroom. When he spotted me, Calvin came fully out into the open.

"Amaya! Thank god!" He tucked something into his belt as he rushed toward me.

That was a gun. I'd seen enough of them to know that was a damn gun.

"What the fuck are you doing here?" I yelled. I didn't know why—it wasn't as though any of my neighbors' houses were close enough to hear me scream as I got murdered.

His steps faltered—he genuinely looked confused. I saw my opportunity and ran back down the stairs.

"Amaya!" he called after me.

I didn't turn to check if he was chasing me. I just ran for the front door. I flipped the lock, grabbed the handle, and yanked. It opened an inch before Calvin caught up and slammed it closed again, and I screamed.

He backed up, hands held up in front of him, eyes wide. "Amaya. Amaya! I'm not going to hurt you."

"Then why the fuck did you chase me down the stairs?" I screeched.

"Because I need to talk to you. I'm trying to keep you safe." He glanced out the window next to the door.

"Oh, like you kept Mom safe?" I gritted out, breathing hard. Now that flight was no longer an option, my body seemed to be preparing for fight. Too bad there was nothing close by I could use as a weapon. I'd just knee him in the balls.

But Calvin deflated before my eyes, his shoulders slumping and his head falling to his chest as he stumbled backward—away from me. He leaned heavily on the banister.

I glanced at the door. This was my chance to run, but . . . was he crying? His shoulders shook, and when he wiped at his cheeks with the back of his hand, I realized he was indeed crying.

"I didn't think she'd go this far," he said under his breath, but I still heard him.

"Who? Mom?" I took a step closer, no longer interested in running away. Not if he could tell me something about where my mom was. "Where's Mom? I know you know."

He looked at me with a devastated expression. "I swear I don't. I wish I did."

"You have to know something," I spat. "You're Raine's son, aren't you? You run illegal shit for her. Don't deny it. I saw you with Shady. BestLyf took my mom, and you're going to tell me where the fuck they took her so I can get her back."

Calvin slowly straightened, steel entering his spine as his tears dried up. He fixed me with a much calmer look. "Yeah, I'm her son, but I've been slowly pulling out of the illegal shit, *all* of the shit." I scoffed, but he continued. "You don't have to believe me. That's OK. But I do have to keep you safe, Amaya. It's what your mother would want. It's what I want. Now, I want you to go pack a bag. Quickly. I'm going to take you somewhere safe."

I gaped at him. "Are you insane? I'm not going anywhere with you!" I wanted him to tell me where my mom was so I could save her—not take me to her so we could both end up . . . I couldn't think that final thought. I refused to go there.

"Amaya!" It was the first time I'd heard Calvin raise his voice, and it startled me. It was a stark reminder I was alone with a dangerous man.

Before I could even glance at the door, think about running again, it burst open. The glass in the windows on either side of the door rattled with how hard it slammed open as Jet rushed inside, gun at the ready. Within a second, he assessed the situation, placed himself in front of me, and pointed the gun at Calvin.

"Hands behind your head," Jet barked.

"Seriously, Burns?" Calvin sighed, holding his hands out at his sides. "Drop your gun."

"Hands. On. Your. Head." Jet's voice was icy calm.

Calvin gritted his teeth but did as he was told. "This is a waste of time. I hope you have a warrant to enter my place of residence, officer."

"It's detective. And I heard shouting. I had reason to believe someone was in danger." Jet tilted his head to the side just slightly, not taking his eyes off Calvin. "You OK?"

I nodded, then realized he couldn't see me and said, "Yes."

"Anyone else in the house?"

"No," Calvin and I said at the same time.

"Am I under arrest?" Calvin asked, his tone impatient.

"That's yet to be determined." Jet lowered his gun, relaxing slightly as he went to Calvin and searched him. He took the other man's gun and placed it on a side table out of reach. "You have a permit for that weapon?"

"Yes, sir." Calvin seemed to have reached the end of his rope. He turned to address me. "Unless this jerk arrests me in the next three minutes—which he won't—I'm getting out of here. Please come with me."

"No." I shook my head and took a step closer to Jet. I may have been mad at him, but at least I knew I was safe with him. At least I could be positive he didn't have anything to do with my mother's kidnapping.

"I'm just trying to keep you safe. You need to trust me."

"I don't need to do shit."

"She'll be perfectly safe with me," Jet said, angling his body to shield me.

"Now, I'm not placing you under arrest, but we have been trying to get a hold of you since last night."

Calvin scoffed. "Yeah? Well, take a hint. I don't want to talk to any of you. They have the woman I love, and I'm going to do whatever it takes to get her back. Deal's off. Last chance, Amaya." He fixed me with an expectant look. The kind of look a parent would give to a child, expecting them to make the right choice.

"Just leave." I sighed, feeling drained again.

With a resigned nod, Calvin picked up a duffel I hadn't noticed by the door and marched out.

Once the sound of his car starting reached us through the gaping front door, I turned to Jet.

"What deal is he talking about?" I asked.

For a split second he looked as if he was fighting some kind of internal battle, but then he pressed his lips together, and I knew he'd tell me nothing. Just like last night. Just like since the day I'd met the asshole.

I shook my head and rushed back upstairs.

CHAPTER TWENTY-THREE

I locked myself in my room and rage-cleaned. After a good half hour, there was a knock at the door.

"Amaya?" Jet called. "Can you come out, please? We need to talk."

"Fuck off!" I shouted and threw whatever was in my hand at the door. My pen cup smacked against the wood, and pens and pencils scattered everywhere.

"Real mature, Amaya!"

I held up both middle fingers at where I imagined him standing.

After a beat, he let out such a deep sigh I could easily hear it from inside my room. "I'll be downstairs when you cool down."

His footsteps retreated, and I glared at the door. I considered climbing out the window and making a run for it, but he'd hear my car and just follow me to the Meads', so I decided to wait him out instead.

I cleaned my room until it was so tidy it looked as if no one lived there. Then I texted the girls to tell them I was taking more alone time and locked myself in the bathroom. I ran myself a bath and took my sweet time in there. I shaved my legs, washed my hair, did a hair and face mask. I even soaked off my nail extensions. I couldn't stand looking at them, even though I'd gotten them as clean as new. All I could see when I glanced at my hands was the blood that wouldn't come out from under my cuticles.

I ate the three granola bars I'd found in my desk and smoked several cigarettes, but by midafternoon I was starving.

It had been hours since I'd told Jet to fuck off through my door. Surely, he'd given up and left by now. Clean, dry, moisturized, and in comfortable sweats, I poked my head out the door. The house was silent. I made my way downstairs quietly, keeping an eye and ear out for him . . . or anyone else.

He'd really left. I couldn't believe that jerk had actually left! Yes, I'd told him to fuck off, but I didn't want to be alone in this fucking house after the last twenty-four hours. Ugh!

But then, as I made my way to the kitchen, I spotted him. He'd fallen asleep on the living room couch. His shoes were off, one arm thrown over his eyes, his mouth slightly open.

A pang of some emotion shot through my chest. I simultaneously wanted to curl up with him and smother him with a pillow while he was vulnerable. Instead, I saw an opportunity to get away.

Deciding I'd eat at the Meads', I turned to tiptoe back to the front door.

"Don't even think about it." His voice was firm and clear, if a little croaky.

I squeezed my eyes shut and huffed before turning around and heading to the kitchen. If he refused to leave, then I'd just pretend he wasn't here.

As I pulled leftover pasta from the fridge, I could see him out of the corner of my eye—sitting up, rubbing his eyes, checking his phone. Dammit! He really had been asleep for a while, and I might've been able to sneak past him if I'd just come downstairs sooner.

I glared at the microwave as my food turned inside.

"Amaya," Jet said gently, carefully, as he leaned on the counter. The microwave beeped. I grabbed my hot-ass bowl with the lukewarm food inside and made my way out to the patio table.

Not taking a hint, he followed me out after a few minutes with a sloppily constructed sandwich on a plate.

"Sure, help yourself to anything in the kitchen," I deadpanned before shoveling pasta into my mouth.

"Thanks," he said around a mouthful of sandwich. "I'm starving. I've barely eaten all day. I think I needed the sleep more though. I never made it to bed. Just had a shower after I left the station and headed here. Good thing I did too."

I glared at him as he rambled. "Oh my god. I don't give a shit."

He just rolled his eyes, and for a while we ate in silence. The food calmed some of the rage deep in my belly—smothering it with carbs. I pushed the empty bowl away and closed my eyes, enjoying the warm afternoon sun on my face. Well, as much as anyone could enjoy anything after the kind of turmoil I'd had to deal with lately.

"Amaya. Look, I know you're . . ." He sighed. "A lot of things right now. Things I can't even imagine. But I do need to speak with you."

I kept my eyes closed. "As Detective Burns? Or as my ex-boyfriend?"

After a beat of silence, I opened my eyes just in time to see a hint of hurt and uncertainty in his expression. I got a sick kind of satisfaction from knowing that at least some aspect of this mess actually upset him.

"Both," he finally said.

"OK, detective." I sat up straight and folded my hands on the table in front of me—all business. "What's the update on my mother's kidnapping?"

"We ran the plates, but they were stolen. We managed to track the vehicle using CCTV but lost it, so that's a dead end too."

I nodded, pursing my lips. "So that's it? She's gone. Nothing you can do about it? Cool. Thanks for the completely fucking pointless update. Bye now."

"We're exploring other leads. This investigation isn't over."

"What other leads?" I threw my hands up. "We both know it was BestLyf. They're behind this. Why aren't you searching their properties? Why aren't you arresting Raine Clayton?"

"It's not that simple." He gave me a pitying look.

"Don't patronize me," I snapped. "You may be seven years older than you pretended to be, but that doesn't make *me* a child, nor does it make me stupid. I know none of this is fucking simple. And I don't care. Do you get that? They have my mom! What are you doing to find her?"

He didn't rise to my ire, keeping a cool expression and replying in a calm tone. "We have a pretty clear picture of one of the men's faces from a security camera. We're trying to identify him. We're also planning to interview some people."

"Like who?"

"The police officer who was shot, once his doctors permit it. He may have seen something I didn't catch. We're also trying to get in touch with people who were at the party, but it's proving difficult."

"Yeah, I bet it is." Of course Raine and anyone associated with BestLyf would be dodging the police. Bunch of brainwashed assholes.

"We'd also like to speak to the two women your mother spoke to just before she was attacked. Do you happen to know who they are?"

"Yes." I nodded and grabbed my phone. I knew those two bitches all right. I gave him their names and phone numbers, but I didn't know where they lived.

"Thank you. This is helpful." He focused on his phone for a while, probably sending all the information to whoever would look into it.

"Why aren't you guys busting down their doors?" I asked quietly, spinning my phone on the tabletop. "They kidnapped a woman. Isn't that enough?"

Jet sat back in his chair heavily and rubbed his face. "I wish it was."

I scoffed. I wanted to argue more, rage at him, but I knew it wouldn't get me anywhere. I felt utterly defeated.

"Is that all, detective?" I wanted to be alone for a while longer before heading next door.

"Officially—"

I cut him off by pushing my chair back, then collected our plates and headed inside. He followed me.

"I don't want to talk to you about anything else," I said, not looking at him as I dumped the plates in the sink. "If you have any more information about my mother's kidnapping or if I can help in any way, please send someone. You know where the door is."

"Fine then." I could hear the edge of frustration in his reply. "Strictly professionally then, I'm not leaving."

I spun to face him. "What?"

"I spent half the night convincing my superiors that you needed to be under protection. I couldn't convince them to approve a safe house, but they conceded to having an officer with you for the next few days—at least until we know more."

"OK, then have them send an officer to the Meads' place. I'll be staying there for a while."

"I volunteered for the assignment."

I groaned. Of course he did.

I contemplated going to the Meads' anyway and making him sit out in his car, but I didn't want to bring this bullshit to their door. The drama with Jet was irritating, but if an argument really could be made that I needed armed protection, that was a whole other ball game. I couldn't go if there was a chance of danger following me.

Glaring at Jet, I called Donna.

"Hey, girl!" she answered on the second ring. "Was starting to think you'd drowned in that bath. You heading over?"

"Hey. Actually, I'm going to stay home." I gave her a rundown of the situation. Naturally, she still insisted I come stay with them. Then Harlow got on the phone and tried to do the same. Even Emily interjected, taking the phone from her daughter to speak to me. She demanded I put Jet on, and he answered multiple questions politely and professionally. He even recited his badge number.

I had to turn away to hide the smile that brought to my lips. It was nice to have someone looking out for me.

After we hung up, I went back to my room and back to ignoring Jet.

Not even half an hour had gone by when the doorbell rang, immediately putting me on edge. Poking my head out of my bedroom, I was grudgingly thankful to see Jet going to the door with his hand hovering over the gun at his hip.

But it was just Emily Mead. I took a moment to tuck the emotion and amusement away before heading down.

She'd brought over a clearly store-bought pie, saying she was dropping off a home-cooked meal for me while suspiciously eyeing Jet. I reassured her I was OK, and she left.

The pie was from an artisan bakery nearby, and it tasted delicious. I had it for dinner and didn't offer Jet any. He helped himself to some anyway. Jerk.

I went to bed early, determined to avoid him, and tried to read. But I had trouble focusing on the words and sentences. My mind was racing.

I couldn't stop thinking about my mom and where she might be. If she was OK. If I'd ever see her again. Then some alarmed voice in my mind would cut in with horror scenarios that included masked men barging into the house, shooting Jet dead, and taking me.

Every little sound from outside, every shift of the house, put me on high alert. I was a fucking mess inside, and I didn't have the adrenaline crash and absolute exhaustion that had made me pass out the previous night.

A little before midnight, I gave up trying to sleep and slowly padded my way downstairs.

I didn't want to admit to myself I was looking for Jet, but I was. I felt so alone, and he was the only other person in the house.

All the lights were out, but the telltale flicker of the TV in the front room lit up the foyer, so I headed there. This room was a bit more formal than the open-concept space at the back of the house with the kitchen. It wasn't used as often, but it was expertly decorated in creams and royal blues. The TV—normally hidden behind built-in cabinet doors—was on with the volume down. I didn't even register what was playing; I just headed for the couch under the window and folded myself into the corner, leaning against the armrest.

There was a whole other three-seater on the opposite side of the coffee table, and a comfy armchair, but I'd plonked myself down next to Jet. He sat reclined in the couch's other corner, a throw blanket over his lap.

He tracked my movements carefully but didn't try to talk to me. I was more thankful for that than he knew. I didn't want to talk. I wanted to sit in silence and just be. Only not by myself.

I turned my face to the screen but didn't even remotely pay attention to what was on it. Jet was looking at the screen too, but I could sense his focus on me.

After a beat, he sat up, draped the throw over my lap, and leaned back into his spot.

He'd changed out of his slacks and shirt and tie. The sweats and ribbed tank he had on now made his shoulders look even bigger than they were. He looked like the Jet I knew—the one I'd been falling for—in his casual clothes. It made my heart ache.

He was sitting right next to me, and I missed him so damn much.

Life was a fucking bitch sometimes.

I tried to spread the blanket so we could share it, but it was way too small. With a resigned sigh, I scooted closer and draped it over both our laps. Our legs were touching.

The whole thing was ridiculous. Neither of us really needed a blanket on such a warm night anyway. But I was still in the whole self-denial stage. The blanket made it easier to pretend I wasn't trying to get closer to him, because it hurt to have any distance between us.

He draped one arm over the back of the couch and looked at me, still not saying anything. His expression held no judgment, no expectations. He was just . . . open to whatever I needed.

Not allowing myself to think about it, I leaned sideways and settled into his side. After a beat, he gently wrapped one arm around me.

In a corny moment worthy of a Lifetime movie, we both released a small sigh, relief palpable in the sound. Why did it feel so damn good to be in his arms? He made me feel so safe. Despite all the bullshit keeping me up, I actually felt calm. He made something deep inside me, something intrinsic, believe everything would be OK.

But the practicalities of everything going on just wouldn't let up.

"What's going to happen to me?" I asked, my voice small.

He leaned back to look at me. "What do you mean?"

I started fiddling with the hem of his tank. "I don't know. Like, what am I supposed to do now? What if Mom needs to be in the hospital for a really long time? What if they don't find her . . ." I couldn't even go there. "I know I've had to learn to be really independent, but fuck. This is different, Jet. Is the house mine now? What about all the other assets? I don't even know who our lawyer is. I can't do this."

"Yes, you can," he said, not a hint of uncertainty in his voice.

"Jet, what's going to happen?" I asked again.

He stared me down, a million complicated things in his gaze. "I don't know, princess," he finally answered. "No one ever really knows what's going to happen. Life just doesn't work that way. But what I do know is that you won't have to deal with it alone. You have the fiercest, most supportive friends I've ever seen. I have no doubt whatsoever that they'll be ready to do whatever you need. And I know shit between us is . . . uncertain right now, but I'm not going anywhere. Not until I'm absolutely sure you're safe. Not as long as you want me around."

"I don't want you around," I declared, gripping his tank in a tight fist. I appreciated what he was saying. I'd needed the reminder that I had people in my corner. It soothed some of my panic. But I didn't want to dwell on it.

My head was all over the place—wanting to sit in silence one minute, then wanting to talk the next. Wanting him gone, then searching him out. Asking questions, then deflecting when he answered them.

"You sure about that?" Jet raised one eyebrow, glancing pointedly at where I was clutching his clothing.

"Positive." I met his eyes, still gripping the fabric in my fist.

"Then let go, Amaya."

The challenge was clear in his intense stare, but I didn't want to let him go. Not really. Not in this moment or in the bigger-picture context.

So instead of pushing him away, I pulled him closer and kissed him hard.

CHAPTER TWENTY-FOUR

His hand threaded into my hair, and he met the challenge with gusto. Our tongues battled for dominance, teeth clashing.

We were both desperate—maybe for different reasons, but the resulting intensity only amped up. I poured all my desperation, all my frustration and uncertainty, into him. He took it all and then some, giving me exactly what I needed. As he always did.

I yanked on that tank top, and he helped me get it off, putting his glorious body on display. I straddled him as I took off my own pajama T-shirt. He was already hard for me, and I ground myself on his erection. Lightning sparks of pleasure shot through my body, driving me to keep rolling my hips, keep chasing that feeling.

Jet sat up, his hands splayed on my back to keep me from falling backward. His hot mouth trailed messy kisses and scrapes of teeth down my neck until he reached my breasts. They weren't big, but I'd never had any complaints, and Jet groaned as that mouth of his closed around a pert nipple.

He grabbed my ass with one hand, his other holding me close to his mouth as he got his fill of my tits. His hips gyrated, moving with me as I rubbed myself on his hardness, getting that friction right on my clit.

It was heady, this feeling—addictive—having him hold me as I chased my pleasure on his lap. But I'd never been one of those girls who could come from dry-humping. Fun as it was, there were still too many layers of clothing between us.

I angled his head back so I could kiss him deeply, then scooted backward. My core clenched at the loss of friction, but I dropped to my knees on the soft carpet anyway. A wet patch showed on his sweats—a darker spot of gray right over the outline of his dick under the fabric. Evidence of how turned on we both were, how hot we were for each other.

Jet sat up, his body following mine, but I stopped him with a firm hand to his chest and shoved him back against the cushions. He looked so damn fuckable, lounging back with his knees wide and his smooth chest heaving, those eyes dark and needy.

I did that to him. I had him looking dazed and crazed with lust, and that made me near euphoric. It was proof I still had control over some things. I still had agency.

Seizing the hem of his sweats, I pulled, and he lifted his hips for me. He wasn't wearing any underwear, and his cock sprang free, slapping against his toned abs. I shoved his pants down to his ankles, and he kicked them off.

The hair on his legs was coarse as I ran my palms up his shins, then added more pressure as I moved up the thighs. His dick twitched when I dug my nails in closer to his groin. I caressed his thick length with my palm, from base to tip, spreading the bead of pre-cum with my thumb. His cock felt so hard in my grip, hot and firm, and I wanted to lick it.

I'd never really been into sucking dick. It was fun to read in my romance novels, but anytime I'd come face-to-face with one, I'd turned my nose up at it. I just didn't see the appeal. But I wanted Jet's cock in my mouth. I wanted to taste him so badly my mouth watered.

Gripping him firmly at the base, I slid my tongue up the underside all the way to the swollen head. That part was softer against my mouth. I ran my lips over it gently, then licked the salty pre-cum off them. Raising my eyes to watch him, I opened my mouth and sucked Jet's hard cock into it.

He struggled to keep his gaze locked on mine as his eyes rolled and he released a low groan.

The sound made me clench my thighs. The sight of how much I could affect him with nothing more than my mouth sent a rush of desire shivering through my body.

I sucked him off slowly, taking my time and absorbing every hitch of his breath, every twitch of his abs, every little reaction to what I was doing to him. I may have been the one on my knees, but he was at my mercy. There was something perversely gratifying about the knowledge that I could clench my jaw and bite into his cock at any moment, that he trusted me enough not to. Something addictive about learning which movements elicited the best reactions.

"Fuck, beautiful." He groaned. "I'm gonna spill down your throat if you don't stop that."

I sat back, licking my tingling lips as I contemplated the idea. I wanted him to come in my mouth. Just the thought of being able to make his body do that had more moisture seeping out between my legs.

Jet just sat there, breathing hard, his swollen, glistening cock on his belly as he waited for my next move. He was totally letting me take the lead.

I decided to indulge in my newest fantasy another day. I needed him inside me *now*. We'd waited for so long, and I didn't want to wait any longer.

I got to my feet and pushed my sleep shorts and underwear down in one go.

Jet's head tipped back against the cushions as he gazed up at me. I stood before him completely bare.

He'd made me feel stripped bare more times than I could count—completely emotionally exposed. This time, I'd bared myself to him intentionally. It was *my* choice. And he was just as bare for me. He was spread open and willing, waiting for me to take what I wanted from him—body and soul.

I moved to straddle him at the same time he leaned over to grab his wallet off the coffee table. He ripped a condom out and rolled it onto his length while I caressed his shoulders, letting my tits hang in front of his face.

He darted his tongue out to lick a nipple, then leaned back once more and gripped his dick at the base.

I shifted closer, holding on to the back of the couch for balance as I positioned myself. With our gazes locked, I sank down onto Jet's cock. I was so ready, so wet, that he slid in easily. I sighed at the feeling of stretching, the welcome intrusion of his body into mine.

Jet sat up and wrapped his arms around my back, and I spread my knees as wide as they'd go. For a few moments we just stared at each other, not moving, just feeling this wonderful sensation of togetherness. Our foreheads touched, and we breathed each other's air. The pressure, the urge to move, built up and up inside me until it was impossible to ignore.

I rolled my hips.

A surprised gasp of pleasure escaped my parted lips at how fucking good it felt. I was hyperaware of every inch of him inside me, every little twitch of his legs, every shift of his body against mine.

I tilted my head to the side, and our lips met in a deep, all-consuming kiss. We started to move, our mouths and bodies flowing in rhythm. His tongue licked at the inside of my mouth just like his cock was caressing the inside of my pussy.

I'd never had sex like this. The position, sure, but not this intensity. With the deep emotions between us, it felt as if he was reaching places deep inside me— places no one else could reach.

I guessed sex was like that when you loved the person you were having it with.

The realization made me gasp, but Jet didn't notice. He leaned back on the couch and gripped my hips, his eyes fixed on the spot where our bodies connected.

The new angle made me moan, and I decided to ignore the realization about the man between my legs. Just for now. Just while I enjoyed these feelings in the most physical, carnal way.

I grasped the back of Jet's neck with one hand and propped the other on his knee as I started to fuck him in earnest.

He caressed my body, dug his fingers into my hips, and thrust up to meet my movements. But for the most part, he lay back and let me take what I needed. I lost myself in the feeling—yes, the pleasure between my legs, but also the satisfaction of being in control. His strong body was splayed out below me as I rode his dick harder.

My entire lower body started to tingle as his pelvis slammed against my clit with every stroke. I ground myself on him, feeling him deep inside me, and surrendered to the pleasure. The heat at my core burst, carried by those tingles up my chest and into my head, running down my arms.

The orgasm seemed to go on and on but was no less intense for its duration. I moaned and writhed through it while Jet kept thrusting upward, shoving me down onto his thick cock with a bruising grip on my hips.

I released a sound somewhere between a sob and a laugh as it finally faded.

"You are so fucking beautiful when you come," Jet whispered, his voice strained. He brushed messy hair off my sweaty forehead and peppered gentle kisses all over my neck and shoulders.

I couldn't speak, so I just hummed as I struggled to catch my breath.

Jet gave me a few moments to recover before he moved. He held me tightly to his chest and stood up from the couch with ease. As if he wasn't tired from the sex so far—as if I weighed nothing.

I gasped in surprise and wrapped my tired limbs around him. Still buried inside my dripping core, he walked across the room, through the foyer, and up the stairs to my bedroom.

By the time he lowered me onto my bed and settled himself on top, I was writhing against him once more. The way he'd carried me through the house, his strong arms keeping me safe and still firmly on his dick, was sexy as hell. And the movement of him inside me as he'd climbed the stairs had me squirming.

He hitched one of my legs up high and let the other fall open on the bed. Then he positioned himself just so, one knee bent higher than the other, and pulled almost all the way out. His eyes did that fluttering, rolling-into-the-back-of-his-head thing again as he slid all the way back in. He did it a few more times—all the way out, then all the way in—slowly, feeling every inch as my pussy clenched and pulsed around him involuntarily.

His hips started to pump faster and faster. I was so wet and messy the sound coming from between us was obscene as it mingled with our moans and grunts. I clawed at his back, feeling his lithe muscles move, wanting to draw him closer.

He kept pounding into me until his movements became as sloppy as the sounds of our fucking. Then every muscle in his body went tense as he moaned long and loud, his hips slamming home one last time as he came hard.

My second orgasm took me by surprise. It was just as intense as the first, but it burst through me with such unexpected force that I screamed.

It took us a long time to catch our breath. We were spent and sweaty, but we remained tangled together, kissing and nuzzling and holding each other. It was downright fucking romantic, and it made me think of my earlier realization that I loved him.

Thankfully, I was too tired to freak out about it. Even more thankfully, Jet was alert enough to go to the bathroom and clean up, then return with a warm, damp towel. He gently and lovingly cleaned me up too. Then he crawled into the bed and covered us with the sheets.

"I love you," I murmured before I could stop myself. I was half-asleep, and the words just tumbled out onto the soft sheets between us. I kept my eyes closed to give myself an out. If he mentioned it the next day, at least I could pretend I had no recollection of saying it.

Jet placed the softest, gentlest kiss on my cheek before replying. "I love you too."

There was no doubt or uncertainty in his voice.

I snuggled into his side and smiled against his warm, bare shoulder. I was terrified to say it to him with my eyes open, in the stark light of day, but even more, I was excited. Because I did love him, and as scary as it was to say, it was worth the risk to hear him say it back, to know he meant it.

CHAPTER TWENTY-FIVE

I woke up with Jet's arm draped over my waist, the sheets tangled around our legs. Maybe it was the comforting presence of a strong body at my back, or maybe just that the trauma was no longer so fresh, but I didn't jerk into wakefulness in a panic as I had the day before. I had that hazy moment of blissful ignorance. My brain was slower to wake up and, therefore, slower to remember the situation I was in.

I thought I'd wanted this moment of respite when I woke up yesterday, but now that I was having it—and the crash of emotions that came when the memories rushed back in—I realized I'd been an idiot. This was so much worse. It was like experiencing it all over again.

Jet must've felt my body stiffen, because he tightened his grip on me and kissed the back of my head. *I've got you*, he seemed to be saying without words.

"Are you supposed to be sleeping on the job?" I asked.

He yawned before answering. "There was a patrol car parked out front until six. I've been on shift and awake since then. Don't worry, you're safe."

I didn't know what to say to that. I didn't feel safe—physically or emotionally. I had no idea where we stood, and I didn't have the emotional bandwidth to even think about it.

Instead of trying to come up with a response, I got up and headed for the shower.

My bedroom was empty when I got out, and as I headed downstairs, I could make out several voices coming from the kitchen.

"Bullshit!" Harlow dragged the word out as she yelled it. I could make out Donna's voice next but not what she was saying.

Keeping my steps light, I crept toward the kitchen. As I rounded the corner, the scene and conversation came into focus.

Jet was sitting at the island, and Donna, Harlow, and Mena stood on the opposite side with their arms crossed and their stares lethal. They were tearing him a new one.

I almost felt sorry for him.

"Do any of you seriously think I intended for any of this shit to happen?" Jet asked, sighing deeply. My friends remained silent. Only a brief glance from Mena told me they knew I was there. "I was supposed to go in, make friendly with the students, and dig up information. My assignment wasn't to single out Amaya, or to fucking fall for her. Jesus, they could have my badge for this if they really decide to throw the book at me. The only thing that's saving me is the fact she was eighteen before anything happened—and that everyone's too damn busy to worry about ethical gray areas right now. I didn't set out to hurt anyone. Especially her."

"Yeah, well, you did," Donna declared, her no-bullshit lawyer face on. "And it would serve you right if you did lose your job."

Jet laughed, kind of maniacally. "I'm not sure I even care anymore. All I've ever wanted was to make detective, and I did it with this task force, but all I can think about is Amaya—being with her, seeing her safe and happy. I love her, and I just want this bullshit to be over."

"So, what do you expect us to do now?" Harlow popped her hip, full of attitude.

"Leave," Jet said, sounding impatient. "None of you should be here right now. And since we all want the same thing—to be there for Amaya—maybe cut me some fucking slack."

"Don't use that tone with my friends," I snapped, walking into the kitchen.

Jet sat up ramrod straight, his eyes doing a quick scan of my body. "You should've heard how they were talking to me earlier."

"They're protecting me." I shrugged, getting a bowl of cereal ready.

"*I'm* protecting you," he argued.

"I don't need your protection."

"You just said your friends were protecting you!"

"I meant it figuratively. Like, emotionally and shit. You're saying it literally, and I don't think it's necessary." I'd spent my entire shower thinking about this. "I don't think I'm in any danger. They must have taken Mom because of whatever she got mixed up in at BestLyf and maybe because of Calvin. They might be after him too—he was pretty twitchy yesterday—but I don't think they give a shit about me. I've had nothing to do with anything. I didn't even connect the dots that Mom was mixed up with these whacks until the other day." God, was that only the other day? It felt like a year ago, and it wasn't lost on me that my panic in that moment had been warranted.

"You sound like Hopkins," Jet grumbled. The girls and I exchanged glances at the mention of the detective Harlow had dealt with after all the craziness with Irene. At least we could be sure Jet was reporting to Detective Hopkins now and was on the same task force.

"So, Hopkins didn't think I needed protection either, huh?" I shoveled cereal into my mouth, slurping and crunching it obnoxiously.

"No. No one thought it was worth our limited resources." He scoffed.

"But you convinced them otherwise?" Mena pushed.

"Yes. Because I refuse to leave Amaya unprotected and vulnerable."

I sighed and gave the girls a pleading look. *What am I supposed to do? Yeah, he lied, but he has a pretty good excuse for it. And he loves me.*

Donna raised a single eyebrow, only slightly. *He's definitely saying all the right things, but I still don't like that he lied to you.*

I rolled my eyes. *I know! Same. But . . .* I bit my lip and glanced at him. *He's so cute though. And he's being all protective. And I think I love him too.*

Mena bounced on her toes and grinned as she gave me a meaningful nod. *Aww! You love him? I think you should forgive him. I think you already have. You guys are so cute.*

I bugged my eyes out at her. *Stop!*

Harlow slowly crossed her arms and stared at me until I met her gaze. Her lips rose into a smirk, and she glanced between me and Jet before fully grinning. *You guys totally did it.*

"Shut up," I said out loud, pointing a finger at her.

Jet looked between us, a deep frown on his face. "What have I missed?"

The girls and I burst into laughter, which made Jet even more confused. It was a wonderful little release of tension.

"You're in luck." Donna put him out of his misery. "We discussed it, and we've decided you're forgiven."

Harlow came around the island and sat down next to him, giving him a pat on the shoulder. "We just want what's best for our girl, and you seem to be it, so yeah. You're forgiven but not off the hook."

"Think of it as a probationary period." Mena leaned on the counter. "Don't fuck it up."

"Huh?" Jet pinched the bridge of his nose. "You discussed it? Discussed what? And when?"

Harlow tapped her temple and bugged her eyes out at him. "We have ESPN."

The girls chuckled at her joke and Jet's continued confusion, but I couldn't find it in me to be happy. Even the laughter from a few moments earlier—the laughter I'd been so grateful for—had me feeling guilty. I had no business laughing while my mom's life was in danger.

Jet's warm fingers wrapped around my hand, pulling my attention back into the room. He gave me a tentative tug, and I went willingly into his embrace. He held me tightly for a moment, his strong arms around my back, his knees on either side of my hips where I'd stepped between them.

I breathed him in, let his fresh, bergamot-tinged scent ground me.

"Amaya." He tenderly brushed my hair back from my face and opened his mouth, no doubt to say something comforting. Some bullshit placating comment I just didn't want to hear.

"I need to do something," I rushed out before he could. "Please, Jet. I know you can't tell me any of your super-secret, classified cop information or whatever, but I can't just sit around and worry. It's killing me."

"I can only imagine how hard this must be, princess." He gave me that puppy-dog face—the one that told me he wasn't going to give me what I wanted, but he also didn't want me to be mad at him. "But I won't do anything that will put you in danger."

I stepped out of his embrace but kept a hand on his shoulder. "I'm not asking you to. I'm just asking you to talk to me. We've been dealing with BestLyf bullshit all year. There has to be something we know, something we can do to help, even if it's the smallest little detail . . ." I wasn't even sure what I was saying anymore, what I was asking.

"Why have no arrests been made?" Donna asked. She could tell I was floundering, and she got right to the point. God, I loved her.

"They don't have enough evidence or something." I huffed. Jet had explained this yesterday.

"What does that mean?" Donna pressed.

"We've been building a case against—" Jet stopped himself, clearly fighting an internal battle. He wanted to tell me more, but his sense of duty was strong. "We've been building a case. This has been in the works for some time—over a year. Those in charge don't want to make a move—and alert *anyone* to the level of the investigation—unless we are positive that what we have is airtight. Do you understand? We want to do this once, do it well, and make sure it sticks."

"Kidnapping isn't enough?" Donna asked. "It happened in front of two police officers. How is that not enough?"

"It's a crime, certainly, and it's being taken seriously. It's being investigated."

"And off the record?" Harlow leaned forward, and we all held our breath, waiting to see if he'd break and give us more info.

Jet pressed his lips together so hard they went white. Then he released a massive breath and hung his head, and I knew we had him.

"Off the record, we know this was BestLyf, probably at the direct order of Raine Clayton, but we don't have enough to tie it all together. It's not like Raine jumped out of that car in her cocktail dress and shoved your mom into the trunk herself." I winced at the visual, and he gave my hip a squeeze. "Sorry."

"It's OK." I waved him off. "What would be enough? What do you have now? Maybe we can help you find the evidence you need."

"I can't go into specifics of what evidence we already have." Four feminine, exasperated sighs filled the air, but Jet just raised his voice slightly and kept speaking. "And not just because of legal reasons. It's too complex, too many different angles and connecting stings to go over. Some of it may be related to your mom's kidnapping, but none of it may be. The best approach is to find her—solve this crime—and see if we can connect it back to BestLyf."

"How would we connect it back to BestLyf?" Mena asked.

"You wouldn't do anything. We—as in, the police—would need solid evidence."

"Like . . ." Donna made a beckoning gesture that invited him to go on.

"Like tracking down the car and having it be registered to someone in Best-Lyf, but the plates were stolen and we can't find it. Like arresting the two assholes who grabbed her and getting their confessions, but that's been a dead end so far. Like getting confirmed correspondence between Raine and the kidnappers saying, in no uncertain terms, 'go steal this person.' Like finding your mom in a building owned by BestLyf or Raine Clayton."

"Can't you just search all the properties owned by BestLyf?" I asked.

"On what grounds?" He gave me a desperate look and shook his head, dejected.

"What if you knew where Vivian was being held?" Donna suggested. I could see the wheels turning in her head.

"Then we would be able to go get her, assuming the information was solid."

"How solid? What if it was from an anonymous source?"

"It would need to be a very reliable source or come with very convincing information. Especially if the property happens to be tied to BestLyf."

"What are you thinking, D?" I asked.

"I'm thinking we know a lot of people in high and low places, and it's time we start getting in touch."

"I have a list of BestLyf-owned properties," Harlow announced, pulling her laptop out of a bag on the floor. "And those owned privately by BestLyf members. Although that second list is still being compiled."

"What?" Jet gaped at her. "How? Compiled by whom?"

"I can speak to Jayden. I don't think he'll know anything, but it's worth a shot," Mena said.

"Mena, no. You don't have to do that." I shook my head. He was her bully, and she'd just offered to casually call him and ask about a major crime that had recently been committed.

"I know I don't. But it's OK. I'm OK. I got this." She gave me a confident smile and pulled her phone out, walking over to stand by the window.

"I'll try Will. He fucking owes me." Donna pulled her phone out too, ready to call her piece-of-shit ex.

Harlow clicked away at her keyboard, probably talking to some hooded figure in a dodgy corner of the internet.

My throat got tight as I watched them go into action. For me. I'd lost track of the number of times I'd cried or held back tears in the past few days. I truly had the best friends in the world.

I made a fresh pot of coffee and called Nicola. Our friend's mom was a famous actress and had been involved with BestLyf for years. Nicola herself constantly talked about the youth program. They may have been too entrenched in the whole web, but I figured it was worth a shot.

For the rest of the morning, we made phone calls and had unpleasant and sometimes boring conversations.

Jayden didn't know anything, but he did give Mena the number of one of his dad's friends who used to be at BestLyf but was firmly in the "they are the devil" camp now. We couldn't get through to him, but Jet took the information and passed it on to his colleagues to look into—anyone who hated BestLyf could be helpful in providing information to bring them down.

Will was a dick on the phone. I could only hear Donna's side of the conversation, but I could tell she was losing her patience. In the end, he gave us a few addresses in the surrounding Devilbend area—places that had been used for the illegal fights his dad ran.

My conversation with Nicola was pointless and painful. She'd heard about my mom's kidnapping and was being a supportive friend—asking questions, offering to come over. I didn't know how to come out and say, "Hey, does your mom know any places where her self-improvement cult might be holding my mom hostage?" and I couldn't figure out how to bring up BestLyf in a roundabout way.

Harlow had a whole army of hackers using definitely illegal means to look at security camera footage around the list of addresses she had. But there were a lot of addresses, and it was taking forever.

Jet had moved to the other side of the room and would cover his ears anytime Harlow opened her mouth. His attempts to avoid seeing or hearing anything illegal would've been amusing if I weren't in an almost constant state of panic.

"Thanks for trying, guys," I said, feeling defeated as I passed around the Chinese takeout we'd ordered for lunch.

"We're not done." Harlow covered my hand with hers. "I still have my guys checking the addresses."

"Lalalala!" Jet covered his ears and yelled over her. I smacked him, and he got back to slurping his noodles.

"I do have one more idea but . . ." Donna chewed her lip. "It might be more trouble than it's worth."

"Then it's probably not worth it," Jet supplied unhelpfully.

I sighed. "Shady," the girls and I all said at the same time, and I nodded at Donna. "Do it."

At this point, I'd make a deal with the devil himself to get my mom back. Shady couldn't be any worse.

CHAPTER TWENTY-SIX

Donna typed out a message, and we all tried not to watch her phone as we ate. By the time we finished, he'd replied, and another half hour later we were pulling into the parking area of Oak Hill Park to meet him.

"This is so dumb. I can't believe I'm letting you do this," Jet grumbled, gripping the wheel tightly.

I huffed. "You're not *letting* me do shit. I was going to do this with or without you."

"I know," he gritted out. "That's why I'm letting you do it."

He'd insisted on coming but tried to talk me out of it the whole way there. We'd been bickering the entire drive, but I was secretly glad to have him by my side. Every time we interacted with Shady, we walked away with one of us owing him something. Being in debt to a criminal like him was stressful as fuck.

It took us a while to find a spot in the almost-full parking lot. It was a beautiful summer day, if a little hot, and people were out enjoying it. Several groups had picnics set up in the shade of the tall trees, and a couple walked up the hiking path and disappeared around a bend.

The five of us wandered over to the main path. I did my best not to run and look as frantic as I felt. Harlow still had to grip my arm hard a few times to stop me from rushing ahead.

Where the hell was that deviant?

All I could see were families and groups of friends having a fun day. No tracksuits as far as the eye could see.

"Donna." I sighed.

She gave me a small smile. "I already texted him."

Jet mumbled some more about what a bad idea this was.

A few minutes later, Shady emerged from the same path that the hiking couple had gone down. He was in shorts and sneakers but still wore a loose-fitting, lightweight tracksuit on top. Even with it zipped only halfway, the sky-blue garment looked out of place in the heat of the afternoon. No more than the two chihuahuas he was walking, though.

He sauntered up to us, two diamanté-encrusted leads clutched in his fist as the little dogs pranced obediently by his side.

We all gaped at the tiny dogs. Shady's unimpressed glower didn't waver.

He also didn't stop. Just walked right past us toward the parking lot.

"Shady! What the hell?" Donna called after him, and he stopped, looking over his shoulder.

"Hey, girl." He gave Donna a sleazy smile. "You looking fine, but I gotta get these two rats home. They need their nap."

One of the "rats" yipped, and they both wagged their little tails as they stared up at him.

"You said you'd talk to us." Harlow huffed.

"I said I'd talk to *her*." Shady pointed at Donna. "Now, I expected her to bring you three. But you should all know better than to bring a cop along for a ride with me."

For a moment, no one spoke, and the corner of Shady's mouth quirked up into a satisfied smirk.

"Jet? He's not a cop. He's just my boyfriend." I laughed, hoping I wasn't laying it on too thick.

"Yeah, he goes to our school," Mena added.

"You four should know not to bullshit me." Shady shook his head like a disappointed parent, but I didn't miss the malice in his gaze. He was pissed. I wasn't too proud to admit that scared me. He was a dangerous man.

"It's OK." Jet waved his hand dismissively. "Yeah, I'm a cop. But the reason why Donna reached out to you stands. My occupation is irrelevant."

Shady scoffed. "The fuck it is. I've got nothing to say to any of you." Both the chihuahuas barked. Then one of them sniffed the ground and squatted to start pushing out a poo.

"I'm not interested in whatever petty shit you've got going on," Jet snapped. He stood with his hands in his pockets, casual to anyone looking over from a distance. But his shoulders were back, his feet planted, his eyes hard. The air of authority about him had my heart skipping a beat. "I'm not here to arrest you. We just want some information. Give it to us, and we can all get on with our days and pretend like this little picnic never happened."

Shady folded his hands in front of his body and cocked his head to the side. The two men shared an extended stare-off, sizing each other up or whatever. The girls and I shared exasperated looks.

"What's in it for me, pig?" Shady finally asked, licking his bottom lip as if he could taste the leverage he was about to have over a cop.

"How about I don't arrest you?" Jet said.

Shady threw his head back and laughed. "For what? I'm just out here walking my buddy's dogs, enjoying this glorious day."

"Refusing to assist a police officer."

"I'll be out before dinnertime."

"Not picking up after your dogs." We all looked down at the little pile of poo next to Shady's foot. The chihuahuas cocked their heads and started wagging.

"Not an arrestable offense." Shady produced a poo bag from his pocket with a flourish. He bent down, scooped the poop, and tied the little baggie off expertly.

"True. You clearly know the laws." Jet nodded, and Shady shrugged with a smug smile. "And since you're so knowledgeable about the laws, then I'm sure you're aware of the ones around carrying a concealed weapon. How about I arrest you for that handgun tucked into your ugly shorts? Hmm?"

Shady ground his teeth.

I had an irrational urge to drag Jet into the bushes and get him naked. The way he was handling a man who scared the crap out of me was such a turn-on.

"Have you got a permit for that weapon? Anything else on your person I should be aware of before I search you? How about that black SUV with your two buddies sitting in it watching our every move? Anything inside that vehicle that might be illegal?"

"What the fuck do you want?" Shady snarled, glaring at us girls.

Jet removed his hands from his pockets and got in Shady's face, any semblance of casual calm gone. "Don't look at them. Don't even fucking think about them. Look at me."

Shady glared at Jet instead but didn't step back. The dogs barked and growled, getting worked up.

"Call off your dogs," Jet demanded.

Shady clicked his fingers. "Sit." The little doggies sat and calmed down immediately.

"The other ones."

With a sigh, Shady gestured dismissively over Jet's shoulder. I whipped my head around just in time to see two men climbing back into a black SUV.

"Now, you give us some information, and you're free to go. It's as simple as that." Jet stepped out of Shady's space and stuffed his hands back into his pockets.

"What information?"

"Two nights ago, a woman was kidnapped from downtown Devilbend. I want to know where she's being kept."

"Are you out of your goddamn mind?" Shady scoffed. "You know how many people get snatched every damn day? How am I supposed to know where one bitch is?"

"She was taken from outside Raine Clayton's private residence. She's dating Raine's son, Calvin Clayton."

Jet didn't spell out the obvious, and Shady's expression didn't give anything away. But we all knew that Calvin owned Davey's—the dive bar where Shady conducted a lot of his "business"—and that Shady had connections to BestLyf.

My heart hammered in my chest as Shady stood there with a stoic expression, probably weighing up who he feared more—BestLyf or the fucking police.

Without breaking eye contact with Jet, he pulled his cell out of his pocket and called someone. After two minutes of speaking in some kind of code to whoever was on the other line, he hung up and gave us an address.

As soon as Shady was gone, Jet called his superiors to report the "anonymous" tip regarding my mom's whereabouts. Then he went into full boss mode, ordering the girls to go home and declaring I was coming with him "for my own safety."

Of course, the girls wanted to come with me, but Jet wouldn't budge. He insisted they get an Uber, then waited until they were safely on their way before walking me back to his car.

He took us to a squat building in Devilbend near the police station. With his hand on my lower back, he rushed me inside and up to a second-floor apartment. He'd told me on the drive over he was taking me to the base of operations for his task force, but I hadn't really thought about what to expect.

At least a dozen people were bustling around the apartment when we walked in, and after a moment, another three walked out from a back room. Desks and computers had been set up everywhere, and a fraying couch sat near the dated kitchen.

Detective Hopkins spotted Jet, glanced at me, and marched over to us. "Burns, what the fuck are you thinking?"

"She needs protection." Jet stood his ground against his boss. I did my best to look confident and not in the way. This was the closest we'd been to finding my mom—the closest I'd been to seeing BestLyf finally destroyed—and I didn't want to miss it.

"You just compromised this entire operation, bringing a civilian here!"

A few of the other detectives turned curious glances our way, but no one stopped what they were doing to watch. An air of business, of urgency, permeated the air.

"With all due respect, sir, she already knew of the existence of this operation, mainly due to your contact with Harlow Mead recently. We are on the precipice of a major breakthrough here. She's not going to get in the way of that."

"I want her out of here. Immediately." Hopkins put his hands on his hips, starting to go a little red in the face.

"Sir, please," I blurted, sick of just standing there like a naughty child while the adults talked. They both turned reproachful expressions in my direction. I squared my shoulders and channeled the kind of confidence Donna had when putting someone in their place. "They have my mother. I won't get in the way. I won't jeopardize this in any way. I'll just sit on that couch and be quiet until you tell me where to go."

"We have good information that Vivian Ellis is being held in a BestLyf-owned property," Jet said. "This could be what we need to get the rest. Amaya is the least of our worries right now."

With one last death glare at us both, Hopkins walked off. Was that a yes? Jet must've thought so, because he led me to the couch.

"Take a seat here. Let me know if you need anything, OK?" He rubbed my shoulders. "I'm going to head out with the others to get your mom. I need you to promise to stay here. You'll be safe."

"By myself?" I frowned.

He shook his head. "The analysts will be here. They're not trained to go in the field, but they're trained enough to protect you."

"OK." I nodded and looked around, wide-eyed. The buzz of activity was ramping up as people leaned over monitors, strapped vests to their chest, and checked weapons.

This suddenly felt too real. There were a lot of guns in one room, a lot of very determined-looking police officers.

"Hey." Jet caressed my cheek, drawing my attention back to him. "I love you."

"I love you," I whispered back as he gave me a kiss on the forehead. Then he rushed off to get ready.

I sat down heavily on the ugly couch and tried my best not to panic—or at least not to let it show. I must've done a good enough job, because no one paid me any attention as they rushed around.

In a matter of minutes, most of the people cleared out—on their way to save my mom. Only two officers remained. The man and woman sat at desks next to each other, each with three screens in front of them. They were across the room with their backs to me.

I updated the girls but was too nervous to read or even scroll social media. I kept glancing at the door, as if the police could have driven two towns over and returned with my mom in the ten minutes they'd been gone.

I sighed deeply as I realized I was in for an excruciating wait.

Unable to sit still, I got up and went to the window, moving the curtains aside to peer down at the street below. Everyone was just going about their business as if it was a normal afternoon. I supposed it was for them.

"Hey! Get away from the window!" the dude analyst barked, making me jump.

"Shit!" I pressed my hand to my chest. "Sorry. God."

"Be a good little girl and stay away from the windows, OK?" He gave me the most patronizing look I'd ever been subjected to before turning back to his screens.

I gave his back the finger but stepped away from the window. All the windows had the blinds drawn, and I figured there was probably a reason for that. But I still couldn't sit still, so I wandered around the dingy room, looking around. There wasn't much to see. Just peeling wallpaper and dirty coffee mugs. Not a personal item in sight.

One of the desks was a total mess of notepads and folders, with mugs and plates on top of them. I stacked the plates and straightened the folders.

"Don't touch that!" This time it was the chick analyst telling me off. "Jesus Christ, what kind of idiot are you? That's classified, important information you're messing with."

"I was just tidying up," I gritted out.

"Well, don't. Just sit on your spoiled little ass and don't touch anything." She turned away without waiting for a reply. I flipped her off too and headed back to the couch. Why did they have to be so fucking mean? The hostility was next level.

I took my phone out to message the girls and complain about the bitchy analysts, but a text came in before I got a chance.

It was from Calvin. I sighed, not in the mood for more of him trying to convince me I should go somewhere with him for safety, but I opened it anyway.

And my stomach plummeted.

It was a short text, and a photo came through right after.

C: I have your mom. Come now and DO NOT tell your cop boyfriend about this.

There was an address at the end. The photo was of Mom. She had on the same dress she'd worn that night—the one I'd cobbled together for her—and bruises covered her face. She was lying down on some bed, passed out.

CHAPTER TWENTY-SEVEN

I called him immediately. He didn't pick up. I called again, and again no one picked up. Then another text came through.

C: Stop calling. Just come to the address. Alone.

Fuck that. Fuck him!

I sprang to my feet and ran across the room to the two analysts.

"Can you get in touch with Jet and the others?" I slapped my palm down on the chick's desk. She looked at it pointedly, then glared at me.

"What now?" The dude sighed dramatically as the chick flicked my hand off her desk as if it were a bit of moldy pizza crust.

"You need to call them and tell them they're going to the wrong place. I just got a text. My mom is not there anymore. Calvin . . ."

They weren't listening. They were laughing at me. At first trying to contain it, then outright laughing.

"Just wait for your boyfriend and let us do our jobs, little girl." The chick waved me off as if I were an irritating fly. They were clearly too far up their own asses to listen, and I didn't have time for this bullshit.

Without another word, I turned on my heel and rushed to the door. The dude called after me, swearing, but neither of them chased me down the stairs or out of the building. I called Jet on my way down, but he didn't answer his phone. Of course he didn't. It was probably on silent while he stormed an empty building with the other cops.

Out on the street, I looked up the address. It was a good hour drive out into the hills. I needed a car, but I'd come here with Jet. Dammit!

Pulling at my hair and growling, I turned on the spot in search of a solution. I could get an Uber home and grab my car, but that would add another forty minutes to my drive. I could go to the police station one street over. If the dickheads upstairs weren't going to take me seriously, maybe they would. But I dismissed that idea almost as quickly as it came. There was a reason the BestLyf task force was in a shitty apartment with the blinds constantly drawn—the police couldn't be trusted. Raine almost certainly had the local police in her pocket. What if they tipped her off? What if they tipped Calvin off? I couldn't risk him taking Mom away again—or worse.

Think, Amaya! What else is in the area? A few friends lived in the apartment buildings nearby, but the closest familiar spot was Exert—the gym where Turner worked. I jogged around the corner and up the block to the gym.

The young girl in activewear behind the counter smiled at me. I was a regular here, and most of the staff knew me.

"Is Turner here?" I rushed out before she could greet me.

"Uh, no." She looked worried now that she'd taken in my panicked expression, my labored breathing. "He's not working today."

"Fuck. OK. Julie, right?"

She nodded, looking more uncertain by the second.

"Do you have a car?" I asked. "Is it here?"

"Yeah . . ." She frowned.

"Good. Can I please borrow it? It's an emergency."

"Um . . . I don't know . . ."

I resisted the urge to scream "IT'S AN EMERGENCY" into her face and took the pragmatic route instead. "Look, how much is it worth? Your car."

"Like . . ." She looked up to the ceiling. "Three grand, maybe?"

"OK. I'll give you five right now if you hand over the keys."

"What?" She bugged her eyes out.

"Five grand." I pulled my phone out and navigated to the payment app. "Right now, for your keys. And you can have the car back when I'm done with it."

When she continued to stare at me, wide-eyed, I waved my phone in her face. Finally, she snapped out of it and gave me her account details. After I'd transferred the money, she slid her keys over the counter to me, and I snatched them and ran for the back door.

"It's the red Mazda!" she called after me.

I found the red compact car, set my phone up on the holder and turned on navigation, then got the hell on the road.

All I could think about was getting to my mom.

Once I was out of downtown traffic and on the freeway, I tried calling Jet again. It just rang and rang until it went to voice mail. I left him a message, but—feeling paranoid—I didn't say the address or allude to what he was currently doing. Hopefully, my urgent tone and insistence he call me back immediately would be enough.

Then I called Donna.

She answered right away. "Hey, girl. What's happening?"

"Hey!" I froze, my mouth opening and closing, unsure what to say or how to say it exactly.

"Have they found your mom?"

"No, there's still no leads on that."

Donna paused for a beat. We both knew there was a very strong lead on that—we'd heard Shady give it to us just a few hours earlier.

"That sucks." Donna picked up what I was throwing down. "Let me grab Harlow and we can talk for a while."

She was telling me without telling me that her computer-nerd sister would know if my phone was tapped. Spying wasn't out of the ordinary when it came to our interactions with members of BestLyf. Harlow diligently checked our devices for spyware and whatever else, but it had been a while.

"No, that's OK." I was coming up to my exit and needed to focus on the road. But I wasn't dumb enough to go into a dangerous situation without someone knowing. Fuck Calvin and his demands that I come alone and tell no one. I was coming alone, but I'd make sure I wouldn't stay that way for long.

"I just wanted to check in, hear your voice. But I don't have time to talk. I'm on my way to that *appointment* I've been *avoiding* and I'm running late. They messaged me last minute, and I figured I'd go before someone else *took* it."

"Oh, OK. Do you want me to come meet you?" I could hear the edge of worry in her voice.

"Nah, but I can't get a hold of Jet to tell him I'll be late for our date. Can you try calling him when he gets off work? His phone is on silent, and I don't think he'll get my messages."

"Consider it done."

"Thanks, D."

"Love you, A." It sounded as if she was saying, *Be careful.*

"Love you too."

I hung up and concentrated on the winding roads. The address Calvin had sent was kind of remote, nothing but trees and the occasional driveway on either side of the road.

Finally, the GPS told me to turn into one of the driveways. My heart hammered in my chest, and I gripped the wheel even harder than I'd been clutching it the entire drive over.

The driveway was long and overgrown. I had to slow down to a crawl as the little car bumped along seemingly endlessly. Eventually, the road ended at a cabin that looked abandoned. Boards covered the windows, and weeds grew through cracks in the little porch. A pickup truck was the only sign there was anyone other than me here.

With a shaky breath, I got out of the car and walked up to the front door.

CHAPTER TWENTY-EIGHT

The door swung open, revealing a disheveled Calvin clutching a gun. He was wearing the same clothes he'd been in when I saw him last. His hair was a mess, his eyes bulging.

"Where is she?" I gritted out, painfully aware of the weapon in the unhinged man's grip. He scanned the area behind me.

"Amaya!" Mom called from somewhere within the house.

Acute relief slammed through me, mixed with the fear that had been a constant companion. The strange combination of feelings made me a little dizzy.

Calvin stepped out onto the porch, and I instinctively took a step away from him. But he hardly looked at me as he moved down the steps, still surveying the woods all around the dilapidated cabin.

I darted inside, desperate to get to my mom. It was dark, but a lamp provided some light in the far corner—right next to a couch where my mother was struggling to stand up. I sprinted to her and dropped hard to my knees.

She pulled me in for a hug. "A hug" didn't really encapsulate the way we clutched each other though. It was too mild a term for the level of intensity, for all the unspoken things contained in the space between our clasping arms.

I was wary of hurting her, but she squeezed me fiercely. It gave me some comfort to feel the strength in her grip.

"Mom, can you walk?" I asked in a harsh whisper, looking at the open door behind us.

"Yes, honey. It's not—"

"We have to move now. Before he comes back." I got to my feet and pulled on her arm. At the same time, I inspected the cabin for something I could use as a weapon. The open-plan space wasn't as shitty on the inside as it looked on the outside. There was a small, clean kitchen, a quaint round table with four chairs, and a fireplace next to the couch and armchair. Two doors on the adjacent wall probably led to a bedroom and bathroom.

"Before who comes back?" Mom got to her feet with a wince. I didn't know what hurt, but I winced too.

"Calvin." There were probably knives in the kitchen, but the fireplace was closer. I grabbed the poker from the pile of fireplace tools and wrapped an arm around Mom's waist. "He wandered out toward the driveway, but I don't know how far he went. We need to move."

But Mom didn't budge when I tried to get us hobbling toward the front door.

"Oh, honey, you scared me." She sighed, then lowered herself back down to the couch.

"What? Mom! Get up!" I yelled.

The door slammed, and I spun around to see Calvin standing inside. The gun was no longer in his hands, but I brandished the fire poker in front of myself anyway.

"Stay the fuck away from us!" I screamed.

He just stood there holding his hands up as if I were mugging him, a confused expression on his face.

"Amaya," Mom said gently. She covered my hands with hers, gently pushing until I lowered the poker. "Calvin is not going to hurt us. He saved me."

Breathing hard, I let her words sink in. Now I was the one confused.

"What?" I shook my head and let Mom take the poker. She dropped it to the floor with a clang, and Calvin relaxed.

"I thought you messaged her and told her," Mom said to Calvin.

"I did." He dragged a hand down his face. He looked exhausted as he moved to the kitchen and put the kettle on—the old-fashioned kind that you heat on the stove.

"He sent me a photo of you looking banged up and dirty and told me to come here and not bring the cops." I started to take in more details as I spoke. Mom was no longer in her dirty dress from the photo. She had on baggy sweats and looked clean. Her hair was even still damp.

"Calvin." Mom sounded reproachful. "I told you to reassure her, not send her a ransom note!"

"I thought I was. It's been a very stressful fucking couple of days." He sighed and leaned heavily on the counter. "I'm sorry, Amaya."

"He saved you?" I asked Mom. I needed to have it confirmed again. "You're OK? He's not keeping you here against your will?"

"No, honey. We can leave if we want to."

"No, you can't!" Calvin sounded panicked. My anxiety spiked.

"Calvin!" Mom barked.

"Sorry, sorry. I just meant it's safer if you don't. I don't want anything to happen to you. We have to be very careful about our next move. But, no, I'm not holding either of you hostage or whatever."

"What the fuck is happening?" I collapsed onto the couch next to Mom. She brushed my hair over my shoulder, and I leaned into her touch.

"Cal and I have been planning to get out. With you finishing high school and going off to college or traveling, we were putting things in motion to move away from Devilbend. The business I mentioned was a new chapter of BestLyf—somewhere the organization doesn't have a lot of members," Mom explained.

"Why? Mom, BestLyf is a cult. Please, you have to believe me. They're dangerous and they do all kinds of illegal shit."

"I know." She patted my arm, then frowned at me. "Wait, how do you know?"

A bitchy comment about how she'd know if she'd paid any attention to me over the last year was on the tip of my tongue, but I held it back. Old habits die hard. "Doesn't matter. How did you end up . . . here?" I gestured vaguely to her banged-up state and the time capsule of a cabin we were currently in.

"The new BestLyf chapter was supposed to be just a stepping stone. Once we had some distance from the headquarters in Devilbend and from Raine Clayton, we were planning to pull back from it and eventually separate ourselves from it entirely. We spent a lot of time making a plan, thought it out carefully, but . . ." She looked at Calvin.

"But my mother is a fucking psychopathic megalomaniac," he gritted out. The kettle started making a high-pitched noise, and he turned to take it off the heat, busying himself with making tea.

"Raine somehow got wind of our plan, and she didn't like it. She's very possessive of her son. And he knows a lot of things that could threaten BestLyf."

"Oh, you mean how they run a bunch of illegal businesses and kidnap and kill people regularly? Yeah, I can see how she might be worried about that getting out." I huffed.

They both gaped at me, and I shrugged, unfazed. I wasn't the one who needed to explain herself right now.

"So, what's the new plan then?" I asked.

Calvin placed two steaming mugs of herbal tea on the side table. "We lie low for a while. No one knows about this cabin. We take some time so your mother can recover, and we plan our next move."

The sound of footsteps on the porch had us all swinging our heads toward the door. There was a knock, and Calvin pulled his gun out.

"I told you not to tell anyone," he hissed at me. "Who did you tell?"

Before I could even reply, another knock sounded on the rickety wood. Then a woman's voice came through the cracks.

"Come on, Cali-boy, open the door for Mommy. I know you're in there!"

We exchanged looks, the blood draining from all our faces. It made the dark bruises on Mom's cheek and eye appear even more stark.

"Calvin! Open this door right now!" Raine shouted.

Cal held his finger over his lips in the universal sign for silence and went to the door. "Mom?" he called, putting on a surprised voice.

"Amaya," Mom whispered as she pushed me away. "Go to the door on the left and hide. Go now."

I got up from the couch, but instead of hiding, I picked up the poker again.

Calvin hid the gun behind his back as he unlocked the door and opened it a crack. He said something I couldn't make out. Then Raine laughed.

"You should know better than to lie to me, my stupid, sweet boy."

Loud banging and glass breaking made me jump. I brandished the poker in both hands, swiveling around. The sound was coming from all sides, and I didn't know which way to face, where the danger was coming from.

People flooded into the house. They came from all directions, shoving past Calvin through the front door, climbing through broken windows, rushing in from the bedroom. Some were women but most were men. They all wore casual clothes and wielded guns and menacing expressions.

I counted at least a dozen. Where had they even come from? How did we not hear a car coming up the drive? Did they creep up through the woods? Did I lead them here?

Too many questions to even process flashed through my mind.

Mom was suddenly standing, her back to mine. I leaned against her and swung the poker in a wide arc. The two mean dudes closest to us just laughed, pointing their guns at my head.

They had a point. What the fuck was I going to do with my stick against their guns?

I still held on to it though. It felt like the only thing giving me any strength in this fucked-up situation.

The intruders easily disarmed Calvin, outnumbered as he was, and one of the men shoved him. He stumbled and caught himself on the edge of the table, sending one of the dining chairs clattering to the floor.

Raine walked into the cabin calmly, her wedged heels thudding on the wooden floors. She was in blue linen pants and a loose white shirt with a chunky necklace, her hair neatly styled in a low bun—an ensemble that paired perfectly with her smug, beatific smile. It was as if she'd been on her way to brunch with other obscenely wealthy women of a certain age and had just popped into this remote, crumbling cabin in the woods on her way.

She paused just inside the door, took in the scene, and wandered over to the dude who'd shoved Calvin. Swinging her arm wide, she smacked him on the side of the head.

The armed man, who was twice her size, just stood there and took it.

"Do not lay a hand on my son," she said, authority heavy in her voice.

"Sorry, ma'am." He hung his head, looking miserable and frightened at the same time.

"Are you OK, Cali-boy?" she cooed to her grown-ass son and caressed his head as if he were a toddler.

Calvin jerked away, disdain and hatred clear in his eyes.

She just folded her hands in front of her. "You're mad at me, I know. But, darling, I'm very disappointed in you too."

She looked at him expectantly, slowly raising one eyebrow. Calvin just kept glaring.

My arms started to shake from holding the heavy poker up in front of myself.

"Not ready to apologize then." Raine sighed. "I shouldn't be surprised, I guess, considering the lengths you went to in order to run away from home." She chuckled. "And here I am ruining your fun."

Was this a fucking game to her?

"Now, come on, get your things. It's time to go home." She smoothed the front of her shirt, unaffected by the deadly weapons in the room or how fucked up this situation was.

"How did you find us?" Cal asked. He sounded defeated.

Raine released one harsh laugh. "I thought you'd learned your lessons a long time ago. There is nothing you can hide from me. I know everything there is to know. I am everywhere, and my will is absolute. Now, you're trying my patience, and I really don't want to have to punish you."

Cal winced. It was the slightest little tic in his face, but I caught it. He'd suffered at the hands of this woman.

"Having you as a mother is punishment enough," he spat. "I've been living in purgatory my entire life."

"Watch your mouth." Raine suddenly looked furious.

"No!" Calvin yelled, and she seemed genuinely taken aback. "I am a grown man. All I'm trying to do is build a life with the woman I love. And your reaction to that is to kidnap her? To show up here with armed goons? What the fuck is wrong with you? This isn't normal! I can't live like this anymore!"

"We do not acknowledge that word in my world. Have you forgotten the basic principles of BestLyf already?"

"Normal! Normal! Normal!" Calvin shouted, going red in the face.

"That's it. I've had enough." Raine was starting to go red too, her perfect mask slipping. I could really see the resemblance now. An identical vein in their foreheads popped out as they shouted at each other. "I told you when you came to me yesterday that I was willing to let that woman live." She gestured vaguely in our direction, making a disgusted face. As if the mere mention of my mother tasted rotten in her mouth. I bared my teeth at her, gripping the poker tighter despite my shaking arms. "I've always been a reasonable parent, Calvin. I was willing to let you keep her as long as you understood that your place was by my side. But now I see just how far this insubordination has gone. How deeply she's dug her claws into you. She's corrupted you, my boy."

"She *saved* me," Calvin said, squaring his shoulders. "We are each other's salvation. You'll never understand what that's like—to have someone who truly understands you and accepts you for all your flaws. I pity you, Mother."

For a beat Raine just stood there, staring at her son, that vein in her forehead pulsing faster. I wanted to scream at him to stop antagonizing the homicidal megalomaniac, but the multiple guns pointed at me kept me silent.

Raine cleared her throat and completely ignored what Cal had just said. "As I was saying, I was willing to indulge you and let you keep her. But I've changed my mind, and now she, and that brat of hers, will have to die."

As if Raine had dropped a grenade into the little cabin in the woods, everything erupted into chaos.

My mom screamed and, with strength I didn't think her beaten body possessed, shoved me to the side to put herself in front of me. I stumbled but managed to stay on my feet.

Calvin dropped to his knees, clutching his mother's pants as he pleaded for her not to literally kill us.

Mom was yelling, threatening the people with guns, cursing out Raine.

Raine's lackeys got jittery and started barking instructions too. They glanced to Raine for guidance while closing in on us.

All logic fled my mind, and I went into pure fight or flight.

I swung the poker at the shoulder of the man closest to us, and it connected with a sickening crunch. He bellowed in pain and dropped his gun to the ground.

The others all sprang into action, diving for us.

I was shoved again. This time I fell to the ground with the wind knocked out of me. Someone kicked me in the ribs, and the pain was so intense I saw stars.

My vision returned just in time to see two of the lackeys smacking my mom down onto the couch. The man was shouting something while the woman punched her over and over and over.

A gun went off, the sound so loud it cut through the chaos already filling the small space.

Everyone crouched and looked around for where the shot had come from, but I didn't bother. I just stared at my mom's limp body.

"Mom," I wailed as everything started to go blurry. "Please . . ."

She wasn't moving, her face a bloody, pulpy mess.

From my position, I couldn't see if her chest was rising and falling. Every time I tried to drag myself closer, my vision would waver from the pain in my stomach and ribs, and I'd collapse back to the hard ground.

More gunshots went off. Boots pounded on the wooden floors. More shouting and violence.

It wasn't until Jet's face appeared in front of mine that I realized I'd been screaming hysterically.

I stopped screaming, but my overloaded mind still struggled to make sense of anything. Jet's mouth was moving, his hand stroking my head gently, but I had no idea what he was saying.

I used his steady gaze to ground myself. I focused on his dark eyes, then his lips, as everything around me started to register.

Cops swarmed everywhere. Raine's goons were either being handcuffed or prone on the ground—dead or knocked out? I didn't really care.

There was no sign of Raine or Calvin.

Mom.

So many people stood crowded inside the small cabin now. I couldn't see her between all their bodies.

"Hey, hey. Focus on me." Jet's gentle hands guided my face closer to his, and he locked his gaze to mine. "Eyes on me, princess. Just listen to my voice. We're gonna get you out of here."

"Mom . . . ," I croaked. I tried to look again, but he forced me to keep still.

"I know. There are ambulances coming. There are people with her. I need you to focus on you right now, OK?" He nodded slowly, and I found myself nodding along with him. "Can you tell me where it hurts? Did you get shot?"

I shook my head. "No. I . . . I don't think so." Panic welled once again, and tears started pouring down my face. "Fuck. Jet, did I get shot? Am I OK?"

I sobbed and he hushed me, stroking my head again and murmuring soothing things.

By the time the wail of ambulance sirens was so close it sounded as if they were inside, I'd managed to tell Jet I'd been shoved and kicked, and he'd poked at my ribs and run his hands over every inch of my body. He spoke to me the entire time, keeping my focus on him and away from the bustling activity where my mom's bloody body lay.

Even when the cops started clearing out the cabin, Jet still wouldn't let me look in her direction. He crouched right by my head, blocking my view with his body as two EMTs came to examine me.

The emergency workers whisked Mom out to an ambulance, and then the wail of the siren rent the air once more—this time getting fainter.

Not long after, I found myself in the back of another ambulance, Jet right by my side. As we prepared to leave for the hospital, I caught sight of Raine Clayton. She was leaning against a car, handcuffed, as she shouted something over her shoulder. Just before the ambulance doors slammed shut, she caught me watching and sneered.

Jet stayed with me through all of it, keeping me tethered to sanity with his touch, his voice, and his very presence.

Whatever the EMTs had given me seriously numbed the pain in my body. It made my head feel kind of fuzzy too, but the absence of pain made it easier to think.

"Jet?"

"Right here, beautiful." He gave my arm a squeeze.

"How did you know? I tried to call you so many times but . . ."

He smiled down at me. It didn't reach his eyes. "You have some very clever friends."

Donna had read between the lines of what I'd said on the phone as clearly as if I'd shouted the information at her. The rest was easy enough to guess. Harlow had tracked my phone, they'd gotten through to Jet, and he'd come to the rescue.

After a stretch of silence, I asked another question. "Is my mom going to be OK?"

When he didn't immediately answer, I tried to turn my head to look at him, but they'd put me in one of those neck brace things and I couldn't move an inch.

Maybe he hadn't heard me? But I knew he had—he'd started stroking my arm right when I asked it. He just didn't know how to answer.

I couldn't find the strength to ask again.

EPILOGUE

The teal silk felt cool to the touch, despite the warmth of the day. I ran my hand over it, smoothing the fabric over my lap.

My ribs still hurt if I took too deep a breath, but I could sit up on my own and walk, and that was all I needed to cross a stage and graduate with the rest of my class.

Despite everything, despite how recent all the pain and chaos was, I refused to miss this. I refused to let that evil woman and her corrupt organization take one more thing from me. I was going to wear the silk gown and silly cap and graduate with all my friends if it was the last fucking thing I did. It wouldn't be, of course. I was going to be fine.

I had one cracked rib and some gnarly bruising, but I was OK otherwise. Unlike Mom . . .

A round of applause went up, and I belatedly joined everyone in clapping along to whatever Headmistress Perry just said. Once she started speaking again, I found the back of Donna's head, several rows in front of me, and focused on her perfectly smooth, short hair for a moment. Then I turned to look several rows behind me. Mena caught my eye immediately and gave me a small smile.

"OK?" she mouthed.

I nodded and turned back to the front.

The stage was set up in the middle of the football field, the bleachers packed with the graduating class's loved ones. My peers and I sat in alphabetical order, ready to go receive our diplomas.

Donna's last name—Mead—should've put her behind me, but she was seated in the front because she was valedictorian. Because *of course* she was. I was so proud of my friend.

Fulton being about as exclusive as you could get for a school, the graduating class wasn't massive. No one had last names that started with *F* or *G*, so Hendrix (Hawthorn) sat right next to me. As much as I was determined to be here for this rite of passage, it had been a rough few weeks, and it felt good to have someone beside me who knew what it had been like, who had been there for me right along with my girls.

He leaned sideways slightly and whispered in my ear, "You know, for a while I thought I'd never even finish high school, let alone graduate with half-decent grades."

I covered my mouth as we both chuckled.

"I guess you never know what life's going to throw at you," I whispered back. I was painfully aware we should've been too young to fully appreciate that sentiment. We'd seen too much. Experienced shit no one should have to.

"You'd think I'd be a bitter asshole after everything I've been through, everything I did." He shifted in his seat, his silk robe rubbing against my own. Hendrix was clearly in a reflective mood. I couldn't blame him. "But I guess I've also learned that life has a way of working out if you let it. Like, everything is OK in the end, and if it's not OK, it's not the end."

"It's because of who you are as a person deep down, Hendrix." I kept my gaze forward. "You didn't let that shit define you, and you worked to learn from it. That's all any of us can do."

He cleared his throat. "Thanks, Amaya."

"You're not bitter." I shrugged. "But you're still an asshole."

I could see his grin out of the corner of my eye. "And you're still a bitch."

"Thank you." I let my grin break free and clapped along with everyone else as Ms. Perry finished her speech and walked off the stage.

More people spoke—inspiring words from former students, the class president, and of course, my valedictorian bestie. Donna's was the only speech I paid real attention to.

And then it was time. Guided by the teachers, my fellow graduates and I made our way forward in neat alphabetized rows. One by one, names were called, and students in shining teal robes proudly walked across the stage to accept their certificates and flip the tassel on their cap to the other side—a sign they'd officially graduated.

I cheered each one of them on, right along with the rest of the crowd.

Then it was my turn.

Ms. Perry called my name, and I took a breath as I stepped forward. I kept my gaze on my feet as I climbed the few stairs in my heels, then focused on Ms. Perry and reaching her.

I could feel all their gazes on the side of my head, hundreds of people staring at me and wondering just as many things as they already knew. It was all anyone in Devilbend had been talking about for weeks.

The tangled web of Raine Clayton's crimes was still unraveling, but it was clear to anyone she was done.

She had spent years perpetrating more crimes than I cared to tally up—everything from tax evasion to straight-up murder. Because they'd caught her in the act of kidnapping and attempted murder in the cabin that day, the police had more than enough to keep her locked up while they gathered even more evidence against her, BestLyf, and multiple members of the organization.

She had immediately surrounded herself with an entire firm of high-profile attorneys, but even they couldn't get her out on bail. Due to her resources and connections, she was too much of a flight risk. But they were doing their damnedest to get her out of paying for her crimes. They had their work cut out for them.

Even if Raine somehow managed to avoid life in prison, she was ruined, along with BestLyf. The organization that had been growing since the nineties—one of the most powerful corporations in the country—was crumbling for the whole world to see, as if it had been constructed from dust and lies. TMZ was reporting on it constantly, sometimes hourly. With that many high-profile people involved, there was a constant stream of scandals, news, declarations of innocence, and scrambling to get distance from a ship that had already sunk.

The police had already gathered a good deal of evidence against multiple members of BestLyf, but recent developments had given them access to more information than they could realistically process in the short time that had passed. But even preliminary reports—the little that they'd speak about—made it clear they had enough to throw the book at Raine.

Jet had barely left my side at the hospital and had practically moved into my house when I was discharged. Since then, he'd relaxed his staunch rule against telling me anything to do with his work; I knew more details than anyone outside the investigation. They had enough to prove Raine had her hand in multiple horrific crimes. Most notably, she was aware of the murder of Chelsea—one of Mena's coworkers at the diner—who had gone missing and turned up dead. Raine had personally ordered the murder of Irene Richards in prison, and she had directly ordered my mother's kidnapping.

More broadly, she was well aware of all the illegal dealings connected to BestLyf—many of which Calvin had been in charge of. There was a massive criminal underbelly to BestLyf, a huge network of drugs, guns, and human trafficking. And she was behind it all, had built it all.

And now she was going to pay for it.

I knew the law was anything but straightforward and the process could be painfully slow, but I also knew in my gut Raine would not get away with it. She'd hurt too many people, and there was too much evidence to prove it.

Not to mention all the people suddenly willing to talk, to give evidence and even testify—most of them in an effort to distance themselves from this truly horrifying shit show. To save their own asses. High-profile people, like Nicola's famous actress mom, were falling over one another's designer shoes to speak against an organization that had been as useful to them as they had been to Raine Clayton.

I didn't care. As long as the real monsters paid for their evil deeds.

"Congratulations, Amaya." Ms. Perry handed me my high school diploma and shook my hand. I returned her smile and reached up to flip the tassel from one side to the other.

Then I reminded myself I didn't give a shit what all those people were saying or thinking about me, and I turned to face them with my head held high. I knew what really mattered to me, and their opinions weren't it.

I held my fists up in triumph, my diploma clutched in one, and everyone cheered a little harder. Maybe I'd been imagining some of the whispers and judgment. The whistling and clapping seemed to get a little more intense and last a little longer than it had for the students before me.

Maybe I was imagining that too, but whatever. I'd been through a lot to make it to this point, and I enjoyed the applause.

My focus zeroed in on a particularly rowdy group in the crowd.

In the first row of the audience, the people I loved most in the world—at least the ones not graduating with me—all sat together in the same section. They must've arrived extra early to grab those seats, although they were on their feet right now, whooping and cheering and clapping like crazy people.

Jet stood front and center, beaming at me as he held his hand up to his mouth and wolf-whistled. The sound carried over all the rest of the noise.

Turner was next to him. His graduation had been the week before, and we'd all gone along to support him, just as he was doing for us today. His dad and little sister were right behind him.

Harlow alternated between clapping and wiping away the tears streaming down her face. Easton had an arm around her while he cheered. Easton's brother, Ford, was on his other side, whooping as though he were at a football game and not a graduation. Harlow and Donna's parents stood next to Mena's mom and dad, and Hendrix's aunt and her boyfriend were beaming. His parents had come too, but they must've been seated elsewhere.

Calvin was at the end of the row, standing and clapping with the others.

The only reason he wasn't behind bars right along with his mother was because he was fully cooperating with the investigation. And because he'd been working with the task force for months before. He'd been serious about wanting to get out from under his mother's sick influence, to help stop her once and for all. The only time he'd wavered had been when Mom was kidnapped. He'd been terrified for her life and had done what he thought was the best thing to save her. He really did love her. There was no way I could deny it or question it anymore.

I was just sorry it had taken all this for me to really see it—to accept him for the genuine, kind man he was.

The only person not standing was my mom. She sat in a wheelchair at the end of the row, clapping and sobbing.

The doctors had kept her in a coma for several days, but she'd made it. She had several broken bones and horrific damage to her face, but she was alive. She was going to need a lot of plastic surgery to regain even a semblance of her beautiful face, and there was a strong possibility she'd never walk again. *But she was here*. She was here for me, and I'd never been more thankful for anything in my whole life.

I looked away from her quickly. If I didn't, I'd start sobbing as hard as she was, and I refused to let all these people see me cry.

The applause settled, and I moved to the other side of the stage to make way for Hendrix and all the students behind him. The rest of the diplomas were handed out, another speech was given, we threw our caps up into the air, and it was done.

Despite all the odds, I'd graduated high school.

The crowd dispersed all over the field, families searching out their graduates. People hugged and cried all over the place.

A body slammed into mine from behind, and Harlow wrapped her arms around me. She bounced and squealed at the back of my head: "I'm so proud of you!"

"Fuck, you're strong for someone so small." I chuckled, extracting myself from her just enough to spin around and return her hug properly. I didn't even care that it made my ribs ache.

Before we could separate, another set of arms wrapped around us, then another. Donna and Mena had joined us. We adjusted our grip so we were all hugging, then held one another for a long time as people milled around us.

"I love you girls so much," I whispered into our little bubble.

"Me too," Mena said.

"Me three," Harlow added.

"Me four," Donna declared, closing the circle of love.

"Come on, let's go get day drunk. We deserve it!" Harlow declared as we finally pulled apart.

"You didn't even graduate," her sister griped.

"So?" Harlow shrugged. "I survived this hellscape of a year, just like everyone else, didn't I?"

"She's got a point, D." Mena nodded.

"I don't give a shit what we do or where. As long as we do it together," I declared.

With our arms around one another, we walked toward the edge of the field and our waiting loved ones, our teal gowns and Harlow's pink dress billowing out behind us.

The girls teased me for being sentimental, but I just smiled because I knew they were only teasing. And I knew we would be just fine, as long as we had each other.

#DevilbendDynastyForever

THE END

ABOUT THE AUTHOR

Kaydence Snow has lived all over the world but ended up settled in Melbourne, Australia. She lives near the beach with her husband.

She draws inspiration from her own overthinking, sometimes frightening imagination, and everything that makes life interesting. She believes sarcasm is the highest form of wit and has the vocabulary of a highly educated, well-read sailor. When she's not writing, thinking about writing, planning when she can write next, or reading other people's writing, she loves to travel and learn new things.

To keep up to date with Kaydence's latest news and releases sign up to her newsletter here:

kaydencesnow.com/#newsletter

Join her reader group here:

facebook.com/groups/KaydenceSnowLodge

Or follow her on: